THE OTHER SIDE OF
Paradise

London 1937. When the brilliant young doctor Kit Masters is forced to leave the country, he sets sail for the fabulous island paradise of Koraloona in the South Seas. He is immediately enchanted by the place, and responds eagerly to the island's medical needs, as well as to the charms of the beautiful Aleena, daughter of the Koraloona princess. But as Kit's feelings for Aleena become ever more passionate, so the turmoil of the outside world impinges more and more on their life, first with the onset of a widespread polio epidemic, then with the coming of the Second World War, and finally with the threat of a catastrophic natural disaster from the wrathful island gods.

THE OTHER SIDE OF
Paradise

'Noel Barber could revive the Darned Good Read all on his own with THE OTHER SIDE OF PARADISE'

Daily Mail

'If you enjoyed TANAMERA and A WOMAN OF CAIRO, you'll love this one – his best yet'

Prima

'Mr Barber is an expert at evoking atmosphere and a stickler for technical accuracy, and this book is as good as anything he has produced'

Hull Daily Mail

'What a splendid storyteller Noel Barber is . . . his latest novel is peopled with characters that spring to life and engage the reader to the very last page . . . masterly'

Hamilton Spectator

THE OTHER SIDE OF
Paradise

'Noel Barber has worked out the elements of his blockbusting success. Not surprisingly, his latest novel has them all . . . and we keep on turning the pages'

Yorkshire Post

'Very readable'

Illustrated London News

'A story of vivid reality'

Evening Advertiser

'His latest novel will cement his reputation as a storyteller of the highest calibre'

The Portsmouth News

'A new and compelling blockbuster. Barber is a master storyteller, a craftsman in the truest sense of the word. He makes any scene, any incident, any character, come vibrantly alive. His story lines, too, are well drawn and make compulsive reading . . . thoroughly entertaining'

The Citizen

THE OTHER SIDE OF
Paradise

'Adventure, intrigue, smouldering passion, drama
. . . if you enjoyed TANAMERA and A WOMAN
OF CAIRO, this book will delight you'
Woman's World

'Always enthralling'
Yorkshire Evening Post

'A sparkling tale of romance and revenge . . .
another international success'
Middlesborough Evening Gazette

'Barber's tale of love, friendship and heroic courage never flags'
Capital Magazine

'His latest and most absorbing novel'
Brighton Evening Argus

'A splendid colourful novel. Ideal for the grey,
cold winter days'
Barnsley Chronicle

THE OTHER SIDE OF
Paradise

'A tremendous climax. Good, readable stuff, all of it'

Evening Sentinel

'Noel Barber fans will not be disappointed'
The Western Morning News

'Full of drama, intrigue, and passion'
Evening Press

'May well qualify as the best "read" of the autumn. The book is laced with colour and the author has an inbuilt talent for narrative drive . . . the story fairly rattles along and, once you get involved, you are unlikely to lay it down. Entertainment that is hard to beat'

Glasgow Evening Times

Also by the same author,
and available from Coronet

TANAMERA
A FAREWELL TO FRANCE
A WOMAN OF CAIRO

THE NATIVES WERE FRIENDLY . . .
(Autobiography)

About the author

As with his previous bestsellers, TANAMERA, A FAREWELL TO FRANCE and A WOMAN OF CAIRO, Noel Barber has based THE OTHER SIDE OF PARADISE on a part of the world he knows well. In his days as an internationally acclaimed foreign correspondent, he spent many months in the Pacific and visited dozens of islands like the Koraloona of the novel.

THE OTHER SIDE OF
Paradise

NOEL BARBER

CORONET BOOKS
Hodder and Stoughton

Copyright © 1986 by Eton Books A.G.

*First published in Great Britain in 1986
by Hodder and Stoughton Limited*

Coronet Open Market Edition 1987

Coronet Edition 1987

*The characters and situations in this
book are entirely imaginary and bear
no relation to any real person or
actual happening.*

This book is sold subject to the
condition that it shall not, by way of
trade or otherwise, be lent, re-sold,
hired out or otherwise circulated
without the publisher's prior consent
in any form of binding or cover other
than that in which it is published and
without a similar condition including
this condition being imposed on the
subsequent purchaser.

No part of this publication may be
reproduced or transmitted in any form
or by any means, electronically
or mechanically, including
photocopying, recording or any
information storage or retrieval
system, without either the prior
permission in writing from the
publisher or a licence, permitting
restricted copying, issued by the
Copyright Licensing Agency, 33–34
Alfred Place, London. WC1E 7DP

for
GEORGE GREENFIELD
– a wise counsellor,
a true friend

The Island of
KORALOONA

Author's Note

My most grateful thanks to Alan Wykes for his enormous help in research and in other ways when I was writing this book. Alan himself has written more than forty books – a feat which makes his assistance doubly welcome. My thanks also go to John Bright-Holmes for his suggestions on the text.

I would never have been able to write the medical aspects of this book had my travels in the South Pacific not been elucidated by the local knowledge of Dr Raymond Walsh and Dr John White, both old friends, still practising in the South Seas, who were unsparing in sharing with me their specialised knowledge.

Finally, my grateful thanks again to Pippa Esdaile for her patience in typing out the four versions of this novel.

NB
The Savage Club
1986

PART ONE

1

When, sometimes, I think back on the beauty of life on a South Seas island, I start to wonder how fate could possibly have propelled me from the rain and bedraggled leafless winter trees of England to such distant enchantment.

And when I daydream of its beauty I think, too, of the people I met on Koraloona, of Doc Reid, the eccentric, wayward medic who first taught me about the island; Bill Robins, the captain of the *Mantela* when our ship was attacked, and who before that was to become my first real friend; Jason Purvis, the starving beachcomber and would-be great novelist who at last did achieve a kind of fame; Paula Reece, the beautiful American with cold, appraising eyes who so loved the island – and several of its free and happy inhabitants. Then there was Tiare, named after Polynesia's whitest flower, who had inherited a secret hoard of paintings from her artist father, paintings that were to be a turning point in the history of the island.

Above all, there was Tiare's daughter Aleena. I can still see her as I first met her, a skinny, energetic schoolgirl with a flower in her shining black hair, who quickly grew into a beautiful woman and whose life became entwined with mine as together we triumphed over disease, over prejudice and even over war. Our travels led us to places as far apart as Sanderstown, San Francisco, New York, and London – all in search of an 'insurance' that would guarantee for us peace and tranquillity on Koraloona, the most beautiful island of the whole beautiful Moto Varu archipelago.

There was no reason, except chance, why I should ever have travelled to live in a remote island on the other side of the world, for my future in England had been mapped out. Our family, which lived in Renishaw Road in Nottingham, was always well off, if never rich. My father, Herbert Masters, was an electrical engineer, and enlisted in the army soon after I was born, in 1914. He saw service in France, the Middle East and England as a captain in the Signals Service of the Royal Engineers, and learned his future trade well. By the time he was demobbed he was the nearest thing to a genius when handling the military gadgetry of radio signals and wireless telephony that the army produced. I suppose it was inevitable that in 1918 he should capitalise on his expertise at a time when the post-war craze for the new-fangled wireless sets was at its height. Before the year was out my father had invested his small gratuity, his savings – for my mother had worked while he was at war – and opened a shop near the Market Place, specialising in selling components for those who wanted to build their own sets. It sold spare parts that were never stocked in larger shops. More important, my father had learned the theory as well as the practice of 'wireless telephony', so he was that rare individual, a man who could offer practical advice on how best to use the components he bought from Marconi's, Cossor, Edison-Swan, Oldham Batteries and other suppliers. He was astonishing. Why, he even once built me a tiny crystal set in an empty match box, saying, 'Here, Kit. That'll give your friends something to talk about.'

Early in the 1920s, Father opened a second shop, then a third, this time in Mansfield. He was so successful that 'Masters of Notts' seemed almost as much of a neighbourhood byword as 'Boots the Chemists'.

One thing my father instinctively knew: I would never join his firm unless events forced me to. I don't think he minded, for once he said to me, 'You can't do a job like mine unless you're fascinated by it', and I wasn't. Though I spent my outdoor time playing any game I could, from cricket, tennis, football or boxing at the local gym, all my indoor time was spent buried in books. I was an insatiable reader, and whenever I *did* visit Father at one of his shops, I invariably managed to wheedle a couple of batteries out of him – so that I could read in bed under the bedclothes.

One day, after a particularly good school report, Father took me for a walk past a second-hand bookstore where I often browsed enviously.

'I saw a book here that might interest you,' he said.

It was a heavy leather-bound copy of *Don Quixote*, dramatically illustrated by a man whose name meant nothing to me at that time, Gustave Doré. But the full-page pictures brought the heroic figure to life.

'Let's call it an extra prize for this term.' Father carried the parcel as we walked back. 'Because I've been thinking, Kit. If you agree, I'd like to send you to Oxford. Your headmaster says he can get you a place. And Oxford! – it was something I was never able to do myself. How do you feel about it?'

I did not hesitate. 'I'd love to,' I cried.

By now I had a baby sister Clare, and it was something that happened to her which helped to shape my destiny and provided the first step on my road to Koraloona.

Clare had been born in 1919, and by the time she was twelve she had grown into a tomboy, excited by all sports – not only hockey, but sometimes she even helped out if we were short of a player for an improvised soccer game in the park.

Mother disapproved. She was a loving mother, tall and thin and delighted at the social success of 'Captain' Masters, the polite way the bank manager doffed his hat to her, and that she was not the only mother who was sending her son to Oxford.

But as for sending Clare Masters to play football! 'It's undignified and unladylike,' she said. Even worse, Clare, with her ruddy, apple-red cheeks, used successfully to beg Father to get stand seats at Meadow Lane for her as well as me and himself when Notts County played at home. I sympathised with her for, after all, Notts County was the oldest league club in the world, and this was the season when Tom Keetley scored a record thirty-nine goals and we came top of Third Division South.

'It'd be like missing part of the world scene,' cried Clare.

'It's like behaving in an unladylike fashion,' sniffed Mother, for, of course, Father could refuse us nothing, and Mother did add, 'Well, let's forget it. Sit down all of you in the dining-room, and have your tea. The muffins are hot and buttered and sprinkled with salt.'

Clare had such a sense of adventure – and it was this love of an active life that made what happened doubly hard to bear. That was the year – 1931 – when the Youth Hostels Association was formed, and Clare went on one of their first trips, organised by the local school, to a hostel in the Dukeries, not far north in Lincolnshire. This despite another sniff of disapproval from Mother.

The trip was supposed to last a week. After three days, the schoolmistress in charge phoned. Mother answered, then she came into the sitting-room and announced, 'Clare's coming home.'

'Coming home?' Father echoed. 'Has she done something wrong?'

'No. She's got a bad cold or 'flu and she's running a temperature,' said Mother in an 'I told you so' voice. 'One of the mistresses is driving her back. She says do not worry, but it's wiser to be on the safe side. She'll be home this evening.'

When she did arrive, my parents at first thought it was 'flu. Hundreds of thousands had died in the post-war 'flu epidemic, so anyone who caught it – especially children – was bundled off to bed, as Clare was, with a hot water bottle, some aspirin, and a glass of hot milk with an eggspoonful of whisky in it.

There was no improvement; she continued to have a temperature. The usual 'flu stiffness and aching in the muscles didn't go away as it should have done, so Father sent for Dr Allott, our family physician, a patient, gentle old man who always arrived in an Essex sedan and – more

6

important to us – always carried a pocketful of toffees to give away to children.

I wasn't present when Dr Allott examined Clare, of course, but I could sense the worry in my parents. Clare was told she was in for a long stay in bed, and Mother moved in a divan to sleep next to her. Dr Allott came every day. He, too, looked grave, and I caught snatches of meaningless (to me) words . . . 'cerebrospinal fluid . . . lumbar puncture . . . muscular reflexes'. All these phrases occurred frequently.

Fascinated, I finally waylaid Dr Allott in the street one day, just after he'd paid us a visit, and I plucked up courage to ask him what these strange words meant. I shall always be grateful to him for not giving me the usual reply of an adult to a curious child's questions, 'You're too young to understand.'

'Well,' he said, 'it's not too easy to answer without giving you a long lecture on the structure of the body.' He handed me a toffee, climbed into his car, beckoned me to sit on the other front seat for a few minutes, and removed the celluloid sidescreen to give us more fresh air.

'What it amounts to,' he explained, 'is that your sister has a mild attack of a disease we call infantile paralysis. It's an illness we don't know much about, but sometimes it affects the muscles of a leg or an arm. Perhaps if it's a bad case the patient has to wear a special boot or keep the leg held straight with iron braces.'

'Will Clare have to wear a brace?' I asked – with, I must admit, rather more clinical curiosity than compassion.

'I hope not. I'm going to send round a nurse who'll massage the affected muscles and help her with exercises. In the present state of medical knowledge, there's little more we can do.'

'It's a funny sort of name,' I said.

'Well actually,' said Dr Allott, 'infantile paralysis isn't its real name. When we're among ourselves we call it by its proper name, which is poliomyelitis. That's been its name since 1880, but it's a bit of a mouthful, even when we

7

doctors call it polio for short. And it means nothing to the layman, two Greek words meaning "grey" and "marrow", so we've given it an easier name, infantile paralysis, which at least is English.'

I didn't take in all he said, but I learned something. And I felt anger and bitterness. I jumped out of the car with a polite 'Thank you, sir', but when I went in, I kicked our gate shut with a burst of temper. How could they do this to Clare, who loved to play games? Father shook his head sympathetically, but said, 'Temper, Kit, never did anyone any good.'

Clare never fully recovered. She had to wear a brace for many years before she was well enough to walk with two sticks, and I still carry in my mind the picture of her trying to walk around the room and on the landing, hobbling in her iron braces. When she got back into bed I used to cry 'Poor Clare!' and almost burst into tears as I hugged her.

'Don't worry, I'm going to get well,' she said spryly. 'Dr Allott has promised me I will.'

'Well, I'm going to see that this sort of thing never happens again,' I said.

'You are?' She managed a smile. 'How?'

'I'm going to become a doctor. A famous one. And I'm going to find out how to cure polio.'

Though I was only sixteen, it was a decision from which I never wavered. I was at Nottingham Grammar School, I always came top in science, and literature, and I loved reading and learning, which I knew would be vital to become a doctor. Perhaps it was one of those impetuous decisions that were always earning me reproaches, but it was also a logical step because of my interests. And it delighted my father. Apart from other considerations, he – and specially Mother – believed that my becoming a doctor would be a step up the social ladder. Dr Allott advised me to be entered for Wadham, Oxford's 'medical' college, and I arrived there when I was eighteen.

The trouble with Oxford, as Bernard Shaw has written, is that it is the only place where you can both have your cake and eat it. I loved the cake and ate it all. The university opened up for me a freedom I never knew existed. From one friend I learned to appreciate classical music played on his HMV portable. Many of the records – 'pinched' from or discarded by his musical family – were scratched and worn, but it was Music with a capital 'M' and the first time I heard the Chopin first piano concerto, we nearly had a fight because I insisted on playing it right through four times. Another friend was equally enthusiastic about a new kind of 'pop' music, the lilting sound of Hawaiian guitars. A third introduced me to the delights of the art world, which meant cheap day-trips to London to browse for hours in the Tate or the National Gallery. All these were treasures unrevealed to me by my doting father who was more concerned with induction coils. And I was fortunate in that I had friends – musical and artistic – who knew so much more about these subjects than I did, and enjoyed sharing their knowledge with me. They were two loves which never deserted me.

With equal excitement I entered into the sports side of Oxford. Perhaps because I was hot-tempered at times, I became what used to be called a 'natural' as a boxer. Bashing one of my peers in the ring released a kind of spring inside me. I didn't enjoy hurting friends, but each blow did in some way help me to cope with a temper. And in the end, to my father's real pride, I got a Blue.

But one thing was niggling away at my conscience (for want of a better word). I was enjoying Oxford so much that I sometimes forgot that moment in Clare's bedroom when I made my decision about my future vocation. I wasn't doing anything to speed up my role as a would-be doctor, so during my last year at Oxford, where I had planned to stay for three years before going to London for the real hard medical training, I arranged (again through Dr Allott) to spend my final long vac helping out as a general dogsbody at the National Hospital for Nervous Diseases in Queen Square, central London, where there was a special unit investigating Heine-Medin's disease, the original name for polio, and – especially in the 1930s – doing research into the spinal aspects. The team was led by a remarkable man, Dr Harvey Cushing.

It took me only a few weeks to realise that the medical world would never come to grips with polio until it could isolate the virus which caused it.

Finally I was enrolled at the Royal College of Physicians. My father paid for my digs in Paddington and gave me a pound a week pocket money, together with what he called 'travelling expenses' for my regular visit home (home and a good, square meal), and to spend some time with Clare who was fifteen and slowly, very slowly, improving.

Usually, to please Father, I would also go on a quick visit to one of his shops and sometimes I wondered if they were doing as well as he pretended. Trade seemed slack. The Depression didn't help. But he shrugged off falling receipts. 'It'll pick up,' he said.

I didn't give the matter much thought, specially when Clare remarked that same evening that she had heard Father tell Mother, 'Don't worry. We can weather this bad period.'

And, of course, when you are young, you are always looking forward, and I had all the answers ready when Clare asked me, 'But what about your plans?'

'Well, Father's promised to buy me a small practice when I'm qualified, which will be in a few months. Of course, I'll have to do an internship first, then a stint as a registrar before I can even think of looking around for a practice of my own.'

'But that's wonderful. It'd make you happy.'

'Everyone likes to be his own boss. That's always been one of Father's maxims. And, of course, a practice of my own – maybe somewhere in the East End of London to start with.'

'Why not in Nottingham? Why the East End of London?'

'Cheapest,' I laughed. 'I want to stay in London, because

only then will I get the chance to do some research into polio, like I did during that long vac.'

We were all so busy making plans, living dreams, that somehow Clare and I – and perhaps Mother too – were blinded to the truth, so evident around us: the unemployment figures, the era of mass production, a new industrial revolution in which machines did the work of thousands of men; even the fact that 'wireless' was no longer a novelty. Wireless had become radio – an item of furniture, often bought in a big store together with a fridge. We never noticed it during the time it took for me to qualify and start work as an intern at St Andrew's in Marylebone. The first warnings of impending disaster arrived in a letter from Clare who wrote, 'Poor Father is feeling very down, he's had to close the Mansfield shop'.

By the time I had been an intern for a few more months, doing my rounds in my white coat with stethoscope dangling round my neck (and feeling very important), Father had had to close down the second branch, leaving – for the time being – only the original shop which he had opened near the Market Place where the annual Goose Fair was held.

I went up for a weekend. Father was very quiet, Mother was dejected beyond words. She had never been a snob in the unpleasant sense of the word, but she *had* always set great store by Father's material success, and later by my having been to Oxford and then on my becoming a doctor. Now the world seemed to be crumbling around us – her world especially.

'I don't see how we can carry on much longer,' Father admitted to me. 'It's the end of an adventure that I thought would last for ever. Thank God *you're* qualified. If this had happened a few years earlier – '

'But if you do close the whole business down,' I asked, 'how . . . what will you do for money?'

He gave a wry smile. 'It's a funny world,' he said. 'Financially I won't be too badly off. I can realise my stock

11

and pay twenty bob in the pound if I go into voluntary liquidation now, before Masters of Notts gets deeper into trouble. And I've already been offered a job as buyer for a group of chain stores which have each got a radio department. It won't pay as much, but we won't starve. But it's the nasty business of disposing of stock, and having to fire men who've been with me for years. I can do nothing to help except give them good references and a few quid to tide them over. But,' with one last sigh and a brave smile, 'there's nothing quite like being your own boss. Thank God you'll be your own boss as a doctor.'

A few weeks later Masters of Notts went into voluntary liquidation, paying twenty shillings in the pound as Father had said they would.

In a way the actual liquidation brought with it a curious sense of relief. The prospect had been hanging over us for so many months that once Father ceased trading, it was as though the weight of worry was lifted. But Father's new life did have a few problems. The promised job with the chain stores was cancelled at the last moment 'due to the Depression', the standard excuse. Father had to draw on his modest savings. He applied for job after job, unsuccessfully, for weeks: he was in his early fifties, and this was the era of 'too old at forty', let alone fifty. We had to move from Renishaw Road to a smaller house in Thorne Road at the other end of Nottingham, a move dictated by financial considerations, but which in a way pleased Mother as it helped to distance her from her old set of friends. In the end Father landed a job that wasn't too bad, working as a technical engineer for Marconi's, whose goods he had bought for so many years.

There was no money left over for me to live in any 'style'. But I moved into cheaper digs near the hospital and did manage to keep the second-hand Austin Seven I had bought five years previously.

But slices of bad luck never come singly. And when I recall the shattering consequences of what happened one night a month or so later, I think of Hamlet, saying 'When sorrows come, they come not single spies, But in battalions.'

I had no premonition of disaster when I was sent off to answer a call from a Mrs Dunston.

I looked up her address on our hospital street map in the reception room – Rockingham Gardens, just behind the Elephant and Castle; and it was a hell of a drive across London, on streets glistening after a day when heavy rain had hardly stopped. The local doctor had sent for St Andrew's (hardly expecting me) because the patient had been bringing up blood, and St Andrew's had a specialist unit dealing with internal bleeding. I was no expert, but I would know enough to make a preliminary diagnosis and summon an ambulance if I had to arrange for her to be taken into hospital.

In fact, there was nothing really wrong with her, and I did what I could to soothe her. She had been spitting blood after a bad bout of coughing, but one look at the sputum told me it was clean blood. She had probably broken a tiny blood vessel in the lung area and it was bleeding, but not seriously. All the same, heavy coughing always meant the possibility of water on the lungs which in turn could lead to pneumonia, so I gave her an injection of vitamin K, to thicken the blood, a sleeping pill, some linctus which contained a tiny amount of morphine, and also told her, 'Take one of these pills every morning for a week.' They were diuretic pills to encourage patients to get rid of excess water quickly. 'And if you don't feel any better in a couple of days – if the bleeding doesn't stop when you cough – let us know.'

I set off back to the hospital – not in the best of tempers after a foul drive in filthy weather – and it was on the way home, as the wet lamps marched towards me, that it happened. I was driving through the warren of small, mean, shop-lined streets towards St George's Circus where Lambeth Road meets Blackfriars Road, leading to the bridge.

In one small street – later to be identified as Keyworth

13

Street – I saw what seemed to be a fight ahead of me outside a shop.

My first instinct was to back the car and find a different way round, but then in the headlights I saw that three or four men were all dressed in black shirts. And they were attacking one man, while a woman, presumably his wife or daughter, was crying by the side of the street.

I knew immediately who they were – Oswald Mosley's Blackshirts, indulging in their favourite pastime of Jew-baiting.

I still hadn't actually thought of doing anything until the woman ran towards me and cried, 'Help, please. They're going to kill my father.'

'You run for help,' I cried. 'There's always some police by the Circus,' I knew they were there because of the Jewish population around the area – and the frequent Mosley British Fascist parades.

She ran off. I jumped out of the car, still not knowing quite how to argue with those toughs a bare twenty yards away, until I arrived; but the sickening sight settled my course of action.

Instinctively I had carried with me my heavy medical case; perhaps I might need it. But then I saw the victim. He was old, bent, bearded, and one man was holding him back while the other two kicked and thumped him.

Without a second's thought I swung my medical case straight into the face of one of the thumpers. The case burst open, the contents flying all over the place, and with a cry of astonishment the man fell, his face bleeding.

The other man turned with a snarl to attack me, while the third grabbed the Jew.

I had dropped my bag as I hit the first man, but that didn't matter. With my boxing Blue, I wasn't afraid of a thug. As he tried to grab me, I feinted, slipped back to make him follow me, knowing he would think I was afraid, and then I let him have a classic straight left that hit him on the point of the jaw. He fell on to the pavement, out like a light. And as I started to go for the third man, I heard the sound of police whistles, and then two policemen arrived with the woman, and the third thug ran for it. The old man had sunk to his knees, so, ignoring the Blackshirt on the pavement, I tried to rescue what I could from my medicine case and give him some first aid. I laid him further along on the pavement, under his broken and smashed shop front, which proclaimed his trade: Rabinowitz Tailors.

The shop owner wasn't too badly hurt and as the policemen arrived and asked me, 'You all right, sir?' I replied, 'Thank you, Officer. I'm a doctor. I was driving past and tried to stop this poor devil getting beaten up. I hit this man in the face.'

'And this one here?' asked the policeman.

'I gave him a straight left. He'll come round soon. Thanks for coming to my help. If you get a basin of water from the old man's shop and pour it over the man, it'll help.'

I prepared to collect the rest of my medicines and make for the hospital, when the policeman said to me, 'Excuse me, sir. Don't you think you'd better take a look at this fellow you knocked out? His 'ead's hanging in a funny sort of way.'

It was the first time I had taken a close look at him. I lifted his head gently with my right hand – and felt the hot, sticky blood covering the back of his skull. I knew instinctively what had happened. As I hit him he must have fallen and hit the back of his head on the edge of the sharp pavement. With the help of one of the policemen I turned the man over. The back of his head was split wide open. I didn't need any further examination to know that the man was dead.

'Better send for an ambulance,' I said heavily, taking in the scene as I wondered what to do next. It had started to rain again, not heavily but miserably. A few yards away, sitting on the pavement, was the thug whose face I had hit; he was shouting, 'You killed him, you bastard!' The other policeman was helping the man and his daughter into their shop. On the left lay a corpse. And facing me was a thoughtful policeman.

'I'll have to report it to the station, doctor,' he started.

'Of course you must,' I said. 'It was an accident, but you must do your duty.' I gave him all the particulars he needed – my name, address, the hospital where I worked, and the number of my Austin Seven.

'Let's hope for the best, sir,' he said. 'As far as I'm concerned, I'd like to see all these bleeding fascists dead. But – '

'Don't worry,' I said more cheerfully than I felt. 'Can I go now, Officer, while you summon the ambulance? Or can I help you?'

'Thank you, sir. Don't worry. The station's only five minutes away along Waterloo Road.' And turning to his colleague he said, 'Charley, keep an eye on these buggers while I nip round to the station.'

'Do you think I could go now? I'm only anxious that the hospital might wonder what's happened to me.'

'I don't see why not. We know what's happened. I'm afraid someone from Waterloo Road Station will contact you. They'll want you to make a statement. After all, a man has died, sir.'

'Of course.' Then, at last I went. And the next morning told the hospital authorities in full exactly what had happened.

Three days later I made a statement. The police were very sympathetic, but as the inspector in charge told me, 'I'll have to hand over the papers to the Director of Public Prosecutions – or one of his staff. To decide what action to take, whether to charge you.'

'You think they might?' I was only asking for confirmation of what I expected. They would have to charge me with manslaughter.

'I'm afraid so, Doctor. It's a bit of bad luck for you, getting entangled with a group of bastards, and if it's any comfort to you, I'll lay a pound to a penny that you'll go free if there's a trial.'

'That's some consolation,' I said wryly. 'But it's the publicity that worries me. You know what stuffed shirts the medical profession are. Especially the older doctors.'

'We'll do everything to keep it out of the press,' he promised me.

But no one could. Even before I was charged, one of the evening papers – there were three in London then, the *Standard*, the *News* and the *Star* – had a front-page headline: BLACKSHIRT DIES IN FIGHT WITH MYSTERY DOCTOR.

No name was mentioned at the time, and ten days later I was formally charged with manslaughter. The case was adjourned for ten days, and I was allowed bail, but the hospital governors thought it best for me to be suspended on full pay until after the inquest had been held. So after giving details of my 'movements' to the police, I drove up to Nottingham to spend a few days with the family.

Even that provided little consolation. Over the years we had become so attached to Renishaw Road that our new, smaller house in Thorne Road seemed cold and indifferent to our worries. The only good news to offset my 'disgrace' was that Father had proved such a success at Marconi's that he had been appointed an assistant manager in the research department dealing with radio materials. It did his ego a power of good.

'All the same,' he sighed, 'you're so impetuous, Kit! How often have I begged you to keep that temper of yours in check. You're so impulsive.'

'I think he was brave to do what he did.' Clare stood up for me. 'You're a hero.'

'Not to Mother,' I said sadly, for she was taking the 'disgrace' very badly. 'After all,' she said, 'you didn't have to help. The police station was only five minutes away.'

On the other hand, the inspector's belief that I would never be punished proved only too true when I returned to London and the inquest was held.

The evidence that it was an accident brought about by bullies was overwhelming, especially at a time when 9 out of 10 Britons were engulfed in a tide of hate for Hitler's British Mosley stooges.

But what really made it impossible for anyone to convict me was when, to my astonishment, a frail, bent old man appeared in the witness box. At first I didn't know who the bearded man was for (as I realise now) I had been too busy participating to see. But this was dear old Mr Rabinowitz himself, spruced up, a new suit, who told in a quavering voice how this perfect stranger had come to his aid after the Blackshirts had smashed open his tailor's shop.

'Sir,' he said to the court, 'I would be a dead man by now if it had not been for this gentleman.'

Added to that, the policeman gave evidence, mentioning my concern, and also adding that 'It was a clean-cut blow to the jaw, sir, as you would expect from a man who got an Oxford Blue for boxing.'

I was found Not Guilty.

That was fine, but I had not reckoned with the excitement the case aroused in the popular press. They seized on every detail of the evidence and plastered them over their front pages.

Clare, walking with a stick now, though still in braces, had come to London to lend me moral support – Father, of course, couldn't just leave his job at will. And it was she who brought me the first evening paper.

'Oh God!' I groaned over coffee at Lyons' tea shop. 'That's ruined me!'

'Ruined you!' Her eyes were sparkling. 'You're a hero!'

'Not to the hospital.' I managed a smile as I read the page-one story: OXFORD BLUE BEATS MOSLEY THUG SAVES LIFE OF JEWISH VICTIM.

And underneath the story started: Gallant young Dr Kit Masters, Oxford Boxing Blue, beat off a gang of three Blackshirts when he found them attacking an old man who ran a tailor's shop. He hit one so hard that he later died, and

18

injured another so badly that he is still in hospital. The victim he helped said he owed his life to . . . and there was more of the same.

'They'll fire me for this.' I paid the fourpence for two coffees, and after I had seen Clare to her train back home, went to St Andrew's to make a few notes of plans to defend myself, for I knew it would not be long before I faced a new 'trial' – by the hospital's board of governors.

Two days later I was summoned to appear before them. I had never met the head of governors, Dr Arnold Barton, though I had seen him at several functions, a thin, tall, stern-faced, lantern-jawed streak of a man who rarely seemed to smile. After I had been kept waiting for a few moments in an ante-room, I was ushered into the main boardroom where Dr Barton and six colleagues were seated around a long, rectangular, polished table. One chair at the bottom of the table was empty, and as I came in Dr Barton, with hardly more than a nod in my direction, indicated the chair and said sternly, 'You may sit, Doctor Masters, while we ask you a few questions.'

I sat without a word.

'Though I appreciate your bravery in going to aid an old man,' Barton began, 'the medical profession cannot countenance the kind of newspaper scandal and unsavoury publicity that you have brought to St Andrew's.'

'But, sir,' I protested almost angrily. 'You wouldn't want me to let an old man get beaten up and do nothing.'

'Why didn't you call the police instead of getting mixed up in such an event?' one of the governors asked.

'Because I didn't know where the police station was,' I retorted. It seemed so unfair to have faced one trial to prove my innocence, and now to face a kind of drumhead court martial as though I were guilty.

'Sir,' I addressed Dr Barton. 'I have had my trial. I have been declared innocent. Just as there can't be one law for the rich, one for the poor, there can't be one law for men, one for doctors. It's not fair, sir.'

For a moment the expression of the stern-faced Dr

Barton softened and he said more gently, 'I'm afraid you are wrong, Doctor. There *are* two sets of laws. You have proved your innocence, and you are not on trial to prove that again. What is at stake here is not innocence of a crime, but your *reputation*, and by a medical, not a legal tribunal.'

Another member of the panel added, 'We have nothing but admiration for the way you tackled those thugs, Doctor. But please remember what Doctor Barton has pointed out – you are not being judged twice for the same crime. There are two different problems, and we all know that in order to gain the confidence of patients, every doctor has to be *seen* to behave in an impeccable manner. The medical profession is guarded by the confidence of its patients.'

'And in this case,' said Dr Barton, 'you struck a man with such force that he was killed.'

'He slipped. The court accepted that.'

'He died, and as a direct result of your intervention.'

For another hour the inquisition continued, almost, I felt, as though the 'judges' were scraping for any dirt they could find. One member asked for details of how my father had gone into voluntary liquidation. On the other hand, one did try to come to my aid.

'Aren't you the young man who spent some weeks with the research unit at the National Hospital for Nervous Diseases?'

'Yes sir, I did.'

'I thought I remembered your face,' he said.

'Why did you do this?' asked Dr Barton. I was able to explain my interest in helping with polio following Clare's illness.

'I see,' said Dr Barton. 'That will be all, thank you. Will you wait in the ante-room while the governors discuss your case.'

I knew the answer before I was recalled twenty minutes later, and Dr Barton pronounced judgment.

'It is the considered opinion of the board of governors,' he said, 'that in the interests of the good name of the medical profession, and' – he gave a diplomatic cough – 'of St Andrew's, it would be much easier for all concerned if you were to resign.'

'And leave medicine!' I cried.

'Please moderate your voice, Doctor,' the chairman rebuked me.

'But, sir,' I begged. 'The only thing I want in life is to be a doctor.'

'You *are* a doctor,' he said. 'You are free to practise anywhere – only not here.'

'It's grossly unfair,' I insisted. 'Why should I be penalised for helping someone in trouble? Isn't it part of a doctor's work to help the sick?'

'It is *not* part of a doctor's work to become involved in brawls,' he said firmly.

The verdict was delivered with such casual brutality that I flushed with the shame of it – being kicked out like a clerk caught pinching pennies from the till. I was about to shout those very words out when, for once in my impetuous life, Dr Barton prevented me, for as the other members of the board filed out, he said, 'Doctor Masters. Will you remain behind, please? I would like to talk to you for a minute or two.'

Sulkily, and seething inside, I remained.

'Now, sit in this chair next to me,' he said, and with a sudden change of tone and manner, said, 'You must not blame us for keeping up such high standards of public behaviour. And I want to help you if I can.'

Somewhat mollified, I remained silently waiting for him to talk. What could he do – what could *anyone* do – when a doctor was blamed for something of which he was not guilty?

'I know how you feel,' he said. 'But I was particularly interested in one thing: the interest you have shown in the treatment of polio. And the extra-curricular work you did when you were a medical student. Tell me, have you ever heard of a place called Koraloona?'

Slightly bewildered, I said that I hadn't.

21

'I didn't imagine you had. It's a small island, barely twenty miles long, one of the seven South Sea islands in the Moto Varu archipelago. Moto Varu, by the way, is Polynesian for seven islands.'

'But what has this to do with me?' I asked, still feeling bitter.

'There's a vacancy for an assistant doctor there. Appointments are in the hands of the St Stephen Sisters of Mercy Mission which operates in the South Seas.' He coughed. 'I happen to be chairman of the medical panel.'

I had never thought about the South Seas, beyond the instinctive yearning to escape the treadmill of an office desk, the clanking trams, the yellow fog, the rain. And even now I really didn't want to go. I wanted to succeed in a normal way.

'There's one thing I haven't told you.' Dr Barton judged his words carefully. 'It's a beautiful place, a real tropical island, but it has a drawback. It has regular outbreaks, for which we can find no reason, of one particular disease. That disease is polio.'

My mouth must have dropped open.

'You see, Doctor Masters,' he continued, 'we have been placed in a difficult position, but that is no reflection on your qualities as a good doctor. And I became interested when I heard of *your* interest in polio. In return for your resignation, I am offering you the opportunity to study a dreadful disease in a living laboratory. You'll never get another chance like it – if you really mean what you say.'

'How would I – well, get there? And when would I leave?' An inner excitement gripped me as I saw in my mind's eye an image of Clare trying to hobble round her bedroom.

'By ship to Australia, and then the authorities will arrange your passage by schooner to the islands. I'll cable if you accept and you can sail in about a month.'

2

Normally a twice-monthly passenger and cargo ship, the *Island Princess*, sailed from Sydney to Tahiti, calling on the way at Sanderstown, the capital of the Moto Varu archipelago, and also on the return voyage to Australia. From Sanderstown a local vessel would take me to Koraloona.

As it happened, I was given an alternative. The Australian representative of the Mission, who drove me to the Southern Cross Hotel in Sydney, explained that the *Mantela*, a Sanderstown boat of 5,000 tons which normally plied between the islands, had just finished a refit in Sydney and was about to sail two days after my arrival. I jumped at the opportunity of travelling on her. I was fed up after weeks of playing deck quoits and shuffleboard, and the *Mantela* appeared to be the perfect introduction to the South Seas for, instead of going straight to Sanderstown, she would call at Rarotonga, and spend a day or two there, so I would be able to fit in a visit to another island and see something of it at a leisurely pace.

I knew nothing really about the behind-the-scenes activities of missions working in remote islands, but the Australian representative, Brian Parker, explained that he worked for several missions of different denominations, arranging facilities, transfer of funds, booking hotels for newcomers and whatever might be needed. He was a short, precise man with a small moustache which reminded me a little of Hitler's, but he had none of the German leader's belligerence. He couldn't do enough to help.

He laughed when I asked him if he was a clergyman. 'I'm just a businessman,' he said. 'My experience of Christian missions has proved that they may be very good at saving

23

souls, or bodies if they're medical missions, but for the most part they're not very good at business. I just run local affairs for a dozen or so missions.'

'But is there much business to attend to?'

'I'm also in the import-export business. But in answer to your question, yes. For example, I've received a request from the doctor on Koraloona for a large parcel of drugs. It's much easier for me to centralise all requests, arrange the shipping – or, in this case, give them to you to take to the island. You'll like the *Mantela*. You'll be sailing under Captain Robins and you'll like him too.'

I did, from the moment we met, almost as soon as the first throb of the *Mantela*'s engines announced that we were on our way.

Captain Robins was a Yorkshireman in his fifties who had long since lost his accent amidst the welter of a dozen dialects. He was a tall man with a craggy, rubbery face which twisted and turned, often into a sardonic grin. He had a mop of grey hair and, under it, steady grey eyes.

The *Mantela*, which had berths for six passengers in moderately comfortable cabins, boasted no luxuries like private bathrooms or toilets. But the saloon, where we ate, as well as drank our apéritifs, was spick and span, and shone with the polished mahogany and brass of a house-proud owner.

She might not have been as glamorous as the great vessels loaded with equally glamorous cargo, but she was just as important in her own way. Not especially gracious, but squat and workmanlike, plodding with tenacity from port to port. The *Mantela* was an honest ship, with no frills, but ready to take on all comers. Besides myself there were three other passengers, but they all disembarked at Raro-tonga, and after that, for the three days at sea before we reached Koraloona, Robins and I were more or less on our own. The first mate and the ship's engineer took their meals at different times, and did not use the saloon as a sitting-room.

Occasionally I would join Robins on the bridge; at other

times, when all was going well, he would come into the saloon to join me in a drink served by a Cockney steward called Tomkins; the choice was limited, but I didn't drink much anyway.

'Ever try this after dinner?' He pointed to a bottle of Crème de Menthe. 'Best after-dinner drink in the world,' he pronounced, 'I call it Sticky Green.'

When I shook my head, he said, 'I suppose it's not a young man's drink. But it does wonders for dyspepsia.'

'An expensive kind of medicine,' I said. 'I can give you something that doesn't cost a quarter of that.'

'Mebbe, but don't forget I get my drinks duty free.'

After Tomkins had served the second glass, Robins looked at me almost quizzically, and said, 'I've seen a few doctors come and go in the islands, but you don't seem to fit into the usual pattern.'

'Too young?'

He searched for the word he wanted then said, with a grin, 'Too posh!'

'That I'm not,' I laughed.

'No insult intended. But you'll find your new boss, Alec Reid, a very different proposition. He's a real character. He certainly fits into Koraloona. A made-to-measure Scotsman.'

'Not even posh?'

'In one way, yes.' He didn't rise to my teasing. 'He's a good doctor, and he's in love with the island. He'll never leave it.'

'Is it that beautiful?'

'You'll see for yourself before long. In the meantime, while I check on the bridge, read this, I brought it down from my cabin to show you. It's the cheapest adventure story in the world, and it'll tell you more about Koraloona than I can ever put into words. I'll be back in an hour, then we'll have a final Sticky Green. What say?'

Captain Robins left the saloon, I peeled a couple of the red bananas that grow wild on the islands – my dessert – and picked up the book. It was a tattered copy of *Sailing Directions*.

KORALOONA, eighteen miles long, eleven miles wide, is one of the smaller islands in the Moto Varu (Seven Islands) archipelago, of which Sanders Island is the largest (pop. 94,000). The capital is Sanderstown which contains a major British naval base. Koraloona is 130 miles west of Sanders Island and is dangerous to shipping because it is encircled by a coral reef at times fifty miles long, marked on all Admiralty charts. Two passages through the reef, both navigable for vessels up to 5,000 tons. Main town of Koraloona is Anani. Smaller town to east is Tala-Tala. Several small villages, unnamed. Regular vessels bring supplies from either Sanders Island or Apia, Pago Pago or Rarotonga. Abundant water supplies, fruit, vegetables, staples, fish plentiful. *Note:* The Lords Commissioners of the Admiralty feel that pilots should advise would-be visitors that Koraloona has only one small hospital and one doctor.

In that respect their Lordships were wrong; by the time the *Mantela* docked Koraloona would have gained, at the ripe old age of twenty-four years, four months and seven days, their first assistant medical officer.

There is something about the sea that invites the exchange of confidences. You meet perfect strangers, listen politely to their life stories and then, when they cock an inquisitive ear, you need no encouragement to answer their unspoken questions. On land it can take years for two people to become close friends, yet at sea the years are telescoped into hours.

Maybe the huge wilderness of the sea helps. A man feels so insignificant against its vastness that confidences no longer seem something to keep to oneself. And, of course, in most cases you know you never will meet again. With Captain Bill Robins, though, it was rather different. He told me that he called regularly at Koraloona, and that I probably would run across him from time to time. In my case it was also different, for though I had done no criminal act I had by force of circumstance set sail for Koraloona to build a new life there.

True, Bill Robins had started the confidences. Perhaps because he spent so much of his time alone, he told me all about his wife, his two children, the home they had bought in Sanderstown, how long he had been married, where the children went to school – all the details of life in a town of about 60,000 people. Especially on the second night, I had the feeling that he *wanted* to talk, and what made it the more interesting was the variety of his experiences and the mature way in which he alluded to them. He was a man of books as well as of the sea, and knew his history as well as his geography.

Leaning forward in the rattan chair, on the after deck, he said, 'I tell you, Doctor' – he always addressed me thus, showing the respect of one professional man for another – 'in over thirty years at sea I've become a specialist in islands. Funny lot, the people on 'em. There's the Andamans, where they never talk, just converse entirely in song – a sort of chant. It's like being in a permanent opera! And Zanzibar – now there's a place. That's where the Arabs prohibited the import of jasmine because the scent depresses the men and excites the women. And once I spent three weeks on Thursday Island. Lived on one of the world's most expensive delicacies – turtle. I never want to see turtle soup again as long as I live.'

'You've talked about several islands,' I said, 'but there's one thing I can't get straight.'

'What's that?'

'My bearings. The Moto Varu group. How big are they? How far is one from the next?'

'Come into my cabin and I'll show you. The *Mantela* doesn't boast a chart room so we may be a bit cramped.'

His room was indeed tiny, all brass and mahogany, a bunk bed with a red blanket on it, a wash basin that folded away, a desk. There was little else, except a small bookshelf from which he took one of several charts.

Spreading it on the desk, he showed where we were, steaming due north from Rarotonga.

'Of course, all the islands are volcanic in the sense that they've been thrown up from the depths by submarine upheavals thousands of years ago; but only one of them's got a crater. We'll come to that in a minute. First and most important is Sanders Island, to the east of Koraloona,' he explained, pointing. 'As you've read, the population is around sixty thousand in Sanderstown itself. It's a city. Flourishing. Aided by the naval base, of course. The island's got five towns as well as the capital.'

'And Koraloona's – what? About a hundred miles to the west?'

'Give or take a few sandbanks. But I won't dwell on her. You'll learn all about the island in half an hour once you're there.'

He pointed again to the chart. 'Almost due north of Koraloona is Hodges Island, named after the painter who accompanied Captain Cook on his second voyage, then went on to paint India for Warren Hastings. It's only thirty miles away, but there's no direct method of getting there because of the reef. You've got to sail south, then half way round the reef. As a result, nobody ever goes there. Anyway, it consists of one enormous coconut plantation to make copra – from which you get coconut oil. It stretches for nearly fifty miles, and the entire population cultivates copra. Stinks to high heaven. I don't land there unless I have to. The copra company has its own ship.'

He showed me a speck on the map to the left of Hodges and said that it was named Banks Island, after Cook's naturalist friend. 'There's already one Banks Island just north of Australia, but Cook must have liked him to name another after him.'

'And inside the huge lagoon of Koraloona?'

'There you have an oddity. It's called Penal Island, thirty miles from Koraloona. A launch calls there regularly. The name tells you everything. It was founded, so to speak, as a sort of Devil's Island – but not so tough: you can't be tough in the South Seas. But trouble-makers in the old days used to be left there until they died. Always plenty to eat. There are few prisoners that I know of, and a hundred people live there, including two or three who are official security guards. Cushy job, if you ask me.'

'That's five.'

'Only two left, and they're simple. High Island isn't far away, inside the lagoon to the west of Koraloona, and is uninhabited. That's the dormant volcano. Low Island – thirty or forty miles long and near High Island – is the richest. Centuries ago the birds themselves chose Low Island as a sanctuary and the droppings over the years made it rich in guano – a fertiliser. Ten years ago a New Zealand company was given a licence to dig it out. The five hundred locals who live there are better off than any of us, because they get a percentage of the profits.' His rubbery face twisted into an unpleasant sniff, as he added, 'I wouldn't recommend it for a honeymoon. The smell is terrible. I've only been once. Never again.'

'But that, I take it, doesn't apply to Koraloona?' I was laughing, but I sensed his sudden excitement.

'You'll find it's like Paradise, or the Garden of Eden,' he said. 'As though it's just been created and hasn't had a chance to get fouled up with so-called "civilisation". I've read my Homer in my time, as no doubt you have, Doctor. And I always remember the Lotus-land in *The Odyssey* where everybody lives in ease and luxury – though not the luxury we Europeans think of as such. That's just material. The luxury in Koraloona is of *contentment*.' He paused and leaned forward again. 'It's something to do with metabolism – eh?'

I doubted it. I expected the Polynesians there to be just as subject to the ailments of the flesh as anywhere else in the world – especially polio – otherwise what would they need a doctor for? But I knew what Robins meant. Somehow time, which in the Europe I had left was always being talked about as 'of the essence', seemed of no account in this part of the world.

One remark he made puzzled me.

'Why did you say I was too posh?' I asked.

'Did I? Must have slipped out. When I was a kid, in Hull, my father and mother took me to Hessle to have tea with his boss, and I remember Mother telling me that she had stayed up half the night making me a new sailor suit and saying, "Behave yourself, Bill. Remember these are posh people."'

'And did you behave?'

'Almost,' he grinned. 'But Mother went scarlet when the boss's wife told me what a nice suit I was wearing, and I told her that Mother had spent nearly all night making it.'

It was very quiet that evening, the steady rhythm of the ship's engines interrupted only by the occasional guttural cry from the deck above. The sea was flat, faintly streaked by a waning moon, and through the porthole of the saloon I could see the Southern Cross and the Milky Way, unblemished by cloud.

The peace and tranquillity of the moment stirred all kinds of memories. I was thinking of Robins' house and then my own before I left home; his mother making a sailor suit, my mother forever – in retrospect, anyway – making patchwork quilts. I suppose that at that moment, the night before I stepped ashore to build a new life, it was time to say goodbye to the old.

Robins interrupted my thoughts by saying, 'Sorry about the word "posh", but I'd heard before we left Sanderstown the last time that a young man had been appointed assistant to Doctor Reid, and I was a bit surprised when I met you. My first impression was that you'd be more at home putting up a brass plate in Harley Street.'

'That was exactly what I did intend to do. You must have a sixth sense,' I said. 'But plans have a habit of coming unstuck.'

It didn't take long to tell him my story. I spared no

details – there was no good reason why I should. It was not criminal to be impulsive; only foolish.

'Not always foolish,' he challenged me. 'It isn't foolish to be right, is it?'

I said nothing. After all, I was only twenty-four and Captain Robins was in his fifties. And though I did hold passionate beliefs, I was a bit young to express them all.

'We were talking about reading Homer,' he went on. 'I remember one line from the *Iliad*, "One principle is for the best, to fight in defence of one's country". That's what you were doing.' His rubbery face twisted into its familiar grin, 'Fighting fascism. Maybe it caused you a few problems, but you might be about to get your reward in heaven. No, I don't think you're going to die yet, rather a paradise on earth.'

'I'll drink to that,' I laughed. 'Yes, even half a glass of Sticky Green.'

'Talking of fascists' – Robins made sure his pipe was drawing well – 'are they going to drag us into a war?'

'I hope not. But it was touch and go at Munich. I'm no expert, but what worries me is that, when you're dealing with madmen, they increase their demands at the slightest sign of weakness.'

'No war would ever reach this part of the world,' said Robins, 'but I remember the last in Europe. And I still have relatives living in Hull. It wouldn't be fun being there, with zeppelins or whatever.'

Again I wondered at myself, only just into my twenties, debating the world with a man old enough to be my father.

'It may never come.'

'I'll drink to *that*!' It was Robins' turn to laugh. 'Just one final nightcap before I turn in.'

That was the last night. The following day, shortly after lunch, we sighted Koraloona on the horizon. At first all I could see was the hazy black outline of a jagged peak, little more than a shadow on the pallor of a dead calm sea, and then, as the air shimmered and danced and drew nearer, I could make out colours, mostly green. Finally I saw shapes of valleys, hills, crags, the white flash of waterfalls and then after Bill Robins lent me his binoculars, even houses, mostly thatched with palms or with roofs of red corrugated iron, the trademark of Polynesia, with the occasional roof of startling white.

'Coral,' explained Robins. 'Usually European. They're expensive but they collect pure rainfall, because coral never gets dirty.'

Within a couple of hours the silence that had wrapped the sea in peace was changed for a distant roar-like thunder.

'The reef,' Robins explained. 'We'll be okay as soon as we're through the passage.'

When we actually reached the reef, with calm water erupting into foaming waves twenty feet high as they hit the rocks, the *Mantela* bucked like a frightened horse, sank into a trough, reared up again, and then, as suddenly as it had started, the old tub was through the creamy foam of the passage and had settled into the lazy waters of the lagoon. The island was spread in front of me, outrigger canoes paddling towards us from the silver beaches lined with tall, bending palm trees and feathery casuarinas, while, behind, the green volcanic mountains rose until they seemed to meet the sky. In the distance I could see two flagstaffs, one with the Union Jack fluttering, the other with the blue flag and stars of New Zealand.

As we approached the ramshackle pier the *Mantela* stopped her engines, waited, then, as though changing gear, trembled into a slow approach. The crew threw out the lines, and those on the pier pulled the heavy ropes attached to them and made fast. I looked out and saw for the first time the main street of Koraloona's largest town, Anani: a dusty white strip of road, a long row of assorted shops, a few cars. One man was carrying a huge bunch of red bananas over one shoulder, another was driving a small open truck loaded with oranges.

At the far end of the beach a dozen kids were running

and splashing into the blue water without a care in the world. All except one, who hobbled after them, hampered by the club foot that is the hallmark of polio.

Apart from that one pitiful figure, the scene looked idyllic. I hoped it would live up to its promise.

3

As the gangplank of the *Mantela* was lowered, an extraordinary-looking man climbed on board. He wore a topee, the original colour of which was uncertain, it was so battered and stained with sweat; a bright red shirt; and a pair of khaki shorts held up with an old red and orange tie. Even I recognised it as being the flamboyant colours of the Marylebone Cricket Club. No socks covered his hairy legs, while on his feet he wore only sandals. He looked to be in his early-to-mid-fifties, and was running to fat, and when he took off his topee it was to wipe the sweat from a pink, bald head. I hadn't the faintest idea who he was, but he looked jolly.

Without hesitation he approached me, held out a hand, smiled and said with a touch of humour, 'Doctor Masters, I presume?'

I smiled in assent.

'I'm Doctor Reid. I wanted to be the first to welcome my new assistant to this benighted spot.'

'Benighted!'

Dr Reid wiped his sweating head. 'I'm known for my feeble sense of humour,' he laughed. 'I shouldn'a make jokes like that. I've put up with the place for nearly twenty years.'

Between shouts to the dock hands unloading my trunks he asked, 'You've got the drugs I cabled for?'

I nodded. They had been my constant care since Mr Parker had handed them to me. As we walked on to the jetty, I was watching carefully to make sure none of my trunks was left on board.

'We've got you a wee bungalow,' said Dr Reid, adding with a touch of pride, 'Two bedrooms.' I soon learned that in the islands a bungalow meant any house, large or small. 'But it might be better to spend a couple of nights with Mollie first.'

'Mollie?'

Laughing from the depths of his shaking frame, he explained, 'Mollie Green. But don't get any ideas. Mollie's nae for bedding. She keeps Green's Hotel – famous all over the Pacific. People who've never even been within a thousand miles of Koraloona have heard of Mollie Green's place.' He looked at my mountain of luggage.

'How much of your clobber will you need for your first two days?'

'This'll do.' I pointed to two suitcases.

'Right then. I'll send the rest to the bungalow, and when you've rested you can explore the town and,' with a sly chuckle, 'go on a shopping spree.'

I laughed politely, my mind mainly concerned with making sure that I would find all my belongings. The islanders in their shorts or sarongs didn't look 'professional'. The jetty was large but needed a lick of paint and its wooden supports were green with sea slime; it also lacked (to my inexperienced eye) any sense of efficiency. And the heat of the day, combined with a natural anxiety, made me sweat, though not as profusely as Dr Reid, who was continually wiping his pink, bald head.

It was true that the happy-go-lucky dockers, working for a few pennies every time a ship came in, were being watched carefully by Captain Robins on the bridge, but it all seemed rather haphazard, as though I would be lucky if I ever found all my trunks. I assumed they would all have been stowed in one corner of the hold and would reappear at the same time. It was something of a shock to see one Polynesian, his face a wide grin, trot down the gangplank carrying a sack of flour on his head and one of my suitcases in his right hand. On the other hand he did, once on the jetty, bend his knees carefully so that he could deposit my suitcase next to another item of my luggage before loping off somewhere else with the sack still on his head.

'Don't worry,' Dr Reid assured me. 'They've got enough method in their madness. Ah!' He spotted one crate. 'Yon'll be the drugs?' He indicated a large parcel and, as I nodded, said, 'I'll send them straight round to the dispensary.'

He gave orders in what I took to be the local dialect. I knew I would have to learn it quickly though, since Koraloona was connected with the Cook archipelago, most people spoke English.

'Shouldn't I keep the drugs?' I asked. 'In case they get lost or into the wrong hands? I could bring them round to you later.'

'Don't worry,' said Dr Reid. 'Nothing gets lost here. And everybody knows everything. They know all about you, where you're going to live. And I've already fixed up a local lass to come and clean up for you every day.'

At that moment Captain Robins, who had been busy shouting orders, hailed Reid. 'Afternoon, Doc. How's things?'

'Fine,' cried Reid. 'You staying at Green's for the night?' When Robins nodded, Reid added to me, 'Bill Robins is one of the best. I'm glad you won't be on your own for the first night. I'll walk you to the hotel and show you round the hospital tomorrow.'

I thanked him, and soon we were making our way along Anani's main street, from which lanes led to the houses in the foothills behind. What struck me immediately was the extraordinary background silence. Cries, laughter, all those, yes. But few motor cars, no big city life: instead, an almost uncanny, disconcerting stillness, the only constant sound the distant boom of waves on the reef. And was there – I could not be sure – a lilt of the Hawaiian music we used to listen to at Oxford, mingling with the waves?

The biggest – and busiest – building was the ship's chandler opposite the pier.

'Jim Wilson runs the place,' said Reid. 'Used to be an engineer in the RFC in the war, so he not only keeps the ship's stores, but knows everything about motor cars – and ma plane.'

'Captain Robins told me you flew a plane.'

'An old Gloster,' Reid said. 'She was once owned by a flying school, so she has dual controls. The flying school went bust. She's an ancient lass, I call her Nellie, but she can take me all the way to Sanderstown if I want a night out with bright lights. She takes off from a field behind the hospital. I had her shipped out from England as deck cargo.'

Not far from the ship's chandler was Mick's Bar, a local pub with green shutters and heavily protected doors.

'They're needed sometimes.' Reid saw me looking at the iron bars. 'There's some wild evenings there when the ships stay overnight. It's about the only crime we get here.' He pointed to the next building. 'Our local cinema. It's open every Friday.' A tattered bill advertised Tom Mix. 'And this is the general store. Come in for a moment and meet Mr and Mrs Johnson. They run the store. They've even got a telephone so you can open an account now, then phone each time you run out of anything.'

'Come on in, and park your bag by the door.' Reid put my other bag there and said, 'Nice day, Mrs Johnson.'

Mrs Johnson was a cheerful woman of enormous energy who was bustling around the shop, despite a pair of huge, heavy breasts which bulged beneath her dress. She was a local Polynesian girl, duskier than most, perhaps with a touch of true Samoan blood. Sitting on a rocking chair in an office at the back, smoking and sipping beer, was a weedy little man with decaying teeth, glimpses of gold fillings, heavily tattooed arms and a cigarette drooping permanently from a weak mouth. That was Mr Johnson. He had a shifty air – as well as an obvious aversion to work of any kind – and I didn't really take to him. But he was polite enough, and got up to greet me.

His 'office' was separated from the main store by a glass partition, and included a fridge with some glasses on top, and an ancient desk.

'Morning, Doc,' he cried. 'This your new assistant? Pleased to meet you, I'm sure.' He spoke with a Cockney accent and dropped aitches, oddly out of place on this paradise with its lilting voices that matched the gently waving palms. As we looked around the store, Reid explained to me, 'Johnson worked on a pearling lugger, stashed a bit of money away, looked around for the healthiest woman on the island, married her and set up shop. He's never done a stroke of work since.'

'Bit rough on her.' I watched her expertly snip off a length of trade cotton, then almost run to a shelf and move a fifty-pound sack of flour.

'Not on your life,' chuckled Reid. 'She's never had it so good. She's aye the envy of every other girl on the island. Overworked? She's even got a girl to help.'

Johnson's, I was soon to learn, was typical of other South Seas stores – more like a warehouse than a shop, with new lines that had just arrived by boat piled up against the shelves of the barn-like building. They seemed to sell everything from bolts of brightly coloured, imported cloth for making sarongs or Mother Hubbards – the island dress that hangs in a straight line from shoulder to ankle – to penknives and a large assortment of tools ranging from chisels to axes, from fishing lines and hooks to pots and pans. There were also large stocks of that old standby of the islands in the rainy season, primus stoves and tins of paraffin, even oilskins, repair outfits, and copper tubing.

The prices seemed more or less the same as those in London at the time I'd left – a box of matches or a bar of Cadbury's chocolate cost a penny. I saw Colman's mustard at twopence a tin. In one corner a modest selection of Penguin books cost 6d each, and nearby were cigarettes at the same price – a tanner for a packet of ten.

The range of everyday articles on the shelves reminded me abruptly of things at home, and I found myself thinking of my last night before leaving London. I spent those final few hours extravagantly, staying the night at the Strand Palace Hotel for ten shillings for bed, bathroom and a cooked breakfast thrown in, with sixpence extra for a haircut at the hotel barber shop – three times as much as the Underground fare of twopence from Paddington to Trafalgar Square, where a Nippy served me at Lyons' Corner House with a sirloin steak for a shilling.

Sitting in his office, Mr Johnson offered us both cold beers from a pail of water in which a few pieces of ice floated. We sipped them gratefully, but I must have been miles away, for Mr Johnson said, 'Daydreaming, eh?' As I said a smiling 'Sorry', he asked, 'Is there going to be a war in Europe, do you think?'

He was the second man in two days to ask me that.

'It doesn't look too good, Mr Johnson,' I said. 'After Munich I thought we'd saved the day. But now it's all bubbling up again.'

'Well, it won't affect us.' Johnson lit himself a fresh cigarette from the butt end of the one he was smoking. 'But it's a terrible thing if it comes. Blimey, that feller Hitler must be crazy.'

'All political figures are mad,' said Reid as he joined us on the veranda. And after we left and were walking into the street, he asked, 'Do *you* think there'll be a war?'

'Yes, I do,' I sighed. 'There's no way of stopping Hitler short of fighting him. If we don't, he'll overrun all Europe – probably England too.'

'You wouldna want to go back?' asked Reid.

'No.' I shook my head. 'I won't deny that if I were in London and war broke out I'd probably join up. But I've signed on as medical assistant with you. And somebody has to cure the sick here as well.'

'Well, you may lairn there's more to cure on the island than ye bargained for.'

I waited for him to go on, but Reid said nothing more and it left a moment of awkward silence between us.

In Main Street a healthy, smiling young man was striding by, effortlessly carrying, as though he hardly noticed it, two baskets of fruit, suspended at each tip of a bending bamboo arched across a shoulder. You could see his muscles ripple, for he was dressed only in a lava-lava, the traditional kind of Polynesian loin cloth. He must have come from the country for the lava-lava was rarely seen in the towns, however small.

He cried, 'Morning, Doc.' So did two or three naked kids playing on the strip of beach. Dr Reid gave them all a wave. The man with the baskets tried to kick a couple of scrawny hens out of his path and they fluttered towards the edge of the road. A dog lay down by the side of the building, its pink tongue lolling out with thirst. My medical eye noticed two things immediately: there were virtually no flies near the children playing on the beach; and the dog lying down was no scrawny, starving mongrel. It was well fed. A couple of elderly men walked past with the slow tread of dignified bishops, their naked footfalls almost silent on the hot dust of the road.

'Well, ye've seen the Harrods of Koraloona,' said Reid, nodding back in the direction of Johnson's. 'Let's take a look at the rest of Main Street.'

The side of the dusty street facing the sea was lined with houses all the way along from the pier, but it was difficult to know exactly why many of them were there. It had only taken a glance to recognise the ship's chandler, the site corroborated by the smell of tarred rope; the same with Mick's Bar and Johnson's store. A little further on there was a sign 'Lee Chong Hairdresser' and underneath the surprising information, 'Ears also pierced'.

Near it was a more imposing building with a sign proclaiming 'Pacific Island Steam Packet Company' and in smaller letters, 'Koraloona Branch Office. Manager, David Truefitt'.

A pink-washed, one-storey, stone building nestled near

to it, looking strangely out of place; it was a prettified building, which might have been transplanted from the South of France. I wasn't surprised when Alec Reid told me, 'It was built by a woman artist from New Zealand. It was her idea to come here each summer, but she hasn't been for three years now. She was of a certain age, so mebbe her painting days are over. It's used now by Mr and Mrs Gilbert. They're from the UK. Retired. Ye'll meet them.'

'It's a bit odd to live in Main Street,' I said. 'I'd have thought that, behind – ' I waved a hand towards the beginning of the volcanic hills.

'Aye, that's where all the nicest bungalows are. Behind Main Street. More space. Coconut groves and lots of flowers. That's where ye'll be living – near our hospital behind Hill Street which runs parallel to Main Street, but a wee bit up the hillside.'

Occasionally a space divided two buildings and then I caught a glimpse of attap huts, children playing, chickens scratching in the dust, pigs rooting, the vivid red of a flame tree, coconut and breadfruit trees, more what I expected than the pink-washed 'retirement bungalow'.

Next to it as we walked towards the end of the street was a two-storey white building, freshly painted, though the old sign was weathered, 'New Zealand Government. Cook Island Land Office'.

'Land?' I asked. 'Is it expensive?'

'Get along with ye!' replied Alec. 'Nobody buys land in Koraloona. Ye take what ye like as long as nobody else lives on it or uses it.'

I must have looked puzzled for Alex went on, 'Ye probably know that the Moto Varu archipelago is a Cook Island dependency.'

But, he explained, it was only a paternal relationship. Sanders Island was virtually independent and so were the other islands of the archipelago, providing they behaved themselves. Reid was convinced that the British Empire had given New Zealand the Cook Islands mandate because the Americans wanted it for their sphere of influence. 'So we kept it in the family,' he said.

'And this is their office?' I asked.

'Aye, but there's nae any real work to be done. They have a staff of three to help administer Koraloona. Ye'll be meeting Colonel Fawcett, ex-Royal Engineers, who's the head man, and his two assistants, Bill Shanks who runs the radio link, and Jack Haslam, general factotum – and the best tennis player on the island. They all live in the houses dotted on the hillside above Main Street.'

We had by now almost reached the end of Main Street, where a group of girls was washing laundry in a stone trough under the shade of two huge, ancient mango trees. They looked up, saw us and, waving to Reid, cried, 'Good morning, Doc!'

'Better be polite to them,' advised Reid. 'They'll be washing your smalls as soon as you settle in. Hulloa ladies!' he returned their greeting.

Taking off his topee, he wiped his head, looking almost comical in his shorts and sandals, but obviously all the Polynesians knew and liked him. There was a great deal of giggling and whispering as we passed by, and then Reid said, 'At last! Here's Green's Hotel.'

At first sight the outside of the hotel resembled a third-rate boarding house in a British resort; three storeys, the white paint flaking off the walls and window sills. I must have looked crestfallen, for Reid said at once, 'It's the heart of a person that counts, Laddie, not the clothes they wear. Same with here. And Green's has got a bathroom on every floor' – as if that settled it.

It was certainly taller than the other buildings in Anani's main street and, despite its shabby exterior, I could sense the air of warmth and welcome the moment I passed through the front door.

The reception room was little more than a hall. Behind the small veneered wooden counter a dozen or so keys dangled from hooks on a numbered board, together with a few dog-eared official-looking proclamations. On the counter itself was a bell, the old brass kind on which one banged a button. By the side of a registration book stood a tray on which rested a bottle of Scotch and four small glasses. As Reid and I put down the cases we were carrying, Reid uncorked the bottle and offered me a shot of whisky.

'Custom of the house,' he explained. 'A free drink for the weary traveller.' Downing his tot in one go, he smacked his lips and said, 'Come on, Laddie, a thimbleful won't hurt you. And it always tastes better when you dinna have to pay.'

I nodded, and at that moment, as I downed my drink, gasping as the fiery liquid burned my throat, a large woman in her late forties emerged from the office behind.

'Morning, Doc,' she said to Alec Reid. Turning to me she smiled and said, 'I'm Mollie Green. And you must be Doctor Masters. My pleasure.' She held out a podgy hand. She had a twang that at first I didn't recognise; it was New Zealand, for though her mother had been local, the late Mr Green, her father, came from Auckland, and had lived there before opening Green's Hotel. However, it was not until she came round from behind the reception desk that I realised how huge she was.

'Come on, sit down and let's all have a beer,' she said, and with a look at Dr Reid added, 'It's better for you than that rotgut at the bar.'

She banged on the bell and shouted, 'Lee Ho, two large beers and three glasses.' A Chinese, wearing none-too-clean ducks and a singlet, appeared with a tray bearing our drinks. A moment later, as he set them down, Mollie patted a chair and said, 'Come on, take the weight off your feet, Doctor Masters.'

She was not gross in any disgusting way, though she had to sit down carefully, for it was a tight fit for her to squeeze into the chair with its wooden arms. She was just cheerfully fat, her obesity partly disguised by the fact that she, too, wore a Mother Hubbard. Two other factors detracted from her massive size: her agreeable, welcoming smile, and her extraordinary absence of wrinkles. She wore no make-up, so that her fatness was disguised by her warmth of character.

'I'll show you your room if you like,' she offered. 'But there's no need really. Lee Ho will take up your bags. The room's clean and tidy and there's only one other guest – Captain Robins. You'll have met him, of course. He usually stays the night here when the *Mantela* comes in. Likes a change from his cabin. But don't worry: I've put him on a separate floor.'

I must have looked puzzled.

'You're the only two guests, so if you're on separate floors it means you've each got your own bathroom. He'll be coming in when the deck cargo's cleared. You'll be staying to dinner. Eight sharp.' Mollie wasn't asking a question, more making a statement, knowing there was nowhere else to eat until I settled in my own home. 'Lobsters do you?'

'Lobsters!' I had visions of London prices.

'All meals included in the tariff,' said Mollie, grinning.

'And dinna get fashed,' said Dr Reid. 'Lobsters are two a penny here. The boys spear them on the reef. When you've been here six months you'll nae want to see another lobster in your life.'

'You don't know how to cook them,' Mollie Green sniffed. 'We have dozens of ways of making lobsters taste different.'

After a second beer, Dr Reid prepared to leave, explaining that he was going to the dispensary.

'When does surgery open?' I asked as we stood outside the front door of Green's Hotel.

'When I feel like it,' he retorted. 'Or in future I'm hoping that on three days a week when *ye* feel like it.' He had half turned to walk to his car, which he had left down by the jetty, when we heard the sound of a horn, pressed just once – not to warn us against danger but to attract our attention. I turned round and saw an old Austin Ten slowly approaching us. It braked as it drew abreast. In the driving seat was a woman in her late thirties perhaps, white, but

43

with the almost stern aquiline features of someone with a trace of Polynesian blood.

I smiled a polite greeting, but the woman hardly acknowledged me. Dr Reid turned to her and said almost formally, 'Good morning, Tiare. May I present my newly appointed assistant, Doctor Masters? Princess Tiare.'

She didn't shake hands – it would have been difficult for her, anyway, sitting in the car – but as I pondered on the word 'princess' and bowed slightly, she said, 'So you are Doctor Masters? How old are you?'

'Twenty-four. Not too young?' I smiled, and taking my cue from Reid added: 'I hope I can be of service to Koraloona, Princess.'

'Thank you,' she smiled back, yet retaining a slight sense of reserve or dignity.

'It's wonderful to be here,' I said, making conversation.

'I was surprised that you came on the *Mantela*.' I could see her looking at the vessel by the jetty. 'I thought you'd have taken the regular boat to Sanderstown and spent a night or two there.'

I explained how by chance the *Mantela* had been in Sydney for a refit. 'And I enjoyed every minute of the trip,' I said with genuine enthusiasm.

'We all love the *Mantela*,' she agreed. 'She's part of our lives. My daughter Aleena travels on her regularly. She goes to boarding school in Sanderstown, but,' with a smile, 'always seems to be coming home for the holidays. You must come round with Doctor Reid for a drink at our home,' she said, again with that slight formality.

'I'd love to, thank you, Princess,' I replied equally formally.

Turning to Dr Reid, she asked, 'Are you going to the cinema on Friday?'

'Aye – unless a new bairn arrives to spoil my weekly fun,' he replied.

'Are any expected?' She didn't ask the question idly, but with the authority of one who expected to be kept informed of everything happening on the island.

44

'There's three on the way,' Reid told her. 'But I hope not for two weeks – and then with any luck not on a Friday, or I may have to ask Doctor Masters to deputise for me.'

The 'Princess' then asked to be told the names of the three expectant mothers. When these were given her she nodded and said, 'Of course. I remember now. I'll go and visit them. Good morning to both of you doctors.'

With that she slammed the old Austin into gear, then almost as quickly put it back into neutral.

'Aleena's got a bit of a cough,' she said. 'Have you any linctus?'

'You'll have some medicine in an hour or so,' Reid promised.

'Thank you.'

As the old car started up again, I asked him, 'How old is Aleena, the daughter?'

'She's a thirteen-year-old. Lovely kid. Ask Captain Robins about her this evening. He'll explain how one day she'll not only be a princess – but an heiress too. Worth a hundred thousand pounds. A bonny sum,' he mused.

'You're joking,' I said. But I could see he was perfectly serious. I thought of the pearl fishers who often visited the South Sea Islands, and of the many who had made fortunes.

'Not pearls!' cried Reid, reading my mind. 'Aye, there *are* pearls in these waters – enough for a king's ransom. But I doubt if they'll ever be fished. If we started that we'd spoil the island.'

'Well, then – what?'

'Why don't you come and join me for dinner tomorrow evening, and I'll tell you then.'

'I'd love to. Thanks.'

After Reid left I went to my room. It was a clean, white, rather clinical-looking room, with its white wooden towel rail, its bowl and pitcher of water for those who didn't have the time or inclination to take a bath. And I noticed that in the wardrobe was a spare pillow. Good – I liked two.

I put away the few clothes I had brought, together with photos of Mother and Father, and another one – a head and shoulders portrait of Clare, looking happy and unconcerned about her legs. I had a couple of books which I had slipped into my light case – Somerset Maugham's novel *The Moon and Sixpence*, which I was looking forward to reading again because it was, of course, based on the life of the painter Gauguin, who'd lived here in the South Seas; and a collection of Guy de Maupassant stories, in English. It suddenly occurred to me that I had been so busy enjoying myself on the *Mantela* that I had never even opened either of them.

Only one thing worried me – my trunks, particularly the one containing all my own medical 'supplies'. I didn't like the idea of leaving them unattended overnight. Supposing someone pinched them – where would I be? To a young doctor like myself, these were my 'valuables' – the Zeiss Ikon microscope in the scuffed leather case, its precious lenses protected from dust by silk covers; the glass-lidded box of stainless-steel instruments – retractors, forceps, hooks, scissors and needles; my much-thumbed copy of that heavy-going but essential tome, Gray's *Anatomy*; manuals of pharmacology and pharmacy; Belding's *Text-book of Clinical Parasitology* and Strong's *Prevention and Treatment of Tropical Diseases*, both of which I'd bought at the last minute in the hope that the young man in John Bell & Croyden in Wigmore Street was right when he assured me that they provided 'the answers to all tropical problems'; and some bound volumes of the *British Medical Journal* which I had picked up cheap in Charing Cross Road.

I decided to return to the jetty and see if I could store them overnight. Perhaps Mrs Johnson could take them in? I went out into Main Street and started off for the pier. Two fishing boats were approaching the small harbour, and at the far end of Main Street I could see the bulk of the *Mantela*. Then I saw the spare figure of Captain Robins walking towards me, bag in hand: even on land after such a

46

short voyage he had the kind of rolling gait that proclaimed him a man of the sea.

'I was on my way to see about my trunks,' I started.

'Don't worry,' he replied. 'Jim Wilson, the ship's chandler, is storing them for you until you get settled.'

'Thank God – that's a relief,' I thanked him.

'I saw you meeting your new boss,' he smiled. 'You'll get on with him fine. Why not let's go back to the hotel?'

'Suits me.' I was eager to talk, especially after the intriguing encounter with the Princess.

We walked back together, and once in the hall of the hotel Robins dumped his small bag, shouted, 'Mollie!' and at once drained a small glass of her whisky.

'I don't really know much about Doctor Reid,' I admitted, 'except that he seems to have a great sense of humour and is – well, perhaps a bit unconventional.'

'He's one of the best. But I'll not bore you with second-hand accounts of the way he lives. He'll soon tell you himself. He loves it. You going to have dinner with him tonight?'

I shook my head. 'Tomorrow.'

'Fine. You and I'll have dinner together then. But how's about a drive round the island – just so that you can see for yourself what it's like.'

'What about a car?'

'Mollie will lend me hers.' At that moment Mollie Green appeared, and both took it for granted that Robins could borrow the car. Her only admonition was, 'Don't be late for supper.'

Robins duly promised, and a moment later we were on our way in Mollie's Ford 8.

There was nothing more to see in Main Street except the eternal fascination of boats bobbing in water as we set off past the ship's chandler – and behind, as casually as an oak or a beech tree in England, dozens of the orange trees which had given the town of Anani its name.

'Next stop Tala-Tala!' Robins gave his rubbery lop-sided grin and added sardonically, 'If you can call it a town, despite its double-barrelled name. At least it had a church there before they built one in Anani. If I'm in port on a Sunday I always go to church at Tala-Tala.'

'You don't strike me as a religious man,' I said frankly.

'I'm not. But I love singing hymns, and the organist is better at Tala-Tala. Going to church is the only chance I get of singing – well, with accompaniment anyway.'

Tala-Tala, he explained, five miles up the road, had the first church on Koraloona because it was built by the first missionaries to arrive on the island. They landed there, and the locals named it 'Tala-Tala' – the Polynesian name for 'preacher'.

It was very pretty, in a picture-postcard way. Coconuts grew almost to the edge of the silver strip of coral beach, which sparkled in the hot sun. Naked children splashed gleefully in the shallow water, trying to catch the occasional sand crab before it scuttled underground. A few scrawny chickens were busy searching for scraps, while half a dozen black pigs grunted among the roots of hedges of sago, or round the slim pawpaw trees bending under the weight of their fruit. The thatched houses often consisted only of a roof of pandanus or coconut leaves on four poles, with rolled-up slats of interwoven pandanus leaves which could be lowered in case of rain.

Tala-Tala even had its own home-made harbour, a kind of inner lagoon in the outer lagoon, obviously a laboriously built, three-sided breakwater, in which I assumed that every stone must have been carried by hand or on rollers to afford protection for the boats it enclosed. For Tala-Tala was the centre of the local fishing 'industry', and its gaily painted boats searched for big fish like marlin outside the reef.

When I told Robins of the effort it must have required to transport the heavy materials by hand he just laughed.

'No, it wasn't that way at all. The New Zealand government transported the rocks by sea and helped to build the breakwater so that the island could start a fishing business. You see, an island like Hodges is so occupied with copra that it produces nothing else. Tala-Tala supplies it with fresh fish – that is, when the chaps feel like fishing.'

In the centre of the tiny harbour lay a sleek white pleasure yacht with, as I could see, one or two white officers in peaked caps and white shorts and shirts standing on the decks.

'Looks a bit out of place,' I said with a smile.

'I'll tell you about that lot in a couple of minutes, but I just want to catch our fisherman and be sure we have enough fresh fish for the *Mantela*'s homeward trip.'

By the time he returned, half a dozen island girls had sauntered past, and their perfume hung in the still air. 'It's like going into the scent counter at Harrods,' I said.

'Frangipani,' explained Robins. 'Nothing like so sophisticated as Harrods. The girls just pick the flowers and twist them into the circlets they put on their heads. The perfume lasts all day. Let's move on.'

I looked away from the sea, behind the sliver of beach, where the hills first rose steeply, then flattened out. I could make out a couple of dozen large buildings. Some were of stone, some of wood. All were a cut above the Polynesian houses. One even had a flagpole and over the top of the trees below I could see the Union Jack fluttering.

'That's the local club,' Robins explained. 'Restricted to expats, preferably British. Must be white or "Caucasian" as the Americans call 'em. Come on – I'll show you round. It's four o'clock – opening time.'

If I had read a dozen Somerset Maugham books about colonial clubs in remote settlements, I couldn't have bettered my first impression of Tala-Tala's Union Jack Club. It was little more than a house, really, with one lounge filled with basketwork chairs and with tables littered with old magazines. There was a bar at one end of the room with a sign above saying 'No thongs. No singlets'. Behind it two men in singlets were serving drinks. Behind that was a billiard table, and near it a couple of bridge tables.

'You'll have to join, of course,' said Bill, adding with a straight face, 'if the committee accepts you, that is. You'll have to be proposed and seconded. But I can't see the local doctor being blackballed.'

It was obvious that the Union Jack Club was, to its members anyway, the local hub of the far-flung British Empire. With the exception of a few New Zealand government officials, the other inhabitants had only come to Koraloona because they preferred it to life in reduced circumstances in a big city. I can't say I blamed them, for though the Union Jack Club might be pretentious, Koraloona wasn't. And the expatriates were happy.

A sprinkling of members was busy ordering drinks and as soon as we approached the bar, there was a chorus of 'Welcome back, Captain!' or 'Good to see you, Bill'. The skipper of the *Mantela* was obviously a popular figure. One man with a bristling moustache that almost twitched at the corners cried, 'What's it to be, Bill? And your friend – what'll he have?'

'This is Colonel Archie Fawcett.' I shook hands with the tall fair-haired man in his sixties, 'and this is your new assistant doctor, Kit Masters.'

'By gad! You look young for a doctor,' cried Fawcett as he handed me a whisky.

'Colonel Fawcett is the administrator of Koraloona for the Cook Islands,' explained Bill Robins.

'No real work involved,' Fawcett beamed happily. 'Just a figurehead.'

'Don't be so modest, Archie,' said Robins, adding for my benefit, 'The colonel is responsible for all manner of things – the daily radio link – "the sked" as it's known all over the Pacific – crime and punishment, what happens if the electricity breaks down.'

'Sounds a tall order,' I said.

'Not really.' Robins gave a sideways teasing look at Fawcett. 'Though, of course, he's responsible for the financial arrangements – sorting out the island's modest economics, including the allowance the New Zealand government pays Princess Tiare to support her honorary status as a princess.'

Innocently I pointed to a sign above the bar and asked Robins, 'What's a thong?' I had never heard the word.

'One of those Japanese-style rubber slippers with a thong between the big toe and the next one – the only way to keep the slipper in place. Bad form to wear them in the club.'

'Strictly for the servants – and Japanese of course,' added a lady who introduced herself as Mrs Fawcett, and asked anxiously, 'Do you play bridge, Doctor?'

I said that I did, if only fairly well. 'Wonderful,' cried one lady member. 'We're always short of a fourth. Can you stay for dinner?'

Interrupting quickly, Bill Robins said, 'We've already been invited, I'm afraid. A sort of semi-official dinner with Doctor Reid.'

'What a pity,' said another woman. 'It's gala night – a three-shilling three-course meal. You can't do better than that, even in London, can you?'

'You certainly can't,' I said, as another member shouted to 'George' for drinks.

'Are both the stewards called George?' I asked a mystified Robins, who explained with a laugh that it had been Colonel Fawcett's idea. He had read that, at the exclusive Beefsteak Club in London, every steward was addressed as George, and the colonel had decided to adopt the same rule to save people from remembering unnecessary names when stewards were changed.

'I'm afraid we have to be on our way, Colonel,' Bill Robins explained. 'But I'm sure that Doctor Masters will be in touch with you about joining.'

'A mere formality, dear boy.' The colonel gave me a friendly pat on the shoulder, and we made for the outside world again.

As he started up the car and we made our way further round the island, Robins explained, 'They're good sports, but every new face is welcome. Some of them were bigwigs in the administration of the islands. And now that they've retired on half pension, they're a damn sight better off than they would be in Sydney or Auckland, let alone London.'

We had gone about a hundred yards when one particular house caught my eye. It was much larger than the others and set in a grove of coconut palms above the beach.

'That's the Villa Faalifu, which means "coconut". It belongs to a rich American, name of Paula Reece. She owns the yacht in the harbour. She's quite a lady.'

The dusty road encircled the island, here and there broken by small fishing settlements – 'village' would be too pretentious a word – the country around us laced with waterfalls on the hills behind, small bays, one very shallow, the next a deep creek where the beach became a small headland, the pale colour of the sea turned indigo because of the depth.

As we turned another corner we came across a few villagers handling copra. Robins stopped the car and we walked towards them.

'What's the difference between – well, how do coconuts become copra?' I asked.

Robins picked a piece up off the beach. 'There's not much difference,' he admitted. 'Copra is the dried-out guts of the coconut, the endosperm and the embryo of the seed. Remember desiccated coconut in cakes? That's shredded copra.'

Several men were splitting the hairy husks on iron spikes driven into the ground. 'Then they put them in the sun to dry out, and when the meat curls away from the shell it's put into sacks. It's one of the staple exports of the islands, especially Hodges. *Cocos nucifera*. For years I used to carry the stuff. It takes five thousand nuts to make a ton of copra, which sells at twenty-four pounds a ton; and that in turn will only produce about a third of a ton of hair shampoo. Looking at these fellers work, it makes you think!'

We returned to the car and drove on until we came to a small wooden bridge spanning a rivulet of water coming from a waterfall not far up the hillside behind.

'Like a walk?' Robins indicated the waterfall. 'This is one of the few private properties on the island. There's a secret pool where Princess Tiare's mother used to swim with her lover. Kind of romantic. When Tiare's mother died Tiare bought the land And now only she and her daughter are allowed to swim there. And me.'

'Why you?'

'Old friend of the family.' He twisted his face into a grin. 'I've been given permission to swim in the pool when the family's not using it. And it's easy to tell if they *are* because there'd be their car by the roadside.'

From the rickety bridge I looked upwards to the waterfall, perhaps fifty feet above us; at the spot where it vanished into ferns and flowers it was frothing like a diaphanous white ball gown. But the pool I could not see. Robins led the way up the sloping path from the roadway, narrow but clearly defined, towards thick undergrowth, ferns, bushes, lined with every flower from hibiscus, tiare and oleander to the bougainvillaea curling round and clinging to the trees behind.

'It's only five minutes' walk,' he said, and sure enough, we soon reached the pool at the foot of the waterfall. Where the fall hit the pool the water threshed as though boiling, but a few feet further on it was limpid, still, crystal-clear, hedged in by banks of ferns and tulip trees, and at the far end was the outlet where the water drained away to the sea.

'We're not there yet – not quite,' said Robins. 'Follow me, it's quite safe.' He led the way about six feet further up where the path ended in a flat ledge, and then I could see what had happened. Immediately behind and above the waterfall, the sloping hillside had become a fifty-foot smooth rocky cliff, so that the water poured not only over the edge above, but out into the pool, leaving a ledge along which Bill Robins now beckoned me. It was as dry as a bone, under a never-ending, roaring waterfall.

'Extraordinary, isn't it?' He stopped to peer at the pool below through a 'crack' in the water, rather as though someone was peeping through lace curtains.

'There's a cave in there.' He pointed to a cliff behind the waterfall. 'Never gets wet.'

He glanced at me. 'Can you dive?'

'Sure.'

'Diving into the pool is like a blind date,' he laughed. 'It's deep. I've dived into it dozens of times. But you have to dive through the waterfall without seeing the pool until the last minute. Game for a try?'

I nodded eagerly. 'Anything once.'

'We can undress here in the cave if you like. No need for a costume in this part of the world.'

It was a curious sensation, diving into water I couldn't see, but once Robins had led the way, and was treading water in the pool, I followed without any fear.

How wonderful it was to be able to stop a car on impulse and bathe in a pool of crystal-clear water! We swam for about quarter of an hour and then walked back to the cave, dried ourselves as best we could on our shirts, and drove on, chests bare.

'It could tell quite a story, that pool,' said Robins. 'Sacred ground, in a way. That's why it belongs to Tiare.'

'You're sure we weren't trespassing?' I felt a touch of the sinister that rules so many of the islands; there was no reason to shiver in that warm spot, but I did, and experienced a slight sense of embarrassment, as though I had been intruding, thinking perhaps not of Tiare but of the great love all those years ago which had produced her: forty years ago when the water was cascading over the same cliff in just the same way as it had today, Princess Tiare's mother and her lover had bathed in the same secret pool and later, perhaps, made love in the cave behind.

It fascinated me, though at first I could not tell why. It was not the beauty alone that had made me draw in my breath. Somehow, even to my youthful reasoning, it was as though the past was speaking to the present, that something of the love between these two people still lingered.

'You're not the first to be affected by the pool.' Robins read my thoughts. 'It's extraordinary, really. The scent of a deep, passionate love still clings to it. I expect it sounds silly to you.'

'No. It might have sounded embarrassing if *I* had said it,' I smiled. 'But I know what you mean.'

'I'm glad,' he said simply.

'I understand this title of "Princess",' I continued, 'but Doctor Reid talked about a fortune. I find that hard to believe.'

'Better let him tell you about it,' Robins advised. 'Alec Reid likes to tell his stories in his own good time. There's no other way of entertaining strangers.' His face creased in its twisted, ironic smile.

'Doctor Reid did tell me about Tiare's daughter.'

'Aleena? Lovely child,' Robins said, echoing Reid's words. 'She goes to school at Sanderstown College, and I've got to know her well because she sails on the *Mantela* every holiday. That's why I'm allowed to swim in the secret pool – a reward because her mother made me responsible for Aleena whenever she's on the *Mantela*.'

Dusk was falling swiftly, as it always does in the tropics, and the silence that had so impressed me by daylight suddenly became noisy with the night life of the jungly-type trees in the mountains behind – the bull frogs, strange bird cries, the never-ending background of the cicadas.

'Too late for any more sightseeing now,' said Robins. 'Let's make tracks for Green's or we'll be late for supper. Mollie's a stickler for punctuality.'

4

The clinic and the cottage hospital were up a small hill at the other end of Main Street, beyond the ship's chandler and the jetty where the *Mantela* was moored. A few fishing boats sat in the lagoon, some outrigger canoes were drawn up on the sand and one small pleasure yacht, which must have come from another island, was anchored to a buoy. In the deck well I could see a couple of girls and two men in bathing suits. Three or four cars wheezed past us on the dusty road.

When Dr Reid arrived to fetch me at Green's he announced that he had left his car by the pier. 'We'll walk there, but no further. I puff too much for mountaineering.' His car was an extraordinary contraption, an ancient Ford truck from which some amateur carpenter (or maybe the ship's chandler?) had stripped off a ten-hundredweight body, and on the chassis had erected a kind of ambulance – with a stretcher bed in it and one chair firmly screwed to the floorboards.

'This is ma private car and ma public ambulance,' Reid announced solemnly. 'No doot ye can drive?'

I nodded. 'Is the clinic far?'

'Nothing's far here. There's a second road, parallel to Main Street, up the hill because it's cooler. The Princess lives at the end of the same road. There's a couple of Mission schools, nothing elaborate ye ken, for the local kids.' As he spoke I could make out the red roofs of the bungalows dotted among the green trees.

'And,' he added, 'there's half a dozen small lorries to carry heavy supplies – stuff like diesel to run our own generator for electricity if the hydroelectric power fails.'

'Captain Robins drove me around the island last night,' I said. 'We stopped for a swim near Tala-Tala. It's a pretty village.'

Reid nodded. 'Most of the fifty or so Europeans prefer to live in Tala-Tala rather than Anani,' he said adding, with a touch of sarcasm, 'They say they dinna want to get contaminated by big-city life.'

We drove up the hill. 'And soon' – Dr Reid waved a hand dramatically – 'you'll be seeing the eighth wonder of the world. My clinic. I call it "Harley Street". Here we are.'

Reid switched off his decrepit Ford in front of a building visible only in patches through the railings of a once-white wooden veranda, over which trailed bougainvillaea, syringa, convolvulus, and hibiscus in a riot of colour. The sun splashed down in patterns of light and shade. Beneath the flowering plants were slats of the veranda half eaten by ants or crumbling with tropical humidity. Above, I saw where a hole in the tin roof had been repaired with a flattened-out biscuit tin that had once contained Huntley and Palmer's ginger nuts.

Inside the single-storey building a leathery-faced, middle-aged white woman hacked with a kind of parang at branches of flame trees which had worked their way through the open windows.

'Miss Sowerby,' Reid explained, 'has been with us for several years. Her father was a missionary and she felt the call to help him. And helping the sick is holy work, eh Miss Sowerby?' She *looked* like the daughter of a missionary; and I don't mean that in a derogatory way. But in this warm and pleasant climate she was dressed in a long black dress which looked as though it had been made at the time of Heathcliff. It had long sleeves; a tightness above imprisoned her neck with its white linen collar. Her belted dress had a piece of string attached from which dangled a pair of old scissors. She was dressed as though ready for church. Everything was there except a crucifix, and I didn't doubt that this was hidden underneath a thick petticoat.

But was her obvious intensity entirely based on religious grounds? I wondered. Most of it, certainly, but – in the way a doctor always judges character as a routine diagnostic procedure – I wondered if she wasn't repressing the normal feelings of a woman. I don't mean sex in any simple way. Many women can ache for the love of a child more intensely than for the love of a man.

It seemed to me that she looked older than she was, using her age as a shield against unwelcome advances which she might secretly long for but would never permit. She could have been any age, for though her face was weathered by the sun, no wrinkles marred her face.

'Pleased to meet you, Doctor Masters.' She put down her heavy curved knife and held out a gnarled hand. 'You'll no doubt find us primitive compared with what you're used to.'

As Reid led me on a tour of the hospital he said, 'She's a po-faced old girl, but her heart's in the right place; and she understands the islanders. Now, here's the ward.'

The 'ward' was scarcely bigger than the waiting-room of St Thomas's teaching hospital, but its six iron bedsteads were meticulously lined up. Every leg of every bed stood in a jar of water to frustrate the ruthless ants, while the 'hospital corners' of the bedding were aligned with a draughtsman's precision – even though the linen, I noticed, was yellowish and patched. At one end of the ward a door led to a bathroom in which the 'bath' was a large caulked wooden tub – the sort one saw in the back-to-backs of the mining villages. There was a flush toilet, and near it what Reid called 'the wash-up'. It had a large earthenware sink and an electric stove where one could heat water in a huge blackened kettle. He led me back through the empty ward to the other end. 'And this, Laddie, is the "admin" section.'

A tin trunk from the Army & Navy Stores tropical department stood there, the lid thrown back to reveal files and cards held together with elastic bands. I was fascinated by it. 'You mean that's all the Mission bought in the way of filing cabinets?'

'Nae, ye mustn'a get it wrong. This house was first built back in the 1890s as a residence for the local missionary. There was nae a doctor there in those days. The missionary looked after the islanders' health as well as their spiritual welfare. Then, when the first priest arrived, he wanted to live in Tala-Tala near the kirk, so this became the first hospital, and this,' he almost kicked the battered old trunk, 'became the first filing cabinet. Tiare's mother gave it to the mission.'

Along one wall was a big cupboard with double doors, warped with heat and humidity and bearing the word *Dispensary*. The doors were fastened with a padlock which a child of five could have picked with a paper clip.

'Another gift from Tiare's mother,' said Reid.

The contents were pathetic. Some four-gallon jars contained different-coloured liquids; these were numbered 1 to 4. Reid nudged me. 'Placebos. But the patients are always fascinated by the colours. I tend to dish out the red for man trouble, the blue for woman trouble, the yellow for baby trouble, and green for anything else. Plus, of course, real treatment if the case demands it. But you'll have 'em buzzing round you like bees at a honeypot if you aren't fairly strict. To them medicine men are like gods.'

The next shelf down contained an array of jars and bottles of proprietary disinfectants and medicines – Lysol, iodoform, Condy's fluid, peroxide, aspirin, Germolene, cough linctus and yeast tablets, together with blue-wrapped packets of cotton wool, bandages, ligatures. Needles were stored in a two-pound Robertson's jam jar; and in a long glass-topped case was a selection of knives, scalpels, forceps, scissors and syringes. My confidence wasn't enhanced by the limited number of blue glass bottles and jars comprising the available pharmaceuticals – chloroform, morphia, prussic acid, cannabis, strychnine, atropine. I noticed that my case of drugs had been opened in one corner of the room, but still, it was a pitiful supply. It was very different from when, during my student days, I had spent some time in the specialised wards of the Hospital for Tropical Diseases at St Pancras, where patients were treated for cholera, yellow fever, elephantiasis, malaria, leprosy, encephalitis lethargica, and a dozen other diseases that might have originated in the tropics.

When I examined the new drugs, I was glad to see some acriflavine – a useful all-round skin antiseptic which has to be used with a bandage to prevent evaporation because of its alcohol base. There was also some gentian violet and Eusol.

Reid saw me examining the Eusol – an antiseptic used since the turn of the century – and chuckled.

'Wouldn't be without it,' he said. 'We discovered it.'

'We?' I must have looked puzzled.

'Edinburgh, the world's finest medical university. That's why it's called Eusol – E for Edinburgh, U for University and "sol" for solution.'

He took my arm and said, 'Now come and see the operating theatre.'

The 'theatre' ran parallel to the ward and we reached it through a short, glass-enclosed passageway. The room contained little more than a long wooden table covered with lino, a barber's chair that had been slightly modified to accommodate dental patients, another deep earthenware sink, and a basketwork bed – mounted on what looked like pram wheels – for patients forced to lie supine. It was used here, I assumed, for transporting the patients from the ward to the operating 'table'.

Reid must have sensed my dismay, for he took my arm in a friendly grip and said, 'Dinna take it too much to heart, Laddie, I've done my "trops" too. I know the perfection of it all, but the ideal and the reality rarely match. It's like life itself – the prettiest girls are always on the Up escalator when you're on the Down. And remember, if we need an urgent op I can fly a patient to Sanderstown in under the hour. I can even fly a stretcher case.'

One patient only was in bed, a pitiful slip of a girl aged perhaps seven or eight. Though she was dry-eyed she looked in great pain.

'Here is another case of the scourge of Koraloona,' sighed Reid. 'And one that I know you have a personal interest in – polio.' Reid drew back the sheet to expose the girl's dropped foot. 'I'm going to operate later on tomorrow. You see – the calf muscle on the left leg just doesn't work, so if I don't do something quickly she'll end up a cripple. No power to keep the foot up like a normal one.'

'How did it start?' I asked as Reid pulled the sheet back over the little girl.

'The usual way,' he sighed. 'Undetectable at first. That's the trouble with this bloody disease. All these viral infections have the same symptoms in the first few days – a patient might have 'flu, measles, hepatitis – ye canna tell during the porodomal period' – he used the technical term for the period of incubation. 'I give them aspirin and hope for the best. Then muscular stiffness suddenly develops, the patient is in agonising pain – just like cramp in the leg – and she shows signs of insecurity when walking. Then you know – and you have to operate.'

I had a sudden flash of memory of one of the most remarkable women I had ever met – Sister Kenny, a woman who had made a great impact on me because of Clare. She was Australian, had no real qualifications, but had created a furore in the medical world by her determination to use unorthodox methods in the treatment of infantile paralysis. Heat treatment, self-help on the patient's part, and rehabilitation of the affected muscles by massage and exercise were the tenets of her faith – and I had to admit that a great deal of what she practised depended on scorn for the accepted methods of treatment with splints, braces, and corsets which only assisted the patients in coping with unhealed limbs, not in any actual sense curing them. Having a strong personality, she had battled her way into the medical profession and convinced many doctors by demonstration that at the very least they couldn't shut their eyes to the possibilities of her treatment.

I had witnessed Sister Kenny's unusual treatment when I went to see her at work at Queen Mary's Hospital for Children in Carshalton, one of several hospitals we had visited during our advanced student days. I blurted out, 'Doctor Reid, could I try to see if I could stop the disease without using splints or operating?'

He looked at me in astonishment.

'Certainly not,' he said. 'You can't just ignore everything that medical science has taught us.'

I would have liked to say that, so far, medical science had taught us nothing about polio, but I held my tongue. He looked at me more kindly.

'You're thinking about the so-called "miracle cures" of Sister Kenny?' I nodded and he continued, 'You've only just arrived on the island. Have a wee bit of patience,

61

Laddie. Maybe soon I'll let ye have a chance to see if you can do anything – but remember, miracles are often caused by good luck.'

'But I *saw* her perform those so-called miracles.'

'I promise you, you'll have the chance. After all, the main reason I asked for an assistant was because of the danger of an epidemic of polio. And I was told of your particular interest in the disease. But – ' he held up a hand to stop me interrupting – 'let's take it slowly. And let's remember that Sister Kenny isn't even a professional nurse. She helped some bairns when she was living in the Australian outback. She did cure them, I grant you. But maybe there they had only a mild form, or maybe it wasn't even real polio. Remember, no one ever saw those bairns until they were cured.'

'But in London I did – '

'I know. And I appreciate your enthusiasm. Just let's get settled in and then I promise to give you a chance. In the meantime, I suppose you've seen an operation performed for a dropped foot?'

I nodded. 'In med school,' I said.

'Come and see it again tomorrow,' he suggested. 'A local anaesthetic will be enough. I'll give the girl quarter of a grain of morphia dissolved in water and inject it to calm her down. Half an hour later I'll inject fifty millilitres of half per cent Novocaine. She'll be out in ten minutes, but I'll pinch some loose skin just to make sure there's no reaction.'

How often I had seen that pinching of the skin! The operation, I knew, was simple enough. It consisted of stretching the Achilles tendon. With a scalpel Reid would cut half way through one side of the tendon, half way through the other a little higher up, then pull the tendon which would stretch and later heal and join up. This would enable him to restore the foot to the proper position of function, and he would keep it like that by strapping it into a right-angle splint, with a kind of plate under the foot attached to splints up the calf.

'Poor kid,' I muttered.

'Aye,' agreed Reid. 'But don't forget she'll be lucky not to have a club foot.'

As we walked back to the dispensary he asked me, almost casually, yet in a way trying to find out how much I knew, 'Tell me, what's the extent of your knowledge of polio?'

'I made a study of it – as much as the medical authorities would allow,' I said. 'You want chapter and verse?'

'It's not necessary,' he laughed, 'but – '

So to impress him I told him briefly of the four stages of polio – first the porodomal, second the muscle pain, then the period of muscle destruction which usually took no longer than fourteen days, and finally the period of repair.

'That's it,' said Alec Reid. 'And that's the trouble. The muscle has the ability to recoil, but when it wastes away, the tissue hasn't. It's like the difference between a bit of cotton and a bit of elastic.'

During our 'inspection tour' I had heard a fair amount of noise from the garden, and now Miss Sowerby announced, 'There's half a dozen patients, Doctor, including one who's hurt his head badly.'

'Let's start work,' Dr Reid sighed. 'There's nae peace for the wicked.'

Outside the front door stood the patients, including two men and three young girls. They all stood up as though on parade, with the instinctive straight back of the Polynesians. One man held a cloth soaked in blood to his forehead.

'You'd better come in first,' Reid motioned to him, and with a wave to the others announced, 'This is Doctor Masters, our new doctor.'

The girls giggled, the other man smiled, and the 'sick parade', as Reid always called it, had started.

The other male patient was very different from the man who had hurt his head. He was white, tall, and wore a scraggy beard. He obviously looked ill, but what I found terrible was the look of starvation on his emaciated body and face. Bedraggled, barefoot, dressed in dirty white ducks, he looked as though he were hovering on the verge of death. Through a tear in the singlet I could see his rib bones sticking out. He might have been forty – or sixty. As Reid led the patient with the bloody head indoors, the white man turned to me, almost stopped me from going inside and said in an educated voice, 'Good morning, Doctor, and welcome to Koraloona. I'm Jason Purvis. I'm a writer.' He added wryly, 'As you can see, not a very successful one. Doc Reid dishes me out a few vitamin pills when I'm feeling lousy.' He was tall, almost stooping, and with a mouth too sensitive for peace of mind. Though I remained in the garden or the dispensary, helping some of the less sick patients, I saw Reid beckon Purvis inside, later, give him some pills, and then slip the man some money.

When the last patient had gone, Reid opened the refrigerator in the dispensary and took out a packet wrapped in white paper. Before I had time to ask about Purvis, he explained, 'My sandwiches for breakfast. They keep nice and cool in the fridge. Want some? Potted meat.' I shook my head and Reid cheerfully walked on to the veranda, munching his 'breakfast' – his day's work apparently done.

'Tell me about the white patient,' I asked him. 'He looked terrible. Purvis, was that the name? And is he really a writer?'

'Aye. Writes all day long, but as far as I can see never sells a word. D'ye ken he's only thirty-seven? He's half starved – and can't do a thing about it.'

'But surely there's everything a man needs to live here – food, fruit, fish, breadfruit? He's surrounded with the fruits of the earth.'

'That may be so, but he canna do a thing to help himself. He canna climb up a tree for a coconut, he canna go up the mountain for wild bananas. Can't even fish. But then, could you, with a spear?'

'No, of course not.'

'So there's a paradox for you. The islanders kill their wild pigs, they fish, they bake their breadfruit. They even make their own liquor without it costing anyone a penny – yet there's this poor devil starving amidst plenty.'

'What's his background. He's obviously educated. Doesn't he have *any* money?'

'He gets a remittance from England once every three months. Then he spends it all at Robinson's store on drink, tinned meat, powdered milk and so on. Once I even caught him buying tinned sardines – with all that fresh fish in the sea!'

While we talked Miss Sowerby had been cleaning up the patient with the head wound and, as the man prepared to leave, Reid cried to him, 'Head feel'um better?'

The patient beamed and proudly touched his bandage. 'Pain out now. No gettum in with mask.'

'Good. Now, be goodum feller and take med'cin along Princess.' He handed the man a bottle and added sternly, 'And no takum along self, savvy? Make better, women; make bad, men.'

'Plenty savvy,' the man said. 'Me takum, make ill.' He loped off cheerfully.

'He probably thinks it's a cure for the curse,' chuckled Reid. 'You'll get used to the pidgin, by the way. It's a language all its own, with rules and a grammar, but it has no definite article. Hence the odd-sounding constructions.'

'Seems very odd to me.' I could hardly understand all the curious words.

'Dinna imagine it's the local baby talk,' Reid went on. 'It's an international language which started so that people who travel between foreign countries can communicate – the Chinese, stevedores, the old-time lascars, and so on. When they load or unload a ship they can understand what's wanted.'

'I'll pick it up,' I promised. 'Incidentally, do you always use your patients as messenger boys?' I couldn't help laughing.

'Always. That's their way of paying for the medicine. One good cure deserves another.' Then more seriously, after he had crumpled up the paper sandwich bag and put it into the waste bin, he said, 'You'll find, Kit – it's Christian names, eh, Kit and Alec? – that the inhabitants of Koraloona are the kindest people on earth. Because they want nothing, they're untouched by the evils of the outside world. Every now and again some of the pearling luggers come this way. They get short shrift. We don't want any get-rich-quick people here. Everyone on the island's got enough to eat.'

'Except Purvis!' I said.

'He's the exception,' said Reid.

'But what about money?' I asked. 'Surely – '

'If they do want something that costs extra, there's always a way to make a few pennies. There's about fifty Europeans on the island – including Americans – and there's plenty of men anxious to do a bit of gardening, or women ready to earn a day's wages doing the laundry – you saw them at work – or sewing. There are fifty times as many Singer sewing machines as motor cars in Koraloona. And the ship's chandler is always needing spare hands when a boat comes in. So is Mick the barman. But they work when there's fun in it, not to live. Since most people own a plot of land, they have everything they need to keep alive. A day's casual work takes on an extra meaning. It's fun, not work; a luxury, not a necessity. What money there is circulates again and again, into the store, out, back again.'

'And drink? Don't they need money for drinking?'

'Not much. They like beer, but only as we'd drink champagne – a treat. They like *kava*. They make it themselves, so it's cheap. It's common all over the Pacific, and they drink it out of big wooden bowls, passing it round the circle.'

'Like palm toddy? Isn't that the drink of South-East Asia?'

'No. *Kava* is made of the ground-up roots of the kava bush. They mix it with water, and it's lethal, I tell you. But though it's guaranteed to give anyone a hangover, I've nae heard of any islanders getting fighting mad on the stuff.'

'I hope it tastes good.'

'Horrible! But for those with a sweeter tooth there's always rum. They make that from sugar cane, which often grows wild here. And then there's orangeade.'

'Doesn't sound too potent.'

'Don't fool yourself. There're so many wild oranges on the island that when they're ripe the boys and girls go out in gangs, pick them by the thousand, squeeze out all the juice and let it ferment in casks until it's ready for a week-long celebration. You'd think they'd bottle it, make it last over the weeks or months, but they're simple pcople, and there's no holding them back. No one would think of hoarding a year's stock for such a free tipple. And they don't.'

'And now come and meet Nellie.'

Alec Reid led the way to a field behind the back door, held out an arm, like a conjuror, and cried, 'There!'

It was a single-engined biplane. It looked fragile, held together by struts that seemed no longer than bits of wire. 'I learned to fly the Gloster before I left England,' he explained, 'though I could never have afforded to buy a plane. But my wife – she's a rich woman, and generous – saw an advert in *The Aeroplane* in 1936 offering one for £1,700. She bought it as a gift on my last trip to the UK. It has a Bristol Mercury radial engine of 840 horsepower. You know, you could pay more for a flashy car.'

'Still – a very generous present,' I murmured.

'Aye, it is that. My wife and I could never see eye to eye on the business of living. She's all for the social whirl of Mayfair or Bond Street, while I like my peace and quiet. So I see her on leaves, and she gives me every so often a new MCC tie!' He went on more seriously, 'So we agreed to follow our different ways. We correspond when we feel like it; there's no bitterness. It's a pity in some ways, but in others . . .' He shrugged his shoulders. 'If you're forced to live in a place you hate, it's the surest way to break up a marriage.'

I didn't know quite what to answer, but he saved me the trouble.

'I think I can say I'm a tolerant man,' he said, not without a trace of smugness. 'I make no judgments on man or woman, perhaps because I make no judgments on myself – or my wife. I've managed to preserve a friendship between husband and wife living thousands of miles apart, and that's nae a bad achievement.'

Alec moved up to the plane and ran a loving hand along its polished propeller blade. 'Nellie, the pride of the islands. She'll do a good two hundred miles an hour, and though she's got dual control you can take out the second seat next to the pilot's to make room for a stretcher.' He showed me the cunning way in which Jim Wilson, the ship's chandler, had hinged the top of the fuselage so that a patient could be lowered into the plane on a stretcher once the second seat had been removed to give the extra length.

'Can you fly?' asked Reid.

'Good Lord, no. The only time I've flown was when I paid five bob for a trip in Alan Cobham's flying circus.'

'You'd better learn,' he said. 'It's dead easy – I'll teach you. It's our only quick link with the islands. She does sterling work, does Nellie, fetching and carrying. And if I have to, I can land on a stretch of roadway. She makes the journey to Sanderstown in under the hour.'

'Suppose you need to make really urgent contact with Sanderstown. You've no phone link, I take it?'

'We've the radio link, twice a day. Very simple. It's up in what we call Cook Island House, where the three government officers work under Colonel Fawcett, or say they do. We can pass or receive radio messages by voice at nine every morning and six every evening.'

The more I had to do with Alec Reid, the more I liked him. It was easy to ridicule him – his battered old topee, his stout figure, the perspiration which never seemed to dry up however often he mopped his bald pate. But beneath this exterior there lived a man who treated the islanders with the affection which a good father bestows on his slightly

68

wayward children. You needed patience to tolerate the at times stupid, hypochondriacal old island ladies, but Reid offered them his placebos with no thought of the unnecessary work such trivial ailments caused him. And you needed even more patience when others ignored danger signals warning of serious illness, such as the stiffness in the joints, dismissed as unimportant, yet because of the background of dirt, possibly resulting in tetanus, which could rarely be cured unless it was caught in time.

Alec Reid had no prejudice. He treated every patient with the same love and care, and so, as I discovered very quickly, he was worshipped by the islanders. He got on with everybody – including me, to whom he remarked with his easy chuckle, 'Here's to ye, Kit! At one stroke ye've halved the white man's burden!'

I think – I hope – that in a sense the relief of having a young assistant was not only that it helped his work, but that he also welcomed the presence of a younger doctor with more up-to-date medical knowledge. For I could tell that he was a little rusty, and I wondered if sometimes this affable and agreeable companion was worried because he knew that he was not keeping up with the strides that modern medicine was taking. I never saw a copy of the *Lancet* lying round his living-room.

After a visit to the cottage hospital one day, Reid said to me, 'There's nothing to do, Kit. Take it easy. I've told you about Paula Reece, the rich American. She's giving a sort of cocktail party this evening and you're invited. And after that you and I are going to have dinner together, so just relax until then and I'll pick you up at six. Tomorrow you can move into your bungalow.'

I did just that. After a cold bath and a trickling shower I fell fast asleep, *before* lunch, on the simple but comfortable iron bedstead. I woke up after an hour or so, and just leaned out of the window looking at the half-empty Main Street. A few small boats gently disturbed the ripples where the water's edge met the beach. A couple of bare-breasted girls in sarongs were returning from the communal laundry, the washing balanced on their heads, their breasts moving gently as they sauntered by, giggling at some private joke. At the far end of the street, where the beach curved into an arc – and where the water was far enough away from the slops of Main Street – there on my right I could see a grove of coconut palms behind the beach, almost bending over the sand like a canopy as they leaned against the trade winds. And high above, at the end of the curve, the steep hillsides rose as high as the rim of the dormant volcano on High Island.

Alec Reid picked me up sharp at six, and gave an approving glance at my clean shirt, spotless white trousers (bought off the peg in Sydney) and the fact that I wore a tie.

'Let's go,' he said and led the way to the car.

The Villa Faalifu was set on the edge of Tala-Tala, and the sight of its opulent exterior almost left me gasping. It might have been transported from the South of France, one of those lush semi-palaces I had only seen in photos. It was all white, with stone steps, instead of the usual wooden ones, and on its huge veranda were several basketwork chairs and tables, and yellow sunblinds.

Every corner of the gardens blazed with colour – bougainvillaea, oleanders, hibiscus and, around one corner of the house, a mass of white tiare. And all immaculately neat. Set in a glade of thinned-out coconut palms, it was breathtaking, but what amazed me most was that, within sight of the most beautiful beaches in the world, the garden contained a large pool edged with white and blue tiles. A pool in such a place! It seemed crazy.

Around the pool a couple of dozen people were chattering and sipping drinks. A butler, a Polynesian in a trim white jacket, approached us with a tray of drinks ranging from champagne to gin fizzes or Scotch and sodas. I took a glass of champagne as Dr Reid whispered, 'Here is our hostess.'

A tall woman came towards us. She had the arrogant walk of people with leisure. She gave Dr Reid, who was wearing a collar and tie and long white ducks, a kiss on one cheek, then turned to me.

She was dressed in an expensive pair of sharkskin trousers, a silk blouse and sandals. She had lean flanks and no tummy, and I could see from the way her breasts moved slightly when she walked that she wore nothing underneath her blouse; I also had the feeling that she knew instantly that I knew. Her hair was reddish – would an actual red have been too flattering a word? I wondered – and I judged her age at about thirty. She carried a pair of sun glasses in her left hand and offered me her right hand, smiling as she shook mine. 'Doctor Masters, isn't it? – or can I call you Christopher?'

'Kit,' I smiled.

'Paula. I'm sorry we didn't meet before, but it's great to have you around. We need every handsome new face we can grab, don't we, Alec?' She smiled, not only with her mouth, but with her very large eyes, a ready smile. And she must have been fabulously rich to live in a house like this. As someone took Alec Reid away I said, 'The house is beautiful. But isn't it a bit unnecessary – a pool I mean, with the beach on your doorstep?'

'It's a salt-water pool. I have it pumped up from the sea, with a small generator of our own. And I wouldn't like to cause the entire population to come and stare at me every day.'

'I don't quite understand.'

'I like to swim in the nude.' She spoke in a matter-of-fact tone, as though all the best people did.

'Yes, I see.' And, of course, I did. It was one thing for the pale brown islanders to swim in their Mother Hubbards, or often, as I had been told, bare-breasted. But for a white American to frolic completely naked . . . 'Yes,' I repeated, smiling. 'I can see it might cause a few problems.'

'I hate to lose you, but we'll meet again soon,' she said. 'You know Colonel Fawcett, I'm sure. He's a bit old for me – I prefer young doctors any day.' She laughed. 'Come along.'

Near me, in a white open-necked shirt with short sleeves was a stocky, rather wooden-looking man, who gave me a rather uncomfortable feeling of only being at the party because he had to be. I understood why the moment Paula introduced him.

'And this is Captain Baker. Ron is the skipper of my motor cruising yacht. There, in the harbour.' She pointed to the sleek white pleasure yacht which I had seen lying at anchor at the foot of the small hill, and chaffed Baker, 'I always have the feeling he'd rather be on the water than on dry land. I had to force him to come.'

The word 'force' embarrassed me. Paula was making it clear that she was the boss and that Baker had to do as he was told – whether sailing her yacht or sipping drinks.

'She's a beauty,' Baker said as Paula moved on to greet another guest. There was real enthusiasm in his voice. 'She's got two 500-horsepower diesel engines which can take the *Nymph* and six passengers in three double state-rooms from here to Hawaii non-stop. You must come aboard and see her some time.'

'Come and say hello to some other guests,' Paula interrupted us.

She motioned to a man I had not seen before, striking in appearance, with a shock of grey hair and immaculately dressed. He smoked through a long amber cigarette holder.

'This is Count Vrinsky,' she introduced me. 'He's an American citizen now, but he comes from one of Poland's oldest and most distinguished families. He collects paintings.'

The count puffed out smoke through his long holder as we shook hands, and then Paula Reece asked him, 'Vrin, be an angel and let's have a little piano music.'

As the count walked into the house, I asked innocently, 'I thought you said he was an art collector. Is he a pianist too?'

'You're sweet,' she smiled invitingly. 'Every year when I come to Faalifu for four months or so I engage a resident

72

pianist from California. It's essential to have those tinkling notes when you feel in the mood. As a matter of fact, I've also got a resident hairdresser and a resident dressmaker. It makes life easier for me, and they don't get overworked, so it's a wonderful holiday with pay for them.'

I already recognised some members of the Union Jack Club, and Colonel Fawcett gave me a hearty handshake while his thin, ill-looking wife reminded me about joining the bridge games. Making up a four was obviously a serious problem. Immediately she asked me when I might be free, but I was able to murmur, 'It's a little difficult, Mrs Fawcett, until I get around a bit more and establish some duty rosters.'

'We're counting on you,' she said archly.

I was still standing by the pool when I saw Tiare, who walked towards me from her parked car and asked, 'How are you settling in, Doctor? Have you got the problem of help solved? It's very difficult in an island where no one really needs to work.'

'I've been lucky.' I told her what had happened, but quietly. I noticed again the touch of reserve about her. A doctor sometimes sees people with a different eye from other people, and I wondered for a moment whether, despite her beauty and her apparently special position on the island, she was really happy. The world is filled with sad women who put a brave face on their unhappiness, even on a tropical island. But she smiled, especially when another girl in her early twenties joined us, saying, 'Hello, Princess. And you must be Doctor Masters.'

'You're sure?' I laughed at the times people had used that sentence to me.

'Well, you're the only white man in Koraloona I've never seen before! I'm Lucy Young. I work for Paula. I'm her general factotum.'

'Faalifu would close down if Lucy didn't run it,' said Princess Tiare. 'How are you, Lucy?'

It's hard sometimes to describe people one only meets casually, one's observations, thoughts even, especially

73

when interrupted by people serving drinks, or other guests barging in. So all I can remember from that first evening by the pool is a general physical impression – of a sweet, typically Californian girl in her early twenties, with long legs, a firm bust, wide-apart eyes below blonde hair and – oh yes, of course! – hundreds of freckles. She looked the sort of girl who is so often a trademark of California – a girl who could dance all night, yet play tennis or golf, ride or swim the next day without the slightest effort.

'Do you like swimming or sailing?' Lucy asked.

'Swimming, yes. Sailing, only if there's an expert around.'

'Lucy's an expert.' Alec Reid had joined us. 'You'd be quite safe with her. Well, as far as the sailing is concerned.'

Ignoring the dig, Lucy said, 'Paula keeps a small sailing boat with an outboard motor, and now and again she lets me use it. You'd be surprised how beautiful the other side of Koraloona is when you see it from the sea.'

'It's a date.' I tried to match her Californian accent. 'If you can fix it with your boss, I can fix it with mine.'

We stayed at the party till eight o'clock, but many others, including several members of the Union Jack Club, remained to play bridge.

As we drove to Alec Reid's house for our first dinner together – and the first sight of his house – I said, 'You know, Alec, I thought this was going to be a simple unsophisticated life on the next best thing to a coral atoll. Instead I've been thrust into the sort of social whirl I never experienced in Nottingham – or in London, for that matter.'

'There's nothing else for people to do.' He carefully turned the corner leading up to the hill behind Anani. 'So they throw parties, with the same people in attendance every time. Thank goodness there's no duty on alcohol!'

'Super house Paula has. I liked her secretary – Lucy.'

'I thought you weren't slow in agreeing to the sailing trip.

But watch your step, Kit.' He stopped the car at the end of his garden. 'Lucy has a job in a million. I'd hate her to suffer, because of you.'

5

Dr Reid's bungalow – half a mile or so up the hill – was a house of character, a real home, filled with the personality of the man himself. This was hard to pinpoint, for as a doctor he was, to say the least of it, a sloppy, unorthodox dresser – a fact echoed by his large airy living-room, with its couple of ceiling fans, lazily turning. I had the impression that there were hands anxious to tidy up, but never succeeding. Large armchairs, with loose covers, looked comfortable, but when I sat in one it had a broken spring. A magazine rack overflowed with rolled newspapers: they had obviously arrived by post, but many were unopened, as though Reid hadn't had time to catch up with news that must have been at least a month old. Even with the drama of Munich and the prospect of war it seemed as though Alec Reid had not found time for the outside world.

No sooner was I seated than Reid shouted out, 'Bubble and Squeak! Old Rarity!' Mystified, I watched a pale brown girl in her teens enter with a tray on which there were two bottles of whisky – one squarish, one round – glasses, and a jug of water kept clean with a small muslin cover edged with blue beads. What happened next was evidently part of a carefully rehearsed rigmarole.

'You'd like what we Scots call a wee dram?' Reid asked.

'Love to.'

'Ice?'

As it happened I didn't like ice in whisky and this pleased Alec. To the girl, he shouted, 'Square!' At which she reached for a bottle of whisky called Old Rarity. He explained: 'I serve ordinary Scotch only to people who like explained: 'I serve ordinary Scotch only to people who like ice. But Old Rarity's my own favourite tipple. It costs thirteen shillings instead of twelve-and-six for the standard brands, so I'm not giving it to heathens who spoil its flavour with ice.'

The girl poured out a generous measure and then, obviously without the faintest idea what she was saying, but had learned by rote, she smilingly asked me 'Saywhen-pleasesir?'

She must have thought she was using some magic pass-word known only to the foreigners who drank this strange golden liquid in preference to kava. After handing me a glass she gave one to Reid, and then, as though unthinkingly, straightened the fringe of hair round the back of his neck.

'Cheers.' Reid held up his glass. 'And welcome to ma modest home.'

'You seem to have your barman – or rather, bargirl – well trained. But I'm puzzled by the "Bubble and Squeak" shout you gave.'

'It's quite simple. A couple of twin girls do for me. Unpronounceable names. As like as two peas in a pod. I can't tell 'em apart, so I call 'em Bubble and Squeak, and whichever one answers it doesn't make any difference.'

We walked out on to the large veranda and sat down with the lagoon spread out below and in front of us. I still couldn't believe I was here, in a different world, all peace and beauty. That and the intriguing touch of intimacy when she had stroked the back of his neck. At first we just made conversation, but after a couple of drinks Reid looked at me thoughtfully, twiddling his half-empty glass, and said, 'There's no reason not to tell you this, Kit, but since we've got to work together, I'd rather explain my mode of living before the old cats on the island – the European gossips – start telling you stories. I have no time for gossips, but in an island like this – ' he called for another round.

'This is not London, you know, and the local girls are happy-go-lucky, so the relationships when you're living in the same house tend to be even more happy-go-lucky.'

76

'I understand,' was all I could murmur.

'Don't get me wrong,' Reid added. 'I'm a happily married man, but as I told you, I've had to compromise. When I get to our house on Wimbledon Common – that's every three years, when I get leave – it's wonderful to be back. But only for the first day or so; after a week I can't wait to return to Koraloona.'

Though I was new to the island, I had read enough – from Henty to the *Boy's Own Paper* – to understand that the spell of the South Seas, with its different tempo of life, must grow on a man until it reaches the stage where it cannot be resisted. It forms a part of a man's life, more deeply ingrained as he matures. So, even though I was young and inexperienced, I felt that I could appreciate some of the feelings of men like Captain Robins, and now this strange and kindly doctor, 'happily' married to a woman rich enough to live in a big house facing Wimbledon Common while he preferred a far-off island; each partner more in love with a way of life than with one another.

'As a matter of fact,' Alec Reid firmed down a new pipeful of tobacco, 'I might ha' made a name for meself had I remained in Edinburgh. I had a guid record, and my wife had it all planned out. She had a tidy amount of money of her own. And she'd have bought me a practice. But then I asked for just one spell of six months as a locum in some exotic place. As ye know, most doctors in the islands get six months' leave every three years, and I volunteered to take one man's place soon after I had qualified. Took the wee wife along too.'

He chuckled again at the memory. 'It happened to be Koraloona. She hated it. I fell in love with it. When the resident doctor whom I was replacing died in Australia during his leave, the missionaries offered me his job. And ye know, I never hesitated. My wife went back to Britain. She said I'd chosen the path to failure. Aye, we're still friends, but she'll never understand that I'm nae a failure, I'm a success. I've discovered the secret of happiness. That's my success. I want nothing more of life. I have no regrets. D'ye ken anyone who can boast of that? But maybe ye'll be different, ye just want a taste of the exotic life and then ye'll go back to the big time.'

I wondered. At that moment I could see no reason for ever wanting to leave Koraloona. I could visualise, as we sat under the rattan shade of the veranda, passing a perfect life on the island – a comfortable house, a garden in which I could grow everything I needed, enough fish to eat. Enough work so that I could enjoy it but not so much work that I would be fed up.

'Ye may stay, at that.' Alec Reid relit his pipe. 'But dinna let me persuade you with a lot of sentimental drivel.'

'I think I'll stay a while,' I smiled. 'As your assistant.'

As though reading my thoughts, Reid added, wiping his sweating head, 'It's the way of life I like, nothing more, ye ken? You'll find out for yourself, Kit.'

He was a strange man. He had had all the advantages of what my father called 'a good family background'; he spoke with an educated voice; he had been raised to respect good manners. Yet this contrasted oddly with his sloppy clothes, his bare knees and hairy legs, for he seemed to see nothing peculiar about a doctor who behaved like a gentleman but who looked like a beachcomber. However, even my limited medical training told me that Alec Reid was good at his profession; his medical supplies might be limited, but he knew his South Seas. In a way, though, that limited him and made him out of touch with modern medicine.

Picking up his last remark, I asked, 'Do all the girls have the same happy-go-lucky attitude to – well, friendships? After all, there are girls and girls, even on a South Seas island.'

'I don't quite understand?'

'Well, the Princess. You told me you'd explain about Tiare and her daughter, where they fit into the island.'

'Oh, Tiare! She's married for the second time. Her husband, Aleena's stepfather, is called Mana. He's half Japanese. He guards both wife and daughter like a samurai. He's a terrible man.'

'What's his full name?'

'He doesn't have a surname, like many men on the islands,' Reid explained.

'And Aleena's real father?'

'Died. For no apparent reason. My belief is that Mana wanted to marry Tiare – maybe for the inheritance – and it's made Aleena very unhappy. That's really why Aleena, who's only thirteen, goes to boarding school in Sanderstown. Gives her a bit of freedom. And of course there's nothing on Koraloona but the two mission schools I mentioned.'

'It all sounds very mysterious.' I was puzzled.

'Look, I've promised I'll tell ye the story of that family, and after dinner I will. But now, I'm starved.'

With a sudden change of voice he gave a roar, 'Bubble and Squeak! Makeum dinner fast!'

'Coming sir,' they both trilled, and soon we were sitting down at the dining table in a corner of the living-room.

'It's only rissoles, I'm afraid,' said Alec, but if I felt a pang of disappointment that the first meal at his house wasn't going to be out of the ordinary I was mistaken. No rissoles ever tasted so good.

I gratefully accepted a second helping. 'What on earth do you put in them?'

'Actually they're meat and coconut, just mixed together with a touch of coriander. Like the sauce?'

I did.

'The Polynesians combine the most extraordinary opposites. This is basically made of mangoes and chopped green peppers. Sounds foul, but it tastes good on meat.'

After dinner, sitting on the veranda, with his pipe well alight and with a glass of neat Old Rarity at his side, Alec Reid told me the extraordinary story of the fortune which he said belonged to Tiare. For the sake of clarity, and since its fate is fundamental to what happened later, I have tried to omit my interruptions and the questions which demanded answers, and reduce it to a simple account based on the facts that Alec Reid told me.

79

Tiare's mother, the hereditary Princess, who received an allowance from the New Zealand government, was called Marama – which in one Polynesian sense means 'woman' but in her case meant 'Princess Woman'. When still unmarried, she met a penniless and obviously sick Frenchman who had lived in the South Seas and had come to Koraloona to paint. It wasn't just the usual liaison: the two of them fell head over heels in love. From stories handed down, it seems that the Frenchman saw Marama, insisted on painting her straight away, and then said she was the most beautiful woman he'd ever seen and begged her to come and live with him. Which she did. Very happily.

Though the artist was ill with tuberculosis and had no money to pay for his keep, Marama looked after him while he painted her over and over again; sometimes nude, sometimes dressed, and nearly always against the background of island scenery – near the waterfalls and the secret pools, in dells that laced the volcanic slopes, in the village market, in the main street of Anani.

The illness – the tuberculosis – slowly worsened, and soon it was apparent that the painter would die unless he received medical attention. He was racked by coughs that almost tore him apart. Sometimes he spat blood. He was undernourished. And Koraloona in those days had virtually no medical facilities. The painter told Marama that if he wanted to live he must go to Rarotonga and receive treatment. He begged Marama to travel with him, but she refused. For one thing, she said, they could hardly scrape up enough money for one deck passage, let alone two, for in two years he had sold only three paintings for a few pounds. There was another reason which Marama didn't reveal, until the day before he was due to sail, when she told the painter that she was three months pregnant.

The painter at first refused to sail. He was, he said, overjoyed at the thought of her having a child. But staying meant dying, and now the painter had an added reason for wanting to live. And he knew that Marama, because of her title, would always be looked after if she stayed on

Koraloona, so it would be wrong of him to be selfish and expect her to live in semi-starvation on a strange island.

The painter promised to return as soon as he was well. And on the last day he led the girl he loved to a shack he had built behind their tiny house and which he called his studio. She was staggered. The walls were a blaze of colour – vivid, exciting, dramatic paintings that all but covered the walls, and she was in nearly every one of them.

'These are for you,' he told her. 'They are a keepsake. There are seventeen of them and a few sketches. If you are short of money, you might get a few pounds for one, but if not, keep them till I return to see you – and our child.'

'I'll never sell them,' cried Marama. 'That I vow.'

In fact the painter never did return to Koraloona – and Marama, his mistress, always thought he had abandoned her, and over the years became obsessed by bitterness at the betrayal, for she never knew that in 1903 the painter had died, after she had given birth to a daughter, a baby girl so white that her mother christened her Tiare, after the beautiful white flower of the South Seas.

By the time Tiare was ten, her mother made the girl promise never to marry until she was at least nineteen, telling her that hasty love affairs never led to happiness. Tiare made the promise which was solemnised by the local 'witch-doctor'. But when Tiare's mother died and Tiare was only seventeen, she broke the vow. The local spiritual leaders warned her that she would suffer, after she fell in love and married – and she did, after the birth of Aleena.

'And I'll tell ye,' Alec Reid summoned Bubble and Squeak for another drink, 'that's a guid reason why the young kid Aleena will never wed before she's nineteen. She knows what happened to her grandma and her mother Tiare, who took a beating and made Aleena take the same vow. Aleena's a serious kid and she's learned the lesson.'

'All that's fine,' I said, though I wasn't particularly interested in the vows of a child who had just gone to

81

boarding school. 'You say that the paintings have been handed down. Is that all there is to the story?' I was a little disappointed. 'Will they ever be worth anything?'

'Aye, they might,' said Alec Reid drily. 'After all, the man who fell in love with Princess Marama and left the paintings to Tiare was a Frenchman you might have heard of – Paul Gauguin.'

Suddenly, sitting there on the veranda sipping whisky, I coughed and spluttered into my glass. 'Heard of!' It was Gauguin whom Maugham had made the hero of *The Moon and Sixpence*. And not long before leaving England I'd read a newspaper item revealing that a Gauguin landscape bought by another novelist, Hugh Walpole, in 1924 for £145 would now in the thirties be worth around £6,000, and that Hermann Goering in Nazi Germany had recently paid Alfred Krupp the armaments boss 10,000 Reichmarks for another of the wayward artist's pictures. £6,000 was double what a Rolls-Royce Phantom III cost, three times as much as Reid's Gloster plane! Thus had values increased.

'Gauguin!' I said. 'They must be worth a fortune!'

'They could be worth a million for all the difference it would make,' said Reid. 'They'll never be sold. The old lady, Marama, vowed never to sell, and made Tiare and eventually Aleena repeat the vow.' With a dry touch, he added, 'They take their vows seriously in the islands. There are native gods and most islanders are genuinely afraid of them.'

'Gauguin!' I repeated. The very name was invested with magic. 'All here on this tiny island,' I said. 'Little more than a coral atoll. And seventeen times six thousand . . .'

'Plus a few sketches he left behind,' added Reid.

'But do you realise what they could fetch one day? Art prices have been soaring. People are buying pictures as a hedge against war and inflation. Who knows, if the Gauguins were left on the island one day they might be worth – ' I drew a breath – 'twenty or even thirty thousand each?'

'I wouldn'a go as far as that,' Reid reproved me.

'But where are they?' And before Reid could answer, further questions tumbled out. 'Are they still in good condition? They must be forty years old, at least. What about the exposure to sea air? Are they properly protected?'

'Don't panic, Laddie! One question at a time. I'm not sure exactly where they're stored, but Tiare told me once that her father' – that sounded an odd description of Gauguin – 'had given her mother instructions on how to protect them. I'm sure they're stored properly. I'm also sure that they're well and truly hidden from prying eyes like yours or mine.'

Of course, it was none of my business where the 'missing' Gauguins were stored, except that I would have enjoyed seeing them, even if prompted only by curiosity. After all, it's not everyone who has a private view of paintings worth £100,000 – a lot of money in those pre-war, pre-inflation days – but which have never been on public view.

'Have *you* seen them?' I asked.

Reid nodded. 'Aye, I have. When Tiare's husband knew he was dying he thanked me and wanted to know if there was anything he could do – a kind of last request. I asked him if he or Tiare could let me see the "inheritance"; and I saw it.'

'Wonderful?'

'I suppose so, but it's a matter of taste. Remember, I'm of Scots descent, and I prefer our own artists like Willie Flint with his pretty titty girls or William McTaggart. Did you know that Queen Victoria put him in the same class as Landseer? I don't take to these modernistic people who just splash on daubs of paint. Whoever saw a beach of red sand, or a woman with a green face? Give me the Monarch of the Glen any day.

'But enough about pictures! Have a wee deoch and dorris afore ye go?'

'You mean one for the road?' I smiled. 'I've never heard the expression before – what did you call it?'

'Ye dinna say! Ye never knew how the other half lives!

Deoch means drink and dorris means door. So it's one for the door if ye prefer it.'

It took me some time to put the fantastic story of the Gauguin inheritance behind me – not out of my mind, but to the back of it, not only because I wondered if they might deteriorate, but also at the bizarre irony of a family sitting on a fortune which they refused to touch.

However, a couple of days later I moved into my bungalow and it was quite a job. In preparation for a long stay, I had several suitcases, a packing case, a cabin trunk, my portable gramophone and records, all my medical equipment. I had help lugging the heavy cases from Jim Wilson's truck, but I had to do my share; and even *thinking* of where to put things was exhausting.

By the time this chore was finished, I was so tired I fell into a doze on the veranda, dreaming of a Gauguin nude of Aleena's grandmother, and then of a painting of Tiare and her daughter, and then how easy it would be if they could all come and live with me and we could just hang the pictures on the walls and enjoy them. Reality was more drab, I thought ruefully when I woke up. The only decoration on the walls of my new home consisted of an old half-used calendar for 1935.

Actually it wasn't a bad bungalow, and I soon settled in. It was impersonal, furnished to the exact specifications of any government building in the islands that goes with a civil servant of a particular grade; the chairs and table in 'ant-proof' hardwood, lacquered a pale brown, three armchairs, one sofa, chairs and table on the verandah, a desk, two bedrooms, a couple of beds, their legs in jars of water, a shower. Impersonal, yes, but quite practical, though of course lacking the warmth and atmosphere I enjoyed at home. Still, I had an overseas news radio set and sometimes at dusk when I turned it on for the BBC overseas news, the light on its dial welcomed me like a beacon from home.

In a way though, the garden was the best feature. By

design or nature, it was on the hill above Main Street and was large and ringed with thirty-foot-high breadfruit trees shading the ground with their thick, dark green leaves. There was a pomelo tree, its fruit tasting like grapefruit, but each one the size of a football. One hedge was of sago. Until I first inspected the garden I hadn't even had the faintest idea that you could grow your own sago as a fence against your neighbour and then eat it! There was one big mango tree, a couple of coconut palms, their tufted branches reminding me of Mother's feather duster. All of this magical garden was set in an acre of tough, fibrous grass on which a boy with a curved knife squatted on his haunches while cropping the 'lawns'. It was wonderful.

If the garden was more exciting than my dwelling, there was a good reason why Alec Reid's house should have a more lived-in feeling. His wife had come out to the island on his first posting and, before she decided to return to London, she had bought the bungalow and furnished it.

'She made a good job of it too,' Alec explained, adding like a good Scot, 'and of course there's a small benefit to me because now I draw a rent allowance.'

In only one respect were my original living arrangements altered, and it was all for the best. The girl who had been selected for me by Miss Sowerby never turned up. It transpired that her family had moved to Tala-Tala and she couldn't face the daily ten miles on foot.

Instead Miss Sowerby had discovered an excellent young half-Chinese man of twenty-two, and like most Chinese he could cook, do the laundry, press and whatever little else was needed about the house. In other words, a cookboy. He was called Toma.

Everyone wanted to help! The feeling of hospitality, of kindness, was warming. When I said goodbye to Mollie Green she announced, 'The next lunch is on me, Doc.' And before Bill Robins left for Sanderstown he gave me his address and telephone number, saying, 'I'll be really hurt if you ever come to Sanderstown and don't look me up.' And then, a few days later, I had an unexpected bonus.

85

The man responsible was Jason Purvis. I had been horrified at his scarecrow appearance when I first saw him at the clinic, and when I met him by chance in Tala-Tala I felt so sorry for him that I asked him if he would like to come for dinner. I'm not quite sure what prompted the invitation. Perhaps it was because I found it hard to define his place on the island. He looked like a half-starved bum, yet he was evidently a man who had known better times. I don't quite know why, but he gave me the impression, without uttering more than a few words, that he had much more than superficial knowledge, and an amusing touch of the sardonic as well.

'I'd love to. I'm starving. Literally.' Then he added, 'Black tie?'

'Not tonight,' I said gravely. 'I think an open-necked shirt.'

'By the way,' he said, 'I was passing by your bungalow last night when I heard you playing a gramophone.'

I nodded.

'Well, I've got loads of records but nothing to play them on. I had to flog mine. Do you like classical music? Shall I bring some round? Do you like piano music?' With an almost sad look that increased the appearance of melancholy, he said, 'I remember hearing Pachmann playing the Chopin B Minor Sonata at the Aeolian Hall in Bond Street in 1929. I can even remember the date, September 29.'

'I'd love it. I'll come and pick you up,' I said, not out of courtesy, but because Purvis didn't look as though he had the strength to carry even a dozen records.

In the end Purvis and his records opened up a new world for me, starting on that very first dinner when we played Beethoven's Archduke Trio, the one in B flat major, 'Opus 97,' he added casually.

'Keep the lot,' he said, 'then you'll have to invite me again to hear my own records. One meal a week with you and I won't even have to go cap in hand to Johnson's store.'

'You don't like Johnson do you?' I didn't either and he knew it.

'I can't stand him,' he said. 'He doesn't do a damn thing for the good of mankind, but makes one hell of a fat living by buying cheap from one worker and selling the same thing dear to another worker. Just a bloody parasite.'

'But still,' I smiled, 'you do need the go-betweens of this world.'

'You know what I mean. You're a doctor with an Oxford education. You do something useful. So does a coalminer who's had virtually no education. I respect both of you equally. But Johnson! He doesn't do a damn thing, he doesn't even pay his wife wages – I give up!'

Another bonus arrived within a week, when I had the first glimpse from the sea of the opposite coastline of Kora-loona, with its empty sandy beaches and the great dormant volcano of High Island rearing up behind it, while in the distance I could even make out Hodges, the copra island. And I didn't see this from the decks of the *Mantela* but from a twenty-one-foot sailing boat, *Faalifu III*, piloted skilfully by a skipper wearing white shorts, a kind of woollen T-shirt and a saucy sailor's cap – Lucy Young. She had promised to take me sailing, and Paula had let her borrow the boat for a few hours, as she had often done before.

I arranged to meet her in the tiny port at Tala-Tala where she was waiting for me. She looked so fresh and happy that I started grinning as soon as I waved to her, standing below me in the cockpit of the boat, where a servant from Faalifu was carrying some packages while Captain Baker looked down from the bridge.

'It's beautiful,' I said as the man stowed the parcels into the tiny cabin. 'But I warn you, I'm a landlubber: I've never sailed a boat in my life. I vaguely remember words like "mizzen mast", but I haven't a clue what any of them mean.'

'Don't worry, we have an outboard motor. We'll forget the sails. Then it's just like driving a car. I've got a packed lunch, a thermos of ice-cold martinis, and some beer and Coke. Welcome aboard!'

As I clambered into the boat, moored near her big yacht, Lucy took the bottles of beer and Coca-Cola and put them into an open net bag which she lowered over the side, tying the net with a long rope to a hook on the gunwale.

'Once we start moving,' she explained, 'the water rushing past will keep your beer colder than any fridge.'

I went below and peered inside the cabin - a tiny fixed table with divan-type seats on either side.

'Supposed to turn into beds,' she said, addingly lightly, 'but not my idea of a honeymoon suite.'

It was a beautiful sunny morning, and at eleven o'clock, after I had done a quick surgery, we chugged quietly out of the harbour, with Lucy at the controls. Once outside she said, 'I've got my costume under my clothes.' She started to pull the jersey over her head. 'You can change into your bathing trunks in the cabin. But keep your sports shirt on until we start swimming. With the sea and sun and wind you'll fry if you don't take care.'

Inside the cabin, separated from this long-legged, tanned Californian girl who never seemed to stop smiling, I felt a tingle of pleasant, uncomfortable tightness in my close-fitting trunks.

What a pretty, unaffected girl she was, full of life and fun. And efficient! The way she sailed the boat. What on earth was a stunning girl like this doing in Koraloona?

'It's a breath of fresh air having you around,' I said. 'What made you come to Koraloona?'

'I met Paula at a party in San Francisco where she lives. She needed a manageress, if that's the right word, three years ago – a sort of paid annual summer vacation.'

'Is it really a vacation?' echoing the American word. 'Is it difficult to get away when you're working? I mean, for a day like this?'

'Sometimes, yes. Paula is a perfectionist and everything is fine so long as there are no snags. Then she *can* be a little difficult.'

'But what exactly do you do?'

She smiled, turned course and steered for the deeper

waters near the edge of the reef. 'I just run the place. Everything. I don't do any *physical* work, if that's what you mean. Dusting or hoovering,' she laughed lightly. 'But I do have to see that the servants do everything, and since they all seem to leave as soon as they've saved up enough money, half my time is spent finding replacements and training them. I have to check on everything: liquor stocks; whether the pool filter is working; is the garden untidy?'

'Sounds tough,' I sympathised.

'It isn't really, though I've got to watch Paula. But on the other hand I get $1000 a month tax free for five months every year, and so far in three years I haven't touched a cent of the money. I'm just about set to realise a dream.'

'Which is?'

'I've already paid down two-thirds for an artist's cottage in Sausolito, a village across the other side of the Golden Gate bridge from San Francisco. Between Mount Tamalpais and the Bay.'

'And then what are you going to do?'

'Invite you to come and see me on your next leave,' she laughed.

'That's a date – if there isn't a war.'

'Will there be?'

'Not here in the Pacific,' I said, 'but in Europe – there might be. The outlook's pretty grim.'

It was a heavenly morning. Half a mile or so out, we swam in the deep water under the lee of the conical shape of the High Island's volcano. Later, we sailed out towards the reef. It was an extraordinary sensation to see the thrashing, churning water on one side while, inside the lagoon a yard or two away, the water was calm. It seems odd, but I was enjoying myself so much that I hardly gave a thought to the fact that we were alone, miles away from anyone, and that the average man in such a situation . . .

But I did get another tingle of excitement when I swam a shade too near a jagged reef, and she grabbed me by the shoulder to pull me away. I must have brushed my back against her breasts, but then the touch of her was over and she shouted, 'How about lunch?'

We swam back to the boat, I climbed up the steps fastened near the stern, and gave her a helping hand. Again I had a sense of excitement as I touched her, holding her hand, then her arm, until she was on the boat, looking for a towel. But within a few moments we were sipping extra-dry martinis from paper cups, then eating cold chicken and tinned ham, with beer chilled by the sea. I said with a laugh, 'You're taking an awful risk, inviting me like this alone with you on a boat.'

She gave me a frank, laughing look. 'I know what you'd like to do – and it may surprise you, Kit, if I admit that part of me may even want to myself. But rushing things is so wrong. Let's wait and see what happens, Kit. Will you?'

'If I must. I'm not a professional seducer, you know. But does that mean – ?'

'I hope so. There, I've admitted it. I hope so. Just give both of us time to get our breath, so that we both feel it's worth it. Do you understand?'

'Not really.'

'Look at it this way. We're not pretending that we're in love with each other. We're attracted – and that's a different emotion.'

As I started to protest, she said, 'No, don't be hypocritical. We're a healthy normal couple. I've had the occasional boyfriend in the past, and I'm sure you've done the same sort of thing. But let's enjoy the pleasure of waiting. Don't let's be seduced by the easy sexual habits of the islanders.'

'I suppose I do understand.'

As we made for home, and reached the tiny harbour of Tala-Tala, the silence between us was almost strained. Neither was angry; perhaps she, like me, was battling with secret thoughts. Fortunately we had other things to occupy us as we reached the spot in the harbour where the boat was normally moored. We edged in. I stood ready with the boat-hook to make sure we didn't bump against the rocks of the mooring. A couple of the crew members from

Paula's yacht, who were waiting for us, grabbed a line and made the sailing boat fast.

I didn't want her to think I was angry or disappointed, and as I helped her ashore, I smiled and said, 'I understand,' and, caught in the no-man's-land between desire and fulfilment, leant forward rather clumsily to kiss her. But she avoided my lips, so that I brushed her cheek, and as I tried to find her mouth she said, 'No, Kit. If you kiss me, I might have to say "Yes".'

Then she added, 'One day, it won't be long, I think, and it won't be contrived, then I'll come knocking on your door.'

6

It was amazing how quickly the weeks passed as I settled into the routine of life on Koraloona. Everything was done at a leisurely tempo. Day-to-day life was governed by the pace of the inhabitants, and there was no point in running from A to B when everyone else walked slowly.

Yet even so, the dispensary was busy every day, and we did have a great deal of work, dealing with the humdrum, everyday ailments – yaws, measles, 'flu and accidents – accepted by the Polynesians with a philosophical resignation, as though they were saying, 'This is the price we pay for living in paradise.' We had our crises too – including deaths from the dreadful tetanus; I had to keep records of all this in the only 'office' I possessed – the old tin trunk bequeathed to us by Tiare's mother so long ago.

But though busy, there was time to swim at least twice a day in warm water, fanned by warm breezes, with an average temperature the year round of between 70° and 80° Fahrenheit, and always against a magical scenic backdrop that never ceased to enchant me. I felt at peace with the world, even though by the summer of 1939 Europe seemed to be drifting closer to war and everyone was glued to the BBC short-wave Overseas Service bulletins, or even devouring month-old copies of *The Times* which had been airmailed to Australia and sent on by ship, together with the *Illustrated London News*, *Tatler*, and particular titles ordered by the expatriates.

There was quite a social calendar to keep me occupied if I ever tired of my own company. I met Bill Robins regularly when the *Mantela* docked, sometimes for lunch at Green's Hotel. Once a week at least Alec Reid and I dined together. I had been so horrified by Jason Purvis' physical condition that, almost unwittingly, I had taken him in hand. It was no use offering him money, for he would immediately spend it on drink, but I suggested that he try his hand at very light work – sweeping the hospital floor, later a little gardening, and for this I paid him in meals cooked by Toma at home. He loved it.

Sometimes I managed to find stocks of surplus out-of-date doctor's forms and he used these to type out rough drafts of his latest short story or chapters of his novel on his old Remington Portable – about the only thing he hadn't sold – and occasionally he would bring one round for me to read. His work wasn't bad, and I had the feeling that one day, if only he would persist, he might write a novel that would be published.

At least his latest attempt was a story on a subject which he knew about. It told the story of a man who had searched for happiness on an island like Koraloona, only to be disillusioned, yet unable to tear himself away.

It was very good – even though it left a nasty taste in my mouth, the same sort of shudder I felt when I first read *The Turn of the Screw*. Was Purvis influenced by the same kind of eeriness when surrounded by beauty on this island? He launched into a long explanation, when I tackled him.

'It *is* beautiful,' he admitted. 'But sometimes events or thoughts or even characters take charge when you're working. No, I'm not being pompous. After all, these islands have been steeped for centuries in everything from witchcraft to ancestor worship. It's still all around us. They're really about as Christian as headhunters. Maybe what I can't help bringing into some of my work is that all this beauty on Koraloona demands a price. And the happier you are, the higher the price you may one day have to pay.

'My God! What balls I am talking,' he laughed. 'For God's sake give me a drink, Kit.'

As I poured out his fourth large Scotch, I wondered, would I too ever be disillusioned with Koraloona? So far, it was love at first sight. It showed no signs of waning. But sometimes there was an uneasy undercurrent to disturb the tranquillity – including, of course, the feeling that I was marking time while great and stirring events were in the offing – war, for instance. If war broke out, would I come to regret having buried myself in some backwater while history passed me by?

These were only occasional solemn thoughts, and there was one easy way to avoid any sense of boredom: go to the Villa Faalifu and see the elegant Paula Reece – with a chance, too, of meeting Lucy. Paula always held open-house cocktail parties on Tuesdays and Fridays, and if you were a friend, no invitations were required. So I often popped in, sometimes alone, sometimes with Alec, for a drink after a day's work. Jason came fairly regularly, and occasionally Baker too was pressed into service. Once or twice Paula teased me about nude swimming, and once she gave me a brief conducted tour of the gardens and the house. But not upstairs. 'Another time perhaps,' she suggested. Upstairs included a bed large enough to sleep ten people. 'My fun bedroom!' she explained. But often she had men staying with her.

I didn't actually *like* Paula very much – she flaunted her wealth as though it was marked with a price tag – but I didn't actively *dislike* her. Hard to explain the conflict in our acquaintance, but perhaps I had an instinctive feeling that she, in fact, wanted me to go to bed with her, and she knew I wouldn't – because if I did make love to her, it would be a victory for her and a defeat for me.

Lucy of course was always fun, and I talked to her at Paula's villa whenever I went there. But I had to watch my step. Paula's eyes could be cold and angry if she disliked something. Once I was talking alone to Lucy in a corner, laughing together and, as I impulsively took one of her hands in both of mine, I heard a sharp cry of 'Lucy! We need some more ice. Tell that damn fool waiter to get some.' And as Lucy walked into the house, Paula looked right through me.

Alec Reid had treated several cases of polio during my first year or so in Koraloona, but there were never any signs of an epidemic. Then one day, when I visited the hospital by chance – Alec was 'on duty' – a boy of eight arrived at the surgery, carried by his father. The boy was whimpering with pain and his left leg was twisted awkwardly. I thought I recognised his face, and I was right, for Alec said, 'Yes, he came in with 'flu symptoms about a fortnight ago. I gave him the standard treatment and told him to come back immediately if he didn't get better.'

'And he didn't come back?'

Alec shook his head in annoyance. 'They rarely do,' he said. 'The trouble is that even when it's a bad virus it always looks like 'flu – and remember, the polio itself dies out in about a week. It's the *symptoms* that are left behind. Look at this poor little devil now.'

The boy's bright face, with its wide, open eyes, was contorted in agony. His twisted left leg was bent at the knee, and though the Polynesians are a stoic race, he was fighting a losing battle to stem the tears.

While the other patients crowded outside and Miss Sowerby tried to keep them in order, Alec motioned to the father to carry the boy into the 'ops' theatre and lay him down on his back on the operating table so that we could make a more detailed examination.

One look was enough to confirm that this *was* polio, and

that the delay in coming to see us probably meant that we had passed the porodomal, or incubatory stage. The patient was probably already in the second stage of muscle pain, leading to the destruction of the muscle, something that could happen in as little as ten days. Then I saw that the disease had also struck the right leg. The muscle wastage had caused a dropped foot – like the little girl who had been treated by Alec. The boy said nothing, only looked at both of us with wide-open eyes, but there were no tears despite the pain.

'That left leg needs bone surgery,' said Alec as we asked the father to wait outside. 'He ought to go to Sanderstown right away and have an operation for arthrodesis by a proper orthopaedic surgeon.'

I knew that – from his point of view – this was the correct treatment. But I had a sudden vision of poor Clare, imprisoned in irons for the rest of her life.

'I don't think it's necessary, Alec,' I muttered.

Almost as though explaining the normal techniques to a med student, he said patiently, 'You know, Laddie, that what I want to do is restore the affected joint to its proper position of function.' He was using standard medical terms. 'Especially if a muscle is wasted. At least arthrodesis is an operation that will immobilise a joint so that the bones grow solidly together.'

'I admit that,' I said, adding bitterly, 'but at what a cost! It usually results in the loss of the muscle below the bone. And then it has to be supported by a brace.'

I looked at the little boy, lying there, and caught a glimpse of the father peeping from the corridor. The father was a tall, straight-backed man, obviously proud of his suffering son. What a tragedy if that son had to wear a brace for the rest of his life.

Impulsively – and straight from the heart – I said, 'Give me forty-eight hours, Alec. At least I'm sure I can relieve the pain – look at that poor kid!' Seeing Alec's dour expression, I added, 'And it won't do any harm to let me try.'

'It could, and both you and I know it, Kit,' Alec replied. 'Come and have another look. Ye ken –' he took the boy's leg again, and with one hand raised the calf muscle below the knee. 'Those muscles are sagging, they're flaccid, and the whole leg is being pulled out of its true shape by the strong muscles surrounding them. The leg must be operated on and straightened, then put into splints or plaster, or the kid'll remain in that crippled position for the rest of his life. Aye, I know that the calf muscles will atrophy, but at least they can be supported by a brace and the boy'll be able to walk.'

'Only with sticks!' I said sharply. 'And anyway, I don't think the muscles *are* flaccid.' I paused. 'At least they might not be. The pain is being caused by spasms – like sudden bursts of uncontrollable cramp. It's agony. Look at the sweat on that little boy's twisted face. And there's no *proof* that the boy's muscles *are* completely dead. Don't you think we should give him the benefit of the doubt?'

'There *is* nae doot – and you know it,' said Alec, not unkindly. 'I know how you feel – your sister's problems – and the fact that you saw this Australian woman perform a kind of miracle. But you have to bear in mind that we *are* doctors, and as such we should really do what we're trained to do – and are expected to do.'

'I know all that,' I began to feel angry and frustrated, 'but Goddammit, the only reason I came to this island was because of my interest in polio. Yet so far I seem to have been treating nothing worse than chicken pox and 'flu. I *know* I'm right. You can't just ignore the fact that people *have* been cured – all right, I agree, they are unorthodox methods. But give me a chance. Have some faith in me – in what I believe in.'

Suddenly remembering a casual conversation, I cried, 'Miss Sowerby! Can you spare a moment?'

She came in through the corridor, shuffling in her thick black clothes. Without waiting, I asked her, 'You told me once that you'd seen Sister Kenny treat a polio patient.'

It was one of the rare occasions when her tight-lipped mouth opened into something approaching a smile.

'It was a miracle!' She was speaking to us both. 'I never saw anything like it. She came to one of our mission hospitals when I was training in Australia.'

'So you'd know how to help me with the treatment – if Doctor Reid allows us.'

'Yes, Doctor, I would. And I hope you can do something for this little lad here. Look at him – the pain.' I caught sight of the boy, trapped in an uncontrollable spasm of painful cramp, and I smiled, took one hand, stroked his face, wet with sweat, and said, 'Be patient and brave.'

'You didn't tell me this,' said Alec to Miss Sowerby.

'Never thought to mention it,' she retorted, po-faced again.

'I may be old-fashioned,' Alec sighed, 'but I hate experimenting in a lonely spot like this.'

'We're not experimenting, Alec,' I cried, my voice filled with passion, 'we're *believing* – Miss Sowerby and me. Yes, even Miss Sowerby –' and breaking the tension I smiled to her and said, 'Sorry about the "even".'

'Well.' I could see that Alec was hesitating. 'If anything does go wrong – '

'You're not afraid of a report on unprofessional conduct? If you are, I'll sign now that I've tried this treatment without your approval.' For a moment another thought crossed my mind – that if I lived in the United States while undertaking an 'experiment' I might be sued if I failed. 'Remember, Alec, the doctor in London who gave me the job did say Koraloona was a living laboratory for the treatment of polio. Do let me have a chance to prove what I believe in.'

'I did promise to give you that chance,' he admitted. 'But it's on your own head. And if you fail – you'll have a cripple for life on your conscience.'

'Can you promise that the boy won't be a cripple for life anyway?'

He shook his head. 'All right – go ahead,' he said quietly.

'And if there's anything you need – ' To Miss Sowerby he said, 'Give Doctor Masters all the help he requires while he tries this new treatment.'

Miss Sowerby nodded – and not with pursed lips.

'Thank you, Alec,' I said, and to Miss Sowerby, 'You know the drill?'

'Only vaguely. You tell me again what to do.'

First I went to find the boy's father and told him, 'There's nothing you can do by staying here. Go home to your village. I will keep your son here – and I hope, cure him.'

'I will stay,' he insisted.

'There's no place here.' I waved vaguely around the hospital. 'It's empty now, but it's crowded every morning. And you can't help.'

Alec overheard the conversation, and said, 'I'm going back to the house now, Kit. You don't need me for the moment, but I'll be back this afternoon. Meanwhile you,' he turned to the father, 'stay along and garden my house.' With a sigh he turned to me, and said, 'Sometimes doctors forget that fathers who love their bairns suffer as much pain of a different sort as the children. Poor man.'

'You're a good friend, Alec.' I returned to the ops room ready to start work.

I knew what I wanted to do, and first of all I asked Miss Sowerby, 'Any spare blankets?' I knew we must have a store of old army-type blankets for use when patients ran temperatures yet their teeth chattered during bouts of fever – malarial or dengue.

She nodded.

'Fetch me a couple to start with, please. And get me some large surgery scissors. Then boil up a big pan of water.'

I went to try to soothe the agony of the little boy, stretched on his back, one leg bent upwards, the other flat, with the foot dropping.

'What's your name?' I asked, mopping his face with some tepid water – the coldest I could find.

He muttered a reply, but I couldn't understand what he said.

'Jimmabibi?' I asked.

He managed a shake of his head.

'Jimbo?'

It probably wasn't, but he was in too much pain to argue, so he nodded, and immediately became Jimbo.

I had to think carefully now – if only to remember the exact procedure. It had been running through my thoughts so often that I knew it by heart, yet now I was suddenly afraid that I might do the wrong thing! For this was not a treatment to be found in Gray's *Anatomy*.

First, while the water was boiling, I had to find some piece of stout wood to hold the boy's dropped foot in the proper position – 'the position of function' as Reid had called it. If I didn't, then that *could* mean an operation for a dropped foot. But where the hell could I find a large straight, flat piece of wood? There wasn't a hope in the hospital. I rummaged around, asked Miss Sowerby, but there was nothing.

'I'll run down the hill and see if Jim Wilson's got anything at the ship's chandler,' I said to Miss Sowerby. It was only three minutes down the road, and Jim always had a storehouse of odds and ends.

Sure enough he came up with the perfect solution.

'How about this old door?' He pointed out a flat, tough door from which he had already removed the hinges and nails.

It was just what I needed to do the job of calf muscle for Jimbo. 'Perfect! Can you spare it?' I asked him.

'Of course. I'll run you up in the car. Only take a couple of minutes.'

'One thing more, Jim,' I added. 'Have you any elastic bands?'

He shook his head. 'Better try Johnson's.'

I ran down the road, bought a packet of large-sized bands and told Johnson to put them on my account.

'Funny thing to ask for on an island like this.' He had

come out of his cubbyhole of an office, adding with a trace of Cockney twang, 'This ain't no place for sending parcels!'

I still couldn't fathom why I didn't altogether trust the man, 'I must be off,' I muttered and returned to Jim. By the time I arrived he had loaded the door on his truck, and I drove up with him.

Once back in the ops room, I laid the boy flat on his back, so far down the mattress that his dropped foot hung over the edge at the bottom, just as I had seen the Australian nurse do when I watched her during her London visit the previous year. Then I stood the door across the end of the bed, so close that Jimbo's right, dropping foot, where the muscle wasn't holding, had no room to drop. His right foot had to remain at right angles to his leg. It cost him no effort, no extra pain. The old door, strategically placed, was doing the work of the muscle.

When I had made him as comfortable as I could – a relative term, since he was in pain with each new spasm – I cut the two blankets into strips, each one two feet or so wide. I then cut each strip into rectangular pieces, two feet by one. I was ready now, for the water had boiled while I was away.

'Take these, please.' I handed Miss Sowerby half a dozen of the strips. 'Now, the water's boiling, put them inside. And give me a pair of tongs so that I can take one out of the water at a time.'

The strong-smelling 'stewed' strips of blanket were hot, and as I wrung out the excess water, I needed tongs to hold them for the first few minutes. Yet when I placed the first hot pad on to the boy's twisted left leg he seemed not to feel any pain; I supposed the pain of the spasms had made him impervious to a lesser pain.

I wrapped one strip around the twisted knee, then a second over the calf muscles below, keeping them in place with the elastic bands. I did the same with another strip around the right ankle and over the foot, so that it was held between the sole of the foot and the wooden backing of the old door. But where the muscles had started to waste was the most important part, and so I asked Miss Sowerby for another square of cloth to reinforce the heat over the ankle.

My theory – 'mine', I say, but the miracle had been wrought in front of me by Sister Kenny – was very simple. Though medical science believed that the muscles affected by polio simply withered and could not be restored, she was convinced that the deformities which followed attacks of infantile paralysis were caused by muscle spasms.

I believed this too. I felt – I could not be more certain than that – that when I had treated polio cases on previous occasions I had actually sensed wasting muscles making slight quivers, contracting with the pain of a spasm; and it was these contractions of muscles which, following normal treatment, so often caused shortening of the leg when the muscles withered. I know it sounds crazy, but even as I watched this little boy, Jimbo, I thought I could actually see a muscle quiver.

'Now, young man.' Knowing that he would speak a little pidgin English, I said to him, 'You trust me, yes? This hot cloth help ease pain, and we put a new hot one on every two hours until the pain has gone completely.'

I don't imagine that he felt any easier immediately I applied the hot blankets, but suggestion is a powerful weapon in the armoury of the doctor, and he did at least manage a smile.

'Don't expect a miracle,' I smiled back.

'How long did you say you're going to keep this compress on?' Miss Sowerby asked.

'A couple of hours.'

'And then, Doctor?'

'Same again. With blankets heated by being wrung out after immersion in boiling water.'

Just then Alec Reid unexpectedly bustled in from the dispensary. 'I thought I'd just pop in. How's it going?' he asked. After taking off his topee and wiping his head, he felt the boy's pulse automatically. I suddenly realised that he was very, very interested.

'Early days. But I've put the first hot foments on the two affected parts,' I explained. 'Actually on the spots where the spasms occurred – and I'm planning to change them – new ones, very hot ones, every couple of hours.'

'For how long?' asked Alec.

'Three or four days,' I said hopefully, trying to hide any element of self-doubt.

'And who's going to do that – every two hours, twenty-four hours a day?' Alec looked incredulous. 'Who's going to keep awake for three days or more? Eh?'

'Alec,' I said, a little desperately, 'I've got to do it the only way I know how to. Just to see if it works. I'll get Toma, my boy, to bring in an alarm clock, or whatever. If it doesn't work because I can't carry the experiment through' – I shrugged my shoulders – 'it wouldn't be worth starting on. But I'm sure it will – *sure*. Only a few minutes ago I felt a slight twitch in the boy's calf muscle. Yet according to you it's supposed to be dead already and wasting away – '

Alec was staring at me hard. 'It could have been involuntary.'

'True. But it *might* not have been. And I have to believe in that "might". There's life in there, I tell you, Alec. As I've explained, I'm going to change the hot strips of blanket every two hours all through the night. And tomorrow. To hell with sleep – '

'It's against all medical teaching,' he said.

'I know, but – '

'I'll come in early – four o'clock tomorrow morning?' Miss Sowerby offered.

'You will? That's marvellous. You've seen us at work. You're part of the experiment. It's imperative to keep the treatment going. And then we'll see – if we can get rid of the muscle spasms, if the pain stops, then I'll go to work on the muscles.'

'How?' she asked.

'Massage. Some manipulation, I dare say, but gentle massage – and then, once the spasms and the pain have gone, Jimbo will be so grateful that I'll easily be able to persuade him to start his own passive exercises.'

'And you think it'll work?' Alec was still finding it hard to hide his disbelief.

'Honestly, I don't know. I only saw that one demonstration. But she cured that child.'

'Getting rid of the pain is one thing,' said Alec. 'I can see how heat, regularly applied, could alleviate that. But that's only a palliative.'

'Maybe that's all I'll be able to do,' I admitted. 'But surely that's something – to a little boy in agony. But you see, the trouble with polio is that once the muscles *are* dead the nerves which serve them are useless.'

At the risk of sounding pompous – for this was very basic medicine – I thought I ought to explain to Miss Sowerby just what I was thinking of.

'You see,' I turned to her. 'In the end it's the muscles that take orders from the brain if they're to work. And the nerve pathways are the messengers between brain and muscle. Once the pain and muscle soreness disappears I'll have to try and restore any muscles that might be in danger – and in doing that restore the nerve routes – the circuits, if you like – that link muscle and brain.'

'Won't we need a trained nurse?' she asked.

'We're experimenting, Miss Sowerby. I know little more than you do about what we're doing.' I knew that would please her, and it did. 'I see two stages ahead,' I went on. 'Once the pains are alleviated, Jimbo, as well as us, will have won a supreme victory, especially if he isn't deformed. You and I'll have to start passive exercises.'

I knew exactly how I would do this and explained in some detail, finding Alec Reid equally fascinated. Whoever was on duty would move gently any part of the affected limb, trying as they did so to persuade Jimbo that now the pain was gone he might – I did not dare to say 'would' – be free soon to walk normally. But I knew that it would be difficult to persuade Jimbo that *he* had to work at the exercises: yet if the treatment were to succeed, it had to be him – Jimbo himself – who, in the end, would reopen the pathway of nerves between brain and muscle.

'And that's out of my hands,' I said.

All of this was in the hours ahead, for I was now to live through one of the toughest three days and nights I ever experienced.

I moved my pyjamas, spare underclothes, a couple of shirts and a few other necessaries from my bungalow and stayed in the hospital bed next to Jimbo's, snatching sleep and meals when Miss Sowerby took over. When, that first night, she went to her own bungalow, I was left mostly on my own, though Alec came in early in the evening to lend a hand.

Alec Reid was wonderful – not only physically, carrying pans of hot water to the stove when necessary, but morally, in allowing me to treat a patient in such an unorthodox fashion. I was dropping with fatigue – mainly because I could not sleep, even for two hours between treatments. Subconsciously I was terrified of missing my two-hourly deadline. I would dip blanket after blanket in boiling water, wring them out almost without realising that I was scalding myself, take off the old strips of saturated cloth, wrap the new ones round each leg and tuck them into the corners of affected muscles, but half the time not really knowing what I was doing.

Yet, despite the desperate fatigue and the fear that I might be making a fool of myself, I was seized with a curious elation that kept me going. For there was no doubt about one thing – after only twenty-four hours the pain was ending. The spasms had gone. Earlier on there had been one or two screams, but no more. And I knew from experience that in the ten to fourteen days during wastage of muscle tissue prior to an operation, a patient should normally suffer intense pain almost every hour of every one of those days. It seemed to me that the hot compresses had not only prevented the pain, but had done so because there must be living matter there which was capable of being alleviated by pain. In other words, it wasn't the spasms that had ended and with it the pain, but the muscle wastage itself.

One of the vital things I had to do – and I was too tired to help him myself – was to keep Jimbo occupied. As the pain decreased, his restlessness increased. It was also essential that he believed he was being cured, because of the need he would face soon for what I can only call 'self-help'.

I telephoned to the Union Jack Club asking for help, explaining the 'miracle' that seemed about to occur. And Mrs Fawcett came rushing up to the hospital with the perfect solution: she lent me a battery-operated portable radio.

'It doesn't have a long range,' she said, 'but it will get the dance music in Sanderstown.'

'Mrs Fawcett, you're an angel.' I think she actually blushed a little. 'Tell me when you next want me to make a four at bridge, and if it's possible, I'll be there.'

Jimbo loved the radio. He was stunned to find that if he turned a knob, music came out of the tiny speaker, and he never stopped playing with it.

On the third day, unshaven and too tired even to eat, I was examining Jimbo while Alec was in the middle of his sick parade. Suddenly I cried out, 'Alec: Come and see this. Quick! Before it disappears!'

He came running in from the dispensary, pulling up his trousers, still held up by his MCC tie, the end of his stethoscope bouncing off his fat tummy.

'Look!' I cried. 'Look at that muscle tendon. It's supposed to be dead, but it can't be because – look! the tendon is moving slightly, the muscle's quivering. Just feel it.'

Very carefully, as though handling a precious object, Alec stroked the affected calf muscle, then took out his handkerchief, wiped his bald pate and said softly, 'Laddie, it's a bloody miracle.'

Even better, the left leg was now lying flat on the bed in a more comfortable position. One of the problems with polio is that the spasms of pain often cause a patient to twist his limb involuntarily into a crippled position and it becomes locked there. That is why surgery is needed to straighten it out as the muscle no longer responds. But now Jimbo was lying on his back, with his left leg almost flat on the bed.

'This makum better,' he pointed to the radio, convinced that it was the radio – not the doctor – which was going to make him walk again!

At the end of the fourth day, after hours of gentle massage by Miss Sowerby and myself, I went to bed for a full night's sleep, Miss Sowerby taking over as 'night nurse'.

I slept with only one dream, exulting in the thought that if I could do this, why shouldn't I one day try to do something to help Clare to walk more easily? But Clare was ten thousand miles away, I was thinking as I woke up, while Toma made fresh coffee and cooked me a man-sized breakfast of local bacon-cum-ham and two of the island's tiny eggs. Perhaps one day I would go back to London, and take up my career where I had left off.

The next day, after sick parade, I said to Alec, 'Let's have a look at the right dropped foot.'

As he watched, I started to drag away the old door that had served us so well as foot-stopper. 'Remember,' I reminded him, 'that his foot has only been held up by the pressure of that piece of wood. There's no mattress underneath the ankle.'

Even Alec couldn't believe the transformation. The ankle muscles were holding the foot in an almost normal position – oblivious to the fact that the joints had nothing to rest on, that this was a classic case of a boy who would normally have ended up with a club foot.

'It's astonishing, that's for sure.' Alec scratched his head, then examined the right ankle carefully. 'There's only the slightest malfunction of the foot muscles,' he agreed.

'I'll put the restraining board back for a couple of days longer,' I suggested. 'Just so that we don't overtax young

Jimbo's powers of resistance.' I rumpled his dark curly hair but gave him a firm 'No' when he asked, 'If I play radio louder, me get better more quickly?'

'Let's hope that's the end of any blanket-brewing,' said Alec, in good humour. 'I never realised what a sour stink wet blankets can make.' Patting me on the back, he added, 'I'm proud of ye, Laddie. And you've done me proud too.'

'We're on the way,' I thanked him, 'but we'll need all the boy's help in getting a permanent cure.' Though I already felt confident of that.

Sure enough, after a week or so the boy's right ankle was responding to more treatment, and the left-leg calf muscles were quivering. I knew we were winning the real battle – a permanent cure – after one particular moment I shall never forget.

I had been trying to produce in Jimbo the necessary mental awareness that the real cure – the reopening of the nerve pathways – lay in the end with him. It was hard to explain to a youngster who was bright but not particularly well educated that I couldn't make a nerve work. He had to do it himself. Miss Sowerby – by now an enthusiastic convert – and I had taken turns at massaging the damaged calf muscles, and suddenly I said to him, 'Jimbo, just imagine it's you that's making the muscles move.' I used the word 'move' because I didn't think he would understand 'quiver'.

He smiled, the dulled eyes of pain now sparkling with the happiness of being alive, and I added, 'Go on! You bloody lazy! Me fed up, doing the work. *You* do it.'

It was a magical moment. I suddenly felt, under my hands, a few quivers of the muscle. I had done nothing. Jimbo himself had made the one effort that only a patient can make. I knew from that moment that it was only a question of time – and perseverance on his part – before he would be completely cured.

I looked up in triumph – to witness an astonishing sight. The dour, austere Miss Sowerby was wiping her eyes with a handkerchief she had tucked under a sleeve. She was crying gently – tears of happiness.

'Miss Sowerby!' I put an arm over her bony shoulder, and she didn't draw back. 'I know how you feel. It's wonderful.'

'A miracle.'

'Did your father believe in miracles?' I asked, in fact to stop the flow of tears, to hide any embarrassment she might feel.

'Yes, he did. He was a good, upright missionary, but like so many Victorians, so stern.' She sighed and composed herself. 'And as a little girl,' the faintest shadow of a smile touched her face, 'I was always naughty and disobedient, and so, under Father's guidance, I learned to control myself – all my emotions – for the greater good of serving the Lord. And now I've given way to my emotions when I swore to my father I never would. I'm so ashamed.'

'Nonsense. It's a good thing to let yourself go,' I said cheerfully. 'This is a great occasion, and it would never have been possible without your help. You shouldn't be so strict with yourself. People can do great good in the world and still smile. May I ask you a question – as a doctor to his invaluable assistant?'

She sniffed, hesitated and then mumbled apprehensively, 'I suppose so.'

'Have you ever been in love?'

With a blush she asked, 'With – a man?'

I nodded.

'Never!' she cried. 'And I will never allow such a thing to happen.'

'And another question – from your doctor. How old are you, Miss Sowerby?' I was thinking in terms of between thirty-five and forty-five. It was impossible to be more precise than that.

She blushed again, and said, 'I don't think – '

'Well, as a doctor to his most trusted assistant – ' I smiled.

Finally, after what was obviously some soul-searching, she said in a barely audible whisper, 'Twenty-nine.'

Astonished, I cried, 'Miss Sowerby, you ought to be ashamed of yourself, masquerading under false pretences. Twenty-nine indeed! You're little more than a girl. Why do you try to look so old?'

'I feel old,' she said and, the tears dried, she walked away.

7

Though I saw Lucy whenever there was a party at Paula's or elsewhere, for several weeks we never seemed to meet alone. I was not sure whether it was accidental or whether she preferred it that way, and I didn't like to phone, although I was now more mobile.

Jim Wilson, the *Mantela*'s chandler, had sold me a reconditioned Ford 8 for £55 – £30 down, the rest at £10 a month. It was a similar model to that of Mollie Green's and though my car rattled a little, Wilson was the kind of man who took such a pride in his work that he would never sell anyone a car that didn't work.

My feelings for Lucy after that day in the sailing boat were strange. My heart wasn't really involved, yet nonetheless it would give me a leap of pleasure whenever she appeared at the Union Jack Club, or at Colonel Fawcett's home, where he gave occasional parties, or even on a Sunday morning, if we both happened to go to Tala-Tala church, where Father Pringle played the hymns on the organ and had trained two Polynesians to accompany him with concertinas.

I hardly knew the good Father until Bill Robins took me to church to sing hymns, warning me enigmatically, 'The Father's background is in the foreground.' It seemed that Father Pringle had been sacked from his living in Australia because he drank too much, and had been 'banished' to

Koraloona where it was hoped he would stay out of trouble. Not at all. Father Pringle – a raw-boned Irishman in his sixties – wore a shabby cassock; his nails as well as his teeth were none too clean. But he also ran two schools, for the islanders, and the children loved him.

He had another extraordinary 'sideline'. Before sailing for Koraloona, he had acquired the sole agency for dealing in several brands of whisky and gin. So he took a percentage on all sales to Johnson's store, even to Mollie Green's hotel. 'And as far as I can see,' Robins had chuckled, 'he manages very well on his free samples.'

I rarely met him unless I went to church in the hope of meeting Lucy, and I was sitting next to her one lucky Sunday when she whispered during a hymn, 'Will you be in if I phone this afternoon?'

I nodded and sang 'Jerusalem the Golden' lustily.

It was just after a quiet lunch when the phone bell rang. I hardly recognised her voice at first – Koraloona's ancient telephones turned any voice into a croak – and I took a moment to respond when she said, 'Are you going to the Anani festival tonight?'

The Anani annual festival was to celebrate the fermentation of the wild oranges which the Polynesians had gathered and left half way up the hill in barrels until the alcoholic content was sufficiently strong for the brew to be drunk. The festival, as far as I could learn, was an all-night free drinking session.

'I thought I'd pop in – yes. I've never been to one,' I said.

'I definitely want to go,' she said. 'Would you take me?'

'What about Paula?' I asked automatically.

'She left yesterday on the *Mantela*, for Sanders. She's had a raging toothache for three days now and that's the one area where she doesn't trust Alec. Would you? Anyway, she'll be away for three or four days. So –'

'So – yes.' I laughed. 'What time?'

'About five? I'll drive Paula's car to your bungalow. Then we'll go in yours to the bottom of the hill. It's a bit of a walk up the hill, but very colourful. And the walk gives you a thirst. Everyone'll be there.'

I had no idea until we parked the car near the beach at the foot of the hill, and started to walk up to the festival, how beautiful and colourful the annual Orange Fair would be. The mountain path, which was not very steep, and perhaps three-quarters of a mile long, was lit with flaming torches on long poles like irregularly spaced street lamps. Scores of people were making their way to the focal point – the vats of fermented orange juice. From time to time more energetic fairgoers passed us, some of them ex-patients who greeted me with a warm 'Hello, Doc!' Women and children jostled by, mixing with the expatriates anxious not to miss what must have been the only funfair in the world where everyone had free drinks.

Where the hillside flattened out, the dales were filled with the wild orange trees, thousands of them, all according to ancient laws belonging to the islanders. I had trudged up the hill once before with Bill Robins, just to see the wild orchards, but now, as the dusk fell with tropical swiftness, I could barely make out a mass of shadows against the moonlight. But in one part the earth had over the years been beaten into an open square. It was ringed with torches, and everyone was cheering, singing, laughing – and drinking.

From one corner came vague sounds of music. Father Pringle, who played the accordion as well as the organ, had brought along his two church accordionists, but as they had been laboriously taught to play nothing but half a dozen hymns, the entire crowd were stomping and singing 'La, la, la' to the only music they – the 'orchestra' – knew, tunes like 'O come, all ye faithful'. I caught sight of Toma dancing in a crowd of boys and girls.

Father Pringle led the choir, encouraging them to sing lustily, but the words sounded strange:

> O come, all ye faithful,
> Joyful and triumphant

111

– not really a hymn at all to those who were singing, because of the unusual intonation, an almost barbaric accompaniment to the drums that were beginning to beat. It was so eerie that I felt Lucy squeeze my arm, almost as though a ghost was wailing on our graves.

Lucy had warned me to bring my own mug, and everyone simply queued up at one of the fermentation vats, into which a helper dipped a ladle and filled whatever container was proffered. When you had emptied your mug you went back for another.

All the Polynesians were dancing, clutching their mugs or in some cases half coconut shells which they used as drinking cups. The women all had flowers stuck in their long black hair, some tiare blossoms, others frangipani, and they wore their most beautiful sarongs. Many of the younger girls were naked from the waist up, their breasts moving with each step as they danced, their skin gleaming in the flickers of the torch lights.

'I'm so glad you came.' Lucy squeezed my arm again. 'I've waited so long for this evening. Only take care of the anani – it's lethal. I don't want you to pass out on me.'

'Don't worry. It's wonderful,' I said. 'And the orange is so frothy it tastes as though it's been mixed with champagne.'

At that moment I bumped into Tiare, accompanied by two leggy schoolgirls.

'Hello, Princess. Aren't you leading your charges into bad habits?' I laughed.

'They're allowed one small glass each.' Tiare returned the laugh and explained to Lucy, 'This is Aleena and her friend Kinawa, who lives in Sanderstown. The girls go to the same school, so Kinawa has come here on holiday.'

As we talked, I looked at the two girls. Aleena was already showing promise of turning into a beautiful woman. The other girl was as well, but she had a more happy-go-lucky attitude compared with Aleena's rather serious one. Aleena, starting to unwrap a bar of chocolate, whispered to me with a laugh, 'I don't really like the orange juice. It's too bitter.'

The girls moved off in search of excitement, for several expatriates and villagers had done their best to provide a little entertainment for the youngsters. Three home-made see-saws, balanced on large tree trunks, were in constant demand; so were a couple of swings, hung from the branches of large, tough, mango trees. There was an added bonus at the foot of the mango trees. Any fruit you could pick was free.

'I don't fancy climbing up for a mango,' I said to Tiare and Lucy.

'You don't have to. Commerce has reared its ugly head, even here,' Tiare laughed as a boy eagerly offered, 'Me get three mangoes for one penny.'

'They'd charge a dollar in California – just for the climbing,' said Lucy. 'The economics are simpler here.'

At that moment I saw a girl precariously balanced on a see-saw – precariously because she wore leg irons, and I recognised her as the girl I had seen the first time I visited the hospital and whom Doc Reid treated for a polio dropped foot. Her mother was doing her best to make sure she didn't fall off, and I made my way towards them.

'Well done,' I said to the girl. 'Let me see your foot.' She scrambled off the see-saw. I could see that the left leg muscles had wasted away, but the foot seemed to be holding up after the operation.

'How did you climb up the hill?' I asked.

'I carry her on back,' said the girl's mother simply.

'Come and see me for an examination,' I said. 'Soon.'

'Thank you. Me feel good.' The girl smiled.

At that moment Tiare came forward, patted her head and told the mother, 'You understand? Doctor Masters says you come to the hospital. Next week?'

It was tantamount to an order, and I suddenly realised that if I ever wanted something drastic to be done, I should enlist the Princess' help.

We walked on. Then I realised that Aleena had been watching the entire scene as I talked to the little girl.

I didn't hear what she said at first, but without warning she turned back – opposite to the way we were walking, and said to Tiare, 'Back in a moment, Mummy.'

Aleena had been literally about to take the first bite of the bar of chocolate when she stopped, the bar half way to her mouth. I saw her approach the polio girl, and give her the bar.

The girl's face broke into a smile as she hobbled off happily. I wondered if she had ever before eaten a bar of chocolate.

'That was a wonderful, spontaneous thing Aleena did,' said Lucy as we moved on, stopping to talk to Colonel Fawcett who said, 'You haven't seen it all yet, y'know.'

'I thought there was nothing but oranges,' I joked.

'Over here, Lucy.' He pointed to the far end of the square of beaten earth. 'Mollie Green's got a food counter. First come, first served.'

Mollie had surpassed herself. I didn't ask how she had carried the contents of a 'stall' all the way up the mountain, though there was never any lack of volunteers for occasions like this. She had cooked hundreds of little meat balls, other plates of thinly rolled pancakes filled with minced meat. Everything cost a penny, though Mollie couldn't resist deserving cases – wide-eyed little boys and girls who had never seen their local food cooked this way – and offering free samples.

One who qualified was Purvis.

'Jason,' I cried, when I first saw him approaching. 'How did you ever make the hill?'

'Determination – and the prospect of free drink, however sweet.'

'Come on,' cried Mollie Green. 'You are in the same category as the kids – free food for those who can't afford to buy it.' She said it with a laugh. 'No offence meant.'

'Reality is never an offence.' Purvis munched away gratefully.

'Shall we dance?' I asked Lucy as the music swirled.

'I'll try,' she said doubtfully. And we did, though not for long. The uneven ground – to say nothing of Father Pringle's uneven music – made it too much like work.

Among the other 'attractions' there was actually (of all things on a South Seas island) an old-fashioned coconut shy. Someone at the Union Jack Club must have dreamed it up, but it suffered through not having any proper holders from which to topple the coconut if you aimed well. So they were impaled on husking spikes. Someone had brought a box of extremely ancient, greying tennis balls, and marked out a line where one should stand. Every time you hit a coconut, you received a garland of mixed flowers – tiares, oleanders, hibiscus – fashioned much in the same way as the Hawaiian *lei*.

'I'm going to make you the most decorated girl in Koraloona,' I vowed, starting off with six tennis balls – six shies in other words – for a penny. In half an hour I had hung fifteen garlands of blossoms around Lucy's neck.

By now the noise was deafening and men and women, and even Captain Baker and the crew of the *Nymph*, were losing their reserve, as they imbibed free anani juice. Father Pringle was playing an Irish medley. Others of the expatriates were singing their own English songs in mock defiance. Drums were being beaten in half a dozen corners. Music of a kind I suppose, but to me drums always held a hint of menace, and soon they began to exercise an almost hypnotic effect on the islanders, both men and women. One by one, lit by the flickering torches and the moon, they started to dance.

Never until now had I seen what the Britishers would have called 'native dances'; they were curiously animal; the hands, the legs, the arms often moving in rapid unison, but though it was sensual, even on occasion explicitly sexual in suggestion, and though the dancers panted with the effort, there was no passion in their movement. It was barbaric in one way, yet as staid and unfeeling as an old folk's dance at the Nottingham Goose Fair. It surprised me at first – until I

115

realised that the dancers were merely enjoying a technical exercise; they were not dancing to arouse a sexual urge. They didn't need to dance to work themselves up. On Koraloona, friendly sex was taken for granted, so there was no need for anyone to simulate it with anything else.

'It's rather boring, in fact,' I said.

'I agree.' She hesitated for a moment as though making a decision, then she spoke.

'Frankly,' she said in a very quiet voice, 'I'm getting tired. What about a quiet drink on our own?'

'Agreed,' I said thankfully. 'The club – or my place?'

'Your place,' she said, still quietly.

For the first time I wondered – was this 'the knock on the door' she had promised?

My tingle of anticipation was fortified when Purvis said, 'You off?'

'Going for a quiet drink,' I said.

'Might pop in on the way back,' said Purvis.

'I wouldn't,' said Lucy quietly. 'We've all had a hard day.'

What made the remark intriguing was that we hadn't had a hard day at all, and it was this that made me say to Lucy, 'Can you hang on for a moment while I find Toma? I must see what he's doing.'

'I'll talk to Mrs Fawcett – just here.' She smiled to the colonel and his lady as I saw Toma on the edge of the 'playground'. He seemed to be involved in some complicated game. A group of men, shouting wildly, were gathered in a circle lit by a storm lantern. It might have been a Victorian illustration of a forbidden cockfight.

'We play for money,' said Toma happily. 'I win fourpence.'

'Yes, but what are you playing?'

'English game. Colonel Fawcett buy it from Johnson's store and give it to us.'

I took a closer look – and burst out laughing. It was a dart board – but nobody had thought to explain to Toma and his friends that it should have been fastened against a tree. It was flat on the ground and the players in turn stood up and hurled their darts downwards.

I thought it better not to try to explain. 'Toma,' I said. 'You carry on and stay along finish. And when the carnival's over you go and see your parents. You don't need to come back to my bungalow until just before surgery.'

Toma was always asking for time to visit his parents – the equivalent excuse of a Koraloona workman going to his grandmother's funeral. He had a girl in Tala-Tala.

'Thank you, master,' cried Toma, 'you make mother-father much happy.' But as he uttered the words, with a perfectly grave face, he was looking straight at Lucy.

Just before we left – saying goodbye to Tiare and the Fawcetts who were also about to leave – I said to Lucy, 'Let me get a bit of food from Mollie's to take back with us. Just in case we're hungry.'

'A very good idea.' She walked with me, and then, having filled a paper bag, we set off down the hill to find my old Ford-8.

'You can get rid of the garlands now.' I tried to help her to take off some of the flowers.

'No fear,' she cried. 'No man has ever given me so many flowers in my life. I'm not going to throw them away just like that.'

I had parked the car by the beach, well out of Anani, and as there was a full moon I suggested, 'Let's have supper on the beach?' I held out the paper bag. I don't know why I thought of the idea, except that now it was my turn to try to make the moments of anticipation last longer.

'Or better still, to work up an appetite,' I said lightly, 'how about a midnight bathe in the moonlight?'

'I've no costume.' Was she teasing me?

'You've got panties and a bra. I've got my underpants. And we can drive home afterwards in three minutes and I've got some spare towelling robes. We can have our dinner and a drink at home.'

We did just that. Deliberately I didn't try to kiss her, as

we almost fell into the shallow water and lay there on our backs, the moon shining on us, her thin panties wet, and so transparent. There can't have been much left to the imagination of either of us.

'Come on,' she said huskily, running up the beach, 'I need that drink.'

As I caught up with her, and grabbed the almost forgotten bag of Mollie's food, and our clothes, I touched her, then leaned against her, her wet body glistening, my face almost touching hers.

'All right,' she said. 'Just one little kiss before dinner – the one I refused to let you have before.' It was dark, as a cloud obscured the moon, and the road was virtually empty, for the dancing and drinking above us on the hill was in full swing. Standing there, I took her in my arms and as I kissed her she opened her mouth and I felt her hands clutching the back of my head, riffling my hair. I heard her say, 'Do we need to have dinner? Can't we go straight back to the bungalow and eat later?'

'Of course,' I said.

I raced the car to the bottom of my garden. The door was unlocked. We walked along the corridor, past the living-room to the bedroom, smelling fresh after Toma's usual evening ritual of spraying the entire house to kill any bugs. Then I found some towels, dried off, and we put on the robes. I locked the bedroom door and the next second Lucy was in my arms, her robe open, standing up by the shuttered window, pressing her breasts against me, arching her back so that I could feel her thighs rub against me. Then she was holding my face in her two hands, kissing me, mouth open, gasping, 'Kiss me! Kiss me!' And almost moaning, 'Oh God! It's been so long – waiting for this moment.'

She almost tore off her robe, then stood as I took off mine. As she let the robe fall to the floor, she whispered, 'There! Do I please you?' She stood in front of me. The cloud had passed by, the moon was shining through the window slats. Her long legs were apart, and as I stroked her beautiful hair above the join in her legs it was as thick as matting. Rubbing her firm breasts against my chest, her thighs against mine, she managed to gasp, 'How beautiful!' Then I carried Lucy to the bed.

The night passed like a blur, a dream of repeated desire – by each of us at different times. It seemed as though we hardly slept. Perhaps we didn't very much. We made love, we satisfied each other, we fell asleep, then she would wake me by gentle stroking or I would wake her by gentle stroking, all through the entire night. I had never known such love-making before.

Some time just before dawn we must at last have fallen into a deep sleep, for when we both awoke the sun was blazing through the slats covering the windows.

Later, sitting satiated but still naked in the living-room, scooping out spoonsful of pawpaw I had found in the kitchen, Lucy said almost dreamily, 'I must have had some sort of brainstorm, I guess. I never felt so wild before in my life, Kit, as though I'd lost all control.' She squeezed a little more lime over the pawpaw and offered me a spoonful. 'Did I upset you?'

I smiled. 'I loved every second of it. *And* you know it. Here, give me another spoon of pawpaw.'

'Such bliss,' she said. 'It's the kind of freedom that only comes from letting yourself go completely. A kind of abandon. But you can't do that with most people. All my body is limp and relaxed as though it doesn't belong to me. Brain too.'

About seven o'clock, when we had put on some clothes, I made two cups of strong black coffee and some scrambled eggs.

'If only I could stay here for ever. I hate the thought of leaving this bungalow, and I don't suppose I'll be able to see you as often as I'd like,' she said.

'Does that mean you'll only be able to see me when Paula's away?'

119

'Of course not. Staying the night might be difficult. What about all the other hours of the day?'

'But darling, I want to see you *every* day. What hours will you be free?'

'Obviously, I can't tell. But I'll make time. Don't worry. I'll give you a call, I promise.'

'I only hope you phone often.'

'I will.' She was dressing by now, back in her pretty candy-striped pink and white dress, all the hitherto secret parts of her body decorously covered for the outside world.

'I'm mad about you,' she said. 'And you're a wonderful lover.'

Then, with one look back, blowing kisses as she walked down the garden to her car, she waved and was lost to view.

That was the end of the most exciting night of my life – up to then. I took a long and cooling shower, and then put my dirty clothes in the laundry basket, and prepared to wait, filled with delicious thoughts and hopes, until it was time for surgery.

In my haste to relive those hours, and the last sight of Lucy waving as she disappeared into her car, I almost forgot that I hadn't washed up the breakfast things. *Two* breakfasts! And at the moment when I *did* remember, I heard the sound of Toma returning, humming a tune as he always did to warn me of his approach. With a quick gesture I hid the plates and cups in a cupboard.

Toma was all smiles and was filled with profuse thanks because I had given him the night off.

Then he departed to the kitchen, and I prepared to wait for another half hour before going to the hospital.

It was then that I smelt what is normally my favourite cooking smell. But not now! Toma was cooking breakfast – and I had already eaten one breakfast. He brought in bacon and eggs, steaming hot coffee, with a smile from ear to ear, and put the tray down on the desk by my sofa.

'I'm not hungry, Toma,' I said. 'I think I'll skip breakfast today.'

'Oh no, master. Very bad. Please eat, or I think you are angry.'

Well, I made a pretence at eating, though I couldn't finish the meal. And I made a mental note to take out the hidden dirty dishes the next day when Toma was out shopping.

Within a week Lucy and I were able to spend another night together. Paula had invited three or four guests from California, and she had decided to spend a night on the *Nymph*. The second night was as tender as the first one, and since I could not give Toma another evening off so soon after the first, I had to let him into the secret – but discreetly. And of course, he *was* fairly discreet, simply because he assumed that what was happening between Lucy and myself was as natural and normal as what was doubtless happening between him and his girlfriends.

We couldn't keep the secret for long after that. I had never expected that we could. But Paula made no mention of it. Reid knew very quickly. I imagine that after the second visit one afternoon Toma must have passed the news directly to his two girls, for gossip was more catching than measles in Koraloona. And within a week or two, after Lucy had been to see me on two more free afternoons, I didn't try to bamboozle Reid. He was too wise a bird in the ways of the islands. In fact we were at my bungalow one day when he found us there together – dressed, thank God. I heard the crunch of tyres at the bottom of the garden.

'That's Alec,' I told her. There were so few cars on the island that I could usually recognise exactly who was coming by the different sound each car made when braking. 'No, don't go.'

'Can I come in?' cried Alec. 'I see you've got company. How are you, Lucy?'

'I was just about to leave.'

Mopping the sweat from his bald head and putting his topee on the table by the door, he said to Lucy, 'Yes, ye look a very pretty lassie. And' – shrewdly – 'very happy.

121

But dinna you go turning the head of our new doctor before he's had a chance to settle down.'

'I won't. And as for happiness – well, I'll let you into a secret, Doctor. I'm mad about pawpaw. Full of just the right vitamins.'

Alec turned to me. 'That'll be the day. When you can take vitamins to guarantee happiness.'

'Anything I can do for you?' I asked Alec, wondering why he had come.

'Yes, as a matter of fact there is. I popped in to say that Katuto, the girl who helps out in Johnson's, has broken a leg and I'm going to have to set it. It's a tricky one. So if you could be on hand during our elastic surgery hours?'

'Of course.'

'And I must be going,' said Lucy.

'Can I give you a lift?' asked Alec.

'Thanks, but I've got Paula's runabout. Bye bye, Alec.' And to me, 'See you the day after tomorrow?'

As Alec looked at his watch, saying to me, 'Meet you in ten minutes, then,' Lucy asked, 'What time is it?'

'Just after four.'

'My God! I promised Paula I'd have the car back by three o'clock.'

She ran down the garden with hardly a backward glance. But as Alec Reid watched her, he sighed, 'Some people get all the luck,' adding cryptically, 'caviar for some, bubble and squeak for others.'

8

The girl Katuto had fractured her leg badly. By the time I arrived, Alec Reid was at the hospital, ready to prepare an anaesthetic and straighten the break before putting the leg in plaster. The girl was in considerable pain.

'It's a simple fracture of the tibia,' said Alec, 'but the

trouble is that she'd just had a meal when she fell, so we'll have to wait a couple of hours before I give the anaesthetic. So would you mind the store?' He was right, of course. Too soon after eating, she'd be liable to vomit into the air passages of the lungs and obstruct her breathing.

The 'store' was Alec's way of referring to the dispensary, which was at the end of the hospital. 'The only difference,' he said, 'is that Mrs Johnson charges like hell at the general store and we give away most of our stock. That's no way to make a fortune.'

There was always plenty to do in the dispensary, and now Miss Sowerby would be kept busy mixing the plaster in the wash-up room, then helping the doctor set the leg in the operating theatre. Apart from anything else, Miss Sowerby and I always fought a losing battle in our war to keep our drugs in some sort of order; for after the day's 'sick parade' Alec Reid invariably managed to change a neat and orderly stock into chaos. He would grab a bottle – anything from Lysol to aspirin – and administer the right prescription, but replace the bottle on the first available shelf.

'It's a wonder you haven't poisoned half the population of Koraloona,' I said to him one day, laughing.

'Sometimes I wonder myself,' he admitted. 'But the Devil has a habit of looking after his own.' Perhaps, I thought, but advancing age often goes hand in hand with carelessness.

Busily occupied, and with Alec and Miss Sowerby in the theatre, I vaguely heard the sound of a car arriving outside the dispensary but thought nothing of it until I heard the short sharp toot of a car horn, pressed down only briefly; once before I had heard a horn sound that way – not as a warning to a stray pedestrian, but as a signal, the equivalent of a shouted 'Hello, there!'

I had two patients waiting at the moment and as I walked out of the door, into the hot air, brushing away the overhanging bougainvillaea, I said, 'Good morning, Princess Tiare. What can I do for you?'

She had switched off the engine, and was stepping out

123

of the Austin. She looked very elegant in a pair of white shorts, a shirt and sandals, almost as though to accentuate the fact that she was 'European'. She was, I thought again, remarkably good-looking, with her very straight nose, almost aquiline. She wore no make-up on her full red lips or her face which, like her legs, was tanned. And her black hair framed her face perfectly. Without thinking, I said, 'You look really stunning, Princess.'

She actually blushed, and I had a sudden recollection of our old professor of medicine saying to us, 'There's nothing makes a woman blush more easily than hearing the truth – a *nice* truth.'

'Do you always flatter your patients like that?' she asked.

'I'm sorry. It slipped out.'

'Nothing to apologise for. With so many beautiful girls on the island it's rare to receive a compliment at my age.' Then, looking around, she asked. 'Where's Doctor Reid?'

'Operating,' I explained. 'A girl, Katuto, she works at Johnson's store. She broke her leg in a nasty accident. Fell down when climbing on some packing cases.'

'Oh! Poor girl. I like her,' she said with genuine concern, and again it struck me that, to her, on this small island, all the population were in a way her subjects. Everyone I met accorded her a special kind of respect, and what's more, she knew most of them. 'I must go and visit her as soon as she's better. But how long will Doctor Reid be?'

'I don't really know. Can I help?'

'It's Aleena, my daughter. Doctor Reid sent her some linctus, but I don't like the way she's coughing, and I have an eternal dread of TB. There's been so much of it on all the islands in the past. I thought that perhaps Doctor Reid could come up and check on Aleena's lungs before she goes back to school.'

'Quite right to be worried. I'll tell Doctor Reid when I see him. Or if you like, I could come up with you as soon as we deal with the last two patients. Come and wait inside. It's cooler.'

We walked into the ward near the dispensary, while the

two patients remained waiting in the garden. At the far end of the ward was an old man whom Reid had kept in for a night or two for observation. 'He wants to check him out for TB symptoms,' I explained.

'Are you sure you can spare the time to come to our home? It would be very kind of you. What about the other patients?' asked the Princess.

'They won't take long. If you don't mind hanging on for a few minutes?'

She moved over to speak to the old man in the bed, and I heard him say deferentially, 'Yes, Princess – ' as I called in the next patient. All he wanted was the standard placebo – a bottle of coloured water which he was convinced would cure his chronic constipation, and he seemed astonished and doubtful when I also gave him some liquid paraffin, warning him, 'Now remember – not all at once. Once a day.'

The other patient had a badly cut foot, and the moment I examined the sole I could see what had happened. Walking barefoot on the shore he had trodden on a stonefish, a 'fish' about six inches long that half buries itself in pebbles and sand. Camouflaged by its natural colours of brown and ochre, and protecting itself by a spiky dorsal fin, it is barely visible on the beach, but the fin is as sharp as needles and injects a poison as potent as snake venom which releases histamine, the substance that transmits nerve impulses through the body. It is intensely painful – and twice Alec and I had encountered death from stonefish poisoning. Yet I was helpless. I could only give him a shot of APC – the combination of aspirin, phenaticin and codeine – as a painkiller and dress the inflammation with acriflavine, bandage him up and tell him to come twice a day to have the wound dressed by Miss Sowerby.

He promised to do so and left, and I walked through the corridor to the ops theatre and said to Alec, 'Sorry to interrupt, but the Princess has asked me, as you are busy, if I'll go to see her daughter who's leaving soon for Sanderstown. I've finished surgery.'

Alec, grunting with the effort of moulding the plaster to the girl's leg, said, 'Carry on. Thanks for helping out. Pop in on your way back.'

'It'll only take half an hour,' I said. And outside I turned to the Princess. 'All ready if you are.'

'Thank you so much. I'll drive you to our home, wait for you, then drive you back to the hospital. Would that be all right?'

'Fine. I'll get my bag of tricks.'

As we drove quietly along Main Street, waving to Jim Wilson standing outside the chandler's, the Princess said, 'I do hope I'm not wasting your time. But you know what girls of thirteen are. Always on the go. Aleena never seems to stop.'

In a way I felt for her, for as we reached the end of the dusty road I was thinking of Clare's energy and tomboy spirits before she was struck down with polio.

'Yes, I do know, Princess,' I said, 'I have a young sister. She had enough energy for the entire family, and even used to play football. But I must say, Aleena looked all right at the festival. She and her friend – '

'Kinawa? They are great friends. Her parents sometimes invite her to their home, but she's a bit of a dare-devil, the daughter. And I'm a mother,' she smiled. 'I'm always worried. Here we are.'

I had never visited their house before, and was intrigued when I did see it. The front door cannot have been more than twenty yards from the beach and, as we approached, the only sound we heard was the splash of tiny waves. On the beach itself, obviously regarded by the islanders as belonging to Tiare, was a shade hut consisting of a roof thatched with spiky pandanus – stronger and more lasting than palm leaves – on four stout posts, but with no walls. Under it were three or four deck chairs, with a couple of striped towels casually draped over them. The beach wasn't large – perhaps a hundred yards long, a curling crescent of silver sand – but it was kept private not only by the will of the people but by a small headland at the far end where a fall of rocks had made a natural barrier.

'What a perfect place for a swim,' I couldn't help saying.

'We love it.' Aleena's mother led the way. 'You must come and have a swim and lunch with us one day, Doctor.'

The house was large, vaguely but indefinably echoing the taste and architecture of the islanders, though with a few notable refinements. It was really a bungalow on one floor, built on stilts as a precaution, I supposed, against sudden high tides but also, as I saw from the water jar traps, to stop the ants devouring the building. We walked up wooden steps to a large veranda on which were several locally made long chairs, common in the tropics, with wooden arms that extended forward by swivelling to support a pair of legs whose owner wanted a siesta. There was also a large rectangular table with half a dozen upright chairs, obviously used as an outside dining-room.

The interior was a curious mixture of ancient and modern – or rather, local and imported. A few indifferent paintings decorated the whitewashed walls; though one was of a striking face which looked as though it might have been a sketch for a mask: a long nose, huge holes for eyes and lips, painted on skin or hide. Not much to my taste. There were several wooden idols – obviously imported from the other islands, for I had seen similar ones during our stop at Rarotonga.

And yet, despite the rather grotesque wooden sculpture, I needed little more than a glance to sense the warmth of a room which clearly reflected the touch of a woman. One side-table held a huge fan-like arrangement of hibiscus blossoms, flat against the wall. They had been arranged in a cunning manner, and I knew they would last for only one day, for the stalk of each blossom had been snipped off and the flower stuck on to the end of the matchstick-thin spine of a coconut frond stripped of its green. Each 'matchstick' had been cut into different lengths. These had then been placed into a wooden block pierced with holes, giving the extraordinary effect of a sunburst – or a peacock, rather.

On another table at the far end of a room stood a huge wooden bowl which I recognised as an outsized communal kava drinking bowl made of ironwood. It was filled with mixed fruits, which looked as though they had been carefully arranged by an artist preparing to paint a still life. Shades of Gauguin, I thought. I wondered whether the Princess had subconsciously inherited any of her father's talent.

At the far end of the room stood an old grand piano, the keys yellow, and when I touched a note, it was sadly out of tune. On it stood a photograph of a tall, rather haggard-looking man and a beautiful young girl dressed in a sarong which was tucked in under her arms, but leaving her beautiful shoulders bare.

'Mother and Father,' Tiare smiled, as I studied it.

'I can see you inherited your mother's shoulders and neck,' I smiled back; then, as I walked to the other end of the room, I heard a rasping cough.

'That's the young patient,' I said. 'We must go and have a look at her.' But first I took in the rest of the room – some rattan chairs covered with chintz stood in one corner and looked comfortable. Next to them was one modern innovation – a practical bar, well stocked, with bottles, glasses and shakers arranged neatly.

'No kava in this house,' I laughed.

'Never. Hate the stuff. Now, let's look at Aleena.'

Tiare led the way to Aleena's room, knocked and said, 'Darling, here's the doctor.'

'Oh!' she exclaimed as I walked into the room. 'Where's Doctor Reid?'

'He's busy operating,' I explained. 'That's a nasty cough, young lady.'

She was lying in bed, and didn't look very ill, I must say; more like the way Clare used to look when she was kept in bed with a cold, filled with suppressed energy; like Clare, this was a teenager with character, energy and a cheerful smile. I hadn't really studied her at the Orange Festival, but I could see, watching her with a 'professional' eye in the daylight, that she had what Dr Allott used to call when describing Clare, 'a woman with a good strong chin'. It wasn't an obvious chin, but it didn't taper away. It showed determination – if only to enjoy herself, which I felt was the way Tiare's daughter wanted to look at life.

I put down my bag, took out the stethoscope, thermometer, and sat down on the edge of the bed, taking her pulse and temperature.

'You're not going to operate?' she asked, with a sense of fun.

'Not today,' I laughed, Tiare joining in, while I said to her, 'All the same, let's check those lungs of yours. First lie on your tummy and let me sound out your back.' I drew back the top of the sheet that covered her. She wore no pyjamas. 'Take a deep breath whenever I ask you to.' I put 'the end piece' (as every doctor has forever called the diaphragm since Laennec invented the stethoscope in 1816) to her back so that I could hear the sounds of her lungs magnified by the vibrations of the tiny ivory disc. It gave back a perfectly normal rustling sound, none of the watery noise which might have indicated pleurisy, nor the sound one gets when the spongy lungs tend to become solid, a dangerous sign of TB.

'Now, take a deep breath and say "Ah!"' I asked her, just because saying 'Ah' is the easiest way known to a doctor of encouraging a patient to let out his breath. Finally I tapped her back, laying two fingers of the left hand in different places on the back, and tapping them with the knuckles of the other hand: a sure way to disturb any fluid so that I could feel it. Before I tapped her I had to move her long, thick black hair – 'island hair', despite her white skin – so thick that it was hard to find a patch of skin to tap.

All the time Tiare watched me without a word, but visibly anxious. A few signals in the stethoscope, a few prods by me on her back, told me virtually all I needed to know. She had a very bad cough, but that seemed to be all. As one last check I probed her left side, below the rib cage, and asked if it hurt. When she shook her head I knew that nothing serious was the matter.

'No problem, young lady.' I smiled as I replaced the sheet. 'You'll live.' And to Tiare I explained, 'There's no infection of any sort.'

'No sign of – well, TB?' she asked.

'None,' I reassured her. 'I didn't even need to examine her chest. It's a bronchial cough, but not bronchitis. I could tell at once if there was any risk. At the same time, I wouldn't let her sunbathe or swim for a few days. Too much sun can be bad for a bad cough.'

Almost as we were about to leave the room, Aleena said, 'Mother, can Doctor Masters look at the tiny mole on my thigh? The one I showed you.'

'Why not?' Tiare turned to me. 'It's nothing, but if it could be taken away – well, teenagers are very conscious of their legs.' To Aleena she asked, 'Are you – '

'Yes Mother,' she said with the resignation of a daughter speaking to her mother, 'I'm wearing panties, if that's what you mean.'

'Well, we might as well check the spot out,' I said. 'Whereabouts exactly is it?'

While her mother watched, Aleena drew down the sheet, and she *was* wearing only panties. She showed me a tiny black mole about four inches up from her knee.

'It could be burned off perhaps?' Tiare asked.

'I don't see why not. Can I examine it a bit closer? Stay in a lying position while I take a good look. Have you had it long?'

I hope I asked the question in a casual way. I didn't want to frighten mother or daughter unless I was sure. But that black mole looked highly dangerous to me. I squeezed it, asked if it hurt, and she shook her head. Then I pressed the skin around it. Did that hurt? Was it tender? I rather hoped she would say that she did feel a little pain, but instead she said, 'No, I only showed it to you because I was afraid it would grow bigger and more ugly.'

'I see. I asked you how long you had had it.'

'It suddenly appeared a few days ago.'

I pulled back the sheet. 'We'll see what we can do about it. Meanwhile, young lady,' I tried to sound avuncular, 'take that linctus.'

At that moment, as I left the girl's bedroom, I heard a noise outside. As I reached the front door of the house, a voice furious with rage shouted, 'Get out! If you're still here in two minutes, I'll kick you out.' Vaguely I saw a houseboy run out of the back garden.

The roar of anger was followed by stamping feet and a huge man, light skinned, dressed in a shirt and trousers and wearing a Japanese-style 'shoe', kept in place by a thong between the big toe and the next one, entered Aleena's room. This must be Mana. He seemed to have an odd cast to his eyes. But what impressed me most was his size, and the set of his shoulders, giving him a hulking, threatening appearance. And the eyes! His face was round and puffy, so the eyes were more frightening because they looked as though they had been folded into his face, like currants in a bun. Reid had told me he was half Japanese. The other half more than made up for it in size. After the peace and quiet of my meeting with mother and daughter it was like being faced with a monster. And my reaction wasn't improved by his manners – especially as I was worried about the girl's black spot.

I had reached the garden by then, making my way to the Princess' car when, without a word to anyone, the man snapped, 'Who's this?'

'Mana, what's the trouble?' asked Tiare. 'Doctor Masters, this is my husband. Mana, who on earth have you been shouting at?'

The man growled out a name I didn't catch. 'I fired him. He's a slacker.'

'But you can't do that,' Tiare cried. 'He's a wonderful servant.'

'He's a bum.'

'But you can't – '

'I can. I've done it.' Then he turned to me, looking me up and down as though inspecting a prospective servant.

'Why are you here?' he asked me abruptly.

'Because I was sent for,' I replied just as shortly.

'What for? Why? Who's ill?'

I looked at Tiare and, deliberately ignoring my questioner, said to her gently, 'I'll be on my way now, Princess, if you can drive me.'

'Of course,' she said, embarrassed. Aleena, dressed in a kimono, had followed us to the garden, but kept silent, though her lips were drawn in a tight angry line. But was it, I wondered, mingled with a touch of fear?

I stalked out into the garden, and Aleena rushed out after me, crying, 'Thank you for coming. We both hope you'll come again.'

Mana followed, shouting, 'Come inside at once, Aleena.' And to me he asked, 'Have you been treating my daughter?'

'Step-daughter,' said Aleena contemptuously.

I could sense the hatred in the way she spat out the word – almost as thought she had been wanting to say it for a long time but hadn't dared to until this nasty scene erupted.

'Go inside,' he roared, as Aleena burst into tears and ran into the house, the Princess following to comfort her. I stood my ground in the garden – apart from anything else, I had no way of getting back to the surgery – and I knew he was sizing me up. My God, I thought, what an ugly brute – and what a foul temper he had! For a couple of seconds, as he stood glowering at me, I caught myself wondering, How *could* Tiare marry such an ape?

I wonder if my face betrayed my feelings, the look of disgust. I saw him clench his fists as though to strike me, and I realised he would have loved to hit me. I wouldn't have minded, for though I knew that he was large and tough, he *didn't* know that I was a trained and expert boxer.

Instead of hitting me, he said, 'You're too young, Doctor. I prefer Doctor Reid. Especially when it comes to treating young girls. I was educated in the United States for

132

two years. I know all about medical ethics – or the lack of them.'

'Are you insinuating? – ' I burst out furiously.

'I'm insinuating nothing. But I want to know why Aleena has to be treated by a young doctor just because she's got a slight cough. And just what exactly did you do to her?'

Suddenly I felt a surge of anger, the sort I suppose that used to cause my father to sigh, 'How often have I told you to keep that temper of yours in check?' Here I was, doing it again! But what made me so angry was to hear another unjust accusation, and from such a surprising source. Was he being simply over protective? Or was it possible that, like so many step-fathers, Mana thought his step-daughter would one day be fair game? I didn't stop to decide. Without thinking, I said curtly, 'What exactly did I do? I had to examine her thoroughly. Especially the chest, around the breast area.' Slowly, deliberately, I added, 'Mostly with my stethoscope, of course, but also it's important to check the breast area with your hands. It's only that way you can feel carefully for any lumps in the breast that might lead to a cancer. I'm sure you understand.'

'You haven't given me the full reason. Cancer? I thought she only had a cough. Just what kind of diagnosis did you make? If any!'

'Don't worry, Mana,' deliberately omitting the 'Mr'. 'I'll give the full details and suggested treatment when I send you my bill.'

I didn't wait for an answer, but walked down the garden path without looking back. Tiare had by now walked to the Austin. I stepped in and she started at once on the drive back to the dispensary.

Tiare had avoided coming out beside her husband, but she must have heard our exchange, and her face seemed to show more sorrow than anger. After a few moments of silence she said, 'You shouldn't have told those lies or treated my husband like that, Doctor Masters – '

'I'm sorry,' I said. 'But you must admit he was insulting

my professional conduct, and I won't stand for that. You saw how correctly I behaved. I made sure you remained in the room. And then, those insinuations – '

'Of course, I understand. But those lies you told – about – stroking her breasts. You never touched my daughter's chest. Why make my husband angry by inventing a situation that didn't occur?'

'I was angry. I'm sorry, but I thought it'd teach him a lesson.' I almost wanted to add that Mana seemed more than usually interested in Aleena, but didn't, because that would have been absurd. Aleena was innocent sexually. She wasn't a flirt. If anything she was young for her age.

'Well, it's done now,' she sighed. 'But be careful. Doctor. You're a nice young man, and I wouldn't like anything to happen to you. And my husband can be very vindictive.'

'I *am* sorry,' I apologised again, for really I was wondering again why a woman like Tiare had ever married such a man.

'I'm afraid that my husband won't allow you to be our family doctor,' she said as we drove along. 'Not after today.'

'I understand, Princess,' I smiled. 'Perhaps it's for the best.' Though I knew that nothing could be entirely for the best when influenced by that sinister and evil man.

I spent the rest of the journey back to the dispensary thinking – and it wasn't about Mana. It was something very different, and I wasn't quite sure how to put it to Tiare. However, as soon as she braked outside the cottage, I said, 'Could you come into the dispensary for a moment? I know I'm not going to be your doctor, but – '

She smiled and said, 'Of course. I'm sorry. It's no reflection – ' She followed me inside.

'No, no,' I reassured her. 'I understand about that. It's something a little more serious. A medical problem.'

I saw the instinctive look of fear that greets every doctor at the word 'serious'.

'Don't be worried,' I said. 'There's a world of difference between "serious" and "dangerous".'

'What is it, Doctor Masters? What are you trying to tell me?'

'It's that mole on your daughter's right thigh. She asked if it could be removed.'

'Oh *that*! In view of what's happened, I suppose it *would* be better to let Doctor Reid do it.'

'It's not "*Oh that*", Princess. If it's only a mole, Doctor Reid could remove it in a few minutes with a local anaesthetic. Only' – I found it difficult to break the news, particularly in view of the recent scene – 'it isn't a mole.'

'A wart, then?'

'No. I made a careful examination because I came across the same symptoms in the Tropical Diseases hospital in London. The technical term for it is a melanoma.'

'And that means?'

If there's one word that terrifies the layman more than any other it's the word 'cancer', so I spoke carefully.

'It's easily curable, if you don't waste too much time. And this one has just been born, so to speak. But I'm afraid, Princess, that it *is* a malignant skin tumour. It often starts quite small, but it's extremely dangerous if one doesn't immediately stop it from spreading.'

'Are you trying to tell me that it's cancer?' she asked, eyes wide open with fear.

'Of the skin – for which we should be grateful. It's easier to detect earlier. But it needs to be treated with all speed.'

'Are you sure?'

'In my own mind, yes, because I know the colour, the black pigment, the sudden growth. But of course we must have tests, blood, skin and so on – proof. As soon as Doctor Reid has finished setting the girl's leg, we'll talk it over with him.' I could hear that he and Miss Sowerby were still in the ops theatre.

'But it can be cured?'

'Without any question. We've got to it so early that

I'd stake my professional reputation that it'll never return.'

'Then – Doctor Reid?'

'He could fly your daughter to Sanderstown. You see, apart from anything else, the laboratory tests must be done by expert pathologists, not just a local doctor. And there is something else. It's not just a question of burning it off.' I spoke carefully. 'I think Doctor Reid would agree with me that it might be better for Aleena to fly to Sanderstown as soon as possible and let her be treated by a specialist at the base hospital. Doctor Reid has colleagues there; he could get her admitted.'

'But why the base? Are you saying it's really serious?'

'No, but it is tricky. Aleena would have to have a general anaesthetic. The operation would take an hour, maybe an hour and a half.'

'To remove a spot?'

'Please don't be alarmed, Princess, but with melanoma you have literally to get to the root of the matter. I've seen the operation performed. It requires a wide excision. All the skin within a radius of two inches round the tumour has to be taken off. That has to be done to make sure there's no recurrence.'

'Poor Aleena.' It was the first time I had seen Tiare give way to her feelings.

'She'll be all right,' I promised her. 'Let's wait and talk to Alec Reid.'

I have seldom seen Alec Reid move so quickly as he did in the next hour. When the patient had been carried out, groggy, but with her broken leg set, I explained, with Tiare listening, everything I knew about melanoma.

'How did you spot it?' he asked. 'Are you sure?'

'Absolutely.'

'Then there isn't a moment to spare. Princess, I'll drive to your house. You follow. Now. Hang on till I get back, Kit.'

'Of course.'

They left in two cars. Half an hour later Reid was back – with Aleena, looking very white and frightened. Tiare followed in her Austin.

'I'm flying to Sanderstown with Aleena in ten minutes,' he announced to me. 'To hell with long trousers. Kit, can you ask Colonel Fawcett to give you an emergency radio-telephone call to the naval base, and tell them to expect me. Ask for Surgeon-Commander Serpell. Explain what's happened.'

I nodded.

'Thanks.' He patted my shoulder, a favourite gesture of his. 'There's not a moment to lose.'

To the Princess he added more gently, 'Don't worry. We've caught it in time, thanks to Kit. I can't get the three of us in the plane, Princess, so you had better follow in the first boat – the *Mantela* is due tomorrow. Don't worry. It'll take a few hours to have the tests checked, and if we have to remove the spot, you'll probably be there before she wakes up.'

9

Aleena went to the naval base hospital in Sanderstown immediately and, as soon as Alec had made sure she was comfortably installed, he flew back in Nellie. That night we had a drink together on my bungalow veranda.

'You've gone up in my estimation.' Alec was pleased with me. 'Spotting that melanoma like that. If you hadn't she'd have been dead within a few weeks. Lots of young doctors would have dismissed it as just another wart.'

'Well, she'll be all right now,' I said, but I, too, I must admit it, was pleased.

'Good doctors at the base. First-class. As a matter of fact, I suggested to Tiare that you might like to go along there and see the op – good experience – also, Aleena's met you, and it's always good for morale to have a friendly doctor visit you in hospital. But there was no room in the plane, anyway.'

'I'd have liked to have gone – for the experience.'

'Well, I thought you might go over on the *Mantela*, but Tiare said no.'

I knew perfectly well why Tiare had vetoed the suggestion, but said nothing to Alec. There seemed no good reason why he should know anything of my row with Mana. He did soon, though.

Two days later Reid heard on the radio sked from Sanderstown that Aleena's operation had been successful. The spot, and all the surrounding tissue, had been removed. Tiare had by now reached Sanderstown on the *Mantela* and I gathered from Alec that his medical colleagues at the base said Aleena would have to remain in hospital for up to two weeks.

But it was before Aleena and Tiare returned to Koraloona – in fact three days after Reid had flown Aleena to hospital – that Alec heard of my row with Mana.

I didn't realise at first what had happened. I arrived at the dispensary to take the morning sick parade and was surprised to find Alec there. It was unusual to find him up so early in the first place, and now his usually smiling, almost cherubic face was as black as thunder.

A dozen patients were waiting in the garden, including the boy who had cut his foot on a stonefish and was waiting for treatment. Miss Sowerby was in the dispensary preparing the inevitable placebos. I was actually calling in the young boy with the damaged foot when, to my astonishment, Alec walked through the ward where two patients were in bed, reached the passage leading to the theatre, looked at me and growled uncompromisingly, 'Come into the theatre, will you. And you, Miss Sowerby, go and sort out the patients waiting in the garden. I want a word in private with Doctor Masters.'

I caught a mystified look on Miss Sowerby's face. Alec

Reid's attitude was quite out of character, and I saw her purse her lips. Since she had helped me to cure Jimbo of polio, she had changed her entire attitude towards me. I was no longer the young doctor on probation, so to speak. So the pursed lips were now reserved for Dr Reid. She walked into the garden, started asking the patients what was wrong with most of them, and then I walked into the ops theatre and stood facing Alec Reid. He didn't waste any time.

'What's all this bloody business about you insulting Princess Tiare's husband?'

I had been half expecting him to question me about Mana, but not with such personal affront.

'I didn't insult him, he insulted me,' I retorted, trying to control my own anger as I remembered the scene. 'I'm not going to allow anyone – even a patient – to imply that I'm guilty of unprofessional conduct.'

He was still glowering at me. I had never seen him like this before. 'All right, he might have accused you, but – for God's sake grow up. You know damn well that doctors of maturity must expect difficult patients – *and* difficult parents of patients.'

He was right, of course. I knew that. I knew too that I had – as so often before! – let my temper run away with me. The patient – or any customer – is always right. How often we had been told that at med school. All the same, I added almost sulkily, 'You wouldn't have stood for such an allegation.'

'Whatever happened, the situation wouldna have arisen if I'd been there,' said Reid shortly. 'I would have prevented it ever getting out of hand.'

I knew that he was right there, too. And yet I was still seething with anger.

'He's an unpleasant bastard,' I cried to Reid, 'and as a fellow doctor, you should be ticking him off, not me. In London I could have sued him for slander.'

'And faced the same problems of publicity the last time you were in London?' He almost sneered.

'That's a rotten thing to say.' I felt myself blushing.

'I know. And I said it deliberately. To make you realise that you can't behave like that on an island – there's no law of slander here. Mana might be an unpleasant bastard, but just remember that I'm the chief doctor here and you're my assistant, and you'll do as I tell you.'

'Or get out?' I asked.

'Or be fired,' he replied. Then he softened his voice. 'It won't come to that, but you did behave like a bloody fool. After all, man, his wife is a princess – and powerful.'

At that moment Miss Sowerby, hearing the raised voices, decided – deliberately, I'm sure – to interrupt; but I waved her back, saying to Alec, 'I thought you told me the Princess didn't have any power.'

Detecting my note of sarcasm, he retorted, 'Dinna try to be clever with me. You know damn well what I mean. She has the power of public opinion. She is revered by the people here. *She* couldn't have you fired, I agree, but if the people of the island knew that you'd insulted her – which thank God you didn't – they could make your life hell.'

'Well, I didn't insult her. In fact she told me herself she understood why I was so angry. She sympathised with me.'

'She may have done. But Mana didn't. And I might as well be straight with you so we know where we stand. I'll look after the family in future. And you'll keep out of the way. Understood?'

'I'd already told Tiare that.'

'*Princess* Tiare.'

'Sorry.'

Reid's face darkened, and he looked at me doubtfully, then asked, 'I suppose what I've heard is the correct version. Can you categorically tell me that your examination of Aleena was ethically and professionally correct?'

'Of course I can.' It was my turn to be really angry. 'Her mother was present all the time.'

'But may I ask since when,' Reid's Scottish voice came out, 'a routine examination of a girl having a check-up for

140

TB includes a prolonged and tactile study of her breasts for suspected cancer?'

'I never – ' I burst out.

'Don't trouble to make excuses.' Reid's voice was uncharacteristically harsh. 'Mana gave me a detailed description of how you told him you had to feel Aleena's breasts for possible tumours, benign or otherwise, and – '

'I didn't,' I shouted. 'Damn it, Alec. I didn't. I never even saw the girl's breasts – if she has any. Are you going to believe the word of a man like Mana against that of your – ' I paused, to lend emphasis to the word – 'your assistant?'

'I dinna ken.' Reid was genuinely puzzled.

'Believe me, I never bothered to examine her chest, even with a stethoscope. I could tell immediately from examining her back that there wasn't the slightest trace of infection. Her mother watched and listened – and anyway I was far more worried about the melanoma.'

'But why should Mana invent such a story?'

I waited a moment to gather my wits, for now I was coming to the tricky confession, tricky because I knew that I *was* in the wrong to have invented the story I did. There was no excuse for that. I took a deep breath, then blurted out a complete account of what I had done after Mana's own outburst.

'My God! What a bloody, bloody fool. How can you be such an idiot, Kit? That's what I can't understand.'

Alec looked astonished at such stupidity, and wiped his bald head more from exasperation than sweat.

'Because – and this is only my guess – I could see in Mana's eyes the reason for his rage at my examination. He was jealous.'

'Jealous?'

'Yes, just that. Jealous because he assumed I had been examining his step-daughter's body, and he wants Aleena for himself one day.'

'Preposterous!'

'I don't think so.'

'You tell me in all honesty that he was jealous because of

that?' Again he wiped his perspiring forehead, before adding, 'All I know is that you're a bigger fool than I thought.' He sighed, more in sorrow than in anger. 'I knew ye were hot-tempered from the reports I got from London before your appointment was confirmed.' His hostility had been replaced by an acceptance that we had to work together, and so might as well behave like civilised colleagues. 'You may not know it, Kit,' he said, 'but the people in London who dole out the jobs were split right down the middle before you were appointed. Doctor Barton, the chairman of the Review Board, wanted you, but in fact, he cabled Sanderstown explaining your problems before appointing you. And,' he put a hand on my shoulder – 'I thought it was time we had a bit of excitement on the island, so I told them to let you come.'

'I didn't know that, and I'm grateful, Alec,' I said, and I could sense that he knew how moved I was at his action. 'I love Koraloona, I really do. As I've said, the life of the islands has gripped me in a way I never thought possible. And I'm really sorry about my stupid conduct over Mana. I *was* stupid.'

'Do you mean that?'

'I do.'

'I believe you. But since you do admit it was wrong, I think it might be wise, for the future tranquillity of the island, if you just say "Sorry" to Mana the next time you happen to meet.'

It was my turn to look astonished.

'Never!' I cried.

'There ye go again.' Alec threw up his hands in mock despair. 'Temper, temper! Come on, Kit, learn to be a man. And I ken the South Seas well. It'll no be a one-way apology. If you make up and say you're sorry – and you don't need to make a big thing about it – Mana'll turn round and apologise to you, and probably insist that it was all *his* fault.'

'On those terms I agree.' I nearly laughed. 'That saves face all round.'

'And it's wise,' said Alec. 'You see, a man like Mana, once filled with hatred, can be a very dangerous enemy.'

'I'm not sure I understand you?'

'Well, odd things happen in the islands.'

I suddenly remembered Tiare's warning. 'Are you talking about casting spells?'

'Aye,' he agreed seriously. 'We may not believe all this nonsense, but there's no normal way certain events can be explained. It's time I gave you an elementary lesson in South Seas life – and death. I'll tell you what we'll do. Let's have a real night on the town.'

'On the town? In Anani?'

'Why not? We'll have a drink at Mick's Bar, and another one at the Union Jack Club in Tala-Tala. Then you can invite me for dinner – I hear you've got a great cookboy – and maybe we'll have a final nightcap at my place. Think of it. Four social engagements on one night. It's a damn sight more exciting than watching cricket at Lord's.'

We started at Mick's Bar, which I had visited once or twice as part of the local doctor's job of getting to know everyone. Robins had taken me there once, and it was quite a popular meeting place, but I had the feeling that Mick, the owner, was trying too hard to reproduce the atmosphere of a London pub because the patrons liked to indulge in nostalgia; whereas all that I, the newcomer, wanted to do was to wallow in the new-found liberty of the spirit which Koraloona had bestowed on me. I felt that I never again wanted to see the inside of a London pub. For years, as a medical student and young doctor, I had spent unending hours with colleagues in London bars. Now, instead, I was passing my leisure time helping Toma to build a new veranda on my bungalow, or cooling off in beautiful clean water on hot sands – with Lucy if I was lucky. Even the medical side was interesting, for it involved virtually none of the sordid side of the visits I used to have to make to deal with drunks and wife-beaters in the tenements of the East End. And instead of eating sausages or pork pies in pubs, I now had my own cook, with foods, especially fruits, I had hardly realised existed outside the pages of glossy magazines like *Tatler*. No, I didn't want to be reminded of London by propping up the bar of Mick's.

On the other hand, I thoroughly enjoyed myself when Alec and I drove along to the Union Jack Club, where I had already been proposed for membership in the traditional way – 'a mere formality, old boy,' as Colonel Fawcett had assured me. I had been seconded by Captain Baker of the *Nymph* who was an honorary member.

The club might be tatty, but it was the casual tattiness of home; it provided the kind of past I had expected to find in my future. Does that make sense? When I set off for Koraloona, I *wanted* to fall in love with a way of life that didn't exist in London. I had expected boring old members of the Union Jack Club, but I liked them. It *was* their yesterdays which I had expected to find in my future, and they all made 'the new doctor' welcome. I enjoyed our games of bridge. And there were also a few younger members, two men from the government office, Lucy of course, occasional visitors, so that we could usually get a game of tennis on the grass court, and I had played enough snooker as a medical student to enjoy a game of Volunteer at a penny a point.

The seedy lounge was strewn with copies of old magazines, such as the *Illustrated London News*, not subscribed to by the club, but handed on by members who had been given a year's subscription as a Christmas present by some relation back home, and who wanted to share it. They were well thumbed, so that I had the feeling that members who knew the contents by heart re-read an issue just to pass the time until the next batch of magazines arrived by the mailboats.

I will say one thing for Alec Reid. After our monumental row he didn't brood on it. After all, I had acted stupidly – I knew that – and he had played hell with me, but now he seemed to have relegated the incident to the past; and this despite the fact that he was more than twice my age.

After leaving the club, we reached my bungalow about eight. I had already warned Toma that my 'boss' was coming for dinner, and he surpassed himself – mango chicken, and then falai fai, a Samoan version of banana fritters.

'Why should you have such a good cook, while – ?' he asked with mock envy.

'What about Bubble and Squeak? They're marvellous,' I said. We were both laughing.

'Well, this mango chicken would cause a wee sensation in the North British Hotel in Edinburgh,' chuckled Reid.

We had originally decided to go back to Alec Reid's bungalow, but in the end we stayed on at mine for our final nightcaps.

When we were comfortably settled I asked, 'The last evening we spent together you told me all about the fortune in lost paintings. What's it going to be tonight?'

'Well, I'll start with one question.' Reid drew on his pipe. 'Do you know what Mana's name means?'

I shook my head.

'Mana is the Polynesian name – it originated in Fiji – for "sacred power". And that's the power that Mana's supposed to exercise over men and women he doesn't like. If that includes you – and it seems that it does – well, you'd better watch out, unless you make that apology.'

'You really mean that, Alec?' I asked.

'I'm no' saying I do. If you can listen seriously, I'll tell you a few simple facts, and then you can judge for yourself!'

Reid studied his glass, then asked, 'Ever thought to ask how Tiare's husband – whose name was Mbindo – died? And so suddenly?' When I shook my head, he went on, 'And ever thought why she then married such a horrible man as Mana?'

'It's incomprehensible, I know that much.'

'All right, I'll ask you another question. Do you ever

cross your fingers if you see a black cat? Or just move a couple of steps to avoid going under a ladder? Or think twice when you're travelling on Friday the thirteenth?' Hardly giving me a chance to shake my head Reid said, 'Of course you don't. But you do know the superstitions I've mentioned, even if you dinna actually heed them. Neither do I. But in the islands – especially the smaller ones like Koraloona – superstition is one of the most dominant features of their lives. Every man, woman and child on every small South Seas island is terrified of people who cast spells.'

'But crossing your fingers when you see a black cat – that's one thing – it's instinctive,' I said. 'Casting evil spells, or witch-doctors – that went out with cannibalism. It's ridiculous.'

'Maybe it is, maybe it isn't. I won't be the judge and jury, I'll just present you with a few facts.'

He started by telling me what Mana had done some years ago – a story that had nothing to do with Tiare or her husband. Mana had had a quarrel with someone about a plot of land. Both people claimed they had inherited it. Finally the argument came to court when the local magistrate from Sanders Island paid one of his periodic visits to Koraloona. The magistrate found that Mana had no title to the land. Within three months, according to Reid, Mana had cast a spell on the other man, made a public announcement to witnesses, and ten days later the other man was dead.

'But how?' I asked. 'It might have been from natural causes – just an extraordinary coincidence. Or if not, it might have been murder – revenge by poison.'

Reid shook his head. 'The poor man just slipped into death – wasted away – and when I was sent for I could do nothing to help. Even when he started vomiting and had terrible diarrhoea. But there was nae a thing organically wrong with him. Nothing I could find. Of course I suspected poison, so I flew the corpse to Sanderstown, where I asked the local coroner to hold a post-mortem.

Again, nothing wrong. There was simply no reason for that poor man to die. He had lost the will to live – or maybe someone had gie'n him the wish to die.'

'But you can't believe that, Alec.' I felt suddenly nauseated.

'But then Mana had a quarrel with Mbindo, Tiare's husband. He was a fine man, everyone liked him, and he adored Tiare. I was worried, because I had looked after both Tiare and the young Aleena and I liked Mbindo. Only this was nae ordinary quarrel: it was deliberately provoked by Mana. In the end the two men had a stand-up fight – and that's rare in the islands. But Mana was the kind of man who loves a fight. *And* a loud-mouthed bully. It's a pity Mbindo didn't kill Mana. He damn nearly did even though Mbindo was smaller. But he almost split Mana's head open when he hit him with a wooden stake in a last desperate attempt to save his life.'

'And then?'

'We hushed it all up. I thought nothing more about it, until one day Tiare came rushing around in a rare state, screaming – and she's normally the most self-possessed of women, as you know – and crying that her husband was dying. I asked her what the trouble was, and Tiare cried, "Mana has cast a spell on my husband. Nothing can save him. Get me a *bonota*, I beg you."'

'What's a *bonota*?' I asked.

'It's the South Seas name for a protective spell. According to superstition, if you can find a good *bonota* you might be able to get rid of the spell. But no one can just walk out and find one.'

'So what did you do?'

This time, and especially in view of Mana's previous victim, Alec Reid took no chances. After examining Mbindo and finding no evidence of real illness that he could diagnose, Reid drove him to the dispensary in his makeshift ambulance, loaded him on to the plane in the field behind, then flew him to Sanderstown. Though Alec was regarded in Sanderstown as something of an eccentric, he knew one doctor with whom he had trained in Edinburgh and who was now a surgeon-commander at the naval base. He persuaded him to admit Tiare's husband immediately.

For three days the best doctors at the base treated the man with varying proportions of opium, morphia, chloroform and alcohol, even minute doses of hydrogen cyanide.

'How much?' I put the question automatically, for I knew how careful one had to be with prussic acid – the popular name for hydrogen cyanide.

'One point five milligrams,' Reid replied. 'It eased the griping pains, but the weakness from persistent discharges long after his stomach had been voided sapped Mbindo's strength. And the frightening thing was that we could establish no organic cause of his death.'

'You think it was the spell?'

Reid shook his head.

'When I was telling my friends about the evil spell they thought I'd gone off my rocker,' he confessed. 'But they weren't laughing when Tiare's husband was pronounced dead. Despite all the expertise at the base hospital, they still couldn't find anything wrong. I give you my word, I was heartbroken. I'm like you, Kit – I canna bring myself to believe in such tosh. But what can ye do – or think – when two men die for no reason? Except that they'd been ordered not to live.'

Despite the incredibility of it all, I shivered.

'I know how you feel,' Reid sympathised. 'Every moment of our medical training tells us to ignore such stupidity, and yet there's no other reason for this happening. That's why I'm sorry you've been involved. Maybe the spell won't work on white men. And maybe Mana hasn't even cast one. Let's drink to that.'

One thing which Alec had mentioned was still unexplained. Why had a beautiful woman like Tiare married such a horror – someone who had in effect killed her husband?

'That's the sad part.' Alec Reid sighed again. 'When I heard that Mana and Tiare were going to be married, I went round to her house at once and told her bluntly she couldn't do such a thing. I said I would do everything in ma power to prevent such an ill-assorted couple from going through with it. Why on earth did she want to marry a devil? I asked her that – point blank. And ye ken what she replied? That she was afraid. Mana had threatened to cast a spell on *her* if she didn't marry him.'

'It's unbelievable,' I said, thinking, even so, did that mean that I did believe these absurd stories of the supernatural?

'But aren't the people of Koraloona Christians? After all, they go to church, and – ' I was thinking of the hymns sung so lustily each Sunday.

'They're Christians all right – but only up to a point. You can't just arrive on an island with a cross and tell people to change a centuries-old way of thinking and believing. Ancestor worship and the casting of spells were a basic part of life in these islands long before Captain Cook arrived.'

'But no more, surely?'

'It's not as easy to change as that. Some of the old men still bury their dead in shallow graves so that, though they are buried according to the Christian religion, they sometimes dig up the graves to give the skeletons of their ancestors a breath of air.'

I must have looked astonished, because Reid laughed and added, 'On the other side of the island I once saw a man who had removed the top soil covering a grave and who was holding the skeleton within in a sitting position. He was pushing a cigarette between the teeth of the skull! Then he reburied it. Only then did he see me. He knew me, and wasn't frightened. When I asked what he was doing, he told me with a happy smile, 'My father always enjoy smoke, Doctor, and though he dead thirty years, I give him pleasure occasionally.'

'My God.' I shivered again.

'You see, when we talk of things like that,' said Reid, 'and of curses and casting spells, it sometimes makes you realise that the whole business of saving the souls of innocent men and women like the Polynesians never *really* makes them Christian. I wonder how many become so-called converts simply because they're afraid, or because at first many missionaries tended to arrive with a crucifix in one hand and a sword in the other. The "heathen" had to accept Christian customs or else – ' Reid left the sentence unfinished.

'But that was decades, centuries, ago,' I cried.

'Aye,' he admitted, 'but you know as well as I do that ye canna blot out past habits just by saying a few wee prayers. Everyone who says he's Christian – who *is* Christian – still has his holy man to guide his spiritual life. Why! Even a modern schoolgirl like Aleena, and her mother Tiare, go to get help to the equivalent of an Indian guru.'

'Sounds incredible,' I muttered.

'It is. And they wield a great deal more power than our Christian priests, though you'd never get the islanders admitting it.'

It was dark now, but a bright moon shone over the lagoon, very still and very beautiful. Alec Reid scraped out the bowl of his pipe, and said, 'Time I was making a move. If ye can find any reasonable solution, I'll be the first to shake your hand.' He got up, stretched his legs, stiff after the long time in the cane chair, and gave my shoulder another pat, his sign of friendship, and I walked him through my garden to his monstrosity of a car.

After I had strolled back, I sat again on the veranda and stared out over the lagoon below, moonlight picking out boats and the silver of the surf on the distant, thundering reef.

There had to be what Alec called 'a reasonable solution'. There *had* to be. And if there was, then I would find it. In the end I did find it, but it nearly cost me my life in the finding.

10

The next few weeks flitted past in a delightful idyll, so delightful that I completely, and foolishly, forgot my promise to Alec to try and apologise to Mana. But 'idyllic' is the only word really to describe the sensation of an interlude whose tenderness contained none of the anguished moments that so tear the emotions of the lovelorn. We were happy together not only because of each other's company, which we found stimulating, not only because we were physically so attracted to one another, but because we had no feelings of guilt. We were doing exactly what the islanders did, enjoying each other's company to the full, without anguish, without jealousy; and all against a background of warm, blue sea, rustling casuarinas, whispering palms and a blaze of flowers and trees everywhere, from the edge of the beach to the mountains rearing behind towards the rim of the dormant volcano.

I worried sometimes about the future. I remember lying in bed one night after Lucy had gone, thinking, There is no love, no real love involved, but what about the consequences? We'd both agreed, without ever saying anything openly, that ours was a temporary love, and we knew that there must be a time limit on all our love-making. Only neither of us knew just what the time limit was – or what it should be.

Though Alec Reid had immediately put two and two together, Paula Reece did not seem to have heard any gossip. Indeed, three weeks or so after the festival, she invited me to lunch at the Villa Faalifu with a couple of her guests.

It was not, of course, the first time I had seen inside her

house. It was not only beautiful, but had been decorated in superb taste. I walked up the few steps to the veranda, then on into the main living-room, at least forty feet long, and which was supported by four massive beams. The room had been smoothly plastered and the walls covered with paintings – scores of them. Sofas and occasional tables were arranged in three groups.

What Alex called the 'usual gang' were there – Colonel and Mrs Fawcett, Tiare, together with a couple of healthy, sun-tanned young Californian men whose names I didn't remember, but who had been invited by Paula. They were chatting among themselves, nibbling the canapés, drinking champagne suitably chilled. Paula, as usual, was immaculate. She had the knack of dressing in a casual manner that still looked as though she had just bought the most expensive clothes in the world and was wearing them for the first time.

'That's a lovely silk dress you're wearing.' I was trying to make conversation.

'Oh *that*!' she laughed. 'I'm so glad you like it. I was in such a rush to be ready that I just grabbed any old thing from the closet.'

A likely story! I thought. She was the sort of woman who probably debated for hours about what to wear, her facial make-up, or the choice of men to be invited to her island retreat.

I had been looking around for Lucy, and then she strolled into the room, greeted me with her special smile, frank, open, unaffected, as Paula said, 'You've met Lucy before I believe. She's my nanny. I'd be lost without her.' And then, as though casually, she said to Lucy, 'I've been looking all over for you! Just check in the dining-room that everything's in order, will you?'

It was curious, the feeling I had, the subtle way in which Paula was showing me the distinct line of demarcation between employer and employee, just as she always did when talking to Captain Baker. It wasn't what she said, more the way she said it. I tried to catch Lucy's eye, but she avoided mine as she said to Paula, 'Sure,' and walked away.

She returned from the dining-room a moment or two later when Paula was showing Mrs Fawcett and me an ultra-modern painting hanging at the far end of the room.

'Everything's fine,' Lucy told Paula. 'We can lunch whenever you say.'

'Thank you. But I think,' she was looking at Lucy as she spoke to me, 'I'll first just show Kit my *pièce de résistance*.'

'What's that?' I asked innocently.

'A room no one can resist,' said Paula. 'My rather special bedroom.'

'I'll be there when you call me.' Lucy turned away.

'Follow me.' Paula turned to the stairway which opened up from the living-room. 'Poor Lucy seems rather out of sorts. Overdoing it, I shouldn't wonder.' Was she having a dig at me? We climbed the stairs, walked along a landing, its walls covered with more ultra-modern paintings, and then Paula opened a door.

I had never seen a bedroom like it. Not only was it almost as large as the living-room, but it had a huge veranda, facing the lagoon. 'A wrap-around balcony,' Paula explained. 'Faces each direction.'

In the centre was a huge bed which must have been all of ten feet across. Certainly it was broader than it was long. She looked at me with a smile, as though taunting me. 'Not bad eh? – but not for sleeping.'

I felt a curious distaste as I walked around, pretending to admire, with Paula always at my side. Any sense of embarrassment was made worse not only because her motives in showing me the room were suggestive, but almost as though she were saying, 'You made the wrong choice.'

On each side of the monumental bed small doors led to two beautiful bathrooms.

'Yes, two bathrooms,' she explained, 'there's one good thing you can learn from having a divorce or two – the joy of sharing a good bed, and the misery of having to share the same bathroom the morning after. Don't you agree?'

'Well, I never have been divorced,' I laughed.

'The bed is quite an experience.' She sat down bouncing slightly, showing beautiful legs above the knee as she almost leaned back. 'Come on – sit on it – try it for quality.'

Luckily I was 'rescued' – for I didn't like the way the scene was being acted – using acting in the truthful sense. I had the feeling that she knew about Lucy and was staging this ridiculous scene either to make me feel stupid, or even worse, to teach Lucy a lesson. Luckily, a sonorous dinner gong sounded from downstairs.

'Damn!' cried Paula. 'Just as I was getting to know you better, Kit, and now I have to play hostess. Never mind.' She jumped off the bed, and said, 'We'd better go.'

'Thank God!' I said. But I said it under my breath and followed her to the dining-room.

Lucy had been invited to lunch – I could guess that she was there as an extra girl to make up the eight. She had told me that she usually ate with Paula and her guests. But this time, Lucy virtually ignored me. I could see that she was angry. But, I thought, why take it out on me?

I had previously agreed to meet Lucy at my bungalow the following Sunday, and she was still cross.

'Darling.' I kissed her. 'Why are you so annoyed with me?'

It was the only time I saw that frank, laughing face really angry.

'I'm jealous,' she agreed as I offered her a drink. 'Here we are, blissfully happy, doing no one any harm, and this bloody woman, who has everything in the world, tries to take you away from me.'

'She didn't even suggest – '

'I know my Paula. She'll get you.'

'She won't, I promise. It takes two – '

'Of course, Kit. I trust you. I'm sorry I blew up. It's just that – '

154

'That's better. Now kiss me and come to bed. We have an hour to play at being Polynesian.' And soon we were lying naked on the bed, stroking each other, kissing gently, the love-making by now more gentle than on that first almost savage night.

As usual, I had taken the precaution of sending Toma to see his parents. I had locked both the living-room and the bedroom door, each of them on the side of the long corridor that led from the front veranda to the back, opposite the kitchen, larder, Toma's room and my bath-room. The attap 'shutters', not unlike Venetian blinds, were drawn so that no one could see inside, yet they gave enough light for us to see each other during daylight. Most important of all, we always knew where Paula was on any Sunday afternoon – for she had instituted a regular bridge club, an offshoot of the Union Jack Club, together with any of her friends who happened to be staying with her.

So we lay there, savouring those delicious moments of kissing, stroking, the anticipation that would last until each was aroused to the point where we could wait no longer.

We had almost reached that stage, so nearly there, that I had to beg Lucy not to touch me, when, lying on my side facing her, I suddenly felt my skin prickle with fear. As Lucy felt me go limp, felt the goosepimples on my skin, she looked at me as if with a sense of shared terror at something unknown. Both of us looked instinctively at the pile of clothes, Lucy's handbag on a chair, as our eyes then watched the door handle.

I put a hand over her mouth and pointed. The inside door handle of the bedroom. It was being slowly, soundlessly turned, as though someone was trying to get in. My first thought, of course, was that it was a burglar – an idea quickly dismissed, for our two cars at the bottom of the garden were evidence enough that someone was in the house.

I gripped her arm – forgetting the warm feeling of her breasts against me as she clutched me. Slowly, soundlessly, the brass handle of the door knob turned back. Lucy still had her arms round me, and I could feel the pounding of her heart as we both watched the door handle, fascinated now by the lack of movement. There was no noise, as though the would-be intruder was barefoot.

All thoughts of passion had vanished. Gently I drew aside the mosquito net, put my feet to the ground, bidding Lucy with a gesture to make no noise, and carefully put on my shorts before creeping across the bedroom to the door. Lucy sat on the bed, half covered with a sheet, biting one corner of it in her mouth, as though to stop herself screaming.

As silently as I could, I slowly turned the key in the lock and then, almost with a flourish, quickly pulled open the door.

Empty. The hall that led to both back and front doors looked just as it had when we'd arrived, as though nobody else had been there, as though I had imagined everything. I ran to the veranda, for no intruder would have had time to reach the lane. Not a sign of anyone. I darted to the other end, the back of the bungalow. The bathroom door was closed, and the only window was made of louvred glass panes sloping at such an angle that you could only see down – and any peeping toms could only see the ceiling inside. All the expatriate bungalows were fitted with similar windows. Only when I ran towards the back door, where a tangled path led to an equally thick hedge of poinsettia, six feet tall and growing wild, did I think I glimpsed a car. But I couldn't be sure, and there was still no noise. It was eerie.

I returned back to the bedroom. 'False alarm,' I cried as I opened the door to our bedroom. 'Don't worry, darling.' Then I bent down. 'Hello, what the hell's this? Is it yours?'

Even as I said it, I knew it wasn't. For I could see that Lucy recognised it immediately, a small, lace-edged hand-kerchief. It bore two initials in the corner – 'PR'. Silently I handed it to Lucy.

'Paula Reece,' I managed to croak.

'That bitch,' Lucy said bitterly, 'didn't drop her hand-kerchief by accident. She was hoping to catch us in bed together. So much for her game of bridge. God, what a bitch!'

'I'll go to Tala-Tala,' I said, starting to dress hurriedly. 'You stay here. I'll have it out with her. After all, we've done nothing wrong. But I'm going to see her before you do.'

'No, no, don't do that,' she pleaded. Lucy was also putting on her dress, then combing her blonde hair. 'Don't you see? She's *proved* nothing. It's just a warning to keep off the grass – her grass.'

'I'd better go and see her,' I insisted.

'Please don't. It could cost me my job.'

'So what? What's so wonderful about working for Paula Reece? You could get another.'

'Not so easily in Koraloona. Not at that tax-free salary. I didn't tell you, but I've borrowed against my earnings to make the last payment on that house at Sausolito. I want to finish my five months here. Only two to go. And she can't *prove* a thing. I've got to stick it out – by being careful. It's my insurance for the future. If you interfere, it's the same as confessing. Leave it to me. Promise?'

I had dressed by now, and Lucy was on her knees searching for one sandal under the bed.

'All right,' I agreed, reluctantly. 'If you insist. But if *you* promise me one thing.'

'Which is?'

'That if you need help, send for me. Promise – a solemn oath?'

'I promise.' And at that the colour came back to her freckled cheeks, and she managed a small smile.

Two days later she managed to phone me to say that everything was normal, and that she hoped to see me in a couple of days. But that was the last message from poor, sweet, freckled Lucy that I received. She did try to enlist my help – desperately. But by then a whole new chain of events had virtually imprisoned me, happening at lightning speed, pulling down on my back until I was on the way to extinction.

It started the following day, when I heard Alec suggest to Tiare on the ancient hand-cranked telephone that he would like to make a quick examination of Aleena's thigh to make sure that the skin graft wasn't being rejected.

'Purely routine,' I heard him say. 'But I'd rather examine Aleena here in the surgery. I've been on the sked to the surgeon who operated on her, and he suggested it. After all, you are my patient,' he added with a chuckle. He knew, as I did, that Aleena had undergone a fairly serious operation and that the dangers of infection in any tropical country are magnified horrendously. A man who sticks some plaster on a small cut in dirty old London will be able to forget it in a week. The same man, cutting the same finger in the tropics, could be infected and die within days. 'So it's always better to overdo the precautions,' Alec was fond of saying.

Following Mana's strict orders, I was not allowed to treat any member of Tiare's family, even though I was the one who had spotted the malignant tumour. I didn't mind, though. I had plenty of work, and though there had been no more polio cases reported, I was studying as much as I could from my few books, and even wrote off to London and Sydney for books on Sister Kenny, as well as making tours of the villages in case I came across children whose mothers hadn't reported any deformities.

I was also worried about Lucy. When she telephoned me she had sounded all right, but just a touch reserved. Was she hiding something from me?

Somehow I just knew that Paula did know about us; and I felt equally sure that Paula realised that I knew. And she was a dangerous woman. Why hadn't she confronted Lucy? Or did she really believe – as Lucy had tried to persuade me – that since Lucy had done no wrong, there was no real problem? No danger of getting the sack, because no jealousy? I somehow couldn't believe that, especially after the more or less open hints when she showed me her bedroom.

But if Lucy felt threatened, then unless we were very careful our private idyll would end abruptly by force of circumstance. It wouldn't break my heart, but I would miss her openness, her sense of fun and her companionship. The occasional evenings playing classical music with Purvis, or talking with Alec, were pleasant enough; but the hours spent playing in the warm and gentle arms of Lucy were far more rewarding, and on a different plane altogether.

When Tiare and Aleena arrived I was in the dispensary, trying to find some papers in Tiare's mother's old tin trunk. Just because they weren't my private patients, it didn't mean I was going to be driven out of the hospital. Alec had told me as much with a casual, 'Don't leave the place on their account. If ye've got work to do in the dispensary, I'm nae going to allow them to interfere with it.'

Tiare in fact gave me a warm 'Hello' and Aleena, somehow looking more grown up than when I had first examined her, said, 'I never had a chance to thank you, Doctor, for dealing with my horrible black wart.'

'I'm glad it's better,' I smiled. So did Aleena – a warm smile. 'Hope it wasn't too painful.'

Alec led them through the ward, through the glass passage and into the operating theatre. I could hear them plainly from the dispensary at the other end of the ward. He said, 'No need to undress, Aleena, just lie down on the table and pull up your skirt. I only want to make sure there's no infection, no sign of festering.'

I heard a jumble of incomprehensible words, the voice of Tiare, and then Aleena saying, 'Please do. It's only fair.'

'Amazing!' cried Alec. 'Really perfect.'

Then he must have stepped across to the corridor joining the ward to the ops theatre for I could hear him clearly as he called out, 'Doctor Masters.'

I popped my head round the corner of the dispensary as Alec beckoned me, saying jovially, 'Aleena and her mother both insist that you should see how the scar is healing. After all, as Aleena just said, you discovered it.'

'All right if I come in?' I asked doubtfully.

'Just for a moment.'

'Come and have a look, Doctor Masters,' cried Aleena.

I did. It was fascinating to see how a circle of fresh skin was growing perfectly into new, clean tissue, largely because the patient was a healthy young girl. Soon the scar would be no larger than one of those early vaccination marks. With a few weeks of sun and sea, it would all but disappear. The only lasting effect would be, if one put a hand on that part of her thigh, one could feel the difference in skin texture; but even then the slight touch of scar tissue would hardly be noticeable to a layman, only to the fingers of a doctor used to 'reading' signs with his fingertips.

With the thought of the diminishing scar, I said to Alec and Aleena, 'They've done a wonderful job at the base. Mind if I feel the scar tissue?'

'Carry on,' said Alec, as Aleena smiled.

I was leaning forward when it happened. As though from another world the quiet of the theatre was filled with a bellow of rage, and a bull-like roar cried, 'No! Damn you, no!'

Unseen, unheard because of our preoccupation, Mana rushed forward, grabbed the back of my shirt collar and jerked me away so that I almost fell to the ground as Alec shouted from the other side of the ops table, 'Leave him alone!'

Tiare tried to grab Mana, but he shoved her aside. Alec, without regard to professional niceties, shouted, 'Get out of my surgery, you bastard.'

As I stumbled, I had a momentary feeling that even Mana realised that he had gone too far by barging into a surgeon's operating theatre and assaulting a doctor, but my feeling was too fleeting to give a second for reflection.

I had kept my balance – by a miracle – and without a coherent thought in my head other than pure reaction – from my boxing days, I suppose – I moved my feet into position. Then, leaning slightly forward, I shot out my left arm, straight to the rib cage by Mana's heart. It had every ounce of my weight behind it, and I swear that the blow, like a piston, hardly travelled two feet. As I hit him he leaned forward, eyes glassy, and I came straight in with a right uppercut. I missed the point of his jaw – vulnerable and unguarded – but it split his left cheek with a weal that within seconds oozed blood.

It didn't, though, knock Mana out. He was a big man, with enormous hidden strength. Somehow he stood teetering on his feet, shaking his head like a puzzled animal. It was at that moment that Alec shouted, 'Stop it! This is a surgery, not a bar parlour. And you, Mana – it was your fault, you attacked Doctor Masters, and he's not to blame for defending himself. Get out – and never come back. Never, understand?'

At least Alec had stood up for me – publicly, too, in front of Tiare. I relaxed my arms, and stepped back.

I wasn't hurt at all, except for a bruised hand – just angry – but I managed to say 'Sorry ladies' to Tiare, who said nothing, and to Aleena, whose eyes were glistening almost as though she had actually enjoyed the encounter.

Attracted by the noise, an astonished Miss Sowerby rushed in from the back of the dispensary where she had been treating one of the last few patients. As she glimpsed the scene, I vaguely heard her shout, 'Stop it, you heathen!' It was a cry straight from the heart – of a missionary's daughter. Then she made a quick dash to the two remaining patients, a man and a woman, waiting in the garden, and cried, 'Unless it's urgent, please come back tomorrow!'

They left – reluctantly, probably sensing that the noise inside promised intrigue. As I walked across the ward, Mana, who was following me, took one look at Miss Sowerby and hissed words that I couldn't understand. They certainly weren't part of the local dialect. More probably Japanese.

I didn't look back, and had reached the veranda door when Alec cried, 'Look out!'

It was too late. I had just reached the shade of the giant

161

flame tree in the garden near the veranda when what seemed like a ton weight hit me in the back. As I fell, my first thought was that something had fallen from the flame tree, but then, as I tried to rise, I was hit again, this time in the rib cage.

It was Mana, standing glowering above me, ready to kick me once more. I tried to roll myself into a ball. I caught sight of his singlet and khaki trousers, and realised that he wore no shoes – thank God, I remember thinking – but all the same he had the power, and appearance, of an enraged ape.

Whatever else I did, whatever new punishment he tried to inflict on me, I had to get up. Once standing, however groggy – and he was just as groggy as I – I felt I could hold my own against him, by skilful defence, by feinting, by ducking, by boxing, by any means I could. But I could only fight on equal terms if I was squaring up to him.

For a moment I pretended I had fainted from the pain – trying to play for time, a few moments of grace – just to gather my wits, to crawl round the tree perhaps. But then he lunged at me again, and though I rolled over and his foot barely grazed my body, I screamed – deliberately.

For that was *his* undoing – because, with all this happening in seconds, it brought Alec Reid on to the scene. I saw him on the veranda, shooing Miss Sowerby back into the room behind, and then he shouted and tried to grab Mana. The sudden diversion from another quarter gave me just the seconds I needed to scramble to my feet.

Tiare, who was still in the theatre with Aleena, tried to get back to the garden. I shouted, 'Go back, Princess – inside. And you, Alec. Take her with you by the back door. We're not in the surgery now.' As he hesitated, I cried, '*Please!* I'm going to teach this bastard a lesson he'll never forget.'

'He deserves it,' growled Alec and he shepherded Tiare back into the building.

The gash on Mana's cheek was streaming blood by now, but it didn't deter him, even though I was on my feet.

162

The garden – the square patch of earth that was our 'waiting-room' – was in a way like a boxing ring, squarish enough, with the veranda fencing which led into the hospital forming one side of the 'ropes'. This is how I imagined it in the split second, as I was thinking, slightly dazed and with my rib cage hurting like hell, 'I must get my opponent on the ropes' – in other words, against the veranda fence.

It was easier said than done, for Mana had no respect for the Queensberry Rules; and as I watched, I could *feel* the way in which the Japanese streak in him was coming out.

With incredible swiftness for such a big and bulky man, he picked up a broom from the grass, normally used for sweeping up leaves, and hurled it at me like a javelin. Luckily I turned so that the side of the broom – not the point – only hit my forehead. Instantly I felt the hot blood flowing down.

As I wiped the blood from my left eye, Mana gave a kind of triumphal roar and – again in Japanese – shouted something. He looked and crouched like a Japanese wrestler as he charged me, not like a boxer, but with his knees bent, one leg in front of the other. I just managed to keep on my feet and as he approached me, fists flailing, I grabbed his vest, without really knowing what I was doing, in order to pull him towards me, and then it was my turn to forget Queensberry. I dug one knee upwards and hit him right in the testicles. He grunted with pain, but still stood, squaring up to me with that terrifying Japanese stance. I almost stumbled – on one of the wooden chairs used by patients waiting to be treated. I grabbed it in my right hand. Then as he hit me again, landing a blow on the cheek, I swung the chair round with all my strength. It hit him across the face, and this time, *he* screamed with pain.

Breathless, I paused. I was very nearly out after the blow to the ribs and then the head, and now the blood was beginning to make it difficult to see with my left eye.

But Mana was tottering too, and with relief I saw Alec Reid in the doorway trying to prevent Tiare from coming into the garden again. I saw, in that split second, Alec push her back into the ward, heard him shout at both of us, 'Stop it, you two. Stop it!'

Mana looked up. So did I. And I thought that was the end of the fight. He, too, seemed to have had enough, but the minute he realised that I was ready to call it a day, he suddenly swung round with that half grunt, half hiss, and charged again.

I was barely ready for him. But I knew that if I didn't want to be killed, I had to get him on the 'ropes'. As he circled round me, still with the stance of a wrestler, I backed away to draw him in. Finally I got him with his back to the veranda fence. I waited. I knew it would be only a few seconds before a slugger would lunge and try to finish me off with one last attempt. That's the difference between a boxer and a slugger. Because you can't advance and slug it out without lowering your guard. Every boxer waits for that moment, and sure enough it came. Mana charged with a roar and did manage to land one punch on my left shoulder as I swayed to the right, and side-stepped; but then I shot out a straight left that caught him full on the mouth. He backed away, spitting teeth and, as he did so, I followed with two jabs, one left, one right, to the chest under the heart. One of the most weakening blows there is in boxing. There was a sound of splintered wood as he smashed down the veranda slats, then he seemed to slide gracefully to the ground.

This time he was out for the count, a tattered hulk of a wreck, his trousers smeared with blood, his vest torn. I myself was not exactly a pretty sight. My face was covered in blood, my shirt torn and bloody.

'Enough is enough,' I managed to croak to Alec.

'Lie ye down,' he said. 'Come on now, let me bathe that cut. It's nothing, but ye're bleeding like a pig.'

Miss Sowerby and Tiare came in, and I heard Alec tell Miss Sowerby, 'Keep an eye on him, and tell me if he shows any sign of coming round.' Tiare came into the room whispering, 'I'm sorry. Oh dear, why did this happen?'

'How did he happen to be here?' asked Alec as I winced when he treated my forehead.

'It's my fault,' Tiare said. 'When you told me that you wanted to check on Aleena, he warned me against Doctor Masters. I was so pleased with what Doctor Masters had done, I never thought anything about allowing him to see Aleena. But Mana must have followed me.'

Aleena peeped at me from the other room, her face half covered by her hands, as though afraid to see what I looked like.

Half an hour, and a couple of stiff whiskies later, I felt better. Tiare and Aleena had gone, and Alec had given Mana an injection to keep him half under. He had promised to take Mana home in the ambulance.

'I'll take him,' I said suddenly.

'Of course you can't.'

'I'd like to,' I insisted. 'A sort of perfect ending to a perfect day.' I tried to smile, but cried 'Ouch!' at the pain. 'You'll have to help me get him into the ambulance,' I said.

'All right then,' cried Alec. 'Thank God you don't need a hearse. But don't be long. I need the car to take me home for lunch.'

Lunch! Was it still morning? The fight had seemed to last all day.

Grunting and sweating, Alec helped me to get Mana's bulk on to the stretcher in the makeshift ambulance. He was an enormous weight, and when he attempted to stand, his legs wobbled like jelly. It was the ambulance steps which proved the most difficult, and it took three goes before we could heave him inside and roll him on to the stretcher. Then I drove off – slowly.

By the time I arrived at the pretty house on the edge of the sea, Mana was beginning to move. Perhaps the jolting of the ride helped. I watched him warily, but he had no intention of doing any more fighting.

Tiare was at the door. 'I'm sorry, Princess,' I apologised, 'but, you know I never started – '

'Don't say anything, *please*.' She whispered urgently, as

165

if anxious to get any words we had to say over before Mana was out of the ambulance. 'And your poor hands, Doctor – look at your hands!'

I looked down. I hadn't realised that my knuckles were red and raw with blood. 'Next time I must remember to use my gloves.' I tried a faint smile.

Mana tried to stumble to his feet, but he couldn't. He was a pitiful sight, the blood on his cheek now congealed, and I knew it would leave a scar for life if he didn't have it stitched straight away. And *we* weren't going to stitch him.

Yet despite his terrible injuries, the missing teeth, the blood around his mouth, he still struggled to stand up, helped by a servant, and somehow he finally managed to speak, slurred words, first in what sounded like Japanese, but then clear enough to make poor Tiare scream, 'No, no!' and cover her face.

'I am laying a death curse on you,' shouted Mana. 'You will be dead within a week. And for the last three days of your life you will be begging to die, the agony will be so great.'

11

I went home for lunch after parking the ambulance. Alec had bandaged and taped my sore knuckles, muttering, 'No serious damage, but for God's sake keep away from that man.' I didn't tell Alec about the death curse because, frankly, I didn't regard it seriously. At first I felt fine, and in three days the only remaining legacy of the fight was my sore ribs. On Monday, though, it was very different. Every Sunday evening Purvis came round for a snack because Lucy was never free because of Paula's new bridge club. Lucy had to be on hand to see that everything functioned smoothly, even to play if (as often happened) a fourth was needed when someone failed to turn up.

I had told Purvis to arrive around six because Bill Robins was in port and I had, as usual, invited him to an early dinner at the house before he sailed for Sanders around midnight. It had become a habit, lunch at Green's Hotel, dinner at home whenever Bill was in port. And Robins, though he disapproved of his drinking, liked Jason Purvis, simply because both were avid readers, and both shared an extensive knowledge of almost every subject under the sun.

I hadn't eaten much lunch, but that was understandable. Combined physical and mental strain of the sort I had experienced often reduces the pangs of hunger for a few days, but I was suddenly seized by a raging thirst. I continued to drink, asking Toma, 'Boil some more water.' We always boiled our water for a minimum of five minutes (though three minutes is acceptable to kill all bacteria). Both at home and in the hospital we always stored our boiled water in empty Gordon's gin bottles because the rectangular shape made them easier to store in the fridge. Our distilled water, which arrived regularly from Sanderstown, came in round jars with screw tops, sealed with tape until we opened each jar.

'Plenty water,' Toma assured me. 'Five bottles full. But I make more, boil.'

I dozed after lunch and must have had a nightmare and shouted for Toma, who ran in, his brown face crinkled with concern, and drew aside the mosquito net to see if I was all right.

'Master, you wet through.' He helped me out of bed to dry me off. Not only were my pyjama tops drenched with sweat, but so were my sheets, reminding me of the sweats I had encountered among malaria patients.

'I find new pyjamas, please sit down.' Toma fussed over me, drying my back, then helped me to a basket chair near the side of the bed.

'I feel damned funny, Toma.' I started to speak as I tried to get up. My legs buckled, I almost stumbled, but worse, much worse, without warning I was violently sick. Thank God Toma had produced the towel. I grabbed it just as I vomited half the contents of my stomach (or so it seemed) into the towel. It was water – a dark green, evil-smelling water.

I managed to reach the chair, gasping to Toma, 'Get me some water!' when I was seized by a different urge. The pain was the first warning. It was excruciating, as though someone had stuck a red-hot poker up my anus, and as I screamed, I managed to make for the bathroom and reached it just as I felt the water pouring out of my bowels. The stench was terrible, though the pain had eased a little. I managed to crawl back to the room as Toma arrived and helped me back to the chair and gave me a drink.

Though the agony passed when I reached my bed and lay there panting, it was immediately replaced by a different emotion: something very akin to panic; a kind of mental tussle between fear and reason, between a doctor's logic and superstition. The violent pain of the burning liquid of renal colic had no rational explanation. My medical training told me that. Poison? I had eaten nothing that could bring about such a swift reaction, and even if I had eaten some poisoned shellfish or over-ripe fruit, or was suffering from ptomaine poisoning, the immediate effects would never be so bad, and would never, I knew from experience, be accompanied by such acute agony.

I didn't dare to voice – even to myself – the awful thought racing through my mind – that if this sudden illness were not normal, what was it? I struggled in my mind to search through my half-forgotten intern cases for a similar case history, but I knew there wasn't one. Yet I *couldn't* give in to something at which I had scoffed – the power of the witch-doctor, of evil men like Mana. But as I looked up gasping at Toma, I saw that there was no conflict in *his* mind.

'It is the death curse,' he whispered.

'Balls!' I said, panting for breath as I felt the beginning of another attack. 'Get Doctor Reid – quick!' I just managed to get the words out before I vomited again, this time all over the floor.

Reid was on the phone of course, but Toma was far too superstitious to use it. He felt, as he had often told me, that only spirits could talk to each other without visual contact, and he never dared even to take the instrument off the hook.

'I run all way to fetch doctor,' he said.

'Leave me some water,' I managed to croak, my voice seeming to disappear with the strain. Even before Toma had left the front door I voided my bowels, this time on the bed. More water. Soon I was sick again – and unable to move. When I tried to get out of my filthy bed, I just couldn't. I had to lie where I was, still panting for breath.

I must have been on the point of losing consciousness, but not quite, for I heard a babble of voices outside, and dimly saw a parade of unknown faces through the open slats of the windows, the faces peering inside my room as I tried to shout 'Go away!'

No sound issued from my throat. All the faces looked through the slats, giving a kind of wail, like a ghostly chorus, a low constant moaning – or did I imagine this? And then, I *do* remember this, one dusky girl, little more than a child, entered the room, went to the bathroom, found a face cloth, and wiped my face with tap water. I could hardly make her out. She seemed to limp, and then I recognised the little girl. She was the one I had seen at the Anani fair, the crippled girl suffering from polio.

I hope I was able to say 'Thank you!' She ran back to the bathroom, I vaguely heard the sound of the tap running, then she hobbled back to my bed and wiped my face again.

Outside, the low wailing continued, a kind of rhythmic moaning of despair, like the wind or the waves.

Dimly I must have realised – especially when the agonising pains returned, burning the insides of my stomach like hot coals – that everyone was looking because they knew that Mana had placed a death curse on me, and they were waiting to see if he had the power of life and death over a white man.

The trouble was that I couldn't control myself. From

169

both ends of my body – by mouth and rectum – I either retched or spewed out filthy water. I could not clean myself up, and I must have slipped into a semi-delirium, for only dimly do I remember Alec Reid arriving, and I have no recollection of what he did or said.

Then, I remember, Mollie Green arrived. News travels fast on a small island, and I remember that this big, strong woman lifted me as if I were a parcel of feathers and carried me to the spare room, which smelt clean – for the moment. Then, as I learned later, she and Toma cleaned up my own bedroom, and sent Lee Ho, her Chinese man of all work, to bring down a couple of new mattresses and some sheets from Green's Hotel. It seems that she berated the onlookers, telling them to go with Lee Ho and help to carry spare bedclothes. Meanwhile (though again I didn't realise it at the time) Miss Sowerby had arrived and was sprinkling the wooden floor with Lysol before dousing it with a mop.

I heard Alec whisper, or it sounded like a whisper, 'I've got some rubber sheets, we'll keep you clean, old boy. Every time ye soil the bed we'll take you to the other room. Dinna fret.'

I was still subject to uncontrollable vomiting or voiding of my bowels, but the effect was less dirty than it had been because by now I was empty. On the other hand I realised that the colic and the sweating was in danger of causing dehydration.

Then – how much longer was it? I wonder – Jason Purvis arrived with Bill Robins and, of all people, Lucy. They arrived in a haze. I do remember saying, 'Lucy. What about Paula's bridge game?'

Poor Lucy was in tears and dimly, between retching, I got the impression that she was saying goodbye.

'What's the matter?' I asked Bill Robins, speech slurred.

'She'll be back,' he promised me. And I thought I heard him say, 'I'm taking her back to Sanderstown tonight.' But that I knew couldn't be true, for Lucy and I had a date the following evening, and anyway, Paula would never let her go away this evening, not on her bridge night.

170

Of course it was ridiculous of me to suppose that this mysterious illness was the result of a malignant spell cast on me by a man I had insulted. And yet, here I was, tormented with spasms, retching. And I could sense, in between moments when I was briefly normal, that the others clustering around me were subtly afraid that they were dealing with something beyond their ken.

Of course they felt compassion for me, but I had the feeling in my more lucid moments that there was a kind of resentment that I had brought this on myself – as, indeed, I had done. And those around me were uncomfortable, almost embarrassed at the thought that they were dealing with a dying man whom no medicine could cure.

I heard later that Toma had even demanded a ceremony of exorcism, hoping to find an animal that could be sacrificed by cutting its throat, but Alec had rightly vetoed the idea. Indeed, first he planned to fly me to Sanderstown, but it was too late now, dusk was upon us, and he had no equipment for night flying. We didn't even have lights available on the 'airfield'. And he would never make a safe landing in the dark. And there was something else. As I heard later, Reid made an emergency radio sked to the naval base, and they strongly advised him against moving me, especially as Reid's previous attempt to save Mana's victim had failed after treatment in Sanderstown.

Only vaguely do I remember the next twenty-four – or was it forty-eight? – hours, the moments of retching, vomiting, the injections to try to blunt the coils of pain that twisted round and round my bowels, the raging thirst, my continual begging, 'Where's Lucy?' and Toma wiping my forehead, and Mollie Green carrying me from room to room every time I had to change beds.

I do remember saying to Alec Reid, in a rare lucid moment, 'Alec, I think Mana's got me, but at least I cured one boy of polio.'

'Ye'll always be able to try and treat it your way, I promise you.' He was talking briskly, trying to tell me that

171

getting well was only a question of time, whereas I could feel in my bones that I was about to die.

Then Mollie Green must have disappeared. Because after one moment when she wasn't there (or was I unconscious at that moment?) she reappeared, and brought with her Tiare and even Aleena who knelt beside me on the edge of the bed and was sobbing, 'Please, Doctor Kit! You saved my life. And now Mana is killing you! Oh! please, Doctor Reid, can't you do something to help?'

'We're trying everything,' muttered Reid.

'Is it fatal?' I dimly heard Tiare ask Alec.

'Nothing's ever fatal,' he replied, 'but the laddie's in a bad way. I dinna know what to do. Except that I'll have to give him a saline injection. He'll die of dehydration if nothing else.'

Tiare held out a hand to touch mine, and said, 'If anything happens to you, Doctor Masters, Mana will die. I swear it.'

'I'll be all right,' I gasped.

'You saved Aleena's life. And – ' in a curiously stilted way, she added, ' – that is a debt that will be repaid. Come, Aleena.'

'I want to stay here a bit longer,' Aleena was crying.

'You can come back later. But Doctor Masters needs medical treatment now.'

I'm not sure how much of this I took in – at one time the picture of Aleena became confused with that of Lucy – but I do remember their visit, and thinking that I couldn't last much longer. I was sinking, just as Tiare's first husband had sunk into death. And now the same fate awaited me in this beautiful island.

Then deliverance came – in the most unexpected and startling way.

Purvis was there, and I remember Alec saying to Miss Sowerby, 'A saline solution is the only hope. Pop over to the dispensary and bring me a carboy of distilled water.'

The hospital was next door. She was back in a minute. And in that brief moment of time I heard a furious Alec

Reid say angrily to her, 'I told you never to undo the taping on a fresh carboy of distilled water because of possible contamination.'

'I didn't, Doctor. There's six carboys of distilled water – and the tapes have been torn off every one of them.'

'What the hell's going on here?' shouted Reid.

I knew as well as Reid that hygiene in the islands was at times non-existent. And distilled water had to be the purest of the pure. After all, it consisted of the droplets of steam from boiling water which were then evaporated into hygenically treated storage jars as the steam turned to water. And it was *always* sealed up.

'I dinna understand it,' repeated Reid, unscrewing the big carboy. 'It looks harmless enough, but why the hell should anyone want to tear the seals off every jar of water?'

'Unless they've put something in.' It was Mollie Green's voice.

At that moment, Jason Purvis of all people, who had gone to fetch one of the last bottles of 'gin' water from the fridge, and was examining it in much the same way as Alec Reid was looking at one of the jars of distilled water, rushed in crying 'Eureka!'

Much of what happened next I only heard later because of my bemused reactions. But it seems that Purvis waved the bottle triumphantly, crying, 'Look at this!'

'Will ye shut up and stop that tomfoolery,' shouted an angry Doc Reid, adding the chilling words, 'Can ye nae see that a guid man's on the point of death. Show a wee bit of respect.'

At that moment I vomited again, unable to control myself long enough to reach a bowl. The filthy green bile slopped all over the bed.

'Don't worry, Doc,' said Mollie gently, wiping my face, peeling off my pyjamas and then preparing to carry me to the clean bed in the next room, as she had done a dozen times. I heard Doc Reid shout to Purvis furiously, 'Ye'd be better occupied cleaning bedpans. That's about all ye're good for.'

As I was carried from the room in Mollie's strong arms, I do remember hearing Bill Robins saying quietly, 'Hang on a minute, Alec. What are you trying to say, Jason?'

What I didn't hear or see, but what I learned later, was that Purvis held up the gin bottle filled with water and cried, 'The mystery's solved! This isn't witchcraft! It's attempted murder. Look inside.'

Pointing out a tiny black speck, no larger than a pinhead, that was floating in the gin bottle, Purvis cried, 'You know what that is? That's a bloody coconut bug that someone didn't squeeze hard enough.'

Cantharides flies – known in the islands as coconut bugs – crawl in their thousands when the sap of the coconut blossom is being tapped to make local toddy. If a couple of dead crushed cantharides are dropped into a bottle of water or toddy, you'd be sitting on the toilet for a week. But if you squeeze out the colourless juice of ten or a dozen cantharides into a bottle of water, it's strong enough to kill any man.

It was so simple to do. You could get all the coconut bugs you wanted, put them in a bag, and they wouldn't hurt you unless you ate them. You could squeeze the insects in secret and make a colourless juice which you could add to every bottle of boiled water.

How had it happened? Was this really the secret of Mana's fearsome ability to cast a mysterious spell that had already killed two men? I wasn't thinking like this, of course, at the moment when the truth was discovered, and neither was Doc Reid whose first task was to save my life. Unless I received urgent attention, I would die. But as I told him later, it would have been the easiest thing in the world for anyone to sneak into the bungalow. If Paula had been able to creep in without being seen, how simple for a man like Mana to do the same – perhaps when I was at the surgery and Toma was shopping; perhaps when Lucy was visiting me and I had deliberately given Toma time off. No front doors or outside kitchens and larders were ever locked in Koraloona. There were a dozen simple alternatives.

Later, I heard what happened. It seems that Bill Robins' first instinct was to charge to Mana's house and confront him. But Alec Reid said, 'His turn will come, dinna worry.' And to Purvis he asked, 'I'm sorry, Jason. Will ye be so good as to tell me how many bottles of water remain in the fridge?'

'That's easy. This was the last bottle.'

'Right,' said Doc Reid decisively. 'You Toma, fill up the empty gin bottles. Mana will have to come and put the poison in tonight. Then we'll be laying a trap. We have to catch him in the act.'

'I'll be gone,' said Bill Robins.

'Dinna fret. Purvis and Miss Sowerby and Mollie and me – between us, we're enough. But all in good time. First we have to deal with Kit. Unless we get him a saline drip, he'll just die of exhaustion.'

I must have drifted off again; it is very difficult remembering the chronology of what happens in those moments when a man hovers between life and death. I heard only intermittent snatches of conversations, shouts from Reid.

Miss Sowerby asked, 'Shall I go ahead with the saline drip?' The words tailed off; I heard Reid shout, 'For God's sake, no! If that distilled water's infected by even one bug, Kit'll be dead in hours.'

It 'woke me up' – a silly phrase, but only now did my medical training warn me that my dehydration was so acute that if I didn't get a drip soon, it would be too late. I think that knowledge – that and the fact that Mana had no occult powers – gave me one tiny, extra spurt of determination to fight the serpents of pain writhing in my belly, as I lay there retching, and now gasping for water no one would let me drink.

'Dinna worry, Kit,' Alec promised me. 'Now we *know* the cause – we'll have ye right in no time.'

'The water. For the saline drip. I daren't.' I knew as well

as Reid did that any contaminated water in a saline drip could easily be fatal.

'We won't use water.'

He shouted to Mollie: 'Boil me a pan of water. A small pan.' Then to Toma, 'Go and get me half a dozen young, fresh coconuts. And make sure they're clean. No bugs on 'em.' And to Miss Sowerby: 'Prepare for a saline solution.'

'No, no,' I screamed. 'No water. He's trying to murder me.'

'Dinna worry, Laddie,' Alec slipped even more into his Scots accent. 'Have faith in your doctor! One thing I *have* learned in the islands is that the purest liquid in the world after distilled water is young coconut milk. I've used it before in an emergency, and it works perfectly – yes, in a saline solution.'

All this took some time. I saw, in a kind of haze, Miss Sowerby fixing the drip apparatus to the bed, and asked her in a stupid way, 'What's your first name, Miss Sowerby?' And she replied 'Lorna.'

And then I gasped to Reid, 'You think I'll be all right?'

'We've caught it in time. Remember it took Tiare's husband nearly a week to die. We've found what's wrong in two days.'

'I'd like to see Lucy,' I said. 'I thought she'd have come back.'

'All in good time,' said Alec. 'First the drip. Here's the coconuts.'

I don't really remember all the details, but I heard Mollie Green shout to Alec that the water in the pan was boiling, and I couldn't understand why they should need boiling water for a saline drip. Hadn't Alec said something about coconuts? As I heard later, Alec had used the boiling water to sterilise a muslin square of cloth used for covering jugs of milk. After piercing the eyes of the coconuts he had poured a measured dose of the pure coconut milk through the 'filter' into the one-litre bottle which would be attached to the head of the bed.

Miss Sowerby stood by preparing the saline solution. 'Half and half?' she asked Reid. He nodded. The salt and sugar went into the coconut water. Deftly she manoeuvred the bottle into its sling and attached the long rubber tube to the valve stopper that controlled the flow of solution to the needle. I thought as I lay there, Thank God for the Miss Sowerbys of this world! She might be a bit stuck-up and goody-goody, but she was utterly reliable, she never flapped, with a character of exactly the right proportions of compassion and practicality. She handed Alec the needle and he raised my arm to plunge it into the axilla, the puffy skin of my armpit. I heard him tell Miss Sowerby, 'Fifty millilitres a minute will be about the right flow-rate.' She adjusted the valve, timing the drips by the second hand of the little Victorian silver watch that was pinned to her dress. When the measure was flowing to her satisfaction she said dispassionately, 'That's it.'

'Rehydration will take a long time; it can't be hurried,' I heard Alec say. 'He'll need at least four litres during the day. But he's through the worst. I'll come back and look at him this evening.'

'I'll look in during the day,' she said. I could see her adding yet another to the mental notes any nurse has constantly to make to remind her of routine checks. 'Thanks, Miss Sowerby,' I managed to mumble with genuine gratitude. 'Your efficiency does me a power of good.'

She wasn't taking any credit for that. 'Any power of good comes from up there,' she said with a lift upwards of her stubby finger.

Alec also gave me a powerful sedative, but it didn't stop me from having mixed-up nightmares, that Mana was coming to try and kill me, and I learned later that at times I screamed with fear; but the most persistent dreams were vague memories of Lucy and Bill Robins coming to see me. And as I slowly came back to a more normal world – temperature dropping, pulse more regular, even a satisfied smile on Alec Reid's face that evening – I asked, 'Can I see Lucy please? Why hasn't she been to see me?'

When I asked Purvis to go and fetch her he mumbled some excuse. And when I asked Alec again he said brusquely that he was too busy to run errands. Miss Sowerby pursed her lips and said nothing. Gradually, I'm not quite sure when or how, it came to me that there was no Lucy. Not on Koraloona, anyway. A disjointed flash of a past conversation returned to me, Bill saying, 'I'm taking Lucy – ' and sudden jealousy. What had he meant? Why had she gone – if she had gone?

Finally Alec told me. Though he couldn't fill in all the details, it seemed that Paula and Lucy had had a major row, and Paula had fired her on the spot, telling her to pack her bags and catch the *Mantela* which happened to be sailing that fateful night. *That* was why Lucy had suddenly appeared when by rights she should have been at the Villa Faalifu.

I was stunned, and in my weak condition burst into tears. We had become such close friends – and such happy lovers – that the abrupt, unhappy ending seemed wicked. I started to curse Paula, thinking suddenly of the first time I had met her at the villa. I had forgotten the moment until now, it had never even registered, but I suddenly remembered that when I was introduced to the long, elegant figure, she had handed me a single flower. 'Pompous old bag!' I shouted out to no one in particular. How could anyone behave so callously, whatever the provocation? That tall, sinuous figure hid an evil soul. In my still abnormal state I cursed her again, my mind indulging in fantasies of how I could revenge myself on her.

While I was struggling to come alive again, and able to take some orange juice and powdered milk, the 'law' (in a very elementary form) was taking its course. Mana had to be put out of the way – safeguarded from any further attacks on me.

And apart from anything else, I couldn't have a man walking round the island who had vowed to cause my death. The fact that the local 'witch-doctor' had failed might only make him more anxious for revenge. Had I died, then no charge could have been preferred against Mana, because I would have died of a mysterious illness.

Mana was, in fact, trapped with almost pathetic ease. It is sometimes easy to forget that most Polynesians are simple, pleasant people with only the occasional villain to disturb their bliss. So they are, for the most part, unused to the devious ways of the Europeans. According to Alec Reid, he and Purvis and Mollie lay in wait after dark, expecting Mana to bring with him a solution of coconut bug poison and pour a few drops into the boiled water in the bottles in the fridge.

He was cleverer than that. Somehow he had collected half a dozen old Gordon's gin bottles, and filled them with water, with the poison in them, presumably so that he wouldn't have to waste time 'topping up' the bottles already in my bungalow. Half way to the garden Reid spotted him, limping from his recent fight, and with a paper carrier bag in one hand. Reid challenged him, and Mana, unaware, of course, that his trick had been discovered, started to bluster. At one point he swung the carrier bag round his head as though to use it as a weapon of attack.

'That's when I realised it was bulky – and heavy,' explained Alec Reid. 'As Mana prepared to hit me with the carrier bag, Purvis, who was by his side, grabbed the bag and wrenched it from Mana's hands.' For a moment Mana prepared to fight, but he was in no fit state. When Alec Reid saw the bottles filled with water, he said sternly, 'The game's up, Mana. We know how ye poisoned the water. You a witch-doctor! You're a phoney – and a murderer.'

Mana's fate was then decided by Fawcett and Alec without my knowing what was happening, as I was still too weak to take any interest in anything but the struggle to stay alive. But this is a simple version of what happened, with the conversations as I remember Alec telling them to me.

Fawcett and Alec Reid met at the Union Jack Club in Tala-Tala.

'We have two options,' said Colonel Fawcett. 'Report the whole matter to the police in Sanderstown and let them make an arrest and hold a trial. Or,' he paused thinking, 'I have enough power as the officer in Koraloona responsible to the Cook Islands to make an immediate arrest on the circumstantial evidence, and put the man away. Obviously we can't have him running loose. He's a menace.'

'I dinna relish the business of a big trial,' Alec said. 'I can see a "witchcraft" story in which poor Kit Masters is involved finally hitting the headlines in London. And it wouldn't be the first time Kit has been the innocent victim of publicity. I do hope ye can deal with it yourself.'

'I'll send him to Penal Island,' decided Colonel Fawcett finally. 'That way there'll be no publicity. I have the powers to do so, and once on Penal Island, he'll remain as a lifer, unless he appeals and the decision is changed later in the courts at Sanderstown. But he won't dare to appeal. Murder could mean hanging. I'll have to make a report to the court authorities there. But once a local has run amok, so to speak, the New Zealand government rarely interferes.'

'Especially as there's overwhelming evidence that Mana boasted of attempting to kill the local doctor. And you're right. He did in fact murder two men beforehand, even if we canna prove it.'

So Mana was arrested and taken to Penal Island which was run by the police in Sanderstown, and staffed by twenty prison officers led by New Zealanders or Britons, who volunteered eagerly for each six-month stint of duty because it carried double pay and free board and lodging. The prisoners were all locked up at night and there was only one large, wooden police launch with a powerful inboard motor on the island which, under strict orders, was immobilised each sunset. Jim Wilson – ship owner as well as ship chandler – had the contract to make the trip to Penal Island once a week to take in supplies, which were ordered by the radio link with Koraloona.

I didn't hear anything about the arrest of Mana, until he had been safely put away; only then did I feel safe. As I began to get better, I remembered how Bill Robins had pointed out Penal Island on the chart the day when he showed me the various specks of land that made up the Moto Varu archipelago, and I had seen it, little more than a dot on the horizon, when we had sailed through the passage. But I had never visited the island. I had no wish to go on a conducted tour of a South Seas Alcatraz.

There were not more than thirty or forty prisoners on Penal Island, according to what I had been told.

The prisoners included several dangerous murderers. One man had killed another with a poisoned spear in a particularly excruciating fashion – one that ignored the myths about trees that possess poison for a simpler South Seas version.

'They just smear the end of the spears or arrows with a lot of pig shit,' said Alec. 'Then shoot or throw them. The chances are ten to one that the victim will die of tetanus. Very painful.'

As soon as I was on the way to recovery, and with Mana out of the way, I received several visits from Tiare, sometimes accompanied by Aleena.

'We owe you a great deal,' Tiare said in her rather stilted English, 'for you have given Aleena and myself a sense of freedom we did not know existed since my first husband died. And the price of my freedom was your unbearable suffering. So,' pausing impressively, she added, 'as hereditary Princess of Koraloona, I would like to make some gesture of gratitude if it lies within my power.'

'You are very kind, but I need no gestures of thanks, Princess,' I replied formally. 'And yet, there is one.'

'And that is – ?'

I hesitated before replying. 'Would it be possible, when I am recovered, for me to see the paintings by your grandfather? The Gauguins.'

'Of course,' she agreed impassively. 'It will be arranged.'

'And I shall go to see my holy man and thank him and pray for you,' said Aleena.

12

For more than a month I was so weak that I found it difficult to try to cure any more polio cases, simply because when new patients needed treatment, I did not have the strength to keep awake all hours of the day and night.

In that month we had three cases – not really signs of an epidemic, but worrying. One girl from an outlying village on the island's east coast had been neglected for so long that even I realised I could not try heat treatment, and so Alec Reid flew her to Sanderstown for an operation. One other I managed to restore to normal health, thanks largely to Miss Sowerby, and stints of hot, wet blanket changing by Jason Purvis who worked like a dog – when he was sober. The other patient recovered partially.

Almost savagely, I said to Alec, 'All this could be prevented if only we had some standards of hygiene. We need a health officer more than a doctor. The sanitary conditions in the villages are appalling.'

It was true. In the villages there was no such thing as a toilet, and only occasionally did some locals dig a trench over which they could squat and throw on earth after defecating. Most just performed where they happened to be, followed immediately by swarms of flies which carried germs from the faeces round the village.

The same indifference prevailed with drinking water. Many villages took their water from the nearest river flowing down from the hills – without thinking that above river someone might have been washing clothes, or themselves, or using the river as a convenient lavatory.

'I know,' said Alec Reid, 'but what the devil can ye do, except pray – and hope for the best?'

'Is there no way the government could employ a salaried health inspector – ?'

'Nae a hope. After all, Kit, even our salaries come from a mission.'

Irritated, I said, 'Well, I can't go round the entire island telling the people when and where to have a crap.'

'It's only the bare essentials we need,' Alec sighed. 'Latrine trenches, ash or earth to sprinkle, specific places for toilets – but the problem is teaching them *why* it's necessary. They'll do it if they realise why, just like dogs can be trained not to pee on your carpet. But the islanders don't reason. So, once outside, they do it as instinctively as a dog does. And they regard polio as a curse from the gods they've displeased. Same with tetanus.'

Tetanus – lockjaw as it was commonly called – was also a killer, specially of newborn babies; and we had case after case caused almost entirely by man's own stupidity. Tetanus was an agonising way to die and the disease was carried almost entirely by germs lurking in horse or pig manure, or chicken droppings ready to infect open wounds. And there was always one open wound after the birth of a baby – the cutting of the umbilical cord. Since nine out of ten village babies were born with no medical help other than a local witch-doctor, the small flow of blood from the severing of the cord was often stemmed by applying a mud plaster to the tiny wound of the squealing baby. And since chickens, pigs and other animals walked in and out of local huts, the chances of a child contracting tetanus were horrifyingly high. We did have an anti-tetanus serum we could inject – one step better than the bewildered attempts to find a serum for polio – but often tetanus wasn't reported until it was too late.

This rather depressing conversation took place during dinner at Alec's bungalow. Our weekly dinners had now developed into a regular culinary challenge. Jokingly, we referred to our evenings as meetings of the Gourmet Club, in which each of us tried to outdo the other.

On this occasion Bubble and Squeak had created a wonderful meal.

'It's from Tahiti, so it's got a wee touch of French – one up on you.' Alec looked pleased.

'What is it?'

'Gin-baked loup. L-o-u-p,' he spelled the word out as the 'p' was silent. 'I first ate it in Bora-Bora. A whole fish, rather like a sea-bass, cooked with onions and tomatoes – and gin.'

After one of the girls had placed the fish on the dining table, she poured another large glass of gin over the dish, then sprinkled it with grated cheese.

'Yes, you win this round,' I conceded.

When later, as we talked over our coffee and Old Rarity, sitting on the veranda overlooking the lagoon, I said, 'I wonder if Purvis could help with the problem of hygiene?'

'Och, no!' Alec shook his head. 'He hasna got the stamina to travel round the island. And he's nae got the will either.'

'He does try.'

'Yes, but only jobs he likes. I canna see Purvis telling the local headman to use trenches as a lavatory. The man's too queasy, he'd be sick at the thought of it.'

'What we need are some volunteer helpers,' I said.

'Ye're right there,' said Alec. 'But who? Have ye ever thought of trying to get Paula Reece to help?'

'Out of the question,' I said shortly. I had hardly seen Paula since she kicked Lucy out. I had never again been to any of her parties, and I only greeted her with polite coldness when we met at other people's houses. I still boiled over with anger when I thought of the way she had treated Lucy.

'She'd pay workers to do what she tells them,' Alec suggested.

'If you fix it, that's your problem,' I said. 'But I'm not going to ask her.'

Alec called for more whisky, and Bubble or Squeak

obliged. I could see from the way he looked reflectively at the golden liquid in his small glass that Reid was toying with an idea. Finally, he said: 'There is one person who *could* help. She's a lassie who has all the authority, and – '

'You mean Mrs Fawcett?'

'God, no! She has no authority, only her position as the colonel's lady. I was thinking of someone very different.'

'Who?'

'The Princess. Tiare. She's not only the titular head of the island, her word is – well, if it's not law, it's one that demands blind obedience. The islanders will do *anything* she orders them to do.'

'What a wonderful idea.' My mind flashed to the evening of the Orange Festival, and how she had ordered the mother of the child with polio to come for a check-up. That mother had brought her daughter in a couple of days later. Had I suggested it, the mother would have forgotten.

'You're right,' I agreed. 'You'd better ask her.'

'Not me,' cried Alec. 'You. The poor woman still feels guilty about the way Mana tried to kill you, and at the same time she's grateful to ye because, however indirectly, ye've given her freedom from Mana.'

'Heard anything of him, by the way?' I asked without thinking.

'He's safely in jail,' said Alec. 'Jim Wilson saw him last week when he was taking supplies to Penal Island. Mana told Wilson that one day he'd escape – to get you. I tell you this only because no one has ever escaped from Penal Island.'

'Thank God for that! It's a pity we can't use *him*,' I laughed. 'And put a death wish on everyone who didn't do as he was told.'

'And ye'd have half the population dead, with the other half spotlessly clean. But seriously, Laddie, the Princess would be the perfect headmistress of a sanitation squad. It's not for me to ask her though. It's for you, Kit. Not out of the blue, I agree. But next week.'

'Why next week?'

'Have ye forgotten? The private view of the Gauguin exhibition.'

It *had* slipped my mind – not entirely, but it had been relegated to a pigeon-hole for future reference. Tiare had phoned to ask me if the following Wednesday would be suitable. I had agreed. She said she wanted to ask Alec to see the paintings again, and of course I was excited. I was, however, a little mystified because though I assumed I would just look at a stack of canvases standing up against a wall, she somehow gave me the impression that preparing to show them to us would entail special arrangements.

'If she gets a wee bit regal, I'll tell her I'm worried about her health,' said Alec. 'That always puts a woman in her place.'

'What intrigues me' – I looked at my watch, we had talked a long time – 'is why nobody really knows about these paintings – gossip, even rumours reaching the outside world. You know what I mean – how can you keep a secret like this from prying eyes – covetous eyes?'

'Very few people *do* know,' said Alec. 'And even though it's common knowledge on Koraloona that the Princess has what she calls "the inheritance", I dinna really think anyone knows what it consists of – except a few of us.'

'I suppose not. Even so, it's a bit rum. You'd think that someone like,' I was thinking aloud, 'someone like Bill Robins might have mentioned the Gauguins leisurely in Sanderstown – and word travels like lightning when there's big money involved.'

'Frankly, I don't think Bill would talk. He's never seen them. No one has seen them since I did. If Gauguin's mistress had been in Tahiti, then it would have been very different, but I don't think people have ever realised he lived here, who he was, let alone had a bairn here. He had his French pension to think of, he was still married, though his wife lived in France. And she wouldna welcome any publicity. Even when Somerset Maugham stumbled on an old painting outside Papeete, he bought it for only a couple of hundred dollars. Gauguin wasn't important – then.

186

Luckily for us, he still hasn't become important in Kora-loona.'

Early on the morning of the 'Gauguin exhibition', Tiare telephoned Alec and suggested that we drive to her home early for a swim at her private beach which I had so much admired on my one visit to her house (apart from the day I had dumped Mana in the garden). Then, after seeing the pictures, we would stay for lunch.

Driving to the house in his car, Alec Reid said flatly to me, 'Ye can swim if ye have a mind to, but I dinna have the sort of figure I'm anxious to show off.'

Tiare was waiting under the shade hut when we arrived. She was already in her swimsuit and got up out of a rattan chair as we arrived.

'I'll sit this one out,' grunted Alec. 'Ye carry on, Kit.'

There was a screen near the semi-hut and I already had my trunks on, so it was easy to slip out of my shirt and trousers. And then I ran into the water. Tiare followed, laughing as she fell into the shallow surf, 'It's wonderful, isn't it? My second dip of the day. But I didn't expect we'd persuade Alec to come in.'

The Princess wore her years well. She had a pale blue one-piece bathing costume which looked as though it had been bought in Paris or New York. When she stood up, saying, 'Ready for a drink?' I could see her straight legs, firm breasts and flat tummy. I didn't say how splendid she looked, but Alec had no such inhibitions.

'Ye're looking in very guid shape, Princess.' He shaded his eyes from the sun as we walked back from the water.

'Speaking as a doctor or a judge of beauty?' She started to dry her shoulders.

'As the doctor who attended ye when ye gave birth to Aleena. And in my book ye'd win any beauty contest. Don't you agree, Kit?'

'Don't embarrass him. What can poor Kit say?' she asked.

'I agree,' I laughed.

187

'And what about a wee drop to drink?' asked Alec.

'I'm sorry. Here it is.' She had prepared a long cooling liquid in a glass jug, resting on the table in the shade of the spiky pandanus roof. The ice clinked in the jug as she poured out three long drinks.

'Delicious.' I sipped mine. 'What is it?'

'Best drink in the islands after a swim,' she said. 'Pure water from fresh coconut, a large measure of gin and some fresh limes. And you don't have to worry about the ice. It was thoroughly boiled before being put into the fridge.'

After another drink, and as we dried in the sun, I asked after Aleena who was back at college in Sanderstown. Then Tiare said, 'Let's go and see the inheritance. In our bathing suits, then we can have lunch on the veranda. Leave your clothes in the shade hut,' she added. 'You can pick them up before you go home.' I had left my trousers and shirt on a spare chair.

'They'll be all right,' I said as we walked up the sandy beach. At the top of the veranda steps stood a large enamel bowl filled with water, and next to it was a small tin basin with a handle.

Tiare dipped the tin basin into the bowl of water and sloshed the water over her feet.

'You next,' she smiled at me. 'We don't need shoes in the house, but sand between the toes can be very unpleasant.' Then she added some surprising information. 'Another person has been here today. Mr Wilson.'

'Jim Wilson?' I echoed. 'I didn't know he was interested in art.'

'He isn't,' said Alec drily. 'But all the same, he was here the last time I saw the paintings. Remember, Princess?'

'Of course I do,' said Tiare. 'When my poor Katuto died. But don't worry,' she smiled at me. 'Actually Mr Wilson has gone. His visit was strictly business, and he'll be back after lunch. I'll explain later.' She led the way into the living-room. I had a clear memory of it from that one visit to her house, the comfortable armchairs covered with

188

chintz, the ornate flower arrangements like a peacock's feathers, the old piano with its single sepia photograph and the curious carvings and wood sculpture.

So I was taken completely by surprise at the transformation when she ushered us both in. For no special reason I had envisaged the paintings as stacked, one against the other, so that you could only see one at a time. Instead, with the sun pouring in, the room blazed with light of a colour I had never seen before. Not on the walls, but a blaze of colour everywhere, for this was no orderly display in some rich collector's home. The pictures had been placed without any thought of showing them to their best advantage but every one was visible.

Some stood on chests and tables, vivid splashes of paint against the darker wood. Others leaned against the walls, with the sun streaming in, so brilliant they dazzled the eyes. Others were hung on the walls next to indifferent paintings, or the very ordinary local South Seas wooden sculpture. Two stood on the grand piano – propped up by piles of books behind the canvases. Three stood against the backs of the chintz-covered chairs.

I was frankly non-plussed – at first anyway – that a woman like the Princess, with her obvious good taste, hadn't bothered to display the paintings a little more formally. It was almost as though she supposed that both Alec Reid and I were so ignorant of art that it hadn't been worthwhile going to any trouble; that she had promised to show them to me, and that the whole thing was a bit of a bore. But *that* couldn't be the truth. She was far too polite and courteous to behave with such studied indifference. Then she said something which resolved any doubts.

'I thought it might be better if you didn't have to stand in front of all of them at once. This way you can pick one up if you feel like it.' She had realised that an orderly array of so many vivid paintings would be too much to take in at once; now, I could only see and really study two or three at a time, because of the angles of 'display', the heights from the floor which differed with each painting.

189

I walked round and round the room, moving from the sight of one painting to the next, then back again.

One painting stood out among all the others as I tried to take in the riot of colour. For I recognised it instantly. It was a large oil canvas of the secret pool I had visited that first day on Koraloona when Bill Robins took me on a tour of the island. And leaning over the edge of the waterfall was a woman with long hair hanging half way down to her waist and a hibiscus over her left ear. The white of the frothing water was accentuated by the rest of the flowers on either side. The girl in the painting, who was leaning over, wore a sarong, her breasts were bare, and in the water of the pool below was reflected the face of the girl.

'That was my mother.' Tiare looked at the painting, adding, unaware that I had seen the actual pool, 'She and Father used to swim there.' Then she made a remark that almost passed me by at the moment, but which was to have profound implications many years later. 'Mother told me that my father often painted from photos, and he had a photograph of the pool taken by a local photographer and asked a boy to stand where my mother is standing, next to the waterfall, so that he could paint the scene in his studio and put in my mother in place of the boy.'

'It's absolutely stunning,' was all I could say. 'And your mother was very beautiful.'

In fact, although the total effect of the painting was one of sheer spell-binding wonder, Gauguin hadn't, to my mind, done real justice to the beauty of Tiare's mother as she appeared in the photo on the piano. For while Gauguin was adept at painting perfectly rounded breasts, his faces tended to be severe and angular; although it was several years before I learned why Gauguin did paint women's faces in this way.

'Do you recognise this?' asked Tiare, pointing to another canvas.

I certainly did. It was Koraloona's Main Street, just as it was today except for the colouring. Only the washing trough near Mollie Green's hotel was subtly different. It was almost the same shape in the same spot, yet it was not a South Seas Island trough, but a French one, as though Gauguin had plucked a half-forgotten memory of a similar communal laundry that one sees in thousands of southern French villages. Obviously Gauguin had mixed realism with memories, perhaps of the time he had spent with Van Gogh in Arles.

'That's my mother again.' Tiare pointed out the figure of a tall woman, standing behind the trough. 'She wouldn't be washing because of her title,' she explained. 'We didn't have much money but we did have dozens of willing helpers. We still do.'

The painting of Main Street was not only recognisable, for most of the buildings seemed unchanged, but the road itself, separating the blue of the sea from the multi-coloured houses, was very different. It had been painted pink. It was quite extraordinary, it looked so beautiful, and the pink in place of the dusty grey street looked absolutely right. It almost hurt the eyes, the pink, but it was as beautiful a painting as anyone would ever see anywhere else in the world. Nothing jarred. Although the picture was filled with sunlight from an invisible sun, the figures cast no shadows – a trick of Gauguin's, I was to learn.

In another canvas, a boy walking along another street (which Tiare said was the road to Tala-Tala) carried a huge bunch of wild bananas on his head against a background of sombre blue mountains, but instead of the dusty reddish brown of the local bananas, Gauguin's bananas were a brilliant crimson; quite wrong technically yet, even to my untutored eye, somehow right aesthetically against the blue.

'He's a wee bit slap-happy, the way he doles out the strong colours,' said Alec.

'You're right there,' Tiare laughed.

'And yet,' I was still stupefied, 'I know it sounds damned silly but, Princess, though I've visited art galleries dozens of times, I've never been so staggered in all my life. Every-thing *looks* right – especially in these surroundings.'

'I'm so glad you like them,' she said.

Beyond the ability to recognise watercolour and oils, charcoal and pencil, ink and wash, I didn't presume to have any technical knowledge, so I took from the piano, where it was almost hidden by a bigger painting, a small square picture of some scrawny farmyard chickens, painted on a roughly cut square of brown wood. The fowls were painted in vivid colours, but the painting had one intriguing difference from the others. Whenever Gauguin had needed a dash of brown, he had left the wood bare. Not until I looked at the back did I realise that the farmyard scene had been painted on the lid of a cigar box. And on the back, written in faded ink, presumably by Gauguin making a reference to the cigar box and his TB, was a message, *'Je sais que je n'ai pas le droit de fumer, mais . . .'*

I walked to one of the rattan chairs to study another surprise – an altogether more formal framed painting: a sketch of a sailing ship, its bow, lettered with the name *Oceanien*, foreshortened as it seemed to sail out of the picture towards me. 'The ship he sailed on to Koraloona,' explained Princess Tiare. It was a good sketch, the heavy charcoal outline filled in with daubs of greyish wash, as if Gauguin had wanted only to make a slight record – as a writer makes a note – of something that might come in useful one day.

'Now there's something I can cope with,' said Alec. 'A ship! Nae doot about it.'

On a chiffonier near the window were three self-portraits. In each the deep-set blue eyes, aggressive chin, narrow, ridge-like forehead, and heavy neck were recognisable; but the backgrounds varied. In one, Gauguin had painted himself as a full-length figure against a vivid red wall, up which climbed a profusion of the heavily podded branches of a vanilla plant. A green sky with a curiously symbolic bird loomed above the wall. It was a startlingly erotic picture, even though it was simple, for the artist had given himself a haunting look of sensuality. Maybe only because I was a doctor, and knew that the medical derivation of medicinal vanilla was from the Latin word vagina, did I detect the slight leer on the artist's face, as if he cherished a secret. The other self-portraits were of mirror-like reflections; but in both there were tiny background figures of island girls placed almost regularly, like the spots on a playing-card, but distantly, as if he had their naked bodies at the back of his mind and wanted to contribute his affection for them, to assure them that they had not been forgotten in his concentration on his own features.

'The man himself,' Reid said, perhaps feeling that he should contribute something as an observer. 'A strong face; but I wouldna call him God's gift to womankind, eh?'

I wasn't so sure. The little I knew of Gauguin – from *The Moon and Sixpence* – suggested that he had a very strong appeal to women. But I nodded in agreement. I had been gripped by the power of the pictures and didn't want to introduce argument as I studied them. Who knew when – if ever – I would see them again? In any case, the next picture I took up from one of the chairs was framed and glazed, as if prepared for a buyer, and was so conventional in subject and style that even Alec Reid said, 'Now that's what I call a pretty picture.'

It was – and what a surprise! It was a snowy scene in an unmistakable French garden, with in the foreground two elegantly dressed girls. The humour of the picture lay in the pretty summer dresses they were wearing and the brightly coloured parasols with which they shielded their cheekily smiling faces from the dour sky that clearly held the promise of more snow.

There were two other portraits – one of a handsome woman wearing a black dress and leaning against a Victorian overmantel, laden with knick-knacks; the other of a boy in a sailor suit posed against the potted palms of a photographer's studio. And I realised now that they were in fact interpretations of photographs – for the sepia prints themselves had been left tucked into the corners of the ornate frames. *Clovis* was written on the back of

193

one print, *Mette* on the other. I did not know then that these were the names of his favourite son and his Danish wife.

Behind the piano, so that I hadn't noticed it at first, was a gem – a large canvas, and a happy picture, of the Anani drinking festival as the islanders raided their tubs of fermented orange juice and sang and danced and made love night-long beneath a climbing moon. Red trees adorned the grove where sensuous figures danced in the foreground, with two white-coiffed nuns smiling benevolently on what they surely saw as a spiritual as well as a pagan occasion. The sarongs of the girls were patterned in bright colours and I seemed to detect the rippling of their skin as they were embraced by youths heading towards couches of leaves and orange blossom. There was little fine detail in the picture, but everything was implied, as if the artist knew that, if anyone liked his work, it would be someone able to match his imagination with their own. The passion Gauguin poured out had to be returned by the beholder.

It was beautiful in a sensuous sort of way. And for a moment I felt a pang of sadness as I thought of the happy evening I had spent there with Lucy. The painting was as truthful as that.

The strangest picture of all was a landscape – an unframed painting on cardboard that had been carelessly, and for no apparent reason, divided into four, the edges fitting – though not precisely – like the bits of a jigsaw. The subject was startling after the idyllic island pictures: The Four Horsemen of the Apocalypse; with War, Famine, Pestilence, and Death painted as raddled Koraloonan girls with youthful figures on which hung shellbursts for War, locusts for Famine, rats for Pestilence, and a skull for Death. And behind the faces of the girls lurked death's heads like the bones revealed in an X-ray picture. It reminded me of a painting in the Tate by Hieronymus Bosch, the work of a man who had seen an apocalyptic vision; in a dream or drugged stupor?

'My bet is that he was a wee bit under the influence when he painted that,' said Alec, with obvious distaste. 'A few sniffs of cocaine, I shouldn't wonder.'

'Could be,' I agreed as I laid the four pictures flat on the piano to get the full effect. I didn't like them, and to get their sour taste out of my mouth I asked Tiare if I could take a further last look at the two I liked best – the girl at the secret pool, and the pink Main Street of Koraloona.

We had spent more than an hour looking at the paintings before Tiare offered us drinks.

'I need a gin and lime,' I admitted. 'I've never felt so mentally exhausted in my life.'

'I'm pleased – that you are pleased. And now – what about lunch on the veranda?' asked Tiare and the three of us trooped out.

'Bring your drinks with you.'

Half way through lunch, Jim Wilson appeared on the veranda steps and said, 'Have a good lunch, all. Okay if I put them away, Princess?'

'Of course. Hope I didn't keep you too long.'

It was then that I learned how the paintings had been kept in such perfect condition.

'It sounds crazy,' Tiare admitted as we ate chicken breasts in pineapple shells, 'but we keep them in a huge aquarium. Empty of course,' she laughed. 'I don't know how or why it ever reached the island but aquariums were all the rage in Victorian times, and someone must have sent this one to a relative in the islands who never received it. My mother bought it second-hand. The case has four legs which stand in water jars against ants, and it stays in my bedroom. It takes all the paintings, and the reason we don't often show them is that Jim Wilson made a top cover of very thin lead.'

'And that's enough to keep them in good condition?'

'No, no,' said Tiare, offering me some more chicken. 'Some years ago he suggested sealing up the tank with putty, and it worked. So when people want to see the pictures – like you, Doctor Reid – he comes and chips off the putty, and opens up the contents. That's why Mr Wilson is here now. To seal up the glass case and make it airtight.'

'What a lot of trouble – I feel awful – '

'It has given me great pleasure to find such an enthusiastic lover of my father's paintings,' said Tiare with her occasional touch of formality.

After we had finished lunch and were having coffee, I suddenly remembered the unsolved problem of the island's hygiene. Tiare *was* in an understanding mood – she had shown her obvious pleasure at my interest – and I thought it better not to be subtle. As simply as I could, I explained why the villagers weren't hygienic and the way in which this was spreading polio and tetanus.

'A great deal of it could be prevented,' I explained. 'Prevention is as important as cure, and a lot of the disease could be prevented, given a few simple rules. But they all say "yes" and do nothing. Now, if you could *order* them to dig trenches, Princess, tell them to make latrines, use specific places outside villages and parts of river downstream, they would do as you tell them.'

'I understand.' She looked thoughtful. 'How are you going to go about it? What exactly do you want me to do?'

'We can't change the island in a day,' I admitted, my first thought being that she might tour the villages with me. But then I had a better idea. 'I'll go to the village of Tabanea' – this was a settlement beyond Tala-Tala. 'That is where the little boy Jimbo lives, so the father treats me like a – well, a miracle man.'

'For Jimbo, you were,' said Tiare softly. 'Go on.'

I would, I suggested, visit Tabanea and persuade the villagers to dig trenches and arrange other simple latrine facilities.

'Even if you do that,' she looked doubtful, 'the villagers won't really understand what you're trying to do.'

'I know,' I agreed. 'But that's where you could come in, Princess. You could call a meeting at Tabanea of every village headman in Koraloona, and you could then demonstrate – and explain *why*. It's the "why" that's most important.'

I must say that Tiare didn't hesitate.

'You tell me the day and time, and it shall be done,' she said.

And so it was that after an art show that would have left the Royal Academy gasping with its heady colours, we laid the preliminary plans to inaugurate Koraloona's first public health service.

Only one thing delayed the arrangements we planned with so much enthusiasm. On 3 September, 1939, England declared war on Germany.

13

The months that followed the outbreak of war were for me – and I'm sure all of us in the South Seas – a strange hiatus. We were bound by ties of blood and longing and past familiarity to share the burden of those suffering in Europe; yet we were onlookers at a drama in which we could do virtually nothing, however dearly many might have wanted to play an active role. For this was the 'European War'; limited by geography and the fight for survival of a distant continent; a struggle which made both the causes and the effects strangely remote.

When Alec Reid said, 'Well, it canna be *our* war,' he was not speaking defensively. He was making an observation about a conflict in Europe as remote to us as the war raging between China and Japan.

Yet September 1939 was even so the signal for an immediate flurry of activity among all of us. The members of the Union Jack Club formed a committee, with Colonel Fawcett as chairman, to organise 'Bundles for Britain'. There was not much we could do though. We read of the increasingly severe rationing in Britain and the obvious need to send food parcels, but that was impossible. We produced only fresh food in Koraloona.

On the other hand Koraloona was sheltered under the economic umbrella of New Zealand, via the Cook Islands, and Colonel Fawcett demanded – and got – supplies of free knitting wool which the ladies of the committee assiduously turned into socks, pullovers, and comforts for the troops. The ladies' knitting needles clicked increasingly as the war became worse. On a personal level, all that I could do was send a money order to Brian Parker, the Mission 'middle man' in Sydney who had arranged my passage on the *Mantela*. With the money he despatched monthly food parcels from Australia to the family in Nottingham.

By April 1940, however, the war was going disastrously. Page one of the *Sanderstown Sentinel* which reached Koraloona by ship – to say nothing of the BBC World Service on the radio – consisted of one recital of catastrophe after another. Hitler was conquering Europe with the ferocity of a madman bent on destroying, humiliating, all opposition. Poland had already been crushed, now the Low Countries were following, a defenceless Rotterdam being bombed mercilessly. Dunkirk was either a disaster or a miracle, it was impossible to judge. The French bolted. On the cliffs of Dover the Home Guard was armed with sticks and staves, with Britain watching helplessly as each country was gobbled up into the maw of a greedy tyrant with an insatiable appetite. The names of each new loss were like stones dropping forever into a pool, leaving the ripples to disappear.

We were safe of course, for even Hitler couldn't reach as far as the Pacific, but we couldn't divorce that safety from our present anguish. What about Father and Mother? What about Clare? I had only received a few letters in months, and meanwhile I had read in the *Sentinel* how Coventry had been obliterated, and later Plymouth crushed. London was bearing up, but on some nights five hundred people were killed by bombs. Whenever the papers arrived, whenever the radio was turned on, I waited for any mention of 'Nottingham'. It never seemed to be mentioned, but this did not allay my fears. Perhaps Nottingham was so unimportant that it had been ignored in the news bulletins? I felt a longing for news, but everything entering or leaving Britain was censored, and even if a letter had been posted, half the ships crossing the Atlantic seemed to have been torpedoed. Had it been feasible, I think I would have taken the next ship home, so great was my desire to see the family. How ironic that I should live in such a happy, sun-drenched community yet, because of the echoes of a war so far away, I should feel homesick for the first time since I had left London.

The war in Europe, however remote, had minor side effects that reached all the way from Whitehall to Koraloona. By 1941 the German U-boats had sunk so much Allied shipping that the larger ships plying from New Zealand or Australia to the islands were pressed into service in what became known as the Battle of the Atlantic, the desperate attempt to keep Britain supplied with food and arms. The *Mantela*, while being invaluable as a runabout between the islands, was too small and slow for such a mission. But with the big ships like the *Island Princess* being used to ferry Australian troops to North Africa, it all meant a heavier work load for Bill Robins; the weekly trips to Koraloona now became fortnightly.

It was that diminishing contact between Sanderstown and Koraloona, however, which led to an exciting prospect for me. It came about shortly after Alec Reid himself joined the sick parade. By now he had to fly whenever he needed drugs because of the shortage of shipping. On this day he couldn't, though fortunately the need was not urgent.

The old boy looked a bit sorry for himself that morning, but he smiled weakly. 'Feel as if I'd been kicked by a horse, Laddie.' The Scottish burr was strong in his speech – always a sign, with him, that all was not well. But his temperature wasn't up much – a degree or so above normal – nor was his pulse rate. I always had a fear of Yellow Fever in tropical areas, but when I raised his eyelids the whites seemed clear enough. It's the doctor's bugbear that nearly all fevers start with mild aches and pains that don't declare their type until they're ready to display symptoms. I turned to Miss Sowerby.

'Probably only a touch of 'flu,' I said. 'Give him a couple of aspirins and some ice to suck; and for heaven's sake call me if you notice any blotches on his skin or if he has difficulty passing his water.'

Reid seemed to be drowsy now, but he was awake enough to hear me warn Miss Sowerby about subcutaneous haemorrhages. 'You're panicking, Laddie. This isn't Yellow Jack; more likely a touch of dengue.'

'All the same,' I said, 'I'm going to be prepared with a couple of micrograms of methyl-naphtho. Having a touch of Vitamin K handy never did anyone any harm.'

'You're the doctor,' I detected a touch of irony in his voice.

As it happened he never developed any signs of Yellow Jack; it turned out to be an attack of sandfly fever – a mild form of dengue – and after a few days during which his temperature soared to 102° and dropped again and he had bloodshot eyes and crippling pains in the back and legs, he reached the convalescent stage.

Bubble and/or Squeak were looking after him; giving him heated powdered milk with 'safe' water, laced with Old Rarity, and I was struck by the concern these two Polynesian girls had for him. It isn't every pair of twins who will cheerfully do all the domestic chores, then happily share the physical attentions of an overweight, perspiring employer, especially as he didn't seem to know, or care, which one jumped into his bed. But their concern was genuine. After one of them had watched him drink his milk, the other would arrive to change his sheets. It was rather touching.

'I'll be up and about in a few days,' Alec promised me. 'I'll *have* to be. I'm not worried about the shortage of drugs

200

for the moment. We've got enough to last two or three weeks. But what *does* worry me is that if we need a special drug urgently, there's no guarantee we can get it – that is, if I can't fly. It's a weak link in our chain of safety. What with the war and shipping problems, the only way is for ye to become Deputy Pilot.'

Alec had said several times that I should learn to fly the Gloster, but it took this mild attack of fever to stir him to action.

'As soon as I'm better,' he said, 'we'll have the first lesson.'

And we did – a week later. Actually, learning to fly the Gloster proved to be surprisingly easy – technically that is, but not counting the millions of butterflies that fluttered in my stomach later, during my first attempts to fly solo and land without Alec Reid's reassuring presence.

Reid was as unorthodox as a flying instructor as he was when doctoring. On my first lesson, as he tightened his MCC tie round his waist, he replaced his sweat-stained topee with a soft leather helmet and goggles with built-in radio, and handed me similar headgear, so that we could talk to each other above the noise. Showing me the step near the wing which I needed to climb in (rather like a stirrup to hoist up a leg when mounting a horse), he said, 'Hop in, and I'll explain what the different instruments mean.' First he showed me how to get strapped into the open cockpit, then the instruments; very simple in what was basically a light trainer plane – a compass, an airspeed indicator, rev counter, altimeter, fuel gauges, one for each tank, and one dial showing that you were flying straight and level. The control column – what Alan Cobham (and countless thousands of other fliers) had called the joystick – was almost between my legs, the rudder pedals like those on any motor car, though with rather different functions. There was also a confusing radio dial, details of which he explained later, so that I could speak to Sanderstown.

The Gloster had a self-starter but, before Reid switched on the motor, he asked me to jump out to pull away the chocks that kept the wheels in position, when he gave the signal. I did so and as the propeller whirred into life, I jumped back into the plane. We trundled along the field, almost as though driving a car over rough ground, with Alec explaining how he used the pedals to change the position of the rudder, and turning round by revving up then slowing down, increasing the speed to make the best use of the rudder, before getting ready to take off into the wind.

Finally we were in position. Alec gave me the 'thumbs-up' signal, the engine roared into life and we moved faster and faster across the field, until suddenly Alec pulled the stick back and almost without my realising it, the ground was rushing past *below* us, and the next thing I was leaning over the side, fascinated by the different-looking shapes of palm trees, like a green carpet when seen from above. And then, as Alec pulled the control stick further back and we soared upwards, he banked and swung almost lazily away from the red rooftops, the green palms, the multi-coloured flowers, the silver beach, and we were over the blue waters of the lagoon, with the pier sticking out like a white finger, and the distant angry line of the reef stretching for miles. We kept flying in a widening circle until we returned to the tip of the island, then slowly lost height, and soon I saw the field rushing towards us as we came in to land.

When flying it was difficult to talk on the intercom, but as we started to come in to land Alec did manage to shout, 'Watch that as we land!' and pointed to the altimeter.

We came down gracefully with only one bump, and as we taxied back to our starting point I thought the lesson had ended; but without stopping, Alec faced the plane into the wind and before I realised what was happening we were airborne again, and as we followed the same course out and across the water, he shouted, 'Take the control column for a minute or two.'

I did. With gestures he told me when to pull the stick towards me – slowly – so that I had the exciting feeling that I was soaring into the heavens. Then as I pushed it down, he yelled, 'Not too much!' and pulled us out of a dive.

When we finally landed, Reid switched off the motor and said, 'Here endeth the first lesson. Can you put the chocks under the wheels, Laddie? On our next lesson we'll work on the rudder pedals and after that you can try to land.'

Despite the apparent simplicity, there was a lot to learn. On the other hand, much of it was common sense in a small plane like the Gloster. It was a wonderful, exhilarating feeling, doing the actual flying; above anything else, the feeling that I was a part of the aircraft, that it was wrapped round me, almost as though the wings were attached to me, a feeling which I am sure never applied when flying in a large commercial aircraft.

Of course there were snags to be overcome. The rudder pedals at first refused to co-operate! If I used the control column to bank, and the rudder pedals as well, the aircraft seemed to slew round, to yaw. And it was much easier to take off than to land, because when landing I not only had to judge the height of the undercarriage (which I often forgot at first as I never saw it when flying), but also I had to get the angle of approach just right, and the speed too. The first time I came in too fast and Reid grabbed the control just in time to slow me down or I would have overshot the field. And yet if I came in too slowly, I started to stall – which meant there was a chance of hitting the ground with one wing tip before the wheels.

But once in the air, I was again seized with that sense of exhilaration and felt a great temptation to throw the plane around, to let her go, even to try and loop. Within three weeks I had made my first solo flight, and from then on, I was 'sold' on flying.

All the expected sense of speed deserted me. The dusty Main Street and Hill Road dawdled behind me like two fat white caterpillars. As I tilted the plane upwards, a new carpet of exotic flowers spread below the top of the jungle trees on the volcanic slopes – flowers never seen half way up the thick trees, flowers forced high above the rest of the island in the struggle to reach sunlight. If I banked the plane outwards to the sea, there was the sensation that I was suspended motionless over the blue carpet edged with white – the foam which looked silent yet in reality consisted of a threshing, pounding roar.

'Maybe I might be able to fly someone vital to Sanders one day, and help the war effort,' I laughed as Alec congratulated me on my latest landing.

'Ye'll need something faster than this,' he said. 'It's a wee feeling I have that the Japanese are behaving aggressively – in speech anyway – since America cut off their oil from the Dutch East Indies.'

'Talking, yes – ' I had read the reports.

'Aye,' he agreed as we walked back to the dispensary. 'Let's hope so, though even their talk sounds to me like the hiss of a snake.'

The distant war affected the people of Koraloona in different ways, even though outwardly we were untouched, and the peace and tranquillity of its inhabitants might have seemed unchanged. Sometimes it was war, plus the unexpected. This is what happened to Jason Purvis. One evening, arriving at my bungalow for a musical soirée (as he ironically called it) and a good dinner, I was astounded to see him dressed in a new suit of white ducks.

'And you've shaved?' I cried, handing him a gimlet.

'You noticed?'

He hadn't shaved his beard off, but he had had it neatly trimmed by Lee Chong, the Chinese barber two doors up the road from Mick's Bar.

'You must have come into money.' I said it as a joke.

'I have. Not much, and in rather sad circumstances, but – ' he shrugged his shoulders.

Over drinks, he told me what had happened. He had depended for his inheritance on the generosity of a cousin whom he had hardly known. The man had been killed in the blitz. And that meant the end of his remittance.

'But – and it's a big but,' added Purvis, 'the old boy left me a legacy.'

It was for £10,000. And it was all Purvis'. It was a staggering surprise.

'There is one snag,' said Purvis. 'Wartime regulations forbid all exports of money from Britain. There is no way I can get my hands on the money.'

'But your clothes?'

'When I learned that I couldn't touch the cash, I said nothing to anyone, but I did have a brilliant suggestion.'

He asked the lawyers in London to send written confirmation that they would be responsible for payment, after the end of the war, for any debts contracted by Purvis to Mr Johnson.

'And Johnson's store are now my bankers,' he said gleefully. 'That old skinflint Johnson is actually *pressing* me to buy. I've got a credit guaranteed for £9,000 – the lawyers wouldn't release the last thousand – so Johnson and I are great buddies.'

'How much is he charging you – interest I mean?'

'I dunno exactly. I think he said something about ten per cent.'

'Ten per cent!' I yelled. 'It's daylight robbery. I'm going to do something about it – and I'm going to limit your spending; yes, I am. Shut up! Whether you like it or not. This bloody war's going on for years, and you'll end being broke if I don't look after you.'

'It's nothing to do with you.' He was half joking, but he did add, 'I knew I shouldn't have told you.'

'It *is* something to do with me. I'm your doctor. I'm not going to have you drinking yourself almost to death and then starving to death. And being screwed for ten per cent for the privilege.'

And I did just that. I went down to the store and confronted Johnson. At first he tried to brazen out the ten per cent charge, but I said, 'Listen, I know one thing about you that you don't know yourself. Your lungs are filled with nicotine poisoning from that chain smoking of yours. One day that cough – and anything else we find – will need attention. Don't come to me for help unless you do exactly what I tell you to do – *order* you to.'

'Guv'nor, I've got to make a living,' he whined in his Cockney accent.

'Balls!' I warned him. 'You make a damned good living, but I don't like the way you do business. And I don't want any crooked business dealings between you and Mr Purvis.'

'I ain't no crook,' wailed Johnson. 'What does anyone mean when they say you're a crook? Only that he's clever enough to make plenty of money. I ain't clever and I won't never make no bleeding fortune.'

'Well, watch it,' I told him. 'You'll make a good investment at five per cent.' I made him sign a document then and there limiting his credit for any debts to twice what he had received from Purvis as a remittance man.

'You're better off,' I told Purvis later, 'than you've ever been. You've got an income that's doubled. And if you stop drinking and get on with that book of yours, who knows, you might have a nest egg after the war.'

Purvis was a changed man, no doubt about that. He still drank, but he did keep the hospital garden tidy and tried to make himself generally useful – up to a point. Then I received help in the hospital from another quarter – help I frankly didn't want to receive. It happened after a meeting of the 'Help the War' committee at the Union Jack Club.

It came from Paula Reece. Since America was not at war there was no reason why Americans shouldn't cross the Pacific in ships flying the Stars and Stripes. And since the Moto Varu archipelago was part of the British Empire, I would have thought that a woman like Paula Reece would have fled the shores of a country technically at war for the neutral haven of her home in California.

Not a bit of it. At the end of this particular 'War Effort' meeting – when both Doc Reid and I, together with Princess Tiare, were present – Colonel Fawcett, the chairman, who sat at the bridge table facing the members, enquired 'Any other business?' and was about to declare, as he always did, 'Meeting adjourned for a month', when Paula Reece got up from the row of chairs and cried, 'Colonel, may I?'

'Of course, dear lady.' Fawcett stood up gallantly, though I saw him cast a wistful eye towards the bar which always opened at the end of a meeting.

I still nursed a kind of hate for Paula Reece, though not actively. I could never forget the shabby way she had treated Lucy, and though I had all but forgotten Lucy herself – I had never heard from her, nor did I have the address of her dream cottage – it didn't lessen the disgust I felt at the way Paula Reece had behaved, even though I knew I was acting in a petty way. But I behaved correctly, and when we had to speak it was with politeness, but no warmth.

'Thank you.' Paula Reece addressed the meeting. 'I know America is neutral, but even so, you've been kind enough to treat me as one of your own, and gee, I'd like to be more practical in my help. Is there anything you'd like me to do that I could do?'

'That's very kind, Paula.' Colonel Fawcett tended to mumble, especially when it was time for the bar to open. Looking towards the rows of expectant faces, he asked, 'Any suggestions?'

It was none other than Doc Reid who finally stood up.

'Well, Doctor Reid, have you any ideas for improving Anglo-American relations?' asked the colonel, adding with a feeble attempt at humour, 'apart from giving the United States the right to establish bases in Koraloona in exchange for Mrs Reece's yacht?' There was a titter touched with rancour, for many people were angry that Churchill had agreed to let 'foreigners' – that is, Americans – establish bases in the West Indies in exchange for fifty clapped-out US destroyers.

'No, Colonel, I would never take diplomatic advantage of such a gallant and delightful lady,' said Reid. Then he paused – deliberately. 'But I do need an assistant – unpaid – to work with Doctor Masters.'

There was an immediate hum of excitement. Everyone knew that I couldn't stand Paula Reece, and several of them disliked her, not only because of the way she had treated Lucy, which was common knowledge; not only for the way she invited available young men, but because she displayed her wealth ostentatiously. She was never really popular. As Purvis said to me one evening, 'It's one thing to accept a lady's free champagne, but you don't have to like her.'

I felt myself blushing, and I kicked Alec on the leg as a warning, because, as everyone looked our way I could only whisper, 'Shut up!' Aloud I said in a bad-tempered voice, 'I'm very grateful for the offer of help,' and avoiding Paulà's eyes, added, 'Miss Sowerby and I can cope quite easily, thank you.'

'No, she can't,' retorted Reid. 'Miss Sowerby is so overworked that a woman less brave would be on the edge of a nervous breakdown.'

'I'd love to help,' said Paula, adding to 'the chair', 'and if Doctor Masters thinks I'll refuse to clean up bedpans, he's got another think coming.'

'It's not that,' I said clumsily. 'It's – '

Then out of the blue Paula Reece – and I must say she looked very attractive against the dresses of the old-fashioned ladies – asked, 'Is it by any chance because you don't like me?'

The crowded room gave one collective gasp. No one in the history of the Union Jack Club had ever dared to say such a thing in front of virtually every member. The gasp was an extraordinary moment, as though the whole room was one huge balloon which had suddenly been pricked, letting the air escape.

I had to hand it to her. I remembered a student in my med school days once saying, 'If all else fails, kick 'em in the balls.'

She'd done that all right.

'No, Paula.' Again I stumbled for words. 'Please don't think that – '

Doc Reid came to my rescue. 'Ladies and gentlemen,' he began formally. 'Thank you, Paula, for your offer. Will ye please bear with me for a few minutes because I've got something to say that canna be said in a few words.'

A sudden excitement replaced the gasp, the kind of excitement that people can sense which precedes dramatic news; but even I wasn't prepared for the next words.

'Kit is nae going to like this.' Alec turned to me, giving me his fatherly pat on the back, 'but our young friend here is also on the edge of a nervous breakdown.'

'I'm not!' I cried.

'Ye are! And for why? No, don't stop me, Kit! I want to tell you something that few of ye know. Kit's cured eleven cases of the dreaded polio – the disease no doctor is supposed to be able to cure – in the past six months, using revolutionary methods that I myself would never have practised.'

'Please!' I whispered.

There was utter silence as Reid continued: 'We have a continuing stream of cases, and the only way Kit and Miss Sowerby can try to cure them is by changing compresses of boiling water once every two hours.' He paused before adding dramatically, 'Once every two hours for three days and three nights without a break. Yes, ladies and gentlemen, seventy-two hours without one wee break. And there are three patients in hospital at the moment. So there's no rest for either of them. Because if ye miss one or two dressings, ye've got a lifetime cripple on your hands.'

'Shut up!' I hissed, furious.

I felt myself blushing like an idiot as there was a spontaneous outburst of clapping. He had made it so bloody heroic! I felt a fool. Then Alec held up his hand for silence before adding, 'I told this story for one reason – not to laud Kit, who's simply doing his job as a doctor, but because it wouldn't be fair to Mrs Reece to take up her offer unless she knew what she was letting herself in for. But we could do with you, Paula!'

'I accept your offer with thanks,' she said.

'Agreed. Meeting adjourned,' cried Colonel Fawcett, leading the dash to the bar, while I saw Paula Reece slide quietly out of the clubhouse.

'Probably prefers her champagne to slumming at the bar here,' I said savagely to Reid.

In his Scottish burr Alec replied, 'An island's too small a place to harbour a grudge, Kit. Don't behave like a wee bairn. Ye're a grown man. And ye dinna have to bed her if ye don't want.'

'Never!' I cried as the first of the guests started plying me with free drinks.

So Paula Reece started as a 'temp' – temporary untrained nurse with no salary. And I have to admit that after a few days of 'training' she became very adept. The subject of our quarrel was never mentioned. We behaved 'correctly'. In other words I called her Paula and she called me Kit. But I still didn't go to her parties.

One thing *was* difficult, however, and it wasn't my fault. Miss Sowerby in her dreary black clothes – the tried and trusted assistant who still addressed me as 'Doctor' – despised the immaculately dressed Paula – who always called me Kit. It wasn't a hostility between the two women which – at the time – manifested itself openly, but I could sense that the two ladies distrusted each other intensely. They were polite – as I was polite to Paula – but it was obvious that Miss Sowerby, who had helped me so much with our case when Jimbo caught polio, bitterly resented the intrusion of this third person.

Alec knew of the mutual dislike, as he told me with a grunt after we had had another case of polio – actually at Tabanea where Jimbo had contracted the disease. I suggested to Alec that we should go and make a few routine checks on the 'Health through Hygiene' campaign which we had finally started successfully, thanks to the leadership and authority of Tiare.

'You must come along too,' I said. 'Your authority – '

'And leave the store in the hands of two women?' he asked jokingly. 'One of them in love with you spiritually, the other physically.'

I felt myself blushing. If only I didn't show my feelings so embarrassingly. Specially as I knew his sly remark was based on a kind of truth. Neither of the women had intimated by so much as a word that they entertained anything but an orthodox relationship between nurse and matron, but as our tiring treatment of polio by Sister Kenny methods continued, Miss Sowerby treated me with dog-like devotion. Paula never said anything, but worked harder and harder in an effort to outrank Miss Sowerby. Yet the harder she worked and the longer the hours she put in, the more she also gave me quizzical looks which showed plainly 'I'm doing everything to atone for what I've done. One day perhaps you'll forgive me.'

And the net result was that they loathed each other.

'Dinna worry,' said Alec when we set off to look at Tabanea village. 'So long as they make themselves useful. Let's see how the locals are behaving.'

We set off after morning surgery, having warned Toika (pronounced toy-ka), Jimbo's father, who was headman of the village, of our arrival so that it would be regarded as a ceremonial visit. It was also a pleasant outing for me, a rare chance, in times suddenly busy, to see the countryside of the island. We drove past Tala-Tala, along the shimmering beach road, with the sea on one side, while on the other, the flat fields and scrub leading to the mountains was dotted with occasional small plantations, some vanilla or coconut, here and there the shadow of a giant mango tree, its dark green leaves studded with pink and yellow fruit giving the appearance of blossoms far above.

Tabanea consisted of a collection of a dozen or so thatched huts several miles along the road beyond Tala-Tala. It lay half a mile or so inland from the beach, with a distant view across the sea of a smudge of land.

'That's Hodges, the copra island,' said Reid, who was

wearing long trousers to signify the importance of his visit.

'Tabanea's an odd name.' I had no idea what it meant.

'Roughly translated it's a cross between dialects for the taro plant and marshland. That's as near as I can tell you. You need marshy land, like this, between the sea and the village to grow taro. The best taro in the island is grown round here – and they need it. It's one of the Pacific's staple foods.'

Everyone, it seemed, ate taro, though it had virtually no fat or protein content. But it did contain plenty of calories, and I had eaten it mixed with coconut cream, then wrapped in leaves and cooked over hot stoves arranged to form a primitive oven. All over the semi-swampy area we could see the taro as we neared Tabanea. The plants were very tall, each one carefully encircled in palm leaf baskets.

'Filled with manure,' explained Alec. 'It sinks through the soil to nourish the tubers which have been planted in what's in effect rich, damp mud.'

As Alec braked the car on the edge of the village a dozen kids ran out to greet us with beatific smiles. One little girl shyly offered us welcoming necklaces of cowrie shells which had been picked up on the beach.

We solemnly put them around our necks, and then one boy ran from behind the others. It was Jimbo.

'Hello there,' I said, 'you're looking fine. No more pain?'

He shook his head, but in place of the smile I expected, he wore a glum face.

'What's the trouble?' I bent down and felt his legs.

'Soon I go back hospital. Soon leg bad again.'

'What on earth do you mean?' I laughed, knowing that one attack of polio does at least guarantee a lifetime immunity. 'What for hospital? Your leg fine.'

Stubbornly he shook his head.

'What makes you say this?' I asked, really puzzled, for obviously he wasn't in pain.

'My cure finish. No more noise.' He took from behind his back the little radio Mrs Fawcett had given him and handed it to me. It was dead. I slid open the cover of the compartment that held the batteries, and, ignorant though I was of radio apparatus (never having absorbed any of Father's expertise), I saw the cause of the trouble at once: one of the thin wires that led from the battery compartment had come adrift from its contact. It was a simple job for Jim Wilson and his soldering iron.

I almost laughed with relief. 'Nothing to worry about. I'll get it mended and you can come to surgery tomorrow and fetch it. Don't worry. You're cured.' I pointed again at the radio. 'I mend, bring back noise. I promise.' He looked at me in wonder. 'I go now to village.'

Jimbo's father Toika was waiting to greet us on behalf of the village. The street was alive with black piglets and chickens. Near the road were a dozen yam huts, each looking like giant wooden dog kennels, in which the season's crop was stored.

By now I knew most of the vegetables, of course, how they grew, how they were cooked, so that when I was occasionally called to a village, I could see their way of life reflected in their produce. As we walked through the main street, one man had filled his small plot with sweet potatoes, which looked like Jerusalem artichokes. I could smell the potatoes which were being baked with coconut milk. Other women were preparing dishes which smelled even more of coconuts, especially from breadfruit being fried in coconut oil.

'Coconuts with everything,' grunted Alec, but he smiled to the women as we continued walking through the village. This was not only a ceremonial visit; never in the history of Tabanea had *two* doctors visited their village together. For me, though, there was another important side to the parade. I was making for the site we had chosen for Koraloona's first public latrine. It was some distance from the village, behind a stretch of wild arrowroot, easily recognisable by the single stems topped with green and

213

brown flowers, and surrounded with threads like puff-balls.

The site seemed all right; canvas screens had, as arranged months earlier, been erected around the trenches, but Reid carefully explained to Toika that this trench was 'used up' and told the headman to have it filled in and to start a new one.

'It shall be done,' promised Toika.

'Meanwhile,' asked Alec as we walked back to the actual village, 'if there is anyone with a bad cold, even a running nose, I want him at the surgery tomorrow.'

'The word of the doctors shall be obeyed,' Toika again promised, the words echoed by sonorous cries from the other men.

Alec knew that they would keep their promise and that the new trenches would be dug quickly. And not for the first time, watching the villagers round their huts and observing this none-too-clean group of humans and animals, I marvelled at the way Alec's years of living in the Pacific had instilled in him an instinctive knowledge of the way to treat the islanders.

It wasn't knowledge alone that made him handle them so expertly; I realised something that had not been apparent at first; it was more than mere know-how. It was knowledge based on love. He loved the indolent, handsome, smiling men and women of the island with all his heart as though they were his children, his own family – a far warmer family than he would have had among his patients had he practised in London, where neighbours hardly knew each other's names.

This was why Alec and his wife chose to live ten thousand miles apart. It was not that he had succumbed to the lure of the islands, nor the ease with which sexual desires could be gratified. He had fallen in love – if that isn't too sentimental a word – with the people. All of them. And over the years he had become their friend and counsellor, as well as doctor; a trifle old-fashioned perhaps, but giving out a warmth that was returned in full measure by an island

214

people who by now almost certainly regarded Alec Reid as the most important person in Koraloona after Princess Tiare.

It was hard work treating the new outbreaks of polio, but even so the number of cases had not reached epidemic proportions; what took up time was that other patients also needed attention; they queued up daily in the garden awaiting their turn for morning surgery. But Miss Sowerby and Paula helped out magnificently. Only when a polio patient had ended his three-day 'blanket' treatment did Paula go home to Faalifu and rest until she was needed again. Then Miss Sowerby came into her own! For a few days she was the undisputed assistant, and I went out of my way to be kind to her.

Then, one day in early November 1941, a girl of ten was carried in by her father, and she was almost on the point of death. One look at her laboured struggle to breathe, and the cries of pain as she clasped her chest, told me that this was polio, but the agonising cramps had not twisted an arm or a leg out of shape, they had struck at the girl's diaphragm. As I carried her into the theatre, and laid her on the table to examine her, I could see that all the muscles of the chest were slowly being paralysed so that she didn't have the muscle strength to get enough air into her lungs – or expel what little she had managed to breathe in. There was only one chance of keeping her alive – if I could borrow an iron lung from the naval base. I knew they had several there.

The iron lung – not necessarily iron, but sometimes made of wood or a lighter metal – was a contraption invented in 1930. It consisted of an almost airtight 'box' in which the patient lay, with one hole so that his or her head could be left outside, and two holes so that the legs could stick out just above the knee. The holes were lined with foam rubber to keep the lung more airtight. It contained a small motor which could increase or decrease the pressure of air in the lung, forcing air through the mouth by pressure on the lungs, then as the pressure lessened new air was sucked into the lungs. Iron lungs were made in various sizes for adults and children.

The trouble for me was that the chest was such a large area that I couldn't use the blanket treatment – not immediately, anyway. This was a case where the first priority was to keep the child breathing. If I could keep her breathing with an iron lung, with its 'bellows' effect, there would come a time when she would be allowed out of the lung for several hours a day, and then perhaps I could test a variation of the blanket treatment.

First, though, I had to get a lung. I drove round to ask Alec for help, and, of course, he did not hesitate.

'I'll get on the sked instantly, and see if Ronnie Serpell isn't using all of his.' Serpell was the surgeon-commander who had studied with Alec at Edinburgh.

'We haven't got much time,' I said. 'She's only breathing with the greatest difficulty.'

'Well, if there's a lung available, ye'd better fly to Sanderstown right away.' He looked at his watch. 'Can the wee bairn hold out till tomorrow?'

I nodded. 'With luck. But couldn't we get back tonight?'

'I dinna think so. It'll be lunch time at the base, and even if ye're lucky and get your lung, it'll take you a couple of hours of red tape to sign for it.' He added ironically, 'Ye'll have to spend the night there. A night on the town.'

'Wouldn't you rather go?'

'No, thanks. You go. I'll get on the sked right away.'

'Would you ask the base to check on the phone if Bill Robins is in port?' I had only spent one night in Sanderstown a couple of years ago, and as Bill had been at sea, I had been bored and friendless.

An iron lung for children *was* available, and Commander Serpell suggested that I fly over, drive straight to the base, sign for it, and a naval car would transport it back to the plane and stow it away, so that I could fly off first thing the following morning. At the same time, he passed along a message that Bill Robins *was* in port, and had asked me to

216

spend the evening and have dinner with him. Robins had also asked for my ETA – estimated time of arrival – and promised to meet me in his car.

It was after lunch by the time I had gassed up the Gloster – the fuel had to be stored in two-gallon tins – and set off into the blue sky for a 'night out' in Sanderstown. It proved to be a turning point in my life.

14

I reached Sanderstown exactly on my ETA and circled over the city with its broad avenues and one big green space, the Savannah, in the centre. I could see, like models, a score or more of naval ships in the harbour, but I flew straight to the civilian airfield, west of Sanderstown, three or four miles across the city from the naval air base, which had its own airfield, used exclusively by planes from the carriers and top brass.

Bill Robins was waiting for me when I landed on the small runway – a pleasant touchdown after the roughness of our grass field. He drove me straight to the base where Surgeon-Commander Serpell, a tubby, cheerful man, but obviously very busy, greeted me with the courtesy of one doctor to another, rang a bell, handed me over to a naval lieutenant, who took me to the iron lung which had already been loaded on a small truck.

'I promised Alec I'd get this lashed down in the plane right away,' I explained to Bill. 'That way I can get off at first light. One storm and I could be delayed a day – and that would be too long.'

We drove back to the clubhouse of the flying-club, followed by the naval truck, then packed the lung into the plane, fastened securely. 'And now,' I said, 'we can forget I'm a doctor until tomorrow.'

It was a curious sensation, moving in an hour from the

lazy beauty of Anani to the comparatively bustling activity of Sanderstown: the hooting taxis, the thousands of uniformed troops, the worried faces, from the seedy but homely Union Jack Club to the elegant Mess at the naval base; and from Mollie Green's hotel, equally homely, to the Southern Cross Hotel, where I took my overnight bag, handing it to a hall porter in a uniform with more gold braid and scrambled eggs than an admiral. Then there was the hotel's Long Bar, with its gently stirring ceiling fans, the barman spick and span, the waiters in the grill room attentive, and, linking the various public rooms, the plate-glassed shops of the arcade selling everything from Dunhill pipes to clothes that in England were rationed.

Sanderstown was really several towns in one. The centre section, facing the sea, consisted of the imposing buildings of the naval base, which was the main employer of labour from admirals to civilian canteen cleaners. It not only had a gigantic dry-dock big enough to stage three football matches, but it was large enough to take the biggest ships of the British fleet. The dry-dock lay behind a natural harbour guarded by the coral reef, so that up to twenty warships could lie at anchor or be tied up to the two miles of wharfs studded with cranes, warehouses, railway lines and, near-by, the barracks.

Behind this warlike conglomeration of buildings and military equipment two main roads led inwards in a sort of 'V' from either side of the wharves – Coast Road West and Coast Road East, lined with flame trees, behind which stood imposing white buildings, the High Court, the City Hall, the Memorial Theatre, and the Cook Concert Hall (after Captain Cook, of course, though heaven knows if he liked music!). They made an impressive and spotlessly clean white façade, looking from the air like icing sugar. Inside the East and West roads was the bright green of the Savannah and the cricket club – a large stretch of immaculate lawns reminding me of Oxford or the calm of a cathedral close. In it were tennis courts, bowling greens, a rugger pitch, all reserved for 'Europeans', with naval

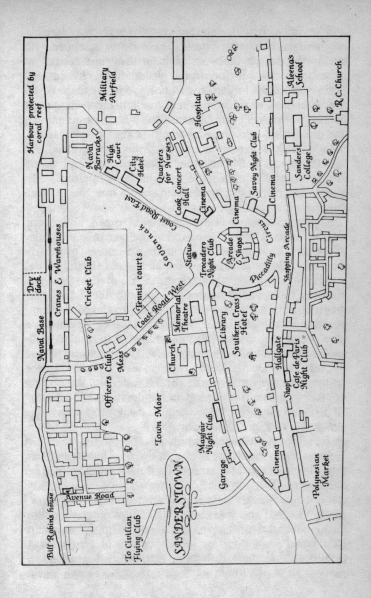

officers automatically elected to temporary membership when in Sanderstown. The cricket club was equipped with an up-to-date pavilion, backing on the wharves so that members never saw the unsightly side of the city. Instead the veranda, the billiard room, the two restaurants, one a snack bar, all looked on to the green of the club: near it were the trim white bungalows of the officers, grouped as if for protection around a larger building which was the Officers' Mess, and at the apex of the inverted triangle, where the two coast roads met, stood the imposing statue of Horatio Sanders, named after one of Captain Cook's oldest friends, a first mate who, like Cook, came from Hull.

On either side of each coast road, ringed with exotic scarlet flame trees, lay the residential areas, rectangular patterns of solid, respectable 'suburban' houses, most with English-style gardens, those facing the sea fetching three times the rent of those facing inwards. Below the statue was Piccadilly Circus, the heart of the city, another large circle of green lined with arcades against the sun and containing a shopping centre, and in or around the arcades were nearly a dozen cinemas, a large hospital, three or four night-clubs and several restaurants, often named nostalgically to give expatriates a touch of homesickness as they ate or danced in the Mayfair, the Savoy or the Trocadero. It wasn't that they didn't love the present in Sanderstown. It was that dreary old England seemed more exciting and enviable when it was a memory of the past.

Bill Robins was taking me on a conducted tour and, just around the corner from Piccadilly – only a few steps down Monument Road – the trim white buildings, the sweating, energetic white-flannelled cricketers or tennis players gave way abruptly to the dignified, leisurely walk of the Polynesians. The briefcase was replaced by a basket carried on the head. The Cold Storage in Piccadilly (the only place where you could buy 'safe' ice cream) was replaced by local produce, the smart European dresses by Mother Hubbards, the predominantly fair hair of Anglo-Saxons by the blue-black hair of the Pacific. The goods in Sanderstown's Piccadilly came from a different world, for in the market huge piles of produce spilled on the pavements. The market place was as lively as anything in Soho's Berwick Street. Bolts of vivid trade cotton, pyramids of coconuts, ragged tapestries of seaweed, foot-long bundles of chives and even longer bundles of beans, mandarin oranges vivid against the green of island cabbages. Other bowls overflowed with watermelons, grapefruit, pawpaws, pimentos, huge tomatoes, pumpkins, limes, and plantains.

On a stool in the middle of the market I saw an old crone selling sugar cane and grinning a toothless smile as she cackled about the wonderful preservative qualities of sugar for the teeth. Next to her another old woman was busy weaving the blade-shaped leaves of pandanus into mats, and carefully setting aside the fruit for later mixing with coconut cream. The heady scent of the fruit permeated the air. Nearby was the fish-market, like any in the world, smelling strongly, so that I might have been in Billingsgate, except that the marketeers were dreamy and smiling instead of loud-voiced and abusive.

By now evening was approaching, and the rush-hour had started, with clerks and other workers from offices or the base making their way home in bright orange, pink and lime-green buses, disgorging their passengers out of the single door like grain tumbling down a hopper. Many of them, I noticed, made for the side streets to eat in the innumerable cheap Chinese restaurants, often little more than holes in the wall around the market area.

I noticed something else before Bill Robins dropped me at my hotel so that I could shower before going to his place for dinner.

'Where are the bare breasts?' I asked.

'I wondered if you'd notice,' he laughed. 'The sailors who visit the outer islands call Sanderstown Titlesstown.'

'But why no tits?' I asked.

'Beats me.' We reached the Southern Cross Hotel. 'Maybe the missionaries – that and the fact that at times there are several thousand randy sailors making for Sanderstown's red light district! Not for old men like us,' he laughed. 'Pick you up at eight o'clock.'

He arrived promptly for my first visit to his house. Bill and Bessie Robins and their two children lived in the oddly named Avenue Road, which seemed as though it couldn't make up its mind whether it was a road or an avenue, for it was broad and straight, but in the centre, running the entire length of the street, was a narrow railed garden filled with tall, spreading bamboo, and oleander, hibiscus and poinsettia. Each side of the garden was lined with three-or four-bedroomed houses.

'With a view of the sea,' said Bill. 'But only from the top-floor bedroom.'

Bessie Robins turned out to be a delightful London-born woman whose age I guessed at around forty. She had kept a good figure and when she laughed, she showed two rows of beautiful teeth in her round and obviously happy face, and dimples at the corners of her mouth below brown eyes sparkling with joy.

'Sometimes I miss London,' she admitted after the introductions, and she had, to my astonishment, shaken a cocktail with dexterity, and poured out a drink I knew, but which I hadn't tasted for years: a White Lady.

'Bill likes his cocktails,' she explained. 'That and a bottle of wine.'

'But you made that White Lady like a professional,' I cried.

'I was a professional – nearly twenty years ago.'

Bill explained. Bessie's father had owned a small residential hotel behind the Cromwell Road and, almost as a joke, he had allowed Bessie to serve in the small, intimate bar reserved for residents.

'So one day when a young Captain Robins stayed at the hotel I served him a White Lady, and he was so impressed that he asked me to marry him.'

The Robins' sitting-room, with flowered chintzy deep armchairs and French windows opening on to the garden, was homely and uncluttered. The paintings were nondescript – especially after the Gauguins! – but they were more than compensated for by a collection of furniture which Bill had picked up all over the world and which he displayed with pride.

'Most sailors have a girl in every port,' he said, 'but I have a parcel in every port.' They included a polished carved head from Bali, a Japanese ceremonial sword from Yokohama, a camphorwood chest from Singapore, a nest of brass tables from Bangkok, and a pair of heavy teak painted elephants from Bombay.

We had a second White Lady and Bessie left to look after the preparation of the meal.

'Don't you think these Japanese are getting very aggressive?' asked Bill.

'How do you mean?'

'Well, I have a good sense of smell, and something very fishy's going on.'

'You mean the fact that America has cut off their oil supplies from the Dutch East Indies?' Alec too had suggested something of the sort.

'Yes.'

'But that's only to stop them from taking the war into China. To limit them.' I had heard that too.

'Well, one thing's for sure,' said Bill. 'The Japs can't take on the Americans.'

At that moment Bessie reappeared, saying, 'I wonder where our other guest is?'

'We've got a girl for you,' explained Bill.

'Really, Bill,' protested Bessie, 'you make it sound so – well, the doctor might be embarrassed.'

'The name's Kit, please,' I said.

'All right,' she smiled, 'Kit.'

'I didn't mean a girl in *that* way.' Bill lit his pipe then threw the spent match into the ashtray. 'I just meant to make up a four.'

'You don't have to do that,' I said. 'I was hoping –.well, we never get much time for a chat and – '

223

'There she is.' Bill got up to open the door. A minute later in walked Aleena.

I have never been able to puzzle out why, in that one moment of my life, when she walked into the room, why Aleena, in my eyes – the eye of the beholder of course – turned from a beautiful leggy schoolgirl into a beautiful young woman.

Her hair was different, that was true. It was done up, pulled up over her head, with a mass of curls on top and a wave in front. It passed through my mind that perhaps this was the first time in her life she had had her hair done by a hairdresser.

There was more to it than that, though. Was it the 'town clothes' she wore? A white sharkskin skirt instead of the usual shorts or sarong? Was it the touch of lipstick? Or was it that, for the first time since I had met her, I had seen Aleena without her mother, and this had released in her a spring otherwise held coiled in reserve? For in Polynesia parental rules, however generous, are there to be obeyed without question.

Or perhaps it was even simpler. It was hard to realise that I had now been living on the island for three years. She had been thirteen when I first attended her on the day we discovered the dreaded black spot on her leg. Then I had treated a schoolgirl. Now she was sixteen, soon to be seventeen and leaving college, with her hair done up, coming into the room with a smile, shaking hands and saying almost teasingly, 'Hello, Kit,' as though to emphasise those extra years by using Christian names.

'Aleena,' I said. 'This is a wonderful surprise.' Then I blurted out the truth. 'But I can't take you in, looking like – well, a fully grown woman.'

'It's the big city life,' she laughed. 'Which do you prefer?'

'This!' I cried fervently.

'Dinner's ready,' Bessie announced.

As we walked into the dining-room, Aleena asked, 'Why did you have to come so suddenly? Bill phoned me at college and told me you were arriving unexpectedly, and persuaded the head to let me out for the evening.'

'I have to get an iron lung from the naval base for a little girl who's got polio.'

'Poor child. Do I know her?' In a curious way her anxious question reminded me of Tiare.

'I don't even know her name myself. But don't let's talk about work and illness on this happy night.'

I *was* happy. It isn't being cold-blooded, but quite normal for a doctor to give his whole attention to a case, yet to be able to banish it from his thoughts when he knows there's nothing that can be done for the time being. Some laymen never realise that life would be intolerable if you couldn't 'switch off' from work when you are away from it.

We had a wonderful dinner. Bessie cooked Australian roast beef, and it was as good as at Simpson's in the Strand, served up with a bottle of wine and afterwards, when Bill Robins was sipping his 'Sticky Green', I said, as casually as I could, but with a sideways look at this astonishingly transformed beauty, 'I suppose when Aleena's allowed out of college like this, you take responsibility for her?'

'That's a promise I made to her mother.'

'Then sir,' I said with mock dignity, addressing Bill officially as her guardian, 'may I have your permission to take your ward for half an hour's dancing on the way back to college?'

'I knew as much!' cried Bill. 'Your first visit to us, and already you're bored! But perhaps Aleena,' with a sly attempt at humour, 'you'd rather not go.'

'Not go!' Eyes shining, she almost clapped her hands as she cried, 'Yes *please*, Bill! The boys who take us out are so spotty and dim, I'd love it if I could go. I promise I'll be back at college by eleven – that's the time I have to be in.'

'I'll make sure she's home in time,' I promised.

'There's a night-club next door to the college in Hallgate,' she said.

'All right! Off you go.' Bill Robins knocked out the ashes

of his pipe, and this time with a mock gesture of resignation sighed, 'What it is to be young. Have a good time.'

I was young – younger anyway. And she was older than she had been. I realised, as we said our goodbyes to Bessie in the hall, that every year of the life one lives diminishes the time zone between two people. When someone is twenty and the other person ten, a world separates you. But when the same two people are seventy and sixty they have become contemporaries. When we first met, Aleena had been a girl of thirteen, slightly frightened at the authority of a doctor of twenty-four.

She had grown. And tonight, with me divested of my title of doctor, I was to her just a young man anxious to go dancing, already (to her, anyway) in spirit years younger than when we had first met as doctor and patient.

As we prepared to leave, Bill whispered, 'I'm responsible for her, remember. Don't let me down.'

'I won't,' I promised.

Bill closed the front door after waving us into Avenue Road, where I soon found a cruising taxi and set off along Avenue Road, then the Coast Road West, skirting Piccadilly until, with Aleena directing, we reached Hallgate which also had a beautiful arcade of shops. Nostalgia took another couple of steps backwards when we reached the night-club near the school. It was called the Café de Paris, after the London club in Leicester Square; but that had been obliterated by a bomb.

Inside the foyer a sign proclaimed, 'Gentlemen are requested to wear jackets and ties'. Thank goodness I was suitably dressed. I took Aleena's arm and guided her to a small round table by the edge of the tiny dance floor, brown wood streaked with white from the French chalk which had been dusted over it.

'Champagne?' I asked casually, as we sat down. 'Are you allowed to drink it?'

'Of course. When Mother's not around. It's wonderful. The boys who take us out dancing can never afford it. It's beer or soft drinks.'

I felt a sudden, quite ridiculous shaft of jealousy at visions of all the young men holding her tightly as they foxtrotted. How absurd of me! I was as young as they were – well, nearly, *and* with a little more wool on my back. But they were in Sanderstown every day!

'Champagne,' I ordered when the waiter came to my table.

'Certainly, sir.' His interest quickened. 'What kind, sir?'

It sounds crazy, but I had only drunk champagne once at Oxford, never in Nottingham, and of course in the early days at Paula's it had always been served in glasses, so I wasn't sure that I remembered any particular make.

Aleena came to the rescue. 'I don't think Doctor Masters has any preference,' she said coolly, and to my astonishment, as the waiter bowed, she said, with a touch of conspiracy, 'I thought the "doctor" would impress him.'

'It did,' I laughed. 'So did you.'

The dance floor was half empty. 'Johnny Fresno and his band' – as painted on one side of a drum – played soft music on a dais near our table, a medley from *Snow White and the Seven Dwarfs* which was being shown at the Capitol Cinema in Piccadilly, almost opposite our night-club. The music was catchy.

'Let's dance, shall we?' I suggested.

She got up. The music was slow, gentle, something about 'some day my prince will come . . .' and she slid gently into the dance as I put my arm half way round her waist and held her close – not too close, but I could feel her body yielding and though I wasn't an expert dancer, she was so professional ('Dancing lessons twice a week,' she laughed) that she made *me* feel I was the most wonderful dancer in the world.

'You're a born dancer,' I said at the end of the number when I took her back to the table. The waiter showed me a bottle of champagne called Taittinger in a bucket and when we sipped it, she confessed, 'I told a fib. This is the first time I've ever drunk champagne.'

How extraordinary. I was still finding it difficult to grasp

227

that I was sitting opposite someone who had already changed from the leggy schoolgirl I first met to this flowerlike vision – and in the short space of time of a year or so when a girl leaves home for boarding school.

'You're a different person,' I said as the band started again. 'I feel I am meeting you for the first time.'

'I hope you approve,' she said almost demurely. 'Oh! I love this tune. Can we dance it?'

'Of course.' It was 'With a Song in my Heart', this time a slow foxtrot, and we danced even closer, more dreamily, and she murmured, 'I could dance with you for ever.'

'How do you think I feel?' I whispered. At the end of the dance I said, 'You're so beautiful, Aleena. I never realised it.'

'More beautiful than the girls in the Gauguins? Mummy wrote me that she'd put on the show for you.'

'They were wonderful – but you – '

Then she made a curious remark. 'Funny to think that one day they will belong to me – to be shared with the man I marry – if my holy man lets me.'

'What on earth do you mean – "holy man"? It's your mother who'll give you permission to marry, surely?'

'Mother is important,' she twiddled the stem of her champagne glass, 'but everyone in Polynesia has a holy man who guides them through their spiritual life.'

I knew, of course, that Polynesia was riddled with superstition and that most people went for advice to 'holy men' – which to me was a polite term for witch-doctor. But a modern, educated girl like Aleena? It seemed crazy.

'Well, you're not going to get married yet.' I laughed off the kind of superstition which I always found rather ridiculous. Then a sudden thought struck me, and I wished afterwards that I had never uttered it.

'Do you realise a curious thing,' I said with an assumed flippancy. 'You and I are nearly seventeen and twenty-eight. My mother and father were exactly the same age when they were married.'

It was a silly thing to say to a girl whose stars showed in

her eyes. She was about to say something, but stopped short and looked me straight in the eyes. Then two large tears filled the corners of her big dark eyes, and in an almost broken voice she said, as she stood up, 'Please, darling Kit, dance with me so that you can't watch my eyes.'

She almost fell into my arms, squeezed me almost fiercely, then deliberately touched my cheek with hers, whispering words I couldn't hear. We were dancing one of the hit tunes of the day, 'You're Driving Me Crazy', and because of her reaction to what I had said, I asked recklessly, 'Would you do me a silly favour?'

'If I can – of course.' She kissed my cheek.

'Let your hair down.'

'Is that all? I can't do that here.'

'It'll only take a moment if you pop into the cloakroom. We've just time for a couple more dances, and I want to see your beautiful hair hanging over your shoulders. Would you mind?'

'Of course not!' Then she almost giggled.

'What's so funny?' I asked.

'If you knew the agony I went through to put it up!' she laughed. 'When I heard from Bill that you were coming to dinner, Kinawa and I spent half the night putting my hair in curlers. She even plucked my eyebrows.'

'You shouldn't have,' I said. 'Forget what I said about putting your hair down.'

'No, no.' She was almost shy as she held my hand across the table, clutching it, squeezing and interlacing her fingers with mine, as she explained, 'I wanted you to see me as a young woman, not a schoolgirl. I wanted to make you notice me.'

'You certainly succeeded!'

'It was such fun,' she laughed. 'Kinawa had lots of American magazines with coloured pictures, and we chose the hairstyle we thought would – well,' shyly again, 'the one we thought would please you most.'

'My sweet Aleena.' My voice was husky, picturing the two girls sitting on the edge of the bed in the small room

229

which she said they shared, trying to copy hairstyles from magazines. 'You and Kinawa must be very close?'

'We are. We've sworn an oath of eternal friendship, in the presence of my holy man. Each of us will always do what the other asks.'

'But will you keep the oath?' I laughed, I didn't mean to cause any offence.

'Life oaths are a part of our lives. Now I'm going to let my hair down.'

'Don't bother – please.'

'I want to.' She untwisted her fingers from mine, saying, 'I just want to do anything that makes you happy.' With that she walked out of the room, saying, 'I won't be a second. I only have to shake it out.'

As I waited, I told Mr Fresno, the band leader, that we had to leave shortly, gave him a five-shilling tip, and asked him to play one particular tune for our last dance.

She returned to the floor, her black hair framing her oval face, the rest falling over her shoulders, looking so beautiful it almost made me gasp, and we started to dance as the band struck up a tune that had become a favourite during the war, 'Goodnight, Sweetheart'.

'Sentimental slush,' I admitted as her cheek brushed mine, 'but I chose it because it's got such a gentle rhythm.'

'It's heaven. This'll be *our* tune. If only I could spend the night dancing instead of having to say "goodnight, sweet-heart" so early.'

'I know. But we'll do it again. I'll manage somehow. Perhaps next month.'

'Please try.' And then she asked me without warning, but a little shyly, 'Have you ever been to bed with Paula Reece?'

'What a question for a young girl to ask!' I tried to laugh off the question.

'A young woman, not a young girl.'

'Sorry!'

'Well, have you?'

'The answer, as it happens, is no.'

230

'I'm so glad.' She squeezed my hand, then said, shyly, 'You've just told me that your mother was seventeen when she married your father. Right?'

'What's that got to do with Paula Reece?' I tried to laugh, but choked as I spoke.

'We're the same age as they were when – well, would you like to go to bed with me?'

'Really, Aleena!' I tried to be 'pompous' but I felt a tingle. 'Please don't – I *am* your doctor – and Bill Robins – you shouldn't be saying things like that, even as a joke.'

'I was half teasing because I'm so happy.' She was still holding my hand. 'But after all, Kit, most island girls – and most of them at the college, and even your mother for that matter – have learned about love-making at my age!'

'Well, don't talk about it, darling.' I pretended to be severe.

'I just thought –' she looked very beautiful as she spoke, 'that it would be nice for *me* if you were the first.'

'It would for me too. Very, very much, because you're a girl in a million. There, I had to tell you.'

'Thank you. Be patient,' and she added gravely, talking rather like Tiare did, 'I will see what can be arranged.'

I looked at my watch again. 'Darling Aleena, let's see what happens,' I said. 'It's time for bed. I don't want the headmistress reporting you – or me.'

I paid the bill, still humming the tune, and we walked out into the warm evening air, hand in hand. The college was only a few steps along Hallgate, in the opposite direction from the Southern Cross Hotel. As we reached the gates of the school, she asked, 'Will you be coming back soon?'

'I hope so. Unless Doctor Reid flies himself.'

'If you do – ?'

'Yes?'

'Can we do the same again? Dance? Only this time, maybe we could have dinner together first – it'd make the evening last longer.'

'Of course, if that's what you want.'

'Promise?'

'I promise.'

'When do you think – ?'

As we stood, with her leaning up against the gates, pressing my body against hers, I was trying to plan out possible dates in my mind.

'The next supply of drugs is due here in early December,' I said. 'I should collect them around the end of the first week in December.'

'A whole four weeks to wait! It's so long,' she cried.

'It'll pass quickly. I'll be counting the minutes.'

'So will I!' she whispered and pushed the gates back. Very naturally, as the church clock started chiming eleven, she stood even closer to me on tiptoe, put her arms round me, and said, 'You're wonderful, Kit.' And without another word she cupped my face in her hands and kissed me on the lips, her lips gently parted, then touched my mouth with one finger and whispered, 'Try not to kiss anyone until I see you again.'

'I won't. I promise. See you in December.'

'Until then it's "goodnight, sweetheart". That's our song isn't it? Early December. I can hardly wait.'

15

All that following month the rumours of possible war between Japan and America increased. We on Koraloona knew very little, except on the rare occasions when we had visitors, such as on the day Surgeon-Commander Ronnie Serpell announced on the radio sked that he would like to visit the island the following day, arriving by frigate.

This must have been during the latter half of November. Serpell, smart in white ducks, with golden scrolls decorating the peak of his cap, jumped ashore on the pier to be welcomed by Doc Reid who was wearing long trousers as a mark of the semi-official nature of the visit. The commander, whom I had met of course in Sanderstown, had indicated on the radio that he wanted to discuss 'military matters' over lunch, and that he would be returning immediately afterwards. As soon as he arrived, therefore, he asked to see the cottage hospital.

I was there treating a patient, and Serpell said, 'Hello, Masters. Good to see you again.' And turning to Alec, said, 'I'm only here to put you in the political picture, Alec.' And as I noticed Alec's puzzled look, Serpell added with a laugh, 'Japan's political picture. Might be a good idea if you've got an extra place at the table for Doctor Masters.'

'Sure,' cried Alec, pleased, I think, to have someone else around if the world situation, of which he was more or less ignorant, was going to be discussed. Not that Serpell was in a hurry to discuss politics.

'So this is your famous Koraloona hospital.' He walked round, and was introduced to Miss Sowerby. 'Not very much spare equipment, is there?'

I agreed.

'You've got oxygen and carbon dioxide cylinders, I see, and a couple of masks.'

'Yes, but still not much,' retorted Alec. 'Remember, we're only a wee mission, not a large government department. What would we want with a deal of new equipment?'

'Nothing,' said Serpell cheerfully. 'You're quite right. What's for lunch?'

We went up to Reid's bungalow, drank a couple of pink gins for which, to my amusement, Serpell brought a bottle of Plymouth, much in demand by the Navy; he was taking no chances with his favourite drink. After Bubble and Squeak had decorously served a lunch built around a steamed fish stuffed with shrimp, Serpell, whose tubby frame and round face accurately reflected his cheerful attitude to life, including good food, explained, 'I thought it was time I came to see you, Alec. Apart from the pleasure of a day off from the routine paperwork – I seem to use my pen more than my scalpel these days – I thought I ought to outline what these bloody Japs are up to. I hope – in my heart I'm sure – they won't start a war with us, but you never know.'

'It's unthinkable!' cried Alec.

'Because of the embargos imposed by the Americans on oil and other strategic raw materials?' I asked.

Serpell nodded. 'Exactly. There's Malaya, Singapore, the Dutch East Indies – they're the riches which the Japanese need but can't get their hands on.'

'But are there any signs of war?'

'Not signs of war – but signs that peace is breaking up.'

'What's the difference?' Reid persisted

'It's the way the Japanese are behaving. They've been cornered – and like any rat that's driven into a corner, there's always the instinctive urge to attack to save yourself, to jump for the throat. They *might* launch an attack on Malaya and the Indies – just to grab their oil, rubber and tin. And if they did – well, they could never *win*, but there could be a hell of a naval scrap.'

'It wouldn't have any effect on us?' Alec was asking a question, not making a statement. 'It's too far away!'

'Not directly. But General Tojo, who gained absolute control of the Japanese government last month, and Admiral Yamamoto, are power-hungry bastards, who will never listen to reason. They could cause a hell of a lot of trouble in Malaya,' said Serpell. 'Yamamoto is a great believer in aircraft carriers. He's now got six fast carriers that can deploy over four hundred aeroplanes. Many of them can launch torpedos that run in shallow water. They're an entirely new device and could sink the biggest ship afloat. Whitehall seems to scoff at Japanese planes, but I've been told that their carrier-based Zero fighters are faster than anything we've got!'

As Bubble and Squeak handed round neat Scotch as a liqueur after lunch, and Serpell glanced at his watch, Reid asked half humorously, his Scottish burr more evident than usual, 'What's the purpose of this visit, then, Ronnie? Are ye trying to scare us?'

'Frighten you? No.' Serpell studied his small stubby shot glass. 'Let's say, put you in the picture. So that if – only if – there *are* any surprises, you'll be ready to absorb any shock. If there's a war, it's unlikely to affect you in Koraloona directly, but still, the east coasts of Japan, Malaya and the Indies all face the Pacific, and though it's a big ocean, the ripples can spread a long, long way.'

'And the Americans?' I asked. 'Do you think they might become involved?'

Serpell shook his head. 'Not a hope. Too far from Japan. Mind you, Tojo and his gang are smarting under what they consider to be an American insult to Japan, and I'm not saying that Yamamoto wouldn't love to have a crack at them, but they can't be such bloody fools as to do that.'

Serpell left after lunch, but a few days later Reid cornered me in the dispensary and said, 'You know, Kit, I've been thinking about Serpell's visit. I dinna think it portends catastrophe, but knowing how governments work – especially when a wee problem like money doesn't count – they'll be stock-piling on drugs. We'd better do the same – just in case we find they've none to spare for us. Get Miss Sowerby to draw up a list, then you recheck the list and double it. Then send a list of what ye want on the radio sked, fly over and collect it. Best get a move on, before they hide what we might need. Nellie's having an engine check but Jim Wilson says he'll have her ready in three or four days. Make a firm date.'

'Don't you want to fly over – and have a night out?'

Reid shook his head. 'Nae, Laddie,' with his sardonic grin. 'I'm scairt – of being shot down by the Japs.'

Miss Sowerby made the list, I amended it, added a few items which might be needed for my special polio treatment – including a new cream which helped to make physiotherapy treatment less painful on swollen joints – and some more blankets for my 'polio strips' as I called them, which by now were stinking with over-use.

And of course there was something else! Commander Serpell's office, after a short delay, radioed that everything would be ready by December 6, a Saturday. And that meant that, if I could let Aleena know, we could spend the evening dancing together.

I didn't dare to contact her at college on the sked. It would be all over Koraloona if I did – dating the daughter of a princess! But there was a better way, simpler too.

Bill Robins was due in port in a couple of days on his way back to Sanderstown. He said he could carry a letter for me. The only thing I felt bound to do was to tell him its contents. During these three years we had become close and he *was* Aleena's unofficial guardian. So I would tell him exactly the truth: that we both wanted to spend the evening of the sixth together, that he had my word that I would behave like a 'gentleman'. In other words he had nothing to fear from an evening to which both Aleena and I had been looking forward for the past month.

'I thought you'd get round to this one evening,' said Robins towards the end of a particularly cheerful evening, 'But don't get too deeply involved, Kit.'

'There's nothing to it,' I assured him, 'Only that I like to have a chance for a dance with a pretty girl.'

'You miss Lucy, don't you?'

'No,' I said honestly. 'Well – in a way, I suppose, but not really. This one – she's different.'

'Be careful,' Bill warned me again. 'And don't hurt anyone – including yourself.'

The evening had been merry because, as always now happened when Bill was in port, he dined with me; and all evening it rained heavily which, curiously enough, gave us an added sense of comfort, eating and drinking snugly in the bungalow while the pelting rain drummed on the corrugated-iron roof.

Jason came round, and drank more than his fair share. After dinner too, Jim Wilson popped in, drenched to the skin.

'I heard the noise,' he said. 'And as I wanted to tell you that I've finished Nellie's engine check, I thought I'd cadge a free drink on a rainy night, especially as I was on Penal Island with supplies earlier in the day.'

'How's your chum, Mana?' asked Bill.

'Alive,' replied Wilson. 'God, he's an unwholesome brute – more Japanese than Samoan, and this morning he was boasting that one day Japan would rule the Orient.'

Then in came Father Pringle, calling, 'I came in because I saw the Light!'

'Literally or figuratively?' asked Jason.

'How about a short one for the road?' asked Father Pringle.

We sat talking and drinking until eleven and only stopped then because Bill had to catch the tide shortly after midnight, his usual sailing time.

'It sounds rough outside,' I said to Bill. 'Are you sure you'll be able to sail tonight?'

'You landlubbers!' he laughed. 'You always think that rain means a wreck. A little rain calms the waves.'

'I'll walk you down,' I said.

'Me too!' cried the others.

'In this rain? Don't be daft,' said Bill.

But we all did walk down to the pier, said our slightly tipsy goodbyes and saw him on board. When we reached Main Street by the pier and started up the short hill towards both the cottage hospital and my bungalow, a shadowy figure appeared through the rain – a female figure, judging by the voluminous, old-fashioned raincoat. It could only be a woman.

'Why! What on earth are you doing out at this time of night and in all this rain, Miss Sowerby?' asked Jason with a laugh. 'You'll catch your death of cold; and anyway it's time ladies were in bed.'

'I had to treat a new patient.' Miss Sowerby ignored Purvis and spoke to me. 'And so I decided to take a breath of fresh air,' adding almost defiantly, 'I like rain anyway. Goodnight.'

As she stood in the rain I asked, 'What was the matter with the patient? Who was it?'

'A little girl was bitten by an adder.'

'You should have sent for me.'

'I heard you all in your bungalow, Doctor. It was nothing to worry about. Adder bites don't kill you. I gave the little girl an antidote injection and then scraped away the skin round the fang marks and put in a little permanganate of potash and bound it up. She was a brave little thing. I told her to stay in the hospital for the night, so I'll go back and spend the night in the ward in case she's frightened.'

'Thank you again. Thank you very much.' I suddenly asked her with a smile, 'Do you ever drink, Miss Sowerby?'

Almost blushing she admitted primly, 'An occasional port and lemon. My father always said that it was the only alcohol a lady should be allowed to drink.'

'Then come and have one, Miss Sowerby. This is the time to take off your wet raincoat. Come and join us all in the bungalow.'

She hesitated, looking at the others with a certain – not exactly distaste, but doubt. Finally she said after some more hesitation, 'Well, thank you, Doctor. I did feel a shiver in my bones. I will. Just one small glass may do me good.'

'It *will* do you good, Miss Sowerby,' said Father Pringle. 'A drop of the good stuff never interfered with the work of the Lord.'

'That's not what my father said,' retorted Miss Sowerby sharply.

'All right,' I said, remembering how my father had always warned me against whisky and gin but considered port respectable.

'Well, port and lemon's okay,' said Jim Wilson.

'Of course it is,' cried Jason Purvis. 'Let me take your arm and help you to the bungalow.'

'It will not be necessary, thank you,' she said frigidly. Once inside I poured out a very modest glass of port with a dash of lemonade in it. She sipped it gingerly, almost suspiciously, and as she took off her shawl I said involuntarily, 'Why, Miss Sowerby, you're wearing short sleeves!'

'I'm sorry.' She sounded flustered. 'It was warm and I never thought I would meet anyone at this time of the night.'

'But there's nothing to be worried about. You should wear short sleeves all the time,' I said. 'So much cooler.'

'And if I may say so,' Purvis was beginning to slur his words, 'you have very beautiful and delicate wrists.'

'Thank you.' Miss Sowerby got up, blushing a little, and made for the door. 'And thank you, Doctor, for the drink.'

With that she left and, as I heard her footsteps walking down the hill to her cottage behind the hospital, Purvis said, 'They are damned beautiful wrists! I'll have to find out if she's got ankles to match.'

'She's a good sort,' I yawned, ready for bed, 'and one day she'll become really human.'

'Care to bet?' chuckled Jim Wilson.

Three days later, just before I was ready to fly off to Sanderstown for supplies on a beautiful Saturday morning, Alec Reid came in, and cried, 'A wee girl with polio spasms in the chest has just come in. She's having great difficulty in breathing. But we can keep her going until the morning.'

'You've got the iron lung?' I asked.

'No. It's being used. But I'll get on the sked right away and order another. If you fly back tomorrow bright and early we should be able to give her treatment soon enough.'

'I wonder if I could get back tonight?' I was thinking not only of a patient in distress, but also of a damsel in distress! How terrible if I had to give up our night in Sanderstown. Fortunately, Alec said, 'Not possible, Laddie. It always takes all afternoon to sign the forms and collect the supplies. Even Miss Sowerby says she'll be all right till morning. So if ye leave around eight, land about nine, it should be all right.'

Relieved – especially as I knew that Doc was right, the formalities would probably make it impossible to fly back that same night – I set off for Sanderstown at eleven o'clock. All went well, my flight enlivened by the tingling excitement of meeting Aleena again, and as I prepared to land around noon, I flew the Gloster over the city and an extraordinary thing happened. Out of the clear blue sky two British fighter planes zoomed up towards me, waggling their wings, and came so close to my tiny fragile aircraft that I could see their faces.

They made one thing abundantly clear: 'Bugger off! Stay away from the naval base.' Obviously because of the jitters over Japan, the naval base, with all its warships lying at anchor, was off limits for civilian planes. It was my fault, because I hadn't bothered to radio the flying club that I was on my way. They knew I was coming anyway, and there was no air traffic in the sleepy little club on a Saturday morning. However I took the hint and turned west to the club airfield. The two British fighter planes flew lazily above, like seagulls wheeling, until I had landed.

'Military secrets,' said the manager of the club sardonically when I bumped towards the edge of the field. 'All the warships have had their names painted out, yet we've been flying over the town – and the base – for years now *and* know the names of every ship in harbour. It doesn't make any difference. You going into town? I'll give you a lift if you like.'

'Thanks.'

The man dropped me at the Southern Cross Hotel in Piccadilly, just below the green of the Savannah and its statue of Horatio Sanders. It seemed a good idea to get rid of my modest luggage before I visited the base and as I made for the reception desk a boy took my small overnight bag while I walked across the cool marble-type floor with its potted palms and gently trembling fans suspended from the ceiling.

'You have a room booked for me,' I said to the desk clerk. 'Doctor Masters.'

'Yes, sir.' He banged on a bell and told a boy, 'Take the doctor to Room 201.' And as I made for the wide stairs, he called after me, 'Oh Doctor – sorry. There's a letter for you.'

'For me?' My first thought was that Commander Serpell might perhaps want to change plans to pick up the lung or the drugs. But the letter wasn't from the base. When I tore open the pale blue envelope I read a short and tender message:

'Kit, I will meet you in the lobby at six. Longing to see you. I am so excited I can hardly wait.

'Love.'

And it was signed – not 'Aleena', not even with an 'A', but with a small heart pierced by a Cupid's arrow. Sentimental I know, but as I read it again I felt my heart pound faster.

I tipped the boy a shilling, put my white sharkskin jacket and spare trousers and a shirt on a hanger in the wardrobe, had a quick shower, then took a taxi to the base. All I wanted to do was get through the hours until six o'clock as quickly as possible.

At the base I had to fill in a form to be given a pass which was made out in my name before I could see Serpell.

'Sorry about the red tape,' he said. 'But the Japs are behaving like mad dogs. Even threatening the Americans! And we've heard that a large Jap convoy is sailing towards the southern tip of Indo-China.'

He indicated the position with a big wooden pointer on a huge war map. 'Hope they don't decide to go any further.' He slid the pointer down towards the Kra isthmus and then the northern tip of Malaya. 'Nothing there. I flew to Khota Bahru once on a proving flight from Hong Kong when I was stationed there.' He showed me where it was on the map. 'The resident was a jolly chap called Baker. He had the only pull-and-push lavatory in the entire province.' Serpell's tubby frame shook with laughter as he remembered. 'It was a great talking-point. But I hardly think the Japs will invade Khota Bahru just to have a good crap!'

I checked on the supply list and at Serpell's insistence returned with him to the Officers' Club for lunch. It was such a beautiful, peaceful spot! Over pink gins at the bar, I watched a cricket match as the commander introduced me to several people whose names meant nothing to me. But just as he signed the chit and we were about to go into the dining-room, an American officer approached Serpell and saluted – something you don't do to an officer who isn't wearing a cap! However, he said, 'Pardon me, Commander, but could you give me five minutes after lunch. I gotta coupla messages you might like to see.'

'Sure, any time.'

'Thank you, sir, see you later!' The man, young and good-looking with blond hair, saluted again.

'Americans in British territory?' I was amused.

'He's a navy lootenant,' Serpell pronounced the rank in the American style with a grin, 'on a courtesy visit. Says he managed to wangle a trip to have a look at the island because he's married to a girl who used to live here. Courtesy my eye! My guess is he's just given our base the once-over. It's amazing how worried the Yanks are. Maybe Roosevelt knows something we don't.'

I was waiting in the hotel lounge at ten to six – a good job I was early, for so was she, arriving five minutes before the hour struck. She walked through the revolving doors towards me with a sensuous grace, and as I got up to greet her she faced me with a perfectly natural gesture, ran towards me, put her arms round me, kissed me lovingly but with decorum, and whispered, 'It's been the longest month of my life. I never thought I could miss anyone as much as I've missed you.'

'Me too.' I held her at arm's length. 'Let me look at you.'

'People will think you're crazy – ' she laughed.

In that month away I had at times thought of her as the girl I first treated when she was at school, but now she looked old enough to be 'escorted'. Her hair was again up.

'Yes, Kinawa was working last night,' she laughed huskily when she saw me looking. She was wearing a white and blue silk dress, very simple, just below the knee, with

242

short sleeves and with a blue belt. It was the first time I had seen her in silk stockings, unobtainable in Britain as I knew from Clare's letters.

'Black market from the American destroyer that came in recently,' she said. 'I know I shouldn't, but for you – '

'It makes the legs look even more exquisite,' I said, but there was something else that puzzled me about her, a different look, an older look – not old, not really old of course, but eighteen or nineteen instead of seventeen or eighteen. A subtle something she was wearing.

'It's these!' She laughed and pointed to her shoes. 'High heels.'

'Of course!' I had never seen her in high heels before and they not only made her look taller, they added to her years as well as to her inches. They gave her that grown-up look.

'Now you're an elegant young lady,' I said as we sat down and she refused a drink, saying, 'I don't want to drink too much too soon. It might spoil the evening. I want to make the evening last for ever.' She had a low voice, an inviting voice, a little husky, sensuous rather than sexy.

'Yes, a young lady,' I repeated. 'Now the young men in Sanderstown will all be after you. Taking you out – gallivanting – '

'Because of the shoes?'

'They help!'

'In that case when you kiss me goodbye at eleven o'clock I'll take my shoes off, give them to you, and you can keep them and give them back to me when we next meet,' she laughed. 'Oh Kit, I'm so happy!'

'And the stockings?'

'If you like.'

'How did you get them?' I was thinking of the young American officer I'd met earlier in the day and what a young sex-starved man like him would hope for if he gave a pretty girl half a dozen pairs of silk stockings.

'Kinawa got six pairs – and gave three to me. Her mother and father took her on board when another American destroyer held a cocktail party two weeks ago.'

Finally she did have a gimlet, begging me, 'Only a single gin, please, and a lot of lime,' and when she had sipped it, as though to give her courage, she held out the long fingers on one hand, the nails unpolished but carefully manicured, and laid the hand on the table, asking without words for me to touch her, just as she had done when entwining our fingers on the table at the Café de Paris the last time.

'It's so long since I've seen you,' she said almost a little desperately, 'and we have to behave like – ' with a laugh – 'like doctor and patient. Is there nowhere I can kiss you? Nowhere private?'

I looked around. 'Of course I want to kiss you too,' I said. 'Of course I do.' My voice was as husky as hers. 'But look around you!'

'We've been dreaming of this meeting for a month,' her voice was almost a moan. 'Kinawa and I have talked over and over about what we'd do, how we'd fall into each other's arms – ' With a faint smile she added. 'You know how girls talk in bed before they fall asleep. I dreamed of you. Naughty dreams – even sometimes – ' she didn't have to put it into words, I knew what she meant. 'It was so lovely sometimes. And now here we are – surrounded by potted palms – it's unfair to a girl.'

'It's unfair to a man!' I squeezed her hand. 'Imagine what I'm feeling.'

'I can imagine it,' she said gravely. 'Oh Kit! If only I could do something to help you – as well as myself. You know what I mean, I've been reading all the latest books and besides, island girls – '

'You're not just an island girl. You're the daughter of a princess. And I promised Bill Robins – '

'That's not a fair promise for anyone to ask you to make. We're both young and we're both – well, in love, I hope.'

'Maybe we are,' I said gently. 'But thousands of young people fall in love every day – and they don't jump into bed right away, darling. I want to – perhaps more than you do.'

'Oh yes, oh yes!'

'But – we can't. Not yet,' I said. 'Don't think I haven't

been dreaming of you all this month, of taking you into my arms. And wondering if one day you'd like to be my wife. If you agree, and if your mother gives her consent, then of course we won't bother to wait for the marriage licence before we go to bed together. But for the moment, darling Aleena – '

'I know!' and with a sad smile added, 'but – at least a kiss. Lovers are kissing each other all over the world at this very moment.'

'But where?'

Squeezing my hand even harder she whispered, 'Can't we go to your room – just to kiss?'

'No!' I cried sharply.

'Just to kiss, I promise!' she begged me.

'I'd love to. But it's not *your* promise I'm thinking about. It's mine. When we dance later, I'll hold you in my arms – closely. But it's too much to ask of human nature to take you into my bedroom and then – do nothing.'

'But why?' She stamped her foot under the table in frustration. 'I just want to hold you in my arms, to let you tell me that you love me. I won't tempt you, I promise.'

'You couldn't help tempting me – just by being close to me alone in a bedroom.'

'But I won't. I'm Polynesian. Polynesians make love when they want to.'

Then hesitatingly, as though confiding in a doctor, she said, 'And if we can't, if there's a proper reason and yet we're in love – then – well' – she gave a tiny trill of shy laughter – 'well I'm sure men do the same as we do when the lights are out and we're alone.'

'I know,' I said. 'But it's a poor substitute.'

'That's why in the islands, when we are forbidden by the holy men to take a man as a lover, we don't like to see him suffer from frustration, so we lend him one of our best friends to give him pleasure. It's better than – '

'And whom do you propose for me?' I ordered another gimlet and then I looked her right in the eyes after a long pause, before she had time to reply.

245

'My sweet Aleena,' I said finally, 'I want to take you in my arms every bit as much as you want me. I'm mad about you. But if you *promise* that we won't even *sit* on the bed –' then almost roughly I said, 'Come on, let's go to my room – just for five minutes, understand?' I signed the chit for the drinks and I heard her give a gasp as she stood up.

I had kept the key in my pocket. We walked the two flights of stairs in silence. I opened the door, let her in first, latched the door behind me, and then, she was in my arms kissing me wildly at one moment, riffling her hands through my hair, and the next, pressing my back so that she had to feel the size of me in my trousers. She said nothing, just moaned, then opened her lips until our tongues touched. I stroked the outside of her dress, feeling the tight nipples under it, thinking inconsequentially that she was wearing no bra and then, still standing kissing each other gently, she gasped, 'I know we mustn't do it but just do one thing. I want you to look at me – something to remember me by until we're allowed –' and before I could stop her she had lifted her skirt. She was wearing nothing underneath and I was stroking her long brown legs and there in front of me were her beautiful thighs and at the heart of them the large damp patch of jet black.

'Oh no!' I groaned.

'Don't. I want you to keep your promise but let me see you – and then –'

She helped me to undo the buttons of my trousers and then stroked me gently, kissing me too until there was no point in touching any more and then she dashed to the bathroom and I heard the tap squelch as she washed her hands.

Released from the prison of frustration I almost laughed as she was washing in the bathroom – not for love but because for the moment I was thinking, My God! It's the first time in my life that a girl has done that to me.

And when she returned she said, gravely, 'It was love, real love, Kit. I knew it wasn't the real thing and I did promise not to let you make love to me, but I'll never let you suffer like that again. And I wanted us both to have a memory of each other when you go back tomorrow.'

'Thank you.' I still had in my mind the picture of the thick, glistening, strong black hair between her thighs.

'I won't forget. One day,' I spoke thickly, feeling myself beginning to grow strong again, 'we'll be lovers. And again, thank you, darling. But my dear Aleena – what about you?'

'Couldn't you tell that I was,' she searched shyly for the right word, 'contented?' Adding, 'As soon as I touched you I didn't *need* touching.'

Almost amused, but feeling very tender towards this lovely flower, I noticed the absence of any explicit words. She was half girl, half woman. Fully grown sexually, fully informed from the magazines that she and Kinawa read. She regarded it as perfectly natural to enjoy erotic waking dreams with a happy climax under the sheets, yet she was half-girl.

'You shouldn't have done this,' I said to her, 'but I'm glad you did.'

'It didn't hurt anyone and it is a woman's greatest pleasure to please a man.'

I couldn't help laughing and said, 'You certainly pleased me.' As she smoothed her dress and retouched her lips, she said first in a studied voice, 'I'm in love with you, darling Kit, and the next time I return to Koraloona I'm going to ask my holy man when we can get married.'

Before I could, with a certain irritation, even think of saying, 'Tell the holy man to mind his own business!' she threw her arms around me, didn't kiss me but cried, 'Gosh! It's wonderful! And I'm so hungry I could eat a horse.'

I couldn't help laughing. She was a beautiful girl trying to grow up and yet very young in one way.

'How about two big steaks?' I asked.

'With lots of *pommes frites*. We were taught some French cooking last week.'

'You shall have them at the Apéritif Grill. That French enough for you?'

Her laughter was infectious. 'But first another drink and

247

after dinner back to the old Café de Paris, for a bottle of champagne. What kind did they give us?'

'It was Taittinger.'

'I remember. It tasted wonderful. Then I can order a bottle with a bit more authority!'

The evening passed like a tender dream, without any false moments to mar its exquisite happiness. I had booked a table at the night-club, in my own name of course, and when we reached it after dinner the head waiter even remembered, saying, 'Good evening, Doctor. Your usual bottle of Taittinger?'

'You see,' Aleena sat down opposite me, 'you're already famous. You'll end up in the famous doctors' street – Harley Street.'

'Never. My home is Koraloona. It's not everyone who has the luck to fall in love both with the place he works in and the most beautiful girl in it.'

I was thinking that, even if I *wanted* later in life to go to live in London, what would happen if I tried to transplant this tropical flower to the fogs and rain of England. How criminal it would be! She would wither, pine for the sun and the sea, be terrified of the bustling traffic. No, no, if – no, *when* – I married Aleena, I would be content to be a big fish in a small and beautiful pond.

There were only a few people dancing. In one corner a couple of young American officers, obviously from the visiting destroyer, were drinking, and I could see one of them eyeing Aleena, and finally he came up to our table and said, quite politely, to me, 'Sir, could I ask your permission to have just one dance with this lady?'

Before I could answer, Aleena looked at him and said, 'I'm very flattered, but you see – '

'Sure, I get it,' he answered. 'But gee, ma'am, you're a mighty beautiful young lady.'

'Thank you,' she said prettily, as he walked away.

That was our only interruption. The evening ended much as our first encounter had finished, beautifully gentle, subtly sensual, dancing cheek to cheek, holding each other more tightly than we had done on the first evening, and finally, back at the gates of the college, kissing even more passionately than we had earlier.

'I want you so badly,' she whispered, 'but at least, beloved, we'll meet again soon. It's already the end of the first week in December, and soon Kinawa and I will be sailing back to Koraloona for the Christmas hols.'

'Of course!' And I loved the way she said 'hols'.

'How long do I have to wait?' I asked.

'Only two weeks this time. And then I'll be in your arms – *somehow*! Leave it to me.'

'And Kinawa? It seems an odd time for her to leave her mother and father – at Christmas.'

'They won't be back at Sanderstown in time. Their oldest son lives in California, and they have two children, so this time Grannie's going to California to spoil them. Will I ever be a grannie?'

Laughing, always the easiest way to lessen tension, I said with assumed gravity, 'I don't know if I'm any good with children. But I'm certainly going to enjoy making them.'

'You do say the funniest things.'

All this time we had been talking outside the college gates which faced on to Hallgate, with the college a few yards behind, and way behind it, the tall, stark outlines of the Catholic church in its churchyard. As we prepared to leave a few minutes before eleven, she said again, almost shyly, 'I want you to have something – a keepsake.' She was twisting a ring from her finger.

'You mustn't,' I said.

'I'm going to.' She took off the ring, showed it under the lamplight, though I had noticed it before, three separate circles of gold like the links of a chain, so that when she pushed the ring on to my little finger – the only one it would fit – they seemed to slide round each other, each time in a different shape, with a different one overlapping the other.

'It's a Russian ring,' she explained. 'It belonged to my grandfather, who gave it to Grandma. She left it to me in her will.'

'It belonged to Gauguin?' I was fascinated.

She nodded. 'You wear it – and promise me one day that, when we have babies, you will leave it to our daughter.'

'I promise,' I said. 'And now, darling, off to bed – your bed. And in only two weeks we'll meet again.'

'I shall always love you, Kit,' she whispered as she kissed me and closed the gates behind her.

'Me too,' I promised her before I walked back along Hallgate and into Piccadilly.

At the Southern Cross Hotel I had a large Scotch and soda at the bar, then made my way up to bed – no longer a lonely, impersonal room, but one in which the love of my life had stood almost naked in front of me, leaving me an image to remember as I lay down to sleep.

16

Nothing could have been more tranquil than that Sunday morning. Lazily thinking of the lovely evening, I woke, ordered toast and coffee in my room at about seven o'clock. When it arrived I stood by my window. I could see Piccadilly Circus with its pretty arcades, and the Savannah, with the sun stretching golden fingers on the early morning tennis players. A file of girls – younger than Aleena – were leaving their boarding school near the hospital to attend Mass. All dressed in white, they carried posies so that no unseemly movement of swinging arms would mar their sedate walk as the nun in charge led them to morning Mass.

The shops presented their blank Sunday morning faces, unobtainable goods behind sunstreaked glass and crudely lettered signs proclaiming CLOSED. To the right, where the bottom of Piccadilly ran into Hallgate, I caught a glimpse of a man who looked like the American sailor I had seen at the Café de Paris. He leant against the façade of the night-club, trying to adjust himself to the morning light after what must have been a monumental hangover. I felt so happy, so content with life, so much in love, that I almost shouted out a cheery 'Good morning!'

The only visible work being done that placid Sunday morning was at a garage near the hospital beyond Aleena's college, where a Samoan mechanic was tinkering with a wrench inside the raised bonnet of an ancient Studebaker. The Southern Cross Hotel itself was coming slowly, reluctantly, to life. Outside the front door, Charlie the porter was unenthusiastically beating the doormat on the pavement, raising a cloud of dust. For the rest, all was still. Nothing seemed amiss as I poured myself out another cup of coffee and looked out of the window. Then suddenly my eyes turned to the sky to judge the weather for my flight back – with the lung for the little girl whose existence I had almost forgotten during the evening. The weather looked perfect – nothing more ominous than a few cumulus clouds like a line of fluffy pillows in the sky.

Then came an unknown sound – and an unknown sight – which puzzled me. The sound resembled the buzzing of bees or hornets; the sight some high, black specks – the type you see when your liver is out of sorts. People in Hallgate and Piccadilly looked up almost idly, in no way put out until the noise started getting louder and took on a more ominous quality.

I heard a voice, it might have been that of Charlie the porter, shout to someone I couldn't see, 'Bloody disgrace, holding exercises, making all that noise, on a Sunday when most people want to lie in.' Yes, of course, they were planes. Charlie was right! Some people stood still, straining their eyes, gaping out to sea over which, in a few seconds, the faint black spots had materialised unmistakably into planes.

By the time the first men and women started screaming, the planes had reached a piercing shriek. Still some distance out to sea they seemed to soar up higher in the sky in the same formation as a flock of geese, pointing their

251

noses upward until they reached the top of their climb, and then were suddenly in screaming descent.

A strange kind of paralysis seized me. I was so fascinated by the sight I could do nothing – not that there was much I could do from the second floor of the Southern Cross. But then the scream became hellish – the only word I can think of. And then I could actually see, in the clear blue sky, bombs which seemed to fall with contrasting slowness out of the aircraft, dropping almost indolently, as the planes shrieked over the rooftops and were gone. I can only remember muttering to myself, 'Dive bombers!' and then 'Christ! Aleena!' But it was as though I were detached, a part of another world – that world of the blitz back in England, of which I had read so much.

As the first bombs hit their targets, I instinctively threw myself flat on the floor – just in time, for half the wall of my bedroom – in fact as I learned later almost the entire front of the hotel – collapsed, hit by a bomb that landed almost in front of us, in the middle of Piccadilly. It felt – I felt – as though everything was reeling drunkenly. My mouth was filled with plaster dust and acrid fumes. I tried to find the bathroom, forcing open a broken, jammed door as another explosion rocked the building. I managed to get to the washbasin, but as I turned on the tap it blew up from some hidden force and a column of water shot towards the ceiling, drenching my boxer shorts, the only clothes I was wearing. I staggered out, drenched, scrabbled along the floor on my hands and knees, searching for some clothes – *my* clothes. I knew that I had to get out of this room in case the damage to the structure brought the ceiling down. Already a hole gaped above my bed.

Suddenly, again without warning, a glaring light showed me where my trousers were in the wreckage of what had been my small wardrobe. It was daylight, of course, but this was a different, searing light, one strong enough to blind a man had he looked at it directly. And it was accompanied by an almost unbearable roar – as though the light itself was speaking. I realised that a petrol tank must have exploded at the docks.

I managed to find my slacks and moccasins, but there was no sign of my shirt or jacket. I would look for them later – if there was to be a 'later'.

Somehow I managed to pull my trousers on, then slid into my moccasins, and stood swaying, my face wet with water from the smashed tap, but also with the sweat of terror and – though I didn't realise it at first – with blood. I held on to my end of the bed and looked out of the torn wall, just as my senses absorbed another noise, and this time it wasn't an explosion. It held a more sinister note, a long-drawn-out kind of whistle, as though a giant was audibly drawing in his breath.

I knew from newspaper reports what it was. The dive bombers had gone, now was the time for high-level bombing. The whistling sound increased in intensity until again I thought my ear drums would burst, and then the sound ended abruptly with the crump of an explosion. In one split second of lucid vision, as I clutched a girder, looking through the hole where the wall should have been, I saw the statue of Horatio Sanders jump into the air and, as though in slow motion, stay up there for a few seconds, then disintegrate into a million pieces as bricks, mortar, lath, plaster, shot upwards with the symmetry of a gigantic fan, only it was not a flat fan, but one in depth so that, almost as I saw it, rubble hurtled into every direction including mine. The corrugated-iron roof rattled under a shower of stones. The blast actually lifted me, as painlessly as though on a cushion, out of what was left of my bedroom into the landing. It was the most eerie sensation I have ever experienced. I *floated* out of my bedroom – the door had long since gone – for twenty feet or so, floating on a cushion of blast, which must have been formed by compressed air, I suppose. I was hardly hurt, the movement was so 'gentle'; it was as though unseen hands had carried me from one spot to another.

I struggled to make my way down the two flights of stairs,

thinking, I must find Aleena! The stairs were clogged with girders, broken in parts, but I managed to climb down. As I stumbled, I passed a man making his way warily against the far wall of the Z-shaped stairway. His pyjamas were spattered with blood and his progress had a certain curious dignity about it, as though searching for a rational explanation for an unseemly nightmare. At least that was what I thought at first. But he was climbing down the stairs carefully because he was carrying a cup in his hand and didn't want to drop it. It contained a set of false teeth.

'They're my wife's,' he cried. 'I can't find her.'

As I scrambled through the hall to the front door, all my thoughts were hammering into my brain, I must get to Aleena, I must find her. I was beginning to formulate my thoughts. If – no, *when* – I found her, I'd get her into the Gloster – if the Gloster hadn't been destroyed – and fly her back to her mother. And me.

Once outside, it was a struggle even to fight my way an inch towards her. Inside my hotel, I had been terrified, but it had been a private terror, confined to my room. Now I had to share terror, fear, panic with screaming, bewildered men and women shouting, 'Japs! Japs!' They were trying to run – but where to? From the last bomb to the next? Death was hurtling down blindly without any chosen targets – except, of course, the docks and ships. Around me a dozen buildings were on fire, flames licking greedily around corners as though searching for petrol or oil or dry wood. But the worst flames of all were at the other end of the Savannah, at the long line of the naval base, now engulfed in a backdrop of fire stretching from the west where Bill Robins' house was, past the dry-dock, the giant cranes, to the store houses and ammunition dumps in the east. It was a curtain of fire, the flames leaping above thick, oily, black smoke.

As the warehouses along the front were hit, different sorts of fires started, different kinds of explosions. Rum barrels exploding, grain burning; rubber with its stinking black smoke almost covering me. I could smell paint, see where it left its blistered surface covered with what looked like treacle; gouts of sea water shot up from the harbour and swayed like cascading fireworks. It was all so close, so intimate that, for a ridiculous moment, I was reminded of the famous Thursday firework displays at the Crystal Palace which I had sometimes visited when I wasn't puzzling over Gray's *Anatomy*.

I could hardly cross Piccadilly because, at the corner of Hallgate, half of a tramcar lay on its side, straddling the street. In it were a dozen bodies, immobilised at the moment of death into grotesque burned sculptures. Still coughing from the smoke and dust, eyes watering, I stupidly looked around for the other half of the tram. It had vanished, blown with its occupants into such tiny fragments that no one would ever be able to trace them.

Then there was the hotel itself. When inside, I had been a witness of the scene outside; now I was outside, facing the façade of the Southern Cross itself, as I looked back. The entire front had been sliced away, just like a slice of bread, leaving the rooms behind open like those of a doll's house. I glimpsed a girl, naked, her clothes blown off by the blast, and a child buried standing up in a pile of rubble, dead. The sudden stench of sewage hit me as a main drain fell apart. And in the middle of the street, near the wrecked tramcar, a black and white cat picked its way fastidiously across the rubble and paused to massage its whiskers with a moistened paw.

As I finally crossed Hallgate near the beginning of the shopping arcade, suddenly I stopped in horror. There in front of me was a vast hole in the ground, filled with twisted, smoking rubble, all that was left of our beloved Café de Paris, smelling with the horrid mixture of smoke and water and charred wood and plaster dust. I grubbed round, thinking of the previous evening. Near the top of the hole I saw two or three bodies. I recognised one as the corpse of the head waiter who had remembered my taste in champagne. At least I recognised his face, but the body itself had been torn away.

And then, sitting on the rim of the counter, next to what was left of the bar, was the American who had seemed to cross my path regularly, who had asked to dance with Aleena, who was now nursing a hangover; and who had now found the remains of the bar and was sitting there, drinking directly from a bottle.

Aleena's college was on the other side of Hallgate, and there was no way I could force my way through the mass of crying, screaming wounded people, all moving in a tide going the other way, making for the fields, the open spaces, away from the smell. To force a way through them, against them, was like trying to swim against twenty-foot waves. I decided to try to get behind the arcade shops, through the smaller streets – and pray that I could reach the college at the other end of the arcade, and that it would be intact.

I managed to skirt the hole where the Café de Paris had stood and reach the narrow streets behind the arcade. It was easier to move there. Nearly everyone had fled, impelled to run from their homes and make for the wider streets, as though imagining that extra space would offer such protection.

At the far end was the Roman Catholic church, set well back – a hundred yards or more – from Hallgate, and I could make out its reassuring strength above the small houses. *That* stood. Between the church and the college lay the cemetery, so that the college – against whose gates I had kissed Aleena so recently – was almost flush with Hallgate, facing Piccadilly. But though I could see the church, I couldn't see the college which lay behind the end of the shopping arcade. I could only pray – until I reached the corner, turned left and looked aghast.

Half the college had been torn away. Not all of it; most stood, but, as with the Southern Cross, it was as though someone with a pair of giant scissors had cut a piece away.

Terrified of what I might discover, I looked at the pile of bricks and mortar that was once Hallgate, the twisted iron gates leading to the college, and I fell on my knees – with fear, anger, despair – every emotion, as though my heart would stop, and then I looked up at the sky, the blue showing through in patches between the smoke of war, and clenched my fists and screamed, 'Bloody Japs! Bloody, sodding, yellow, stinking Japs!' I was screaming abuse, an invocation against the enemy, when the 'all clear' sounded, a steady wail on the sirens.

Reason grabbed me – a doctor's reasoning. Why was it so silent? Why were there no screams from the twisted tangled metal girders? Why were no bodies littered around the debris, as they had been everywhere else? Because, I realised, with hope returning, that the building had been empty when the bomb passed by. The silence really was golden – comparative silence of course, because the wailing of grief and fear engulfed the whole town – but as I peered at the half-hit building, which had not received a direct hit, but had been 'shaved' like the Southern Cross, it was the absolute silence that reassured me.

And yet, how could I be assured that even if they *had* all left the school they might not still all be dead? Not far away stood the hospital, and it too had been 'shaved', like the school. But there was movement there, in the hospital, screams, bodies. Had the college students sought refuge in the hospital, only to be bombed?

A British sailor, his face bloodied, looked at me curiously, and thinking I was also a sailor, cackled, 'Don't you know no tits are allowed in Sanderstown? That applies to men too. You could be on a charge for indecently exposing yourself.'

I hadn't realised until that moment that I had only been able to find my trousers. My filthy, bloody chest was bare.

'Help yourself!' Again the man gave that horrible cackle as he pointed to a men's outfitter, its windows long since broken. Behind were dozens of shirts, ties, socks – anything you wanted. At the risk of being caught looting I grabbed a sports shirt. It didn't fit but it was good enough.

At that moment the fear that was tightening my heart like a steel circle, was replaced by a miracle – the sound of young voices, boys and girls, dozens of them, talking, chattering, crying with relief, coughing with smoke, an almost unearthly sound because at first I couldn't take in what had happened, and kept looking stupidly at the partly bombed college, puzzling how on earth the sounds could come from the wreckage.

Then I turned round. A procession of boys and girls, led by the teachers, was emerging from the unharmed church, walking along the path between the gravestones that led the hundred yards or so to the college.

As I stood there I heard a voice cry, 'Kit! Kit darling!' And then a figure ran out from the file of boys and girls, stumbled towards me and there was Aleena, crying, tears of relief streaming down her face, crying, 'Thank God! Oh, Kit! How awful! I was so afraid you would be dead!'

She threw her arms about me, kissing me, oblivious to the rest of the pupils, hardly noticing at first the blood on my face and clothes until I whispered, 'It's me who has to thank God.'

She was crying gently, and whispered, 'Have you a hanky, please?'

I shook my head, still under shock.

'This'll do.' She pulled the tail of my sports shirt, and reached down so that she could dab her eyes.

'I'm sorry. But seeing you – '

'Darling Aleena,' I said. 'We will never be parted again. Never.'

'We're alive, that's all that matters. These poor people all around us, so many killed for no reason. But we're alive.' She looked at me, her tears stopped, and tried to straighten my tousled, bloodstained hair with her long fingers, and whispered, 'But what have they done to you? Your face? The blood on your chest, your shirt. You're covered with blood.'

It looked worse than it was. My wounds on the head, where I had been grazed by a beam, had poured out blood because the head bleeds easily, but it had dried up now, and the knocks on my chest and arm were not even worthy of treatment.

258

'I saw the wreckage here, of the college – ' I began.

'When the first bombs hit the base, the teachers made us run to the church and take shelter in the vaults. We were just filing in when the college was hit.' She was still coughing and retching from the smoke, dust and oil.

'I've got to get you away,' I urged her. 'Apart from the little girl who's waiting for me to keep her alive, this is a war now, Aleena, a full-scale war, and this is just the beginning.' I explained that I had left the Gloster at the flying club as usual, and as far as I could tell, the raid, which had only lasted a few minutes, had been concentrated on the base, and the town itself had only suffered because it was so close to the base and the military airfield.

'Nellie has been refuelled. All the drugs and the iron lung for the patient are stowed away. She's ready to fly – now, before the Japs come back.'

She hesitated, saying in a faltering voice, 'I want to come – but I know there's only room for two – and there's Kinawa.'

My nerves were already near breaking point, and I cried, 'What the hell's Kinawa got to do with it? We're supposed to be in love – and all your school friends must know it by now, after what they saw. And I'm offering you a lift to see your mother and get out of this hell.'

'But Kinawa – '

'She's got her own mother,' I said almost angrily.

'Not at the moment. They're on holiday in California. I can't leave Kinawa alone. That's why Mother invited her for Christmas. Now it's even worse – can't you squeeze her in – for me. She *is* my blood sister.'

I hesitated, thinking of overweight – but they *were* thin: the two of them would weigh no more than Alec!

'All right.' I squeezed her arm, and shouted towards the boys and girls who were preparing to go off somewhere with the teachers, 'Kinawa!'

She ran across, saying, 'I'm so glad you're all right, Doctor.'

'Where are you all going?' I asked.

'To the Officers' Club on the Savannah. It wasn't hit. We're all going there for breakfast and then we'll wait there until the parents of the other girls come and find them, only mine aren't here.'

Breakfast! I thought. To think of breakfast at a time like this! But shock is one of the commonest things a doctor has to treat and it takes many strange forms – stricken silence, manic laughter, fugitive visions of nightmare landscapes like Gauguin's 'Four Horsemen', irrational speech, lunatic requests. And of course the word 'breakfast' might have meant just hot coffee; so perhaps it wasn't so surprising.

'I know. Aleena told me.' I forgot the 'breakfast' surprise. 'You'd better come to Koraloona then,' I said almost roughly. 'You're both so skinny, I suppose I can count you as one.'

Other parents, who had managed to reach Hallgate before the pupils arrived, were crying with joy and excitement, hugging their sons and daughters, surging round or over the ruined building. I managed to find one of the teachers and told him, 'Don't worry about Aleena and Kinawa.' I explained what I planned to do and he seemed delighted that his burden was about to be reduced by two. 'Fine,' he cried. 'Thanks for looking after them. You're sure they'll be safe, flying?'

'Safer than here,' I said, and turned to Aleena.

'Are you both all right?' I asked the girls. 'We've got a long walk.'

'Frightened, that's all,' said Kinawa.

'And you, Aleena?' I asked.

'I can't understand.' Aleena was close to tears again, bewildered as she asked over and over again, 'But *why*? Why us? What have *we* done to the Japanese to deserve this?'

Of course, we all asked the same question at this moment of our lives, for the simple reason that none of us could understand why the Japanese had picked us out to launch this unprovoked air attack. I suppose our thinking was so fuddled, we were under such great stress, that it never entered any of our heads that we were only one of many targets being bombed in the Pacific – until one of the parents standing next to me asked, 'Have you heard that the Japs have bombed Pearl Harbor, the American naval base in Hawaii?'

'America? It's impossible.'

'It's true. I heard it – and Singapore. And they've landed troops in Malaya. I heard it just before the radio went dead.'

'Impossible,' I repeated. Then, hardly able to believe it but suddenly aware of the world-wide implications and the need for urgency, I turned to Aleena. 'Come on, let's make a start.'

Both girls were unhurt, thank God, both were young and strong, and the only difficulty lay in trying to force a way through the crowded streets leading to the edge of the city – and eventually the flying club.

Fortunately there was a big common not far from the end of Monument Road called the Town Moor, and it was soon obvious that everyone regarded it as a safe haven, which in a way it was, unless the Japs decided on indiscriminate, low-level machine-gunning. Once there, where everybody congregated, the crowds of panic-stricken refugees thinned out. Some continued to try to reach country areas, but it was easier now. But as my early worry – whether we would make it – diminished, another worry took its place: would the plane be fit to fly?

As we trudged past the edge of the town, and the herd instinct that had driven so many to the Town Moor faded, we were able at least to walk more easily. Here and there we had to skirt impassable blocks of human beings, or a crater made by a stray bomb, but right at the edge of the town limits – after passing the Town Moor – we came along a small road; I remember the name, Silver Street – thinking how unsuitable it was for a day like this – and found a half-demolished shop, the island equivalent of a delicatessen, with a Polynesian man and wife moaning bitterly, heads in their hands, 'We've lost everything.'

'You've got your lives,' Aleena tried to comfort them gently. 'Be grateful for that,' she soothed, adding, 'Can we buy something to eat?'

'Take anything – never mind the money,' cried the man.

I insisted on leaving a couple of notes and the girls, with ravenous appetites, grabbed a large Tonga-type pineapple and coconut pie, and what looked like a cold meat loaf, but which I recognised as one that Toma sometimes cooked, *Kapai Holo*, a tapioca cake. I too was hungry. We ate as we walked and then, out in the open, we all started to run as we saw the tiny airfield and the outline of the half dozen or so planes of the flying club.

Just before we reached the flying club we came across one of the few Jap planes that had been shot down. It was still smoking but didn't seem to have been badly damaged except for its nose. We joined a small crowd of gaping sightseers. The crew of two men was dead but still sitting in their seats; they must have been killed by the shells of Bofors guns. One of them had his flying gear half undone, and underneath it he was wearing the traditional red shirt to show his disdain of blood, and on his head he wore the *hashimaki*, the cloth headband which I knew symbolised a man's readiness – indeed eagerness – to die.

'Come on,' I cried. 'This isn't the time for sightseeing. Poor devils.' And smiling at Aleena, I added, 'Now that I know *you're* alive, I feel almost sorry for them. I don't suppose the poor bastards had the faintest idea who had told them to do it – or why.'

We reached the airfield a few minutes later. 'It looks all right!' I shouted. The handful of light aircraft was standing by the small hangar and repair shop and I don't suppose the Japanese had ever seen them as they came in from the west, along the coast, their eyes fixed on the important targets ahead.

A man gave us a shout as he emerged from the office. I knew him from my occasional visits, a tall rangy Australian who helped to manage the flying club, a man called

Fellowes, and he beckoned us in with a twangy, 'Hello girls. This is a right bonus!' Then he added in his Australian accent, reminding me a little of Cockney, 'Come and listen to the latest news.'

He had a big short-wave battery-operated radio, and an American voice was announcing, ' – and it is estimated that between 300 and 400 planes attacked the base at Pearl Harbor with staggering losses in men, ships and planes, though so far we have been unable to confirm the extent of the losses. The attack, from carrier-based Japanese torpedo bombers, took place at five minutes of eight, when the base was not on full alert. In the meantime other Japanese aircraft have bombed Singapore, the Philippines and the British base at Sanderstown, which was attacked just after 0700.'

'You can say that again,' said Fellowes.

'Shut up,' I cried. 'Listen!' The radio voice continued, 'Reports of damage to American warships are extensive. According to a Pearl Harbor spokesman, the first attack wave consisted of "Val" dive bombers, each carrying a 500lb-bomb, then "Kate" torpedo bombers, and others, carrying 1,000lb-armour-piercing bombs.'

'Jesus,' cried Fellowes. 'They must be darned crazy.'

Still shocked by the news – the confirmation of the vague story I had been told at the bombed school – I said, 'This means global war.'

'You can say that again,' said Fellowes, and looked longingly at the girls still munching their coconut pie. 'You kids got any grub to spare? I'm so hungry my stomach's hitting my backside. I've been here all night.'

'Why on earth?' I asked.

'I never expected *this* to happen – or Hawaii. But I'm a bachelor, I was listening to the radio warnings about the Far East, and I've fixed up a bed here in case of urgent early calls. Then of course I couldn't get home.'

'But you normally go home for breakfast.' I couldn't help laughing.

'You bet. It's bacon and eggs and Australian lager for me

every day of the week. But I reckon it'd be a waste of time today.'

Aleena gave him the rest of the meat loaf, as I asked him, 'Can you get Koraloona on the sked?'

'There's no electric circuits, of course,' he said. 'Everything's gone haywire, but we've got a generator same as you have on Koraloona, so there should be no sweat.' He looked at his watch. 'Ten o'clock, I reckon that's a dandy time.'

He twiddled knobs, finally got a message through, 'Sanderstown to Koraloona. Do you read me?'

In a minute I was talking to one of Colonel Fawcett's assistants, asking him to get a message to Doc Reid that I was safe, and that the iron lung should be operating in an hour and a half.

But I also knew that if a Drinker respirator (the medical slang term for an iron lung) is to be effective, quick action is necessary, and I had originally planned to be in Koraloona by 9am. I was hours late, and worried that Alec Reid might be up at 'Government House', as we sometimes facetiously called Colonel Fawcett's home. There must be near panic on the island.

So I asked on the sked, 'Can you please take this down carefully? A message to Miss Sowerby to give the patient oxygen with a seven per cent mix of CO_2. I knew that we had cylinders of both gases in the stores, and an oxygen mask. I also knew that Miss Sowerby was capable of administering a mixture of oxygen and carbon dioxide through a tube and mask. There was also one other instruction, in case the girl's condition was weakening. She would need hand pressure on the chest, so I added the instruction, 'Ask Miss Sowerby to keep hand pulsating till I get there with the Drinker.' And finally, I asked, 'Would you please get a message to Princess Tiare telling her that I'm bringing her daughter and a friend back with me. Over.'

'Will do. What's your ETA?'

'I don't know the time, the electric clock's stopped. But say, one hour and five minutes from now. Over.'

'Message received. Will pass on to Doc Reid and the Princess. Over and out.'

With that we went to find Nellie. She had not been even superficially damaged.

'No problem,' said Fellowes.

'Now ladies,' looking with joy and affection at Aleena, mingled with some reservations about carrying an extra passenger, 'we're overweight, so it's going to be tough getting Nellie off the ground. We'll throw out the seat, that's going to save a bit of weight, and the stretcher too; you'll have to sit or lie on the ground. Very uncomfortable.'

'Will you be able to make it?' asked Fellowes, adding wistfully, 'I'll look after one girl if you leave her behind, I promise you, mate.'

'I'd better take them both,' I laughed. 'I always take two girls when I'm flying.'

I won't make a long – or a tall – story of the take-off. The girls crouched, one grabbing the back of my pilot's seat, the other inside the iron lung to save space. It was the only way to prevent them from sliding backwards, and disturbing the balance of the plane, when we started to climb. 'If we ever do climb,' I muttered to myself as we trundled across the grass from the hangar to the strip.

'Hold tight!' I cried and gave her the throttle.

We started slowly, lurched, bumped, finally rose a few feet off the ground, but then lost height and bumped again. But we *were* gathering enough speed, and almost as we reached a hedge that marked the perimeter of the airfield, I pulled the stick back really hard.

Nellie faltered for a second at the change and the jerk, like a horse on the verge of refusing a jump, and for one second or two I thought we wouldn't make it. But we did. We cleared the hedge with inches to spare and then I circled round to gain height before setting course for home.

As we circled, gaining height, I looked over the side at the appalling sight, truly appalling, below. Inside the harbour walls a dozen or more ships, ranging from

8,000-ton cruisers and 1,800-ton destroyers to frigates and motor torpedo boats, lay in a jumble of wreckage, some half submerged, some with masts only above the water line. In the dry-dock, which stuck out from the dockside, the pumping station and the lock gate had both been shattered. A grey iron mass of metal in the dry-dock had received a direct hit – we learned, later, from a kamikaze pilot. One of the huge 100-foot tall gantries capable of lifting a hundred tons, with wheels on rails so that it could move along the dockside to any ship, was smashed, obviously beyond repair. So were two jib cranes. Only one building in the vicinity of the yards seemed to have escaped damage: the ugly rectangular three-storey naval barracks and the near-by storehouse. Despite the shattering sight below me, I couldn't help smiling that the storehouse had escaped, and how thankful the naval ratings would be that they still had their 'British' favourites, such as Cadbury's cocoa, whipped cream walnuts, Woodbines and plum jam, sometimes unobtainable in local shops.

Even at 2,000 feet, I said, 'That's enough,' and told the girls who both looked ill, to lie down as best they could. They were feeling sick – probably the fumes of oil that came into the plane from the smoke, together with the circling of the plane, and above all, the terror they had experienced.

'We're on our way home now,' I said to both of them. 'Try and lie on your backs. You'll feel better.' They were just able to manage it. 'We'll be landing in an hour,' I said, adding, 'God willing' – but I said that silently.

Once I had taken a compass bearing, there was nothing to do for an hour except keep a look-out, and stay on course: and as the girls dozed fitfully on the floor and we droned steadily towards Koraloona, I was reflecting how stupid it was, with hindsight, that we should not have had some inkling of the terrible events in which we were all now engulfed. Not so much the bombing of Sanderstown; more the fact that, from the viewpoint of a small overcrowded island like Japan, with America denying them their raw materials, the only way was for them to grab what they could, to fight for it, even if they lost. And they had always regarded suicide as an honourable death anyway.

I was thinking that American newspapers were common enough in Sanders (they even drifted into Koraloona) by way of the naval base. And even I, with an ear cocked only for news in Europe, had seen regular if vague references to the war of words between America and Japan. I had even heard rumours that an American cryptoanalyst had, in 1940, cracked the Japanese cipher system, warning the State Department of a possible attack on the US Fleet. Most of the warnings had been ignored.

Finally I saw a dot on the horizon.

'Wake up,' I cried. 'We're almost home. Look. There!'

Slowly the dot became larger, greener, and I could see movement, life – and no bombs.

Exactly an hour and five minutes after take-off, we were bumping our way on the grass airstrip of Koraloona, as the girls held on for dear life to anything they could grab to prevent themselves from being thrown about as we hit the deck.

'Home,' I said, 'home and safe.'

'And happy.' Aleena squeezed my arm when at last we'd scrambled unsteadily to the ground.

'Yes.'

I kissed her gently.

PART TWO

17

A large crowd had gathered to meet us as I switched off the engine and the propeller idled to a stop. Tiare's Austin Ten and Doc Reid's car-cum-ambulance stood at the edge of the field. As we clambered out – the two girls stiff from their cramped positions – all thoughts of 'Tell us what's happened!' and 'Thank God you're safe!' were halted by the urgency in Doc Reid's voice as Aleena fell into her mother's arms.

'We may be just in time to save the wee girl if I hurry,' said Alec. To him the saving of a life was more urgent than details of the war news. 'The lassie's going fast despite everything Miss Sowerby's done. It's the delay.' He said it almost as though I were responsible for the Japanese attack, though I knew he didn't mean it that way.

'I'll take it along, Kit.' He helped to unload the iron lung. 'Never mind the rest of the drugs. We'll collect them later.' Carrying the contraption to the back of his Ford, he laid it down carefully and jumped into the driving seat. 'Ye must have had quite an experience,' was all he said. 'Miss Sowerby'll get the wee bairn into the lung, and when ye're ready, come in and tell me all about what happened in Sanderstown.'

'I'll be with you in a few minutes,' I promised him.

The impatient crowd, anxious for eye-witness news, must have heard some details on the radio, for though one bomb in Sanderstown had knocked out the local radio station, everything was working normally in Koraloona, including the radio, so we were able to get the BBC and Australia. Purvis ran forward and clutched my arm asking, 'It's terrible. Are you all right, Kit? Your shirt – blood – '

271

I told him that I had only been scratched as Mollie Green put an arm round me, and asked, 'Is it true that the Southern Cross Hotel was hit?'

'It was, and I was in it at the time.'

I laughed – it helped to ease the tension, and the apprehension for the future which I could sense among the crowd.

'Do you think it'll spread to Koraloona?' It was Jim Wilson who shook my hand.

'I know no more than you, Jim, but I don't think so.'

Question after question was fired at me – and I could provide no real answers. Finally Tiare came to me with Aleena, Kinawa remaining on the fringe, and, as so often happened on the island, the crowd made way for her. She said to me very simply, 'Aleena has just *started* to tell me how you saved her during the bombing raid and how you brought her to safety – '

'It was nothing,' I smiled. 'I was so worried – '

'Come and have lunch soon, Kit,' said the Princess. 'I have the feeling that all of us have a lot to talk about.' I didn't quite know what she meant at first but then I saw her looking intently at my hand – not even my hand, but my little finger on which I was wearing Aleena's gold ring, the one she had given me just before the end of the dance the night before. Was it really only last night?

'It would give me great pleasure.' I returned her somewhat stilted way of talking with a touch of formality of my own, wondering what she was thinking, and then Aleena shook hands with me – that was all she dared to do in front of the other people – but as she, too, thanked me, she gave me a secret, fleeting smile that both of us knew was the equivalent of a kiss, and everything else that had happened last night.

Jim Wilson helped me to transport the drugs from the aircraft. Then I went to take a look at our patient, who had been fitted into her lung, given an injection, and she offered me a small, wan smile. Already she was breathing more easily.

Then I went with Alec to my bungalow and lay down on the bed. He sat in the basket chair and I said, 'I'm not sleepy, Alec, I'm just so bloody overwhelmed by what's happened that I'm exhausted. I'm – well I never imagined *anything* like this could happen. I was so shattered – and so scared – that I completely forgot I was a doctor. I don't suppose I even helped anybody, though the dead and dying were all around me.'

'Aye, I can see ye're all done in, Laddie. Rest a wee bit.' And looking at the stubble on my chin, added, 'Have yourself a sleep, then a good long shower, before ye take a razor to your face.'

Lying on my back, I said to him, 'It's incredible to think what happened. Just before I took off I heard on the radio that Pearl Harbor has been bombed. It's not possible. How dare Japan attack America?'

'And Japan's going to draw in Germany against America too,' said Alec. 'Remember, Germany's part of the Axis. We'll be having American soldiers not only in Japan – if they can ever get there – but in Europe too, ye mark my words. And,' turning from the world scene to a more local one, 'did ye have a chance to see Ronnie Serpell?'

I looked at him in amazement. 'Don't you realise just how big this raid was, Alec? It would have taken me a day to make my way from Piccadilly to the naval base – or what's left of it.'

'As bad as that?' Alec still couldn't grasp the ferocity of the attack. 'And I hope the Southern Cross Hotel's in good order?'

I laughed, almost hysterically. 'Alec, it's *gone*!' I cried. 'It's all gone!'

Everything changed with the war. It hadn't affected us physically, yet it had killed hundreds of innocent people in the neighbouring island of Sanders, where the British Navy, it appeared, was in a state of great emergency. Within days decrees started pouring in to Koraloona from Sanderstown. A black-out (of sorts) was enforced on all the islands. A kind of voluntary system of rationing was imposed, though there were not enough officials on Koraloona to enforce any regulations. But Colonel Fawcett was warned to husband supplies of imported goods, because no guarantees could be given about the next shipment of items like diesel or petrol, cigarettes or liquor. Then the skeleton police force had to round up the half a dozen or so Japanese who had lived most of their lives peacefully on Koraloona. They were interned on Penal Island.

Regulations sprouted everywhere. Everyone seemed to be working at frantic speed to do what in effect amounted to virtually nothing. Sanders Island was now under the strict control of the British military, who were understandably afraid of another Japanese bombing attack. Their anxiety inevitably gave minor officials a golden opportunity to build up little empires that had suddenly become invested with pomposity. We received totally unnecessary orders to compile complete lists of all drugs and medical accessories, even to the number of stretchers, via Colonel Fawcett.

'They say it's in case the Japanese bomb Koraloona or invade it,' Fawcett told Reid and myself apologetically, to which Alec replied, 'We've only got three stretchers, and if we need any more, we'll make our own out of tree branches and blankets. We've done it before and we'll do it again,' he snorted, adding afterwards to me, 'They're building a wee molehill into a mountain. Who in God's name would invade an island like this?'

Inevitably I hardly saw Aleena in those first few days of anxiety – and they *were* anxious and busy, for though there was no reason for an enemy to attack our little island, the speed of Japanese advances and Anglo-American retreats set everyone's nerves on edge. If the Japanese, within a few days of Pearl Harbor, could successfully invade the small American island of Wake – almost due north of Koraloona – what hope would there be for an undefended island like Koraloona itself?

*

It took several days before we learned the full extent of the Japanese onslaught. To us, Sanderstown was 'our' war; and though newspapers had started printing within two days of 'Black Sunday', they were not reaching Koraloona. The radio, however, was functioning, and we were all glued to it.

Losses at the British Pacific base of Sanderstown were horrific: fifteen British warships sunk or seriously damaged, including three heavy cruisers. The gantries, cranes, stores, all suffered appalling damage. The huge dry-dock, which had taken three years to build, was flooded, its pumps, its sides wrecked. It would need rebuilding completely. In the ships themselves, twelve hundred sailors had died, entombed for ever in the warm waters of the South Seas. The figure would have been higher but for the fact that the barracks, where the married ratings lived, was not hit, and many of those on normal duty were not on board because they had weekend passes.

There were few details of the damage to civilian buildings in Sanderstown, but first accounts said that 518 civilians had been killed, and another 1,820 injured, a figure which took no account of the missing – men and women who lived in the country areas and were visiting Sanderstown at the time of the attack.

But even worse than the local attack was the news from the outside world. The fact that the Japanese had even dared to challenge the might of the United States was one thing; the fact that they had succeeded at Pearl Harbor was incredible; for with the one blow at Pearl they had crippled the American Pacific Fleet. Five mighty battleships – the *Arizona, California, Nevada, Oklahoma* and *West Virginia*, had been sunk. The *Pennsylvania* and *Tennessee* would be out of action for months. Ten other warships lay either at the bottom of the sea or were seriously damaged, and 188 American aircraft were destroyed and 2,403 Americans killed, and 1,178 wounded. The Japanese lost only 29 aircraft and 56 men killed.

It was almost impossible to grasp the arrogant nature of

the attack, especially as Pearl Harbor and Sanderstown were only two prongs of a far-reaching offensive. Day after day we listened to fresh details on the radio. While Singapore was being bombed, Japanese army forces were landing at Patani in Siam and Kota Bharu on the north-east coast of Malaya. My ears pricked up as the impersonal voice intoned 'Kota Bharu'. Where had I heard that name? Of course! Ronnie Serpell had mentioned it – the township with only one lavatory. Now the lavatory and the surrounding countryside were in the hands of the Japanese. Other Japanese forces had taken Kowloon and were starting to attack Hong Kong, and also the Philippines, hundreds of miles away.

According to one American radio report, the Japanese had nearly 1,500,000 men, around 4,000 planes, 10 battleships, 11 carriers, 41 cruisers, 129 destroyers and 67 submarines. It was a formidable array of strength. And then came the worst news so far. I was listening in with Alec, when the BBC World Service announced that we had lost two of Britain's most modern warships, sunk off the coast of Malaya: the *Prince of Wales* and the *Repulse*.

'That's the end of Britain in the Far East,' said Alec as we sat on my bungalow veranda sipping beer after surgery. 'They're mad! Our only hope is that they canna keep up the momentum against both the might of Europe and America. Why man, that's half the civilised world!'

'Against half the uncivilised world!' I said bitterly.

'Germany's nae uncivilised.'

'Maybe you're right,' I admitted, 'but Germany bit off more than she could chew when she took on Russia. Stalin has ordered a general offensive outside Moscow and the Germans have been halted.'

That same evening Jason Purvis, looking spruce in one of his new white duck suits, came round and we played the fifth symphony of Mahler.

'The same haunting music of Polynesia,' I said, for

though no one could compare the ukulele with an orchestra, the uncomplicated music of the islands was always haunting.

'I know what you mean – treacly, but it *is* haunting.'

He dusted each old record, changed the needle with each new side. When the 'recital' (as he called it) was over he asked, 'By the way, I've been meaning to enquire, any news of Bill Robins?'

'No.' I shook my head. 'I hope he's all right – and his family. I'm sure I'd have heard if anything had happened to them or to the *Mantela*.'

'You mean enemy action?' Jason refilled his glass before waiting to be asked.

'Well, we *are* at war,' I said. 'But no, nothing like that can have happened. If any ships in the area had been sunk, we'd have heard. I think the *Mantela*'s due in Koraloona in a few days. Jim Wilson will know. He always gets advice of what stores are required, and so on. But I can't use the radio link to check on whether his wife and children are all right.'

'Not as a special concession?'

I shook my head. 'No, it's strictly reserved for the military, and emergencies. For medical supplies I suppose I could. Not that there can be *many* medical supplies left. But for private messages – well,' with a sigh I added, 'I only hope nothing has happened to Bessie and the children.' I didn't add that the Robins' house in Avenue Road was not far from the sea and that, from the moment I had started to fly back, I had been tormented by the fact that the Japanese flight path must have taken them right over the built-up area west of the base. Yet there was no way I could find out, nothing I could do.

'Keep your fingers crossed,' Purvis consoled me, adding enigmatically, 'And also for Paula Reece.'

'Paula? Why? What's happened to her?'

'Nothing really.' We sat down for dinner. 'Except that on the night you were in Sanderstown the two ladies – she and Miss Sowerby – had a monumental row. I haven't the foggiest idea what about.' He looked at me sardonically. 'Not you by any chance?'

'Me! Are you serious?'

'Oh, I didn't mean literally – or physically. She wouldn't know how to start,' he admitted. 'Jealous perhaps. I don't know. But I do know one thing. It's strange, but the presence of Paula has brought hidden depths out of Miss Sowerby.'

'What on earth do you mean, you're talking in riddles.' Purvis *was* – well, loquacious, the way people get after a few drinks.

'Well, hate, for example. I don't suppose dear Miss Sowerby has ever hated anyone except heathens in all her missionary life. Now she hates Paula. And that, coupled with – what shall we say? – her *admiration* for you, has added a new dimension to her character.'

'You're talking balls,' I laughed.

'No, I'm not. It's extraordinary, those two women are mortal enemies. In a way, it's like this war that's tearing us all apart. It'll bring out facets of character in millions of people who otherwise wouldn't ever find their own characters out. Yes, I must remember that – a good argument for my next novel.'

'But what was the row about? What did Doc Reid say or do?'

'He didn't know. And I've no idea. I just heard them shouting at each other.'

'Well, I hope the row – whatever it was about – and it certainly wasn't about *me* – has blown over.'

'I hope so too,' said Purvis. 'She almost threatened to leave, and I'd hate to see Miss Sowerby go. You know, I'm beginning to like her. She's not exactly a bundle of fun, but she's got a good heart and now that she's learnt to smile occasionally she's improved beyond all recognition.'

'Smile and hate. Quite a contradiction. Remember that too when you write your novel. Come on, let's eat.' We attacked the main course of dinner, but after Purvis had gone, and in the next few days, I thought no more about his

278

words, until after surgery one day I called out, 'Miss Sowerby! How's the little girl?'

She came out on to the veranda – which is what I had intended. 'Much better, thanks to the lung. I hope we can take her out now and again for a couple of hours.'

'I think you're right. But we will give her a thorough examination first.'

She smiled – I knew that she loved the 'we', which I used deliberately to flatter her. But the fleeting smile vanished, turned into a hard, straight line the moment I asked casually, 'By the way, Miss Sowerby, I heard that you and Paula Reece had a few words the night I was away?'

She said nothing.

'Well?' I asked. 'I'm sure it wasn't important, but what was it all about? Since' – more deliberate flattery – 'you work so closely with me on our polio cases, I think I should know all about it.'

She pursed her lips, and for a moment I thought she was going to refuse to reply, but finally she muttered, 'It wasn't important, Doctor. Your description was correct – it was just a few words.'

'I see.' Purvis had been unable – or unwilling – to give me any details, but I persisted. 'There must be some reason. I even understand that you threatened to resign.'

Finally she blurted out. 'I did, Doctor, when she started to try to tell me how to run the ward. But I didn't mean it.'

'Thank goodness for that.' I smiled again. 'I don't know how we'd manage without you.'

She almost preened herself as I asked, 'But how exactly did she upset you?'

'I don't like to speak badly about anyone, Doctor,' she said, though I could sense that she was aching to unburden herself. 'But she's so – hoity-toity. She thinks her money can buy anything, but it can't buy nursing skills. That only comes from experience. And when – ' I could see that her normally stony face was lined with anger – 'and when she told me – yes, Doctor, she *ordered* me – to clean a bedpan – I just said that if I had to take orders from her I would rather leave.' Anxious to make sure that she wasn't misunderstood, she added, 'I was going to clean the bedpan anyway, of course. But I didn't like being *ordered* to do so by an amateur help. Then she demanded the keys of the old tin trunk. Why? There are only records inside. I'm afraid I lost my temper.'

'Very understandable,' I murmured. 'And then she left the hospital?'

'No. The noise attracted Mr Purvis and I must say, Doctor, he saw in an instant what the situation was.'

'That was fortunate. My sympathies are entirely on your side. As you know, I'm not particularly fond of Miss Reece myself. So Mr Purvis arrived. What did he do?' I prodded her gently.

She had relaxed considerably by now; the anger which had shown in her face was replaced by her usual dour look, but there was the hint of a satisfied smirk when she said, 'Mr Purvis is a very forthright man, Doctor, he soon sent her packing.'

'Did he, now?'

'I don't know what the words he used meant, obviously some dialect or slang, but I remember the words exactly because I had never heard them before.'

'Well, they worked! Whatever they were.' I was about to regard the discussion as ended when I asked almost idly, 'What on earth did he say, then?'

With complete innocence, and without the faintest knowledge of the words which Purvis had used, the prim and proper and praying Miss Sowerby said, 'I recall them exactly.' Then making sure she had got them right, she repeated his words, 'Why don't you bugger off, you old fart.'

For one second I was lost in startled surprise, for the way Miss Sowerby repeated Purvis' words, almost rolling them round her lips, made them sound as though she had said them herself. I burst into laughter, I couldn't help it. And wiping the tears out of my eyes, I said, 'Good old Jason!'

'You know the words?' she asked.

I had to cover up as quickly as I could, for I was still struggling to keep a straight face. 'It's a kind of military slang,' I said. I could certainly imagine the speed with which an insulted Paula had left the hospital.

'I never had a chance to thank Mr Purvis. Perhaps, Doctor, you could thank him for me. You know,' she was searching for the right words, 'I think there's a lot of good in Mr Purvis, and he's very polite. If only he wouldn't drink so much. Is there no way of helping him get rid of that curse?'

18

For the time being I thought no more about the problems of Miss Sowerby – nor for that matter about the war – because a few days later Tiare phoned me at my bungalow. She had never done that before.

'Princess,' I started, my heart sinking, remembering how she had stared at Aleena's ring on my finger. 'Is there anything I can do for you?'

'Yes, Kit. I'd like to talk to you.' Obviously she had been questioning Aleena about our friendship, but at least she didn't sound angry. And I couldn't be accused of going to bed with her daughter.

'Yes, of course,' I said rather lamely, adding as a joke which she didn't appreciate, 'your place or mine?'

'If you don't mind, yours,' she said. 'I'm very grateful for what you've done for my daughter – twice now – but I *would* like to talk to you. A friendly talk, Kit. I hope you regard me as your friend.'

I wasn't sure whether she was my friend or not – I wasn't sure what her attitude would be to the fact that I had fallen in love with Aleena. 'Of course, Princess,' I replied. 'Would tomorrow after surgery be convenient?' Then, thinking that a good meal might help to keep the conversation relaxed, I added on the spur of the moment, 'What about lunch?'

To my surprise she accepted. It seemed with pleasure, and I told Toma who, swollen with pride, prepared to excel himself for what he regarded as a royal visit, which in a way it was.

The following day she arrived in her Austin Ten and, as she parked the car, I walked down the veranda steps to meet her. She was dressed, as so often, in white sharkskin slacks, the crease immaculately pressed, and a blue silk blouse; and as there was a slight breeze, she had a matching blue cashmere cardigan thrown casually over her shoulders.

She was smiling and relaxed as she said, confidentially, 'Paula gave me these clothes!' Then, 'I hope the surgery wasn't too difficult today.'

'All over in a couple of hours,' I replied cheerfully. 'Come and have a pre-lunch drink.' I led the way to the veranda. 'I seem to remember that you like gimlets?' And when she nodded, I cried, 'Toma! Ice, please!'

Toma came in with the ice bucket and glasses, put them on the drinks tray, and bowed so low that he nearly fell over.

When I had mixed the gimlets, she gently twiddled the mixture of gin and fresh limes with a finger which she then wiped with one of the paper napkins Toma had placed on the arm of her cane easy-chair. Tiare couldn't have been more charming but even so, when we sat down for lunch I was still slightly apprehensive. She hadn't accepted my invitation merely to repeat her thanks for helping Aleena, and sure enough, half way through the main dish of fresh prawns cooked in coconut milk with rice, she sat back in her chair, sipped the chilled Australian white wine, and with an almost quizzical look said – and it was a statement, not a question – 'So you're in love with Aleena.'

'Very much so.' I didn't hesitate in my reply. 'I'm hoping that you'll give us your blessing to marry one day soon.'

She didn't say anything for what seemed like a long, long

282

time, and then she repeated part of my last phrase in th form of a question, but omitting the final word.

'So you want to marry one day?'

'I do. Though I expect this – this has come as a shock – '

'Not really,' she smiled. 'But all the same – ' She paused and for a moment my heart sank.

'All the same?' It was my turn to repeat a statement as a question.

She waited while Toma cleared away the plates, and I looked across the lagoon and sighed; watching me looking out to sea, she said, 'You really love this island, don't you?'

'I never thought any place could be so wonderful.'

'Even with people like Mana?' she asked.

'That's in the past. Forgotten.'

'Not by me.'

I hesitated, anxious to guide the conversation back to Aleena and myself. Yet I didn't quite know what to say. Tiare was hardly the woman with whom I could discuss my future prospects or professional standing – the usual preliminaries, I suppose, to an English confrontation with prospective in-laws. Tiare had to make the running. This she did before long by saying, 'I like you, Kit, and I think you and Aleena would be very happy. I know she loves you. I asked her after I saw her grandfather's ring on your finger, and I felt that it was no sudden infatuation, just because you're,' she smiled slightly, 'an eligible bachelor.'

As she toyed with her sliced mangoes, I waited for the one word which, from the careful choice of her language, I knew she would use. 'But – '

That was the word!

'But what?' I asked. 'If you approve, Princess – '

'Don't get excited,' she smiled again. 'All I suggest is that you and Aleena don't rush things. Aleena is only just seventeen, and her birthday's on March 8. You both have a whole world ahead of you.'

'But we're in love!'

'All the more reason to wait – to make sure it *isn't* just an infatuation. After all, to you, life on Koraloona must be an exciting adventure, a new experience. Many of the girls are beautiful and – ' again choosing her words carefully, 'accessible. You may be swayed by your surroundings.'

'I'm not!' I cried. 'I've never touched a Polynesian girl. Apart from any other considerations, as a doctor, I have to be very circumspect. And with Aleena, it's not an infatuation. It's for life.'

'I think you're right,' she agreed gently. 'I certainly hope so. But the equivalent of an engagement is not a bad thing. And apart from that, I think our wise man – he's called Tiki, you must have seen him around – '

'Yes, I have.' I tried not to sound angry. Tiki was one of several 'wise men' who wielded, I felt, a sinister influence. I had seen him, dressed in European clothes, though I had never met him.

'But what's *he* got to do with love and marriage?' I burst out.

'Everything,' she said quietly. 'We are always advised by him, and we believe his advice is right and just.'

I was on the point of asking whether the redoubtable Tiki had advised Tiare to marry Mana, but thought better of it. Such a remark – the sort of retort that always came naturally to me – could turn an ally into an enemy for life.

'And what advice does he have to give to you?' I tried to keep the sarcasm out of my voice.

'He approves of Aleena's choice – and mine – but – ' again that bloody word! – 'but, he feels that you should wait for two years before marrying.'

'*Two years!*' The words hit me with the force of a blow in the solar plexus. 'What on earth for! *Two years!*'

'You *are* impatient, and you get angry so quickly.' The smile robbed her words of annoyance. 'Is it so long? Is it so dreadful? Aleena's only seventeen.'

'I know her age,' I replied, 'but remember, Princess, I've also known her for years, I've watched her growing up, turning from a girl into a young woman. For me, falling in love with Aleena has been – well, a natural progression. That's why nobody can ever say that it's an infatuation. It's

284

absurd to talk about waiting until she's nineteen. And especially,' I had to be careful not to give offence because I was really angry, 'especially when it's not *your* decision, or Aleena's, but – '

'A witch-doctor's?' She could read my mind. 'Isn't that what you really think?'

'I didn't say that. But a decision by *you* – that's one thing. On the other hand, you can't really mean that you'll let this wise man run Aleena's life for her?'

'If we believe that he's honest, then we think his wishes should be respected. Why not?' the Princess asked.

For a few moments I sat there, absolutely dismayed. Two whole years to wait! I had expected some delay, perhaps three months to arrange the wedding at a time when the island spirits were favourable, but two whole years. And on this island of peace and tranquillity. How easy it is for human beings to mess up paradise. All kinds of wild thoughts passed through my mind. Maybe we could elope? Perhaps I could try to get a job on another island, or on the east coast of Australia near the Barrier Reef, which was reputed to be as beautiful and unspoiled as the South Seas. But I knew I was just toying with ideas that could never materialise for one insuperable reason: Aleena also believed in the advice of the wise man. I sensed it would take some cataclysmic event to make her break her vows. But I did have one sudden idea – why not volunteer for the Army? Take a commission in the RAMC? Then, surely, we would get a dispensation to marry. But that, I reflected, might mean being parted for three or four years, whereas this way, it would at least be only two years.

Desperately, I said to Tiare, 'I know you have faith in these things, but when it comes to the lives of other people, is it fair to take their word as gospel?'

We had reached the coffee stage by now, and she looked at me across the cups on the veranda table and, almost with a twinkle in her eyes, asked, 'Tell me, Kit, do *you* believe – in Christianity?'

'Yes, I do.'

'Fervently? I mean, do you go to church every Sunday without fail?'

'Well – no, not that way – '

'But' – was she laughing at me? – 'you do believe that the principles of Christianity are worth following?'

'Of course,' I said, knowing she was leading me into a trap.

'And is there such a difference between following the advice of your missionary, and Aleena and me following the advice of ours?'

I really couldn't say what was passing through my mind – that this witch-doctor was trading in superstition, whereas our church, our Christianity, was in the hands of – well, trained theologians and not crackpots.

'I know what you're thinking,' again she repeated, 'witch-doctors?' As Toma hovered around, I tried to cover my embarrassment by saying, 'Yes, please. More coffee.'

'I didn't mean that,' I added lamely. 'I'm really sorry if I gave you that impression – if I offended you.'

'I know what you mean. But you see *I* agree with the wise man. And if you were back in England, probably *your* mother would tell you to wait until your career was launched before you decided to get married.'

She was quite right! I could just see Mother warning me back in Nottingham, 'She's a very nice girl, Kit, but take your time. Don't rush things. A long engagement is a wonderful way to make sure that you really love each other.' Those would have been Mother's actual words, and now, though employing a different kind of adviser, here was Tiare saying exactly the same thing about her daughter.

Tiare glanced at her old wrist-watch with its leather strap looking as though it would fall apart any day, and said, 'Let's see what happens. I've no objection to what I believe in Europe is called an understanding. But take life slowly and,' she smiled slightly as she got up to leave, 'what's the American word I read the other day? In the meantime, no hanky-panky.' Then she said something which brought a flush of anger to my cheeks. 'Because,' she said it quite gently, 'we don't want a repetition of the Lucy business, do we?'

'That's unfair, Princess!' I cried.

She sipped her, by now, cold coffee, gave the smallest of sighs and said, 'I wasn't being unfair. I was trying to show you how fragile happiness is – and how much better if people wait until they've built up a solid foundation. That's all. If you hadn't – forgive me – rushed into bed with Lucy, she might still be here. And you were so happy together you might even have married her. Instead she's been dismissed like a servant – and – '

'But Lucy and I never were really in love,' I cried. 'I liked her and, perhaps we were both lonely, but we had a lot of fun together. I'm *in love* with Aleena. Can't you tell the difference?' I didn't say so, but I was thinking of the difference between Tiare's first and second husbands.

'All the more reason to wait – and not let your impatience lead you up the wrong path,' she said. 'And think, too, of Aleena. Now!' Tiare stood up, smoothing her beautifully cut white slacks, 'I must go. And Kit, I trust you; and remember what your famous Captain Cook told his men when he first set eyes on these islands, "You'll be all right as long as you always obey the rules."'

After thanking me for lunch, she shook hands and, on the steps of the veranda, as though about to make for her Austin Ten she turned back and said with a smile, 'We have a custom of our own on the islands, when there is an understanding. We don't get engaged in Polynesia, as you know – but when there is an understanding between a couple, the mother-in-law sends the prospective bridegroom a gift.'

'That's a bonus!' I laughed, even if ruefully at the thought of two years' wait. 'I didn't think mothers-in-law ever sent gifts before the actual marriage.'

She laughed too. 'I think it originated as a bribe to win them over. Sometimes it's a goat, sometimes chickens, it all depends on your social status.'

'Well, even though I'm depressed at the thought of waiting, I don't need any gifts to be won over by,' I said and she could see that I meant it and was pleased.

'Thank you,' she said quietly. 'I believe you. But as I just said, or rather as Captain Cook said, we must obey the rules. And so' – she jumped into her car – 'I shall send you some gift as – what is the English phrase? – a token of our esteem.'

This was the start of our 'engagement', and it meant that we could go to the cinema, dine at Mollie Green's or with other people, swim on Tiare's beach. The physical side was limited to kissing, what the Americans called 'necking' and the occasional adventurous stroking. At times I *did* miss the liberation of a complete physical love – especially after that tantalising sight of her in the Southern Cross; but it was replaced by an extraordinary tranquillity. We were deeply in love – quite different from the attraction I had felt for Lucy – and in a way I find hard to describe, her mixture of a young girl and a growing woman gave me a protective feeling towards her. I did want her physically, but I didn't want to force her to give in, although I feel sure I could have done.

The 'token of our esteem' arrived a few days later. I had just returned to my bungalow from morning surgery and was sipping a cold Australian beer – one of the few welcome wartime exports that we were still able to enjoy – when Toma said, 'Parcel arrive master. Very large.'

'For me, Toma? Where?'

He nodded in the direction of the spare bedroom and when I went there, carrying my pint mug of beer topped with enough froth to give me a white moustache, I found a roughly wrapped flat package leaning against one of the walls.

'From Princess Tiare,' Toma announced importantly.

So here was the token! A token of acceptance from a prospective mother-in-law. A very good omen for the future – provided I could control my impatience. The package was tied with sisal, and it was large – about five feet long and four feet deep, I judged without giving the matter much thought. And for a moment my imagination toyed with what it might be. Flat – so a mirror perhaps, or a typical Polynesian hand-woven rug, the sort the locals often stretched and used as a wall decoration.

Putting the beer down on the bamboo table next to my bed, I fumbled with the thick, rough sisal, finally shouting to Toma in exasperation, 'Bring me a pair of scissors!' Even then, as Toma came shambling in, I hadn't the faintest idea what the parcel contained, because its real nature lay beyond my wildest imagination.

'What are these?' I asked almost crossly as he handed me a pair of nail scissors.

'Only ones can find,' he said. 'But no worry.' And then to my astonishment he picked up the package and was about to bite his way through the sisal with his strong teeth when I cried, 'Hey, be careful, it might be glass.'

It wasn't difficult to cut the sisal in a couple of places and then, almost before I had handed it to Toma and laid the package on the spare bed, I caught my breath with a sudden excitement that made my heart pound with premonition.

It couldn't be! I thought, and yet I was suddenly convinced in my mind that the unbelievable was about to happen, that a casual matter-of-fact promise of a gift by the mother of the girl I loved wrapped in ordinary paper, tied with ordinary sisal, brought by a house-boy as though it were unimportant, contained a prospect so exciting that I hadn't even *bothered* – let alone dared – to imagine what the shoddy brown paper might contain. And yet, sense told me that, if I were honest, the package had to contain a picture. And then, breath coming quicker as I started to tear off the paper, who should peer through the door but Alec Reid.

'Och! I didna know it was Christmas time!' he chuckled. 'People in Koraloona dinna go distributing wee gifts except on special occasions.'

'This *is* a special occasion!' I breathed, my hand about to tear the last remnants of the paper away. 'A very special occasion.'

'Well, why the suspense, man?'

I stood the packet, still covered up, against the back of the iron bed. I could feel the hard touch of the wood on which the canvas had been stretched.

'Will ye get me a beer, Toma?' Alec asked, and Toma went off to the kitchen.

'Ready?' I asked.

'Steady, go!' laughed Alec.

Almost with a flourish I ripped off the paper, and there it was – like a dream come true, my favourite painting in all the world. I gasped as the drab, rather ordinary spare bedroom, with its 'standard' furniture, sprang into colour, life, movement, excitement – every word in the dictionary I could think of.

'Why! It's "Pink Street".' Even Alec cried out with astonishment.

Yes, it was, the painting which I had told Tiare I thought the most beautiful of all – that and the picture of the pool. I almost forgot the others, hardly heard Toma's muttered, 'Real street no pink, master. Painting no good!'

I stood there gloating, yes, that's the only word, *gloating*, drinking in the beauty of this astounding mix of paint which, through the art of a tormented genius, had somehow transformed an unimportant street on Koraloona into one that was a blaze of extravagance.

'Will ye nae read the message?' Alec was not *that* impressed by the painting itself, but no doubt impressed by its value, as he pointed to an envelope attached to a corner of the back of the rough frame.

I opened it, hearing with sudden clarity the sound of the drawing pin which had held it in place dropping on to the wooden floor. Tearing open the envelope I took out a card. Reid craned over my shoulder to read the clear, almost squarely formed schoolgirl letters. The message was very simple but (as so often with Tiare) a little stilted, using the royal 'we', although, I think, unintentionally. It read:

> Our thanks for saving our only daughter and for the pain our family inflicted on you. Here is to your happiness in the future.

Reading the message again Alec said wryly, 'I canna deny you seem to be well in with the Princess. Ye'll be taking my job next!' But it was said without rancour, and I clutched his arm, I was so excited, and cried, 'Never!'

'Ye really like this tosh?' He pointed to what I considered to be one of the most beautiful Gauguins in the world.

'Tosh? Oh, Alec. It's genius! As much in a different way as the genius of poor old Mahler. The same ability to turn a man's pain into someone else's pleasure.'

'It's everyone to his own tastes. Worth a bit of money, eh? Not a bad fee?'

'A fee!' I had a sudden sinking feeling. 'If it's a fee is it unethical to get such a huge present? Do you think I should return it?' At the back of my mind, always, was the way in which my career had nearly been destroyed once before.

'Git away with ye, Laddie.' Reid burst into laughter. 'Have ye ever heard of a Scot refusing money?'

'I trust you!' I cried.

'But dinna forget to write the lady a bread and butter letter. It's nae everyone gets a Gauguin for a fee.'

In the end I took the picture to Jim Wilson who made a strong frame and then cut a piece of glass to fit. In the hope that the glass would protect the painting from the salt air, I asked him to put a few dabs of putty around the edges making it virtually airtight. After that I hung it on the wall facing my two armchairs – the wall that never got a full flood of sun on it so that the colours of the painting would never fade.

*

The Princess was as good as her word about the 'understanding'. While I was still staggering mentally over my glorious Gauguin, Aleena phoned me a few days later.

'I'm so glad Mummy gave you that particular painting,' she said. 'I was wondering – could we go to the pictures tomorrow evening?'

I knew the idea had probably been suggested first by Tiare, and I was delighted, even though the Ritz Cinema was open only every Friday evening and the films they showed were so old and so knocked around that the screen often flickered with spots and numbers, followed by a faint flapping noise in the dark, until the film finally stopped – temporarily, until the fault was repaired. The grandiloquently named 'Ritz' was always referred to by the same nickname as thousands of seedy English provincial cinemas, 'the flea-pit'.

'What's on?' I asked. It was almost a weekly ritual to go to the cinema every Friday, but nobody really bothered to find out what was being shown.

Aleena knew, though. 'It's *Goodbye, Mr Chips* with Robert Donat. I've read about it. It's a weepy. Wonderful!'

'What about a quick bite of dinner afterwards?' I asked. 'At home? Toma's a wonderful cook.'

I could sense the hesitation in her voice as she whispered, almost as though afraid of being overheard, 'I'd love to, Kit, but don't rush Mummy.'

'I know what you mean. Well – Mollie Green's then?' adding with a laugh, 'That's quite safe and proper.'

'Perfect. I'll tell Mummy. You do understand, don't you?'

'That I'm not to be trusted?' I asked almost crossly.

'Oh no!' she cried. 'I'm the one who can't be trusted. Mummy knows that. She says I take after Grandma. Look what happened with Gauguin! And remember what happened at the Southern Cross!'

'Mollie Green's it shall be!' The cinema always started at seven, so I added, 'I'll pick you up at ten to seven.'

The film, as it happened, was good, and a bit newer than

292

I expected. We held hands when it was dark, cuddled when we dared, but 'The End' came far too soon and before I knew what was happening we were standing to attention for 'God Save the King'.

We drove back to Mollie's, and over dinner I broached the subject of Tiki, and Tiare's qualified approval of our love.

'I still don't understand why we shouldn't get married right away,' I said as we toyed with fresh mangoes. 'We love each other – and that's all that counts.'

'You *must* understand, darling.' Once again she had put her hand out on the table to grasp mine. 'If we *weren't* going to get married after our – well, I suppose the word *is* engagement – then we could go to bed together and no questions asked. But marriage is different from happy-go-lucky fun. If I didn't *want* to marry you – to be yours *for ever* – then I would give myself to you tonight.'

'Sounds damned stupid to me.'

'It isn't. If it's for life it's worth testing each other. If it isn't, you don't need any tests. I just happen to be a virgin, but if I weren't, if I had just had fun with the local boys without love, nobody would have minded. Look at Kinawa. She's the same age as me. She's a good girl, like a sister, she's been to bed with three or four local boys – but it meant nothing serious. So it doesn't matter.'

'It's a refreshing philosophy.' I couldn't help laughing. 'Do you mean that Kinawa – ?'

Aleena smiled. 'You find it odd?'

'I do.'

'But you see, my Kit, one's for fun and there's no harm in it. But for love it's different. You have to be sure.'

Lee Ho, Mollie's Chinese factotum, brought us coffee, saying, 'Very good coffee, lady. Straight from Australian black market.'

It *was* good – though the words 'black market' jarred, but I imagine that Lee Ho – or rather Mollie – had really bought it quite legitimately.

'I do try to understand,' I told her, still clasping hands

293

across the table. 'But what does sometimes annoy me is that it's not your mother who's taking the decision, but – '

'Our witch-doctor?' she laughed, using the same words as Tiare had done – a description obviously used by generations of missionaries.

'I wasn't going to say that.'

'But that's what you meant?'

'Your adviser,' I hastened to explain. 'You take everything he tells you as gospel. But Aleena, what right has he to run our lives? Especially when we're at war, when there's nothing permanent left in the world – '

'But he's a wonderful man,' Aleena interrupted, taking her hand out of mine and starting to drink the coffee. 'I believe him – just as I was told in college to believe the Archbishop of Canterbury.'

I burst into laughter at the thought of the Archbishop of Canterbury driving to Nottingham to tell my mother what to do, only to have my laughter interrupted as Mollie wobbled in. 'I thought you'd choked on something,' she said.

'I never choke on coffee,' I laughed.

'I'm trying to tell Kit,' explained Aleena, 'that Tiki, our wise man and adviser, is a wonderful person.'

'I believe you,' I said. 'You don't have to sell me on the idea. It's just that it affects us.'

'He *is* a remarkable man,' Mollie said. 'He's much better educated than Father Pringle. Have you never met him?'

I hadn't.

'You should,' persisted Mollie.

'Why not?' asked Aleena. 'Would you? Just to please me? He knows we love each other. Will you go for my sake?'

'I might,' I half agreed, 'if only to ask *why* – what are the reasons behind the decision to wait for such a long time.'

'He'll never tell you *that*,' Aleena warned me, almost gravely. 'He never gives reasons – he never argues or discusses, he just says yes or no.'

'Go, anyway,' said Mollie. 'He might unburden his soul

to you. Meantime, you lovebirds' – with difficulty she got out of the chair into which she had all but jammed her enormous frame – 'I'll send Lee Ho up with a couple of Sticky Greens – on the house.'

In the event I didn't see Tiki, the wise man, for several weeks, partly due to pressure of work, partly because I didn't want to, but also because Tiare very soon started to treat me as one of the family. After the first invitation to swim with Aleena, she sometimes drove off on some errand, returned and we all lunched together, and she said, 'Whenever you want to come and see us, Kit, all you have to do is ring up. You will always be welcome so long as we have no other engagements.'

I loved that unaffected way in which she used the royal 'we'. She wasn't referring to mother and daughter, but more to herself. And I was intrigued by the fact that she seemed to trust me. Of course, the unobtrusive presence of servants acted as a kind of chaperone; and then there was Kinawa, who planned to remain in Koraloona until her father and mother were able to return – and with the Japanese occupying island after island, that could be a long wait.

In a way it suited us, for Kinawa was a delight, who regarded me as a brother-in-law, and was the soul of discretion. If I went swimming, she stayed indoors or set off for a walk along the sands, climbing over the rocky headland that made Tiare's beach so private.

'If you weren't spoken for, as the missionaries used to call it in college, I'd fancy you myself.' She gave a laugh – and a sexy laugh too, as though all life was meant to be an experience of fun, to be lived to the full. But whereas Kinawa was sexy with a look of mischief in her eyes, Aleena was sensuous; she didn't only want to live life to the full, she wanted to love to the full; she was more serious, and I think the difference between the two girls was summed up by the different ways each remembered that awful morning when Sanderstown had been bombed.

'It was such a sunny day,' Kinawa remembered that Sunday morning, 'and I wonder when we'll see all the boys again.' Aleena said, 'I shall never forget the day. It was as though a curtain had been drawn across our beautiful island and the sunlight blotted out.'

In the end I did go to see the wise man, perhaps because I felt that, as Tiare had been so kind, I should repay her hospitality. I knew she would be pleased if I went.

She was so excited that she even made the appointment, and when it was arranged I made my way to Tiki's house half a mile behind the cottage hospital.

The room was small, with very little furniture. A faint scent of incense hung in the air, and a thin but very English voice said gently, 'Come in, Doctor, come in.'

I moved to the other side of the room. Tiki sat relaxed in the chair – a bearded man of uncertain age, dressed in a European suit of white duck, neatly pressed.

'Perhaps you are surprised at my clothes? You expected someone more exotic? I can assure you that I am as native to Koraloona as Tiare.'

'The Princess,' I said, stiffening at his familiar use of her name. Even old Alec Reid, who had known her far longer than I had, consistently used the title Princess.

He shrugged. I noticed that so far he had kept his eyes closed. Was he, perhaps, blind? If not, it wasn't very polite to keep your eyes shut when talking to a doctor, for the first time.

'"Princess," if you prefer. We have known each other all our lives. In any case, we are equal in the hierarchy of the island.'

'Sorry,' I said – not really meaning it.

'Oh, it's all right. I wasn't meaning royalty in the accepted sense; there are parts of our heritage that are difficult to understand for those who have lost their knowledge of the primitives beneath a veneer of sophistication.'

I thought of the primitive quality of the Gauguins; but

this was no time to edge towards irritation: I needed his help. Then he opened his eyes. Immediately I saw that he needed *my* help. They were bloodshot in the inner corners – a common result of the small capillaries breaking after a bout of coughing or sneezing, or even the rubbing of the eyes with the back of the fists while asleep. But something told me to keep my knowledge to myself. For the moment anyway.

His eyes, despite their affliction, gave life to his face. It was a lean face with high cheekbones and a beard that matched the black hair which, island style, was caught by a ring in the nape of his neck.

'No doubt you're surprised to find someone so – English?' He rephrased his question of a moment ago. 'I was adopted by one of the wealthier patrons of the Mission and sent to the New Zealand University College at Dunedin. I was thought to be an outstanding scholar. I wasn't; but I made the most of what I had. Wealthy patrons are easily impressed – they want to be, you know; it confirms their perspicacity. In return it seemed to me a courtesy to adopt the dress style and some of the manners of my benefactor. Hence the European suit that so surprises you.'

I hadn't said a word about being surprised, but he was right: I was, faintly.

'No doubt you are also surprised that I have advised against your marriage to Aleena – until her nineteenth birthday.'

'It seemed to me,' I said with mounting indignation, 'that you had *forbidden* it.' I added with an edge to my voice, 'We are not children, you know.'

Tiki smiled. ' "Forbidden" is not a word we need to use, Doctor. I am adviser to Tiare and her daughter; just as you, as a family doctor, would advise the parents of a young girl not to tempt fate. For you can be sure that if you break the laws of the islands, fate will always demand revenge. I am concerned – shall we say? – with the health of her *inner* life.'

297

I said rather sarcastically, 'Her spiritual needs are well taken care of by the nuns at the college.'

He smiled enigmatically. 'I was not meaning that kind of spirit, Doctor.'

'Then what – ?' My temper was beginning to rise.

'If you are asking me the reasons for my advice, Doctor, then I'm afraid I have nothing to reveal.' He rested his hands on the arms of the chair, as if weary. 'I, too, am a doctor of a kind, you know.'

'A bloody witch-doctor!' I said explosively. Then, hastily, I apologised.

'No need,' he said with dignity. 'I understand your feelings. But ethics are not the exclusive property of the Royal College of Physicians, you know.'

I paused, realising that I needed some sort of lever to prise from him his *reasons*.

Suddenly it came to me. 'Ah, well,' I said, as if accepting his refusal and dismissing the subject. 'No harm done. Except to your eyes.'

'My eyes?'

'Being bearded you probably don't look in a mirror very often. Here.' I took from my pocket a small polished metal shaving mirror that had been my father's during the Kaiser's war. 'Look at yourself!' As he did, I could see his reaction of horror as he saw the blood suffusing the whites of his eyes. 'You have done this to me – '

'No, no,' I said. 'Of course not. I bear no malice.'

'Then – I must have offended – '

'Some Polynesian god. Possibly. Fortunately I can assure you that my medicine is stronger than his.'

He was very quick on the uptake. 'You mean you can cure – ?'

'Oh, yes. In three days. But,' I added, 'my fee will be the information I want.'

I could see him struggling restlessly with his need to keep in with his gods, his uncertainty as to whether he had offended them. 'Blindness is a terrible thing,' I said almost casually. It was cruel, for I knew perfectly well that in a

couple of days the ruptured capillaries would heal themselves and the blood would have dispersed of its own
accord.

He returned the mirror to me and made a gesture of
despairing resignation. 'Thank you, Doctor.'

I went out to my car and returned with my 'bag of tricks'.
From it I took an eye-dropper, filled it with a few drops of
distilled water from the bottle I always carried for diluting
linctus, dissolving aspirin, and similar routine needs.
Telling him to hold his head back for a moment I squeezed
a couple of drops into the corner of each eye. It wouldn't
help his eyes in any way, but it was to him a practical
demonstration of my powers. 'There,' I said. 'Three days.'

'Thank you,' he said again.

When I returned in three days his eyes were as clear as
they had ever been – as I had known they would be. He
made no bones about paying me his 'fee'. Evidently he was
satisfied that he had offended his mysterious 'gods' by his
refusal to co-operate with me. 'You see?' I said.

He smiled gently. 'In every sense of those words – thanks
to you, Doctor.'

We sat together in another small room that I supposed he
kept as a sort of sanctuary. Carved masks adorned the
walls, some of them quite hideous. I had, basically, the
usual Englishman's indifference to superstition – though I
automatically crossed my fingers, or threw salt over my
shoulder; but I had an underlying respect for the ancient
folklorists who manifested symbols of fertility, offerings to
the gods, pleas for rain, or propitiation of evil spirits. Even
in England there were countless customs that were celebrated as rather jolly festivals but had deeper significance
underlying them – well-dressing, the phallic symbol of the
maypole, the proverbially lucky symbol of the horseshoe as
a mocking representation of a woman's vulva, the black cat
as the companion of witchcraft, the exhibition of the
wedding-night sheets to prove the rupturing of the hymen –
even if the stain was made by chicken's blood. All these and
countless more were as frequently sneered at as celebrated.

For some people scorn was their only defence against deep-seated bubblings of fear. Their 'veneer of sophistication', as Tiki called it, was used to subdue those inmost feelings.

'A bargain is a bargain,' he was saying. 'The gods must approve of my meeting your "fee" or they would not have allowed you to cure me.' (He clung to his conviction, I could see, that their 'medicine' was stronger than mine!) He went on: 'You will not know, but there is a goddess of the island, Hine-nui-te-po, who is of the moon and is therefore one to favour her kind. You understand?'

I suppose I must have looked a bit blank; but suddenly the significance hit me – of course! The moon, the monthly association with menstruation. 'Of course.'

'In times gone by, before mankind spread over the earth, it is said that Maui, her lover, tried for twice twelve moons to penetrate her and thereby make men immortal. But she resisted and so they remain . . . mortal.' He smiled. 'From that derives the rule that Hine-nui-te-po must be consulted by a wise man' – he touched his chest with his fingertips – 'whenever a pair of lovers wishes to marry; for they will not be happy unless their love is tested. I wish you both to be happy, Doctor. It was my duty to give you the secret advice of Hine-nui-te-po without revealing its source. But – ' he spread his hands and put them to his eyes – 'you swayed me with your help. I hope I have done right.'

'I'm sure you have, Tiki; and thank you.'

'Physical contact is, of course, all right. Hine-nui-te-po knows the needs of lovers. But love-making and marriage . . . twice twelve moons.' He paused. 'Think of it as ensuring happiness!' Then he added, 'You may scoff at these things but I can assure you that they are true. Have you ever read the Larousse *Dictionary of Mythology*?'

I shook my head.

'I recommend it to you. I can assure you that what I have told you is fully documented in that remarkable volume.'

'But mythology!' I protested. 'How can you take that as gospel truth?'

'Gospel is an apt word for you to choose. Can you tell me where truth and mythology are separated in the gospels of the Bible?'

19

Nothing makes the time pass more slowly than being part of a war in which you are not involved, so inactive that the world passes you by, and when the only knowledge of the momentous events around you is gleaned from newspaper headlines or radio bulletins. If anyone had tried to discover for me an escape from war they could have found no more peaceful haven than Koraloona, safe in its vast placid lagoon guarded by the reef. Yet all around us, from one end of the Pacific to the other, the fighting raged.

Like Pearl Harbor, Sanderstown had never been bombed after the first attack, and I had almost forgotten what the place looked like – or, for that matter, the actual *sounds* of war – until one afternoon, months later, I was having a siesta, dozing on the veranda when an ear-splitting screech pierced the afternoon heat and brought me to my feet, as though I had been jerked upright. Like everyone in Koraloona I rushed into the garden at the sound of planes flying at treetop height round the High Island volcano. I just had time to see them flatten out west of Anani, then they came tearing in – three of them – sweeping over us, so terrifyingly low that, as I ran towards the pier, I could see people ducking instinctively, as though to avoid being hit by the wings, each one with its Japanese marking – a white circle, its centre filled with solid bright red.

I had only one thought – bombs were about to hurtle down, machine-guns about to stutter, and I braced myself to re-live the half-forgotten horrors of the Sanderstown raid.

Before I could marshal my thoughts or think coherently,

the planes had flashed past, zoomed up and away, climbing high and harmlessly into the bright blue sky like gulls. As I shielded my eyes against the brightness, I saw them turn as though to take a last look at the rim of the volcano, then they flew west, in the direction of Penal Island, near the thunder of the reef, and then on, presumably, to their Japanese carrier.

I ran down the hill towards Main Street. Every man, woman and child seemed to have gathered near the pier, the focal point of Anani, impelled by a mixture of fear and curiosity. I made out the figure of Mollie Green lagging behind the others, as she waddled past Lee Chong's barber shop and Mick's Bar.

'Will they come back and bomb us?' Mollie finally panted, grabbing my arm. 'Oh my God! What are we going to do? They'll torture us.' More and more stories of Japanese atrocities were filling the newspapers.

'They didn't drop any bombs on us,' I reassured her. 'We're not worth wasting bombs on. Maybe they were just on a routine flying mission and wanted to see what a volcano looked like from above.'

'How did they get here?' asked someone from Mick's Bar.

'Must be from a carrier.'

Tiare and the girls had arrived. 'They're not going to invade us?' asked Tiare.

Alec Reid was followed by Bubble and Squeak, both so terrified that each clutched one of his arms. When he had disentangled himself, he raised a fist to the heavens, shouting, 'Damn them! Curse them! I willna have my beauty sleep disturbed by a bunch of yellow pygmies.'

It was left to Jim Wilson to calm our fears. 'They weren't bombers,' he pointed out, asking me, 'Did you notice a funny-looking lump under the belly of each plane?'

Notice them! It had all happened so quickly that nobody had noticed anything except the Japanese markings.

'Who could see anything?' said Mollie. 'They went by in a flash.'

302

To me – as to most people – a lump on a plane was *part* of the plane, and they all looked the same apart from the number of engines.

'What does it mean?' I asked Jim, who, after all, had been in the RFC in the Great War.

'Those bumps were automatic cameras fitted underneath the fuselage of the aircraft,' he explained. 'The Japanese version of the RAF's PRU – Photographic Reconnaissance Unit. They were taking photos of the island.'

'But what on earth for?' asked Tiare.

Nobody had an answer, but the thought that flashed through my mind was: why should they take photographs of Koraloona unless they were checking out possible invasion beaches?

In the event, I think, most people felt, as I did, that the Japanese were probably on a routine training flight and took the opportunity to look over the rim of a volcano. But within the hour – by which time many of us were at the Union Jack Club – Bill Shanks, the radio operator, telephoned Colonel Fawcett, who was at the club, with startling news which had been transmitted from Penal Island to Koraloona on their own radio link.

The chief police official in charge of Penal Island announced that the planes which had skimmed so casually across Main Street had spent an hour photographing Penal Island, over and over again in what seemed, according to the information we could glean, a kind of rectangular pattern.

'I know what *that* means!' Jim Wilson explained. 'If you do it accurately, you can build up what's almost like a three-dimensional photograph, which can be enlarged to show every building – indeed every window in every building.'

'But they wouldna be interested in a wee speck of rock like Penal,' said Alec Reid.

'Unless they're planning to land there – ' It was Tiare's troubled voice.

303

'No one could do that,' said Mollie. 'It's like a fortress.'

'People have tried to organise escapes even from places like Devil's Island,' someone said. 'Why not Penal?'

'Especially the Japs. After all there are over half a dozen Japs in jail there,' I pointed out.

'Interned,' corrected Fawcett.

'They might try to free their comrades,' said someone. 'I will say this for the Japs: they're not scared of certain death.'

'Neither would ye be if ye regarded death as an honour,' said Reid.

'And,' said Tiare bitterly, half afraid, 'I know one man who would stop at nothing, but who has no wish to die – Mana!'

No one knew more than we had been told. But Colonel Fawcett, who had already advised Sanderstown about the Japanese flight over Koraloona, didn't even stop to finish his drink, saying, 'I think I'd better get through to GHQ at Sanderstown personally. Puts a different complexion on the whole business, eh?'

He did fill in Sanderstown with all the details he could, and it had an immediate effect. Early the next morning, half a dozen RAF planes flew over Koraloona on a 'goodwill' visit, their British roundels plainly visible. They flew over the entire lagoon, waggling their wings in a traditional salute over Main Street where everyone in Anani had gathered, some in terror because they did not know one plane from another, others cheering as they recognised the friendly aircraft.

Though it was a goodwill visit, Colonel Fawcett explained when next we all met, 'It's not so much a fear of invasion that worries GHQ, as the fact, by God, that Japanese aircraft are able to fly anywhere they like and cock a snook at us. We need an early warning system – like in the Battle of Britain, but we don't have the machines or the specialists.'

Later that day Commander Serpell managed to get Alec

on the radio sked, and told him that Sanderstown was trying to persuade Whitehall to release specialist operators to man a string of stations linking all the islands across the Pacific to track Japanese air movements.

'But he doesn't hold out much hope,' Alec told me later gloomily. 'They dinna have even a couple of WAAFs to spare – and they'd make a welcome change.'

In the end though, something was done – but from an unexpected source.

One Sunday morning a month after we had been buzzed by the Japanese planes, Colonel Fawcett convened an extraordinary meeting of members of the Union Jack Club for eleven o'clock – neatly timed, I knew from experience, to allow Father Pringle to offer prayers and a few hymns to his flock, but earlier than usual for the meeting to be followed by the usual pre-lunch Sunday drinks – the Koraloona equivalent of England's national pastime of Sunday morning at the pub before sitting down to roast beef and Yorkshire pudding.

For a few moments the members talked among themselves. Paula Reece was trying to be affable, and Tiare was talking to Alec Reid and Jim Wilson. I heard a snatch of Tiare's conversation, 'The car just doesn't seem to start as well as it did,' and Jim's 'I'll have a look at it'. Then Colonel Fawcett stood up in front of the bridge table, his back to the bar, and announced, 'Ladies and gentlemen, please – will you all be seated,' and when everyone was sitting down and waiting expectantly he said, 'Thank you all for coming to this meeting at such short notice. The matter in hand concerns you all as the leading members of our community. I did explain to Father Pringle that I didn't wish to interfere with any churchgoers but as you know he held his service earlier to enable us to meet.'

He took a deep breath, and with that sense of importance which he wore with the pleasure of putting on a smart suit he said, 'As we all know, our gallant allies the Americans are fighting magnificently, and,' with a dramatic pause, 'I am delighted and proud to announce that they are going to help with the defence of Koraloona.'

There was a gasp. Daisy Gilbert, who lived in the pink house in Anani, called, 'Why on earth should *Americans* be needed to defend Koraloona?'

'If I may explain,' the colonel added hastily, seeing the look of amazement on everyone's faces. 'Not – ahem! – to *fight* here. But as part of the, er, defence strategy of the entire area.'

'Meaning what?' asked Jason Purvis. 'Why the hell talk in riddles?'

'Really, Purvis. Please moderate your language. Especially on a Sunday. I was about to explain. A small force of American troops is going to be stationed on Koraloona to help with the overall defence of the archipelago.'

There were more gasps of disbelief. I heard someone mutter, 'This is British soil!' Questions were shouted: 'How many?' 'Where will they stay?' 'Aren't our own soldiers good enough?'

Colonel Fawcett held up his hand, '*Please*, fellow members,' he cried, 'there's no cause for alarm. There'll only be between fifty and a hundred soldiers to man an air station equipped with plane-spotting apparatus.'

Most of the members looked nonplussed. 'It's all part of a link which, when properly used, will give headquarters in Sanderstown vital information on enemy air movements,' explained Colonel Fawcett.

'But why no British troops?' asked one member.

'We don't have enough British troops in the area – and aeroplane detection is a highly specialised job. We lost a lot of skilled men when the Japanese attacked Sanderstown and British forces are fighting all over the world. We are very grateful that the Americans will help us out with such specialised technical skills.'

A few minutes later the colonel explained that the American troops would bring their own prefabricated huts. Their rations and equipment would be supplied by sea, and three officers would command the unit.

'It shouldn't make any disruption to our way of life on the island,' said Fawcett a trifle sententiously; but I knew it would. There was no way you could put a hundred or so randy American men amongst a bevy of bare-breasted, willing and eager girls without causing a lot of 'disruption' as the colonel rather pompously called it. Horizontal disruption, I thought and caught sight of Paula Reece who had a gleam in her eye. Even she couldn't cope with fifty at a time, I reflected.

A few days later the American commander, a naval lieutenant, Sam Truscott, arrived by frigate to make an inspection, choose the site, and, as he announced casually, construct a small strip for aircraft. He anchored off Tala-Tala and a crane hoisted up two small open four-seater runabouts of a kind I had never seen before, and landed them on the tiny pier of the Yacht Club. I had driven down to Tala-Tala more out of curiosity than for any other reason when I saw the frigate making its way past the reef and into the calm waters of the lagoon.

'Looks a useful runabout,' I said to a sailor.

'Sure is,' he said cheerfully. 'Four-wheel drive. Great little performer. It's called a jeep.'

At that moment the man I took to be the commander of the proposed contingent arrived in his khaki uniform and I noticed that he had wings on his chest, showing that he was a pilot. As he approached the jeep with half a dozen soldiers, he looked at me and I looked at him, puzzled at half recognising each other. I knew I had seen that face before – somewhere – but I couldn't put a name to it.

'Hope I'm not in a military zone,' I laughed, shaking hands. 'I'm one of the local doctors.'

'I'm Lieutenant – ' he pronounced it Lootenant, of course – 'Truscott. Glad to meet you, Doctor Masters.'

Rather puzzled I asked him, 'You know my name?'

'Sure. Recognised you immediately. We met at the Officers' Club in Sanderstown with Commander Serpell.'

Of course! The young blond officer who had asked Ronnie Serpell to meet him after lunch.

On this first day, Truscott inspected a stretch of flat ground near Tabanea, and a cigar-chewing military engineer who was with him said that this was the longest possible strip for a proposed airfield. Round the corner, beyond Tabanea, they would build their camp and erect four scanning towers and what were called 'dishes'.

Three weeks later, the smudge of a strange vessel appeared over the horizon. A 10,000-ton grey-coloured cargo ship with no name but with large numbers painted on its stern made its way through the reef and, as soon as it docked, started disgorging an incredible assortment of cargo unloaded by grinding winches at Anani pier, including more jeeps, bulldozers, tractors, all handled by a bunch of khaki-clad Americans who kept up a ceaseless banter as they worked, especially when the word went round among the locals. Soon a crowd was watching curiously and the GIs, as they called themselves, were admiring the bare-breasted girls, and giving wolf whistles and shouts of, 'She's for me, baby!' And when any of the girls laughed a lot – which meant a lot of movement of their breasts – the wolf whistles doubled and it seemed as though the real work of unloading and transporting would never get done.

I didn't then know anything about the Americans' brand of disguised energy, the way in which they approached work with a casual air, giving at first an opposite impression to the discipline of British troops.

In fact they worked – as many would fight – equally well; only they went about their chores or fighting in a different way, with a grin, with no *apparent* regard for rank, so that often I heard shouts of 'Hi, Sarge!' or 'Where do you want this, Lootenant?' They didn't salute, they seemed to smoke all the time, often chewing cigars, addressing an officer without taking the cigar or cigarette out of the corner of a mouth.

308

'No wonder they were caught on the hop at Pearl Harbor,' said a disapproving Colonel Fawcett.

'Well, Colonel, we too were caught on the hop at Sanderstown,' I said.

He didn't answer.

Lieutenant Truscott did not come back on this first unloading trip, but within three days the little pier at Anani was as empty as it had always been, and within a week an entire village of wooden huts for seventy American soldiers was being assembled from parts that only needed nuts and bolts and floorboards to transform flat pieces of wood into sturdy dwellings. There was everything – from a cookhouse to latrines, and on the other side of Tabanea another miracle was performed. It was an airstrip which seemed to have been constructed from huge sections of metal with holes in them, like pieces of a gigantic Meccano set.

I took Aleena to see the new village springing to life. She was as fascinated as I was by the speed of the construction gangs creating this prefabricated settlement out of nothing except what they had brought with them.

'Why can't we do that with an island village?' she asked.

'It would cost a fortune and people only waste fortunes in time of war.'

'Don't worry, ma'am,' said one sergeant who was standing near, showing us what was happening. 'When we've kicked these goddam Japs out of the Pacific, you can have the lot, free, gratis and for nothing. We won't take it back. Cost too much.'

'It would make a wonderful cottage hospital,' I said without thinking. 'The one we've got only has six beds.'

'You're the local doctor, sir?'

I nodded and Aleena, who was dressed in a sarong, with a scarlet hibiscus in her black hair cascading over her shoulders, said very seriously, and with a touching pride in me, 'Doctor Masters is the best doctor in the islands. And we're engaged to be married in a few months.'

'You don't say! Lucky man, sir.'

'I know.' I said goodbye and we walked across the flat ground, arms round each other's waists, feeling the warmth of her body through the thin island cotton of her sarong.

I drove towards home, then stopped the car on a lonely stretch of road and kissed her. 'Don't you think we're crazy?' I asked huskily for the hundredth time, 'not going all the way. We must be the only two adults on Koraloona who – '

'I know,' she whispered between kisses. 'Don't you think that, at this moment, it's almost as though we've done it. I get so excited when you kiss me, but – '

'Then *let's* do it,' I said desperately.

She hesitated, kissed me again with her lips open and then said almost gravely, 'If you really want me to, I'll break my vow. If you really want to, I will. Only – well, the months are passing by so quickly and soon – '

At this moment I could have possessed her. And yet something stopped me. The one thing I didn't want was for her to think that I had forced her, because the kind of vow that she had taken was as important to her as a similar vow would be to a religious-minded Catholic.

Looking back now to the times when such terrible things were happening in the war, and when I nearly lost her, I sometimes find it hard to remember that in the 1930s and 1940s millions of young people thought it wrong to sleep together until they were married. And long engagements were considered right and proper. Now –

'Yes,' I repeated with a sigh, 'you are right.' I stopped stroking her long legs under her sarong and sat back in my normal driving position. 'Only I *am* healthy and young, and if I didn't love you so much I'd be going to bed with all the local girls.'

'If I didn't love *you* so much, I'd be going to bed with you.'

'Ah, well, it's another cold bath for me. Or else a night of lonely love.'

'It's better than nothing. But just remember – I love you with all my heart and, whatever happens, I always will. And soon I'll be loving you with all my body as well as my heart.'

In fact we were very happy together, our 'understanding' had given us the status of an engaged couple – happier in many ways when we were *not* alone with each other because the presence of others helped me to stifle my physical desire; and, as Toma was recognised as one of the finest cooks on the island, we held more and more 'respectable' parties, dinners to which I invited Tiare with Aleena, sometimes Purvis, sometimes Alec Reid, even occasionally Paula Reece, and some of the other expatriates. Alec was always welcome, for I felt that he was beginning to show his age – not seriously yet, but there were tell-tale signs and sometimes I caught him staring vacantly into space. But he certainly gave the impression of enjoying himself when dining at my bungalow. And he loved good food.

'What banquet are you preparing for tonight?' he asked before one dinner which was to be graced by the presence of Colonel and Mrs Fawcett as well as Tiare and Aleena, Alec, and Jason Purvis.

'The main dish is *gari vakasoso*,' I said. 'Originally a Fijian dish, but you've had it here before, I'm sure – basically it's crab cooked in coconut cream. At least we know the crabs will be fresh.'

'Aye, that'll do fine,' he agreed.

Almost at the last moment Tiare cried off with a touch of cold and, although I wasn't particularly fond of Paula, I was on the point of asking her, when Jason, who happened to be passing – as he often did when he was thirsty! – said, 'Why not ask Miss Sowerby?'

'Miss Sowerby?' I looked at him incredulously.

'Why not? She works damned hard and she doesn't get much of a break.'

At first I dismissed the idea, for though I occasionally

met Miss Sowerby 'socially' at the Union Jack Club, she *didn't* – in Jason's words – get much of a break. 'Why not?' I asked finally. 'But she'll never come.'

She nearly didn't. In the dispensary I asked her and she actually blushed – if that weatherbeaten face could be said to blush – and after a bit of humming and hawing, I appealed to Alec who said, 'Good idea, Miss Sowerby. Ye'll come!'

The one thing that I had never expected from Miss Sowerby was the age-old lament of every woman in the world, 'But I've got nothing to wear.'

'What about the dress with the short sleeves?' I suggested. 'You remember? The one you wore the night of that storm. I liked it.'

So Miss Sowerby came, behaved decorously, of course, but was not afraid to speak her mind. And, with a touch of amusement, I noticed that, whenever Jason Purvis was about to help himself to another drink, she looked at him, pursed her lips and folded her hands across her lap. And more often than not Jason took the hint.

The evening gave me a great deal of tenderness, especially when I watched the way Colonel Fawcett treated Aleena as a grown-up – almost eighteen, playing the role of hostess, and doing it very well.

Perhaps the evening was also helped by a bottle of Sticky Green which I bought from Johnson's, and particularly when I persuaded Miss Sowerby to try a thimbleful (though, of course, Alec stuck to neat Scotch). In fact when the party broke up at midnight – a sign of success! – Purvis offered to escort Miss Sowerby home, and though her bungalow was only three minutes from mine, Miss Sowerby said primly but pleased, 'Thank you, Mr Purvis. I shall be delighted.'

Normally I would have driven Aleena home, but I had to visit the hospital to check on the condition of a young boy who had hurt his leg. So I asked Alec to take Aleena home, and then returned home to bed. A very successful evening, I thought.

But for how much longer would I be doomed to spend the nights alone?

Two days after that 'formal dinner', and when the American camp was finished, a dot appeared in the sky, a plane circled the island, and Lieutenant Truscott arrived. He was flying, as I learned later, an AT6 Harvard, the training plane for Mustang fighters. It had a speed of 300 mph at 20,000 feet and could land on a 500-yard-long airstrip. Though only a two-seater trainer, its speed meant that it could cut the trip from Koraloona to Sanderstown to under half an hour.

Realising what was happening, I drove to watch the plane arrive. Truscott made a perfect three-point landing, trundled up to the control tower – another prefabricated hut with a wind-sock next to it – and seeing me, called, 'Hiya, Kit! Come over and have a drink and maybe a swim.'

He was a likeable fellow, but I took to him particularly because there was really no one else on the island of the same age. We had a long swim that afternoon and then he took me to the 'Officers' Mess' for a drink – 'Old Methuselah', he said. 'It's standard Navy issue whisky, not to be confused with Scotch' – and after the second or third he explained that he was a Navy flyer – as opposed to the US Army Air Force – and asked me to stay for dinner, which consisted of typically huge American steaks, each one weighing more than half a pound. I thought of my family in Nottingham, rationed to about a shilling's worth of meat and, officially, one egg a week, when here there was everything that anybody could want and enough to spare.

'How do you like them – normal?' asked Truscott, and when I nodded he shouted to the Mess steward, 'Joe, the doc'll have the same as me – medium rare.'

'Why the need for a plane?' I asked.

He looked surprised. 'I'm Navy but, seconded to the Army as I've done a course in radar.' He noted my puzzled look, and added, 'It's a sort of aeroplane-spotting gimmick.

313

We've got a liaison officer with the British in Sanderstown –
and, of course, all the outlying islands. Flying's just the
natural way to communicate. Besides,' with a cheerful grin,
'I think I told you I've got a girl who once lived in the
islands. I'm going to get permission to have her come over
to Sanderstown. So I'll need my plane to go over every time
I can. By the way, talking of girls – and nothing to do with
my girl! – how much clap is there in Koraloona?'

I couldn't help laughing at his directness.

'Like your steaks,' I replied. 'Medium, rare.'

'Thank God! I'm responsible for my men and I don't
want them all reporting sick. I guess I'll have to indent for
things like rubbers and so on. But I want to ask you
something. Could you become a sort of honorary medical
officer for our outfit? It's too small to warrant a hospital or
medical facilities of its own, specially as it's a joint Army
and Navy enterprise. I don't know whether anybody can
pay you – '

'But what about Doc Reid?' I asked. 'After all he is the
senior doctor.'

'Sure, but,' Truscott hesitated, 'he's kinda old, isn't
he? The boys'd like you. Pardon me if I speak out of
turn, Kit, but people like old Colonel Fawcett and Doctor
Reid – gee, I can't understand half of what they say. You
behave natural – why goddammit, you could almost be an
American.'

'A compliment! I'd love to help if I can, but I must clear it
first with Alec.'

'I expected you to say that. But you will. In fact I told the
liaison officer whom I wanted, and we talked about some
arrangement for paying you for your services when necessary and he made a suggestion.'

'He did?'

Truscott nodded. 'Yeah,' he said. 'All this question of
keeping accounts is a load of bullshit. He suggested that if
you'd help out where necessary, he'd arrange for the next
transport ship, due in a couple of weeks, to bring an extra
item of cargo – a jeep. Just for you. Mind you it'll be on

loan – but we'd write its value down so that when the war's over you could buy it for ten bucks.'

A jeep. I had been fascinated by this sturdy little workhorse ever since I first saw one, and of course by now the jeeps were a common sight, while my clapped-out car was nearing the end of its life. On the edge of the beaches or parked outside Mick's Bar – doing a roaring trade now of course – I had seen jeeps at almost every corner of the island, and I would have loved to own one.

Alec put no obstacles in my way and said 'Yes' immediately, but, generous though he was in spirit, I detected a sign of the passing years when he said, 'Och aye, there's nothing like a war to make an old man feel older.'

It was the first time I realised, I think, that Alec Reid had spent nearly half his life on the island which he loved among the people he loved; and I wondered what he would do, how his life would change, when he no longer had the urge to work. Do missionary doctors get pensions? Would that chain him to the island? Or would he go back and live with his wife a world away in Wimbledon?

Being co-opted on to the 'staff' of the US base gave me several privileges including the right to buy goods from the PX, the name for military Post Exchange, a dry canteen specially opened all over the world for Army and Navy personnel. There they could buy cigarettes, chocolate, Zippo lighters, casual off-duty clothing – such as sweat shirts, sports shirts, and slacks – and quite a few foods which were beginning to be in short supply. I didn't want to use the PX too often – it seemed unfair to the other expatriates on the island – but I *was* able to get plenty of tobacco for Alec Reid and the occasional box of chocolates for Aleena and Tiare.

The camp also provided another treat which Aleena loved – a good film. The Ritz was a cinema of habit – you went there every Friday, irrespective of what was being shown, simply to pass an evening. At the camp cinema, however, they showed up-to-date films in good condition, and I was allowed to take Aleena. The first film we saw together there was *The Road to Morocco* with Bing Crosby, Bob Hope and Dorothy Lamour.

I remember that she wore her hair down over her shoulders, on that first visit, and she was dressed in slacks, with a white silk blouse.

The camp cinema was held in the Mess Hall, and all the tables, which had folding legs, had been stashed away, and the hard chairs arranged in neat rows. The first row was for officers – but since there were only three, it included VIP guests – such as ourselves. NCOs sat in the second row, and the back two rows were kept for local civilian workers and their families – though no one under twelve was allowed.

In between there was plenty of room for all the GIs; and there was an outburst of wolf whistles when Lieutenant Truscott led in Aleena, with me following. There were uninhibited cries of 'Wow!' and 'Gee! What a babe!' and no sooner had Sam Truscott shown us to our seats than the wolf whistles started all over again, this time for another guest who had been invited – Paula Reece. For she, as usual, looked as though she had just stepped out of the most expensive dressmaker's in the world. She gave me a polite smile, which I returned – I felt warmer towards her now that everyone in Koraloona knew that I had become the 'official' escort of Aleena. Sam motioned her to a chair between his and mine.

Looking at Aleena, pleased with the wolf whistles, which a grinning Sam Truscott made no attempt to check, I couldn't help thinking again of the difference between the American and British soldiers. I was astounded at the way in which American officers made no attempt to quieten their men. I still didn't understand their codes of discipline which we found hard to accept, but which made them just as efficient fighting forces as ours.

Paula leaned across me to ask Aleena, 'Is this your first visit to the camp cinema?'

Aleena nodded. 'Better than the flea pit!' she laughed.

316

'And the film is so new. Much later even than the ones we used to see in Sanderstown.'

Turning to me, Paula said, 'So you're the official camp doctor?'

'Yes,' I said briefly, feeling Aleena's right hand squeezing my left one between our two chairs. 'And in love?' she said, with a touch of mocking irony, as though to say, 'Puppy love! You'll get over it.'

I didn't think the question needed an answer, but luckily Sam leaned over to ask her something. Aleena, squeezing my hand more tightly, whispered so quietly that I could only just make out the words, 'I'm so glad you never went to bed with her.'

'So am I,' I whispered back. 'She thinks she's God's answer for all men.'

'And me?' The tinkling laughter was back in her voice.

'You're God's answer for me,' I replied, and we settled down to watch the film.

Once the film had ended, the makeshift cinema emptied with amazing rapidity. There was no playing the 'Stars and Stripes', the equivalent of 'God Save the King', just some nostalgic Hawaiian-type music. Nor was there any attempt to let the officers file out first.

'They're thirsty,' explained Sam's number two, who was introduced as Lieutenant J. G. Dixon – which at first I assumed to be his initials until I discovered later that 'JG' meant 'Junior Grade', an American Second Lieutenant. 'Thirsty and – hungry,' he said with a grin.

'I thought they'd already eaten dinner,' said Aleena innocently.

'Not chow hungry, Miss,' said Dixon. 'If you'll excuse my directness – girl hungry. But it's like standing in the chow line, if you get my meaning. First come first served.'

There were other changes as time passed, not all for the good of the island, once the small American military unit was thoroughly established. The Americans had created a new township out of thin air and at some distance from

317

Anani and Tala-Tala. But the islanders were used to long walks or cycling, and the American attractions – not only of sex – were too wonderful to resist.

Girls who had regarded fermented orange juice as a free annual alcoholic binge, and soft drinks as a treat, suddenly discovered Americans offering them unlimited Coca-Cola. Cigarettes, never a female vice in Koraloona, were distributed to girls without second thought; and many of the girls whose ideas of sexual morality were cheerfully naïve would take cartons of cigarettes from an American, make love if he wanted to, partly because she enjoyed it, but also so that she could supply her special island boyfriend with cigarettes. I don't think the men ever encouraged the girls to 'earn' cigarettes for them. There was no suggestion of 'pimping', but they didn't mind encouraging a girl to give herself to an American so that she could get a free carton of Camels.

I must say that, when I first heard about it, I didn't like it. I'm no prude, but one of the most delightful aspects of life on Koraloona had always been the innocence of its people. There might be the odd villain like Mana, but he was an exception, and even the few Japanese who lived on Koraloona and had been interned as enemy aliens on Penal Island seemed harmless and in the past had always been happy. The prospect of this idyllic life being soiled by an influx of unattached males might pose disagreeable problems. I only hoped Truscott could keep his men in check.

Yet it was hard for the men and women of the villages to resist temptation. Money had never really interested Polynesians, each of whom had enough to eat and drink and a roof over their heads – but that was largely because wages were so low that money was no attraction. With the exception of the staff employed by Paula Reece, and the barmen at the club, most men and women in Koraloona had only done the occasional day's work when it suited them.

Now it had all changed. The Americans were big spenders, and men and women clamoured for regular jobs because of the perks that went with work in the laundry, or washing-up in the military canteen, or, for the men, gardening, cleaning out the 'honeybuckets', as the latrines were called. For the favoured civilians attached to the tiny base were given luxuries never before known on Koraloona – the flat purple-wrapped packets of Hershey chocolate bars, so much food that half-finished steaks which would have been thrown away in America were now grabbed by eager Polynesian hands; there was even food which had never been served because too much was always cooked, and often this was taken home to feed entire families with hitherto unknown delicacies.

A smart girl working in the military canteen could often take home enough food to feed her family for days. She wasn't stealing it, she was allowed to take left-overs. They even took home tins or cans of milk or – with supreme irony – tinned fruit. To many families, a can opener was now for the first time an indispensable item of their kitchens.

And over the weeks (and later, months) I noticed the beginning of a trend among many families, especially in the Tabanea area, close to the base. No man had ever been overworked in Koraloona, but now they were growing positively lazy. In a world of abundant food, men had only worked to grow what they needed – and even that had not been arduous since the good earth provided most of everything they needed. But now, as Jason said to me one evening, 'It's as though tins of corned beef are growing as profusely on the trees as coconuts or breadfruit.'

Yet we enjoyed one blessing on our island: peace. Since that first fright, when the three Japanese planes flew over, we had not seen any more for months, while in strange contrast to the brutal and global war around us, Singapore, the Philippines, Java, dozens of smaller islands were gobbled up by Japanese to form their co-prosperity sphere. Even Singapore, where I had stopped on my way to Australia, had been re-named Shonan. Hundreds and thousands of Allied prisoners were now dying after being

319

tortured in forced labour camps in the sweating jungles of the Asian mainland, while we lived in peace.

It was with supreme irony, therefore, that death suddenly came to Koraloona on a horrifying scale. Not death from war, though that would come later too; but death from peace, a peace that would kill almost as many people as those who died in the frightful bombing of Sanderstown.

20

Early one morning in September 1943 before the first patients arrived for surgery, I suddenly saw a woman approaching whom I recognised as Jimbo's mother. Though she was hefty she was carrying the boy with difficulty as he seemed to be in pain.

'Trouble!' said Alec. 'I thought it was too good to be true, this cure of yours for polio.'

'We don't know if it *is* polio,' I retorted almost crossly. 'Probably he only wants his radio battery renewed again.'

Mrs Jimbo (as I always thought of her) unhooked the boy's arms from around her neck as Miss Sowerby, who had been brushing the veranda before the morning surgery, came forward to greet the boy with a smile. After all, she had helped greatly with his recovery.

'Jimbo!' she began – but her pleasure vanished when she saw – as we did – the agony in the boy's face.

Alec and I moved automatically into the 'theatre'.

'Sit down.' I indicated the table. Jimbo seemed unable to speak.

'Is leg.' Mrs Jimbo pointed to her son.

'Leg?' I said blankly. There were no signs of wounds or breakage.

'Pain.' She touched the limb. 'Leg jump, it makes pain.' She indicated spasmodic movement.

As Alec and I looked at each other across the table, I felt

my heart sink. Alec's eyes were saying as clearly as any words, 'I told you so. You and your new-fangled methods. A temporary cure, perhaps. But in the end you've got to fall back on the proper treatment.'

Though Alec hadn't said a word, I felt as if my guts had been wrenched from me. All that faith and work and midnight blanket-wringing; the triumph, the boy with his infected muscles set to rights. And now, 'Start all over again,' I muttered to myself.

All this passed through my mind in a few seconds as the healer's carpet on which I had so proudly set my feet was whipped from beneath me.

But – had it? I suddenly recalled one of the old professors at St Andrew's saying, when we were note-taking at his lecture on what he called 'Diagnostic Doubts': 'And write this down in capital letters: TAKE NOTHING FOR GRANTED.'

A few more seconds passed.

'Where's the pain, Jimbo?' I asked. I took his hand, which was clammy and seemed to be shrivelled like a washerwoman's. Alarmingly. I could feel almost no pulse in the wrist. He muttered something I could scarcely hear, his voice was so gritty.

I looked to Mrs Jimbo for enlightenment. 'What's he say?'

She shook her hand and held up a finger. 'He make no water. One day no water, make pain inside.' She described with a single finger what I guessed to be a distended bladder.

'I see,' I said flatly. Again my glance crossed with Alec's. Was he, too, thinking back into the distant days when he'd done his 'trops'? I was trying to drag the details from the back of my mind. Minimal pulse, cramps, husky voice, suppressed urine, clammy skin . . .

Suddenly the boy on the table began to make awful heaving noises. He struggled to raise his body, his skin had taken on a bluish tinge and he began to vomit rackingly – a thin colourless explosion with a filthy smell.

Miss Sowerby rushed for a basin, but it was too late. The

flood of bile was all over the boy, splashing on to my trousers and Alec's who had attempted to support Jimbo as he raised his body. Our glances interlocked in horror.

'Christ Almighty!' I said. From the corner of my eye I saw Miss Sowerby's shocked reaction. But this was no time for niceties. Alec's head was nodding in confirmation.

Cholera!

My first feeling was one of shivering fear, not for myself, but for the island which suddenly, without warning, faced – unless it could be checked – one of mankind's greatest scourges, a plague that could decimate the 3,000 people of Koraloona with the devastating speed of a hurricane.

I know all doctors are trained to repress their feelings, but there are certain plague-type diseases that act so swiftly, kill off so many, that the prospect wipes out all dispassionate feeling. Cholera was one of these.

Looking at poor little Jimbo, retching as he lay in his own vomit, I suddenly felt sick myself – not because of the foul smell that filled the room, but daunted by the way the water-borne disease could be transmitted – a disease which doomed people not only to die, but to live the final hours of their life in unimaginable agony.

I stole a look at Alec. His face had sagged with despair. He had lived through one cholera epidemic many years ago, and knew what to expect now. What frightened me was that I thought I detected a look of resignation in his usually cheerful face; as though the blow was too much to bear, that he knew what the consequences would be – death everywhere because of one vital factor: there was no way we could inoculate the entire population of the island.

I looked at Miss Sowerby, as though hoping against hope that she could provide me with good news.

'How much vaccine do we have?' I asked.

Before she could think out a reply, two figures staggered into the garden. One was a big, broad man, the other a frail woman. Both looked on the edge of death. The woman's eyes stared out of a sunken face which had turned a pasty

322

grey. As they half stood, half fell, both vomited on the ground, again that filthy, colourless liquid. The man stood for a while, but the woman keeled over as Miss Sowerby rushed to help her.

I recognised the two faces, though I couldn't place them. 'From Tabanea – like Jimbo.' Alec almost vomited himself.

I felt as badly as he did. But I asked Miss Sowerby again, 'How much vaccine do we have?'

She let the woman gently down on to the ground. 'God rest her soul,' she said. 'She's already dead.' And to me she added, 'Vaccine? Perhaps enough for about five hundred inoculations.'

'Dear God!' I said. 'Five hundred for three thousand people.' And, staring at the shrunken face of the dead woman with a kind of fascination, I added, 'Let me think for a moment.'

Thank God, I reflected, Alec, Miss Sowerby and I, together with Jason Purvis and Paula Reece and the expats had kept our inoculations up-to-date – for the cholera vaccine has a life of only six months and you needed to have a booster shot twice a year.

I was trying to get some semblance of order into my thoughts. I knew that one great danger of cholera is the dehydration which follows the first attacks, so I told Miss Sowerby, 'Put the boy on an intravenous saline drip right away. And keep the tap on in the ward to encourage him to pass urine.' You had to make a patient urinate, otherwise he could die of uraemia – the accumulation of poisons normally evacuated with urine.

But that was only one problem. What of the larger problems? The woman dead. The man was past saving, I could see that. And as I tried to formulate my thoughts, two more patients arrived. We had to treat them, we would have to bury those who died – and we had to inoculate the island. But with what?

Tabanea was near the American base and it was obvious that the disease had started in Tabanea. What if it spread to the base? The troops would have been inoculated, of course, it was standard military routine, but inoculations don't always prevent a carrier from bringing disease to someone who should be safe.

As though shaking off this mental shock, Alec came up with a suggestion.

'Let's at least use the vaccine to keep cholera away from Anani.'

'Good idea,' I said. 'Miss Sowerby – please get hold of Jason and Paula Reece as soon as you've fixed up Jimbo. We'll organise the mass inoculation of Anani. I'm going to telephone the base and warn them what's happening – and to ask for help.'

'What sort of help?'

'It seems to me,' I said, 'if you agree, that Sam Truscott could fly right away to Sanderstown for vaccine supplies and bring them back – as much as he can get to start with – then Alec, why don't you, as the boss, go round and see Colonel Fawcett and alert him. And maybe he could radio Auckland and have supplies flown out from New Zealand. Or even small supplies from islands like Rarotonga. After all we *are* isolated. An island is like one huge isolation hospital.'

There was another point which I had to attend to before I saw Sam. I must be absolutely sure that this was the more virulent of the two types of cholera. I was sure in my own mind, yet I needed proof that this wasn't the milder *cholera nostras* – known as 'summer diarrhoea' – instead of *cholera morbus*, known to every laboratory expert as 'the comma' because that is the shape of the bacillus of cholera. The symptoms are the same for both. So I had to take a sample of Jimbo's stool, seal it up, so that I could send it to Sanderstown. Only after I had done this did I phone Sam Truscott.

There was another immediate problem. If the disease spread quickly, we would need all the saline drip solution we had – and containers for the drips. We would have to treat every single patient with a saline solution to compensate for salt loss. Had we enough distilled water? Perhaps we would have to use Alec's once-tried successful method of using pure coconut water – which had saved my own life. And what about syringes? And yet, all this was nothing, compared with the urgency of preventing the spread of disease, almost invariably caused by contamination of water supply by human beings. That is a far more important transmitter of the disease than flies or dirty food.

And if – as now seemed obvious – cholera had started in Tabanea, I had to warn Sam that the disease was on his doorstep, and villagers using infected water could act as carriers every time they came into the camp.

I managed to get Truscott after some delay and took a deep breath before I said to him, 'Sam, we're in deep trouble. We've got an outbreak of cholera. Two deaths ten minutes ago.'

'Jesus wept! On the island?'

'Even worse. In Tabanea. That's where it's started. Must be infected water.'

'What can we do?' I could detect a note of near-panic in his voice, even over the crackling telephone.

'Three things – first a minute's job: confine everyone to barracks. And second, send all canteen labour home until we've licked the outbreak.'

'Hell, what a step. But still – will do. And next?'

'Get on that plane of yours pronto – to use one of your favourite words – and fly to Sanderstown for me. Don't leave the airfield when you get there. Every minute's delay is dangerous. During the time you're airborne, Alec will get on the sked to Commander Serpell who'll contact your liaison officer, and collect all the vaccine there is in Sanderstown, together with spare syringes, bottles for saline drip and so on. We've got to inoculate three thousand people if we can. By the time you arrive at Sanderstown airfield, the medical boys at the base will be waiting for you with supplies. They'll have to hurry to beat you – even allowing for the time it'll take you to gas up before flying back here.'

'Is it really that urgent? I mean – only two dead, it's not what you'd call an epidemic.'

'That's what we've got to stop – if there's time. Two dead now could mean twenty-two dead tomorrow, two hundred and twenty-two dead the day afterwards. Cholera can kill a healthy normal man in twenty-four hours.'

'But *how*?'

'Infected water. But Sam, don't waste time asking questions. I'll give you all the reasons you want when you return.'

'Sorry.' Sam still sounded frightened, but added, 'I'm on my way. My God! Cholera! It doesn't bear thinking about. As if I didn't have enough trouble without that.'

'Meaning what?' I asked.

'Girl trouble. Not to worry. You get on the sked to Sanderstown and I'll get on the plane right away.'

I dashed up to Colonel Fawcett's house. The colonel and Bill Shanks were already trying to make contact by short-wave radio to Australia – a major transmitter, nothing to do with our local radio link. Alec had already arrived there and alerted them.

'Sam's almost on his way to Sanderstown,' I explained. 'And when he gets there he'll be ready to turn right round if the supplies are ready. So can you persuade Serpell to have materials ready at the airfield in Sanderstown so as not to waste time?'

'I'll do it right away.' I could see that asking Alec to act not only pleased him, but stopped some of his earlier depression. 'We'll need all the phials of vaccine they've got in Sanderstown,' he said.

'And make sure the Americans help – maybe they could fly more supplies in from Hawaii,' I interrupted. ' 'Specially if Serpell tells them that the outbreak is right next door to the American base.'

'That'll scare them,' said Alec.

By now Jason and Paula had arrived. Paula Reece was as grey as a bucket of ashes and the sight of the contorted bodies lying in the garden horrified her, but I will say this for her, she didn't flinch. A dozen more patients, some not seriously afflicted – not yet, anyway – crowded the gardens and it was Miss Sowerby who muttered, 'This is ridiculous, no space, even in the garden. What we need is an isolation hospital.'

'But where?' I asked, looking at the discoloured bodies on the grass.

There was a moment of silence. In fact I was thinking of how I could set about ordering – literally – every man, woman and child in Anani to be inoculated. At least it would protect the largest township on the island. So my mind was on other things when Paula, still visibly shaken by the sight of the corpses, spoke in a voice she managed to control only with difficulty.

'I have an idea,' she offered tentatively. 'Why not use Faalifu? As an isolation hospital, I mean. It has large rooms, and a big garden which could deal with an overflow of patients.'

For a moment I was so astonished at the generous gesture of a woman I had never regarded as generous – a taker rather than a giver – that I didn't answer. It was left to Miss Sowerby to speak first.

'That's a very practical suggestion,' she said in her precise voice. 'It's the largest house on the island and the gardens are huge. If this outbreak spreads into an epidemic we'll need space – space and air. And isolation.'

'That's a wonderful gesture, Paula,' I agreed. 'At least we can help the other patients here without too much risk of infection.' I was thinking of the two or three 'normal' illnesses which we were treating, including one man with a bad foot after treading on a stone-fish, and another boy receiving 'blanket treatment' for polio.

As the assistant doctor, I obviously couldn't make the decision to use Faalifu myself, though I knew that Alec would be delighted to agree. And when he returned from his session with Colonel Fawcett in the radio room, agree he did.

'Ye're a great girl, Paula. We'll make a Florence

327

Nightingale out of ye yet. Ye ken that it was cholera that she had to treat, eh?'

We now had to deal with practicalities – and in the right order, for by the evening there were nearly thirty patients, most of them sleeping on mats or blankets in the garden, each bout of vomiting or diarrhoea accompanied by groans and cries.

'Let's have a council of war in your bungalow,' Alec suggested to me. 'It's – well, it's cleaner there, and we can have a wee dram to help us get our priorities right.'

This we did – briefly. First Alec phoned Tiare to come round quickly. 'We need your help urgently,' he said. Then he sent Paula to prepare the villa.

'I'll give ye an hour and a half to turn a villa into a hospital! Can ye do it? Then Kit'll transfer the sick to Faalifu in our ambulance, and new patients will be taken there directly.'

Transport posed no real problem. I had the jeep, so Alec could use my old car, and Jim Wilson was pressed into service as emergency ambulance driver. He had plenty of time for that because, once cholera had been notified, no ships would be allowed to sail into the lagoon – including the *Mantela*.

When Tiare arrived, without the faintest idea of what had happened, she blanched at the sight, then the tears sprang to her eyes.

'I understand ye well.' Alec put an arm round her shoulder to comfort her, for he knew that to her everyone in Koraloona were her 'subjects', and she had a deep sense of grief for anyone in trouble. Her voice had a hollow ring of misery to it when she asked, 'What do you want me to do? Anything special? Of course I want to help in any way I can.'

'Princess, we're facing the prospect of an epidemic.' Alec spoke frankly. 'I hope and pray I'm wrong, but there's no sense in ignoring all the danger signals. And we've only a wee stock of five hundred vaccine inoculations. My plan is that we inoculate everyone in Anani. I want ye to exercise

328

your power and *order* everyone in the township to line up and be inoculated. Now. This afternoon.'

'But how?' she asked.

Alec suggested that Wilson and Tiare should set off immediately and tour Anani, which wouldn't take long, though there were some agricultural settlements behind the township. With the aid of a loud-hailer, she would order everyone to report to the hospital immediately, where Miss Sowerby would start inoculating the township's entire population. And at the hospital, Purvis would be deputed to marshal the queue of people waiting for Miss Sowerby to give them their jabs.

A couple of hours later, after I had visited the US camp and Paula's villa, borrowing every spare mattress from the camp, I returned to the cottage hospital to see an astonishing tableau. With typical stoic indifference to pain, there was a queue of perhaps a hundred men and women, the mothers carrying babies in arms, other small children tugging tearfully at their mother's sarongs as they wondered what was going to happen. The queue moved forward slowly, stretching all the way through the garden and into the road outside. One woman was breastfeeding her child which she cradled with one arm. The child seemed to be asleep, but perhaps it was just closing its eyes with bliss. The older men shuffled nearer the queue with the same indifference that they displayed towards work – a job that had to be done.

Only the teenagers laughed and treated the whole thing as a joke. They weren't worried by the brief prick of the needle. Nor did they really understand what cholera meant. Two bare-breasted girls were giggling with a couple of boys who tried to fondle their breasts – jokingly; not, I thought, with any particular desire. Then one of the boys quickly lifted up one girl's sarong to peep at her genitals. The four laughed as she let them. Then the other girl pointed with a laugh to one boy's trousers and teased him by slapping the obvious bulge.

This was too much for Purvis, who was trying to keep the queue in order.

'Have you no respect for the dead?' As he shouted, he grabbed one teenager and showed him the corpse near the queue. The boy muttered something, but only out of politeness to a white man with a beard who obviously held some authority; and it occurred to me that, in a way, they took death with the same innocence they displayed towards life, towards love. It all had to come to an end, and so long as you had ancestors to worship nothing else mattered. Ancestors were happy. Death was only the same as turning a page. I heard Miss Sowerby call, 'Come along, next please!'

One other problem would need urgent attention. The bodies in the garden would soon begin to show signs of putrefaction. They must be buried, but where and how?

On the veranda Miss Sowerby was dabbing arms with ether then dipping her syringe into the standard-size phial as she measured the vaccine, holding the syringe up to the light and with the practised eye of one who had stuck needles into thousands of patients, squirting out the excess until the measure was correct.

I lingered with her for a moment, though she didn't stop the inoculations, except for one moment. She *looked* busy, but one corner of her eye must have been on the garden, for to my astonishment, I heard her cry, not angrily so much as reproachfully, 'Jason! Not on duty!'

I looked up. Jason was taking a swig from a flat half bottle which he had carried in his pocket. But it wasn't *that* which staggered me. It was Miss Sowerby's use of the Christian name. Jason! She had called him Jason, at which he had quietly pocketed the bottle. *Jason!* I wasn't aware that this strict, severe daughter of a missionary even knew Purvis' Christian name.

She must have seen the look of astonishment on my face and, as though needing to explain because I was a doctor, she said hurriedly, never once interrupting the flow of jabs. 'Since Mr Purvis came to help here, I've been trying to force him to keep at writing his novel. I've tried to make him do at least a page a day.'

For a moment I had a picture of this strong-minded determined religious woman standing over Purvis until he had written his day's stint. Not literally. I knew no one could write a novel to order. But she did explain, 'At first he only pretended he'd written a page, but now I read each one when it's been written. That way I can check that he's been working.' And then, as though dismissing the matter, she turned to a little girl with huge staring black eyes, and said, 'Don't be afraid, my dear. A tiny prick, that's all. It won't hurt.'

'You're very good with children, Miss Sowerby,' I said.

'I'm very fond of them,' she said in that prim voice of hers.

'You should have some of your own,' I said, without thinking – but moved into the dispensary before she could make a retort, or blush, as I am sure she did.

21

By late afternoon, after Truscott had returned with the drugs and material from Sanderstown, 15 people had died. And the awful thing was that we were powerless. We could only try to contain the outbreak, while watching the advanced cases hopelessly, knowing they would die. The next day 42 people died.

'It's an epidemic all right,' Alec admitted. 'And there's nae a way of burying them. We dinna have the time nor the manpower to dig pits and give them a decent Christian burial. Every putrefying corpse is a danger – and ye know it.'

'But we can't – '

' – We'll have to get Jim Wilson to bury them at sea.'

Though I realised that this was the only way we could dispose of the corpses – and I realised there would be many more – I caught a look in Miss Sowerby's eyes and I knew we were thinking the same thing: the people of Koraloona were devout ancestor worshippers. Normally they even buried their dead in shallow graves so that from time to time they could open the graves up and look at the grisly skeletons of men and women long since dead. But if they were buried at sea, there would be no ancestors to look at.

'Aye, I know what ye're thinking,' Alec sighed. 'But can ye gi'me a better solution?'

In the end we did bury the first batches at sea. We all had to help. The emaciated bodies, with their sunken eyes and cheekbones almost protruding through the pallid skin, lay in rows in the garden. We had to wrap them with as much gentleness as we could muster, in anything we could find – mostly sail-cloth, on this first burial. We bundled them into the ambulance which carried them to the pier. A solemn crowd watched as we put them into every available space in Wilson's launch.

Then, with Father Pringle, we left the pier. Jim manoeuvred the boat through the gap in the reef and into the open sea, for we could not risk the possibility of bodies being washed back into the lagoon. We travelled a mile out beyond the reef, then tied the bodies together, adding a sackful of stones so that the combined weight would prevent them floating back to the surface.

Father Pringle conducted the funeral service, continually muttering his prayers and drawing the sign of the cross as we pushed the bodies over, like so many sacks of copra. He recited part of the service used for the burial at sea: 'The Lord shall stand at the latter day upon the sea as upon the earth. And though after the sea shall destroy this my body, yet in my flesh shall I see God and the sea shall deliver up its dead to Him.'

Then we went back to the pier to collect the next batch of corpses.

'There'll be a devil of fuss at Tabanea,' said Alec. 'I think one of us should go and try and explain to them.'

'One of us' was a hint that I should go. I didn't relish the prospect, but of course Alec was right – someone in authority, like a doctor, should try to explain why the villagers would never see their ancestors. It wasn't a very pleasant task. The groans of pain that had filled Faalifu were replaced in Tabanea by the wails of anguish from men and women who had been robbed of the visible evidence of the departed souls.

When I reached the village I found piles of food arranged in the dusty streets, as votive offerings, together with carved masks and idols – often hideously ugly – displayed as though to placate the mistreated dead. Alec had warned me that I would find a reversion to the primitive – not because of the death all around, much more because the dead could not be buried.

I tried to explain that there was no one to dig trenches, no one to bury the dead, that there was nothing dishonourable in being buried at sea. To no avail, and after nearly an hour I drove to Faalifu, to see if I could help Miss Sowerby – and Paula Reece, who came in occasionally.

Faalifu was an excellent place for an isolation hospital, but we had a lot to do to get the place in order. Alec drove over and we decided that Miss Sowerby should stay at Faalifu, as she was the more experienced, and Paula would look after the cottage hospital. Jason would move from one place to the other, as need dictated.

We had just started opening the cases of materials which Truscott had brought from Sanderstown, when I heard a sudden rumbling noise that seemed to come from nowhere. It was astonishing, and for a second I thought it was gunfire – the terrifying sound of a hundred guns firing simultaneously – and as I stood with Alec in the grounds, I said, 'What the hell's that bloody noise?'

At that very moment the rumbling sound was transformed from sound into sight and smell. Gaping with disbelief, I saw a huge gout of smoke spurt out from the crater in the conical mountain that was High Island. As I watched, spellbound, it shot out like a bullet, leaving a sinister, slowly expanding black cloud.

I gasped. 'The volcano!'

I stared fascinated. The mighty clap of noise had ceased, as though a giant had belched once. I waited for the second internal explosion – or whatever it was – to break my eardrums, but none came. The plume of smoke that had shot straight up flattened out at the top, and gradually, as I watched, was transformed into a cloud that darkened the sky. It brought not only a sinister darkness, but a horrible stench.

'Dinna fret, Laddie.' Alec wiped his head, then tightened the knot in the MCC tie that held up his trousers. 'She blew her top about ten years ago. And once before that – but it's a dormant volcano.'

'Doesn't sound like it!' I cried.

Nor did it sound like it to the crowds of dying in Koraloona. Wails and cries, screams of supplication, filled the house and garden of Faalifu, where most patients had by now been transported.

Paula Reece, who had come over, rushed out crying, 'The volcano's erupting! Where can we go?' She was crying – real tears of absolute fear.

'Ye'll be all right,' said Alec. 'It's nae going to explode if that's what ye're afeared of.'

I knew that noted volcanologists in New Zealand and Australia had pronounced High Island as safe as Mount Egmont, once the most fearsome volcano in New Zealand.

'Every ten years or so all the gases build up and explode, and that's all there is to it,' explained Alec.

A little girl, half dying, screamed and tried to run down the path to the road. Paula chased her and Alec turned to me and, when Paula was out of earshot, said, 'It's just nature's way of having a really good fart. And it smells like it too!'

It certainly did. The sulphur cloud started me coughing and spluttering, and the stench was like the one we used to

334

have in the lab – H$_2$S, or rotten eggs. Almost as bad was the way in which the sky darkened, as the ever-expanding cloud blacked out the sun. I was convinced that at any moment the volcano would roar again, to be followed by flames and then the awesome river of moving, red-hot lava. I could see it in my mind's eye – I had seen it on the films often enough to invest the scene with reality – and I felt the palms of my hands clammy with fear.

'Get a grip on yesel', Laddie,' Alec's voice held an unaccustomed note of sternness, not used since I 'misbehaved myself' when taunting Mana. 'There's one thing I think ye should do, Kit. Go back and show the flag in Tabanea. There are scores of dead – yet there are few bodies to bury. That's the worst thing. They're going to think the volcano is caused by their gods. Go and show them that you are their doctor, and that you're not afraid of sharing their fate.'

I hated the idea, but I knew I had to return, because in some cases entire families had been wiped out. And the volcano seemed like an omen even to me.

I had barely reached the village when I heard a car approach at speed, and saw Jim Wilson, who shouted, 'Come quick! Doc Reid sent me to fetch you.'

'Why on earth – ' I began.

'It's the lad you cured of polio. Doc says he won't last long.'

'*Oh no!*' I jumped into my jeep, revved up the engine and shot out of the village without another word.

Jimbo was alive – just – by the time I reached his bedside and took his hand, trying to comfort him – and trying to force back my tears.

I had watched over him day and night to save him, to prevent his being crippled, when every instinct told me he might never recover the use of his legs. Doctors may be known for their clinical detachment; 'hard' is a word people often use and in a way it may be justified. But you need to be hard to do battle, and we were battling all the time – short sharp battles in emergencies, protracted battles against lingering enemies, grim battles against folly and ignorance.

Of course, our emotions have to be subdued. But they tend to creep back in moments of defeat. It wasn't easy for me to subdue them now as I thought of Jimbo's stoicism as he had lain on the operating table when we'd first examined his legs, his eyes wide open and denying tears, his teeth clenched, and of his delight in the tinny music of the little radio that he associated with his cure – his belief that playing it louder would hasten his recovery; his response to my demands for self-help; his whole innocent faith. And now, overcome by the anuria wrought by cholera, his faith must have been waning. I had let him down.

How high our hopes had been after we had beaten his illness, and he had started playing in the streets of Tabanea like any other kid; such a splendid boy. And now? He opened his eyes once or twice, and once I thought he tried to squeeze my hand.

The battered little radio was near his pillow. I switched it on. Something my father said flickered across my mind from my own childhood, aeons ago, it seemed: 'Marvellous thing this wireless. It's in its infancy, y'know.'

It was growing dark when Jimbo died, and night crept softly over the garden. The music went on in the darkness, tinny and puerile. I told myself, in the fading daylight, that I had seen a smile flicker into his darkening eyes. But I could never, now, be sure.

With a heavy heart I prepared to drive up to Tabanea the next day, but this time I did not go alone. Tiare had asked what more she could do to help and to announce that, with so many people dying, she had requested Tiki, her adviser, to go up to Tabanea. Suddenly, turning to me, she said, 'I know how you felt about Jimbo, Kit. I'll come with you.'

We drove up together in my jeep, turning down a rough rutted road, little more than a path through the taro plants, flanked by creepers and thick undergrowth, almost like a natural fence for the village and, as we reached the village, I saw men supplicating the gods by offering more food – and jars of water – all probably infected. With the dead lying in the streets it was a pinpointed picture of everything that made cholera such a dreadful disease. An old man tottered towards me. I vaguely recognised what was left of him, for with terrifying speed the radical dehydration had shrunken him into a wizened figure with his ribs standing out. He looked like an exhibit in a museum. His skin was turning black or blue – due, I knew, to ruptured capillaries. He clung piteously to me, and as I lifted him to the side of the road to rest – and die – I hardly noticed the feather-weight feeling of his frame. His breath fluttered, and he tried vaguely to croak words that were trapped in his throat.

'The gods are angry,' was all I could catch. I knew, when his eyeballs became suddenly fixed in the instant of death, that he had reached his last drab passage to eternity.

The village looked like a desert of the dead: skeletal figures, the dirty streets, the refuse, the filth, piled up despite all attempts to keep the place clean. I determined to ask Sam Truscott to detail some troops to help to clean up all the places. Some islanders had lit fires – not against cold, but for some more deep-seated meaning. Fire, like earth and air and water, had to them an almost elemental force. What were they hoping for? Or repelling?

Suddenly I saw Father Pringle at the end of the village. I had no idea he was going to be there, but I soon found out why. He had brought his two accordionists to provide hymns, the ill-matched chords straggling down the primitive main street as he conducted funeral services, one after the other, with almost indecent speed. When a man or woman died, all neighbours who were well enough rushed to help – by digging shallow graves near the village where they could bury their dead before they were clutched from the land by the sea and buried outside the lagoon.

Even more macabre was the sight of helpers preparing

graves for those still alive yet marked for death. Father Pringle was comforting them. I heard him say to one old man, 'You will die before long, my son. But you will be lucky to meet God so soon and save yourself from pain. When it comes it will be a matter of minutes.'

How, I wondered to myself, can you measure a few minutes of pain? Aloud, I said, 'But they can't do this! They might look dead, but they might have a spark of life in them.'

'They're dead – and better off,' said Tiare bitterly.

'I hope you're keeping Aleena at home.' I suddenly thought of her.

Tiare nodded. Aleena had pleaded several times to help with the nursing, but I had told her on the phone to stay at home – for the moment. Like her, all the servants had been inoculated of course.

At that moment Father Pringle conducted yet another service and I saw that he was in tears. One of the servants at the Union Jack Club had died. 'He was a good man,' said Father Pringle when the body was being lowered into the grave, 'I'm sorry for the tears. Being a Christian makes cowards of us all.'

I was about to give some consoling advice when Tiki arrived, but it was a different Tiki from the one I had talked to when he had been dressed in his neatly pressed white duck suit.

Now he wore a ceremonial robe decorated with shells sewn on in intricate designs and girdled with a belt of carved stones; and towering over his shoulders was one of the masks I had seen on the walls of his house. Hideous enough there, it was now even more terrifying when being worn. It was carved from wood. The lower part looked like the open jaws of a shark. Above sharply pointed teeth were nostrils that flared.

I knew that according to Polynesian legend, the waters which formed the seas round their islands came from the nostrils of the gods; and 'Tiki' was the Polynesian word for 'idol'. Above the nostrils two bulbous eyes represented the

338

sun and the moon. And in the wooden skull, hundreds of tiny spikes had been driven, each one representing an ancestor claimed by death.

The islanders stopped wailing at the sight of Tiki, who crossed to me as I stood on the fringe of the crowd. His voice sounded sepulchral as he spoke from within the mask.

'This no doubt seems very strange to you, Doctor,' he began. 'But we believe that the world began here in the Southern Seas. We are attached to our ancestors as by an umbilical cord. My task now is to set their souls and their minds at rest. They are distressed because many are not being buried in the earth. I have to reassure them that the sea is the primordial element.'

It made an odd scene. Tiare standing there, clasping her hands, Father Pringle with a slightly baffled look on his face, and me, a doctor, caught up in 'witchcraft' as Tiki tried his best to give a message of hope to the dying men and women around him.

I stayed for a few minutes longer and then both Tiare and I went back.

'That was a guid helping hand ye gave me in Tabanea,' said Alec when I returned. 'To tell the truth, I canna stand all that bloody mumbo-jumbo.'

'I know. Neither can I.' Then I told him how both Father Pringle and Tiki had each been at Tabanea at the same time. I even told Alec that for a moment I hadn't known whether to laugh or to cry, but in the end I realised that in a strange way the people were accustomed to death, to the act of dying, but that they wanted it witnessed by one priest or another. They could at least then tell their children that their ancestors had died with a prayer on their lips.

'They both believe in what they preach – but,' said Alec with unusual bitterness, 'it's damn difficult to believe in *anything* when you see men and women dying like this. I'd like to know what god has ordered human beings to be sacrificed like this?'

'I certainly don't know,' I said.

Alec Reid sighed. 'God knows I've seen enough of it. And I'm beginning to be afraid of growing old and the manner of my dying. Not death itself, but suffering. I sometimes think that the only thing I will ask of the guid Lord is that when I die and the *Scotsman* prints my obituary, it'll read, "He died peacefully in his sleep".'

'Don't be so morbid,' I said. 'I'm going to have a Scotch at my bungalow before I drive over to have a look at Faalifu. Care to join me?'

'Aye, I'll drink to that,' he agreed.

Once in the bungalow, with Toma serving our Scotches, I made one phone call to thank Sam Truscott for the bountiful supplies which I had been too busy to examine thoroughly. There was one other thing: would he help us out – as I explained, in his interests as well as ours – by sending sanitation teams of GIs all over the island to try and contain the infection?

'Sure. We've got sprays with insecticides and all that crap,' he said. 'I'll get the boys out tomorrow morning. And I've got some good news. I received a signal that substantial supplies are being flown over in a Liberator from Pearl. Barring a Japanese attack, they should be in Sanders in four days. That'll give me an excuse to fly over and pick them up. And see my girl there who's going to fly home to the West Coast soon.'

'I thought you were having girl *trouble*,' I laughed – for the first time that day.

'Yeah, kinda difficult problems.' He didn't volunteer any more information – not that I was interested.

After a last drink with Alec I drove over to Faalifu. I planned to sort out any hospital problems, and help Miss Sowerby with the inoculations of the new patients as they streamed in. Jason had already arrived to start sorting out the drugs we had received.

When I arrived after dark, the place presented such a Dantesque scene that I could hardly recognise the once elegant house and gardens where the guests had so often

340

sipped champagne. The sky was ghostly, only one star loitering in the sky, still mostly overcast with fumes.

The sick and dying lay on the landings and terraces and in every corridor where they could be squeezed in and where a bed of sorts could be arranged. The lucky ones did have beds, but the rest often had mattresses, or nothing. Because of wartime restrictions, the generator only worked at half speed during the night, and so there was very little light in the corridors. A few night-lights floating in oil threw out shadowy, faint beams. The smell was overpowering, in stark contrast to the heady perfume of flowers that normally Paula Reece placed in Meissen bowls and Venetian glass in every corner.

On my last night round, as I helped to empty containers of excreta, I met Paula at the turn of the stairs. She had come to collect some clothes. Her face was drawn in the light of a hurricane lantern she carried.

'The lady with the lamp,' she said.

Later, as I moved into the garden among the patients lying under awnings, the lights in the garden shone dimly, the black night around the garden guarding the grounds like a wall.

When I had made my final rounds I turned my attention to the one task that remained: sorting out the drugs.

The most important item was the vaccine, obviously, and I found Jason in the kitchen, ripping through the sealing tape that closed the flaps of the cardboard boxes.

'Damn stupid to deliver life-saving stuff in plain brown boxes like bottles of ink,' he said sardonically.

They were regimented in compartments of a dozen – tubes no thicker than a fountain pen, each containing a few millilitres of cloudy liquid drawn off from the intestines of choleric fowls and diluted for immediate use. Life-savers, yes – but only if the long-drawn-out task of inoculating the entire population was begun at once.

Irritably, I said, 'Why the hell do they have to seal them up?' Each tube had a twist of wire holding its cork in, and was sealed with a laboratory seal. Each would have to be snipped with pliers. Since we could muster only three or four pairs of pliers from car tool kits, there would be further delay. But it was no good panicking – just hand each batch of ampoules to Miss Sowerby and let her get on with it: a swab of ether to clean the flesh, a 5-millilitre jab with a syringe, and hope for the best.

The saline drip posed more problems. The worst cases of dehydration needed at least four or six litres a day of salt solution, fed intravenously from the standard one-litre bottle positioned above the patient's head, and with the usual rubber tube running from it to the needle. But though we could just cope – only just – for the night, I would have to improvise, because more and more sick patients were bound to flow into Koraloona's makeshift isolation hospital.

That was my last thought before I tried to snatch a few hours' sleep.

22

I woke just as dawn was breaking, with the promise of a beautiful morning, and as the first light of the day drifted curling across the lagoon, stealing over the awakening township, I walked outside. There was a touch of dew sparkling on the rough ground; the sulphurous smell of the volcano cloud had been blown away by the night wind – almost as though the sky had been washed clean – and there was a new smell, fresh and green, to the world.

And yet, remembering all the bodies I had seen, and tried to care for, let alone bury, even the good clean air seemed to me a wicked irony. How could the sun be allowed to shine so benignly on gasping men and women, waiting only for a merciful release while their lives ebbed away in agony?

After a shower, a change of clothes and some breakfast, I

decided to have a quick word on the phone with Paula Reece before going to see Alec. A man answered the phone; not surprising since the resident pianist and others had been 'trapped' on Koraloona by the war. But I didn't recognise this voice.

'I'll go and fetch her,' said the man. 'May I ask who's calling?'

'Doctor Masters.'

'Oh, Doctor,' replied a languid voice, 'you won't remember me perhaps. Count Vrinsky.'

'Good Lord! Of course I do, but what are you doing here?' I was thinking of that drawl, those beautiful clothes, the amber cigarette holder.

'I'm in the army, Doctor. An officer in the Education branch. To be honest, I only popped in to see Paula to beg a square meal. I can't stomach Army food. What I wouldn't give for a big plate of *bigos* washed down with ice-cold Polish vodka! But I shouldn't talk about food, Doctor, not with this terrible epidemic going on.'

'Yes, it is very bad. But, Count, don't bother to fetch Paula now. I'll have a word with her later. I must get to the cottage hospital and see Doctor Reid.'

Once there, I asked Alec, 'How was the night?'

'Twenty-three dead. It's a bad business, Laddie,' he said, seeing my look of depression as well as fatigue. 'There's only one way to treat tragedy on a grand scale. There's nothing ye can do about private feelings. It's like the sea. One natural cause follows another. That's what the Polynesians think. Look over the lagoon.' He pointed to the waves breaking lazily on the shore. 'There's one wave, there's another, it's not the same wave, yet each one influences the next. There's nothing ye can do about it.' Changing the subject he asked, 'D'ye think ye'd better go to Tabanea and inoculate everyone in the village?'

'I was intending to spend an hour or so with Jim Wilson and see if we can improvise some stuff. At the rate this is going we'll be short of drips, bottles, even tubing for the saline drips.'

'Ye do that, then – but be quick as ye can, for we'll have to have a new burial at sea afore long. Meanwhile' – he drew a deep breath – 'I'll drive Miss Sowerby to Tabanea and inoculate the village – or what's left of it. Purvis can come here. In case of emergency, he can get ye at Jim's. And Paula can keep an eye on the isolation hospital and phone ye at Jim's if *she* runs into trouble.'

I walked down to the ship's chandler, wondering how Jim could help. If anyone could, it would be Jim, who was a master of improvisation.

That was what we needed now. With Paula's house overflowing, the only place where we could put the sick was out on the lawns; but though there was plenty of space in the grounds, we had long since run out of beds.

As I reached Jim's, I had a sudden thought. I would go to Johnson's and buy up their old bolts of cloth, the material they used to make up Mother Hubbards. It was brightly coloured, but as new lines arrived, the old patterns often remained unsold for years.

'Remember, Johnson,' I said to him in the store, 'this is an emergency, so no bullshit about charging us.'

'I've got to make a living, Doc, like anyone else, but you can 'ave it at 'alf price.'

'Too expensive,' I said. '*Give* me stuff you know you'll never sell. And I mean *give* it. All the old unusable material you've got.'

'I don't like the way you're threatening me. I'll tell you straight, it ain't fair,' he said. 'You've called me a crook once before, and you don't 'ave to go after me. I 'asn't 'ad no experience of givin' me profit away.'

'Now's the time to learn,' I said cheerfully. 'You'll get paid in heaven.'

In the end, grumbling, he gave me quite a lot. Jim sent some of his boys to carry it to the chandler's workshop. Then I asked Jim to find a few sewing girls. When they appeared, they started sewing the cloth into long bags into which we stuffed anything we could find – grass, shredded paper, soft leaves, and then waited for Alec Reid to return from Tabanea so that he could transport our makeshift palliasses by ambulance.

Drip feeds for saline solutions were another problem. The bottles containing the solution had to be suspended over the patient – simple when the patient was in bed, but requiring ingenuity when he was lying on the ground. Some mattresses could be placed under tree branches, to which drip feeds could be tied. For where there were no trees, Jim invented a holder. He ripped the spokes from discarded bicycle wheels in the back of his store and soldered them together into tripods from which the drips could hang. When the supply of spokes ran out, we turned branches of palm trees into arches that spanned the beds, and made cradles of old wooden scraps, nailing or glueing them together to support the feed bottles, for we had an endless supply of Coca-Cola bottles from the American camp.

Jim also solved an apparently insuperable problem: rubber tubing to link the drip bottle to the patient. For we had no rubber tubing. Jim raided his stock of oilskin sou'wester clothing used by ships' crews. He cut these into strips, rolled them into tubes, sealing them with the type of glue used to seal the seams of the oilskin coats. While the stock lasted Jim also used small-gauge brass and copper tubing which he stocked to supply ships' engineers needing to replace cracked steam or petrol inlets. They could be flexibly linked to the bottle and the patient's needle by short lengths of inner tube.

The days and weeks as the epidemic took its course seemed to be endless. Only rarely was I able to see Aleena, and when I did it was usually at Tiare's house for just a quick bite of lunch. One day we almost had a row, for time after time Aleena had begged me to let her help with the nursing and I had always refused.

'I'm supposed to be going to marry you,' she said almost crossly, while Tiare listened with a slight smile of amusement. 'And I *want* to help. If Paula Reece can help, so can I. I'm not a girl any more you know.'

I did know. But I was adamant.

'If we needed help, or if you were a doctor, I wouldn't wait to ask you,' I told her again. 'But we don't need nurses. And the American army is doing a wonderful job cleaning up the mess in the villages.'

Slightly mollified, she said, 'But I *like* to be by your side when you're in trouble.'

'That's sweet of you. But coming to see you both here for an hour is the finest way I know of recharging my batteries. I must confess,' I added, 'that my biggest problem is keeping awake. I haven't been to bed properly for nights. I feel I could sleep for a week without waking up.'

'I wish I could help you there.' Aleena kept a straight face and looked her mother right in the eyes, but Tiare pretended that she hadn't heard – and Aleena didn't help; I saw to that.

For nearly two months, until the end of November, the epidemic raged, and there seemed no stopping it. The trouble was that sometimes it only needed *one* new patient from an outlying area to start a resurgence. Even in Anani, with every person carefully inoculated, there were five deaths – showing that even inoculation wasn't always a guarantee that you wouldn't contract the disease.

In the third week the first expatriate died. She was Daisy Gilbert who, with her eighty-year-old husband, had lived in the pink-washed house near the shipping offices in Main Street, which I had noticed the first day I arrived in Koraloona. I did not see much of them as a rule unless they visited the club, because they were old, frail and obviously completely satisfied with each other's company and the love they had for the island. It was, she had once told me when I went to treat her for a touch of bronchitis, the idyllic way to grow old.

But not the idyllic way to die. I happened to be in Anani, near the pier, when I saw what at first sight looked like a madman screaming as he stumbled along Main Street towards me. I ran forward to help, and near Lee Chong's,

346

the barber shop, the man collapsed into my arms, crying, 'She's dead! Daisy's dead!'

Mick had run out from the bar and I shouted to him, 'I'll go in and see. You look after Mr Gilbert.'

I pushed open the pink door surrounded by bougainvillaea, and facing the lagoon. Daisy Gilbert was lying on the floor, so emaciated that I swear I could have lifted her up with one hand. I needed no second glance – or second smell – to realise she had been dead for some time.

I left her there and rushed back into the tiny front garden to steer old Mr Gilbert into Mick's Bar where I shouted for some hot tea. He was sobbing pitifully, as a child sobs when he knows that he can never have what he wants, and it struck me, watching him try to steady himself on the brass rail of the bar, that he *was* a child again. I noticed he was wearing new check woollen carpet slippers. Daisy had probably bought them for him as a present.

'Come on to the club,' I said to him, trying to help. 'You can't go back to the house until – ' I hesitated – 'I've sent someone in to tidy it up.'

He looked at me with wide, staring eyes and cried, 'No, no! I'm going to see Daisy – dead or alive. I can't live without her.'

'Now listen to me please – ' I started.

'What shall I do?' He was suddenly quiet, his eyes glazed, staring into a future he couldn't understand without Daisy. 'I want to go home,' he mumbled.

'You're not going now,' I cried firmly. 'Doctor's orders. I'll take you home later.' I had in mind that I would try to get Jason Purvis to help me lay out the bag of bones which was all that was left of poor Daisy Gilbert, perhaps in her bed, decently covered, so that a devoted husband's last sight of his dead wife would be a happier one for him to remember. But there was no stopping him – and I had no power to stop anyone so long as they had been inoculated.

I was still trying to argue when suddenly, as though invested with a sudden, hidden strength, Gilbert butted me

347

in the stomach and before I could stop him he ran out of Mick's Bar and was stumbling up the street. A few people looked at him in amazement as I followed. He was too quick for me and reached his house seconds before I did, and banged the door in my face. I heard the bolt pulled back, then the click of the key in his front door.

I banged on it furiously. He refused to answer my pleas. Before I could even think of what to do next, Mick arrived, panting with the unaccustomed exercise. At that moment the problem of an old man obviously afraid of being left alone was solved – by him, for him, poor devil. By a shot.

Mick gave one heave of his large shoulders and burst open the door. And there, in the small sitting-room with its lace curtains, which had been their pride and joy, was Gilbert, leaning over the dead body of his wife, a revolver in one hand. He had shot himself almost through the heart, but not quite, and was thus given a few seconds of extra time to live.

As he lay dying, his last words, when his eyes flickered open, was a gasped, 'I couldn't bear the thought of living alone without Daisy. You understand, don't you?'

I had to confess to myself that I did.

In those eight or nine weeks 411 people died, but by the ninth week we could sense that the epidemic was on the wane. This was due to several factors. Huge supplies had arrived in Sanderstown by a twin-engined flying-boat, which had then been flown to Koraloona by Truscott. At the same time the Americans had, as I had told Aleena, done a truly remarkable job of 'cleaning up' the island. They had sprayed almost every house, visiting even the tiniest settlements, where only three or four families lived off their land – and a bountiful nature. The GIs not only dug latrine trenches, they installed portable American toilets after I had asked Truscott to see if he could fly in some Elsan toilets, used all over the world by the British Army.

'What the hell are Elsans?' he asked.

I explained that Elsan was the name of a chemical toilet for use in country places which had no sewerage.

He chuckled. 'You ever read a book called *The Specialist* by Chick Sale?'

I hadn't.

'Been a bestseller for years in the States. This old guy, the specialist, devotes all his talents to the construction of outside privies – one-holers, two-holers, family size. I guess that's what you mean by Elsans. Sure I can get something similar. Chick Sales with quick lime added are standard issue in all army camps. We don't have any fancy names for them like you do though. Just "crap cans" or "honey-buckets".'

Educating villages to use the 'crap cans' was a different problem, but Tiare, with her houseboy, toured every village they could find, sometimes taking Aleena with her, and explaining, as best she could, the advantages of sanitation.

Finally, by the end of the ninth week, the number of new cases was reduced to single figures; and these were almost always caught in time, so that if someone had escaped inoculation the patient could be treated and put on a saline drip and so cheat death. Occasionally a rogue would upset our calculations. He would look healthy, but be dead the next day – for no apparent reason; even if he had been inoculated. This is what happened to our second white expatriate, who died – without warning.

Several of us were clustering round the bar that day for a midday drink. Mrs Fawcett was asking me, 'We stopped having our bridge sessions after the poor Gilberts died. I wonder when we can resume them?'

'Right away,' I said. 'Everyone needs all the distraction they can get to take our minds off things.'

Colonel Fawcett interrupted. 'I also felt that it was unseemly to play cards in front of the Polynesian staff. Most of them had relatives who had died.'

'Very right and proper,' said Father Pringle, who had come in for company as much as for a drink. 'I may not be a very good Catholic, I agree,' he added wryly, 'but the best thing you can do is set an example. The club has been a great consolation to all of us. And the church, and the church hall, have been the sort of meeting places where people have gone to comfort each other in times of trouble. In some ways it's the best method of teaching religion I know.'

Father Pringle was right. The fear engendered by the epidemic had brought many members of the club and the church together more often, as though to share the misery which enfolded the entire island. Even the colonel's two assistants – Bill Shanks and Jack Haslam – who rarely appeared normally until it was time for evening tennis, started coming. So did Alec and I, for that matter. My own bungalow suddenly seemed lonely and empty because we could never make any plans. How could I ask Alec or Aleena for dinner when the only two doctors on the island were faced with scores of deaths every day and had to work nearly twenty-four hours at a time, snatching a drink over a snack as best we could?

At least the club offered a sanctuary where you could swallow a beer between Tala-Tala and Anani and exchange a few minutes of gossip, often with Sam Truscott, who popped in almost daily.

'Gives me a chance to be a civilian for a few minutes,' he confided to Fawcett.

'Ah – yes – oh! I see! Good show! American humour eh?' said the colonel, and when he had moved to the other side of the bar to re-tell the American joke, Sam turned to me and almost apologetically said, 'Gee, I get real upset because the colonel's a helluva nice guy, but I just can't understand what in hell he says.'

'Don't worry,' I chuckled. 'The colonel's accent would sound just as difficult in Nottingham as in Nebraska.'

'I feel better,' said Sam. 'What'll it be? Sorry I can't offer you a Budweiser.'

350

At that moment I happened to look up, just in time to see Bill Shanks, the New Zealand radio operator, clutch the side of the bar in sudden agony. His glass dropped, shattering like an explosion as it hit the ground. The youngster appeared to hesitate, look around as though beseeching help, and as I began to move towards him, his legs buckled, he seemed to fall as though drunk and then, before anyone could help, he vomited. One look at that evil-smelling colourless liquid was enough.

'He's got it! If we get him to Tala-Tala – ' I cried.

'Jesus wept!' Truscott looked horrified.

As the barman rushed to clear up the mess, Shanks, a healthy youngster in his early twenties, gasped, 'I'll be all right,' and tried to get up. He couldn't.

'Help me to get him into my jeep, Sam,' I shouted as the drinkers around us suddenly grew silent and afraid, seeing for the first time the ugliness from which most of them had been cocooned. 'Every minute counts.'

I was worried. Normally there would have been earlier symptoms such as cramps. I knew Shanks had been inoculated, like all travellers to tropical areas in those days. And I had personally given most of the expatriates big booster shots. But now Bill Shanks looked as though he was past the primary stage. He was unable to walk. When I got him into the jeep, I noticed his hand was clammy and he was beginning to look shrunken.

We had him up to Tala-Tala within five minutes. His pulse was very weak. He was almost unconscious, vomiting again and again, and I noticed that bluish tinge in his face – the sure sign of broken capillaries.

'Miss Sowerby,' I shouted. 'Come quick! Have you got a spare bed and a saline drip? It's urgent!'

There was one bed available – in the corner of Paula Reece's living-room. It had just been vacated by a woman who had died. But the fact that it was a bed with a back meant that I could speed up the vital process of installing a saline drip, so that Miss Sowerby would be able to inject intravenously within a matter of minutes.

'Poor Mr Shanks,' she whispered as she jabbed the needle into his vein. 'Any hope?'

'Afraid not.' I shook my head. 'I'm dashing to see Doc Reid at Anani. There's nothing I can do here for the moment. But I'll be back as soon as I can. Just make the poor devil as comfortable as possible.'

In the event I met Alec just as he was reaching his bungalow so I stopped him there instead and told him. Bubble and Squeak poured out two glasses of Old Rarity unasked.

'A sad business,' Alec sighed. 'There's nae a way of telling the innocent from the guilty.'

An hour later I went back to see Shanks – just in time. He was gasping in agony. His face seemed to have sunk as acute dehydration set in. Even after the death of men and women all around me for days, it gave me a fearful clutch of the heart as I stared into the eyes of a man in such pain that he wasn't even afraid or resigned, for he knew that he was about to die.

At that moment, just before he died, Paula Reece, who had been helping at the cottage hospital, returned to Tala-Tala for (as she told me later) a change of clothes and a shower. At first she showed little hint of the emotions other than the tiredness which made all of us feel like zombies, but she did have an added note of sadness when she stood by the door and Miss Sowerby told her that a white man was dying.

As she approached she said to me, 'Isn't it terrible. I know there's no difference because he's a white man but still – '

'Yes,' I sighed, 'and this is one of those lightning strikers.' It was a term we had started using for those who died with great speed.

Approaching death meant so little to so many that her voice hardly changed as she reached the bed and asked, 'Who is it?'

'Bill Shanks.'

She gave an almost animal cry, half stifled. I looked up.

352

Her face was contorted, as white as a sheet, and for a moment she swayed and I thought she was going to fall over.

'What on earth – ?'

'Bill Shanks! Oh my God! Is he really dead?'

'If not now, within a few seconds,' I said sharply.

'Let me look.'

The man's face seemed to have fallen in. I whispered to him, and finally he tried to look at me, opening his eyes slowly, very slowly, as though he could hardly summon up the energy required to lift his eyelids. Then he saw Paula, smiled weakly, and gave a grotesque attempt at a wink just before he gave one fearful convulsion and his eyes glazed over. Only a few hours ago he had been playing tennis as hale and hearty as I was. Now he no longer looked like a man, more like one of those masks of death that littered the streets of Tabanea as offerings.

Paula stood there wringing her hands, the tears streaming down her face, as I covered the body and called to Miss Sowerby. By now we had enrolled a couple of orderlies who carried out the dead on stretchers, and laid them in rows at the bottom of the garden.

'Miss Sowerby, please arrange to take the body away,' I said. 'I'll phone Colonel Fawcett and ask him to collect it, so that he can make the proper funeral arrangements.'

As Miss Sowerby went to call the orderlies, Paula Reece stood there, almost with a look of terror. She was still racked with sobs.

'Come on, Paula,' I tried to console her. 'I know being a white man – but,' adding with a deliberate brutality to try to bring her out of shock, 'it's sad – but it's just one more dead man.'

'But you don't understand,' she gasped. 'Come into the garden where we can talk – quickly.'

I followed her until she stopped near the gates – as far away as possible from the nearest patients and corpses. Then, standing there, she clutched one arm and asked me, in a hollow, frightened voice, a question that staggered me.

'Is cholera catching? Is it – what's the damned phrase? – can it be sexually transmitted?'

'Paula!' I grabbed her shoulders. 'Are you telling me – ?'

She nodded, speechless.

'You bloody fool,' I said harshly. 'When?' Then, I thought, she *would* try out Bill Shanks, a good-looking young man. He was exactly the kind of stud she was always looking for. *But at this time!*

'How often?' I asked, 'And when?'

'Several times,' she admitted.

'And the last time?'

'Two days ago.'

'My God. It's not impossible.' I was thinking, how the hell could *anyone* get sexually aroused when involved in wholesale death, with misery, agony, pain, and the stench of vomit all around us, like a blanket that covered us all? How *could* a sophisticated woman like Paula Reece stoop to such an act at such a time? And then I thought, it's going on all over the world all the time. I remembered once we had a case when I was an intern in London of a man who had slept with a prostitute for months even when he knew she had clap. The sudden urge makes everyone take a chance, like poverty-stricken, starving Indians in besieged villages who lie down and somehow get an erection and do it in the street, not caring if the passers-by see them, not caring if it hastens their death, nothing mattering where the strongest urge in the world is concerned.

'When was the last time?' I asked again.

'I told you! Two days ago.'

'Oh God! How in *hell* did you let it happen?'

She had been to bed and was in the hospital ready to go home when Bill Shanks happened to pass by after she was ready to leave.

'Happen on purpose?' I asked sarcastically.

Ignoring the question she said, almost as though reciting, 'He invited me to Mollie Green's for dinner. We had spent a few evenings together in the past, and after the meal and a

354

few drinks he asked me back to his bungalow near the radio shack for – '

'For a quickie?' I interrupted brutally.

'If it pleases you to put it that way,' she said angrily. 'After all, we weren't doing anything wrong, were we?'

'I suppose not,' I replied. 'No, you weren't. You had every right to do what you did. The only thing I cannot understand is – how you *could* – at a time like this?'

'Well, I did. I needed it, if you want to know the truth. Just a few minutes of pleasure – and release – after everything I've been through. God knows I've tried to help.'

'Yes, you have. And magnificently, we all know that. And the other thing – well, let's forget it.'

'You didn't answer my question,' she said in a small voice. 'Is it – '

I was so disgusted with her – realising that her nymphomania ruled all her actions – that I spoke carefully, using medical language to shock her. 'The actual insertion of the penis into the vagina cannot transmit the disease.'

Stunned by my words, she said, 'But if – ?'

'I suppose you mean, does ejaculation make any difference?' I asked coldly. 'The answer is no.'

'Thank God.' She breathed a sigh of relief.

'But there's one other thing I should warn you about. Cholera is transmitted by water – any water that's infected, and that includes the water that's inside the body.'

'Well?'

'Well – in addition to the sexual act, did you,' I looked at her intently, 'did you kiss?' She nodded dumbly, again too frightened to speak.

'What kind of a kiss? And for God's sake Paula, be frank. I'm sure you can see what I'm driving at. Was it – what's the usual name? – a French kiss?'

Again she nodded.

'Well, I don't want to alarm you,' I said, 'but it does mean that if poor Bill's tongue played with yours it must have had some water on it. It doesn't mean you'll catch it,

355

you probably won't because the incubation period is from one to three days, so you're lucky.' I drew a deep breath. 'Only one day more without kissing anyone.'

I left for my bungalow soon afterwards. I felt dirty – in body and in spirit – and not least by that final, unnecessary, crack I had made. Back home I took a quick shower, hoping to shake off the depression I felt. The shower refreshed my body for a few moments but it did nothing to refresh my spirit.

23

The death of poor Bill Shanks in early December was the last case of the epidemic. It was ironic that, though the white population had been the most careful to have their inoculations, a white man should be the last to die. For the expatriates had been anxious to a man to take preventative measures, whereas quite a few Polynesians had (I was sure) slipped through our inoculation net. And some of those had escaped the disease.

The end came abruptly. On the last day of the ninth week we had only two cases, both curable, and the following day Alec and I braced ourselves for the usual exhausting morning – with Alec mainly concerned with the general problems at the cottage hospital, while I was at Tala-Tala. It happened that surgery at Anani was quickly over, so Alec drove to Faalifu for a cup of coffee. Although I was trying to file a list of deaths in the old tin trunk given us by Tiare's mother, I had hardly realised there were fewer patients in the house and grounds. I had become so used to seeing rows of suffering people – and rows of corpses – that one day's scene blurred with the one before and the one after. Time, suffering, death night and day, were all telescoped into one exhausting emotion.

But on this morning as we sipped our coffee there wasn't one single case, and when, towards evening, I drove over to my bungalow for a shower and clean clothes, I noticed a smell of cleanliness in the air.

It was a windless evening, so still and warm and soft that it seemed almost tangible. You could feel it wrap itself around you like the warm water of the lagoon. I rang up Alec Reid to report the good news.

'That's deserving of a toast. Come round, Laddie,' he cried, and when I came, Bubble and Squeak had already prepared a tray with the square-shaped bottle of whisky and two glasses.

'We licked it! We deserve our drink!' Alec held out his glass to me, then corrected himself, 'Nae, Laddie, not "we" but "ye". It's your youth and energy and bloody hard work that did the trick. Ye fought it wi' might an' main. I couldna ha' done it alone.'

'Neither could I,' I retorted. 'I could never have coped on my own and you know it. I'd have had to radio for an assistant.'

'Well, let's have a mutual flattery session. Bubble and Squeak! More square – an' fill the glasses to the brim.'

One of the girls had just offered us a glass – with her one-word, parrot-like formula 'Saywhenpleasesir' – when I saw Sam Truscott jump out of his jeep and walk up towards the veranda.

'Come in,' called Alec, crying to Bubble and Squeak, 'More square!' While to a slightly mystified Truscott he said, 'Like a snort? Isn't that what you call it?'

'I guess you could say that.' Truscott grinned and, as a reply to Reid's teasing reference to America, he added with a laugh, 'and I guess I'll never say no to a Scotsman who offers me a drink!' Then as we all laughed, he opened a large manila envelope and said, 'I flew to Sanderstown today and I brought back a batch of clippings from the American newspapers. Doctors! You are famous!'

'For giving ye a drink?' asked Alec.

'Seriously! Look at this.' Truscott held out with both hands a clipping with startling headlines so large that we didn't need to peer to see:

BRITISH DOCTORS SAVE AMERICAN BASE IN CHOLERA EPIDEMIC

'That was from Los Angeles. Here's another one':

DOCTORS BEAT CHOLERA EPIDEMIC IN PARADISE ISLAND

There were a dozen more in the same vein, though the clipping from the *Sanderstown Sentinel* dated that morning, 14 December, 1943, struck a less dramatic note. It read:

KORALOONA ISOLATED BY CHOLERA EPIDEMIC

and the report went on:

Doctor Alec Reid and Doctor Kit Masters have been fighting a winning battle to end a cholera epidemic in Koraloona which has so far claimed over 400 victims. Aided by massive supplies of drugs – some flown by the US Navy from Pearl Harbor – the two mission doctors have worked round the clock, inoculating the entire population of approximately 3,000, and are now believed to have the epidemic under control.

There followed details of our two careers, including one paragraph:

Doctor Kit Masters, before coming to Koraloona, saved the life of an elderly man who was being attacked by thugs in the East End of London. An Oxford boxing blue, Doctor Masters took on three thugs single-handed and fought them until the police arrived.

'You didn't tell me you were a boxer!' cried Truscott. 'You're a hero!'

358

'You didn't tell me you were flying to Sanders today,' I retorted, embarrassed by the newspaper reference to my fight in London.

'It was very sudden,' Sam confessed. 'My girlfriend had a rare chance to fly back Stateside, so I went to give her a goodbye kiss. Now, I'll have to find a way to fiddle a trip to California, and meet her there.'

'Want anyone to carry your bags?' I asked facetiously.

'Could be! Or if not you, Kit, Doctor Reid. How'd you feel, Doc, if I could fix up a free trip to California?'

'If ye'll give me what you in America call a raincheck till the war's over, yes. But with the Japanese shooting down everything in sight – no thanks.'

'How's about you, Kit, as assistant?' He turned to me.

'If I knew what the hell you're talking about I might be able to decide more easily.'

'Sorry. It's a hunch I'm working on. I got a message from one of the big boys in the medical corps of CINCPAC' – he pronounced it 'Sinkpack' – 'the Commander-in-Chief Pacific Fleet at Pearl. They're very impressed at the way you handled the cholera outbreak, and if there's another one – '

'God forbid!' I interrupted. 'I couldn't stand it – let alone the patients.'

'Let me finish! It seems there's been a big breakthrough in the treatment of cholera. It's a new sulpha drug, and I guess that as a mark of their admiration they'd like to meet you.'

'A new drug?' asked Alec. 'What base? What constituents?'

'Don't ask me,' laughed Sam. 'I'm a flier, not a drug addict.'

'Then how do ye come into it?' Alec persisted.

'I guess they want to show their appreciation for the way you both saved the American base from a fate worse than death,' he said almost slyly.

'We never treated a single case at the base, and you know it.'

'Kit, you don't understand the mentality of us Americans,' said Truscott solemnly. 'The fact that the epidemic involved three thousand Polynesians doesn't interest the States. The fact that you saved – in quotes – seventy Americans is big news. Just look at those goddamn press clippings.'

'But where do we come in to it?' asked Alec.

'Maybe you don't,' confessed Sam. 'But there's gonna be this major conference of top brass medicos in California in January to discuss the best way of combating health hazards in the Pacific War – not only cholera, but problem diseases like VD – and the treatments are one hell of a high priority. Especially cholera, with this new, unproven, but apparently great, drug.'

'Fine,' I said cheerfully, 'but I still don't see – '

'Neither do I.' Truscott was equally cheerful. 'I read all the dope on the conference which is being held in San Francisco early in January 1944 – and when I was in Sanderstown today, there was a kinda suggestion that you two *might* – only might – be invited. A sort of reward,' he added, trying to keep a straight face, 'for saving the lives of so many gallant American soldiers.'

'It's not actually fixed?' asked Alec.

Truscott shook his head. 'Nope,' he admitted. 'The question of danger, the long flight and so on comes into it. I wouldn't invite you without warning you that it could be a dangerous mission. It's a hell of a long flight all the way to California. Anyway, you know how top brass works. It takes one hell of a time to decide if they all agree, and when they do, they want you there the day before yesterday.'

'Well.' Doc called Bubble and Squeak. 'One last round of square! And Sam, dinna count on my attendance. I'm nae coward, but I dinna relish the prospect of flying into a pack of Japanese aeroplanes. And anyway, both of us cannot be away from Koraloona at the same time, particularly just after an epidemic.'

'Well,' Sam Truscott sighed, 'if you refuse, we'll have to send your assistant to represent you.'

Did I catch a gleam of satisfaction in his face? A touch of self-satisfaction in his voice? I had a sudden feeling that he had skilfully manipulated the suggestion so that he had just given Alec enough warning of the perils of wartime flying to discourage him from making the trip.

'Ye can go. I wouldn't gie a fig for a hare-brained flight like this. But if ye want to go,' Alec turned to me, 'do so by all means, only dinna get yourself shot down. Otherwise,' with one of his typical sly digs, 'I'll find myself working all alone – me a Scot born and bred – to nurse a camp of sick Americans!'

'They're not sick.'

'Not even home-sick?' asked Alec drily.

Both Alec and I were dropping with fatigue, ready for bed, too tired even to eat, so after we had drained the last drop of Old Rarity, Sam and I walked together to our jeeps.

'You been up to something?' I asked suspiciously.

'With luck. I've almost fixed up a hell of a jaunt for us.' He could hardly conceal the glee in his voice as he said, 'Do me a favour. Come over to the club for just one drink, I'll put you wise to what's happening.'

In the Union Jack Club he steered me to a quiet corner of the veranda where we could talk undisturbed and over two whiskies he explained what he hoped to do. The American doctors *had* sent a message of congratulation to Alec and myself, and they *were* holding a conference in San Francisco to discuss disease in the Pacific, and there *was* talk of a new drug to combat cholera.

'But apart from that,' said Truscott with pride, 'I've cooked up the whole scheme myself.'

'Explain please!'

'Sure.' Truscott sipped his drink thoughtfully. 'I need your help, Kit.'

'With a girl?'

He nodded.

'If you've got her in the family way, forget it,' I said. 'I wouldn't touch an abortion for a million dollars. An abortion is classed as a felony, and if you're found out, the penalty is penal servitude for between three years and life.'

'I didn't mean that,' he cried. 'But the girl – and me – do need help. I knew from the start that Alec Reid would never want to make a big flight like this to San Francisco, that's why I suggested it. And the flight *does* have an element of danger – but then so does all life. But I knew that wouldn't stop you from coming to the big city for a change.'

'Go on.'

'So I guess I played up your part as a hero – well, godammit, you *did* run Faalifu – and I suggested that they ought to invite a hero.'

'You mean,' I said sardonically – but I couldn't help laughing, he was such an ingenuous man – 'you mean the man who saved the American base from a fate worse than death?'

'Yeah!' He laughed too. 'I guess that was the line I took. I gave you such a helluva build-up that they regard you as one real brave guy. So don't chicken out on me and say you won't go.'

'What do you mean chicken out on *you*? I'd love a break in the big city. So long as you don't try any illegal tricks! I've a feeling you're using me.'

'Sure, I am. What in hell's name do you think I am – a godamn philanthropist? But no medical monkey business – you have my word. We'll be flying together.'

'You, at a medical conference?'

'Yeah – me. As an American guide to help show a limey around. All you gotta do is shake hands, listen to a couple of speeches – '

'And you?'

'I'm going to see my girl who's got a deep problem, and I'll tell you all about it if and when the deal comes through.'

'*If* it comes through.' I called for refills.

'I'm sure it will.' He crossed his fingers.

'You really think so?'

'Yeah,' he nodded. 'There's one helluva lot of cholera

and clap and so on in the East, and my bet is that if there *is* another outbreak of cholera in the Pacific they'll want to test these new drugs. And so they really *want* to put you in the picture at the conference in January. I think they'd like to have a session in which you can tell them what happened in Koraloona – and then they'll tell you what easier method you might be able to try out if the epidemic breaks out again.'

'I'm ready,' I laughed.

Now that the worst was over, I telephoned Aleena two days later with the intention of asking her if we could have a quiet dinner together. Tiare answered the phone, and said, 'Aleena is swimming with Kinawa. I'll go and fetch her.'

'No, don't bother. I wondered whether Aleena could come and have a quiet dinner with me tonight, at home,' adding slyly, 'you trust me, I'm sure.'

'Of course I do.'

'And did Aleena tell you that I mentioned that I may – only may – be going to a medical conference in San Francisco.'

'Yes, she did. It must be exciting for you – and such an honour.'

'Undeserved. But I can't say no. If it comes off.'

'Of course you can't.'

'I thought that if Aleena and I could spend a few hours alone, it would help me to relax. I'm so dog tired I can't face the prospect of talking to anyone.'

'I understand, and of course I trust you. Have a quiet dinner together.'

We *did* have a quiet dinner, but when it was over, and we were sitting on the rattan sofa kissing, I laid my head on her lap – and fell asleep!

She must have sat there, cradling me in her arms for at least an hour before she stroked my face and whispered, 'Darling Kit, I must go.'

'I didn't fall asleep?' I groaned as I sat up with a jerk. 'My God, how awful!'

'You're exhausted,' and leaning forward to kiss me, said with a laugh, 'I think I'm going to send you to Doctor Reid for a check-up.'

'I *am* exhausted. I'm sorry, darling. Behaving like an old married couple. It's the classic married situation – a nap at home after a good dinner.'

'Won't it be wonderful when that day comes? Next March I'll be nineteen.'

'And already we bore each other?' My tone was still bantering.

'Never that. Now, darling, drive me home, and then go to bed.'

I did, kissing her at the door, like any normal provincial engaged couple, but the sleep had so refreshed me that, when I saw a light in Alec's bungalow, I peeped through the window, saw him drinking alone and asked if I could come in, for a nightcap.

'I did a terrible thing,' I explained ruefully when Bubble and Squeak had given me a Scotch, 'I had dinner with Aleena – just the two of us in my bungalow – and then I fell asleep.'

'Just like an old married couple,' Alec echoed my words. 'Ye'd have been better off if ye'd taken her into your bed.'

'I know,' I sighed. 'It won't be long now.'

'Well, I think ye should have raped her – with her consent – months ago. And if that's not possible, well, take a look around and pick up a wee bit of fluff to pass the time. There's a lot of it around in the daily tit parade.'

He poured out a second drink, and with a chuckle said, 'What beats me is how a healthy young man like you, surrounded by beautiful girls, canna – well, canna have a wee fling now and again. Like ye used to have with Lucy. Ye appreciated her!'

'Lucy was different,' I said.

'Aye, I'll grant ye that. But this mumbo-jumbo chastity vow that Aleena's made – it's agin human nature – especially a man's nature. Why, man!' Alec mopped his bald and sweating head. 'Ye should be panting with desire twenty-four hours a day at the sight of that beauty!'

I couldn't help laughing.

'Maybe I am,' I admitted. 'But you know, Alec, there are two reasons why I don't.'

'Ye're not going to become a nancy boy?'

'Never, I promise you. But Lucy and I were never in love with each other. I've never *been* in love until I met Aleena. The girls I took to bed now and again in London – I don't know, you can't really say I'm fastidious, but often it all felt sordid. That's the only way I can describe it. Or degrading. Especially afterwards. Except with Lucy, I always lost much more than I gained.'

'Mebbe ye're right. But what's the second reason?'

'Aleena's young, and sometimes I forget that she's grown up. I still see her as she was – the day I spotted the black mole on her leg. Just a kid, and I forget that she's no longer a kid. And Koraloona itself has a part to play in the way I think.'

Alec Reid took another sip of Scotch. 'I dinna get the drift.'

'The South Seas has taught me patience. I've been learning that art from you. I don't *mind* waiting for Aleena, for a young girl to grow up a little more – and be more ready for marriage. If that pleases her, that makes me happy, and in this part of the world the question of time doesn't seem to matter, not really, for she's little more than a child.'

'Her grandmother was hardly more than a child when Gauguin seduced her,' retorted Alec.

'That was different. I have all my life before me. Gauguin was a dying man and he couldn't *afford* to wait.'

'Ye've got a point there, I'll grant,' admitted Alec, adding as though it explained everything, 'and anyway, he was French.'

I knew that Alec was trying to understand the feelings I held, why I didn't try to persuade Aleena to go to bed with me. For I *could* have persuaded her, I've no doubt. But it was even more difficult for him to understand *why* I didn't really miss sex. If Lucy had been on the island, things might have been different but, apart from the possible exception of Kinawa, I hadn't really fancied any of the local girls. And so, silly though it may sound, however randy I sometimes felt, I didn't want to do anything that would hurt Aleena. In a way, to delay the pleasure was only going to increase it.

A couple of weeks after Christmas Alec and Jason Purvis were having a late dinner with me when I heard the sound of a car brake outside my bungalow, then a shout from a voice I recognised.

'You there, Kit?' It was Sam Truscott. 'It's arrived.'

As he walked into the living-room and greeted the others, I looked at him with assumed nonchalance in order to disguise the fact that my heart had missed a beat. 'What's arrived?' I asked.

'Godammit, you British always refuse to get excited! The invite from San Francisco, that's all. Here – open it.'

'If it's not already been opened, how do you know – ?'

'Because I got a copy, dope. A military operation was needed to get you to California. How's about a snort?'

'For all of us.' Purvis, who had already been drinking quite a lot, slopped the whisky as I asked him to pour out a drink for Truscott.

'Ye's right. Unlimited drink tonight – it's a celebration,' cried Alec. 'Never mind the bawbees!'

'Don't you drink too much if I have to leave Koraloona in your hands,' I laughed.

'I'll nae do that,' promised Alec, giving Jason a sly look. 'Unlike Purvis, I can drink and no be drunk.'

'Aren't you going to read the letter?' asked Sam impatiently.

I tore open the buff envelope. The letter-heading, typical of the curious American habit of giving personality to

inanimate objects, read: FROM THE DESK OF THE
DEAN OF THE FACULTY OF EPIDEMIOLOGY, and
said:

Dear Dr Masters,
The outbreak of cholera in the Moto Varu archipelago
group being the latest recorded in world epidemiology,
and your and Dr Reid's treatment and prophylaxis
therefore being of special interest, we extend to you an
invitation to attend our convention in San Francisco
opening on 13 January, 1944, so that we may have the
benefit of your opinions in a full seminar, devoted to
current medical problems in the Pacific.
Accommodation, travel, and all expenses will of course
be met by the University. The date will be cabled
separately to the US forces in Sanderstown.
I look forward to hearing soonest so that we may
share your experienced opinions in the cause of medicine.
Cordially yours,

Underneath was a flourish of a signature which I made no
attempt to decipher. For I was feeling stunned with
excitement. I re-read the letter, this time aloud for the
others – and with curiously mixed feelings. I loved Koraloona, I knew I always would, but I couldn't help bursting
with excitement at the proposal of visiting, if only for a few
days, sophisticated men and women, taxis, fresh faces,
large, luxurious hotels.
'But January 13! That's three days away. We can't make
it.' I downed another Scotch in one gulp.
'Of course we can. It's only the tenth. We leave
tomorrow morning.'
'*What!*'
'Sorry. There was a delay in the mail which should have
reached us a week back. I got a military cable today, so I
sent a message back that we'd go. I told you, these guys
don't waste time. You can pack tonight.'

'If I can stand up – we're on the second bottle.' In fact, though I felt heady, it was with excitement as much as alcohol. 'But I must see Aleena first.'

'Not tonight, Josephine,' Purvis hiccuped. 'It's nearly one o'clock.'

'What time do we leave tomorrow?' I asked Sam.

'Eleven. You'll have plenty of time. We're going by flying-boat to Pearl, then pick up a new crew and plane for the second leg.'

It meant a rush, but at least I would only be away for less than two weeks, of which four days would be spent flying.

'You're sure you don't mind,' I asked Aleena the next morning when I took the jeep up to Tiare's house. 'I'm going to miss you terribly, but it won't be for long.'

'Of course I don't mind if you go. Only,' she looked at me with those sultry eyes, 'be careful. It's dangerous. And you won't be tempted by the big city? It's almost our time – and then,' almost slyly, with a catch in her voice, 'one bed for two people. Can you wait for that moment? You won't be unfaithful in San Francisco?'

'Do I look the unfaithful type?' I laughed.

'Well, if you can withstand the lure of Paula Reece,' she smiled. 'I suppose I can trust you.'

'Don't mention her,' I said almost angrily. I could never obliterate from my mind the picture of Bill Shanks dying in agony and Paula's face twisted with terror.

'I wonder sometimes if I was stupid to ask you to honour the vow,' she said. 'But you know that, if you *do* feel that you really can't wait – if you become – what's that funny word you use? – randy, I'll – '

'We have waited so long,' I said a trifle ruefully. 'I suppose we can wait until March 8.'

'I hate to see you go like this – and so suddenly.'

'I know. But now I must go, darling. The plane takes off in half an hour.'

She went with me to the garden where my jeep was waiting – at the very spot where, so long ago it seemed, I

368

had all but thrown Mana out of the ambulance – Mana who was now incarcerated for life in Penal Island.

I kissed her on the lips, mouth slightly open so that the tips of our tongues stroked each other, and then I felt the surge of awakening desire, and almost roughly pushed her away from me.

'We'll get married as soon as we can after I come back,' I said. 'You're right. I *am* randy. And I don't know how long I can hold out.'

Climbing into the jeep, I backed, ready to drive along Main Street to the military airstrip near Tala-Tala, but as I turned for one last look as she waved, I saw that she was beginning to cry.

Jumping out, running back the few yards, I kissed both of her wet eyes, tasting the salt of real tears.

'My darling heart,' I said. 'Don't cry. It's only for a few days. Don't cry. I can't bear it.'

'It's silly of me. But I suddenly thought – suppose you don't come back. And you left without telling me that you love me.'

'Didn't I? But you know I love you. I love you, I love you, I love you. There!'

'Now I feel better.' She wiped the tears away and forced a smile. 'Because, Kit, I love you with all my heart and if anything happened to you I would die. No, I'm not being hysterical. I couldn't live without you. I wouldn't want to. So take extra special good care of yourself.'

24

I had never been on a flying-boat before, and when I first saw the giant on which Sam and I were to fly non-stop to Hawaii, my first thought was, 'How the hell can that huge great weight ever stay up?'

The flying-boat, explained the captain, a naval officer

369

called Franks, was a PB-M3, powered by two Curtis Wright engines. She carried a crew of thirteen and bristled with guns. She also carried nearly nine tons of fuel, giving it a range of up to fifteen hours because of its extra wing tanks. There was room for thirty passengers – but no seats. All of us had to sit on the floor most of the time.

'I call her the flying flophouse,' grinned Franks, an engaging young man with grey eyes and sporting a crew cut, 'because I've fixed up eight canvas bunks so that everyone can take turns to get a small kip.'

I looked the aircraft over. It had a lower deck, which included a makeshift kitchen with a three-burner electric stove on which one crew member could cook rough and ready meals – corned beef hash or chili con carne heated up in tins.

The journey was uneventful but so exhausting – eleven hours in the air until we reached Pearl Harbor and spent the night there – that I didn't have the time, or the inclination, to go and see Honolulu itself. We spent another twelve hours in the air until we finally reached Alameda Naval Air Station in San Francisco Bay. We taxied across the water and moored at the foot of a ramp. Wheels were hooked on to the hull, then we were winched up. A few minutes later I was on dry land – and in a different world.

I loved Koraloona. And I loved and missed Aleena. But it would have been abnormal if I hadn't breathed excite-ment as the car provided by the medical conference whisked Sam and me from the Alameda base to the skyscrapers of San Francisco, round Union Square, up streets which meant nothing to me – not then – Sutter Street, Montgomery, and Telegraph Hill, to a glimpse of what looked like a slim lighthouse which, as the doctor explained, was called Coit Tower. 'We've reserved a room for you at the Mark Hopkins Hotel,' he added. 'It's convenient because the conference is being held in the Fairmont Hotel, just opposite. Would you care to make a short detour, Doctor, to show you Fisherman's Wharf – the greatest abalone steaks in the world?'

We careered up and down the incredibly steep hills, the normal sounds of a busy city interrupted by the clanging of bells from the cable cars which trundled up and down, loaded with passengers, teetered for a few seconds at the brow of a steep hill, and then plunged down the other side, the passengers hanging on to the steps of the platform.

'You're not too pooped for a short tour?' asked the doctor who was called Greene. In truth I was – absolutely exhausted, even though I had slept an hour or two on the plane – but I hadn't the heart to deny him the pleasure of showing off his beautiful city. Finally we arrived at the Mark Hopkins.

'On Nob Hill,' explained Dr Greene. 'So-called because that was where the first nobs lived when they made their pile in San Francisco.'

I had never seen anything like the Mark Hopkins Hotel before. A battery of lifts, or elevators, decorated the foyer. All had winking light signs before them. Dr Greene pressed one which said 'Non-stop 1–18'. And when we got in, it shot up without stopping. 'You're actually on the fifteenth floor,' explained the doctor. 'I've got you adjoining rooms, and it's only three floors below the top of the Mark. I thought you'd like to stop by and take a look at the view.'

This was San Francisco's most famous bar, a circle of plate-glass windows around the central array of bottles clustered in an inner circle. From the windows I could see the entire cityscape, sea and land – a breathtaking series of views. On one side stood the Oakland Bridge, stretching across the bay, with Treasure Island half way across it; on the other side the elegant fingers and dull red beauty of the Golden Gate Bridge led from San Francisco to Mount Tamalpais – the bridge under which thousands of naval officers and ratings had passed on their way to live or die in the Pacific.

One chunk of rocky island stood in the bay, rather lonely and forlorn.

'Alcatraz,' said Dr Greene laconically.

'Penal Island,' I said without thinking.

371

'Pardon me?'

'We have our own Alcatraz in our lagoon,' explained Truscott. 'Not quite so important as yours, Doctor Greene, but equally escape-proof.'

We had a dry martini served in a huge glass after the barman had asked, 'Straight up, sir?' Baffled, I turned to Greene who explained that 'straight up' meant a drink without ice in it, otherwise it would be 'on the rocks'.

Then he added, 'I guess you boys'd like a little shut-eye after the drinks?' We would. We descended three flights by lift but I hardly noticed the luxury of an American hotel in war-time – free soap, sachets of shampoo, spare razor blades, boxes of tissues, together with fluffy pillows and more breathtaking views. I took them all in in a kind of daze, and though I must have removed my shoes, I had no recollection of doing so. I rolled on to the bed, and slept for six hours without budging.

All through the period before Sam Truscott had arranged for me to attend the conference I had been vaguely concerned by two things: first, that he *had* skilfully arranged for me to attend the conference – me, not Alec Reid; and second, that he was deeply worried about a problem which centred around his girl, and hoped that in some way I could help her. He never talked about her; but he had spells of moodiness, and at those times I had the feeling he was on the verge of a confession; but he never could quite bring himself to the brink and, since it was not really any concern of mine – I had had enough battling with cholera to last me a lifetime – I did nothing about it. I was delighted to get a free holiday and let the future take care of itself.

But the first evening, after we had had a good sleep, Sam Truscott did finally unburden himself – and ask me for help.

I had walked across from the Fairmont to the Mark that evening after being introduced to several of the doctors discussing arrangements for future conference business. In the lobby I found a note from Sam saying that he would like to take me to dinner at Trader Vic's, one of the best restaurants in San Francisco, and noted for its South Seas cuisine.

'It's hell to get a reservation, but they know me and I've managed it,' he wrote in his note. 'If you can make it, see you in the bar up top at 6 p.m.'

'Up top' meant, of course, the top of the Mark, and Sam was already sitting at a window table when I arrived.

'Look at that view!' he cried, and indeed the view was even more spectacular than before as the first lights of the skyscrapers twinkled, and a few wreaths of sea mist hung above the Golden Gate Bridge and the tops of tall buildings – fog, they called it in San Francisco, little knowing what a London pea-souper was.

'Just one drink,' Sam advised me when I joined him. 'The drinks at Trader Vic's are lethal, but one Old Fashioned will give you a solid foundation.'

I liked Old Fashioneds, and stirred the mixture of Bourbon, Angostura, orange, a few specks of sugar, and a dash of soda. Then I took a sip.

'You look worried, Sam.' I was watching him, as he blew his nose, tucked his handkerchief into the sleeve of his jacket, stared out of the window, then took his handkerchief out and blew his nose again when he didn't really need to. 'Your girl let you down?' I asked facetiously. 'Is that why you're taking pity on a lonely doctor in a strange city?'

'No way,' he said. 'Gee, I hate to be so goddamn depressing, but I'll be even with you. I *am* depressed.'

'Tell your Uncle Kit – no charge for consulation,' I said with mock resignation.

He sighed. 'I will. I need your help – medical advice. And I'm going to bring my girlfriend along to have dinner with us in half an hour.'

'At last!' I cried. 'About time. She must be a real beauty for you to hide her like you have done!'

'She is. A beaut is the word. But what I'm going to tell you first, now, is to prepare you in case you can help – '

'No monkey business – I warned you.'

'Nope.' He knew what was passing through my mind for he added, 'I told you – no abortion. Not to worry. What I want is for you to mix with all these top doctors and find someone who can help my girl – a specialist. A surgeon. Especially as some of the finest gynaecologists in America are attending the conference to discuss clap and related social diseases.'

'They are. But is she so ill?'

'She's not sick in the accepted sense of the word. But she – and I – both of us – need help.'

All sorts of possibilities flashed through my mind as they always do when a doctor is faced with embarrassing questions from a man who is shy of revealing all. Many doctors face this problem. Perhaps Sam was unable to make love. Or suffered from premature ejaculation? Obviously not, though it happens more often than many people realise; but one thing was already clear in my mind: he wouldn't have kept this illness a secret had it been concerned with TB or polio or even the dreaded cancer. It had to be concerned with sex.

'Before you unburden your soul,' I said, still trying to ease his embarrassment with a touch of flippancy, 'will you answer a couple of questions – honestly? This girl of yours. Do you want to get married to her?'

He never hesitated. 'I sure do. She's deeply in love with me, but doesn't want to marry me.'

I immediately jumped to the wrong conclusion. 'You mean, she's already married?'

'Hell, no,' cried Sam. 'She's as free as a bird. And so am I. And well,' with a touch of shyness which I found appealing, 'we're so great in bed together that I never want to get up. She's pure magic.'

'Well then, what's the problem?'

'Aw shit, let's have another drink.' He signalled to the barman. 'Same again, please. Kit, you'd better prepare yourself for a long, long story, but I'll make it as short as I can. I don't want *you* to do anything. But I did want you to come to the medical conference in the hopes that you could find the right specialist to operate on her.'

'For what? Why do you keep talking in riddles? The next thing you'll be telling me is that she suffers from VD!'

'Jeez, no. You may not know it, Kit, but Sam Truscott is a home-loving guy whose only dream in life is to fall in love, get married, and raise a family.'

'Very laudable! So what?'

'There lies the trouble. She can't have any children. And she won't marry me because she says she knows I want a family above everything else. I'm *willing* to forgo the prospect of having a family – adopt some, or whatever. But she just gives me the flat no-go sign. She'll be my girlfriend for as long as I like, but as for marrying – not a hope.'

'There's a lot of men who'd give their eye-teeth to have an attractive girlfriend who'll never get into trouble!'

'Don't joke, Kit. It's deadly serious.'

'I'm sorry. But where do I come in? Presumably she's been to her family doctor. I don't see the reason for all this mystery just because a girl can't have a baby. Millions of women the world over are barren.'

'It's not so simple as that. You see, she wasn't always barren – gee, that's a horrid word. I hate it.'

'I don't understand,' I said, and I didn't.

'Well, you'll meet her in half an hour and you'll see what a helluva great gal she is. But the answer is simple. First of all, her old man is a High Court judge in San Francisco. So she has to be very circumspect – especially as she had a boyfriend before I came on the scene and he *did* put her into the family way. And then,' he gave a sigh and gulped at his highball, 'he obviously didn't feel the urge to get married like I do, so he packed her off at a moment's notice from Sanderstown and – '

'And then?'

'She had a botched-up back-street abortion, got rid of the baby, and then met me!'

'And now she's – barren?'

'That's what she tells me. I don't know the gory details,

375

but whatever happened, the doctor told her that the price of the abortion was that she might be sterile. I met her a year ago, we've been trying ever since to have a baby, and she's sure proved her point.'

'And the man? You know who made her pregnant?'

'No. Only that he's a shit and I'd bash his brains in if I ever met him. If he'd given her the right kind of money – well, I guess you can do most things if you can pay enough. But he didn't feel that way about it, he packed her off and she had a back-street job, and the bastard who put her in the family way apparently didn't give a damn. I don't know the details – only that he shipped her back from Sanders-town to San Francisco pronto, and, well – I guess you know the rest. I haven't mentioned her name because her father's a kinda bigshot in these parts, and so, as they say in the British Army, no names no pack-drill.'

I was still vaguely puzzled by this confession, and I asked him, 'But how can I help?'

'It's very simple – and very honest. Thanks to you, if you'll help. I'm told that there *are* gynaecologists who are also surgeons – who specialise in gynaecology – who can perform goddamn miracles in what you might call restoring the balance of nature. As far as I can make out, my girl's lost nothing vital, I mean that back-street sonofabitch didn't take out her ovaries or whatever they call them. But though he sure fucked her up, the doctor did say that she might be able to have a major operation one day to restore – as he put it – the balance of nature. What a shit to do a thing like that.'

I finished my Old Fashioned and said, 'I'm still baffled, Sam. What the hell's the problem? Get the best doctor. That's all you need if it's possible to do anything at all. You don't need me.'

'You don't understand. Let's walk to Trader Vic's. It's downhill all the way towards Union Square.' He was silent while we stepped out of the lift, out of the door, and braced our knees against the steep downward pavements.

'You see, I met this girl a year ago when I was already in

the Navy. There's just no way I can look around for the kind of specialist we need. She won't consider any operation in San Francisco because everyone there knows who her old man is. I'm told there's a great specialist in Harley Street in London, for instance – but there's no way she can get there during a war. Now, don't get this wrong, but I've got a spare cent or two floating around. In fact, Kit, my folks have got enough oranges on our estate near Carmel to sink the entire Japanese navy in their juice. So money doesn't matter a damn. Contacts do. As VD is a major problem in the Pacific, there must be a lot of gynaecologists here. You find me the right doc at the conference who doesn't live in California and persuade him to operate, and I'll pay any fee he demands and you'll be the best man at the wedding – with a lifetime supply of free orange juice.'

'And the girl?'

'She's the best. She agrees. Godammit, she *wants* a husband and kids, but no doctors in her home town.'

'And me?'

'I told her the truth. No names, of course – as I said, no names no pack-drill, because you may not be able to do anything. But I've told her that you're attending the conference and – even though you haven't promised yet – I've told her that you'll use your influence to help if you can.'

I was thinking, wondering about some of the specialists I had met on that first day, as we reached the courtyard leading to Trader Vic's.

'There are one or two tricky bits, you know,' I warned him. 'I can't approach a specialist unless I do so in the role of a consultant asking advice about an operation.' I stopped him before we passed through the front porch. 'It's a question of medical protocol, you understand.'

'Not quite, but – '

'Well, that's the way it goes. This afternoon I was introduced to a man who's supposed to be the most brilliant gynaecological surgeon in America. His name is Morris.

Lives in Boston. But I would have to ask him officially. That's the difficulty. There's no problem if I ask him officially. But one thing you must understand, Sam, I'll help if I can, but I have to give him all the details of the abortion, what the doctor told your girl, dates, everything so that I can put it in writing. Otherwise any specialist surgeon would just laugh at me. And the higher they charge, the louder they laugh.'

'You're the doctor,' Sam said, adding, 'maybe you think you'd have to examine her?'

I shook my head. 'Probably not necessary. The case history is what a surgeon needs. Details, the date of suspected impregnation, the number of periods the patient missed before the abortion. That sort of thing. All very humdrum, but it has to be put in writing before a surgeon will even think of giving a preliminary examination, never mind an operation.'

Poor Sam! He must have been deflated, for I said with a laugh, 'Don't worry! We don't have to talk about it over dinner and spoil your appetite. And of course I'll have to have her name, address, phone number, and make an appointment to get down to the details so that I can pass them on to the surgeon.'

'You could meet at the Mark tomorrow.'

'Fine. It won't take long, but let's meet the lady now and then tomorrow, if I get a chance, I'll have a word with Morris. By the way, what is your girl's name?'

At that moment the entrance door burst open as the doorman welcomed us with a flourish, 'Ah! Lootenant Truscott. Great to see you, sir. The sooner we get rid of all these bloody Japs sir, the sooner you can get back to your oranges – and Trader Vic's.'

Truscott laughed, handed in his peaked cap and we walked into the restaurant, all soft lights, pretty flowers on the pink tablecloths, obsequious waiters, and the manager bowing us towards one of the best tables in the room. We had just sat down and started to sip a 'Tahitian Special' through straws dipped into enormous glasses when Sam's girl appeared, hesitated, then, as he waved to her, walked towards him with her face partly hidden.

The first thing I saw was a radiant, beautiful, freckled vision, and my mouth dropped open. Dumbfounded, I was unable to do anything but look at her.

It was Lucy.

25

Lucy Young! Of all people! She was a part of my life that had passed, and I had never expected to see her again. Yet we had shared the happiness of physical love; and it was a happiness followed, for me, by a long stretch of time without sex. Perhaps that was why my heart leapt at the sight of her: because although we had never loved each other in the sense of despairing each time we parted, the memories of our light-hearted happiness constantly haunted my memory like a volume of old photographs.

'Why it's Kit – Doctor Masters!' Lucy was the first to recover her composure and with such astonishing speed that she had been able to add the 'Masters' in order to give a note of formality to the shock. 'How are you?'

'You two seem to be acquainted?' said an equally astonished Sam, as I shook hands with her, again almost formally, and said, 'Lucy Young! Well, yes we are acquainted.' I turned to Sam, careful to say nothing until Lucy gave me a lead.

'Of course,' she said. 'How wonderful to see you, Kit. I hear you and Alec Reid had a terrible time with the cholera outbreak. I read all about it.' And to Sam she said, almost reproachfully, 'Really, Sam! You and your mystery doctor! You might have told me it was Doctor Masters.'

'I didn't realise you knew him,' said Truscott. 'Where did you meet?'

'On Koraloona.' With hardly a moment's hesitation

Lucy explained to Truscott, while the waiter hovered around proferring enormous menus. 'Paula Reece invited me to stay there for a spell. You *must* have met Paula, Sam?'

'Oh, sure. A red-hot momma!'

'You sure you didn't go to bed with her?' Lucy was teasing him – perhaps to change the subject.

Truscott went quite pink for a second or two, which confirmed a suspicion I had long held.

'Not that it matters if you did,' laughed Lucy. 'You'd be one of the dozens of men in her life.'

'Not me,' muttered Sam, lying like a trooper, as Lucy deliberately planted a 'casual' remark to me. 'I heard you're engaged to Aleena. Lucky you. I knew you'd fall for her. She's so sweet, and beautiful.'

'Sure is,' said Truscott. 'I'd have asked her myself if I hadn't met you first.'

Apart from that, the only other 'casual' reference came when Sam said to both of us, 'I've explained Lucy's problem, and I'm sure grateful to Kit here for helping out. I told Kit I've got to drive to Carmel tomorrow to see my folks, so maybe you, Kit, can tell Lucy the sordid details.'

'Anything you say. What time and where?' she asked.

'Lobby of the Mark Hopkins?' suggested Truscott, looking at me as he asked me, 'Eleven o'clock okay by you?'

I shook my head. 'No, I've got to report to the conference first thing in the morning, but I should be free by noon, so I could meet you then.'

'That's fine,' said Lucy.

I can't really remember that dinner, it was so embarrassing – though fortunately for all of us, Sam was so worried about Lucy's reference to Paula Reece that he had little time to think about my friendship with Lucy.

As he told me after dinner, when he had put Lucy in a cab and we had returned to my room for a nightcap, 'Gee, the shit really hit the fan when she mentioned Paula Reece! I felt myself going bright red. Did you notice? Sure I did have a quickie or two with Paula, it didn't mean a goddamn thing, just letting off steam, but I've got a black mark against me.' That was all Truscott said, except for a perfectly normal, 'Damn funny, you two meeting. I knew you'd like Lucy and get along.'

'She's a great girl,' I agreed.

Though I had never had the faintest idea that Truscott's girlfriend was Lucy Young, I could see how it had come about. Sam had talked over and over about his girl 'who was mad about the islands and wanted to return'. Yet it was only now that he explained *how* she had returned to the islands – always 'the islands', never had he mentioned Koraloona, because she had never mentioned the island to him, perhaps because of a touch of guilty conscience. But how had she returned – in the midst of a war?

'I do remember Lucy Young of course.' I was searching for an explanation. 'And I remember you told me she loved the islands. But during the war, how could she do it?'

Pouring a drink from a bottle in my bedroom, Truscott chuckled, 'I'm the world's greatest fixer – and I have one helluva lot of contacts. Look what I did for you!'

It seemed that the two first met in San Francisco, and when Truscott was posted to Sanders, he arranged with some of these contacts in high places to send Lucy to Sanderstown on a temporary civilian mission for which I had to admit she was well qualified – as a consultant to give advice to women serving with the American forces, in the Pacific. I didn't know it until this moment, but Sanders had been selected as a staging post for the army WAACS and naval WAVES, because it was considered 'safe', yet nearer to the Pacific battle than Pearl. 'And of course,' added Truscott, 'the British were so short of dollars that they accepted the American offer on the spot. At times there were up to three thousand nurses, WAACS and WAVES, at Sanders. And I was as pleased as hell to have Lucy, even when I was transferred to Koraloona. I couldn't get her *there*. I just didn't dare fly a civilian girl in a US plane. One bit of gossip and I'd have been court-martialled. But I went over to see her whenever I could.'

I asked, 'Then why did she leave?'

'The location of the staging posts was moved forward as we started over to the offensive. Lucy didn't want to go, and as she was a civilian she could refuse. But they wouldn't let her stay in Sanders because she was part of an official mission and had to sign off where it started – in San Francisco. And we,' with another chuckle, 'followed her.'

After the final drink Truscott changed the subject. 'When you went to the john I explained to Lucy that you had a famous surgeon in mind and that she'd have to tell you all she knows about what happened,' he said. 'You can rely on it, she'll be at the Mark at noon.'

'You'd better come along too,' I suggested. And I meant it. I didn't really want to see Lucy alone. I wasn't sure that I could fulfil the role of doctor to a patient with whom I had spent so many nights of love. Jason had once called me a prude because I ignored the local girls on an island in the South Seas where there was nothing wrong if a girl agreed. But I had never lusted after any of them. I *had*, though, enjoyed every second of my relationship with Lucy, and even the first sight of her in the restaurant had sent tingles of excitement through my body.

'I think you should come along,' I insisted again.

'Not me.' Truscott made for the door. 'I don't want to go through all that stuff again – times, dates, details. And anyway, I told you, we've only got a few days here and I must go to Carmel to see my folks. They'd never forgive me if I didn't.'

'As you like, but in a way I'd rather you *were* here.'

'No sweat. The most important thing is to persuade the right man at the conference to look after her. Number one priority.'

When Dr Greene first met me, he had said, 'Here's the "skedule", Doctor,' and had handed me a list of the speeches, functions, and entertainments. I noticed that the first full day of the conference was not very arduous. A speech of welcome at 10am, followed by, according to the schedule, 'lunch free, afternoon, optional sightseeing tour. Cocktails in Fairmont ballroom followed by dinner.'

So I would have no problems meeting Lucy at noon, and in the meantime I would make a point during the morning of meeting Mr Morris, the famous gynaecologist. After meeting Lucy, I would probably lunch alone at the Mark and sleep all afternoon. I still needed sleep badly, because of the change in hours.

I reached the lobby of the Mark just as Lucy did, looking stunning, in a pale pink dress, gathered in at the waist, exaggerating her figure which I remembered so well. On her blonde hair she wore a large pink straw hat with flowers on it – the sort I had seen in pre-war pictures of Ascot on a summer's day.

All this I noticed only vaguely, for I was agonising over one question which had been uppermost in all my thoughts and had tormented me from the first second we set eyes again on each other: was I the man responsible for the abortion? It was the first question I asked her as we sat down in the Mark. I saw the answer in her face as she lowered her eyes and nodded.

'Oh Lucy! How *could* you?' I cried. 'How could you have done such a thing – knowing it was me? Why didn't you tell me? It was wicked of you. You ought to know me better.'

'And you're unfair to say such a thing,' she cried. 'You're a doctor – you *must* realise – it's obvious – that I didn't know I was pregnant when I left. I was kicked out of Koraloona at a moment's notice – and I thought you were dying. Darling, you *were* dying. And I wasn't even allowed to stay with you.'

'But when you *did* find out that you were going to have a baby – and that I *was* alive – then you should have written to me. We could have married – and been happy, I'm sure.'

'We didn't *want* to get married,' she said with a touch of sadness. 'I remember you saying that – and I felt that way too. And I'm not the sort of girl to force any man into a shotgun wedding.'

'But when you *did* find out that I was alive – don't you think it was very unfair of you not to tell me?'

'You would never have known – you'd never have been any the wiser if dear old Sam hadn't blundered into our private affairs – a love affair that was all over and done with.'

I still couldn't grasp the enormity of what had happened, not even after a sleepless night in which I had tossed and turned, waking with dreams of Lucy as I remembered her at the Anani festival and afterwards, the long lazy nights of love, stolen from Paula. They *were* all over and done with, as Lucy had said, but when without warning the clock is turned back, you can't erase a memory as though it had never happened, you only heighten it, want to relive it. Yet, as I looked at her sitting there on the banquette in the lounge at the Mark Hopkins, her pretty, open-looking freckled face as sweet and as gentle as before, I felt a vague astonishment that she seemed to show no visible scars of the trauma through which she must have passed – and for which I had been responsible.

I had thought – and this had passed through my mind all night long – that even if we didn't 'love' each other, she must have loved me enough to tell me what had happened. She might have been worried (wrongly) that I would be upset – or even blamed me for, after all, it was my fault. Instead she had given me no chance to tell her my feelings. Yet this was long before Aleena had grown into a woman and if Lucy had told me she was expecting a baby, I almost certainly would have married her, for Lucy had certainly awakened in me a physical happiness I had never known before. And I would probably have been quite happy married to Lucy. It wasn't as though I was a struggling medic trudging around a warren of East End streets, bag in hand, worried by new responsibilities. I was Assistant Medical Officer of what I thought the most beautiful island in the world; I had a good boss in Alec Reid, I had gained

384

the respect of the community who relied on me to help keep them healthy, and I wasn't even hard up, for in Koraloona two people *could* live as cheaply as one, even three! Perplexed at what I thought was Lucy's insensitivity, I said as much to her.

'Apart from anything else, didn't you even care enough about me to discover whether I had died?' I asked.

'How can you say such a thing?' she replied in a low voice. 'Of course. You can imagine the agony I went through that night on board the *Mantela*. I spent most of the time in the saloon drinking with Bill Robins, who got on the radio as soon as the *Mantela* docked and found out from Colonel Fawcett that you were out of danger. Bill told me immediately. He was very fond of you, Kit, and just as upset as I was.'

'Not *quite* as upset.' I couldn't keep the sarcasm out of my voice. 'After all Bill wasn't expecting a baby!'

'Oh, Kit,' she cried, 'how *can* you say a thing like that! I told you – I didn't know – I had no idea.'

'I'm sorry,' I said. There was an awkward pause, which she broke by looking at her watch.

'I think it's time I told you the details. It's twelve-thirty. Could we have a drink? It's been a pretty eventful few hours since you walked back into my life.'

'Of course. Shall we go to the top of the Mark?' I got up.

'No.' She shook her head. 'Let's go to neutral ground. Let me drive you to Fisherman's Wharf and if you've got time, you can have the best fish lunch in the world – yes,' with a smile of real affection, she linked her arm in mine and said, 'even better – or at least as good – as in Koraloona.'

Scoma's restaurant on Fisherman's Wharf had a pleasant bar overlooking a crowded basin of small fishing boats and a few pleasure yachts, and beyond that, glimpses of the famous Golden Gate bridge. 'And there's the ocean – ' Lucy pointed beyond the bridge. 'But you can't see Koraloona.'

I ordered a gin fizz, but she said to the barman, 'Vodka and orange please,' and when she sipped it, she gave me a toast. 'I ordered this because the orange reminds me of the Anani Festival.'

'I should have ordered the same.' My voice had suddenly gone husky as I remembered that evening. 'It was such a wonderful festival. What happened the rest of the night was even more wonderful.'

'I know.' She slowly sipped the drink. 'In some ways the love we had for each other is the best kind in the world. All the love in the world, but without jealousy, without bitterness, without anger, only the joy that makes happy memories.'

'Sometimes they can be very, very real memories,' I said, 'and it's very hard not to bring them to life again once you stir them up.'

She sighed. 'Let me tell you what happened, and then we'll have lunch, and after you know the whole story you can go and see if there's the right doctor around.'

The story was quickly told. 'I wasn't quite honest with you,' Lucy admitted. 'I didn't tell you about my family – they're well known and they have old-fashioned ideas on – well, sex and so on. Paula knows them. I *was* telling you the truth about trying to earn money because I hoped to buy a little studio. I wanted that independence. But Paula was so jealous of you preferring me to her that she told me to get out that night, and threatened to tell my parents about us if I didn't go.'

'But surely,' I interrupted, 'you weren't afraid of your parents? They couldn't eat you just because you had fallen for a man?'

'I wasn't worried for *myself*,' Lucy said quickly. 'But for *you*! Paula warned me – and she meant it – that she would tell my father how the local doctor – that's you – had seduced his only daughter. And you'd already had a little trouble in London. *And* you were a mission doctor. I was afraid for you, not me. It wouldn't have looked good for you. So for *your* sake – and not even knowing that I was

386

pregnant – I grabbed the boat that night. It broke my heart, because I was afraid that you might be dying.'

I ordered two more drinks before asking, 'And when did you find out you were pregnant?'

'Five weeks later. I was in Honolulu then, and decided to stay there for a bit. I had a few friends and I searched around when I found I was pregnant. I was a long way from San Francisco – and my parents. I found a doctor – and he botched the job.'

'And,' I said bitterly, 'Sam's convinced that the man who made you pregnant is a bastard who walked out on you.'

'I know,' she sighed again. 'But it doesn't really matter, because he'll never know that it was you. I *know* that you'd never do a thing like that. And I suppose I did behave badly. I should have written to you. But I did it for you and we *had* agreed that we would never get too involved. Well,' with a laugh as we walked through from the bar to the restaurant, 'you can't become more involved than suddenly becoming an unmarried father.'

'It might have been for the best,' I said as we sat down and ordered abalone steaks, soft and succulent and breaded like veal escalopes.

'All past.' She leaned across the table. 'I'm so happy for you, but you know I feel a twinge of jealousy at the thought of you making love to her. Is she very beautiful in bed?'

'*Really* beautiful, but there's no need for jealousy because we've never been to bed.' I ordered some strawberries and cream. 'We're engaged – and I adore her – but – we're not lovers. You know what these Polynesian taboos are among the so-called upper classes? We'll be married, but Tiare insisted on no rushed wedding.'

'You poor dear,' she cried impulsively. 'How awful to be in love and do nothing.'

'I know,' I laughed. 'With us it was the other way round – we weren't really in love yet we did everything!'

'Not quite true. There are different kinds of love.' She

sipped from a glass of local white wine – 'I love Sam very deeply and this is why I won't marry him unless I can bear his child. Because that's part of my love for him.'

'And with me – ?'

'Well,' she looked at me very steadily, those big grey eyes staring into mine, 'it was a physical delight – a joy – an experience that I'll never forget.'

She gave me a sidelong glance that seemed equally an echo of that joy, and an invitation. For a moment I was tempted. When a girl who once loved you looks at you steadily, the signals are out. Danger signals! I could feel a tingle of desire – or were they goose pimples of warning? 'Careful, Kit!' I said to myself. 'You can't trifle with girls like Lucy. They're too attractive.'

Of course I loved Aleena with all my heart, and with a love far deeper than that I had ever held for Lucy. I would be faithful to her, of course. But where past love is concerned – especially one that was happy – it has tentacles as strong as those of an octopus. Any healthy man feels an urge to translate the past perfect to the present tense.

What nonsense I was thinking!

'Will you give me the information you said you'd written out?' I deliberately broke the train of thought.

She nodded. 'If you drop me at the St Francis in Union Square where I'm staying, I'll give it to you straight away. Then if you need to ask me any questions, I'll fill in any missing gaps.'

The sudden spark of that moment of temptation had passed, and after I'd paid the bill she drove me from Fisherman's Wharf up and down the hills, past the cable cars, and finally parked in the back of the St Francis, facing the green grass and the shops that lined Union Square.

'We'll go in through the parking lot,' she explained. 'Come to my room to get the list.' She pressed the button and the elevator then took us both to the tenth floor.

'It's all prepared for you.' She had kept the key of her room and unlocked it quickly. 'Here it is. No, don't read it now. And, it may sound silly, but as we are two engaged couples, perhaps it would be better if we didn't meet alone again.'

My voice was trembling as I agreed, 'You're right.'

'So – goodbye Kit, and happy memories.' She held out a hand, almost formally, then suddenly she gave a cry, 'But we *can't* say goodbye like this!'

'We can. We must.'

'You're right,' she whispered. 'But – just one goodbye kiss.'

'That's all right,' I said lightly. But it wasn't, for without warning she put her arms round me and cried, almost plaintively, 'Our love affair was so beautiful and we never said goodbye. We did love each other, didn't we?'

'In our special way.' I tried to disentangle her arms. 'And the memories were beautiful. Don't let's spoil them.' I kissed her gently on the lips – and I was reaching with the pieces of paper in one hand for the bedroom door, when I dropped them. And then, at the moment I touched her lips, she opened hers and kissed me – just as she used to do.

'I know we shouldn't – '

'We shouldn't – and we won't.' I half opened the door and said, 'No, Lucy dear. Don't think only of Aleena, think of Sam.'

'I am, I am.' She banged the door closed. 'I'm thinking of both of you. Just stay for a few moments more.' Then, almost desperately, she asked, 'Would you like me to order some coffee?'

What an odd request! 'No coffee. No – anything,' I smiled.

'All right. I know. So it *is* goodbye. After we've kissed goodbye, we'll never meet again.'

'No kissing.'

'Once more – and then – '

I had forgotten how beautifully she used to kiss in what seemed like a distant past, and then she gasped, 'Just a *real* goodbye, just this once. When we parted we never had the chance to say a real goodbye.' She almost tried to pull me to the bed.

'We shouldn't,' I said, wavering.

'I'm not jealous because Sam went to bed with Paula.'

'That's different. You and I are going to get married to Sam and Aleena.' Yet even as my voice went hoarse, I was weakening. Everything in my prudish Nottingham upbringing told me I was behaving wickedly. I mustn't. I shouldn't. But there is no more demanding mistress than a past and happy love. Yet I swear that deep inside me I was afraid – not of making love to Lucy, not of being discovered, but of myself, of the guilt I knew I would feel when the moment of ecstasy had passed.

'But we're hurting no one,' she whispered. 'And I want you to make love to me, Kit. And you want me really, don't you?'

And we did. Half undressed on the bed, and that's all I can say about it. It was heaven while it lasted; it was a kind of perfection born out of our traumatic separation, and I left after an exquisite hour of yesterday and today jumbled together.

'I'm sorry, Kit, I'm sorry,' she said. 'But only in one way, for you gave me something I needed. Go now.'

I opened the door, moved across to the elevator and pressed the 'down' button, thinking, I shouldn't have done it. What I did was wicked. I must be mad. But though I knew the guilt from time to time would haunt me, I knew what Lucy had meant. We never *had* said goodbye.

As I waited, I heard a voice cry, 'You forgot your pieces of paper. The details!' I ran back along the corridor to the door where she handed them to me. 'No, I'm not going to kiss you,' she smiled. 'But I do want to say that if the operation is successful, you'll have helped, and I'll marry Sam and be happy with lots of children, and you'll marry Aleena and have lots of babies. And yet only the two of us in the whole wide world will ever know that we did finally say goodbye – properly.'

26

It never ceases to amaze me the way women whom you last met locked in passion can put on entirely new faces when you meet them a few hours later. There was Lucy, who had in a way been fighting with me, her loins wrapped around mine, panting with desire; and here she was now at the top of the Mark, looking as though butter wouldn't melt in her mouth.

We met the following morning and Lucy arrived looking, as Sam put it admiringly, 'as fresh as paint'. And she did look newly painted – with innocence, her unregistered trademark.

'How are you this morning? Was your medical dinner terribly dreary?' She turned to me as though asking whether I had enjoyed the food.

'As dull as hell,' I replied cheerfully.

'Oh dear!' Her face fell. 'No luck?'

'On the contrary,' cried Sam. 'Tell her, Kit.'

Lucy had given me, in the two sheets of paper, her written record of what had happened – the dates of her missed periods, where she had had the abortion, with all the details she could remember – except, of course, the doctor's name.

'Apparently,' I explained now to her and Sam, 'judging from the information which I passed on to Mr Morris, hers is quite a common problem. And Mr Morris – he's a top specialist in this kind of surgery and a very pleasant man – says he'll agree to be of assistance.' I hesitated. 'But he lives in Boston and he won't operate except there. And he won't even meet you to arrange for a preliminary examination unless Sam goes along with you first.'

'But of course,' said Lucy. 'You *are* clever, Kit. Thank you so much. And you'll come, Sam?'

'Sure!'

'Why does he want to see Sam?' she asked.

'Nothing sinister. He wants to make sure that any operation is being done because you really intend to get married,' I laughed. 'It seems – it's an unpleasant subject but there it is – that these botched operations are pretty common, and sometimes things are done in a bit of an underhand way.'

'Goddamn bastard!' muttered Sam.

'Hush,' said Lucy, avoiding my eye. 'Go on, Kit.'

'Nothing really to add. He's got a strict sense of whatever it is – decorum? – and feels that if he undertakes the preliminary examination here in San Francisco – which is not his home territory, so to speak – he'd have to borrow a friend's consulting room and he wants everything to be above board. It's not easy,' I apologised, 'to persuade an eminent surgeon to take time off from a conference just to examine someone he's never met.'

In fact I had arranged with Mr Morris to meet Sam and Lucy at the Mark the following day and then, if he agreed, he would use the surgery of a doctor friend, a fellow gynaecologist called Griffiths, who lived above his consulting room in San Francisco. He and Morris had been at medical school together, and were old friends. Griffiths was away and had lent his flat to Morris for the conference.

If Morris saw that Sam and Lucy were serious, he would conduct a preliminary examination and say whether or not he could operate. After that, Lucy would have to travel to his clinic in Boston.

'No sweat, so long as her life's not in danger,' said Sam and, patting me on the shoulder, turned to Lucy as I squirmed and said, 'Didn't I tell you that Kit's a true friend?'

After Lucy had gone I had to tell Sam, 'There's one other thing I didn't mention.' I squirmed a bit more. 'Morris has borrowed this surgery of his friend Griffiths, but after all, he's in strange consulting rooms, he's a bit suspicious about the need for secrecy and so on, and since I've involved him in examining a stranger – through my recommendation which was strictly necessary – he doesn't want to hold a preliminary examination without a second doctor being present. I must say I understand. Being asked out of the blue – '

'Sure. What's the problem?'

'He suggested that I should be there,' I explained. 'You see, I had to tell Morris – in order to persuade him – that I knew both of you, I even pretended that I was going to be the best man at the wedding – and as I am a doctor – '

'That's OK by me.' Sam gave a hearty laugh. 'I guess that, to you doctors, one pussy's much the same as any other.'

'You have a point,' I agreed gravely. 'But if you feel that, as we're friends, Sam – '

'No sir. If you're instrumental in giving us a baby,' he said, 'I tell you, I'll travel to the end of the earth to ask you to deliver the child. That's a promise. So you might as well do your homework on my future wife first.'

I felt decidedly uncomfortable, embarrassed, guilty, becoming involved as I had done, and my first instinct had been to give a flat 'No' to Morris, but he was an expert in his field and, when I hesitated, he shrugged his shoulders and said, 'Of course if you prefer not to do it, I'd quite understand. But then, to be frank, Doctor, it would be better for me to have a preliminary examination of the patient in my Boston surgery. Suit yourself.'

I couldn't very well argue, especially as Lucy flatly refused to see her usual family doctor – or for that matter, any doctor in San Francisco. *That*, I realised, was the real reason for Sam's contriving my visit to San Francisco. But the price I had to pay was pretty high – to watch the girl with whom I had been passionately involved being examined in an intimate but clinical manner.

For the most part, the conference was a bore – largely because it dealt with problems which I could never resolve, for the suggested cures required expensive equipment, and our mission hospital had only six beds!

On the third day, though – the day after Morris had met Sam and Lucy, and the day before he was to examine Lucy – we did have two fascinating sessions. The morning one was devoted to the new drug to combat cholera, the afternoon session to venereal diseases.

The morning started with a highly embarrassing speech after I had described the way in which Dr Reid and I had coped with the epidemic – embarrassing because the chairman of the sub-committee on cholera followed me to the podium and – almost in tears, it seemed – told the hardened assembly of American doctors that it was not too much to say what an honour it was for him to give thanks to 'this young British doctor'.

'This seminar on epidemiology has brought together the loftiest capabilities of the medical profession from all over,' he said. 'And Doctor Masters – yeah, Doctor Masters – has come at our invitation, to unburden himself of the experience he's gained in the cholera outbreak in the South Seas, which sound so idyllic but ain't so when *vibrio cholerae* is on the rampage, hey? – '

He paused for a laugh which didn't come – understandably; then he proceeded in complex clauses and sub-clauses and at last came round to his point, if he ever had one.

'And so, gentlemen of the Hippocratic persuasion, we thank Doctor Masters for the manner in which he helped our boys – our boys fighting out there and defending these great United States – to subdue what might have become a pandemic – I repeat, a *pan*demic, sir – ' He looked at me benevolently. 'Right, Doctor Masters?'

It wasn't, but I wasn't going to lengthen his speech, so I gave a vague smile.

The doctors gave me what the evening papers later described as 'a standing ovation'. They printed a photograph of me across two columns under the heading, TRIBUTE TO A MEDICAL HERO.

During the session, however, came something of considerable interest to me – a long discussion of a new drug, sulfaguanidine, referred to as Drug X. It was made by Du Pont and it was hoped it could be used to treat cholera. According to the doctor giving the address, the Americans had already experimented with it, 'but,' he had added to the audience, 'so far we have only proved its efficacy in the laboratory. However, if there is any suspicion of the *vibrio* – ' he used the technical term for the organism that causes cholera – 'and if the serological agglutination tests confirm that it *is* cholera, we would be delighted if our distinguished colleague Doctor Masters would test our new drug in the field.'

In fact, he arranged for me to take supplies back to Koraloona, together with the chemical details of the formula.*

The session also included a brilliant address by Mr Morris; and though there wasn't much venereal disease in Koraloona, one always had the feeling that it could break out (as it had done in Tahiti) in islands where morals were lax.

'But please do not go too far into the realms of self-experimentation,' said Morris, 'we do not want the highly acclaimed Doctor Masters to follow the example of Otto Obermeier.'

'I promise!' I interrupted with a laugh, for I remembered from medical school the classic case of the German Dr Obermeier who in 1831, in his efforts to find a cure for cholera, injected himself with blood from an infected patient and died.

So it was with interest that I listened to Morris. The first few minutes were devoted to historical failures, including the efforts of John Hunter, who had lived in Jermyn Street in the eighteenth century. Of course, as a medical student I was also taught his history.

* The drug was later marketed under the trade name of Sulfasuxidine. The chemical formula was $H_2NC_6H_4SO_2NHC$ (=NH) NH_2.

'He was another Englishman, like Doctor Masters, who was not afraid of trying out cases for himself,' said Mr Morris. 'The audience is no doubt aware that Hunter was the most famous of the autoexperimenters, whose study of VD led him to inoculate himself with matter obtained from the penis of one of his patients who thought he had only contracted gonorrhoea. Oh dear! Unfortunately the patient had syphilis as well and Hunter drew the erroneous conclusion that the two diseases were one and the same.'

After a pause, Morris added, 'We are on the brink of a new discovery for combating venereal diseases – though again I beseech Doctor Masters not to follow the example of either Obermeier or Hunter and test the new drugs on himself!' Again I laughed and the rest of the audience tittered and turned in my direction with signs of appreciation.

'It seems a long time since Ehrlich produced his Salvarsan 606 in 1910,' said Morris, referring also in general terms to the numerous other arsenical preparations as well as to mercury and bismuth. 'But now comes a new drug – penicillin – which barely a year ago in 1942 was scheduled for trial as a killer of the *spirochaeta pallida* virus. We are having some production difficulties – it is manufactured here in the USA – but I'm convinced in my own mind that it will eventually revolutionise the treatment of gonorrhoea and syphilis. It is not a painful cure, but it is a boring one, for we have discovered that to achieve a proper cure, the patient must be injected with penicillin once every three hours for three days and nights.'

I had, of course, read papers on *penicillium notatum*, discovered by Professor Alexander Fleming in 1929, and I remembered rumours about work with him and Professor Howard Florey during the thirties at the School of Pathology at Oxford, while I was a student.

'Penicillin is harmless even in enormous doses – the only chemotherapeutic agent that is,' said Morris. 'And it can be given in powder or pill form by mouth, or by injection into a muscle, so that it's rapidly absorbed into the blood and reaches every part of the body. Even so, parenteral treatment is very wasteful because it's rapidly excreted by the kidneys and the dosage has to be maintained every three hours. It's like trying to fill a bath with water with the plug out. But as it's harmless to the body tissues the dose can be enormously increased.'

At the end of the session I congratulated Morris on his address and when he thanked me he said, 'I met Miss Young and her fiancé yesterday. They are a delightful couple. We'll meet tomorrow as arranged. I'll pick you up in my car at the Mark at eleven o'clock.'

I had, of course, told Morris why Lucy was afraid of her family finding out.

'But my dear Masters,' he said, 'doctors don't gossip, you know that. They're bound by an oath of secrecy.'

'Some gossip among themselves,' I said wryly.

'That's true,' he admitted.

'That's why she's grateful to you for arranging to go to your colleague's surgery,' I said. 'It doesn't matter even if Miss Young is seen going there. She could be visiting a doctor for any one of a dozen reasons. But if it ever came out that a local doctor was conducting a post-abortion examination – well, Mister Morris, you'll appreciate – '

'I don't really,' said Morris almost crossly. 'As a rule I'm against any cloak-and-dagger stuff. No San Franciscan doctor would *talk*, even if they knew.'

'I know how you feel, but – there you are – '

'So long as Mister Truscott pays my fee,' said Morris sardonically, 'I don't suppose I should complain!'

'He'll pay,' I laughed. 'He's loaded.'

'You're beginning to talk like an American,' Morris laughed. 'I never heard an Englishman use the word.'

It gave me a certain sense of relief that Morris should regard examination with such a casual approach. Of course, all of us treat an approaching routine operation in the same way – life would be intolerable if one worried about the operating dangers that face any surgeon – but I *had* been through a very special hell of my own during the cholera epidemic, and it was a pleasant change to be with a man who joked and laughed. And after all, I wasn't going to be involved in the actual operation later in the year. I was only there as a witness to what was a perfectly normal examination.

The receptionist was there when we arrived, and when she announced that Miss Young was in the waiting-room, Morris came out to welcome Lucy, 'Ah, Miss Young. Good morning.' And with a typical American gesture asked, 'Lucy, isn't it?' Then he ushered her into the surgery. When Lucy saw me she paled and stood for a moment, even though she had, of course, known I would be present. The sight of me there must have embarrassed her – as it embarrassed me.

'This'll only take a few minutes, Lucy,' Morris reassured her. 'You go behind the screen, my dear, and take off your skirt and stockings and so on and put on the white cotton dressing gown you'll find behind the screen. Then I'll give you a local anaesthetic.'

She came back in the loosely fitting open-at-the-front hospital dressing gown and I looked the other way while she lay on the couch as Morris prepared to give her a local anaesthetic, explaining, 'There's nothing to worry about. The examination won't really even hurt, but I like to give a spot of ether to make you relax. Your flesh will feel very cold for a moment when I inject but that'll soon wear off.'

I kept my head averted as he gave her an injection in the groin. 'Now – or in ten minutes – you'll *know* that nobody's going to hurt you. It gives you a kind of confidence,' he smiled. As Lucy lay on the couch waiting for the anaesthetic to take effect, Morris explained to her, 'Doctor Masters and I are going to wash up.'

In the adjoining medical bathroom we washed, put on gowns, masks, gloves, caps, already hanging there sterilised and presumably normally used by the gynaecologist Dr Griffiths. While there Morris reiterated what I had told him – that the abortion had been done with a probe and scissors.

'That was the normal way in the thirties and even now,' said Morris. 'Typical of these butchers. They puncture the uterus with the probe, and then enlarge the puncture with scissors to a size large enough to allow the abortionist to extract the placenta and the foetus. It's old-fashioned but I dare say that in a few months, when the war is over, abortion methods will be improved.'

'It isn't really risky, is it?' I said.

'Not if it's done in clinical conditions. And normally you can have all the kids you want afterwards. But even before looking at the girl I'll bet a hundred to one that I know what's happened to her, and why she can't produce children. I'll bet she's got a highly active G-spot.'

I had wondered about that too. The 'G-spot' – named after its discoverer, the German Dr Ernst Grafenberg, who was born in 1894 – is an area about one and a half inches deep into the vaginal entrance which produces an orgasmic fluid (not a lubricating fluid) which is the female equivalent of the male semen (just as the clitoris is the female equivalent of the male penis) though not, of course, in any way fertile – and not by any means ejaculated by all women.

'Are you sure?' I asked.

'We'll know in ten minutes.' He pulled on his gloves and as we walked back to the large consulting room he added, 'You only need to look at some women to know that they have the sexual excitement that's caused by a G-spot.'

Dr Griffiths' consulting room was divided into two parts by a white curtain. Morris drew this aside to reveal a complicated examination couch and said to Lucy, 'Now, Lucy, let's have a look at your insides.'

For a moment Lucy looked with embarrassment at the complicated contraption in front of her. 'These nuts and bolts are called a stirrup,' said Morris. 'Lie down on the table please and I'll help you to get into the right position. If you feel a little dizzy, don't worry. The examination table is

adjusted so that your head is a little lower than your body –
just to make sure that an adequate blood supply is
maintained to the brain.'

On the other side of the table, the stainless-steel struts of
the stirrup rose vertically with adjustable padded clasps on
each one. I hadn't seen one of these since I was in London;
we didn't have one in Koraloona.

'Now,' said Morris, 'here's how we'll do it.' He was a
very gentle man, particularly as he drew up Lucy's knees
and forced them apart so that the knees could be placed in
the padded clasps. She could feel nothing, of course. Then
he carried a curtain rather like a home cinema screen on tall
legs, adjusted it so that the curtain was the right height to
keep Lucy's face hidden from the rest of her body.

'Now you won't feel anything,' said Morris. 'But I'm just
going to have a look around.' He picked up his speculum –
an instrument like a slim torch with an illuminated mirror
which, when inserted, clearly shows the walls of the vulva,
cervix and uterus.

After a few seconds Morris turned round the screen and
said to Lucy, 'Feel anything?'

'No.' Lucy actually smiled.

'Fine.' He then asked, 'When you and your fiancé make
love do you find that you need a towel or a tissue very
quickly after intercourse?'

She couldn't see me, thank God, so she didn't have to be
embarrassed by answering – an answer which I knew
perfectly well from the times we had made love together.

'Yes, I do,' she said in a quiet voice.

'Exactly,' said Morris. 'That's why you can't conceive.
The spermatozoa never reaches the egg to fertilise it.' To
me he explained, 'It's as I thought. She's got a highly
developed G-spot which gives out a lot of fluid when she's
sexually aroused, and, of course, it's a slight irritant. The
careless manipulation of the probe caused a small abrasion
in the cervix. I'll let you see it in a moment. It's resulted in
infection by the fluid, causing a subcutaneous cyst. When
Lucy is aroused, it expands and blocks the passage of male

semen. There's no problem – but she must have a surgical excision of the cyst. Here, take a look for yourself.' Morris handed me the eyepiece of the speculum. 'You see what appears to be a small calcified nodule in the cervix?'

'Yes.'

'Well, it's not calcified. It's extensile.'

'Ah! I see, it swells.'

'Exactly, when moistened by the G-spot fluid. It's like lowering the portcullis, shutting the gate – however you like to put it. And since she can't have intercourse without arousal – G-spot women like Lucy can't anyway – that's it. The chances of conception are at a minimum.'

To Lucy, he turned behind the screen and said cheerfully, 'You can get dressed now, my dear.' He helped her carefully out of the stirrup and, while Lucy was dressing, Morris said to me, 'It's a minor operation. I could do it almost blindfold and it seems damn silly for her to travel all the way to Boston – '

'Still, that's what her fiancé wants.'

'Okay by me.' He shrugged his shoulders and, after a few moments, called through the curtain, 'You ready, young lady?'

'I'm presentable,' Lucy managed a laugh, 'though I'm a bit sore.'

'I know,' he sympathised. 'It's the stretching – but I can tell you, young lady, you'll be stretched a damn sight more when you have your first baby.'

'You mean – ' she caught her breath with excitement and went quite pink. 'You mean I *can*?'

'Not yet. But later – yes. The operation is quite simple.' He explained some of the details. 'And I would say that the chances of you becoming fertile are ninety-nine-point-nine per cent.'

I felt a curious pang as I looked at her excitement and radiance. Was it latent jealousy? I watched as she leaned forward and grabbed Mr Morris' hand impulsively and cried, 'Thank you – Oh! Thank you.'

I was thinking that, if our lives had turned round

different corners, she might already have had a baby – mine; and what a mother she would make! Her face was lit with happiness. She was always a happy-looking girl, but there was an added dimension of contentment that I could hardly explain or understand. Not for the first time since I landed in San Francisco did I feel happiness for her mixed with sadness and jealousy for myself and the thought that I would probably never see that freckled face again. She was as different from Aleena as chalk from cheese; one living life with the joyous laugh, the other with a sultry, inviting, irresistible smile of pure love. Certainly I loved Aleena more than Lucy. But I don't suppose I was the first man in the world to think how wonderful it would be to love two girls at the same time!

'And you should thank Doctor Masters,' said Morris. 'If it hadn't been for him – '

'I do!' she turned to me. 'I thank you – ' she hesitated, 'for *everything*.'

Before we left, Mr Morris outlined what few details he had to discuss. Normally, as he pointed out, arrangements for the operation would have to be made after consultation between him and me – dates, times, the booking of a hospital room: but since by then I would be back in Koraloona, the normal arrangements leading to surgery would need to be bypassed. Instead Morris fished in his wallet for a visiting card and said, 'This once, you can deal directly with me. Phone me in Boston when you and your fiancé are agreed. I'll make the arrangements for you, book the hospital room, and the time of the operation.'

Soon afterwards, the conference drew to a close. I did meet Lucy several times with Sam, but never alone, except by chance for a few moments on the very last day when we were almost ready to be driven to Alameda to catch the plane to Honolulu.

Lucy had promised to come and say goodbye to us at the Mark and, as Sam was delayed on his way back from Alameda, I was able to spend a short time alone in the foyer with her, in which both of us were trying to say 'sorry' to each other. We were sitting there drinking coffee – not even holding hands or anything – until Lucy leaned forward impetuously and *did* grasp my hands in hers as she said, 'I'm so sorry for what happened. And yet – '

'I know – don't say any more, Lucy dear. I feel so awful in one way for what happened.' Out of the corner of my eye I saw a man at the registration desk point to us, and as he approached I whispered, 'Someone's coming to see us. Behave yourself.' She took her hand away just as a man with the pale brown skin of many Polynesians approached and asked, 'Doctor Masters?' I stood up.

'I read about you and saw your picture in the newspapers.' He smiled politely to both of us. 'I am Kinawa's father.'

'Oh!' I cried with genuine pleasure. 'I'm so glad to meet you. This is Miss Lucy Young. She lives here but we're old friends from Koraloona.'

The elderly Polynesian hesitated and then said, 'I just wondered if you could tell me how Kinawa is. We miss her so much. As you know she has a brother here and we are torn about whether to stay in California or go back to Sanderstown.'

'Don't worry,' I reassured him. 'Kinawa's got a wonderful home with Princess Tiare and she and Aleena are such good friends. I thought you lived in Southern California,' I added.

'We do. But my wife and I have been visiting the Redwoods north of San Francisco and we decided to stay on,' with a slight bow to Lucy, 'in your beautiful city.'

'I'm so glad you like it,' murmured Lucy, while I gave the man as much information as I could about Kinawa, hoping all the time that he would go soon so that, however innocent and public our meeting, Lucy and I could at least have a few minutes alone together before Sam arrived.

Instead, the old man prattled on, and I had to ask him to sit down. He promised to visit Koraloona after the war, he asked whether he should offer Tiare any gift, he asked if he ought to buy Kinawa a present. In short, when all I wanted was to be alone with Lucy, he never stopped talking, and he was still talking when Sam bustled in, crying, 'We leave in half an hour. Sure glad to meet you, sir. Will you excuse me if I go upstairs?'

He shook hands with Kinawa's father and then turned to me and said, 'Have a quick drink while I go upstairs.' To Lucy he added, 'Darling, be an angel and help me pack.'

She gave me one last look and nodded, with a final sad smile, and I said, 'Of course,' and with a sudden shaft of something near to jealousy, I knew what would happen during that last half hour upstairs. Especially as our bags were already stacked near the exit on the ground floor.

27

Koraloona seemed like home when I returned from San Francisco. Home, and peaceful too, for the last agonising echoes of the cholera epidemic had receded from everyone's memory – helped in my case, I suppose, by the complete change of a few days in California. All traces of the epidemic had been removed – the last makeshift palliasses in the villages had been burned, the last Coke bottles which had proved so effective for the saline drips had been dumped in the open sea beyond the reef. Life had returned to its normal routine with, in Alec's words, 'nothing but bruises, bones and babies'. We could enjoy a regular night's sleep, and once again, Toma could prepare a meal for us, safe in the knowledge that we would be there. At the Union Jack Club it was drinks as usual, bridge as usual, though the quality of tennis had suffered since the death of Shanks.

His name was never mentioned; it was almost as though he had never existed, probably because everyone wanted to erase the memories of what had happened. It was the same with the Gilberts. 'Koraloona wants to wipe the slate clean,' was the way Alec put it. 'For aught they ken it might never have happened.'

There were other changes. Though we could handle the ordinary radio sked between Koraloona and Sanders, we needed an expert to replace Shanks and deal with short-wave radio traffic to New Zealand. A replacement for Shanks set off in a Royal Australian Air Force plane, but he never arrived. Alec was told privately that the plane had been shot down by the Japs, though no official announcement was ever made. Three weeks later, just after I had returned, another RAF plane flew the dangerous route and landed another replacement at Sanderstown, a radio expert stationed in Auckland who had been seconded from the Army. He was Sergeant Dick Holmes, born in Yorkshire, who was delighted at the appointment and at not having to wear uniform because he had been seconded to a civilian job. As it happened he was an enthusiastic bridge player, and so any references to his rank of sergeant were quietly forgotten.

'Damn it all,' said Colonel Fawcett, 'this may be a club for officers and gentlemen, but there *is* a war on, and that feller's risked life and limb to come here.'

'I'm so glad he's British,' confided Mrs Fawcett. 'They transfer more easily to the tropics than foreigners.' Adding with practicality rather than sympathy, 'We will always miss the Gilberts, but we're very lucky that Mr Holmes plays bridge.'

'Very important,' said Alec, who was there, and gave a thin smile, almost derisive. I had the feeling that though he *was* there in person, he wasn't really listening. Long experience as a doctor had told him, by the inflections of patients' voices, when to be sympathetic, when to laugh, when to say yes, when to say no. Advancing age has curious side-effects. I sometimes felt that Alec had acquired a new set of values since I first landed on the island nearly five years ago.

*

In many ways the epidemic had kept us all so busy – and so frightened – that we had hardly had time to think about the war. We had rarely seen a newspaper, no ships had called, and we were often too exhausted to listen to the radio, so that we hardly realised that in the latter part of 1943 the first American successes indicated that the tide was turning. In Guadalcanal, an American landing force killed 24,000 Japanese, and inflicted crippling losses on the Japanese navy – sinking a Japanese aircraft carrier, two battleships, four cruisers, eleven destroyers, six submarines and sixteen transports. Another 9,000 were killed in the New Guinea campaign.

In Europe and North Africa the news was equally heartening. The RAF had launched its first heavy bombing raids on Berlin; in North Africa Monty had routed the Afrika Corps and a defeated Rommel had been switched to command the German armies in Europe; and by January 1944, the Russians had raised the German siege of Stalingrad after 872 days, displaying heroism at a terrible cost of a million and a half Russian civilians dead, mostly from starvation.

There was no doubt that the tide of war was turning; and not only was there wonderful news from the battlefronts, there was an item on my personal agenda that was even more wonderful. In a few weeks I would be getting married. With the date fixed for March 8, Aleena's nineteenth birthday, Tiare was already starting to plan celebrations that would involve the entire island. Yet even the plans for our wedding took a brief back seat because of another 'social' event.

Soon after my return, early in February and barely a month before the wedding, the Union Jack Club decided to hold a 'Thanksgiving Dinner' in honour of Dr Reid and myself for what Colonel Fawcett described as 'the heroic efforts of our two doctors to rid our beloved island of the scourge of cholera'.

'They've been wallowin' in the trashy newspapers yon feller Truscott brought us.' Alec's voice was heavily sarcastic or was it tinged with a slight annoyance at the publicity about me which my trip to San Francisco had aroused?

There was nothing I could do except say cheerfully, 'Well, if there's a speech, you'll have to make it.' Aleena told me that the idea had started with Tiare. The dinner would be preceded by a service of thanksgiving which Father Pringle would conduct in the Tala-Tala church. And once the idea took root, everyone joined in with suggestions to ensure that it would be an evening no one would ever forget. The best musicians on the island practised their songs accompanied by the ukulele. They would provide 'background music' during the dinner. Sam Truscott would lend us American long-playing records, from the army mess, together with a new record player – at which point the dinner was immediately upgraded to a 'dinner dance'. Sam had also arranged with the PX for what was described as 'a gift from the grateful camp' – a dozen sides of beef – a gesture beyond price, as Australian beef was becoming desperately short.

Although naturally, being a guest of honour, I had nothing to do with the preparations for the party, Jason Purvis kept us informed. He displayed an amusing gift for mimicry, and would sometimes drop by after surgery and nurse a drink while regaling me with details of the latest developments. Fawcett was the Chairman, and he made a great to-do about the formalities.

'Can't have a committee without a gavel and hammer,' he boomed. 'Symbols of office, eh? Might as well try to beat retreat without a flag to salute.' I could see his moustache twitching.

'Now I can bring the meeting to order,' said the colonel via Jason. After that an agenda had to be discussed, a minute book prepared, Mrs Fawcett being appointed Hon. Sec. to keep the record – 'Well, you write a pretty good fist, m'dear,' said the colonel.

'Now then,' he boomed at the first meeting, 'first things first. Plan the campaign; detail the forces; issue the orders.

407

That's it. Plain enough if you do it in an orderly fashion.'

It wasn't by any means as simple as the colonel indicated, unfortunately. The longest job was arranging the place sittings.

'You'd think we were discussing a dinner at Buck House,' Jason said. He mimicked Mrs Fawcett: 'Really no, Archie, I hardly think – '

'All right, m'dear,' the colonel replied. 'I'll give way to you as CIGS on that point.'

'There was even a china-and-cutlery subcommittee,' Jason said, with laughter lurking behind his deadpan expression, 'with Jim Wilson in charge. It was realised we wouldn't have enough dishes and knives and forks to go round, and would have to borrow them from the Yanks.'

Eventually, it seemed, after several meetings going on well into the night, things were more or less straightened out. There would be ten tables with six places at each, and Mollie Green would be in charge of the catering. Fervent assurances were given by the colonel that 'Everything'll be all right on the night, if every man does his duty and no slacking.'

But to me, the best news of all was that the date hadn't been chosen haphazardly. Unknown to Alec or me, February 12 coincided with the arrival of the *Mantela*.

'That'll make the night,' I cried when Jason told me the news. It was nearly three months since I had seen Bill Robins, not only because of the epidemic but because, after the quarantine on shipping had been lifted, Robins had sailed to New Zealand for a special cargo. So the dinner would be a reunion too; Bill and I had always been close friends from the time I arrived, and the friendship had been strengthened because he regarded Aleena like a daughter and was delighted about the approaching wedding.

When the *Mantela* arrived it brought a batch of mail, the letters and parcels being delivered by one of the ship's crew to Jim Wilson; by tradition the ship's chandler doubled up as Koraloona post office from which everyone collected the mail. I received three letters from home. The family was in good health, the letters said, but the censor's blue pencil seemed to rob each letter of any personality. Reading them, I had the feeling that someone must have been looking over Mother's shoulder when she wrote them. Mother and Clare were helping out with the Red Cross and Father was working at – the blue pencil obliterated the name – so I imagined he must be engaged on secret radio work or perhaps even radar. They had received several parcels of food from Australia which was good news. And that was about all. They might have been written by strangers. That and the passage of time – and I realised many must have been lost at sea – gave them a curious quality. Though I always tore them open eagerly, they inevitably left me with a feeling that disturbed me.

I felt a kind of guilt – my cloudless present compared with my father and mother's clouded life, which was something I found hard to imagine; and when my father told me of how he had spent an entire day sweeping up glass after an air raid (the name obliterated, but was it Nottingham?) I could only compare the sound of men sweeping up broken glass and debris with the lazy sea breaking on the pebbles in one corner of the lagoon.

I had returned home to read my letters while Bill Robins superintended the unloading of the cargo; but my slight feeling of depression lifted as soon as I saw him walk up the garden path.

'Welcome back! It's been far too long!'

'I know.' He walked in and I offered him a cold beer. 'But here I am, all ready for tonight's shindig. Yes, I've heard all about it. How's Aleena? One week it's a dance, the next a wedding.'

'She's getting excited as the great day arrives.'

'On her birthday – right?'

'March 8,' I confirmed. 'Any chance you'll be here?'

'I doubt it. We're due in next at the end of the month, I

think, but dates have a habit of changing these days. It all depends on where we have to call and pick up or discharge unexpected cargo. After all, I *am* only a tramp – well, the skipper of a tramp.'

'A very special tramp to all of us,' I said.

The Thanksgiving dinner was an occasion none of us would ever forget. For one thing, there was an astonishing surprise which all the committee members – even Jason – had kept a deadly secret. Just before the party was due to start, the colonel had 'ordered' Alec and me to let the others reach the club first – it was only a short walk anyway from the church to the club – 'so that we may welcome you in the traditional way, eh?'

'It's a load of tosh,' muttered Alec. 'But if they want to play games, why not let 'em?'

When all the guests were assembled in the lounge we entered to a burst of clapping; a bevy of pretty girls with ukuleles were trying to play 'For they are jolly good fellows', while everyone sang. But that wasn't the *real* surprise. What made me gasp was far more breathtaking! The lounge was a blaze of colour, for Tiare, to celebrate the occasion, had taken the ten best Gauguins out of the fish tank, and hung them on the walls as a decoration for the dance.

'That's why we closed the club for lunch, old boy,' chuckled Fawcett, adding with some vague memory of the Royal Academy, 'It gave the hanging committee a chance to say where the exhibits should go. Good show eh?' He didn't *need* to ram the point home, but he was so pleased that he couldn't help adding, with a guffaw, 'A good show in both ways, eh? Damn good, if I do say so meself.'

I was too entranced – for this was only the second time I had seen the Gauguins – to do much more than give a polite grin. I was thinking: whoever, in any great city the world over, would believe that a group of people on a tiny island could hold a dance for sixty friends, surrounded by

410

priceless works of one of the greatest painters of his age? I just stood and gawked.

'Godammit, they must be worth a fortune!' Sam Truscott was just as staggered, but his reaction was more down to earth. Most of the people at the club had never seen the paintings before, of course, but now, with plenty of drinks at hand, they were able to examine the treasures leisurely. As I peeped outside I could see that the tables for dinner were laid out on the veranda, with an overflow on to the surrounds of the tennis court behind the club house, but still close to the veranda. Ten tables in all, I counted, with six at each table.

No one was wearing a dinner jacket, of course, but we had been asked to wear ties and jackets, and it had been suggested that the ladies might wear long dresses if they wished.

The seating had been carefully arranged so that married couples were split up at table. I wasn't married – not quite – so Aleena was seated at my table. Jason arrived escorting Miss Sowerby, Purvis immaculate in newly pressed white ducks, but the real shock was Miss Sowerby – almost unrecognisable in a long white and gold dress, and so attractive that I had to look twice to recognise her.

'Why, Miss Sowerby – you look stunning!' I spoke from the heart as I greeted her. 'I've never seen you in this dress.'

'I made it myself,' she went slightly pink. 'It's a copy of a dress I saw in the *Tatler*.'

'She's a dab hand with a needle,' said Jason. 'You should see how she keeps my shirts in order.'

'This – and our private view of the Gauguins – calls for another round. What'll you both have? Miss Sowerby?' Though she could still purse her lips at the slightest feeling of disapproval, I must say she looked a different woman, perhaps due to the new dress. And she had good arms, rarely seen.

Jason gave a look at Miss Sowerby, as though seeking permission.

'A port and lemon for you?' I asked her, remembering the past.

'Thank you, Doctor. And on an occasion like this I don't think we can refuse to' – she hesitated before saying – 'allow Jason to have a whisky or two.'

'Fine!' As I called for drinks, I heard Miss Sowerby whisper to Jason, 'Just a couple. And of course a little wine with our meal.'

Alec, who had joined us, said to Jason, 'Ye're a reformed character, man. But dinna go too far and sign the pledge. Whisky and aspirin are the best medicines ever invented.'

'In moderation, Doctor,' Miss Sowerby dared to reprove him. 'And – Jason, you tell the doctors. Go on – '

Jason hesitated.

'He *is* a reformed character,' said Miss Sowerby. 'He's becoming a real writer.'

'Meaning what?' I asked as I felt Aleena tuck her arm into mine.

'It sounds incredible, but when the *Mantela* brought the post, there was a letter for me,' said Jason. 'It took two months to reach Koraloona, but it's from a publisher. He's – *interested*.'

'My God!' I cried. 'Jason, *another* drink. Yes, Miss Sowerby, I insist. This is an *occasion*. What happened?'

'I sent him the first hundred pages and an outline of my novel after Lorna' – I was startled at his use of her Christian name – 'after Lorna forced me to write something every day. So they've made me an offer of fifty pounds on account, and some more when I've finished the book.'

'I say.' Colonel Fawcett had joined us. 'Damned good! Are any of us in it? You know, the way Somerset Maugham used to put real people in. Want to take care on a small island like this!'

'Have you read it?' Alec asked Miss Sowerby.

'Yes, I have,' she said almost shyly. 'And it's all about Koraloona, but not about our friends.'

'It's about sex!' Jason had sneaked in a third Scotch.

412

'Don't you ever say such a thing,' cried an angry Miss Sowerby. 'It certainly isn't. If that disgusting subject is ever mentioned in the book, I'll tear out the pages.'

'That's nae a recipe for success,' remarked Alec to me. 'A book wi'out a wee bit of sex is like strawberries wi'out cream.' He added, whispering, to Jason: 'Ye'd better hide *those* pages in the old tin trunk in the dispensary.'

The dinner seating had of course been arranged in advance. Mrs Fawcett was next to me. The rest at our table comprised Aleena, Bill Robins, Jason and Mollie Green.

Half a dozen girls, dressed in identical Mother Hubbards, but with bare shoulders like a décolleté dress, sang to ukuleles. As a rule I never really enjoyed the pure Polynesian music – it was actually rather like a melancholy conversation in song which was still popular in the Andaman islands – but a great deal had changed since 1917 when someone heard the small Portuguese four-string guitar, imported it to Honolulu, patented and mass-produced it. After that, the ukulele craze swept across America, then Europe. It soon reached the South Seas, so that by now, as we ate our first course of filleted flying fish, to be followed by roast beef, we were listening to the lilting tunes of sentimental American music.

'Very charming,' said Mrs Fawcett, watching the girls strum while looking at the sheet music, 'and really very clever of these girls to learn to read music.'

'They're not reading *real* music,' explained Purvis. 'There's no formal music for the uke. It's called *tablature*.' He showed Mrs Fawcett a sheet. The 'music' consisted of squared diagrams which showed where the fingers had to be placed on the strings to get the right notes, a series of basic chords really. 'I often play it.'

'How did you learn?' asked Mollie Green.

'From one of the island's best ukulele players. It'll all be in my book, but don't tell Miss Sowerby yet.'

'Why not? Is it a secret?' asked Mrs Fawcett.

I had a premonition of what was coming.

413

'Not really, Mrs Fawcett. But my instructor did name a price.'

Falling into the trap, as Jason knew she would, Mrs Fawcett asked, 'How much?'

'A couple of hours in bed with her.'

'Oh! Really.' Mrs Fawcett gulped at her white wine. 'You shouldn't say things like that, Mr Purvis.'

'I'm sorry.' Keeping a straight face, Purvis apologised, 'but it was only in the course of research.'

We had more music – better, up-to-date rhythm – when the dinner was over and we started dancing to the gramophone in the lounge.

Sam Truscott had brought along all the latest music and the difference in reproduction of long-playing records played on a modern gramophone was incredible. Apart from two or three duty dances – including the first one with Mrs Fawcett when the colonel asked Tiare for the first dance, I danced once with Kinawa, but spent every moment I could on the floor with Aleena, who was looking more beautiful than I had ever seen her. She was wearing an ankle-length dress giving her an almost ethereal look, for it was made of blue chiffon with what (to my masculine eyes) looked like lots of white bubbles. The material was dark blue at her ankles, gradually becoming lighter as it reached her beautiful, bare, honey-coloured neck and shoulders. The blue and white suited her perfectly.

All our favourite tunes, which had leapt into world-wide favour since the American Forces Network started broadcasting in the Pacific, kept us dancing, hugging, squeezing close as we danced to 'Red River Valley', 'Cocktails for Two', 'Chattanooga Chu-Chu', 'As Time Goes By', 'Sentimental Journey' and 'I'll Never Smile Again', which was to become a favourite Frank Sinatra number. There were songs sung by Dinah Shore, Bing Crosby, and then Judy Garland, singing a British song – 'our song', 'Goodnight Sweetheart'.

'Do you realise,' Aleena was holding me very tight

414

during the slow foxtrot, 'that it's over two years since we danced to that tune? What a lot has happened since that wonderful evening in the Café de Paris!'

'All the waiting and frustration will soon be over,' I whispered.

Tiare had the biggest say in the preparation for March 8. Not only was she the hereditary Princess of Koraloona, it was her daughter who was getting married. She had every right to run things her way (though at least she allowed me to buy the ring in Sanderstown).

It was to be an island-wide celebration. School children were to be given a holiday, and bars of free chocolate provided by the American PX. Everywhere would be decorated with whatever bunting, flags, ribbons and festive novelties were available.

Only Johnson, the storekeeper, showed his usual mean streak. He knew he was the only source of supply – and he tried to corner the market. Jim Wilson told me that Johnson had several unopened boxes containing souvenir mugs that had been made in anticipation of the coronation of Edward VIII, who had abdicated.

'Just the thing to please the kids,' I said to Jim. 'They couldn't care two hoots whose picture's on the side. We'll get him to donate them to the cause.'

'I wish you joy,' Jim said. Apparently when Jim Wilson suggested this to Johnson, the Cockney sat in his rocking chair, whining refusal as he chain-smoked. 'Can't afford it,' he said.

'But they're lying there doing nothing,' Wilson reasoned with him. 'You've lost your profit and your capital anyway. You might as well give a bit of pleasure to the kids.'

'Tell you what,' said Johnson, holding a cigarette between finger and thumb, 'make it a tanner a yard for the bunting and a penny each for the mugs and we'll do a deal.' And with that Wilson had to be satisfied. Tiare, who had maintained a dignified aloofness in this wrangling, came to discuss with Jason and me the matter of the music.

'It will be, of course, the traditional English church service; but there's the matter of Tiki – ' she hesitated.

I intervened. I knew exactly what she wanted, and that was for the more esoteric rites of Polynesian mythology to have their place.

'Believe me, Princess,' I said. 'Both Aleena and I are agreed that the last thing that should undermine any wedding is differences of opposing – well, religions.'

'Thank you, Kit,' she said gravely. 'I knew I could rely on you for that – concession.'

'Hardly a concession: more of a privilege.'

A week before the wedding, Aleena and I dined together at Mollie's for a change – 'a night out' we called it laughingly.

'Well, we're all set,' I said. 'And soon you'll be leaving home to come and live in mine.'

'I'm not going very far!' she laughed back. 'I'll easily be able to run home to Mother if you beat me.'

'No fear of that.' After dinner, I stopped the jeep at the gate of her garden, with the water on the lagoon shining like silver behind. I kissed her and whispered, 'Goodnight, Mrs Masters.'

'Don't ever say that,' she cried with a sudden burst of anger.

'Darling – I'm sorry. But it's only an old wives' tale.'

'It isn't. Remember, I'm a Polynesian. And I know. It's bad luck to use our name before we're married.' She suddenly shivered. 'I'm cold!'

'Please darling – ' I began.

'I'm cold – I'm freezing. It's bad luck. It is, it is. *I know*.'

For no reason in particular, the words of that old man at the roadside, as he was dying of cholera, came back to me: 'The gods are angry . . .'

28

I now came to a sequence of events that led to the most tender night of love imaginable, shrouded at first in mystery, yet giving Aleena and me an hour to treasure even though, unknown to me, there was a secret background of events that would have terrible consequences.

The evening started in a very simple way. I had to perform a minor operation, but one that took me away from Anani for several hours, so that during my absence, I had no idea what had happened; indeed, I knew nothing of those events until the following morning.

Around five o'clock that evening, I was having a drink with Alec when Toma, who had been to see his ailing mother, rushed back on a borrowed bicycle, crying, 'She dead, Master! My mother she dead.'

I knew it couldn't be true. But she *was* suffering badly from diabetes, and she might have taken a sudden turn for the worse.

'Is she conscious?' asked Alec.

'No, sir. All dead.'

'Might be a diabetic coma,' he suggested. 'I'll go.'

If only I had agreed! Instead I offered to drive to the old woman's village, and Alec said, 'Well, just in case we need the ambulance, why don't we both go? And take Miss Sowerby with us.'

There were no other patients. I took my surgical instruments and 'bag of tricks' and we set off, Miss Sowerby and I, in my jeep, Alec Reid following.

I was glad to have Alec along. His understanding was always of the most sympathetic kind. We were in the same trade, though I sometimes smiled to myself at the difference between 'dramas' like this evening and the popular idea of medical drama, with ambulance sirens screaming through the night, rare drugs being rushed by special messenger to dying patients, and everybody's eyes watching the hands of ticking clocks. My case was almost farcical in its comparative simplicity. There was, it is true, a rush to the village in my jeep, but that was all.

When we reached the village, I wasn't surprised that Toma thought his mother was dying. She *was* in a diabetic coma. While I examined her, Reid puffed at his pipe.

'Between you and me, Laddie,' he said, 'I've often wondered that there isn't more *mellitus* – or diabetes – on the island. All that sucking of sugar cane and the way some of the old 'uns get grossly overweight. It plays havoc with the metabolism.'

The trouble was, I had no idea what sort of diet Toma's mother had been on or if she'd been passing excessive urine. So I had to depend on guesswork. The coma was easy – well, relatively. I risked a shot of glucose and she came round fairly quickly. Toma thought I was God Almighty!

Alec looked at me. 'There might be a complication,' he said.

'Retinitis?'

'Exactly. But that's long-term. She'll develop a cataract, no doubt.'

'What worries me,' I said, 'is that she's got a fairly advanced sepsis.' I had been examining her feet.

'Ah! A case for hack work, eh?' He still used the slang student term for surgery.

'Her left big toe is showing every sign of it – bad colour, and I can't feel any pulsation of the artery.'

'Ye need an oscillometer for that, Kit.'

'I know what I need,' I said tetchily. 'But if you can find me an oscillometer this side of Australia I'd be bloody surprised.'

There was no doubt about it. She had to lose the toe. I tried to explain to Toma that gangrene sets in with terrifying speed in the tropics and that delay might mean amputation above the knee. Of course, he wanted to see his witch-doctor. But I managed to persuade him that there mustn't be any delay – though by the time I *had* convinced him there had already been too much.

'Why don't you go home, Alec?' I suggested. 'This is routine, and with Miss Sowerby to help – '

'I will,' he agreed. 'Ye dinna really need me and I don't like both of us to be away from the shop for too long.'

'Don't worry,' I said, and I knew when he left that I didn't have to worry. The danger of gangrene if I did nothing was much, much more serious, and I only had one problem: I had to wait doing nothing for a couple of hours before I could give the anaesthetic because neither Toma nor his mother could agree on the time she had last eaten.

Two hours later, the operation successful, I prepared to drive home, Miss Sowerby having agreed to spend the night in the village in case of any post-operative complications – not that there would be, but she insisted.

Thus it was that, when I got home, I was in total ignorance of the cataclysmic events that had taken place in my absence. As I poured myself a much-needed drink, still blissfully unaware that anything was amiss, I heard a soft, feminine voice call from the doorway, 'Kit.'

It was little more than a whisper. I heard the front door being pushed open, and then in walked Kinawa, a piece of paper in her hand.

'I'm not supposed to be here,' she whispered. 'But the Princess will explain everything tomorrow. I've come from the *Mantela*. We have to leave suddenly.'

'But why on earth – ?'

'Ssh! I only have an hour.'

'An hour?' I asked, puzzled. 'An hour for what?'

'This is a letter from Aleena. She wants to try and make you happy.'

'But *why* are you and Aleena leaving so suddenly?' I was stupefied.

She hesitated, standing by the bed. 'Don't worry,' she said. 'It is for the best. The Princess came to see you with Aleena and me, but both you and Doctor Reid were away. You must have been on a call because your boy was away too.'

'Yes, but Aleena can't just – just walk out on me.'

'The Princess had no time to warn you. And I'm only a guest in the house. Aleena will return soon. We had to board the *Mantela* early. The Princess left, and I sneaked back when I saw the faint light. I knew you had returned. Because Aleena wants me to make you happy.'

'But I don't understand,' and then added, 'Sorry, do sit down.'

'It is the custom, as you know. When women of high rank cannot make their men happy because the wise man prevents them, they have the right, at times of parting, to nominate a substitute.'

'But you?'

'I am very proud to be of service. I shall enjoy myself trying to make you contented so that Aleena will be happy, when I tell her every detail.'

'But I'm not sure that – '

'Hush, there is nothing wrong in what Aleena has asked me to do.'

'But *why* – why are you *going*?'

'Tiare will tell you. There is a moment of crisis and Aleena must leave the island. As for me – Aleena has honoured me by choosing me to take her place with you. And I'm not so bad, am I?'

It was all so fantastic, it was hard to know right from wrong. Aleena, of course, had taken a vow of chastity until her birthday in March – but still! Should I take advantage of what I knew was a normal Polynesian habit? And Aleena had told me that she was experienced. Nor could I deny that Kinawa was, as I had often said, 'a fun girl', but I was still on the point of saying no when she smiled, 'You must not insult Aleena by refusing her gift.' She had a trace of the stilted language common to so many missionary-educated girls. But there was nothing stilted about the next thing she did. 'Read this letter.' She offered me the piece of paper. It was the most astonishing letter I had ever read, written in Aleena's squarely formed letters – another legacy of missionary schools – and it said:

'Beloved, I BEG YOU to accept a special gift from me to you on the night when I must leave you. I wish to enjoy it with you, but I am on the *Mantela*, preparing to sail, and Mummy will explain why tomorrow. Kinawa is travelling to Sanders with me, but she has slipped secretly off to see you and spend an hour in your arms. It is my farewell present to you, for I love you and feel that it is wicked of me to deprive you of man's greatest pleasure just because I have taken a vow of chastity. Do not think me wanton, I love you, but her hour in your bed will be my farewell gift to you, and in another way a gift to me, for later, when she returns to the ship she will tell me all about you and what it will one day be like for us, when our problems are resolved. And you will be able to pretend that it was me you were loving.'

What an incredible letter! What an astonishing mixture of folklore and innocence. Of course, I knew that to a Polynesian there was absolutely nothing wrong in what Aleena had suggested. In many islands – even in Koraloona – pregnant women approaching their 'time' insisted on lending unattached girls to husbands who could not make love to their wives. The wives genuinely felt that they were helping their husbands to relieve the tensions of their enforced abstinence. The truth lay in the fact, as I had realised, that to the Polynesians, the physical act was one of pure enjoyment, a physical exercise, best of all naturally with someone you loved, but if that were impossible, well, why not take second best?

Still, I vaguely felt that the whole business verged on the disloyal, and I still might have refused, had not Kinawa made one simple gesture. With one movement – or so it

421

seemed – she let her sarong drop to the floor in a pool of coloured silk around her feet.

'There,' she said demurely, standing stark naked, 'Do I please you?'

For a moment I wondered if maybe Aleena was testing my strength of will to refuse such a gift. But no, she wasn't devious enough for tactics like that. She had the frankest, most open of faces, with only the rare glimpse of her secret smile. No, this was no test, no mean trick. This was pure generosity of spirit.

After that (and I make no excuse) I accepted the fact that I would be a fool and perhaps even hurtful if I spurned such a gift, especially one made to me by the woman who was to become my wife.

'So you mean it,' I whispered, suddenly growing excited.

'I want to make you content,' she said simply, 'because I know it will make Aleena happy.'

She had the same firm young breasts as Aleena, the same long, silky hair as Aleena.

'Are you sure you want to?' I whispered.

'I promised Aleena, who loves you' – she never hesitated, spoke almost gravely – 'that I would be the receiver of that love; but please – put out the light. If I were discovered, nothing serious would happen to either of us of course, but I might miss the *Mantela*, if we are questioned. We have an hour, let us enjoy it, even in the dark.'

She was right. We now had a squad of ARP volunteers anxious to investigate anyone showing too much light. Air Raid Precautions had become a big thing in Koraloona.

As I switched off the light she whispered, 'I'll put my clothes in the bathroom. Aleena asks only one thing.'

'What is it?'

'That you pretend I am her. To the best of your ability, I mean.' In a few seconds she was back from the bathroom which led off my bedroom, and then, wordless but sighing happily, she slid under the single sheet, and – as I had so often dreamed of Aleena doing – she lay on one side against me, fully stretched out, so that her feet were touching mine, her lips, her soft breasts pushing against my chest, her thick secret hair – and I could imagine it, what the boys at med school used to call the Maidenhead Mountain – and it was entwined with me, and my loins. Kissing me gently, her hands at first stroking my hair, feeling my face, and then later, as I touched her she cried out only one word, 'Wonderful!' Her hands were exploring my body, as I stroked the calves of her legs, the knee, stroking ever closer to her flat tummy where her legs parted, and I remember crying, 'Oh Aleena! Oh, if only it were you!' And I could even feel the salt taste of a tear. She said nothing, just stroked me with what, even to me, seemed an excellent simulation of love instead of just love-making.

'If only,' I repeated and pulled her legs across me as I stroked them, moving slowly up to her thighs. My heart pounding as I whispered, 'There's plenty of time, we have a whole hour.' I remember saying that to comfort her – and then suddenly, almost as I said them, it was as though my brain seized up, the gentle and considerate approach to love-making turned into a frenzy of unshackled desire and *real* love.

It happened in a second – the second my hand travelled up her right thigh, already damp and exciting; the second it took for my hand to move upwards towards the join of her legs, all done so swiftly as my excitement increased, Thank God she could not realise what I as a doctor could recognise almost automatically: the faintest indentation of scar tissue in the one spot on the thigh where, years before, I had diagnosed the disfiguring 'mole', a scar unnoticed to anyone but a doctor with knowledge of the case. Thank God I did not hesitate in my swift exploration of her body. Thank God I did not cry out, as I almost did, or switch on the light and cry, 'Aleena! It's you!'

A strange lover in the dark would no more have noticed the faint mark than that of a vaccination, just the merest ridge of different flesh, but *I* knew. Because I knew her body as a doctor knows the contours of a body. Yet, I realised in a flash that I must not let her know that I knew.

She had slid between my sheets in secret, and I must respect the secrecy of someone who has vowed to remain chaste. The game of pretence had to be played to the end, and even if she realised that I knew she had changed places in the bathroom, I had to 'pretend'.

Almost hoarsely, I cried, 'You asked me, Kinawa, to pretend you are Aleena. I shall, even if I am rough with you and call you Aleena.' Turning her over so that she lay on her back, I cried, 'Aleena, Aleena! I can't wait any longer.'

Inside her I forgot that as a virgin she might be hurt, until she gave one small cry of pain. Then I smothered her with kisses, and she gave herself to me, pressing her hands over my buttocks, scratching with her nails as she tried to force me deeper into her body, all with the abandon of one who knows it has never happened before, that it can't last for ever, but is so wonderful that it is worth dying for.

I moved again, holding back with an effort, as she moved with me, and then she was panting, the movement of her hips ceased as we both came, and I could feel the wet tears, but on *her* cheeks this time, from her eyes, as she kissed and kissed me, mouths opened, all but biting each other, touching her breasts – those beautiful firm breasts – so that what happened was like a miracle.

I hadn't come out of her to rest and draw new strength. I grew strong inside her, and as she felt me growing and I started to move inside her, she too started moving again, all in love, in silence, all in rhythm, all in blackness, kissing, squeezing, pressing, crying – both of us in different ways – her silky hair spread out over the pillow and my right hand searching through the equally silky thick hair between her legs until I touched the spot she needed, and she gave a long-drawn sigh of pure content.

'Aleena, I love you,' I cried again. 'There'll never be anyone but you. If only – ' But at this, still moving, she kissed my lips smothering all talk, almost suffocating me with love, moving her body up and down, one moment arching her back, the next sinking, gasping, uttering little moans of pleasure or pain until again she seemed to gather herself for one final moment, and suddenly drooped, spent and tired, on the bed.

We lay there, silent except for the panting and the pounding of two hearts banging against each other, her breasts rubbing against me as though deliberately trying to stimulate me. I thought perhaps it was a way of saying goodbye, that she was frightened and thought she should go, but then, shyly, she spoke the only words of that night and that was the merest whisper, in an assumed voice, 'Once more and then I must go. I know Aleena would wish it.'

It was more gentle this time, for I knew now that, whatever happened to us, whatever the future held for us, we were joined as lovers, and this time she didn't come, but gave herself to me as a moment for me to enjoy, to control, to wait until I was ready so that, instead of ending in a wild, uncontrollable tumult, this time it ended so that she could feel, as much as I could, what happens when a man in control reaches the supreme moment of his love-making.

She lay for a few moments more, then disintangled herself while I needed all my willpower not to switch on the light and confront her. But I couldn't do that.

'One last kiss for Aleena,' I said huskily and she leaned over, unable to see in the dark, so that at first her breasts were over my face, then she moved downwards, flattening them against my chest, soft and pliable and beautiful, unseen in the dark, she kissed me with a passion that bruised my lips. After that she stumbled into the bathroom muttering, 'My clothes,' and two or three minutes later she reappeared, only it wasn't her. As though to underline the deception, Kinawa whispered, 'I can't find the front door. I think we can risk a tiny shaded torch, please.'

Half covering the torch I switched it on. 'Over there,' I whispered, and Kinawa turned and smiled, turned so that I could see Kinawa's face for a fleeting moment, then said, 'Thank you. I hope you have been happy.'

It was not for me to reflect that, for a woman who had thrown abandon to the winds, who had torn my flesh with her nails, so great was her frenzy, she seemed to have recovered her breath very quickly.

Did I hear a faint scuffling sound from the back outside kitchen door, faint sounds of footsteps in the back? Perhaps, but it was not for me to enquire. A minute later, though, I peeped out of my window, and I *thought* I could make out the faint outline of two figures – not one – walking near the end of the garden path towards the road leading to the jetty. But it was a watery moon, and I could not be sure.

Then as she or they disappeared from view, I rolled over into bed, praying that I would dream of her. The exhaustion of a sated lover should lead to a tranquil sleep undisturbed by anything but images of love – and the beloved. But strangely, I was visited by a nightmare of which I could recall no details except that I awoke to the sound of my own hoarse screams. But I was quickly asleep again.

29

I did dream of secret love for most of the night, waking only occasionally, happy in my memories, yet troubled by one worrying question: what on earth could have prompted Tiare to send Aleena away so suddenly? The decision – for whatever reason – had been made so urgently and for so important a reason that it had made Aleena break her vow of chastity, even if by deception.

And this in turn had given a strange quality of tenderness mingled with passion when I realised that it *was* Aleena and not Kinawa. Looking back on that night I felt that it was almost as though she was breaking her vow because she had no other way of telling me that she could not know when next she would lie in my arms. Our love had a touch of suppressed anxiety in it, and yet – since I was not to know 'officially' that it was Aleena – I had not been able to ask her even the simplest question. The only time I did stop kissing her to start posing a query, she had put a finger on my lips.

As I showered and dressed I was feeling so hungry that I forgot I had told Toma to stay the night in his village. Just when I was ready to eat six rashers of bacon and three eggs, to say nothing of toast and marmalade!

Instead I had some bread and butter and marmalade and made some coffee. Perhaps it was for the best, for the sooner I finished breakfast, the sooner I could go to see Tiare. Because that was what I had decided to do. Before anything else, I would drive along Main Street and ask Tiare why she had sent the girls away so suddenly.

There was a slight rain, more of a mist coming in from the sea, and so I had my coffee in the living-room, looking at my Gauguin on the wall facing me. I could almost picture my darling Aleena walking along the pink street. What love I had for that girl! And how tenderly she had shown her feelings for me. The secret night of forbidden love had been so wonderful, the waiting, I thought, had contributed to the tenderness. Had we jumped into bed that first night in Sanderstown, our love-making would by now have taken on a quality of familiarity, an equally tender love, but one between a couple already used to each other's bodies. Instead, there was last night! The thought of it, the memory, made my trousers pleasantly tight and I was enjoying thoughts and possibilities that only another cold shower could dampen when Alec Reid poked his head through the window and asked, 'Any chance of an extra cup of coffee?'

And as I said, 'Of course – come in,' he pushed open the door after saying, 'That must have been a tough night. Is the old girl all right?'

'Yes. Sorry I'm late for breakfast. I overslept.'

I could see that Alec was puzzled, and when I looked at him questioningly he asked me, 'I don't see your guard.'

It was my turn to look baffled as I laughed, 'What guard? Don't tell me I'm under arrest!'

'Get on with ye, man,' he replied. 'But where in the devil's name *is* the guard? When I phoned Lieutenant Truscott an hour ago he said he'd have the man at your home right away – at least that's what I assumed he meant. He used his favourite word: pronto.'

'But *why*?' My amusement at some obvious misunderstanding was for the first time linked with an unaccountable fear. No, it wasn't really unaccountable, but was this 'misunderstanding' somehow linked with Tiare's decision to put the girls on the *Mantela* without so much as a goodbye? Had I done something wrong? Was Aleena being sent away in disgrace? Of course not. The idea was preposterous and I knew it, but what *was* it all about? Why had Aleena given herself to me?

My thoughts were interrupted by a gasp of astonishment from Alec Reid.

'My God!' he cried. 'Ye've been away most of the night. Ye mean to say ye dinna know what's happened?'

'You're talking in riddles,' I answered almost sharply.

He took a deep breath and then said in a sombre voice, 'Japanese parachutists occupied Penal Island yesterday.'

My jaw dropped open, my coffee cup nearly fell to the floor and the coffee spilled out.

'It's not possible!' I cried, but just to look at him sitting there made me realise that, however ridiculous or astonishing it might seem, the news *must* be possible.

'I can't believe it! But how? It's incredible! Japs on Penal. What about the guards? What about – ?' The questions tumbled out.

The sudden news was made more horrific because in my mind's eye I could see Penal Island, every detail of its harsh, tiny landscape. I had visited it once to attend to a sick prisoner, and even then it had given me the shivers. It was just one chunk of flat rock, with only a few stunted trees struggling to survive, and one small street encircling the island, lined with houses for the workers and their families, and at one end the prison block. Because of the rocky nature, and because the prison was surrounded by

428

water, it had always made me think of Alcatraz. Hostile, escape-proof. And now it was in Japanese hands.

'But surely the guards were armed?' I repeated. 'They must have put up a fight?'

'Not against Japanese armed with sub-machine-guns,' said Alec. 'Ye'll hear the whole story from Jim Wilson.'

'Why Jim?'

'He picked up the only survivors.'

'Survivors?'

'All the guards – and their wives and kids – were butchered.'

'Oh my God.' I could hardly take in the news, it was so shattering. Now, though, I could begin to see why Aleena had been shipped to safety. Finally, dragging the words out of my mouth, I asked, 'Were they all killed?'

'All but two who were picked up by Jim.'

'And what about the prisoners?'

'All the Polynesians were shot in their cells.'

'It's not possible.' I had heard stories of Japanese atrocities, but they always seemed so far away. A sudden thought struck me.

'And? – ' I didn't dare to ask the question.

'The Japanese were freed. Yes, including Mana.'

'So that means Mana must still be on Penal Island?'

'No,' said Reid heavily. 'As far as we know – and it's hearsay – the Japanese parachuted down not only with sub-machine-guns, they also carried small collapsible rubber dinghies – or else they parachuted them down separately, I don't know. Jim saw some of the Japs paddling in the sea. But he doesn't really know the details. The only thing to remember is that Penal Island isn't far from the western edge of the reef and I wouldna be surprised if the Japanese had some sort of rendezvous there. Maybe a submarine. But I dinna know for sure.'

'And Mana?'

'Bad news, Laddie, so best brace yourself for it. That's the reason for the armed guard. Mana was last seen heading for Koraloona with one other man. They took the

429

police launch, and the survivors who pretended to be dead and were rescued later by Jim Wilson saw Mana setting off towards Koraloona.'

The news was so overwhelming that, without thinking, I was just about to say, 'Thank God Aleena got away!' but almost bit my tongue off just in time. Because of course the girls had boarded the *Mantela* while I was attending to Toma's mother, and they had only crept out when, seeing the light in my bungalow, they had come to visit me secretly.

Tiare, as Alec now confirmed, had come round with the girls to my bungalow to say goodbye when she heard the news, and had decided to put the girls on the *Mantela*. As Alec explained it, 'But of course we were both away with Miss Sowerby. So there was no way they could let ye know what was happening.'

'I see. But what about the Princess? How is she?'

'There's a guard there too – an American soldier,' said Reid. 'Thank the Lord Aleena and her girlfriend were safe on board the *Mantela* with Bill Robins.'

'I second that,' I was able to say – and mean it, for by now the *Mantela* would have docked in Sanderstown. I added grimly, 'I see now why you wanted to post a guard. You think Mana'll come after me?'

'That's one thing ye canna rule out. He'll be hell bent on revenge.'

I was thinking hard, only slowly realising that my trousers were wet through with cold, spilled coffee. I was trying to digest the astonishing turn of events.

'Of course we don't actually *know* that Mana ever reached Koraloona?' I asked. 'If he is on the island, he must have come, as you say, by the Penal Island motor launch. You say that's what Jim thinks. But has the boat been found?'

Alec shook his head. 'But that doesna mean a thing. There's scores of nooks and crannies along the coastline and a man like Mana would know every wee one.'

At that moment Miss Sowerby arrived back at my

430

bungalow. She had borrowed a bicycle from Toma's village and looked very out of place as she wobbled dangerously to a halt.

'How's the patient?' asked Alec.

'Fine. The after-effects have worn off, Doctor.'

'That's good news,' he said. 'And ye – did ye get any sleep?'

'Not much,' she admitted. She looked exhausted, but still her eyes had not lost their look of intuition. She could see, looking round the room, that something was wrong. 'Is anything the matter, Doctor?' She looked at both of us.

Alec took her into the kitchen and whispered the details to her. Then I heard him tell her, 'Ye go to bed, Miss Sowerby, I'll share the surgery with Kit.' And, with a smile which I could imagine, and which I knew would please Miss Sowerby, added, 'Paula Reece can do the dirty work.' She was about to start to the house when Reid added, 'I'll take a drive later to see how Toma's mother's getting along.'

Then I heard the sound of a car I knew well – Tiare's Austin Ten.

As she braked and jumped out, she cried, 'Kit! Are you all right?' Then she ran up the garden followed by an American soldier with a rifle. Tiare looked a different person. Her long black hair was uncombed, she had no lipstick or make-up, and wore a pair of stained old khaki-coloured slacks – the sort I'm sure she used if ever she did any gardening.

'I'm so thankful you're safe,' she said. 'And that the girls got away. I'm so sorry we couldn't say goodbye. This is so terrible, Kit, and now the *Mantela* is overdue. Have you heard anything about her? When I told Colonel Fawcett that Aleena was on board,' she rushed through her words, 'he radioed through to Sanderstown and got them to promise to let him know the moment the *Mantela* docked. Then he would phone me. But she's two hours overdue now – and no news.'

'Perhaps Colonel Fawcett's phoned you – and you're not at home.'

'I told him I was coming here.' She shook her head. 'Oh dear, I do hope the girls are all right. I'll never forgive myself if anything has happened to them. And what about you? If Mana is on Koraloona, it'll only be for one reason – to kill you.'

Trying to reassure her, yet vaguely apprehensive myself, I said gently, 'But Princess, we don't even know Mana *is* on the island.'

'I *know* he is,' she muttered bitterly. 'I know Mana. And what terrifies me is not my safety – but yours. It's revenge he wants – on you.' Almost harshly she asked, 'Haven't you got a guard?' Turning to the soldiers she said, 'I thought someone was being sent to guard Doctor Masters.'

'I'm sorry, ma'am.' The GI took out a packet of Camels and lit up a cigarette with one of the shiny new lighters which had never been seen on the island before the Americans arrived, but which were now the most popular buy at the PX – the Zippo. 'Want me to check with the lootenant, ma'am?'

'Never mind. It's not your problem,' she agreed. 'This is PFC Dunhill.' I held out a hand as he gave a 'Hy'a!' and I said, 'I'll talk on the phone to Lieutenant Truscott.'

Private Dunhill sat on the veranda and I offered him a beer which he gratefully accepted as I motioned Alec and Tiare to follow us into the living-room.

'I've got an idea,' I began. 'Sam Truscott is always saying that his men don't have enough work to do. He's always sending them on exercises to keep them on the go. Let's ask him to mount an amphibious exercise to find Mana's boat . . .'

'Go on,' said Alec.

'Sam's outfit has a couple of launches and a dozen or so jeeps. I'm sure that if I drive over to his camp he'll organise a search for the missing boat – as an exercise. His men'll love it. The launches could examine the coastline from the sea. And soldiers in jeeps could make a tour of the island road to keep a look-out for anything suspicious.' I knew that one jeep would be able to keep in radio contact with one of the launches. The launches might not be able to see inside a deep rocky cave – the sort where a boat could be hidden – but if they could find where the cave was, the troops could check it out from the beaches. I looked up for approval.

'Aye, that's guid thinking,' said Alec. 'Because there's no possible way that the boat could land Mana and leave the island drifting, unmanned, and not be seen.'

'You're right. We'd see it,' agreed Tiare. 'Oh Kit! Do try and persuade –' for the moment her worry over the delay of the *Mantela* was forgotten.

'He'll do it,' I promised. 'He owes me a favour.'

There was no problem in arranging the sea and land search. In fact it started within an hour; even before that an American soldier arrived at the hospital and introduced himself as, 'Corporal George Minter, sir. I'm your guard, at your service, sir.' He was armed with a sub-machine-gun instead of the usual rifle. As he saw me look at it he grinned. 'I guess that's because you're the number one target for this crazy Japanese guy!'

'Well, I *do* think he'd rather like to kill me,' I admitted.

I asked Tiare, 'Are you sure Colonel Fawcett will be able to find out where you are?'

'Are you worried?' She paled with sudden fear – which I shared – but I smiled and said, 'No. Only we *are* at war. And though I'm sure there are no Japanese ships in the area, the *Mantela* has had to go through the open seas. There's always a possibility of trouble.'

'You're right,' she agreed. 'No harm will ever come to the *Mantela* but still, I'll go up to Colonel Fawcett's place right away and wait there, if he'll let me, until we have firm news.'

She drove off with Private Dunhill while I offered Corporal Minter a cold beer and prepared to hang on for Tiare to return with news; good news, I felt sure.

Alec said, 'Ye wait here a wee while. Paula will be at the surgery by now and she can look after it. I heard her car when she arrived. I'll tell her I'm going out to Toma's village to make sure the old girl's all right.'

'I'll go if you like.' He could sense that I didn't really want to go until I had news of the *Mantela*. 'But Miss Sowerby did say she's out of danger.'

'Aye,' he agreed. 'I've no doubt ye're right, but nothing is ever sure in our line of business. And I could do with a whiff of fresh air anyway. I'll be back in half an hour to take surgery.' And as he walked down the garden path he cried a cheery, 'Dinna worry, Laddie! There's more people die of worry than any other disease in the world.'

Which might not have been strictly true medically speaking, but did at least cheer me up. Never worry about something that hasn't happened! Unless it *should* have happened and hadn't.

But one thought insisted on intruding. The *Mantela*. She was *never* late. Though she always kept up ten knots, she only went at that speed in order to economise on fuel. She could make fifteen knots easily if she hit bad weather or if the trade winds threatened to slow her down. Why, she had even arrived on time – a trifle battered, to be sure – in the legendary storm of 1936, before I came to the island.

I was waiting on the veranda, explaining some of our problems to Corporal Minter, including a description of Mana's attempt to murder me, when the telephone shrilled in the living-room. Corporal Minter followed me into the room. He was the sort of man who, knowing there was a maniac on the loose, wasn't going to let me out of his sight.

It was Tiare. Colonel Fawcett had been on the radio link again and the *Mantela* still hadn't docked.

'Don't worry, Princess,' I said. 'Maybe she's had an engine breakdown or something like that.'

'But they've tried to reach the *Mantela* on the ship's radio. It's dead. Sanderstown can't get through to her.'

'Give us all a little more time.' I tried to cheer her up – but my heart missed several beats. Why had the *Mantela* lost radio contact with her base? 'I'm sure there'll be a logical explanation.' I hoped so, but however hard I tried to hope, fear was beginning to gnaw at my stomach: and for one special reason which I hadn't thought about before. If the Japanese paratroopers had, as Jim Wilson believed, been picked up after making their way to the reef, they must have had some mother ship waiting for them outside the reef. Where was she? Where had she gone? It might even be a submarine, the most silent, the most secretive of all the predators of the sea, and even in its shape, as deadly and swift to strike as a shark.

My growing fears were allayed, if only for a few moments, by Corporal Minter who had been steadfastly looking at my Gauguin, chewing his gum reflectively, and now he said, 'Sir, I like that painting.'

'I'm glad, Corporal, so do I.'

'Kinda amateurish, all that pink stuff, but I guess the natives don't always have much choice when it comes to buying coloured paints.'

'It isn't a painting done by an islander, Corporal,' I smiled, 'but by a European.'

He clapped the palm of his hand against his forehead, crying, 'Jeez! Trust me to land in the shit. Did *you* do it? It's great!'

'No, I didn't do it,' I laughed. 'My fiancée's grandfather did it.'

'You don't say. That makes it old. In my book any painting that's old is usually worth more than any of this new stuff.'

'You could be right.'

That was about the only time I laughed as the hours of the morning dragged by. Before lunch Toma returned from his village beaming, because his mother was slowly recovering, but I could only peck at the food he prepared. Purvis came to see if there was any news of the *Mantela*, and Sam Truscott arrived to say that every inch of the coastline and the surrounding shallows had been searched without a trace of the police launch.

'I'll lay you a grand to a dime that if a motor launch did ever land on Koraloona, she's nowhere around now.'

'Thanks a lot, Sam. But maybe she never *did* go there. Maybe this is all a lot of nonsense. We've only got one witness.'

'Two, no?'

'Yes. That's true.'

'And of course if this crazy guy is really out to kill you – and he sure doesn't seem to like you from what I hear – then there'd be nothing to stop him anchoring in the surf, tying the boat up to a log or even a palm tree not far from where you live.'

'And then – ?'

'Well,' said Truscott, 'he might have come looking for you, discovered you were away, had to get back in the only fast launch available to keep his rendezvous with the others. It's the only reasonable explanation I've come up with. If he ever *did* land here.'

It did sound plausible, but to me it was too pat. It was true that Mana might never have reached the island, but if he *had* came looking for me, he might be hiding out on the island, waiting.

'And the boat? It won't untie itself from a palm tree, will it, sir?' asked Corporal Minter.

'It only takes one man to kill another. If Mana is determined to get me, his companion – a serving soldier in the Japanese army, remember – might have agreed to carry Mana here on condition that the Japanese soldier left to keep his rendezvous with his fellow parachutists.'

'That's on the cards. Yep, I'll buy that as a possibility.'

That was the last time for many, many days that I gave even the slightest thought to Mana, for that was the moment – 'Yep, I'll buy that' – when I heard the sound of a panting man, half running, half stumbling towards the garden, and a moment later the fat, perspiring figure of Reid, holding up his trousers where his MCC tie seemed to be coming untied, almost fell over the veranda steps.

His voice little more than a croak, his round, sweating face contorted with grief, he begged me, 'Come Laddie, come right away to the colonel's.'

436

Appalled, afraid, I could see the lines of anguish etched on his face. Even though in a way I had been preparing all day for possible catastrophe, I still hadn't feared the worst until this moment. Finally, Alec, the tears running down his florid face, said, 'It's bad tidings, Laddie. Bear up, I know ye will.'

'Dear God, no!' I cried. 'Not – '

He paused, sat on the veranda steps, cupping his hands in his face, then looked up with a kind of hopelessness.

'Aleena?' I whispered.

'It's the *Mantela*,' he said. 'She's been sunk. Forty miles off Sanders Island. All hands lost. According to reports, at least it was – ' he hesitated – 'over very quickly.'

30

The next hours were the worst I had ever lived through. Not only was the entire island stunned by the death of 'the Princess' daughter' but, because the Polynesians love the sea as much as the land, they mourned the end of a ship that was part of the life and history of Koraloona. So Tiare must have felt much the same as I did: that we had been plunged into hell. For the islanders the grief was more widespread – though we shared in it too; a kind of communal grief at the loss of a beloved daughter, but also of the captain of the *Mantela*; for Bill Robins was known and liked by everyone.

No one was spared. Alec Reid's face sagged in creases and folds and he looked twenty years older, as though he had lost a stone in weight in a day. He slumped in a rattan chair on the hospital balcony, a bottle of Scotch on the table beside him, looking vacantly over the bay and the pier where so often the *Mantela* had docked. The death of Aleena was a sorrow he found it hard to bear, but I could see that in a different way he felt even more desperate about the fate of Bill Robins; just as Jim Wilson did. His entire life since coming to Koraloona had been bound up with that of the *Mantela* and her master. The same with Mollie Green. Even Father Pringle held a special service, and was sober for the occasion.

For me – and for Tiare – the death of Bill Robins had sliced away a staunch friendship formed on the very first trip out from Sydney; but the loss of Aleena meant the loss of half of my life, and half of Tiare's too. I could not imagine carrying on without that happy smile.

There was even a kind of bitter irony after Aleena's death, one which doomed her mother and me to live a lie to the end of our days. For after Tiare's first breakdown, and then the short service at Father Pringle's when he intoned, 'In the midst of life we are in death . . .' and the congregation had dispersed, Tiare confessed to me, 'I feel so sad for you, Kit, I wronged you so much by not letting you become lovers. I robbed you of life's greatest happiness.'

And I could say nothing, could only lie by omission, for only Aleena and I knew that we *had* been lovers, if only for an hour, and I could never tell a soul. And already I knew how quickly life is woven into legend in the South Seas. In a few months I would already be known as the doctor who had been robbed of unconsummated love by the sea.

I could not really learn anything of Tiare's deepest feelings of grief because, after the service at Tala-Tala, she said, deathly pale and holding my arm for support, 'I want to drive home. And please – nobody come to see me. I will let you know when I am brave enough to meet you all again.' Then she had climbed into the Austin Ten and the guard had driven her home.

The entire island was wrapped in gloom, for this was their Princess who was suffering. Even the sea seemed to have turned grey and the sun was half obscured by cloud. Down by the communal stone washing trough, standing under the shade of the two giant mango trees, the girls wrung out their laundry silently, as though Koraloona was a graveyard where it would be indecent for anyone to make any noise.

Side by side with the grief was the irritation of not knowing any details of what had happened. Try as we might, through the radio sked, Sanderstown had no news to give us beyond the fact that a reconnaissance plane had seen irrefutable evidence of the sinking – oil slicks, smashed-up lifeboats, floating debris, lifebelts, all identified as belonging to the *Mantela*. I even tried to listen to the World Service of the BBC and the short-wave Australian news bulletins, but I knew before I heard the crackling voices that there would be no news of the *Mantela*'s fate. Why should one small coastal steamer count in the statistics of great ships sunk day by day all over the seven seas? Besides, the names of lost ships were never given now for security reasons.

Wallowing in self-pity I thought it was all my fault. All the fault of the same bloody stupid aggressive nature that had cost me my job in London years ago. And now, I reflected bitterly – unwittingly in medical terms – it was the mixture as before. If I hadn't behaved in a thoroughly unprofessional manner towards Mana in the first place he would never have noticed me, let alone tried to murder me. And if that had not happened, he would never have harboured revenge against me. So when the other Japanese had escaped from Penal Island he would probably have joined them and left to join the Japanese army. Instead, and because of me, he was thirsting for revenge, and once that was known Tiare had, quite rightly in the circumstances, sent Aleena away while I was absent. And thus Aleena had lost her life. But I had *started* it all, just as I had started it all in London years ago when I hit the man across the face with my doctor's bag. On that occasion if I hadn't hit him – if I had stopped and shouted, 'I'm a doctor! Leave this old man alone or he'll die!' who knows what might have happened? The bullies might have taken fright and bolted. Perhaps not, but at least there would have been an alternative. And now I could picture nothing but the long black tresses of Aleena; I could, in my imagination, see them floating on the blue sea.

Finally, just after lunch, I could stand solitude no longer and drove to the Union Jack Club, not so much to drown my sorrows, but to share them, remembering the old proverb that a sorrow shared is a sorrow halved.

The club was empty except for Sam Truscott, who came up, gave me an American-style sympathetic squeeze on the shoulders, and simply said, 'It's tough, kid. I wish I could do something to help. That was one helluva fine girl.'

'I know,' I sighed as he ordered a beer. 'It's such a waste, such a bloody waste.'

'If only – ' he mused.

'If!' I retorted harshly. 'The nastiest word in the English language. If – what?'

'Nothing really.' He stared into his glass as intently as if he were looking for insects in the froth. 'It was a nasty thought, unworthy. But we had a GI on the *Mantela*. Sending him home on compassionate leave that he didn't deserve. He wasn't much of a guy really, a con man if you ever saw one, but I was thinking – if only Aleena had been saved instead of the GI – and the steward.'

I looked at him, stupefied.

'What the hell do you mean, Sam? I was told there were no survivors.'

It was his turn to look astonished at me, but then as the barman, without asking, refilled our glasses, he said, 'Of course you *wouldn't* know. I heard on the military sked.'

'What do you mean?'

'There were two survivors,' Sam said quickly. '*Men*. Don't build up any hopes, Kit. There's been an air search of the entire area all day. Nothing else on the water but this one raft.'

'But I didn't know about this. How do – ?' My heart had jumped with excitement for a moment, until Sam shook his head.

'Forget any false hopes, Kit. It's all over.'

'I know but – '

'We have our own military radio link with HQ in Sanderstown. As soon as I knew one of my men was on the *Mantela*, I radioed Sanderstown. Matter of routine. They radioed back that a Carling raft – that's the new-style raft being used on merchant vessels – had been sighted with two men on board. It was pretty simple after that – the Brits sent out a motor torpedo boat and picked the two men up.'

'You're sure it was men – girls in pants look like men?' I almost begged him for help which I knew was hopeless.

'No, Kit, we identified the other man.'

'It wasn't,' I hesitated. 'Not Bill Robins?'

Truscott shook his head. 'I wish it had been. Afraid not. Don't know the guy's name because it's not military business, but I did ask if it was the skipper and they said no, it was the steward.'

'Oh!' I felt like crying. 'I knew him, name of Tomkins. Served me on my first trip on the *Mantela*,' I said. 'And no more details?'

'Nothing.'

'I understand,' I said and after a final drink, drove home – and got maudlin drunk.

Half way through the night, with all thoughts of Mana long since chased from my mind – if he was on the island and if he was going to kill me, I didn't really give a damn, I thought – there was one person I did want to meet: Tomkins, the steward. Just to discover a little more of the silence that shrouded the death of a ship and all who had sailed in her. All but two men, that is.

There was only one way to do it, I realised. Though I was allowed to fly Nellie between the islands inside the lagoon, there was no way I could get clearance to fly such a slow plane to Sanderstown. But there was another way.

After breakfast I took twenty minutes off and jeeped along the coast road to see Sam Truscott, and ask him a direct question, giving a direct reason: could he on his next flight take me as a passenger so that I could hear from Tomkins, the steward, about the last moment of Aleena's life?

'No sweat,' he agreed. 'So long as I'm not contributing to your unhappiness. As far as the flight's concerned, you're the company doctor, so you can fly under military orders. How does the day after tomorrow suit you? 6am start for the twenty-minute flight, returning at 4pm?'

So, two days later, having asked Alec Reid for a day's holiday, I flew in Truscott's 'souped-*down* Mustang' as he called his trainer version of the American fighter. It might not have been souped *up* – but travelling at three hundred miles an hour was quite a thrill, expecially when taking off; and in a way, since I loved flying next to doctoring, the flight blew away some of the tears and scattered them into the tiny cotton wool clouds around us.

Not all the tears, however; but I knew that, when I saw Tomkins and asked him for details, I wouldn't break down. Nor, after I had seen Tomkins, would I break down when I had to face up to another painful ordeal: I would have to go and see Bessie Robins.

We landed at the military airfield instead of at the old club from where I had flown so long ago with Aleena. How much history had been relived since those days!

A surprising amount of cleaning up or rebuilding during the years since the attack had helped to make Sanderstown reasonably presentable. As I drove along Aerodrome Road to Piccadilly there were many gaps of rubble – most of them already sprouting exotic wild flowers, their roots taking a grip whenever a wind had blown the seeds in their direction and where there was enough soil to nourish them.

The hospital lay at the south-east corner of Piccadilly just past the nurses' and doctors' quarters, and though it had been badly damaged, temporary repairs had kept it functioning. Tomkins, I had been told, was spending a few days there recovering from shock.

The US military – always lavish with equipment – had given me a jeep and a driver and on an impulse I asked him to drive round Piccadilly and to take a look at the Southern Cross Hotel.

It was astonishing, really. I was forgetting that two years

442

had passed since Aleena and I had embraced in my bedroom there and since the following morning when that bedroom had been demolished. It seemed like yesterday – until I looked at the newly built façade. It might have been a rush, but the builders had made a good job of it, all the same. Taking advantage of the demolition, the front of the building had been set back to allow space for a garden terrace with striped umbrellas and a kind of pavement café – something totally new in our part of the world.

'It's a great improvement!' I said to Charlie, the porter. 'You're about the only thing that hasn't changed!'

'I 'ave,' he said with a grin. 'I get more tips now the Yanks are 'ere.'

We drove along to see Tomkins. Here, too, the amenities had been improved, faster lifts operated, the rooms seemed to me to be larger, almost as though to prove that at least some good could come out of evil. American largesse!

Tomkins recognised me the moment I stepped into the room, and I of course remembered the little Cockney steward.

'Why, if it ain't the doctor,' he said, still rather weak in his speech.

'I just wanted to see how you're getting on, Tomkins,' I said, but it took me quite an effort to make small talk, for what I *really* wanted was to hear of the last few moments of the life of the *Mantela* and of course I couldn't start on the details too quickly. I had to give him time to settle down.

'The Yank and I were saved because I was 'aving a quiet Woodbine on the after deck. When the first torpedo 'it us, blimey, what an 'ell of a bang! The bleedin' bridge went right up into the bleedin' air. I never saw anythin' like it. I saw the skipper and the first mate shoot into the air – I remember, it reminded me of that music-hall trick when you shoot a man out of a cannon.'

'And you?'

'I was explainin' about one of them new-fangled life rafts – the Carlings – and this Yank and I was actually turnin' one over – with our hands on the straps, when we was both blown up like bleedin' matchsticks right out of the water. I thought we was gonners, but we both landed together – with the raft. It were a bloody miracle, sir, beggin' your pardon. The blast lifted us straight into the air and then into the sea next to the raft.'

I could imagine it – for I, too, had memories of the blast that had blown me, as though on a cushion, half way across the Southern Cross.

'And then?' I prompted him.

His voice took on a sombre note, as though to emphasise the sense of personal loss that affects all men of the sea. 'The old girl sank like a stone,' he said. 'She went under the waves inside of five minutes.'

'And no survivors?'

He shook his head. 'All below decks, Doctor. No one never 'ad no chance when those bleedin' Japs struck us without warnin'.'

'I know how you feel,' I asked, adding as delicately as I could, 'and Princess Tiare's daughter, Aleena? How many times she's travelled with you, Tomkins! Did you know that we were engaged?'

'Bless you sir, I 'adn't no idea. Congratulations, Doctor. I've seen that beautiful girl grow up from a leggy kid at school to a woman. I'm delighted you're engaged.'

My face turned red with suppressed anger. To talk like that about a dead woman, and a dead romance! He could see my fury as I almost made to leave the room, for he asked me anxiously, 'Sorry Guv'nor, 'ave I said somethin' I shouldn't 'ave said?'

'It's a bloody awful thing to speak of the dead like that,' I almost shouted at him.

'Jesus. I'm sorry, Doc. I didn't know as 'ow the lady was dead!'

I looked at him. Obviously the ordeal had gone to his head. 'You must be mad,' I said shortly. 'You're the one who should be telling *me* how she died. I wanted you to tell me about the last time you saw her on the *Mantela*. And you come out here with this slobbering nonsense.'

444

'It ain't my fault.' He suddenly sat bolt upright in his bed, his eyes stricken with a puzzled frown. 'What are yer drivin' at, Doctor?'

My look of astonishment must have puzzled him further.

'On the *Mantela*.' I tried to say the words but they stuck in my throat. 'Aleena and her friend Kinawa. When they left Koraloona on the *Mantela* – '

It was Tomkins' turn to think that I had taken leave of my senses.

'You're crazy! No disrespect meant, Doctor, but' – taking a deep breath – 'there weren't no Miss Aleena on the *Mantela* when she sailed. Nor her friend. Nor any passenger for that matter, 'cepting the Yank.'

I looked at him – I knew how shock can derange men – and I couldn't stop leaning forward, almost as though to strike him. I grabbed his bony shoulders, forgetting that he was just coming out of shock, and cried, 'You're lying, you're lying! Why?'

'I ain't lying,' he shouted and cried, 'Nurse, 'elp!' and to me he shouted, 'Take yer 'ands off of me.'

'What do you mean?' I said harshly.

'What I said,' he retorted angrily.

'Explain what you mean – please,' I whispered, hardly daring to let go of his shoulders. 'I'm sorry I hurt you, but – I don't understand. *What were you saying?*'

'No offence intended, Doctor, and no offence taken. But ask the American GI. After all, I was the steward on the *Mantela* and the only extra person on board was the GI. There wasn't no wimmin aboard, that's the gospel truth, Guv'nor, strike me dead if I lie. And do you think I'd 'ave Miss Aleena on board and not see 'er? She's travelled on the ship dozens of times. Cripes! She always 'ad a good word for me – and a good tip. No, there weren't no wimmin aboard.'

I felt my head spinning for a moment, and I almost fell over. Tomkins who was watching me closely, slightly afraid, must have seen my ashen face, for he said, 'You look as though you've seen a bleedin' ghost! I'd better call the nurse.'

'No, don't.' I knew the symptoms well enough – loss of oxygen and blood to the head in moments of mental stress. God knows I'd seen enough cases in my medical life of fainting caused by dilation of the blood vessels. Sitting normally on the edge of the bed, passing my head over my hands, I could actually feel the blood returning to normal as I said, more to myself, my whole being filled with a surge of excitement in which all other thoughts of what might have happened were forgotten. The only thing I could think of was that maybe she wasn't at the bottom of the sea!

'You're absolutely sure?' I asked hoarsely.

'My word's my bond, Doctor,' he insisted in his Cockney accent. 'Mind you, I ain't denying that the Princess, with the two young ladies, did come aboard, but I could 'ear them all talking, and at first I thought the Princess had only come to say goodbye to Captain Robins. Sure enough, she does get off the *Mantela*. But I 'ad no idea that the young ladies was going to get off later, after dark it was. Mind you, I wasn't that surprised.'

'Why not?'

'Well, Doc, they was walking round the deck one moment, the next they was 'opping down the gangplank. And at that moment I thought to meself, obviously they wasn't going to sail because they'd brought no luggage.'

'No luggage of any sort?'

'Not an 'andbag! That's what made me think that after all, they was just visiting the skipper. Cap'n Robins was mighty fond of the Princess's daughter.'

No luggage! In a way it was understandable. In the mad rush of getting on board, Tiare must have panicked and, determined to make sure that Aleena was safe, had driven the girls without a second thought to the *Mantela*. Luggage didn't matter in a crisis of this sort. The only thing was – safety from a madman let loose from his cage.

'And they didn't return?'

I was so stunned – the automatic reflexes of doubt when

446

faced with the impossible – that I couldn't take in the unbelievable, and it must have been this that made me ask Tomkins harshly, 'And what about later? Come on, Tomkins – the truth, or I'll send for the police. Both girls returned on board. I know they did.'

His own anger, following the way I had grabbed his shoulders impatiently, was beginning to boil over. 'And I'll shout for the nurse to kick you out if you threaten me. Was you there, Mr Know-All?'

I shook my head, miserable instead of hopeful, miserable because I knew Aleena must be dead, and this was like a dream.

'Well, I *was* there,' he said angrily. 'All the time until the gangplank was drawn up, so don't you go h'accusing me and callin' me a bleedin' liar.'

'I'm sorry. Try to understand what I've been going through,' I begged him and made to hold out a hand to touch him, but he drew back, afraid. 'You're sure? I realise now that you say they didn't return to the *Mantela*.'

''Ow many times do I 'ave to tell yer?' he asked angrily. 'Where I come from, we don't boil our cabbages twice.' He slipped into Cockney slang, and I could see that I was beginning to make him nervous, a bad sign in a patient barely recovering from shock; he wiped the sleeve of his striped hospital pyjama jacket across his sweating forehead.

'Of course I believe you, Tomkins,' I tried to be conciliatory. 'And I'm sorry I acted as I did. You see, perhaps you don't realise that the two girls *were* supposed to have sailed that night.'

I could hardly bear to spend another moment in the hospital room. Apologising once again, I said goodbye as quickly as I could to Tomkins and drove to the Officers' Club, where I had arranged to meet Sam Truscott. The most important thing was to send a message to Tiare right away.

Truscott immediately arranged to do this by sending through the military channel a message from himself to

Lieutenant Dixon at Tabanea camp. Truscott was as excited as I was, and together we sent a message of hope to be taken by jeep to the Princess and Doc Reid. It read:

> Don't be too optimistic but it seems that although Aleena has vanished she was not repeat not on board the *Mantela* and so am hopeful that both she and her friend Kinawa might still be alive. Will explain this evening. Sent on behalf of Doctor Masters.

'That okay?' asked Truscott.

'Fine. Thanks,' I said.

It was then that Truscott asked, 'But what's the answer to the million-dollar question? Where is Aleena?'

'That's something we'll have to find out,' I sighed, for amidst the flurry of excitement and happiness Truscott had put his finger on the key question: if Aleena was alive, where had she and Kinawa vanished to?

There could, unfortunately, only be one answer to that.

Horribly, and with the prickling sensation that accompanies cold sweating, I now realised that what I had believed to be a nightmare after that wonderful hour of love had been no nightmare at all, but the real thing. The scream I thought I had voiced myself had been uttered by Aleena – at the moment when Mana and his Japanese accomplice caught the two girls on their way back to the *Mantela*.

31

Truscott had to get clearance to fly back, and I was so bewildered that I begged him, 'I need a stiff drink. Take me to the Officers' Club.' I had forgotten about visiting Bessie Robins. He needed no second bidding, and once in the neatly furnished, cheerful bar we had a couple of double gin and tonics.

'I prefer dry martinis,' he explained, trying to take my mind off things, 'but the English just don't get the hang of making them cold, and dry. Their dry martinis tend to come up slightly yellow and just off the boil.'

At that moment Ronnie Serpell saw me, gave me a wave and came across, recognising Sam.

'So the poor old *Mantela*'s gone,' Serpell sighed. 'It's bad enough in the Pacific, but we're in even graver danger of losing the Battle of the Atlantic. Last year alone – 1943 that is – we lost 597 ships – over three million tons. We *did* sink more than two hundred German U-boats, but still – ' he ordered another round – 'I hear there's some puzzle about the *Mantela*. A couple of men survived, but no one seems to know how many passengers were on board.'

I explained the story briefly.

'But the two girls who were supposed to be on board? Why did they walk off so suddenly?' It was not my place to explain *that*, so I just matched his baffled look. 'And if they *weren't* on the *Mantela*, where the hell were they?'

'Don't think I haven't been imagining every answer to that question,' I said bitterly. Indeed I was tormented with awful possibilities – torture, rape, even that they had been killed. One minute they had been there, the next, two beautiful girls had been wiped off the face of the earth as easily, and as finally, as someone wipes a name off a blackboard.

'The only thing I can reckon is that the Japanese have abducted them and that they're on Penal Island,' I said. 'I presume you've read the reports of the massacre.'

He nodded. 'You're probably right. As far as I know – though it's not my line of country really – the Japs control Penal. Our first reports gave the impression that the Japs had somehow escaped across the reef to rejoin some mother ship – perhaps the one that sank the *Mantela*. But then we sent out a reconnaissance plane over Penal, and the pilot could see several figures in what looked like khaki uniforms. We're sending a Catalina flying-boat, which has heavier firepower, later this afternoon to come down lower.'

'God! I wish I could go along,' I said.

'Not a hope.' Serpell shook his head. 'First, you're a civilian, and second, there's about as much co-operation between the Navy and the RAF as between an egg and a spoon. They only come in contact when they have to!'

'I was only dreaming.'

'But I wonder – ' Truscott was thinking aloud. 'Penal is a dependency of Koraloona, in the same lagoon, and Koraloona's garrison, such as it is, consists of American soldiers under a Navy flier. Okay, I'll admit we're not a fighting force, because we're there for a specialist function. But,' he turned to Serpell, 'maybe I'll go have a few words with the US officer here and tell them that as an American is, in theory, responsible for Koraloona, I want permission for my plane to have a look-see at Penal.'

'You'll never get it,' said Serpell. 'You'd be strangled with red tape.'

I was inclined to agree with the surgeon-commander. Much as we needed American help in the Pacific – to say nothing of Europe – the overall command of the archipelago lay with the British, and the Americans had been engaged solely on specialist duties because we lacked trained personnel. But even the American representative in Sanders – Truscott's boss – would have to ask permission from the British C-in-C, a title guarded jealously.

'I guess you're right,' Truscott agreed. 'Still – I'll give it a whirl.'

'He's young and inexperienced in military diplomacy,' Serpell turned to me jokingly as Sam left, 'but then, the Americans' – he shrugged his shoulders and added a trifle enigmatically – 'they *do* like playing Cowboys and Indians.'

Half an hour later, Truscott returned to the club and as soon as he saw me, gave me a 'thumbs down' down signal of failure.

'You were right, Commander,' he said. 'Never got to first base.'

450

'Don't worry.' Serpell turned to me. 'I promise you, Kit, you'll be kept fully informed of every scrap of news as soon as I hear it.'

Oddly, Sam didn't seem as downcast as I had expected, for he wasn't the kind of man who liked refusals. With almost a twinkle in his eyes he said to Serpell, 'I shoulda known better, sir.' To me he said, 'Time for us to return to base.'

'Come back as soon as you can.' Serpell shook hands with us and Truscott gave him a laconic, 'Be seein' you, Commander.'

As we jumped into the jeep to drive to the airfield, Truscott cried, 'Step on it, soldier! We're in one helluva rush.'

'What's up?' I asked.

'We're going to take a quick look at Penal, that's what's up,' he chuckled.

'But I thought – '

'So did I. And I knew before I left you that if I made any official approach, my immediate boss would *have* to refer it to the Brits. So I made an *informal* off-the-record request.'

I didn't understand, but then I didn't have any real knowledge of the way in which American officers bend the rules if it's in a good cause, whereas British officers regard rules as sacrosanct. But I had certainly seen how the system had been bent to send me to San Francisco.

'But how?' I asked.

Truscott explained. 'As you know, every flight has to be logged, okayed, the ETA planned, together with objectives of the operation. I can't even fly between Koraloona and Sanders without informing base and getting the okay. So I told Major Maxwell – he's my immediate boss – all about you, and, of course, he'd read all about your heroism in the cholera epidemic, and when I told him about your girl – and that we wanted to take a peek at Penal, he, well – '

'Well, what?' I asked impatiently, as we turned on to the apron of the airfield.

'He's kinda smart. All he said was, "I heard nothing,

Lieutenant, but I've been meaning to tell you that you have a tendency to stray off course. You should improve your flying." Goddammit, he looked at me with a glassy stare, and I knew we had it in the bag. Penal! Here we come!'

I shook my head with disbelief as we climbed into the plane.

Before we fitted our flying helmets with their intercom, Truscott told me, 'The RAF Catalina plans to inspect the island at 16.30. It's now a quarter after one. So we can fly straight to Penal in under a half hour, dip low and take a quick look, then return to Koraloona before any other planes are in our air space.'

We were airborne within five minutes. Just over quarter of an hour later, flying at 8,000 feet, we passed over Koraloona, looking like a peaceful picture postcard below, a mountain clothed in a dozen differing hues of green, surrounded by the pale gold or white of the sand, and beyond, the thicker white ring of the reef – and next door to the picture of peace, already visible in the distance, a vile and wicked speck of rock where beasts who couldn't be called human had slaughtered innocent men and women and – who knows? – were about to kill my beloved Aleena; if, that is, she was still alive. The contrast was almost unbearable.

Luckily, action overtook thought.

'Hold fast!' yelled Truscott, more from habit than warning for we were securely strapped in. Then he pushed the stick forward and my stomach seemed to leave my body as we suddenly nose-dived, dropping like a stone, the wind screaming towards the earth at such a speed I thought the strain would tear the wings off. Sam gave me a 'thumbs up' sign, and then suddenly, as the stubby chunk of rock, with its pattern of red roofs, and the narrow street, seemed to rush towards us, Truscott pulled the aircraft out of the dive and we flattened out, and Penal was behind us. Almost lazily, Truscott banked, and with the whistle of the speed gone, he shouted into the intercom, 'Just thought I'd give those yellow bastards a lesson in flying.'

I could imagine his grin. He throttled back as much as he dared without stalling, and by the time we were approaching the island again, I could see startled men running out of buildings, waving into the air. Every man was in uniform, running like brown ants towards the tiny village 'square' and the house of the chief prison warden, above which flew the Japanese flag.

We banked again, turning as Truscott yelled, 'We've got time for one more run, but then, as you English say, it's Home, James, and we ain't going to spare the horses.'

Again we turned lazily, and prepared to approach the island at zero feet. This time, though, as we slid in above the small main street, a dozen or so Japanese opened fire with rifles. We couldn't hear the sound, but we could see the figures with rifles pointing upwards, and the tiny puffs of smoke, like balls of cotton wool. It all happened in five seconds, and we were right over the 'target area' when I heard a kind of hiss, a wham, and on Sam's intercom a yell of pain and rage.

'The Japanese shit's hit me!' he cried.

I could see nothing, but I knew that if Truscott passed out, we would crash. The trainer plane, now on active service, no longer had dual controls. I gulped as the aircraft lurched, swerved to the right, and I cried, 'Okay?'

'Yeah! Just a nick on one leg, though I'm flying by the seat of my pants, but I'm going to give 'em one last run and pepper those bastards with machine-gun fire.'

I knew the plane carried the standard light machine-gun that is timed to fire through the revs of the propeller.

I leaned over as best as I could. I could see a small stain – blood – oozing through the left leg of Sam's flying suit.

'No sweat, but by God, I'm going to grab me a couple of dead Japs before I go home.'

He soared upwards, swung round, gave the customary trial burst to test the machine-gun, and prepared for the run towards the island. Suddenly, all thoughts of Sam's injury were forgotten – in a moment of terror.

'No, Sam!' I tried to grab the stick. 'No shooting.'

'Don't panic,' he shouted back. 'You scared?'

'The girls. Aleena.' I was sure my gasp of fear came through the intercom. 'If they're on the island they must be hostages.'

Truscott was understandably livid with anger, and his right thumb was on the button on the top of the stick. All he had to do was press it – and he wanted to. Badly. I thought he hadn't heard me, and I lived a thousand deaths in the two seconds of our approach. I could see that for a moment he clutched his left leg as though in pain.

Then suddenly, his finger still on the button of the stick, we approached Penal, and the figures started firing, their puffs of smoke around and below us, but then he took his thumb off, pointed down and yelled, 'My God – look! The girls!'

I had a fleeting glimpse as we approached of a ring of Japanese soldiers firing blindly upwards and in their centre, as though in a cage, two girls standing. The sight was over in a flash, but we both knew that if Sam had gunned the Japanese soldiers, the girls would have been in the bull's eye of the target.

Even as Truscott spoke, even as thoughts and agonies spilled into my brain, through my mind, Sam was zooming upwards, long since out of range, soon all but out of sight and heading for home, only minutes away.

'Thanks pal!' I yelled above the crackle of the intercom.

'Close thing!' he yelled back. 'If you hadn't shouted, I'd have given them a burst before we reached the target.'

We landed soon afterwards. As American mechanics, realising that Truscott had been hit, helped him out of the tight-fitting seat of the aircraft, Truscott said, his voice shaking with fury, 'Those bloody yellow shits! Do you realise they brought those kids out deliberately – talk about honour of the bloody Samurai or whatever they call them. Bushido! Bullshit!'

As the mechanics lifted Truscott down carefully, Sam grinned. 'Lucky you gotta doctor around. That's real service!' He winced between grins. His suit, like most others, was zipped acrossways all the way from the hip to the shoulder, so apart from some difficulty in taking off his boots without jerking the bad leg, it was comparatively easy to examine him on the spot; his trousers were soaked in blood.

'Thank God for the padded suit.' I took a look at the wound. 'Everything conspired to inflict minimal impact. It's only a flesh wound. It'll be better in a few days, but we'll drive to the hospital and fix you up properly.'

Truscott hobbled over to look at the single bullet hole. 'Imagine if it had hit me in the balls – with Lucy almost set to start the production line.'

I laughed – but almost a 'professional' laugh, used to help a patient to steady his nerves after a shock – and there are few shocks more unpleasant than being shot when you can't shoot back; I too was feeling shock, for I couldn't wrench my thoughts from the split second that had flashed by – the ring of Japanese soldiers with the two girls in the centre, the picture all over so quickly that I couldn't see any detail. Even as I drove Sam to hospital in Anani, where I decided to put in a couple of stitches in the thigh, I could hardly keep my mind on my job as we arrived and Miss Sowerby made the preparations.

'Stitches!' cried Sam. 'What the hell for? You saw me walk. I don't need any bloody stitches.'

'True,' I admitted. 'You'd live, even if I didn't stitch you up. But you'd always have a nasty scar. This way, by pulling the skin together, you won't be able to see anything by the time you get married. It's cosmetic.'

When I had finished bandaging him up I was still befuddled by a mixture of anger, fear and frustration, but by then Sam had become the practical officer again, and prepared to report his findings to his immediate superior in Sanders, who would obviously alert the British. And I would make my report to Colonel Fawcett and drive over to see Tiare.

'But don't let's mention that we were hit – or what happened to me,' said Truscott.

'Why on earth not?'

'Hell, if I'm even only slightly wounded, it'll start off all sorts of fireworks – enquiries, why was I there, who was with me – you know! Instead, I'll just say I strayed slightly off course and confirm that Penal Island is now in Japanese hands. I guess *that's* important enough – the fact that the Allies have lost another chunk of territory.'

'And the girls? You can't hide what we saw.'

'God, no! We've *got* to let Sanders know that pronto. Before anyone else. If they don't *know* that we've actually seen Aleena, the first reaction in Sanders will be to bomb the hell out of Penal Island. Especially as there'll be no Japanese air opposition.'

'They couldn't bomb an island knowing there are innocent civilians there,' I muttered.

'Hope not. But it didn't seem to worry your Bomber Command in Cologne.'

'Just let's concentrate on getting the girls out – whatever the price,' I begged Truscott.

'Sure. But how? And the price might be sky high.'

I was in a mood of black despair after I had seen Tiare and returned to my bungalow. There Alec came in to try – without avail – to cheer me up. The danger to Aleena didn't bear thinking about – and yet I could think of nothing else, minute after minute, second after second. How was it possible that this beautiful island – one that stood for joy and happiness in the sun – how could it have become enmeshed in the grip of such stark terror? The swaying palms, the splash of waves on hot sand, the girls with their ukuleles, they had all been signals for happiness.

'It was paradise,' I cried to Alec. 'And now it's all changed, though we've done nothing to anyone.'

Alec was silent for a few moments, refilling a pipe almost as though to gain time to think.

'I'm nae saying that the Japs might not have invaded Penal to free the Japs interned there,' he said carefully, pausing to hold the flame of his match over the bowl of his pipe, 'but ye canna deny, Kit, that there's an extra dimension – a vendetta between Mana and you.'

I felt myself go cold all over.

'Maybe Mana wants Aleena for himself.'

'Not a bit of it, Laddie. You said once before that Mana lusted for Aleena. I didna contradict ye at the time, but there's nae a morsel of truth in that. It's against all the codes of Polynesia – it always has been. Incest, even once removed, is always punishable by death. Ask Tiki. Nae, ye can set your mind at rest on that score.'

We were on the veranda, standing there smoking, looking out over the flat sea as glistening as a burnished tray, and as I thought of Aleena and the agony of *her* terror, I blurted out, 'I know, I know. It's all my fault. If I'd never insulted Mana' – I put my hands to my face, unable to say another word.

'Dinna fash ye'sel', Laddie,' Alec put an arm on my shoulder in an almost avuncular way, 'It's ye the madman's after, not Aleena. Dinna worry on her account. She'll nae come to any harm. He's just holding her to make ye suffer.'

'She's *there*!' I shouted. 'A prisoner – at the mercy of a madman. And it's my fault.'

'Keep calm,' Alec urged me. 'Everything's being done that can be done.'

'Such as what?' I asked, bitter with frustration.

I felt so *helpless*. If Aleena had been marooned on a desert island or trapped on the ledge of an inaccessible cliff or – any of this kind of mishap, I would only have had to pit my wits against the elements, against odds which with luck could be overcome. But the *Japs*! They were sadists, they took a perverse pleasure in torture. And Mana! I supposed that he must have been working with the Japanese for years (though I had no proof, not then) but he was motivated by an even stronger urge than that of a warrior's victory. He wanted a victory of revenge; he wanted to make me suffer an ultimate degradation by taking prisoner the girl I loved. He probably knew, and enjoyed the irony, that Aleena was about to marry me.

457

All these jumbled thoughts passed through my mind as I walked back to my bungalow, more frustrated, more dejected even than I had been when I thought Aleena was dead.

I was walking up the veranda steps at home when I heard the jangle of the phone bell in the hall just behind the swinging, flapping netted door which was not really necessary during the day but kept the moths out at night.

It was Colonel Fawcett and he wasted no time on preliminaries or sympathy. 'Spoke to Sanders on the sked. Damned bad business,' he grunted. 'Can you come round? Right away? For a confab before I try to contact the Japs on the sked between Koraloona and Penal.'

'I'm on my way. Where are you? At Holmes' place, I presume.'

I knew that Holmes, the replacement for poor old Shanks, lived in a bungalow which was both home and office combined, built on higher ground than most to make reception easier, and with two extra rooms. One room contained the paraphernalia for short-wave transmissions between Koraloona and New Zealand or Australia, which needed expert knowledge; and the other also possessed a desk and filing cabinets together with a stock of spare parts. The second room housed the two 'local' sets – radio telephones of what Jason always called the 'Over-to-you' type. One radio was beamed permanently to Sanders, the other to Penal. Each was fitted with warning alarms by Holmes' bedside in case of emergency, as well as the 'alert' signals in the shack itself.

Conversation between Koraloona and Penal (as between Koraloona and Sanders) was normally restricted to specific scheduled times – hence the term 'sked' – and most people in Anani or Tala-Tala knew the regular times, so that if anyone needed to pass on a message to other islands they would come to the radio shack and hand it in, much as they might send a telegram – but as this was a free service only important messages were accepted.

458

It was by now almost five o'clock – the time for the regular sked to Penal, but as Holmes opened the line, 'Koraloona calling Penal. Do you receive me? Over,' there was only silence. He persisted, patiently repeating the question over and over again.

The talking, the waiting, was exhausting, and the repetitive nature of the call sign suddenly made me feel desperately tired, not only with fear but because I could see no solution to such a terrifying problem. What solution *could* there be? Mana now held Aleena a prisoner on an island guarded by units of the Japanese army, and which could never be freed except by attack – and that one fleeting glimpse, as our plane soared over at almost zero feet, indicated with grim clarity what the fate of the girls would be if the armed forces tried to overwhelm the Japs. We *could* easily liberate Penal by bombing, but every person there, including Aleena, would die.

My thoughts were almost suicidal as I listened to Holmes' droning voice, articulating clearly, 'Koraloona calling Penal. Can you read me?' when, as though electrified out of a torpor, a guttural voice replied with unintelligible words, and Holmes' voice seemed to rush up the scale from its steady tone as he cried, 'Colonel! Quick. I think they're on the sked.'

Fawcett bounded – really, the only word – across the room. Curious, I thought with a kind of medical detachment, he looked ten years younger as he grabbed the mike and since he had been 'on active service' again.

'Koraloona to Penal,' he cried. 'Over.'

Crowding round the mike, we listened for the next words. Through the crackle of the speaker, a guttural, accented voice cried, 'Who is speaking?'

'Colonel Fawcett. Am I speaking to Mana?'

'This is Major Mana Sagawaki, of the Japanese Imperial Army. I have taken my mother's name and am now in command of Penal.'

'But Mana?' interrupted Fawcett.

'In future you will address me as Major Sagawaki.'

459

'All right. But Mana – the – '

I couldn't actually *hear* the hiss across the airwaves, but I could sense it – Mana's fury as he cried, 'I ordered you to address me by my rank. If you wish to talk to me you will do as I say. Otherwise I refuse to keep the line open.'

'I'm sorry, Major,' spluttered Fawcett, puce with fury.

'That is better,' said Mana and this time I fancied I detected the trace of a sneer. 'What do you want, Fawcett? My time is limited.'

'The girls. Aleena, the daughter of the Princess, and her friend – '

'What about them?'

'They have done you no harm, Major.' Fawcett hesitated, the word sticking in his mouth. 'I hope that you will allow them their freedom.'

'So that you can invade Penal with bombs and return it to the British Imperialists?' Mana asked sarcastically.

'But, Major – '

'No buts. By rights the two girls should be sent to Japan to work as prisoners of war. But I may keep them here for the moment – as a guarantee against any attack. I will decide later. For the moment they are safe. The next radio schedule will be in three days at the same time. Long live Japan!'

There was a click and that was that.

32

For the next three days I was in a state of shock. Though Mana had promised – for what it was worth – that the girls would be unharmed, my jumbled thoughts were only concerned with their freedom; but all I could manage was a series of empty ideas, strung together by a thin thread of inactivity. I just didn't know what to do; it was as simple as that. Wild thoughts crowded upon me. Could I land on

Penal undetected? Perhaps the rock was honeycombed with secret tunnels, so that I might be able to land by dark and squirm my way through dark holes to the summit? Absurd, of course, reason argued, but even so, in one desperate moment I actually went to see Tiki, who had once lived on the island for several weeks, and doubtless knew its history. There were no secret tunnels, he assured me. He would have known if there were any. Penal was sheer rock with hardly a crevice on which to gain a foothold except at the tiny bay and the small road leading to the summit.

Poor Tiare was also in a state of shock. I went to see her not only as her prospective son-in-law, but professionally, for her face was pinched and haggard, her outlook so hopeless that I immediately gave her an injection of dextroamphetamine, containing dextrose, caffeine and amphetamine.

'That'll help you to face up to it all,' I tried to reassure her, though God knew whether a jab would help.

'Next Monday you would have been married.' She was in her living-room, sobbing quietly, while I tried to console her. 'God help us, what'll happen next? You see, I know Mana.'

'So do I,' thinking of our painful encounters.

'Yes, but I know him in a different way. He is a man whose evil knows no bounds.'

It is impossible for anyone who was not in Koraloona in those fateful days to realise the curtain of gloom which covered the island. In my darkest moments I did at times think of the nights which must have struck cities like London or Coventry, but their disastrous slaughter of the innocents (no more, no less innocent than Aleena) in some way stiffened the spirits of the British people, gave them an urge to fight back. And though nothing could bring back the dead who littered Britain's city streets, those living at least had something to do, like my father spending a day sweeping up glass.

Here, in this idyllic unspoilt beauty, we had no broken glass to shovel away. For Tiare, for me, for all the islanders – there was nothing we could do to help to fight an enemy who was holding hostages, for we knew that one abortive rescue attempt would imperil their lives. We could do nothing but talk between ourselves – Alec, Jason, Fawcett, Paula, all of us – endless, fruitless discussions, conducted in what seemed like island-wide whispers. Everyone was almost afraid to talk loudly. The club in Tala-Tala was like a morgue. The ladies had even stopped playing bridge, and when I asked why, Mrs Fawcett said rather primly, 'There's no reason why we *shouldn't* play, Doctor, but I wouldn't like the Princess to arrive suddenly and see us.'

On the second day of silence the colonel telephoned me, and before I could utter a word said, 'No news of course, but I want to talk to you urgently. I've had a message from GHQ that they're sending some of the Sanders top brass to talk to me.'

Apparently they were already on their way – travelling from Sanders in a naval frigate – and they wanted to hold a round-table conference and then wait for the following day's radio contact with Mana.

'They talked about keeping me in the picture,' said Fawcett, 'and I told them that you should attend, though I'm blowed if I know what they can do.'

The frigate, its name painted out, arrived later that evening, and the chief members of what Colonel Fawcett described as 'the ops committee' met us in a private room, at the Union Jack Club. The leading members were a naval Captain Osmond (not the skipper of the frigate, he outranked him); from the army a Major Marshall, and a quiet-spoken, short, rather gentle man with sandy hair who wore thick spectacles, and introduced himself, 'I'm Ralph Skinner, but everyone calls me "the Prof".'

'No uniform? You are – ?' I asked idly – idly because I was so tired with the strain of inactivity, that I could hardly bear to engage in small talk.

'I'm a – ' he smiled apologetically, 'I'm afraid there are several joke-names for my dreary role in life. Boffin is one. Egghead is another – American I believe.' He seemed to wander off in his thoughts. 'I don't really like the name egghead. Later, perhaps, when I'm bald, but now – '

'I've heard the word boffin – and read it, I suppose in some English newspapers.' He must have seen my drawn and haggard look for, after brushing back his pale hair which seemed to get in his eyes all the time, he peered at me through his thick glasses, and said, 'You're engaged to the girl hostage, aren't you? I know how you must feel. But don't despair, Doctor. Hostages are nothing new in warfare and you'd be surprised how many are freed and always have been throughout history.'

'By boffins?' I forced a polite smile.

'Sometimes.' He sighed. 'It takes all sorts of situations to *make* a war. But it's always the unexpected that *wins* a war. Just imagine – for instance – the prospect of an American invasion of the Japanese main islands. Why! It would cost a million American lives. Unthinkable. And yet we have to bring Japan to her knees.'

'Even at the cost of a million lives?'

'No. That's where war is won by the unexpected. I know that the Americans are working on a new kind of bomb which, if it succeeds, could force Japan to surrender in a matter of days.'

Fascinated, and for the moment forgetting my own misery, I said, 'In days! That's impossible, because the Japanese will fight to the last man. What kind of bomb?'

'I don't know,' he admitted. 'And if I did, I wouldn't be talking about it. But science – well, never mind. I was only trying to give you a little encouragement. In this present predicament about Penal Island, I don't see what any of us can do, but at least we'll do everything we can.'

He smiled rather pleasantly, and for the first time I had a curious feeling of inner strength.

*

I won't dwell on the deliberations that took place in the club, for nothing really new transpired. Both Captain Osmond and Major Marshall were sympathetic, well-mannered and tried to do their best to reassure me. Yet they did make one or two intriguing points after telling Colonel Fawcett that 'for the moment,' as Captain Osmond said, 'we must rule out any possibility of using naval force.' To which Major Marshall added solemnly, 'And no troops either.'

'Guile is the only way,' said Captain Osmond. 'Guile and subterfuge,' adding something that further reassured me. 'Fortunately Penal Island isn't important enough to warrant a military operation that would endanger the lives of the girls. It's got to be a cat-and-mouse game.'

'Patience,' interrupted Fawcett.

'Exactly, Colonel,' said the major. 'Because after all, if we wait long enough, and do nothing, they'll *have* to act. Why dammit, they'd starve if they didn't. When they act – when they move into a different gear – when their demands disguise the fact that they need help – then they might make a slip.'

With these few crumbs of comfort I had to satisfy my appetite for action. Do nothing!

'Inactivity can be a recipe for success – that and the unexpected,' said Ralph Skinner, who, it turned out, was an Oxford professor with a double first who had been seconded to help Churchill plan new ideas for winning the Pacific war.

The following evening at five o'clock, the time for the sked with Penal, we all assembled in the radio shack, together with Tiare who had not previously met 'the ops team'. They couldn't have been kinder to her, and Captain Osmond bent his stiff straight back and his stern features enough to promise her, 'Dear lady, you have my word as a naval officer that everything possible will be done to secure the release of your daughter.'

The air was filled with suppressed tension as we stood

464

there while Holmes sat in front of his transmitter. Colonel Fawcett eyed his wrist-watch, waiting with military precision for the moments to tick by. When the Prof offered me a cigarette I accepted it gratefully. But the hand that held my lighter was shaking. I was overawed by the entire proceedings.

'Right!' Colonel Fawcett's bark broke the silence. '17.00 hours. Carry on, Holmes.'

Holmes switched on the power and broke into his normal routine. 'Koraloona calling Penal. Do you read me? Over.'

Almost immediately came the crackling reply, 'Japanese headquarters on Penal Island to Koraloona. Major Saga-waki speaking. I read you. What do you want to discuss with me? Over.'

Fawcett turned purple again and grabbed the mike, shouting, 'You can release two innocent girls. That's what you can do – Major.'

'Be quiet, Colonel. Let me speak to the officer in charge.'

'I don't understand.' Fawcett looked at the two officers as though appealing for help, for none of us understood until Mana explained, speaking with deadly calm, 'I mean, Colonel, the *real* military, not retired old fools like you. I am referring to the senior British officer who has arrived at Koraloona in a British warship from Sanderstown.'

The gasp – from every person in the room – was so audible that I wondered if Mana could actually hear it. He obviously hadn't, but the shock of his knowing! I stole a look at Tiare. Her face was as white as the flower after which she had been named, and she was biting the corner of a fragment of linen which served as a handkerchief. How on earth did Mana know? Even an astronomical telescope couldn't have supplied the detailed information.

'Short-wave radio,' whispered Osmond. 'We know there's at least one Jap submarine lurking in the area – probably the one that sank the *Mantela* – and it's acting as a mother ship. No doubt it spotted us, and radioed in code to Penal.' Politely he turned to Fawcett, and asked, 'May I?'

And as Fawcett handed over the mike – all of us waiting to hear what he would say and Mana's reply – the naval officer said in an agreeable voice, 'This is Captain James Osmond of His Majesty's Royal Navy.'

'The British Navy that lost the *Repulse* and *Prince of Wales* off Malaya?' sneered Mana.

'Part of the Allied forces that inflicted the crippling Japanese naval losses off Guadalcanal, Major.'

'Do not be impertinent. Anyway, there is nothing you can do.'

'But, Major – '

At this moment Tiare, who had been listening, biting her knuckles, a look of terror on her face, touched the arm of Captain Osmond, and indicated that she would like to talk to Mana.

The naval officer nodded, then said sharply into the mike, 'Here is someone who wants to talk to you.'

'Who? Over,' said Mana.

'Me.' Tiare was weeping softly. 'Tiare. Mana – *please* – give me back my daughter. I am so afraid for her.'

There was a moment's silence, and Holmes, who was next to Tiare, said into the mike, 'Over.'

'What do you mean, woman?' asked Mana angrily. 'Do you think I am not aware of the honour of the Japanese code of conduct. Of course your daughter is safe and well. She will only come to harm if the island is attacked, then all would probably die. So if she comes to danger it will be the fault of the British. That is why I will not speak to the English pigs who are desecrating the good name of Japan by printing lies about Japanese atrocities. Your daughter is all right. And when I have had time to formulate plans, I will discuss further.'

'Oh, thank you, Mana!'

'I have not yet decided. You will hear more later.'

'May I speak to her, Mana?'

'You may. She is here by my side. You can talk to each other for three minutes on one condition: not one word about that man Masters. If his name is mentioned, I

466

switch off the radio. Is that understood? Here, Aleena. Over.'

Then I heard her voice, distorted by the airwaves, yet at the sound of it, so steady, I had to grip the side of the table to keep myself standing; I could imagine her there, surrounded by Japanese, the hidden fear she must have surmounted in order to speak so calmly now. For I could only picture her as I had *last* seen her – ringed by Japanese soldiers firing into the air at our plane.

'Mummy, darling, it's Aleena. Please don't worry. Kinawa and I are all right.'

'Aleena, I am so worried. Are you imprisoned?'

'That's nonsense!' interrupted Mana. 'Do you think I would keep our daughter in a common jail? You fool.'

'I'm all right, really I am, Mummy. Kinawa and I are sharing one of the wardens' houses. Because no one can escape, we're allowed to walk on the island as we like. And we have enough to eat. We cook everything ourselves. The only thing I miss is you and – ' she hesitated, I could imagine Mana's angry warning look – 'and my White Lady.'

'Enough!' cried Mana. 'What lady – brown or white?'

But my heart leapt. That beautiful bride-to-be had managed on the spur of the moment to get a message of love through to me; for it was with me that she had tasted her first cocktail – a White Lady at the Café de Paris so many years ago.

'Enough!' repeated Mana. 'And you, British captain, go home. And pray you won't be sunk like our submarine sank the *Mantela*. We will call the idiotic Colonel Fawcett in three days. But no discussions with the Navy or we close down.'

With a click of finality more telling than any words, the line went dead.

There seemed no way of breaking through the deadlock, especially as each abortive conversation occurred only every third day. Two weeks passed in confrontations on the sked; and though Aleena was able to talk to her mother –

no doubt with Mana ready to switch off if she but mentioned my name – the waiting and inactivity were unbearable.

Finally, it was Tiki, the 'witch-doctor', who suggested a new course of action. When it was time for the sked, Tiki, by prior arrangement, opened the conversation with Mana.

'Mana, this is Tiki,' said the Polynesian. 'No, do not interrupt me, Mana. And remember that you are half Polynesian, and will obey the same laws of all our ancient gods.' As Mana started to interrupt, Tiki said almost wrathfully, 'Silence, man, when your spiritual adviser talks to you.'

'What do you wish to say?' Mana's voice sounded truculent, but at least he was prepared to listen.

'Tomorrow morning I am coming to talk with you. As a Polynesian to a Polynesian. You understand? Mr Wilson will take me to you in his launch, and if you prefer, you can come out in the Penal launch to meet us. But no shooting. I am a Polynesian god, and your spiritual master. I offer protection to Mr Wilson and you will obey what the English call a flag of truce. Is that understood?'

There was a moment of silence, broken finally by Mana. 'I have nothing to say, but if you demand that I meet you, I will do so, as a matter of respect to you. But no other passengers on the Wilson boat. And I will come alone except for the boatman. The girls will remain on the island. This is all right?'

'It shall be so. But remember, this is to talk, not a time for action. I have your word that no one will harm Mr Wilson, you have my word that there will be no concealed fighters on his boat and we will be unarmed.'

'It shall be so.' Mana repeated the words. 'When we sight your boat I shall sail out of harbour to greet you.' Then Mana asked an odd question. 'Tell me, wise man, your guarantees of honour and the Polynesian way of life – do they extend to white men too?'

'The question is absurd. The British Navy and its frigate

468

have long since departed. There are no British troops on the island of Koraloona.'

'Good. But that doesn't really answer my question.'

'The Polynesians were born from the oceans of the world,' Tiki almost intoned, 'and they are a race apart with their own religions and rites.'

'That is all I wanted to know, even if Tiare's father was white,' said Mana enigmatically. 'We meet tomorrow in friendship.'

'Not in friendship,' replied Tiki sternly. 'In shame for your treatment of the daughter of a royal princess of Polynesia.'

'For that I apologise,' said Mana, speaking, remember, to Tiki whom he obviously held in awe. 'I will see what can be done. We meet tomorrow.'

Soon after sunrise the following day we made our way to the pier – Tiki, Jim and I. The sun was just beginning to burn into the hazy sky and the sea broke over the coral with insistent rhythm – pounding warnings of imminent disaster, it seemed to me, for I, of course, was to remain behind.

Some of my shudders were caused by Tiki's presence in the full regalia of what I always thought of privately as his witch-doctorate. We had decided that Tiki's meeting with Mana would be far more effective if Tiki's religious neutrality could be emphasised.

'Psychology, old boy,' Colonel Fawcett had said. 'These orientals are different from Western minds altogether.'

It was true. To play along with the weaknesses of an opponent was something I had learnt in my boxing days at Oxford; and there was common ground between the enemy and the islanders in the mystique of public worship. After all, Shintoism is a primitive religion with its basis in ancestor and nature worship, just as the ancient cults of the South Seas are. And a demonstration of this common ground of neutrality in addition to the token of truce was likely to form a sound basis for palaver.

So there was Tiki arrayed in robes and mask, just as he

had been on that other occasion – the burial of the cholera victims. And as he stepped into Jim's boat, his bulky shadow, topped by the hideous mask with its grinning teeth, fell across the sparkling waters.

'Good luck,' I said; and Jim smiled grimly as he ran the white tablecloth to the masthead. 'Can't say when we'll be back,' he said quietly; and I sensed that he meant 'if' as well as 'when'.

But they returned all right.

To keep my mind occupied, I had done surgery with Alec, trying to keep my thoughts off the possible outcome of the palaver. Of course I was back at the mooring hours before Jim's boat could possibly be expected, and the tension of waiting was about the worst I had ever experienced – far worse than when I had awaited the verdict of the court on my manslaughter charge and the result of the deliberations of the hospital governors on my future.

But at last I saw the boat, still wearing its white flag of truce and moving with what seemed reluctant speed across the shimmering sea. The others gathered on the pier.

As I stood there in the shade of the tiny shed in which Jim kept mooring ropes, marlin-spikes, and boat-hooks, my back and forehead were running with sweat and the inside of my mouth felt as if I had been on a long binge.

At last the sound of the boat's two-stroke engine could be heard pop-popping above the beating of the surf, and within a few minutes, Jim was grappling for the edge of the pier with his boat-hook and tying up.

Tiki had removed his mask and looked grave; but realising my anxiety he came straight to the most important point. Putting his hand on my shoulder he said, 'They are unharmed – guarded of course, but not imprisoned; and well looked after.'

I said nothing. I suppose my relief was too obvious to need words.

'Bear up, Doc,' Jim said sympathetically and took a flask from his pocket. 'Have a shot of Scotch.'

I needed it. And in a few minutes, as Tiki and Jim unfolded the tale of their mission, I needed another one.

The Japs were in complete charge of Penal Island – as we knew. But Mana had abducted Aleena and Kinawa solely for reasons of vicious personal revenge against me.

'But they are all right?' cried Tiare, more a question than a statement. 'Will they be released?'

As we all stood in the circle on the pier, Alec said, 'Out wi' it, man! What are ye trying to tell us?'

For a moment the tall, grave figure of Tiki stood silent, and then he said slowly, 'They have agreed that the girls shall be freed.'

'Thank God!' cried Tiare.

'When?' I asked.

'By gad, well done!' said Colonel Fawcett.

'But,' added Tiki, 'there is a price that must be paid.'

His words were uttered in such a grave way that they acted on me, and I think on the others, like a cold shower on a person drunk – if only with excitement. A price! What was it?

'Mana's offer is explicit,' said Tiki. 'They will release the hostages in exchange for another.' He paused, and I could see the sweat glistening on his brow. 'You, Doctor Masters.' Another pause. 'And no other. Failing acceptance of that offer . . .'

33

The words dripped like ice from the man's lips, each syllable separate, like ice cubes dropping into a pool. There was an utter silence, broken only by the sounds of in-drawn breaths as though disbelief were suspended. Every face turned towards me as the others realised the full impact of what amounted to a death sentence, until the tension was released in a mad wail from Tiare as she realised that, in saving Aleena's life, I would simply be exchanging places with her on the island and put myself at the mercy of Mana.

As for me, I could see no way of winning.

As Tiare ran towards me crying, Colonel Fawcett, his face grave, stood silent; for once, I thought inconsequentially, his moustache was not twitching. Alec Reid, hitching up his stained khaki shorts, and tightening his MCC tie round his waist, came towards me, put an arm round my shoulder. Everyone seemed to have gathered on the pier, but none had a word of comfort to offer, only a silent horror of the inevitable. I saw Miss Sowerby, normally prim and proper, and for the first time in my life, the tears were glistening in her eyes, as she fought not to weep openly. Purvis' face was expressionless.

For a moment the group of normal individuals standing on the pier, listening to Tiki, waited as each struggled inwardly to come to terms with the awful choice they knew I would have to make. There was no choice, really, except the one that meant certain death. Knowing this, I was thinking how pointless life was. All those years wasted in Nottingham, poor Clare crippled by polio which I could have cured had I known then what I knew now; Oxford, the med school in London, the planned future as a steady doctor with a quiet practice. And then an unexpected turn in an East End street, and the death of a Mosley thug. Was I now facing retribution, an eye for an eye? Life had an odd way of catching up with you, but at least I had been given many years of grace in the most beautiful island in the world, loved by the most beautiful girl in the world.

I don't know how long it took for these thoughts to race through my mind; a few seconds maybe, in the way that all one's life is supposed to flash before you at the moment of drowning.

The shroud of silence that enveloped us was shattered by Alec Reid crying, 'We all need a drink. And for medicinal reasons. Come up to the house. All of you.'

The first voice brought the others away from silence.

Colonel Fawcett cried, 'I'm coming, Doc. It's monstrous. The man's stark staring mad.'

'Aye, that he is and no denying it.' Reid started walking up the hill, taking off his ancient topee and wiping his sweating, pink, bald pate. And when we reached his bungalow – with me still in a daze, unable to take in the truth – he shouted, 'Bubble and Squeak, drinks all round.'

Turning to Fawcett, as though he was continuing his conversation on the pier, he admitted, 'The question is – what are we going to do about it? We've got to find a way of bargaining with the man, putting off any commitments, because I'm sure of one thing which Tiki told me: he won't dare to kill the girls.'

'But the feller might take them to Japan.' Colonel Fawcett downed his Old Rarity in one gulp. 'Send 'em to brothels. It's a favourite Japanese trick.'

'You can't bargain with a lunatic,' muttered Jason.

Everyone looked at me as though expecting me to come up with a solution. I was quaking, trying to keep my voice steady, trying also to keep out any vocal suggestion of bravado, any display of false heroism, for I never felt less heroic than I did at this moment when I said, as quietly as I could, 'Thank God we can save Aleena.'

Impassively Tiki, who had come up to Alec's bungalow with the rest of us, said, 'That I can guarantee.'

'But the price!' cried Miss Sowerby. 'Oh! Doctor Masters!'

'Please,' I almost shouted the words sharply, 'don't let's make this more difficult than it is.' And using the words I had employed to myself as the picture of my life was crowding my thoughts, 'No heroics.'

'But ye canna do this, Laddie,' cried Alec, and I could see that he, too, was on the verge of breaking down. Six long years we had passed together starting as colleagues, and it was at moments like this that each of us knew how close that friendship had become since I first met Alec as I stepped off the *Mantela*. 'We *must* bargain,' he said.

'There can be no bargaining,' said Tiki. 'I am more sorry than I can say, but – '

473

'I'm going to call GHQ at Sanders right away.' Colonel Fawcett was spluttering with rage.

'No, Colonel,' I begged him. 'Please!'

'Why not?' asked Purvis.

'Because we know that enemy submarines are picking up our sked conversations and then reporting them back to Penal. And if Mana learns that Koraloona is asking headquarters in Sanders what to do, what bargaining procedures to follow – Mana might call the whole deal off, and then Aleena – anything could happen – ' the rest of my sentence tailed off into a miserable silence.

'Kit's right,' Alec nodded to the colonel. 'At any rate for the moment, until we've had time to think things out.'

'Remember, this is a personal feud between Mana and me,' I emphasised. 'Using war as an excuse, he's man-oeuvred himself into such a powerful position that there's no way we can bluff him.'

'You must do *something*,' Tiare cried to Tiki. 'You have the authority that is invested in only a handful of the wise men. I pray you to test your powers at this moment in the life of our honoured doctor.' Distraught with grief, the words tumbled out, like a waterfall that couldn't be stopped. And then she turned to me and said in a voice of anguish, 'Oh Kit! Oh – that this should happen to you and Aleena.'

'I will go to see him again if I can force him to receive me,' Tiki promised. 'But Princess, please reflect that I am a wise man whose powers apply only to the men and women of Polynesia. I have no power over the men of other races.'

All I could say to Tiare, as I put my arms about her, was a muttered 'Aleena's going to be safe. That's the most important thing of all.'

It answered the unspoken question that haunted every-one in Alec Reid's bungalow: the price! Everyone knew what that price would be; it was as clear as the price tag at a bargain sale. The life of one man for the lives of two girls. And everyone knew, too, that I *must* pay that price, it was based on an insane hatred for me born out of my own folly.

Standing on the veranda, where I had gone for a breath of air – and solitude – I stood looking over the bay, the only sound coming from the small waves on the beach. Fawcett came out and grunted, 'Kit, we can't let this damned Jap get away with it.'

'We can't interfere, Colonel!' My voice had a harshness that came from fear as much as determination. 'It was my fault in the first place. If it hadn't been for my stupidity in goading Mana, this would never have happened.'

Suddenly Tiare cried, again more to Tiki as a 'spiritual' leader than to the others, 'Let me go to plead with him.'

'No!' I still used the same rough voice. 'Princess! Please! Leave it to me.'

This was a problem of life and death I had to solve alone.

Soon afterwards we went to Colonel Fawcett's bungalow, though not to the radio shack, for what he called a 'full-dress conference.'

It did result in a few minor decisions, largely helped by Mana himself who had announced to Tiki that though Aleena and Kinawa would be freed once I became his captive, he would not break radio silence for another two days. Perhaps the delay was his way of exercising a little mental torture.

'Time is of the essence,' pontificated Colonel Fawcett. 'This is a classic hostage situation. We must – ahem! talk our way through it.'

Which was all very well, but not positive; for no one, least of all Mana, had made any plans for the exchange, which would be in the hands of Tiki. If only we could have asked Sanders for advice.

It was Jim Wilson who suggested, 'Doc, why don't you fly old Nellie to Sanders and put the authorities in the picture. That way the Japs would never know.'

Poor Alec almost jumped out of his seat in alarm.

'Damned good idea,' said the colonel. 'Think you could make it, Doc?'

Alec hesitated, but only for a few seconds. 'Aye, I'm

willing,' he agreed. 'But I dinna ken if the old lady's airworthy after lying fallow in a field for so long.'

'I'd go like a flash,' I interrupted. 'But I can't leave the island – in case. And I can't be *seen* to leave the island. Otherwise, Alec, you know that I – '

'Truscott could do it,' said Colonel Fawcett. 'Bit of a problem though. This is a British show and we don't want the Yanks interfering. If they did they'd bomb the island with a dozen Flying Fortresses, just to protect their boys on Koraloona. If we're going to save Aleena – and Doctor Masters – we need tact,' he coughed diplomatically, 'not, well, American brute force.'

'Why not use both men?' I suggested almost nervously. 'We couldn't fly Nellie. It'd take a week to get her ready. Why not ask Truscott to fly the doc – to act as a chauffeur?'

'By gad, that's a damn good idea,' said Fawcett. 'I'd go me'self to report, but my place must be here – at the seat of the operation.'

In the end, that is what happened. Truscott, of course, knew what was happening – the broad outlines, if not the details – but we all understood Fawcett's reasons for 'keeping the show British'. Among other considerations was the secrecy of the negotiations. The British Navy was not called the silent service for nothing. Everything that had so far happened had been secret. No bulletins, no news for the press. But Truscott himself admitted that if the Americans started helping, the American press, scenting a sensational story in their part of the world, would publicise every detail of the entire operation. I knew he was right – I only had to remember the way they had treated my non-existent role in 'saving' the Americans in the epidemic.

But it was a different matter for Truscott acting un-officially. He was a good friend, and could be trusted to keep his own counsel. So the following day Alec flew to Sanders, returning that afternoon. He had not dared to advise anyone that he was coming, but he did see the top brass and reported directly to them.

Back in Fawcett's bungalow that evening, Alec gave all

of us a picture of what had transpired. In essence, of course, it boiled down to what we already knew.

'But Captain Osmond, the Navy bloke who came here on the frigate, told me that ye's got to go through with it, Kit, but to try and not worry overmuch. Ye may be taken a prisoner – ye will be, nae doot about that – and ye may still be a prisoner when the war's over. And I had a long talk with your boffin friend, Professor Skinner, and he gave me a wee bit of heart to pass on to ye.'

Alec rested, mopping his brow. 'He came out with a message for ye, Kit. It was a wee bit spooky. He told me to say to ye, "The hardest thing in life is to face death you believe to be certain when no one can tell ye that ye're goin' to be saved."'

'If I knew what that meant, I'd be happier,' I said a trifle bitterly. 'Anything else transpire?'

'Aye, the Navy captain also said that all sked messages between Penal and Koraloona were being monitored, and so were the messages from the Japanese submarine, though they're in code and it hasn't been broken yet. But in a strange way, Laddie, he gave me a glimmer of hope.'

According to Alec, the Prof had also given me some advice of a different nature. In brief, it boiled down to this: sooner or later Mana would demand to talk to me on the radio sked. I had to play it by ear, but if possible, I had to try and make him angry.

'His words were "Taunt the bastard – that's one thing the Japs can't stand,"' said Alec. 'Dinna forget it.'

I didn't – for Skinner's premonition came true sooner than I expected – that very night. Unexpectedly, the radio sked crackled into life. I was at the surgery at the time, attending a few minor cuts and bruises, with Miss Sowerby helping, trying to hold back her tears, when Fawcett phoned me, and with a tone of urgency, cried, 'Mana is on the radio, and he wants to talk to you in person.'

I hurried round, almost running up the hill. At the front door of the radio shack, Fawcett in a stage whisper said, 'Stall him, Kit. Keep him talking. Remember they're listening back in Sanders, and that's what the Prof demanded – a chance to analyse everything that Mana says, to read into it something we may not know about.'

Even as I picked up the mike, Mana's voice crackled. 'Bring in Masters immediately or I switch off.'

'Doctor Masters here,' I said into the mike, 'what do you want, Mana?'

'Major to you, Masters.'

'And Doctor to you. If you want to talk to me, *politeness*. Otherwise it will be me who switches off. Understood? Over.'

I could almost hear the hiss of indrawn breath.

'You switch off, *Doctor*, and you never see Aleena again.'

I knew that he was making a threat I could never dare to treat as a bluff.

'You wanted to talk to me?' I hoped that my voice sounded cool and detached – in reality it was about as cool as a trip to hell.

'You agree to the switch?'

'Of course. What did you expect me to do?' adding with studied insolence, 'I am British, not Japanese.'

I had been told to make him angry, so no holds were barred.

'The British are cowards. They were afraid to fight for Singapore and Hong Kong. Are you afraid?'

'No,' I lied. 'The only thing I demand – '

'Demand! You are a cowardly Englishman. They have no right to demand anything.'

'I have. Guarantees.'

'You ask guarantees. What guarantees, British doctor, coward? You have my word as a Japanese soldier – '

Mindful of the advice to try to make him angry, I somehow managed to give him the best imitation I could of a derisive laugh. 'Your honour! You are joking! What about Japanese honour towards British prisoners, now working in slave camps?'

'Prisoners are cowards. They should die.'

'And you?' I taunted him. 'You are a brave man? Like trying to murder me?' And then, with a sudden thought, 'Tiki knows. You cannot hide the truth from Tiki. *He* knows you cast no spells. You tried to murder me.'

'Not true.'

'Is true.' Without thinking I relapsed into the tongue of the islanders. 'I will come – but will you have the courage to fight me like you did last time – when I won?'

Again the silence was more telling than words, and I knew that when I went to Penal in exchange for Aleena, there would be no fair fight. I would probably be manacled or bound hand and foot before they started beating me.

I spoke to him again. 'Your silence is the silence of a coward, Mana, not the words of a major. I will come. But only when I have the guarantees through Tiki that you will honour your pledge and let the girls go free.'

'Willingly,' he snapped. 'I no want the girls. I want you. I speak this time tomorrow.'

There was nothing I could do now, except go to the island. All through the night we argued, discussed suggestions, made emergency plans, all to no avail. It was Tiki who made the final arrangements, talking on the sked to Mana.

Jim Wilson would take out the launch at nine o'clock in the evening, when the moon was full. He would carry Tiki, Tiare and me. At approximately the same time, Mana and a soldier would take the two girls out into the lagoon in the large and powerful police launch which the Japs were using.

I had wondered – and even discussed – the possibility with the others, of waiting until the final moment of exchange and with hidden guns shooting Mana and the Japanese soldier. If we could do that, the problem would be solved. But it was too easy – simple enough for Mana to have thought about it. So he had arranged that, when the two boats met in mid-lagoon, Mana would guard the girls while his assistant would jump on Jim's launch and frisk us for hidden firearms. We wouldn't have any, of course, but to make sure, Mana would remain in his police launch with the girls – and a grenade in his hand. Any attempt to shoot him or overpower the other Japanese would cause the grenade to explode, blowing up the boat and killing the girls. When the guard was assured that we were not armed, then the exchange would take place.

'We will make the exchange tomorrow night,' said Tiki.

With dreadful irony, it was a perfect tropical night. The full moon hung low in a sky that graduated from deepest blue on the horizon to a pale azure, twinkling with stars, reminding me of the dress Aleena had worn at the dinner dance a few short weeks back – yet it seemed aeons ago.

The palms fringing the lagoon trembled in the breeze, against the background of the sleeping volcano on High Island behind them. While I summoned what gallantry I could to take Tiare's elbow in my cupped hand as we stepped from the wharf into the launch, I surprised myself by thinking how utterly unheroic and mundane the whole drama seemed to be. I suppose my mind was anaesthetised by the travesty of heroism which the situation presented: to save the life of the girl I loved I had to hand myself over to a maniac.

What a bitter waste of love it was! In a world filled with the hatreds of war, the gods couldn't allow even such a tiny romance to go unsullied.

In the dreamy silence, broken only by the sound of waves lapping against the boat, I was conscious of the presence of Tiare and Tiki. She was a princess; he was a priest; neither would give way to emotion. It made the silence all the more unbearable. Jim Wilson was quiet too. As he cast off, the engine started to putter, and we were on our way.

It is pointless to try to describe my feelings. In retrospect I see that I ought to have felt all the agonies of a condemned man. It was true that no threat had been made to kill me; but for what other reason could Mana have worked out his evil design of the exchange? No doubt torture and humiliation first to satisfy his crazy desire for vengeance, but my death would undoubtedly be the end-product. As I recall, though, the numbness of my mind had simply robbed me of any feeling at all except for Aleena's safety.

The launch chugged on. I was aware of Tiare suddenly shivering as she sat beside me – though certainly not with cold, for the night was balmy. She had heard, a second or two before I did, the sound of the other boat approaching, and it was the tension of menace that made her shiver. Nothing was said, but I rested a hand on her shoulder. Tiki sighed or mumbled something, I wasn't sure which. Perhaps an invocation to the gods. Not that it would do much good at this stage, I thought. The gods were not on our side.

Then across the moon-dappled ocean the enemy boat hove into view, a faint shadow increasing in size and density until it became a dark and ominous hulk. From the bow came a sudden harsh call, 'Stop engine!' and Jim Wilson responded immediately by turning off the ignition. We all of us knew only too well that any attempt at trickery would simply have resulted in a hand-grenade blowing us all sky high.

As the two craft drew together I could see how much bigger the police launch was than our own. It had a cabin superstructure and seating for perhaps a dozen around the low rails that enclosed the deck, which was six or seven feet above the level of our own.

The same harsh voice cried, in a guttural accent, 'Haul in and make fast!' and suddenly a coil of rope landed at Jim's feet. He hauled on it until the slight bumping of our sandbag buffers told us we were alongside; then he twisted the rope round the cleat at our prow. I could make out the shape of a small Jap in field fatigue uniform leaning over the rail above us. Behind him loomed the great bulk of Mana.

'You will all raise your hands and keep them raised while my man inspects you and your craft. I can assure you that I have you covered with a sub-machine-gun and a grenade.'

A short, lightweight metal ladder was thrust over until its

481

foot was in our boat and its top end fixed to the railings of the launch. The soldier climbed down. His 'inspection' took only a few minutes – there was hardly room in Jim's boat to conceal anything anyway. I saw Tiare shudder as he passed his hands over her body, but she kept silent; Tiki stood rigid, as if turned to stone.

'All right,' the man called to Mana, adding in broken English, 'You can now be making the exchange.' His hand moved to his belt and the moonlight suddenly flickered on the gleaming blade of a knife. With exaggerated courtesy he bowed and said, 'You the doctor? Up the ladder.'

I turned to Tiare, a token of farewell, sympathy; but suddenly the man's knife was at my throat. 'No contact!' he hissed. 'Turn! The ladder! Up!' As I put a foot on each rung I could feel the point of his knife just touching my ankles.

On the deck of the launch Mana barked an order and the cabin door was opened by the crewman. A cloud passed across the moon at that moment, but when the light renewed itself I saw Aleena and Kinawa standing motionless in the doorway. Aleena made to run towards me and I heard her gasp, 'Kit! Oh Kit – '

But this was a moment that Mana could savour with racking cruelty. He moved from the rail and placed his great bulk between me and the girls, his sub-machine-gun pointing directly at my ribs.

'Turn about!' he snarled.

It was frustration more than fear that I felt – knowing that if I defied him he would have no compunction about whipping round and shooting even his step-daughter. My back prickled with the cold sweat of the defiance I had to control.

'You bastard!' I said. 'You dirty, cowardly bastard.' I put all the venom I could muster into the words.

I felt that behind me he was grinning. Then I heard him order the girls to the rails; and I had no doubt that the crewman still held the knife as he politely urged them forward.

'More speed,' cried Mana. 'No time for wasting. We

have to transport the eminent Doctor Masters to his place of – ' He left the implication clear.

I could hear Aleena sobbing, and Mana's laughter, almost a maniacal giggle. I could hear the sound of the ladder grating against Jim's boat as first Aleena and then Kinawa must have descended. I heard Tiare cry, 'Darling. Thank God!' and then, 'Okay! Kit!' I clenched my hands as tight as I could, and I could feel blood on my lips where my teeth had bitten through. From the other boat came the continued sound of Aleena's sobbing. Kinawa was crying too and it crossed my mind how, only a few short weeks ago, I had told her father in San Francisco that she was well and happy.

Mana barked orders and suddenly the poignant silence was shattered by the noise of the engines. I couldn't be sure, but I fancied I heard two words from Aleena: 'Goodnight, Sweetheart'.

> *Goodnight, Sweetheart, all my prayers are for you;*
> *Goodnight, Sweetheart, I'll be watching o'er you –*

Noel Coward's line in *Private Lives* about the potency of cheap music also crossed my mind. It amazes me, the attention one could give to a triviality at such a moment.

The boat was turning now, the spume in its wake whitening the moonlit ocean, and we were sailing towards Penal and into whatever unknown hell was prepared for me.

34

From the moment I heard Aleena's voice fade across the still, dark water, I began my own private hell on earth; from the very first moment, as the police launch turned round and set off for Penal, and I, with a groan of despair, stumbled across to the long bench-type seat and flopped on to it, my head between my hands.

Without warning, a terrific swipe from Mana hit my face and nose, hidden by my hands, so that I had no warning. It was like a horse who is thrashed across the head but doesn't know it until the pain strikes. I was knocked off my seat and as I lay in agony, Mana's voice, with a silkiness disguising hatred, said, 'How dare you?'

I looked up, still crouching, blood on my face, and managed to mumble, 'What? What have I done?'

'How dare you sit without permission?'

'Sorry!' I was retching with pain.

'Get up!'

It wasn't easy. The big wooden launch was rocking slightly, and my sense of balance had deserted me, so that when I tried to stand I fell over again. This time it was a kick in the ribs that made me howl. Finally, clutching the gunwale for support, I did manage to stand.

'Let us be clear.' Mana's voice was no longer silky, but openly menacing. 'You are a prisoner of the Japanese Imperial Army. You will be treated as a prisoner of war as an assurance against attack by the British. You are no use to us dead. So you will stay alive – just, and for the time being.' Then he warned me, 'But you will obey orders – or you will be punished. And if you *are* punished, you may wish that you were dead and not alive.'

The sinister warning drummed into my ears, already tingling with pain as we reached the shore and the launch was moored. Half a dozen men in Japanese fatigue uniform grabbed me, manacled me, and all but frog-marched me up on the steep narrow path leading to the plateau on the top of the rocky island. It was a miserable place, with its one narrow street, one lamp-post, and a few stunted trees on a tiny, ragged, ill-kempt plot of garden that passed for a village square. Around it were the bungalows of the wardens, and the long low building, dirty white with a red-painted corrugated-iron roof, that served as the jail.

Once there, I was pushed through a door into a cell which

was locked behind me. The room had bars, but no windows, all facing the same way. I soon discovered that if the sun beat down – or the rain pelted down – I could only shelter from the elements by crouching in the far corner of the room. There was a tap of rain water, a hole in one corner which looked like an old-fashioned Middle Eastern toilet. There was a bucket which I could slowly fill up to use as a flush – or to swill my face or bathe cuts and bruises and wipe away drying blood after my almost daily beatings.

Knowing that I must be prepared for a long stay – if I remained alive, that is – I had at the last minute packed a couple of spare shirts, vests and pants, an extra pair of thin drill trousers, a razor and some soap.

I never saw them. Never. I was not allowed to change my clothing, I was never given a bar of soap. I could not shave. All I could do was to have a soapless body wash with the bucket of water and then wait for a hot, sunny day, rinse my shirt and underclothes hurriedly. But if I faced a so-called 'military inspection' and I was found to be improperly dressed because I wore no shirt, I was beaten. There was no way I could win, for if I did not have the time secretly to wash my shirt, I was beaten for 'dirty habits'.

The first time I was discovered washing my clothes and my shirt was drying, a Japanese soldier cried out to Mana.

'You are using your shirt to signal to the enemy!' he said.

I protested. In vain. I was dragged out, tied loosely by the wrists to the lamp-post on the plateau and flogged. Mana himself administered the punishment. When my wrists had been tied round the post, guards forced me to slide my wrists down until I was first on my knees, then flat on my stomach on the ground. A couple of guards sat on my ankles and feet, so that I was spread-eagled.

There was no point in struggling; I did not dare to, for I quickly learned that any 'disobedience' earned more kicks and bruises, including one of the favourites in which, weak as I was, three or four men stood me against a wall while the other punched me.

When, with my ankles powerless, I was spread-eagled,

face downwards, I was flogged. Mana had made a long bamboo whipping cane, and he used it brutally. Again, because I could not see, I was reminded of an ill-treated horse which could not tell where or when the whip would fall. Each time I was flogged my back was a mass of weals and cuts. The first time I fainted, and the next thing I knew was the shock of a bucket of water thrown on my face to revive me as I was held up, my legs sagging. Then I screamed again as two buckets of water – one after the other – were sloshed across my back. For it was sea water and the salt bit into my cuts with excruciating agony.

To myself, when I could catch my breath, I said, 'Bloody swine!' But I didn't dare say a word to Mana, for I realised very quickly that he had two objectives: the first was to keep me alive as a hostage against enemy attack; the second was to make me suffer physical and mental torture to the point where I would almost be dead. Almost, but not quite.

Every so-called infringement of the rules that followed was an excuse for a beating. Only once did I experience a moment of unexpected kindness. After one beating, I was lying on my stomach on my hard, flat bed when a Japanese who had lived in Koraloona and had been interned, sidled up to the bars of my cage – as I called it – and hissed. Dimly I recognised him. He was married to a local Koraloona girl and I had treated his wife successfully for a broken arm, as usual for no fee.

He said nothing, he was too afraid to make any noise except for that one discreet hiss, but he threw a tiny white packet into my cell. I scrambled on to the floor to pick it up. It was a tablet of aspirin.

The food was almost inedible and in a month I must have lost at least twenty or thirty pounds. A bowl of cooked rice or taro was the basic daily ration with occasionally a piece of old fish, the scraps usually thrown away. At times Mana inflicted a special psychological torture which he thought was amusing. He would order half a dozen soldiers to set up a table opposite my cage, and then they would all participate in a huge feast – lobsters and other fish which abounded in the waters surrounding the island. They would sip drinks while I was half starved and thirsty, forced to stand in their presence and watch during the entire meal. If I couldn't take it, even if I fainted and slipped, I was punished.

One infringement might result in a 'cell beating'; another in the loss of a day's food; perhaps a flogging; or, worst of all, was the denial of drinking water, for I could tell that I was beginning to suffer dehydration. One part of my fuddled brain didn't mind, for I could see dehydration as a pathway to death, but a tiny part of me wanted to take the path to life.

'If I don't have water soon, I shall die,' I croaked one morning to Mana. 'The first time you tried to kill me you failed. This time, if I do die you will have failed again.'

He knew as well as I did that, if I died, Penal would be bombed until every man on the island was killed. For once, I could sense that he was worried. That day I got as much water as I wanted and a tin of corned beef as an extra ration. I wolfed it in one go and was promptly sick into the hole in the corner of my room, so he gave me another tin for the following day.

It was only temporary respite. In a few days I did feel better, but on that afternoon a plane flew over, as planes often did. I could hardly see it, the plane was so high, but because he caught me drying my shirt while the aircraft was overhead, he accused me of signalling, and dragged me to the lamp-post where I was flogged again.

This was the third flogging and all the hope which the 'gift' of the corned beef had given me, and the hope that Mana might after all be human, vanished in the agony of pain inflicted on my back and in the additional spasms as my torn and bleeding back was doused in salt water.

That was one of the nights when he decided he would enjoy a little mental torture of a different kind. Not for the first time I was half dragged to the Penal radio shack to listen to the sked with Koraloona, so near, so far away.

Once there I was forced to listen to the pleas of Colonel Fawcett, even to abject begging from Tiare, to spare my life.

'But his life is not in danger,' Mana said smoothly to her. 'Did Aleena complain when she was on Penal? Of course she didn't. Then why should Doctor Masters? He is a hostage, nothing more.'

'Let me speak to him,' Tiare begged Mana.

'He is resting, sleeping,' Mana lied; but as he did so, and knowing of the fearful consequences, I summoned up from some hidden reserves enough energy to scream so that everyone listening on the Koraloona sked could hear, 'I'm being tortured. I'm dying.'

A Japanese soldier hurled me to the floor and started to beat me.

'You will pay for this,' shouted an enraged Mana. 'I will wait for you to recover then you will be flogged again.'

'I heard you,' cried Tiare. 'Everyone did.'

This time Mana turned on his heel and took a vicious swipe at one of the Japanese soldiers.

'You fool!' he cried, for in the panic of my sudden scream, the man had forgotten to turn off the mike. With a roar of anger Mana clicked off the sked, and I was dragged bleeding to my cell.

A month of hell passed. I was not only ready for death, I wanted it desperately, hoping with all my heart and body for a merciful end to starvation and beatings.

And then the promise of death came from an unexpected quarter, and with a surge of hope I welcomed it. As so often when the sked with Koraloona was operating, I was dragged – if Mana felt in need of a little 'enjoyment' – to listen to the pleadings from Koraloona, including any from Aleena herself. Having once shouted, and paid dearly for it with a beating, I was never given the right to answer.

Sometimes I could hardly take in the words; at others, when my brain was functioning better, the words came through crystal clear – and this time the news from

Koraloona was grim and unequivocal. I gave a silent whoop of joy. For I was going to die – promised a merciful death by the British. And so were all the Japanese.

It was more than an eye for an eye, it was like a dozen pairs of eyes for mine, though I never knew the exact number. But dying would seal the fate of all the hated enemy. It was a cheap sacrifice on my part.

I learned my fate during the evening sked. I heard the voice of Holmes opening up the sked and when he said 'Over' Mana replied, 'What you want? Your heroic doctor is alive. We are keeping him alive. You want to speak to him? You cannot. Speak to me. He is here and will hear what you say.'

'If I cannot speak to him, it doesn't matter. So long as he can hear.' It was a different voice on the mike, that I realised; a new, quiet, resolute voice, and though I was in no state to know or care who it was, I did understand when he announced, 'This is Captain Osmond of the Royal Navy. Can you hear me, Doctor?'

'He can hear you,' cried Mana. 'Why you returning to Koraloona? I told you, don't come. If you attack us, doctor die.'

'He will die,' said the naval captain. 'We know that he has been ill-treated by you and your thugs.' Then he added words that burned. 'So we are going to bomb Penal with a massive land-mine that will kill you all.'

'You do this – your doctor he die.'

'We know. It may sound brutal, but we know that the doctor will welcome it, that it will be a merciful ending to the torture you have inflicted on him.'

'You are stupid. He is in good health.'

'You are a liar, Mana. And stupid. The doctor is not in good health. We know that you have had him flogged publicly as a punishment.'

'It is you who lie,' shouted Mana.

'We have seen it.'

'How?'

'We have taken photographs.'

'I saw no photo man,' cried Mana.

'Of course you didn't, you stupid man. We photographed you from more than a mile high. Many times. And these aerial photos can be enlarged to show up every building, every figure.'

I listened flabbergasted, heart pounding. They actually *knew* of the floggings. The science of modern warfare was a mystery to me, but this naval officer was telling the truth. I *had* been flogged in public. No man could invent such a scene. And as for me – I was now so ill that I would be delighted to sacrifice my life.

For the second time in that month I interrupted. As loud as I could, I shouted, 'Bomb the island, Captain! Bomb it! Never mind me, I'm dying!'

A Japanese soldier knocked me down with the butt of a rifle and I screamed with the sudden extra pain. It must have been heard in the Koraloona radio shack, because in another voice, a man said, 'I am Professor Skinner. We heard and recorded that scream. And we know the reasons behind it. It shall happen, Doctor Masters. I promise that we shall drop the land-mine.'

'You wouldn't dare!' snarled Mana, asking, 'When?'

There was a gasp in the room as the calm voice of the Prof announced, 'Tomorrow morning. Listen! At six am precisely we shall fly over Penal and drop a land-mine. It will have a time switch triggered to go off at eight o'clock – two hours later. That will give you tonight to say your final prayers. There is no escape for you now, Mana, only death.'

There was a pause, while the news sank into the minds of Mana and those of his men and the internees who spoke English.

'This is no bluff,' said the quiet voice of the Prof, 'because we know that you, Doctor Masters, will welcome the chance to end this cruelty. But remember the words that I asked Doctor Reid to tell you.'

'What words are these?' Mana cried to me.

'I don't know,' I mumbled. I didn't. I didn't really know

what he was talking about. What was it that Alec Reid had told me? – something about the fact that certain death was hardest to bear when no one could tell you that there was still hope.

'Listen,' cried Mana. 'I want to know – '

But this time it was Koraloona who switched off after the naval captain had announced, 'Better look up to the skies tomorrow morning. The land-mine will drop on the island and then nothing can save anyone. Doctor, we know you wish it. We shall pray for you.'

There was a click, and though my shoulder was in torment from the sudden blow of the rifle butt, I almost laughed.

Mana was in a rage. Some of the Japanese soldiers were being fallen in, and commands were given in sharp, guttural tones. The internees who spoke English were panicking as they spread the news. Yet Mana was in command, no doubt about that, as he shouted orders. I didn't know what he was saying but I heard the crackle of the short-wave radio tuning in and when Mana spoke in Japanese, it didn't take much imagination to realise that he was talking to the mother ship, presumably the submarine that had been in regular radio contact. But, I pondered, surely the submarine could never pass through the opening of the reef. I knew that at the outbreak of war the entrance through the reef had been netted, in the same way that years ago the Dardanelles had been netted.

The minutes ticked by, and I prepared to face my last night on earth. I was shuffled to my cell and lay down. But sleep eluded me. I was not afraid to die, I really *wanted* to die, but you cannot spend your last night of life all alone with only thoughts and happy memories to sustain you. I would have liked to pray – for Aleena, for Clare. But I couldn't. There was no way I could get on to my bruised and battered knees and ever get up again without help. And there was no help.

Half way through that long night I began to be afraid –

not for myself, but that I might die and the Japs might live. What about the launch? Why shouldn't they make good their escape? I tried to put the thoughts behind me, knowing that the British *must* have thought of such an eventuality, but I couldn't dismiss it.

Not until a quarter to six in the morning did Mana come to me and sneer, 'So you are going to die, Doctor! And you will never marry your Aleena. This is the fate I intended for you all along. To die!'

'And you?' I tried to produce a show of boldness, but tortured by thoughts all night, I was only anxious that the Japanese wouldn't escape. 'You, too, will die when the land-mine explodes at eight o'clock. You can't stop it, Mana. You daren't tinker with the mechanism. If you touch one wrong fuse wire it will blow up.'

I did not know much about land-mines, though a lot had been written about them in the few newspapers we had seen – in some detail, because the fact that the Germans used them first meant that censorship was lax, especially after one had been defused when it fell near Charing Cross station. And I knew that it had a strong outer casing eight feet long and two feet in diameter and strong enough not to release the clockwork mechanism inside when it landed. That was why it was dropped by parachute. And I did know that the timing device consisted of a clockwork mechanism that could be timed to release a hammer and create a spark – like a cigarette lighter – that would set off the explosion of the TNT in the inside of the bomb.

'You British are fools.' Mana actually laughed. 'That naval captain! Does he think we are stupid?'

'Yes,' I cried before he hit me across the face.

'It is you who are foolish. Everything is ready now. We shall wait a few more moments to see if the land-mine *does* land on the island. We shall listen to its mechanism. If it is really ticking, you fool, you will die – but you will die alone, for we shall escape in the police launch. Most of the men are already on board, prepared.'

My heart sank at his boasting, for this was the prospect

492

that had haunted me during the night. But I cried, 'Our aircraft will attack you.'

'Penal is only a mile or so from the reef. The Japanese soldiers crossed it to get in and rescue us. They will guide us to it, and – because we are Japanese too, our mother ship is on the other side of the reef. No, it is you who will die – and alone. When the bomb lands, you will be chained to the lamp-post so that you can watch the time go by. You will die. We shall live – to help to lead Japan to victory.'

Again I was beset with despair. They *were* going to leave. Couldn't the British Navy have realised – especially after the visit to Tiki and the exchanges – that the Japs had the big police launch and that they could reach the reef in a matter of minutes? Even if the wooden launch broke up on the reef the men could scramble across. The RAF might attack the launch – or would they be afraid of being caught in the blast of the land-mine? And even if the RAF chased the launch, could they hit such a tiny target, a small boat bobbing about on a lagoon? What a travesty it would be if I died and they lived.

My thoughts were confused, for I was plunged into a miserable state, half exhausted, bleeding from what seemed like a broken nose where I had been hit. I didn't care any more. All I wanted was to die, and now, at long last, after a month of misery and torture, not even Mana could stop me dying.

'Listen!' I cried suddenly, with a renewed strength. 'A plane!' It was five minutes to six.

I could hear the steady drone clearly. So could Mana. He barked out an order, and the last of the men, a Japanese, came and helped Mana to tie me to the lamp-post on the square, with my wrists behind my back. Then Mana shouted an order and the man ran off, presumably to join the others on the launch.

In a few seconds, or so it seemed, the plane came overhead flying fairly low. I was too exhausted, with blurred vision, to see what kind of plane it was, or to care. It flew across the island, and I had the feeling that it was testing, to make sure of allowing for the wind. What an ironic joke it would be if it missed the target and hit the sea!

It didn't. The plane flew back, and I caught myself thinking, If only the rest of the Japs were scared and decided to bolt for it in the launch, Mana would die too, for he would be trapped on the island. He must have read my thoughts, for with a grotesque parody of a grin, he dangled a key on a chain and said, 'I am the only one who can start the launch.'

Then it happened. As we looked upwards, with the plane roaring across the island, what appeared to be a black shapeless mass hurtled out of the bomb doors. As Mana gasped in disbelief, the black package, or cylinder, burst into what looked like a flower, causing the canister of metal to stop, motionless in the air, for a moment before it started to float gently downwards.

'It's true!' I cried. 'It's arrived.' For at that moment it hit the centre of Penal Island, half burying itself into a pit of soil in the gardens the other side of the square, spraying both of us with earth and loose stones. Even Mana was hit.

'Listen!' I cried, delighted that death was now so close. 'I can hear the ticking. Can you?'

I could, quite clearly.

'You had better be quick, Mana,' I jeered. Yet at the back of my words, uttered out of bravado, was the silent prayer that the Navy would – *must* – realise that the Japs had a boat.

'You hope they will shoot us down,' said Mana. 'They will have no time. I leave now. I will be on the reef in a matter of minutes. I should shoot you like a dog, but I would rather let you suffer for two hours. There is no escape for you now, Doctor, and we shall not meet again. You may like to know,' he extinguished any lingering hope, 'that our submarine will not only look after us on the other side of the reef, but that an aircraft carrier is waiting just across the horizon and planes are on their way to protect us if we should be attacked from the air.'

So that was that. They would escape. I knew that our old aircraft were no match for the Japanese Zeros, and in fact as I waited I could see the black specks of the Japanese planes come in.

Mana made only one last gesture. As he prepared to run down to the launch, with the bomb ticking remorselessly, and with my hands and arms tied round the lamp-post, he hesitated for one second. Then he spat at me, full force in the face.

Without another word he ran off down the hill. In three minutes I heard the sound of the launch's motors start, then the sound as it moved away from the shore of Penal Island.

Trussed up like a chicken, I waited to die.

35

Does it sound mad, impossible, that, as I waited for certain death, I half fainted away? Not from fear, perhaps more from suspense; possibly I didn't really faint, I was so exhausted that with my wrists tied securely but loosely behind my back, I slowly worked them down the post until I was in a sitting position – uncomfortable because of cramp in my shoulder blades and feeling dirty in spirit as well as in body because of the spittle which at first I could not wipe from my face since my arms were powerless. Eventually I did manage to twist my head and wipe some of it off on the cast-iron lamp-post.

It was then that I must have slid off into a kind of semi-conscious stupor of which I can remember only little. I was aware of the inexorable ticking a few yards from me, from the land-mine half buried in the loose earth and covered with the shroud of the parachute, ticking away the last minutes of my life, and I was so far gone that my only real wish was to speed up the process of being blown to smithereens so that I could get it over with more quickly.

This was my predominant frame of mind in the morning sunlight, the world silent except for the sinister ticking. In the distance, towards the edge of the lagoon where I could see the reef, was the boat in which the vile Mana was escaping and so winning the fight against me. One of the things about Penal was that by twisting myself round the post, I could see in almost every direction and, as the reef was not far off, and the morning clear and cloudless, it seemed to foreshorten everything. Of course I could not see the figures on the big launch, but I could make out the shape of the boat, see its wake, as it approached the foam of the reef. Then, barely noticeable at first, I saw something else – a low grey shape like a huge cigar emerge from the sea on the other side of the reef. If only I had been free! If only I could have flown Nellie and crashed her at the cost of my life on the grey hulk that had sunk the *Mantela* and sent dear old Bill Robins to a watery grave. Then something else appeared – three specks in the sky became larger, and they, I knew, must be Zero fighters from the unseen carrier. They had been sent to watch over and prevent air attack during the transfer of the Japanese to the mother ship.

All this tableau was played out in an eerie silence broken only by the sound of the clock – until without warning the silence erupted into the most devastating noise. Without any warning there was a mighty explosion. Sheets of flame soared into the sky. Huge pieces of material were hurled into the air. I was so befuddled that at first I thought the land-mine had blown up prematurely and that by some miracle I had survived – manifestly impossible, as one glance showed me that the mine was still there.

Then I realised – or thought I realised – that I had dozed off and was just awakening from a nightmare; that in my half sleep I was living the future. But I *wasn't* dreaming. I had wakened from semi-consciousness, and as I looked across the plateau and out across the lagoon, the flames were still burning into the sky – to my muddled mind as though the volcano had erupted.

With a kind of inward gasp I realised that the explosion

496

hadn't come from the island. It had come from the sea. From the launch. Looking across the blue water and downwards, I realised for the first time, as I took a grip on myself, that the police launch which I had last seen near the reef – was it only ten minutes since it had cast off from the island? – had vanished. Not disappeared to safety, but *vanished*. It had blown up, and with such ferocity that it had disintegrated, hurling the remnants of the boat into space together with everyone on board.

I was alone – I was about to die – but I gave a cry of excitement. The explosion had died down. A few flames eerily licked the sea on an oil slick, black against the sunlit blue, little islands of oil bursting into sudden jagged spurts of flame. And for me, only one thing mattered. Mana must be dead. I wasn't going to waste my life in vain.

High above me I could see the three Japanese fighter planes pirouetting in the sky. The grey hulk of the submarine slid below the waves of the open sea. Two of the planes zoomed lower over the island for half an hour, skimming the sea, presumably looking for survivors – but there couldn't be any after that explosion. I knew that the flying time of fighter planes is limited and, sure enough, after what seemed like a search over the debris littering the waters, they flew higher and then in a 'V' formation set off for the horizon, presumably to land on their carrier. There were no British planes in the sky.

I was alone then, and I looked at my watch. It was ten minutes past seven. Nearly an hour to wait for death and now again all was silence, broken only by the ticking of the bomb. Even so, I felt an elation never before experienced – because my real agony had been that I would die and Mana would escape. That had been the worst torture inflicted on me during my month on Penal. But now he and all his men were dead.

More than half an hour later – a lifetime in lonely thought – I heard the vague noise of a ship's engines. Gasping with excitement, I twisted round the lamp-post, using my legs for leverage, bumping my bottom on the rough ground as I tried to see where the sound came from. And there, below me, my heart leaping, I could see a ship. My heart was thumping as though it would burst out of my rib cage. The shape grew closer – as my watch told me it was quarter to eight. Fifteen minutes to go.

I *thought* I recognised the kind of boat – a naval vessel, a fast motor-torpedo boat, like the German E-boats I had read about. It must have been the Allied equivalent, but, the time! They could never make it! Four minutes had gone already. Only eleven minutes of life left. There was no way they could reach the island, climb the steep gradient and get me off before I was blown up. Not a hope.

Worse happened now. Unaccountably, when every second counted, the engines were dead, and I could see that the boat was rocking gently – immobile. Engine failure? I did not realise until much later that the captain had ordered the engines to be cut off because he needed silence. Without warning, the stillness of the air – exaggerated now because there was no engine sound, nothing but the ticking – was cracked by a booming voice.

It had an unearthly sound, for the usual ship's megaphone had obviously been magnified by some electrical device so that the brief message seemed to bounce off the sky itself, from the astral plane, and drop on the island.

It was five minutes to eight. Five minutes to live until the disembodied voice boomed out six words: 'Don't worry! It's a dummy bomb!'

I felt the whole world swirl around me. Or was I – though still tied as a captive – swirling round the world? I felt as though I would faint as the ghost-like voice repeated the message twice more, and then, having been told that I would live, but still refusing to believe it, I looked at my watch again. Exactly eight o'clock, and the only noise on the island had ceased. The clockwork device had stopped. And I was alive!

The noise was broken by the megaphone voice again, while I struggled not to lose consciousness. The voice cried, 'Sorry we're late. We had to wait for the Jap fighters to clear off. It's a dummy bomb. We're coming ashore to get you. Doctor Reid is with us.'

I think I heard the last words, or did I imagine them and realise only later that Alec was there? I did hear the roar as the ship's engines restarted, and then I remember no more. I had been able to survive the torture and the taunts, the hunger, the brutality with only an occasional fit of fainting after a particularly bad beating. But the sudden promise of life, after I had been prepared to welcome death, was too much. I lay slumped on the ground, senses gone. It was as though I *had* died in the explosion – except that I was brought back to life by the vague sound of a babble of voices. Unseen hands slashed through the cords that bound my wrists. Unseen arms started to lift me, and I remember moaning as someone who could not see my back because I was wearing my shirt, perhaps handled me a little roughly, for I then heard – and this time more clearly – the Scottish burr of Alec Reid, and I could sense the suppressed fury in his voice as he saw my back, my matted beard, the bruises everywhere, and he said, 'The yellow bastards! He's lucky to be alive. By God, I'd kill the lot of 'em if I could.'

I caught a glimpse through blurred eyes and cried 'Alec!' He cleaned a patch of skin on one unwashed arm with a swab of cotton wool and spirit, and then I hardly felt the prick of the needle, barely heard Alec tell someone, 'He'll be out for a couple of hours. That'll give us time to get him home and put him to bed.'

I was dreaming, wallowing in the depths of a luxurious mattress that fitted the curves of my aching back. My chest was covered with silken sheets, my head rested on fluffy down pillows and Aleena was gently bathing the bruises and cuts on my face when suddenly the dream changed into a terrifying nightmare as Mana burst into the room and made to strike Aleena and then, as she fell, he ripped away the silk sheets and carried me back to my cell, where I crouched whimpering like an animal cornered, waiting to be beaten.

I screamed and tried to scramble out of the cell before he hit me. But the effort of screaming drained away all my strength and I slumped back, powerless. Mana must have taken pity on me for I was back again in the silk sheets, crying.

'Hush, beloved,' Aleena whispered as she leaned over, brushed my lips with her fingers and wiped away the tears. 'No one is going to hurt you, ever again. It was a bad dream. It's all over now.'

She was whispering love words very gently, and I could not tell whether the dream had taken a new twist for I was so tired that, though I was trying with all my reserves of strength, I could not open the heavy lids of my eyes to see whether the gentle touch of lips was real or imagined.

I moved an arm. I carefully turned my head. No one hit me. No one threatened me. Instead, a delicate hand pushed a straw between my bruised lips and a gentle voice whispered, 'Try to suck in.'

I did. A trickle of liquid beauty wet my tongue, a sip of never-to-be-forgotten fresh cold lime juice and water. I managed to force open my eyes and again tears of weakness filled them.

'Hush, my darling Kit.' Aleena leaned over me, stroked my face, my beard, took the straw out of my mouth and put down the glass and I stretched out my arms to touch her, to hold her, to see if she really existed, to make sure the dream came true.

'Yes, my beautiful love,' she said softly. 'We will never be parted again. We are together. Hell is behind us.'

But it wasn't. Afraid to wake up, I tried to talk, my hands stroking her beautiful black hair, and then, just as I thought reality had arrived, I screamed again.

'Hush my darling.' She soothed my brow.

'The land-mine!' I cried in panic. 'I can hear it ticking. Get out while you can. Never mind me. Run – run!' I was bathed in sweat as I screamed again, 'The land-mine! Can't you hear it?' I could – dream or no dream.

'There.' She stroked me gently again, and took away the

clock ticking on a bedside table and with one movement stopped it from working. 'There!' she repeated, her smile wonderful and relaxing. 'It's stopped – and it hasn't gone off.'

'Aleena,' I cried, 'are you all right?'

'I am.' She held one of my hands in hers and kissed them. 'It's you that we are all worried about. Rest, my sweet. Doc Reid is coming round any moment to see you, and if you are strong enough, some of our other friends.'

'Is Alec still alive?' I don't know why I asked such a silly question.

'Of course.' She laughed for the first time. 'We're all alive, waiting to see you again.'

'All of us? You mean that Mana is alive?'

'No. Not him.' Her mouth hardened. 'He is dead. But all the others – we're all ready to look after you, to fatten you up, to get rid of the horrors you've passed through.'

'And then have a White Lady?' My mind unaccountably focused on the secret message she had given me.

'When you're fit – as many as you like.'

'But where are we? Why are we here?'

'You're in the biggest bed in Koraloona. Paula Reece's. Oh, my beloved, if only I could share it with you!'

'But why Paula?' A thousand questions demanded answers. 'What about my own bungalow?'

'You're suffering from delayed shock. That's why I've been here alone with you for hours. Paula suggested that you needed to have the most comfortable place to sleep. Alec Reid agreed. I'm staying in the next room so that if you have a bad dream I can come and comfort you.'

Later, she and Miss Sowerby changed the dressings on my back, then Paula came in to see how I was. She had asked Truscott to get a special frame that supported my shoulders and kept my back clear of pressure.

'Thanks for the bed.' I tried to laugh.

'So long as you get well.' She was more serious than I had ever seen her.

501

'Don't tire yourself,' warned Miss Sowerby with the detached clinical manner that nurses manage to acquire.

'Yes, nurse,' I said in a properly meek tone.

Alec Reid came in mopping his forehead, Purvis and Colonel Fawcett a little later, followed by Tiare.

'And how's the patient?' Alec said breezily, slackening the MCC tie a bit as he sank into a chair.

'You say all the proper things,' I said gratefully. 'I didn't hear any kind words when Mana tried to do me in.'

Purvis said with a twisted smile, 'And now *he's* done in – and good riddance too.'

'Jason,' Miss Sowerby said sternly, 'I will not have you saying these things. However villainous, he was one of God's creatures.' Clearly Purvis wasn't going to have it all his own way with Lorna Sowerby.

'Quite right, m'dear,' the colonel said briskly, 'but not one of the better quality ones, eh? I must say I echo Jason's sentiments somewhat.'

After only a few minutes of small talk I was suddenly tired. Vaguely I heard Alec say, 'Leave him be, let him sleep.'

Aleena came in with a cup of that most welcoming of drinks – tea. She held the cup to my lips – and as I drank it, I started to fall asleep. As simple as that. But this time it was different. The misery of dreams had gone. I slept for five glorious hours, with (as I learned later) Aleena holding my hand all the time. And when I awoke, I not only felt refreshed – but hungry.

'I could eat everything in the house!' I tried to laugh.

'Not too much for the first time,' she said. 'But here's some prawns in coconut milk. I know you love them. And Alec says you can have one bottle of beer.'

The following day, I felt much better and had a breakfast of home-cured bacon – or what passed for bacon from the piglets on Koraloona – and eggs and coffee. Around eleven most of our friends gathered round to fill in the missing parts of the jigsaw.

502

The most fascinating thing, of course, was who had worked out such an incredible plan to get me off the island, and how it had been done.

'It was Professor Skinner's brainchild,' said Colonel Fawcett. 'The Prof, he likes to be called. Pretty smart feller.'

'But they wouldn't go to all that trouble while I was still alive.'

'They believed that you wouldna be alive for much longer,' interrupted Alec who had come along. ' 'Specially when they discovered how badly you'd been flogged, and the fact that we knew you were being tortured.'

'But how? You mentioned that in your broadcast to Mana. How on earth did you know they were *flogging* me?'

'Simple, my dear Kit,' explained the colonel. 'You evidently don't know about the advances in aerial photography since the formation of the PRU – the Photographic Reconnaissance Unit – of the RAF. Two fellers called Cotton and Longbottom developed cameras that can photograph clearly from thirty thousand feet; and another chap named Spender linked the results with that toy which the Victorians used to love – the stereoscope. Put the pictures into a bit of optical machinery called a Multiplex Stereoplanigraph and you can see magnified images that reveal details even down to the buttons on a chap's uniform.'

Alec Reid took up the story.

'I flew to Sanders to examine the enlarged photos with the medics there. I argued to Ronnie Serpell that I knew more about your powers of resistance than anyone else and that ye would not last much longer. And I also wanted to put across to Ronnie that ye might *force* yourself to die, for then ye'd have *won* against Mana because we'd be able to bomb the hell out of Penal. So the boffins came up with the plan.'

'It was a magnificent bluff,' I said. 'Even Mana fell for it.'

'He *had* to,' explained the colonel. 'Even if the bugger had suspected a bluff, he was powerless. He didn't dare to tinker with the land-mine. He couldn't wait to see if it would go off. So he *had* to bolt for it – and we took care of that.'

I shifted a bit in bed. Though already healing, the weals were still painful. 'So?' I tracked back.

'While I was there,' said Alec, 'Ronnie Serpell held a consultation with the sappers and naval "dirty tricks" boys under the Prof. The sappers were willing to take the gelignite out of a land-mine and stuff it with sand instead; with a ticking time-clock in it, the Japs couldn't have known it was a dummy; it was easy enough to anticipate what they'd do next: escape in the launch and leave you on Penal – the very situation we were aiming for.'

'I still don't see how you could be sure the escaping Japs would be killed. It was very convenient that their boat blew up when it did with all hands lost.'

'Not at all,' said Colonel Fawcett. 'It needed a careful bit of timing, no more. The Prof had the very chap: a skin diver with an aqualung and frogs' feet. All we had to do was hang a limpet mine from his belt, take him out at night into the lagoon in Jim's boat, dump him over the side and let him swim to Penal. We knew exactly where the launch was tied up from our aerial photos. The frogman stuck the limpet to the launch below the waterline, wound up the time-clock to fire the fuse ten minutes after the ship's ignition was switched on, and swim back to Jim's boat.'

'But how could a man using an aqualung carry a mine? Isn't it heavy?'

The colonel shook his head. 'Remember I was a sapper! I know these things. It's circular, about the size of a frying pan and only a couple of inches deep. One compartment contains the clockwork mechanism that can be timed to create a spark. The other contains the gelignite – dynamite made into a jelly by mixing it with potassium nitrate and wood pulp. It becomes malleable and can be put into containers.'

'But doesn't it get wet? How did it stick to the launch?'

'My dear chap, easy. If you want to fix it below the

504

waterline, it's got to be waterproofed with Bostick, a water-insoluble plastic adhesive which was invented earlier in the war. Then you stick it to the launch with three suction pads – rather like those things you clear stopped-up sinks with.'

'But the real agony of the whole project,' said Tiare, 'was that there was no way we could let you know that the bomb contained no explosives without arousing Mana's suspicions.'

'That was the most terrible thing about the plan,' Aleena joined in. 'I was afraid you might die of a heart attack.'

'I nearly did!'

'Ye see,' Alec explained, 'that wee quiet man called the Prof tried his best to tip ye off by making ye recall his words that certain death wasn't always certain.'

'I remember that. It did puzzle me – but I was too far gone, I suppose, and I took it to mean something else – that a sudden death was better than a lingering one.'

'The Prof was going to add something else, I dinna know what, but ye'll remember that Mana became angry the moment the Prof tried to talk to ye. Mana obviously suspected something. And if he'd been really suspicious – well, ye wouldna be here today.'

'I only just am.' I managed a smile, I felt so happy. 'Even though I do have a damned sore back.'

'Now, I think it's time we all had a drink,' said Jason. 'And by the most remarkable coincidence I happen to have a bottle handy.'

'Jason,' Miss Sowerby said warningly.

'It's an occasion, Lorna. One that no amount of reproach can allow to pass uncelebrated. I know you don't drink Scotch, but I've no doubt that Paula could manage to dredge up a port and lemon for this special occasion.'

I had always enjoyed Scotch in moderation – a taste which Alec Reid had helped me to cultivate – but the awful thing is that now, when I started to drink, I had to spit it back into the glass.

'It tastes terrible!' I cried.

'Ye'll get over it,' promised Alec. 'Your metabolism has changed. But ye did have a beer yesterday? That went down all right?'

I nodded. 'I enjoyed it. Dehydration, I suppose?' I asked professionally.

Alec nodded. 'Have another beer then. Just one today. Ye've got to have a drink to celebrate.'

'My safe return?'

'That,' interrupted Tiare, 'but equally important, to toast your approaching wedding to Aleena.'

'When?' I lay back against the soft pillow. I was already getting tired again.

'As soon as you can manage it,' Tiare promised. 'When you're ready you'll both be married at the church here in Tala-Tala.'

36

It was so wonderful to be 'home' and free that I had not reckoned with the time it would take to recover from the starvation and ill-treatment. As so often happens in hot climates, some of the weals and cuts on my body were in danger of turning septic. I needed regular treatment. There was always the danger of a blood infection, and I could not contemplate marriage – or sex – until that danger was cured.

Not only was my back sore and uncomfortable, but my mouth had been badly knocked about, causing ulcers. I could move around, I could treat a few patients as long as I had plenty of rest, but unfortunately my recovery was hampered by the lack of rest because, for no particular reason, we had several cases of polio in the next few weeks. I treated them with my 'Sister Kenny treatment' of hot blankets and massage of withering muscles. It was in no sense an epidemic, but the treatment was very tiring.

So I was placed in the odd situation of spending much of my time helping to cure the children of polio while Alec Reid was spending much of his time helping to cure me.

Of course a dietary deficiency lowers the resistance to infection and I had lost a great deal of weight while on Penal; but more worrying was the tendency in tropical climates for flesh to resist the hardening process of the lymphatic tissue, and remain soft and crumbly as in athlete's foot, giving a welcome to various fungoid bacteria. It was because of that same tendency that we had taken so much care of Aleena after the removal of her melanoma.

With the abundance of fish on Koraloona it was easy enough to replace all the protein my body needed; and equally easy to build me up with massive doses of A and B vitamins – 'Ye'll be a tower of strength in nae time at all,' Alec Reid said cheerfully.

As the days passed, however, I could see that he was bothered about the slowness with which the lacerations on my back were healing. I was certainly regaining strength, but the repair of the tissues was not keeping pace. Alec got plentiful supplies of the new sulphonamide powder that every American soldier was issued with to apply to wounds to prevent sepsis, and a daily dusting with it certainly produced an improvement; but it was clear that it was going to be a long job.

Painfully clear, I might add. I thought wryly of the many times I had told patients to 'cheer up' when they cried out as their wounds were dressed. I was getting a dose of my own medicine now, and though I was now in friendly hands, I yelped when Alec took the dressings off and probed in the weals with swabs which he sent off to the pathology lab in Sanders for biopsy. It was months before he was able to give me reassuring news.

'The infection's clear, Laddie; and with those wee bacteria out of the way, the tissues'll start mending,' he promised.

Certainly the suppurating had stopped; and when I looked over my shoulder at my back, I could see, reflected in the bathroom mirror, that the flesh was taking on a more healthy colour. But the pace of healing was infuriatingly slow and interrupted by setbacks when little beads of pus showed that the antiseptic powder was having a tough fight. At length, however, Alec was able to run his fingers down what had once been livid weals and say with satisfaction, 'Clean as a whistle, Laddie.'

By that time 1944 had slid into 1945; and after a further painful delay in the single most important event of my life: marriage. The Germans were on the run now, the Japanese not beaten but retreating; and after the final blood test had been analysed in Sanders, showing I was free from infection, Doc Reid announced, 'I reckon ye're now in a fit state to undertake yer duties as a married man.'

Now that I really was fit and well, I wrote in guarded terms to my family letting them assume earlier letttters had been lost; for all I wanted was a quick and quiet wedding. It didn't take too long – the process of getting married – but quiet it wasn't. Everyone wanted to share in the climax to the love affair that had started soon after I landed on the island of Koraloona six whole years ago, during which time a leggy girl of thirteen had grown into a beautiful woman of nearly twenty.

The 'festivities' started after Jason Purvis insisted that I must have a wedding-eve 'stag-do' as he called it. 'Must preserve some of the ancient laws and customs, Kit. The further from home you are, the firmer you ought to cling to 'em.'

This was a side of Purvis I had not seen previously revealed – that of the lonely remittance man who had never quite severed the umbilical cord binding him to England. It applied to all of us in some degree -- Alec Reid never quite forgetting Wimbledon, myself linked with home by letters that became less heavily censored as the war reached its climax; Colonel Fawcett an ex-Sapper recalling his days at the Royal Military Academy, Woolwich. All of us had 'sold up', as it were, for the tranquil life of the South Seas, but we found our birthright ineradicable.

Oddly, as I learnt from Tiki, there was a Polynesian custom that was not far removed from the ribald wedding-eve clebrations that were supposed to mark the English bridegroom's last fling of freedom before getting married.

The Polynesian traditions varied, but basically the husband-to-be was entertained by the elders of his tribe in a ceremony that was supposed to eliminate the devils of misfortune from his spirit so that he could never pass them on to his bride.

'Just another excuse for a binge,' said Purvis, though there was to be neither revelry nor ribaldry for us. 'Just a quiet meal at Mollie Green's with a few bottles and a bit of man-talk to keep us going, plus a few good-luck toasts,' he added.

The evening, however, did include one poignant scene before dinner when we were having sundowners on Mollie Green's veranda. 'Mrs Jimbo' came lumbering down the street, apparently hiding something in the folds of her Mother Hubbard. As soon as she saw us she made a beeline for me.

'I glad to see you, Doctor; I go to your bungalow but you not there, you here instead.'

'No trouble, I hope?' I said warily, the usual doctor's reaction to a possible interruption to the evening.

'Trouble? No. Plenty trouble enough come and gone. This not trouble-day, nor tomorrow. Tomorrow happy day, you make missus of Aleena – no trouble there, hey?'

'Indeed not,' I said.

'Happiest day of his life.' Alec Reid twirled his glass.

She was still holding her Mother Hubbard as if concealing something. I could see she was embarrassed. 'Weddings where king and queen is – ' I gathered she meant faraway England ' – they give man and missus things for make'um home. Doc Reid's woman' – Miss Sowerby! – 'she tell me this all long time ago.' She paused. She means wedding presents, I thought. It was my turn to be embarrassed. On Koraloona the islanders never gave each other wedding

509

presents; the custom belonged to a much more sophisticated world; they gave each other, that was enough.

'Bless ma wee soul,' Alec muttered as Mrs Jimbo pursued her objective relentlessly.

'You make Jimbo good one time with box of music.' With a dramatic flourish she whipped the battered little radio from the folds of her Mother Hubbard. '*You* have now. Powerful medicine. *You* have now. Mebbe sometimes missus get sick, you do her better with box of music. Mebbe Jimbo inside somehow.' She stroked the plastic frame with loving fingers.

In remembrance of Jimbo, I thought. But I couldn't say the words. All I could manage to say was a 'Thank you', knowing that she sensed my feelings clearly. She lumbered off down the road smiling happily. There was a long pause. Alec made a great to-do of clearing his throat, and even Jason and Jim Wilson were quiet.

Then Jason said, as though breaking a spell, as if nothing had happened, 'Right: first toast coming up. "To the groom – may he ever be strong enough".'

After that it was time to mix the past with the present. To Alec Reid, it meant casting his mind back to Wimbledon, and raising a glass to Rhoda, the rich lady he had married; to Jason glasses were raised to the minor public school from which he had been expelled when discovered gambling. To Jim Wilson it was to Cardiff Bay where he had learnt 'to chandle ships' and to me that toast was to Nottingham and the 'bed-sits' of my London student days.

We all got slightly high and went home cheerily humming after Captain Baker – more cheerful as his 'boss' wasn't present – gave the naval toast, 'To wives and sweethearts – and may they never meet!'

The most excited islanders of the day – apart from Aleena and me – must have been the children. They all had a day's holiday, and the prospect of being away from their alphabets and multiplication tables had doubled their excitement. Not that they minded learning, but as Father

510

Pringle put it, 'They learn all the better for not learning for a day.'

Every shop, house and hut was decorated with bunting and flowers twisting around verandas and over roofs. Many crudely drawn posters were stuck on windows – Father Pringle's idea: 'I thought the kids might be usefully creative in their art class,' he explained. The Edward VIII Coronation mugs, at last brought into use, bubbled with Coke and Pepsi, and even Johnson managed to leave his store and attend the church service. There, what Colonel Fawcett called the 'flower sub-committee', consisting of Tiare and Mrs Fawcett and other ladies, had created a blaze of colour inside and outside the little white building, with its small spire. Children ran in and out, shrieking with laughter in a most unholy manner, playing games round the pulpit and dashing in and out of what was politely referred to as 'the vestry' – a lean-to where Father Pringle kept his cassock and a few bottles of communion wine (plus, no doubt, sample bottles of something a little stronger). Even Miss Sowerby, busy putting out the few hassocks, unbent enough to say that if the Lord heard them He would no doubt be pleased that they were enjoying their time in His house. Since her 'friendship' with Purvis she had shed some of her austerity, and blossomed.

I went along early to the church to 'measure things up', as I told myself. We had planned to combine English and Polynesian customs in the wedding service. Tiki, as Aleena's mentor, would 'give her away' and Jason would be my best man (he still had the ring, which I had bought in Sanderstown and given into his care before the drama of Penal Island); and before bringing the bride to the church in her ancient but gleaming Austin Ten, Tiare and Aleena and selected colleagues of Tiki would attend a ceremony in which the symbolism of offering a virgin to the gods before casting her upon the waters of earthly domestic life was enacted. Naturally I, as bridegroom, was excluded from that ceremony. Not that I wanted to go: I had never quite lost the feeling that the islanders' customs had a slightly sinister side – and Mana's behaviour had reinforced it.

We still had an hour or two to wait before the actual wedding ceremony, and since I couldn't, according to our own customs, see Aleena before the wedding, I thought on the spur of the moment I would take a quick swim in the 'secret' pool to which, so long ago now, Bill Robins had introduced me when he took me on that first tour of the island.

I would not go so far as to say that I visited the pool as a ritual cleansing of body and soul; I am not religious enough (or superstitious enough) for that; but I did have an inner feeling that a secret swim there would in some sense wash away the past – the occasional girls in London, and Oxford, later the affair with Lucy and, more especially, that occasion in San Francisco about which I still felt traces of guilt.

I made my way to the pool in the jeep. With the 'virgin ceremony' ended, Aleena would, I presumed, go home to let Tiare help her dress. I braked the jeep, then climbed up the narrow flower-lined path, walked underneath the waterfall without getting wet until I was in the cave where Robins and I had undressed and left our clothes safe and dry. Then I plunged through the waterfall.

When I surfaced I had the shock of my life.

Standing on the bank, half hidden by ferns and bougainvillaea and tulip trees, stood Aleena. She was turned away from me and the sound of my voice as I cried 'Aleena!' didn't carry because of the noise of the waterfall. She was naked and patterned with the shadow of leaves; and as if magnetised, she suddenly turned and saw me. She emerged from the arbour and stood there like some sprite with the drops of water glistening on her body and catching the reflection of the dappled sunlight. I climbed up on to the bank. We stood looking at each other, not speaking, for a long moment. We moved closer but only close enough to link hands and stand in silence.

Perhaps we were thinking the same things – that one

512

night together, culminating in that terrible scream; the way in which I had suffered at the hands of her malignant step-father. And perhaps she was asking my forgiveness for taking her place on Penal, not that there was anything to forgive. Was she forgiving me – for the past? Or was she thinking now that we had been punished for breaking our vows, and that we must not risk breaking them again?

She said nothing, not a word, we just stood there naked, thinking, yearning, the water glistening on our bodies. Then she smiled – that special smile of hers, radiant yet tinged with a sultry desire, and said very quietly, 'Tonight, beloved.' Then more prosaically, 'You didn't see my car? I left it a bit further on.'

'Your car?'

'Jim Wilson let me borrow his. I just wanted to come to Grandfather's place. I must go now, Mother will be getting excited if I don't have time to dress.'

Suddenly she was gone, vanished with scarcely a rustling of the leaves. In the car behind the waterfall I put on my shirt and slacks and went thoughtfully back to the bungalow to attend to my own preparations.

The church had never seen such a congregation. Apart from the first couple of pews, filled with so-called VIPs, the islanders packed the place to overflowing. Some were crushed around the door, others pressed faces against windows. The older women had put on their most garish Mother Hubbards, the young girls, on Father Pringle's instructions, had adorned their breasts with bras made from twisted chains of hibiscus and frangipani and scarlet salvia.

'Ye'll note,' Alec Reid nudged me as we sat in the front pew, 'that their nipples are not over-constrained by such fragile blooms.'

Music was provided by the Philadelphia Orchestra, thanks to the generosity of Sam Truscott and the American PX, which had installed its record-playing equipment and gone to the trouble of getting recordings of the *Lohengrin* bridal march and the *Midsummer Night's Dream* wedding march, together with a selection of what Colonel Fawcett called 'tippety-tappety' tunes for the island concertina players to join in.

It wasn't exactly a St Margaret's, Westminster, ceremony, as Jason observed very audibly while we waited for Aleena to arrive. Father Pringle and Miss Sowerby did their best to subdue the children and eventually seemed to get them into some semblance of order. In the vestry Dick Holmes was in charge of the record player, awaiting the sound of Tiare's car at the entrance; and like all best men, Jason repeatedly felt in the pocket of his white duck slacks to make sure that the ring was still there.

The ceremonial details had not seemed important to me. The section of the marriage service that joined us in the sight of God had at first seemed to me to be enough. But Colonel Fawcett insisted otherwise.

'After all,' he said, 'apart from birth and death it's the most important event in your lifetime, so you ought to have a bit of regard for traditions and customs. Women are funny about traditions, y'know. Maybe they've got more roots in superstition than we men like to think.'

Then I heard Tiare's car arriving. There was an immediate hush, the children's babbling fell silent as Aleena entered with Tiki, in his highly decorative ceremonial robes and carrying a kind of knobkerrie that he supported on his left hip in the manner of a king. My heart seemed to hiccup and beat faster as Aleena was suddenly there at my left side, with the *Lohengrin* bridal march fading into silence as Father Pringle began to speak the service.

Afterwards receptions were held all over the island, the major one being at the Union Jack Club (where else?), where Mollie Green had laid on what she called 'a do'. There were festivities in and around Johnson's store. Johnson had actually given away a few 'carnival novelties' to the merrymaking islanders; and in the plantations and fields, games and competitions were organised. At Mick's

Bar drinks were to be 'on the house' for the first hour of opening so that everyone would have a chance of toasting Aleena and me. Of course we had to show ourselves by driving to Anani, calling in at Wilson's and at Mick's Bar, before returning to Tala-Tala and the Union Jack Club, and then leaving on our honeymoon.

This had been arranged for us by Captain Osmond of the Navy, the RAF, and the Prof. There were not many places to which one could travel in wartime, but the British forces, as a tribute to the way in which (to use Captain Osmond's words) 'Doctor Masters liberated Penal Island', had offered to fly us in a Catalina to Sanders where we would spend a week at the Southern Cross Hotel. It was comparatively safe now, for the Japanese were operating only far west of our archipelago.

Finally we reached Tala-Tala and the relative peace of the club. There the first surprise awaited us. Not only was there a chorus of 'Good Luck' and similar wishes from all the members, but Tiare had, as she had done for the dance, brought out all the Gauguins and hung them on the walls. It was staggering, breathless, that display of such concentrated colour, together with the knowledge that a loving and courageous man had painted them on this very island so long ago.

It had been agreed that there would be no speeches but there was a good supply of champagne which loosed many tongues as I kept my eye out for the flying-boat that would take us to Sanders.

Truscott, referring to his record player, said with a grin, 'Gee, I sure am great at playing wedding music. My turn next! Best wishes, Aleena. Kit's one hell of a lucky guy.'

As someone turned to shake hands with Aleena, Truscott turned to me and told me, 'I've heard that Lucy went to Boston and had the operation. Morris say it's a hundred per cent successful. I guess all I've got to do is to see her and make sure he's telling the truth.'

Looking ravishingly dressed at the reception was Paula

Reece who still kept on her private dressmaker. Paula came up and wished us 'Best of luck, Doctor and Mrs Masters'. And to me, with a slightly quizzical look, she added, 'And congratulations on resisting temptation.'

As she walked off Aleena asked, looking puzzled, 'What did she mean by that?'

'I imagine she was congratulating me on resisting her charms. Not that it ever needed any effort,' I laughed, but Paula's mind never reasoned as simply as that. She was probably having a sly dig at me for having long ago preferred Lucy to her.

Not until after the champagne had been reduced to a large number of empty bottles, with only a few full ones remaining, did Tiare motion to Colonel Fawcett. To my dismay the colonel announced, 'The Princess would like to make a short speech as the mother of the bride.'

I had only felt a touch of dismay because the flying-boat was ready to leave, and I wanted to get to the Southern Cross Hotel as soon as possible. I was already exhausted! But the dismay turned to a very different emotion after Tiare had spoken.

'It is, as you know,' she said, 'a custom of countries over the sea to make gifts to people newly married. Not here, because everybody has everything they want.' She made a sweeping gesture that embraced the island. 'However, heritage is a different matter,' she continued, and now her glance took in the dazzling array of paintings. 'As you also know, my mother vowed never to sell the paintings which my father gave her, and I in my turn and Aleena in hers have made the same vow. But as I say, heritage is a different matter from a gift. No selling is involved. And it is to my daughter Aleena and her husband Kit that I now declare ownership of these paintings by Paul Gauguin, who died because, in those days, there was none of the medical care and devotion given by people like Doctor Reid and Doctor Masters.'

I hardly heard the rest of the words, I was so shattered by what she said – and said so calmly. I felt Aleena's warm

516

hand clutch mine, and she whispered, 'Does that make you happy?'

It did, of course. It was an enormous gesture on Tiare's part, even though it meant nothing but the transfer of a legacy before it was due, and one which would pass to our children in due course. It meant nothing financially, it was the gesture that gave me such a flush of pleasure; it symbolised something more than money, it showed trust. The paintings had been given to both of us, with the same vow of course, but the gesture meant that Tiare believed our marriage was sacred, and permanent, that we would never part. And on a more mundane level, I couldn't help thinking for a moment that, though we both felt that we *would* never separate, it wasn't often that a mother-in-law had such faith in her daughter's new husband.

The first moment of what I can only describe as shock passed, as I realised that after all the tribulations through which we had passed, we were finally married at long, long last. I was almost stunned, as the last toasts greeted us, the last champagne glasses emptied, and with our bags already packed and the crew waiting, Mr Johnson arrived again with a dozen bags of confetti and started to shower us as we made for the small harbour and the plane rocking at anchor.

'No charge,' cried Mr Johnson for the second time that day. 'It's on the house.'

They were the last words I heard as the engines roared into life.

'What a day!' I said as we squeezed ourselves in.

Aleena didn't answer. She smiled – radiantly.

Then we were away, rising above the fields and huts and dusty streets of Koraloona, and heading for the Southern Cross.

PART THREE

37

As, during the months of 1945 that followed, we started to build what we hoped would be the foundations of a long and happy married life, the two wars ended – first in Germany, then with the atomic bombs in Japan. On the last day of April 1945 Hitler shot his dog, his wife then himself in his bunker in Berlin and a week later, the Germans unconditionally surrendered and May 8 was proclaimed VE-Day. Japan followed. On the morning of August 6 a bomber of the US Air Force dropped the first atomic bomb used in warfare on Hiroshima, destroying sixty per cent of the city by blast or firestorm. Two days later the Americans dropped another atomic bomb, this time on Nagasaki, and on August 15, Emperor Hirohito broadcast that the Japanese must 'bear the unbearable and accept defeat'.

To us, the end of the war brought two strange twists of drama that were to change our lives. First, the Americans pulled out of Koraloona. I knew it was imminent, and Sam Truscott had already left. One morning during surgery there was a squealing of brakes in 'Harley Street' and Alec and I both looked up from the minor injuries we were attending to see a cigar-chewing American major vault like a jack-in-the-box over the side of a jeep and strut into the clinic.

'Hi'ya,' he said with a pronounced Bronx accent. 'Which of youse is Doc Masters?' He rolled the cigar round his generous mouth and eyed me. 'I guess it's you – they said you was the young one.'

I thought Alec might take the distinction amiss, but he only laughed. 'Aye, I'm nae so young as I was. An yon's Doctor Masters, sure enough.'

I straightened up from the bandage I was putting on my patient's arm. 'Yes, I'm Masters. If you're needing treatment – ?' I left the sentence unfinished, implying that he should wait his turn.

'You kiddin? I ain't lookin' for treatment, Doc; I'm looking for the right guy to transfer that battle-wagon to legally.' He jerked his thumb over his shoulder at my jeep parked by the veranda. 'Sam Truscott's say-so. He's in Sanderstown but he reckoned you'd remember that I gotta get ten bucks from ya.'

Of course, I thought: he was the cigar-chewing engineer who had surveyed the island for the camp site; and this was Truscott's way of keeping his promise of a jeep 'marked down' in value when the Yanks had no further use for it.

'Does this mean you're really pulling out?' I asked.

'Sure. Waal, there ain't no war to fight no more. I wanna get me back to Bronxville toot de sweet like the French say! We ain't lingering.'

Nor did they. During the next couple of days knots of islanders gaped in amazement as the Americans stripped their camp of all its possessions, personal and military. The stores, the PX, the canteen, the cinema equipment, the kitchens; only the prefabricated huts remained like empty shells.

On the last day or so I met the cigar-chewing major again. I was looking at the forlorn remains of the once bustling camp, with its cinema shows and American food, and almost innocently, I asked, 'How are you going to transport all these prefabricated buildings to America when you finally close up?'

He looked at me with astonishment. 'You joking?' he laughed. 'These buildings ain't going nowhere. No way we're going to waste men carting this junk Stateside. It's all yours if you want it. Otherwise use it for firewood.'

'There's no shortage of firewood on Koraloona,' I smiled.

'Waal, take it if you want it.'

I hesitated for a moment, thinking of the time so long ago

when Aleena and I had watched the men assembling the huts, and even then a sergeant had told us they would leave them on the island. I had said then what a wonderful cottage hospital they would make after the war. On the spur of the moment, I asked, 'But you're the one who arranged the details of selling me the jeep.'

He nodded. 'So what?'

'Well' – I hadn't the faintest idea how it would turn out – 'but could we buy the camp for ten bucks?'

'You can have it for free, Doc.'

'But the purchase would make it legal,' I insisted. 'I got a receipt for the jeep. A proof of ownership. I think that one day we might be able to use the camp. But I don't want to run the risk of it being regarded as communal property.'

'I guess you're right there. Sure. Will do, if it makes you happy. You and the missus wanna come into what's left of the office and live in the place?'

'No.' I laughed again as he made out the legal sales document. All kinds of wild ideas were racing through my mind. It would make a wonderful hospital, or a school, or *something*, rather than let it rot. I said as much to Aleena that evening. Of course a hospital was out of the question, the Mission back in London would never have money of that kind – equipping a hospital, even if we had free premises, would be an unsupportable financial burden. But perhaps a school?

When I told Doc that I had become 'a man of property', and said what a wonderful hospital the building would make, he laughed.

'Aye, but that notion belongs to cloud-cuckoo-land. The Mission's a worthy body, but its government grant and the income it gets from charities and legacies has to be spread around a muckle of activities. Ye can forget it, Laddie.'

I gave the matter only very little thought, but the second 'pull-out', which followed the Japanese surrender, was far more serious. Surgeon-Commander Ronnie Serpell told

Alec that, as there was no prospect of further war in the Pacific, the naval base at Sanders was closing down.

'And that means,' he said when he flew over to tell us both the news, 'that the hospital and so on is closing down too. Of course the privately run New Zealand hospital isn't military, so that'll remain. But it isn't a patch on our modern building and equipment.'

'Could you loan us some of the equipment?' asked Alec, not with much enthusiasm.

'Serpell shook his head. ' 'Fraid not,' he said. 'It's all being embarked for a big new defence base in Singapore. Whitehall feel that we've already had troubles with Communists in Malaya. They're going round boasting that *they* won the war. And there's always Commie troubles in South-East Asia.'

'What a pity,' sighed Aleena.

'And how ironic,' I said as Toma brought in dinner. 'Here in Koraloona, we've got wonderful barracks given to us as a present, and a hundred miles away is all the equipment for a modern hospital. What a pity we can't buy it and make Koraloona a big hospital centre for all the islands in the South Pacific, a back-up to the cottage hospitals which already exist.' I was thinking aloud. 'With two or three more doctors, and with Miss Sowerby as matron,' I laughed. 'She's the stuff of which all matrons are made.'

'She's got a heart of gold behind that defensive coldness,' said Aleena. 'But it's beginning to melt.'

'Think so?'

'I know so. And she'd never admit it, but the man who's kindled the flame that's melting her is Jason.'

'He couldn't even light a fire, let alone kindle a flame.'

'Don't be so sure.'

'Well, I do know what you mean – up to a point. She's certainly done a lot for him. She keeps him working,' I said.

'He's done a lot for her. Without realising it. He's brought out a kind of – well, she's more *human*.'

'I never met a human matron when I was at med school.'

When, I wonder, did we first think seriously about equipping a real modern hospital, whether we could ever do so, where would the money come from? We must have talked about it, but, hardly realising what we were doing, the vague thoughts then began to crystallise into less ephemeral dreams. It happened after an extraordinary scene in which Aleena was the central character.

By now – it must have been the end of August or September 1945 – with the world at peace and the two of us blissfully happy – our bungalow had become a kind of home from home for those who liked us as much as we liked them. Aleena was the perfect hostess. Toma was the best cook on the island and proud of his reputation. Living was cheap, and if Aleena wanted a new dress, Paula Reece and Aleena thumbed through the latest magazines and asked her resident dressmaker to get busy. And so the few friends gathered together. Alec – who was lonelier than he pretended to be – and Jason Purvis often came round. So did Dick Holmes, who had elected to stay on as a civilian and run the Koraloona sked. I felt, I suppose, a special relationship with Dick Holmes because I had so often been on the receiving end of the sked when I was almost dying on Penal.

We didn't all meet for dinner every night, of course. Nor only by invitation as they say. Aleena had somehow gathered around her a cloak of happy informality, so that our house became a meeting place when someone needed company – including three men who had no wives. And perhaps it was enhanced because life was so simple; that was why people popped in to 'say hello' and perhaps have a drink.

If I weren't doing surgery, Alec would drop by of an evening and sip an Old Rarity as we watched the sun go down. Without any embarrassment, Miss Sowerby – more and more she was 'Lorna' now – would also pass the time if she was in the vicinity – and everywhere and everyone was 'in the vicinity' in Anani. She could still purse her lips as sharply as any missionary's daughter, but not as often. She had a wonderful way with children, and so this once unlikely nursing sister was slowly approaching middle age with a mellowness hardly revealed before. I suppose we had all changed. Jason drank less and worked harder. Even Paula Reece had less aggression, for the war had turned her from a rich holiday-maker into a resident. During the long years of the war she had been unable to get home to the mainland – only clever boys like Sam and I had done that! – and so she had gently come to terms with the life that war had forced on her.

None of us drank too much and so we faced no social problems anyway.

Sometimes we would have a semi-formal dinner, in which Aleena would arrange a carefully chosen menu. This happened the night that Jason and Lorna, Alec Reid and ourselves had a dinner which Toma had cooked for Alec's birthday. It included one of his favourite dishes, 'chicken in pineapple ships' – quite simple if it is well done, for it consisted basically of slitting pineapples in two, scooping out half of the fruit and cutting it into cubes, then cooking chicken also cut into cubes in – inevitably – coconut milk, with a touch of gin, and serving the whole lot piping hot in the pineapple 'ships'.

'That's why I came,' declared Alec solemnly. 'Ye can hae all yer raw pineapples. I'd rather have a Granny Smith, but when pineapple's cooked – ah! That's a different proposition.'

Sipping coffee on the veranda afterwards, Aleena asked an odd general question – but one with a hidden meaning.

'Can you think of anything more useless than a fish tank?'

'But if you've got fish to fry?' Jason cocked an eyebrow and winked at me.

'Fish are to be eaten – or left in the sea,' she said. 'But an empty tank – '

526

'Darling, what are you driving at? The fish tank Tiare inherited turned out to be quite useful.'

'You really think so?' she said slowly. 'If there's one thing duller than a fish tank, it's to use it to keep a treasure which nobody ever sees.'

'You *are* a crosspatch,' I teased her. 'What's eating you?'

'You'll nae be expecting?' asked Doctor Reid shrewdly.

'Doctor!' Miss Sowerby reproved him.

'Just an informed guess,' said Alec.

Aleena gave her special tinkle of laughter. 'Not yet!' But with a sly look at Alec she whispered, but so that we could all hear, 'But it's not for want of trying.' Then switching the subject she said, 'No, I was talking in riddles. Because I was listening to Kit dreaming about his cottage hospital. And I've got an idea, but it's so revolutionary that I daren't talk about it.'

'Come on, out with it,' cried Purvis. 'What's on your mind – divorce? Already?'

'Silly.' She looked so radiant that I got out of my rattan chair and put an arm round her shoulder, and parted the back of her long shining black hair, then kissed the nape of her neck. 'What is it, my sweet?'

She turned round, took my hand as though clutching it for reassurance, and then, after a deep breath she said quietly, unemotionally, 'It's the Gauguin inheritance.'

'What about it?'

'I think we should sell the Gauguins.'

The gasp of collective astonishment really *was* audible; as though we had all drawn in our breath, held it, then expelled it at precisely the same moment. For a few seconds there was silence – utter, bewildered silence – at such a heretical thought.

'She's got a wee touch of the sun,' said Alec.

'What are you talking about?' I asked. 'Sell the Gauguins? First of all you can't – it's a heritage handed down by your mother. And they were painted by your grandfather. It's unthinkable.'

'Is it?' she asked. 'I'm serious. I mean it.'

527

'But why?' asked Miss Sowerby.

'It's not a sudden idea,' Aleena said, almost defensively, still clutching my hand as I stood beside her. 'It came to me after overhearing you dreaming with Alec about starting a big new hospital now that Sanders is going to close. All of you – just answer one thing. What good are they to us, the Gauguins, sealed up in an old fish tank?'

'But they're priceless!'

'Paintings are meant to be *seen*, not hidden, darling. Except for "Pink Street" they're hardly *ever* seen. What good are they to us? We should sell them.'

'And live happily ever after with a huge fortune which we could never use?'

'No, no,' she cried. 'I know we don't need money.'

'That ye dinna need. I'll say that, even if I am a Scot. But tell your Uncle Alec – '

'It's for you, Alec – and you, Kit – and you, Lorna – and all the people who need your help. Listen!' Aleena, still sitting down with me at her back, lowered her voice almost to a whisper, as though about to impart some information that was secret. 'I want to sell the Gauguins to build the big new hospital you've been dreaming about.'

This time there was a babble of excitement.

'To take the place of the military hospital which is going to close in Sanders,' she continued. 'We've already got buildings for a hundred beds if we use the old camp Sam Truscott gave us. If we could buy medical equipment from the hospital in Sanders – what a chance we'd have to start a big hospital for almost nothing.'

'And my hospital?' asked Alec, almost sadly. 'Will I treat the left-over patients?'

'No, no, Alec, of course not. You'll be the doctor-in-charge. Kit will be chief assistant. We'll hire more nurses and Miss Sowerby will be matron.'

How odd that only the other day we should have been summing up her virtues as a matron!

'But it will need a fortune,' cried Purvis.

'We *have* a fortune,' said Aleena. 'But it's hidden in a fish tank.' And she put an arm round my neck in front of the others, 'Oh, my darling Kit. You have my heart. Now take the paintings and put them to good use.'

I had been so flabbergasted at the idea that I had not even had time to think of the practicalities. Of course the Gauguins would be worth a fortune. But we couldn't just send them off to auction – and hope for the best. Even if we were *allowed* to sell them. The Gauguins were a family trust, even though the trust was given to Aleena and me. But not to sell. There was the small matter of a vow – small to some unscrupulous people maybe, but a vow was *never* unimportant to the Polynesians – to families, to mothers, and above all to Tiare, and to the Tikis of the islands, and their gods.

'Don't worry, my sweet,' she reassured me, as Alec asked, 'Are we ever going to get a nightcap? All this talking and we've nae had even a wee drink.'

'Sorry.' I felt nonplussed. 'Toma!' I shouted. 'Drinks, please.' Toma had long since learned that he never interrupted a discussion unless called for. Then Aleena said something that surprised me. She announced, 'I'll admit that I'm not at all sure that Mummy would agree if *I* ask her.'

'Oh no,' I groaned. 'After trying to make our dreams come true!'

'But she still *could* be persuaded – and so could Tiki.'

'More riddles,' cried Purvis. 'How – by whom?'

'By my adorable and persuasive husband.' She gave a shy, delightful, low laugh. 'There's only one person who Mummy's been in love with – in a respectable way! – since she first met him. It's you, Kit. She knows that you've saved my life – twice. She adores you. And she *is* practical. You could ask her. You could tell her and Tiki what really is true – that by selling the Gauguins you'd be letting other people see them for the first time; and that the Gauguins would provide money to help keep her subjects healthy, and make sure we never had to face again a time as terrible as the cholera epidemic. You are the one.'

I looked around a trifle helplessly.

I didn't relish the task. I was thinking that 'Pink Street' came in a different category, it had been given to me, and whatever happened to the legacy, I wasn't going to part with *that* – a beautiful painting, long since behind glass and in its puttied airtight frame made by Jim Wilson.

But as for selling the heritage so carefully preserved for nearly fifty years, I couldn't see any hope. And yet, if only I *could* persuade Tiare and Tiki to agree – I could almost visualise a modern hospital growing in front of my eyes.

'But how shall I do it?' I asked Aleena after the others had gone.

Then, warm in bed, and together, she explained.

'Yes, dear Kit,' Tiare said, when I visited her house later in the week. 'It's very laudable, it's a wonderful idea: but I don't think you realise the sanctity of a vow taken in the presence of one's – well, *priest*.' She glanced towards Tiki, who sat stiffly on an upright chair in the curve of the piano, his hands clasped over the knob of a polished cane. He looked grave and dignified.

'I'm sure we don't have to question Doctor Masters' understanding of sanctity, Princess. It was simply that for a moment his heart overcame his head. Most laudable, as you say. But hardly to be considered seriously.' He paused and gave a gentle smile. 'Any more than one would consider asking the Archbishop of Canterbury to renounce the Thirty-nine Articles.'

I had come prepared for stonewall opposition but Aleena had insisted that I point out to Tiare that, but for the skills acquired in teaching-hospitals, her daughter would by now probably be the victim of the melanoma that had been so carefully removed at Sanderstown; and I saw her wince at what really amounted to moral blackmail.

Nor did I stop there: I convinced both Tiare and Tiki that, with better hospital facilities, there would have been far fewer deaths from the cholera outbreak. They glanced at each other. They were wavering, I could sense that, even though, as Tiare said, 'worse disasters could befall the islanders if the gods are mocked.'

'I understand,' I admitted, then switched the conversation with an idea worked out in advance by Aleena.

'Princess,' I said after a suitable pause, signifying by a gesture my acceptance that I agreed it was impossible to rescind the vow, 'my most treasured material possession is the picture you gave me – "Pink Street" – because it symbolised an act of friendship – of love even. I am sure that your love for the people of Koraloona – '

'Ah,' Tiki broke in with a faint smile. 'I begin to see the deviousness of Doctor Masters' mind. Perhaps because I too have been educated to some extent in the sophistries of the modern world.'

I had the grace to blush at my veiled suggestion; but at least it was made in a good cause.

Tiare folded her hands together. 'I see. You mean that as I made you a present of a single picture, the same principle could apply because I made over the entire collection to you both as a gift. It was a gift, with no monetary gain involved. So you, my dear Kit, would not feel the need to observe the fidelities of a vow. Is that what you are driving at?'

'To a certain extent.' I forced a smile. 'But there is one other point. We are *exchanging* the paintings, not *selling* them. It's a crucial difference. It's true that money will have to pass, but every penny will go to the hospital. There will be no thought that we shall benefit.'

'That I do understand,' she said. 'I know that would never enter your head.'

'And,' I added, 'a new hospital would not *really* be donated by Aleena and me, but by your father.'

'Meaning exactly?' asked Tiare.

'If this hospital had existed in 1900 your father would have lived long enough to hold you in his arms and love you. But in those days the medical facilities weren't good enough in the islands. We – Aleena and me, you Tiare and, yes, your father's original gift, are going to be used to make

531

sure that nobody faces the same unnecessary death that Gauguin did. If you want to look at it cynically, we are giving away a fortune. But by this magnificent gesture not only will millions of people be able to *see* the Gauguins, but his spirit will live over Koraloona, the island he loved.'

A little wistfully Tiare admitted, 'It would have been wonderful if I had ever met him.'

Very carefully, I didn't want to push too hard, I said gently, 'If – and I say "if" because the decision is yours and yours alone – if the hospital ever does become more than a dream, we would like to call it the Gauguin Memorial Hospital.'

As tears glistened in her eyes, Tiki, hand still clasped over the knob of his stick, interjected. 'I think we must remember, Princess, that Doctor Masters has already taken what is to him a sacred oath – to aid the sick by any means at his command.'

It was then I knew that we had got our way. From that very moment the Gauguin Memorial Hospital became a practical proposition.

38

So one hurdle had been overcome! We now had the possibility of financing the projected hospital, though, as we talked it over with Alec, we realised we hadn't the faintest idea how to go about it. We couldn't merely wrap up a parcel of paintings and ask someone, 'Can you sell these for us?' We needed expert advice – and time to think.

The first thing I did was to tell Alec the good news – and then ask him, as senior medical officer of Koraloona, to write to the Mission in London and tell them of our new bequest. I asked him not to mention my name, simply to explain that the paintings had been left by the family. In fact I helped Alec to draft the letter because I wanted the money – and the site – to be hedged in with a few express conditions. Though unlikely, someone *might* take advantage of our good fortune unless it were properly protected. So Alec wrote that Princess Tiare wanted a guarantee that he would remain as senior doctor until his retirement at sixty-five, and that then, I would have the automatic right to succeed him unless it could be proved independently that I was unsuitable. The ground on which the hospital would operate – the acres of the old camp site – would remain in perpetuity the property of Aleena and her family, together with the equipment. I arranged with Colonel Fawcett to transfer the land deed from me to her because, though it seemed ridiculous, I didn't want some smart executive coming to the Pacific and lording it over her if anything happened to me. It was Alec who thought of that.

'Ye never know, Laddie,' he said sagely, 'if the Mission ever went bust or someone had an eye on the main chance, the hospital would be Aleena's – at least the site and the equipment, and without that no one could operate. It sounds mean, but it's a way of protecting her investment.'

When surgery ended a few days after I had met with Tiare and Tiki, and had told Alec the good news, I met Alec as the last patient departed, and suggested, 'Let's drive in the jeep to the camp site, and see what can be done with it.'

'Aye, but ye'll nae be forgetting that it'll take a muckle o' money to equip it properly.'

'I realise that. But even if we can't afford all that we ought to buy, at least we can get supplies to combat any possible outbreak of disease. And space!'

'That's true. But it's a great shame that we canna get our hands on any of the equipment from Sanders.'

'There must be second-hand equipment in some part of the world. New Zealand perhaps. Perhaps we could advertise. Let's look round first – and get excited instead of gloomy.'

The deserted camp lay in flat fields near Faalifu. Alec Reid and I strolled round its neatly rolled paths with their borders of whitewashed stones. I had a huge bunch of keys that had been given me by the US major and I jangled them with a proprietorial air that amused Alec.

'I must say, Kit, ye take on the look of a landed laird wi' great ease.'

I smiled as I fitted one of the keys into the door of the largest hut – once the dining-hall, or 'chow house' as the Yanks called it. Then I made an expansive gesture. 'Welcome to GMH – Gauguin Memorial Hospital,' I said. 'One day, I hope it will be on the medical map of the world as a remarkable achievement in the face of adversity.'

Alec put a hand on my shoulder with a touch of gravity. 'Dinna get too excited too soon, Kit,' he said. 'After all ye've been through, one way and another – well, I'd hate tae ken ye disappointed.'

Alec was right to be cautious. I really had no idea of the cash value of the pictures. I had the previous day written for advice to Christie's, the art auctioneers in King Street, St James's. It was the only name that had sprung to my mind, and if they replied at all (by no means certain – they could conclude I was some crank) they might tell me that there had been a slump in the market for Gauguins. Alec was right. It would be as well to control my enthusiasm for the time being.

'This' – I indicated the rectangular room, big enough for all the Americans to eat their meals at one sitting – 'seems to me ideal for a general ward. There's ample space for several rows of beds.'

Alec gave a lop-sided grin as he examined the walls, which had been plastered with pin-ups by Petty and Varga torn from *Esquire* and photos of glamorous film stars like Jane Russell and Lauren Bacall. 'Aye,' he said, 'and ample scope for the imagination too. If ye ask me, those Yanks ate, slept, and dreamed of tits and bums.'

'And why not?' drawled a low-pitched voice behind us. Startled, I turned.

It was Paula Reece.

534

'Hello,' I smiled. 'To what do we owe this honour? What are you doing here?'

'I'm a camp follower.' We laughed at her use of the wartime jargon. 'I'm not intruding? I was in my garden when you arrived. I was so glad to hear that you are to have the camp. *And* the paintings. Yes,' returning my smile, 'it's all over the island. You can't keep news like that secret for long.'

Of course I knew that. Koraloona was like a village.

I don't know why, but even now I still felt slightly uneasy in Paula's presence. Perhaps it was because she flaunted her sensuality; or possibly, despite the compassion she had shown during the cholera epidemic, because she was at heart a rich, spoiled woman with an eye to the nearest susceptible male. I felt it even more as she accompanied Alec and me around the deserted camp, allotting rooms for different purposes – the officers' mess to be a rest room for convalescents, the offices to be our X-ray department, and the stores to be used for Out-Patients. From time to time Alec cannily reminded me, 'We're building castles – or rather hospitals – in the air y'know, Kit. We dinna ken the value of these paintings.'

'I know, I know, Alec,' I interrupted. 'But it's fun throwing caution to the winds for once.'

This time it was Paula who interrupted. 'I hope you realise what you're doing, Kit.' She said seriously. 'The art world's a real jungle.'

'Don't worry,' I said. 'I've written to Christie's, and sent them photos of the paintings. And if *I* know Christie's they must be famous.'

She gave a short laugh. 'Oh, they're famous all right. But terribly old hat. You could use some real up-to-date advice.'

'Advice? Well, pictures are pictures, aren't they? You sell them to the highest bidder, surely?'

She took my hand and squeezed it, laughing. 'Keep an eye on him, Doc! Kit would be taken for a newborn babe by the art world sharks. Not that Christie's are sharks – but why pay them ten per cent commission when you could sell direct to a private collector?'

Slightly irritated, I replied, 'I dare say Christie's will reply if they think my request worth considering.'

'Of course they will. But meanwhile why not take a crash course in art values? It'll put you in the picture – excuse the pun! – and help cut corners if you can talk about art. And I've just the man. You've met Count Vrinsky?'

'Oh, the Pole who's been here once or twice?'

'Polish *aristocrat*, my dear Kit; not a mere Pole.'

I remembered meeting him at one of Paula's numerous parties. The man with the suave voice, who smoked cigarettes through a long amber holder, and had somehow got drafted into the army as a captain in the educational branch to provide food for the GIs' minds when they weren't engaged in battle. Alec had taken an instant dislike to him. 'Bloody charlatan!' he remarked.

'Anyway,' I said, 'much though I'd appreciate his advice, he's not here now.'

'True,' Paula drawled. 'But he *is* coming – next month. To stay with me for a while now he's left the army. So then you must meet him, and pick his brains.'

'It's a date,' I said, 'and thanks. I'm most grateful. I don't suppose I'll hear from London for a month at least.'

It didn't take as long as that, as it turned out. Three weeks later I was contacted by Christie's, by which time, the first enthusiasm over, I had forgotten about Paula's Polish friend. Especially as Christie's wanted to *telephone* me! Even though we didn't have an international telephone exchange in Koraloona.

But just before dinner that evening, Dick Holmes, who ran the sked, phoned me at home saying that a cable was expected for me via Sanders. It had originated in London and Sanders would dictate it within half an hour. The few cables for Koraloona were sent to Sanders and forwarded on the sked. My first thought was one of fear, fear that the cable was from Nottingham and would contain bad news from the family.

Nothing could have been further from the truth. It was from Christie's. It was quite long, and it read:

VERY EXCITED GAUGUINS STOP PLEASE DO NOTHING UNTIL WE MEET STOP CAN YOU BE AT SOUTHERN CROSS HOTEL SANDERSTOWN OCTOBER 1 AT 6 PM YOUR TIME AND I WILL TRY TO PHONE YOU THERE REGARDS IAN PETRIE CHRISTIE'S

A phone call! I stared bemused at the printed letters which Dick Holmes handed me.

'Seems pretty important,' he observed.

'But a phone call!' I cried. I knew, of course, that telephone calls now operated over most of the world, sometimes radio-telephone. Even before the war, in 1938, Singapore had inaugurated the first phone link to California.

I ran round to the bungalow and cried to Aleena, 'Darling, they're excited – that's the word they used. They're going to phone me!'

Trust wonderful Aleena. She might not have had the faintest idea what I was talking about, but she had the rare facility of knowing instinctively when something excited me, and taking the scrap of paper, shouted, 'Hooray! Three cheers for Christie's! You're a genius. Toma, drinks!' Then, kissing me gently but with all her love pouring out of her, she whispered, 'I'm so happy that I feel – well, let's have the drinks in bed and make love – now.'

Later that evening I asked Dick Holmes to dictate a brief cable from Sanderstown to Christie's, saying WILL BE THERE OCTOBER 1 and as I handed him the message, he said with a grin, 'You doctors are in demand. Here's a signal from Commander Serpell to Doctor Reid.' It said:

GRATEFUL IF YOU AND OR MASTERS CAN FIX VISIT TO SANDERSTOWN STOP CHANGE IN

DISPOSAL OF MEDICAL EQUIPMENT MIGHT BE ADVANTAGEOUS STOP SERPELL

I had of course told Alec about the message from Christie's but now it seemed important for Alec also to visit Sanderstown. If there really was a chance of buying equipment at 'advantageous' prices, *and* hear good news of the paintings, we had to act quickly. Since neither of us liked to be away from the hospital at the same time, we worked out the next evening how to plan the trip. Aleena and I would spend a few days' holiday at the Southern Cross, taking the overnight boat – the *Mantela II* – in the last week of September, and then, on September 30, Alec would fly over early in the morning in Nellie, which he had had completely overhauled. We would both meet Serpell, then Alec would fly back around lunch-time.

'Then ye can talk to your fine friends in London on the expensive telephone, and maybe ask your man from Christie's, whatever he's called, to phone ma wife in Wimbledon. I've nae written her even a word for six months.' He hitched up his trousers.

'I'll do that,' I promised, already tingling with excitement at the prospect of a 'holiday'. It might be work in one sense – a vital telephone conversation, and the mysterious request to meet Serpell; but all the same, when you are married, the prospect of a holiday has an added glow of excitement. I had never really been interested in holidays as a bachelor. Apart from anything else, I couldn't afford them. But when you are married, it seems different. I was looking forward to revisiting the city, walking arm-in-arm around Piccadilly, along the coast roads. Alone it would have been dull. With Aleena, back where we had first fallen in love, and where we had barely escaped death in the Japanese attack, it would take on all the quality of a second honeymoon.

The meeting with Ronnie Serpell at the military hospital had been arranged for eleven o'clock, giving Alec plenty of time to fly Nellie over, and we arrived there promptly at the appointed time.

'What's all this aboot?' asked Alec once we had been served with coffee.

'I'll explain.' Serpell held an official-looking airmail letter in his hand. 'This came from the surgeon-general – ' He broke off and explained, 'He's the kingpin medic of the services. A man you don't argue with. "Close down Sanderstown Naval Base Hospital," he says, and you jump to it and close it down. "Transfer equipment to Singapore," he says, and you make ready to transfer equipment to Singapore.'

Alec, beside me, felt me stiffen. He knew only too well that this was an area of medicine of which I was completely ignorant. In training colleges and hospitals you work your stint but the equipment is all there, its cost is not your concern.

Serpell was tapping the letter with a forefinger. 'So what do I do? I jump to it. Then comes another cable: hold it, change of plan. Singapore's working on a grand scale – no bruised-and-used for them. It's a priority project. Nothing but the newest. Await further instructions. And now here are the further instructions. "Close base hospital, dispose of equipment ad lib."'

'You mean,' I said with astonishment, 'that you could chuck it in the sea for all they care?'

Alec mopped his brow. His canny Scots instinct was shocked. 'I canna believe – '

'And you're right,' Serpell interrupted. ' "Ad lib" simply means that the boss man is shifting the burden on to me. He's got the Treasury to account to. Woe betide him if his accounting shows lack of consideration for the taxpayer's money.'

'So what'll you do?' I asked.

'What they'll expect me to do is to ship it all back home. Then they can complain, because that's another charge on the Treasury and the taxpayer's money.'

'But,' I interrupted, 'it's wartime – '

'Not now it isn't. You've no idea what crocodile tears they can weep for the taxpayer's money when there's no victory to be won.'

'In that case – ' I began.

'You've hit it! You start by wanting *me* to do *you* a favour and then the turnabout comes and it seems *you* can do *me* one. I'm selling and you're buying.' He winked. 'And believe me, it's a buyer's market.'

My heart lcapt. To tell the truth, I was thinking how the Americans had been willing to write off a jeep for ten dollars! But I was quickly disabused of that notion. As if he had read my thoughts Serpell continued, 'But don't imagine you're going to have it all your own way. I aim to get a pat on the back as a shrewd officer. So let's start.'

As we toured the hospital I made mental notes and nudged Alec. 'It's the really vital things we're concerned with,' I suggested. 'Admin stuff – filing cabinets and the like we can keep at the back of our minds. Agreed?'

'Aye, Laddie. Nobody's ever yet been cured of anything with a filing cabinet.'

The laboratory, X-ray department and operating theatre were of course the most important for our purpose. The Solus-Schall X-ray machine was an absolute must. Quite apart from its everyday use in revealing bone fractures, I could organise mass X-rays of the islanders and detect the early signs of TB – still a health hazard in Koraloona.

Serpell saw my determined look. He flipped through the Solus-Schall catalogue in his hand. 'Complete with tube, high-tension cables, and fluoroscope – thirty thousand dollars.'

I gasped. With dollars at about four and a half to the pound at the end of the war, that would set us back £7,500.

'Mind you,' Serpell looked at us straight-faced, 'it's had quite a bit of use. How's about a knock-down price – say five hundred?'

'Dollars?' I asked breathlessly.

'You must be joking, Masters. Pounds. I told you, I'm

going to make sure the Treasury thinks I'm a shrewd bargainer.'

Even so, it was marvellous value. And as we looked at one complex machine and instrument after another, Serpell continued to tease me over prices. The anaesthetic apparatus with its flow-meters, ether control, and uni-directional valves (what a contrast to the wire-framed gauze mask of 'Harley Street'!) was a prize that Alec Reid insisted on – even though one of us would obviously need some special training in the use of it.

'Twenty-five thousand,' Serpell said with a flip through another catalogue.

'And the knock-down price?' I asked casually, fingering the re-breathing bag on the apparatus.

Serpell stroked his chin as if pondering. 'In pounds – five hundred again?'

'Done!' I said.

Alec, his canniness overcoming him, quietly urged caution. 'Ye'll soon be up in the thousands, Laddie. Can we noo dispense with the oscillometer?'

'I suppose we could.' I was thinking of the occasion when it would have been a godsend – as when I was attending Toma's mother for her diabetes and could have measured the changes in her arterial pulsations instead of guessing. 'But with the prevalence of mellitus on the island – '

'Aye; I suppose ye're right.'

By the time I had included another Drinker respirator or iron lung and a selection of bronchoscopes and similar instruments we had always wanted, together with beds and other ward furniture, we had committed ourselves to far more than I could be certain of getting – and even that left us with the constructional costs of putting in extra drainage, converting army latrines into proper lavatories, and maybe thinking about air-conditioning. But it was a *fait accompli* now. I must admit Alec and I were more than a little scared, despite Ronnie Serpell's generosity.

'I don't know where or when we'll get the money,' I

admitted to Alec as we drove back to the airfield so that he could fly back to Koraloona. 'But thanks for all your help. I could never have done it without your backing.'

'Forget it. Ronnie'll wait for the cash,' Alec reassured me. 'Governments dinna expect to be paid on the dot. It's the paper transaction that counts – something that can be entered to look good. They're all the same, the civil servants. If Ronnie promises Whitehall that the money's safe, that's good enough. Apart from anything else it'll take at least six months to run the base down and they willna close the hospital till the last soldier, sailor or airman has gone.'

It *would* be paid of course, but as the taxi took me back to the Southern Cross after seeing that Alec was airborne, I was wondering, not greedily but as a matter of interest, how much we *would* get. We now had, in effect, bought some of the finest hospital equipment any doctor could ask for – and we already had a free hospital building. The cost of the equipment was so reasonable that we would never need to use *all* the heritage money, which (as Alec had written to the Mission when announcing the bequest) would enable us to arrange for two or three local girls to be trained as full-time nurses on a modest salary. And as for ourselves, I was thinking, as we approached Monument Road and the public library at the far corner, the Mission would still pay the salaries of Alec and myself and Miss Sowerby together with the costs already borne by it in London. But they could not fail to be delighted with the windfall which Alec had carefully described as a 'gift' from the 'royal' family of Princess Tiare and her daughter.

I broke the news of Ronnie Serpell's generosity to Aleena as soon as I had paid off the taxi and bounded up the old stairs, two at a time, bursting with excitement.

'It's worth a fortune,' I cried as I entered the bedroom. 'Hundreds of thousands of pounds. And Ronnie gave it to us for peanuts.'

'Then let's celebrate.' Aleena patted her black silky hair where I had ruffled it when kissing her. It was a beautiful

542

day and we walked out of the Southern Cross, into the circle of Piccadilly with its characteristic flowering shrubs, carefully tended and pruned, dotting the neatly clipped thick grass, and past the cinema at the southern tip where the circle opened into Hallgate and the shopping mall on the other side of the street.

'Let's go and look at the old school.' She squeezed my hand. Even though we had been to see the rebuilt college on our honeymoon, it seemed to have a fascination for her, perhaps because it echoed that time so many eventful years before when the young girl from the college had first become – to me, anyway – a woman, and then the later moment when Aleena ran from the church to greet me near the ruins of the bombed school and I had taken her and Kinawa back to the safety of Koraloona.

'Yes, it seems a long, long time ago,' she sighed softly. As we walked along the Mall I pointed to one newly built shop.

'That's where I pinched a free shirt from the wreckage,' I remembered.

'You never told me that!'

'Mine was torn off by blast,' I explained. 'So I took one from a smashed shop window.'

'A looter!' she laughed.

'I could have been shot.'

We walked along a few more steps just before Hallgate began to merge into the local market. 'Let's go to the Café de Paris for lunch,' she suggested. 'It was such fun on our honeymoon. And such a change to eat good French food.'

It *was* good food, though I imagined 'French food' meant French food from Tahiti. But we sat down and ordered a bottle of champagne.

'It's becoming a habit!' She had always loved champagne since I bought her her first bottle at the Café de Paris. That was the night I took her out dancing after dinner with Bill Robins and Bessie. The second time we drank champagne had been the night before the night-club had been bombed into a tangled mass of girders and bricks and mortar.

'And now we're a staid old married couple.' She hugged me, as we sat down to a real French meal – a cheese soufflé followed by roast duckling with a sauce of Morello cherries.

'The first time I've had tinned fruit since I left home for Australia,' I laughed. 'But this time I must keep a clear head. The phone call from London is due at six o'clock. I want to find out everything I can. Prices, delays, commissions – how we go about things – you understand?'

'Of course,' she said sweetly. 'So I'll drink most of the champagne and you can do all the talking. I adore you, my handsome young husband.' And then, in full view of everyone enjoying their meal, she kissed me full on the mouth. 'Yes, I do. I adore you.'

'I say! Remember I'm a doctor!' And in an aura of happiness I caught a glimpse of envy on the face of a middle-aged man at the next table as he saw not only the girl's beauty and her youth, but the secret look which showed that we were lovers; and I heard him sigh as his stout wife made some sharp remark.

I had warned the hotel that, as I was expecting an important telephone call from London, I would stay in my room to receive it. They had been suitably impressed. But six, seven, eight o'clock passed without any news despite irate demands on my part. The exchange contacted the international exchange time and again and reported no news. Yet, I did not dare leave our bedroom, so we had some cold food sent up to the room with coffee for Aleena and a bottle of cold lager for me.

It was just as well I did wait. Just before 10 pm, the shrill stammer of the phone nearly made us jump out of our chairs and I spilled my second glass of beer. I grabbed the phone and before I could shout 'Yes!' the operator said, quite casually – for her, but not for me – 'Is that Doctor Masters?'

'That's me.'

'This is the London exchange. Don't hang up if there's a short delay. It's quite a complicated link-up.'

'I won't,' I promised and then waited – silently. Aleena sat next to me, perched on the side of the double bed because the phone was on the bedside table. At last a woman's voice said, 'Doctor Masters, can you hear me?'

'Perfectly. Quite clearly.'

'Good. I'm putting you through now to Mr Petrie.'

I could hardly believe that this woman talking casually to me was so far away, in the city where I had learned to be a doctor. And here was I, half way across the world. A moment later a male voice crackled over the line.

'Doctor Masters? This is Ian Petrie. Delighted we have been able to make contact. It's about eleven o'clock in the morning here. There's eleven hours' difference and we had a job getting through. Delay of up to four hours.' I heard him give a short laugh. 'I had to get up at five o'clock to be ready.'

'I'm sorry. Not my fault.' I toned my voice down, after the initial instinct to bridge those ten thousand miles with a shout. 'I'm delighted you're interested.'

'We certainly are. We face a number of problems, Doctor – authenticity – provenance – '

'Provenance?' I asked, puzzled. 'Do you mean what province did they come from?'

'No, not geographical.' He realised that the word was new to me. 'The history of the paintings. The proof of their – well, what their history has been, their life, and so on. I'll explain it all in a detailed letter. Most interesting. From what you've written, it seems that there is no doubt they're genuine, and if you will allow us to conduct the auction, I can tell you, Doctor, it will be the sale of the decade. Sixteen Gauguins! Never been heard of before. A splendid find. Why – er – did you write to us?'

'It was the first name I thought of.'

'Very gratifying. Very. Lucky we received your letter. Perhaps you didn't know, but our premises in King Street were bombed, so for the moment we're operating from Stratford Place.' 'Sorry about that,' I interrupted, 'This must be costing you a great deal of money, Mr Petrie.'

545

'Never mind that.' I thought I heard him chuckle as he added, 'We'll make all that back and a lot more in our commission at the auction.'

The real problem, as he explained to me, was that though they obviously wanted to conduct the auction, equally obviously they couldn't do this until their experts had actually examined the paintings. Which was understandable.

'I suppose our team of experts *could* come to see you in this island of' – he hesitated – 'Where *is* this place Koraloona?'

I explained as best I could.

'I see.' Suddenly he had to speak louder as there was a curious noise, almost like the sound of sea waves, until he said, 'Ah! That's better. But of course it would be much simpler if we could meet each other half way across.'

'Where would that be?'

'Well, not really half way, Doctor. New York. We are planning a major expansion in America and of course the British government is very anxious to expand all forms of business, so we wouldn't like the Americans to snatch the sale from under our noses.'

'Then wouldn't it be foolish to go to New York?' I shouted back. 'It's a long way.'

'It wouldn't be foolish, because of the publicity we would get.'

'It's a long way,' I hesitated. 'I suppose my wife and I *could* make the trip – but – '

I could sense that he was thinking, trying to formulate ideas.

'Flying across the States presents us with no problems at all. Air traffic across America continued all through the war,' he said finally.

'What *is* the problem then?' My right wrist was beginning to get a bit tired.

'I know that we in Christie's can arrange a priority for crossing the Atlantic. The question is, can you get across the Pacific?'

'I don't know, Mr Petrie. I just don't know. I *have* been to the West Coast once, to a medical conference. But of course the Americans arranged all that. Now, though – '

After another pause, Petrie said, 'I think that we might be able to help you to cross the Pacific to San Francisco or Los Angeles.'

'Then we could meet there.'

I could sense the hesitation again. 'We *could*,' he said finally. 'And our men could fly across the States to meet you.'

'Why not?' It was my turn to be slightly puzzled. 'If all you need to do is examine the paintings to make sure they're genuine, we could do that in California. It doesn't matter *where*, does it?'

'It's a fair question, Doctor – and very simple to answer. Yes, it does make a difference. The world's finest expert on the Impressionists is in New York. And also, both of us hope to sell the paintings for the biggest possible amount. You agree?'

'Of course.'

'We're on the edge of a huge expanding art market,' explained Petrie – and then the line went dead.

'Damn and blast!' I jiggled the receiver up and down furiously, and yelled to the girl on the switchboard, 'We were cut off. For God's sake!'

'Just a moment sir,' she said, and I realised it was not her fault. 'It's the line,' she said. 'It'll be restored soon, I hope. A little patience, sir, and if you don't mind staying in your room – '

The call wasn't connected until nearly midnight, by which time we had given up all hope and gone to bed. Without warning the bell stuttered and I fumbled for the light switch and then the phone, and there was the voice of Mr Petrie.

'Ah, there you are, Doctor. Now where was I?'

I realised that to him it was nearly lunch time. He had probably been sitting at his desk, doing something else while waiting for us to be re-connected, and before I could say anything, he said, 'Ah yes! The expanding market. It's in three centres – Paris, London and New York. We can discount Paris because of the tax on auction sales. That's why it's shifting from France to England. And New York is now chasing London, Doctor.'

'But what's that got to do with your examining the paintings?' Half awake, I tended to be as irritated as when a patient called me out of bed, only to find he was suffering from nothing worse than a bad cough.

'It's very important to go to New York,' Petrie insisted. 'If we arrange it properly the advance publicity which such an enormous art discovery would generate in New York would attract the richest collectors in the world – all hoping to buy your paintings. If the publicity is bold enough, every big collector will know about it – especially if the photos include your wife.'

'You're not going to auction her!' I couldn't help laughing.

'That's where you're wrong, Doctor. We *are* going – as you say – to auction her. You see, we are going to sell the wonderful paintings not merely as Gauguins, but as the secret work handed down by a great painter to the family no one knew existed. If it is handled properly, it will add thousands – yes, Doctor, *thousands* of pounds to the money which you, your wife and your hospital will receive. I cannot over-estimate the value of letting the world know about the romantic connection.'

'If you say so – ' I hoped I didn't sound too doubtful across the thousands of miles, but to me, the paintings were the paintings – and that was all to it. They stood for what they were.

'I *do* say,' he replied.

'Of course,' I hesitated, 'I'm sure she'd love to go. Neither of us has ever visited New York.'

'Remember, we are *always* – ' I could plainly hear the emphasis in his voice – 'concerned with getting the best possible prices. And to do that we must, as I've said, arouse public interest – with the help of your wife. The right

548

photos will be published in almost every country in America and Europe, if we make it discreetly *romantic*. Not just a few paintings, Doctor, but paintings belonging to the grand-daughter of Gauguin – the girl he never saw.'

I hadn't thought about what Alec Reid would surely describe as 'a wee bit of bloody nonsense' but I could see his point. His arguments about publicity did make sense. Then another thought struck me.

'Even if I could cross the Pacific by military aircraft, wouldn't it cost a fortune for us to travel another three thousand miles across America?'

'My dear Doctor,' even across miles his voice seemed to take on an indulgent tone, 'for the moment leave all that to us. Once you agree that we should handle the auction, we will advance you the cost of transport and your hotel in New York, and I'll write to you to make the concrete financial arrangements. Let's say that if you make "x" thousand pounds more than you expect, we'll go fifty-fifty on the travel costs. If they're not as much as the reserve which we will agree on, then we will have to put the charge down to our failure.'

'That sounds a bit unfair – '

'Not at all, Doctor. We expect to make a great deal of money out of you if the Gauguins are genuine. That's the first step. Our experts must verify them. So I suppose that if you insisted, we'd have to come and see you. Look at it that way – by using the money for your trip we are spending no more than we would do if we had to come to you, but we are getting a bonus of publicity. And in the meantime, we can continue working on our other projects. No, Doctor, we're getting a good bargain, persuading you to do our job for us. Let's leave it at that. I will write to you today a letter setting out our terms and so on, and if you agree, you will sign a copy of the letter and return it to us. We shall be very happy to work that way. Meantime, you and Mrs Masters return to your island and see what you can do about crossing the Pacific. That's a bit of a hurdle. Cable me when you have news, will you?'

'Of course.'

'Oh, there's one thing more. Can you make some sort of – well, we'd call it a search. Can you see if there are any old letters or notes that Gauguin made and which perhaps your wife's grandmother might have kept? You understand, of course, the value of any provenance. Something to connect any letters with the paintings would naturally enhance our belief that they were genuine.'

'I've heard talk,' I said, 'but I'm almost sure it was just talk. Otherwise someone would have found them after all these years.'

'I suppose so,' he admitted. 'Pity though. Every little helps.'

'I'll do everything I can,' I promised him. Then I remembered other things which I had forgotten in the excitement, and was only reminded by Aleena pushing a piece of paper under my nose. It bore two telephone numbers – one in Nottingham, one in Wimbledon. I explained to Mr Petrie.

'Of course,' he said, 'it's a pleasure. And now I'll bid you good morning, Doctor. I'll be hearing from you. Have a good lunch.'

Lunch! It was midnight – but the thrill of that long exciting phone call had cancelled all time barriers. The people in London and myself, separated by oceans and continents, had traversed time, encapsulated it into the same moment for both of us. It wasn't night, it wasn't morning. It was just the same second of excitement for all of us, no matter what any clock said.

39

Almost the first thing I did when I returned to Koraloona was to ask Aleena, and Alec Reid, 'Have you *any* idea whether or not there are documents that might help –

whether there might be some letters or notes written by Gauguin?'

Both shook their heads. 'There were rumours of their existence afore I came to the island,' said Alec. 'Personally I dinna believe them, but Tiare swears that her mother told her she had kept the painter's letters. Though I dinna see how she could'a read them in a foreign tongue.'

'And even if she had kept the letters,' argued Aleena, 'they'd have been destroyed or eaten by ants years ago.'

I agreed. 'Even if there ever were any, they'd surely have been lost or burnt by now.'

And frankly I gave the matter no more thought, because two weeks later I found a simple way to cross the Pacific with the help of the cigar-chewing American major from the Bronx who had 'sold' me the camp. Unexpectedly he had returned to Koraloona, with two military policemen.

'What brings you here?' I was astonished. I had never expected to see him again.

'One missing GI Joe,' he explained angrily. 'The god-damn fool's crazy about some local dame and gone into hiding. I've gotta get him home. If he ain't properly discharged, he'll be posted as a deserter.'

The major stayed three days before the deserter was found, but came to have a bite of dinner with us and we told him some of our exciting news, explaining that we had to get to the west coast of America – and didn't have any money.

'No sweat,' he waved a cigar expansively.

'Why not?'

'We've got so many US Air Force planes in the Pacific and way back in Australia that we're running a regular shuttle service between Port Darwin and San Francisco, and because of your dooties as medical officer to the camp, we can easily get you and your wife on the Travelling Junk Shop.'

'The what?'

'The Skymaster plane. It has one hell of a range and can even carry a load of guns or tanks. It makes regular trips, stopping wherever it has to refuel or pick up freight or passengers.'

'Sounds great. And Aleena?'

'No sweat,' he repeated. 'Army and WAVE girls are always on the way home across the Pacific. We've even got separate cans for them. Give me a rough timing on the sked when you're ready and I'll cut your orders and tell you the date and time to report.'

That was the day before Paula Reece telephoned. Her artistic friend, Count Vrinsky, whom I had met so long ago, had arrived on the *Mantela II*. He would be delighted to offer his advice. I had forgotten about his coming, but nonetheless I got Jim Wilson to take the Gauguins out of their fish tank the following day and stood them up against the walls. I wish I hadn't.

Count Vrinsky arrived soon after surgery. Toma, obviously impressed, announced proudly, 'Master, another master come to see you.' Behind him hovered the tall, elegant figure of Vrinsky, dressed casually in fine hopsack slacks and a silk shirt embroidered on the left breast with a heraldic device indicating his nobility. The same device glittered in a ring on the little finger of his left hand, in which he held the amber cigarette holder complete with black Balkan Sobranie cigarette. Across his shoulders he had slung a tailored camel-hair jacket which he shrugged off. He let it fall into the nearest chair.

'My dear Doctor! A pleasure, as always, to see you.'

There is nothing much one can say in reply to such a greeting. He was handsome, in middle age, I thought; excellent features, wide shoulders, narrow hips, his mass of grey hair cut in a way that suited his finely shaped head. No sign of baldness.

As if drawn by a magnet, he crossed to the wall where 'Pink Street' hung, and as if concentrating on serious matters, flicked the half-smoked Sobranie through the open window.

He stood in front of the picture for several minutes then

took it from the wall and held it in the sunlight streaming through the window. 'How interesting! Yes. Very, very interesting.' Both his tone and his manner were reverent – the manner of a connoisseur. 'You have many other Gauguins, Paula tells me.'

I took Vrinsky to see them. He muttered something about the originality of the idea of keeping pictures in a fish tank and one by one studied the paintings with no more than the occasional, 'Very, very interesting'. He examined each one with the same meticulous care he had bestowed on 'Pink Street'. I hovered in the background saying almost nothing for nearly an hour before he finally sat down, crossed his legs carefully and said, 'Truly fascinating. Indeed remarkable.' He looked for some minutes at his grey suede moccasins. The aromatic smoke from his cigarette clouded his face. The pause continued.

'You speak excellent English,' I said fatuously.

'Ah, yes. My parents settled in Boston; I was educated at Harvard.'

I knew little of the social status of the Bostonians, but I did know that his father was a Polish immigrant, and for some reason Alec Reid's explosive 'Bloody charlatan!' echoed faintly in my mind.

'And what do you think of the pictures?' I asked, aware that I sounded the simpleton I was in art matters – though I was certainly unprepared for the revelation to come.

'Remarkable, my dear Doctor. As I said – remarkable.' He idly pushed his cigarette through a perfect smoke ring. 'What do you know of Gauguin's life?'

'His life? Very little, I'm afraid. Most of it is based on what I read in *The Moon and Sixpence*.'

'Ah! An excellent tale, but fiction of course. There is far more to Gauguin's life than is revealed there. Did you know, for instance, that he left the South Seas in 1893 and went to Paris?'

'No.' I shook my head.

'Yes. In Paris he met a half-caste girl of thirteen from the

East Indies called Annah. He nicknamed her Annah the Javanese, and she became his mistress. And she encouraged him to spend all the money he had from a small legacy from his uncle – wild parties and so on. When the money was gone, Gauguin arranged an exhibition of his work at the Durand-Ruel Gallery. It was a failure, and he decided to return to the South Seas. But Annah wanted more money. May I tell you how she got it?'

'Please do.' I called Toma to bring in gin and fresh lime juice.

'Behind Gauguin's back she decided to steal his paintings while Gauguin was in Copenhagen meeting the Danish wife, Mette, he had abandoned. This left Annah the time to organise the theft, and then she left Gauguin.'

I began to see the light. 'And these were the seventeen pictures?' I asked. 'How did Gauguin get them back?'

'He didn't,' said Vrinsky drily. For a moment he gazed at his ring as if seeking inspiration. Then he continued, 'Annah knew that when Gauguin returned to find his studio ransacked he would realise that seventeen pictures had been stolen. So she arranged with Ambroise Vollard, an art dealer and friend of Gauguin, who was a technically competent painter in his own right, to paint convincing copies of the pictures she had stolen. She knew that Gauguin would only give them a casual glance, since he would have no reason to suspect the theft.'

'Copies?' I could scarcely believe my ears. 'You mean – these are forgeries?'

Vrinsky rose hurriedly as if anxious to offer me reassurance. 'Forgeries? No, no, no, Doctor. *Copies* – a very different matter. Oh yes indeed; *very* different. The art of the copyist is recognised, always has been. Many students go to the art galleries and copy the works of the great masters. There are many clients willing to pay modest prices for such copies.'

Suddenly I recovered my wits. It was clear to me that something was unexplained. 'But how do you know,' I asked, 'that these are the copies and not the originals?'

'Very simple.' He paused and fitted another cigarette into the amber holder. 'I know because it is an established fact that Annah was a passenger on the cross-Channel steamer *Princess Alice* which capsized in a storm and was lost with all hands – and, regrettably, the pictures. One of the major puzzles of the art world ever since has been, What happened to the copies? And now that puzzle is solved. Gauguin carried them to Koraloona and he gave them to your wife's grandmother.'

Shocked, I tried to reason. 'But, he was her lover. He wouldn't have given her fakes.'

'He was a very sick man, Kit. From 1896 on he was a wreck. He may have loved Aleena's grandmother but he was incapable of rational thought. He gave her some keepsake,' Vrinsky shrugged, with a hint of melancholy. 'No doubt he simply gave her his portfolio of pictures and told her to take them.'

I was dumbfounded, and I felt as if my world had stopped spinning. The vision of the Gauguin Memorial Hospital had vanished like smoke from Vrinksy's cigarette. 'You mean – ' I pointed at the pictures he had carefully examined. ' – they're worthless?'

He laughed. He really had a very attractive laugh – it matched Paula's deep-throated huskiness perfectly.

'I mean no such thing, Kit. But let me explain in more detail. You asked me how I knew the pictures were copies. I've told you the factual side – all documented of course, my dear fellow. But there are other matters than the recorded, the chapters and verses.'

He took one of the pictures – it was the one of the boy with the red bananas against a background of blue mountains – and stood it where the light from the window fell full on it. Then, using his amber cigarette holder as a pointer he gave me what I must admit was a fascinating talk on the technicalities of painting, of the grinding of pigments, how they were mixed with dilutents, of the stability of certain mineral colours derived from azurite and malachite, how the identity of a painter revealed itself in upstrokes and downstrokes, or even the use of the thumb to spread thick masses of colour.

He dwelt on the absorbent powers of wood and glass and canvas and paper, and of the quality of paints made from synthetic dyes which were just coming into use in Gauguin's time.

'They could not possibly have been available to Gauguin in a remote spot like Koraloona,' he said. 'That sky is done in French ultramarine, which was barely on the market in 1893. Vollard, though, being an art dealer, would have had a supply to offer to his painter clients.'

Dumbly I listened, all hope fleeing with every expert word the man uttered. Then I clutched at one straw.

'But if Gauguin only came to Koraloona once, just before he died, and painted all this – ' I indicated specially 'Pink Street', 'then they *must* be genuine. Gauguin visited France and met Annah the Javanese *before* he lived in Koraloona. So Annah couldn't have stolen paintings that hadn't been painted.'

For a moment I thought that Vrinsky looked taken aback, particularly when I added, 'Princess Tiare told me once that Gauguin had never been to Koraloona before he met her mother.'

Vrinsky gave a deprecating gesture. 'Gauguin was a Frenchman, and every inch an artist, and sometimes,' he coughed discreetly, 'they tend to alter facts to suit themselves. And one can easily understand that a man who has deserted a wife and children has scant regard for the truth.'

'What are you driving at?' I asked, almost harshly.

'The real truth, Doctor, is one that perhaps you shouldn't tell your wife or her mother. Sometimes silence is kinder. The truth is that Gauguin made one, possibly two, visits to Koraloona and visited Noumea and other islands before he fell in love with Tiare's mother.'

'Tiare *knows* that some are portraits of her mother,' I insisted. 'Her mother told her.'

Vrinsky put one or two canvases side by side and then suggested, 'Take a good look at these faces – they each have a similar, characteristic square face, square more than aquiline. Do you know why all Gauguin's faces look alike? Any serious student of his work will tell you one indisputable fact: that when Gauguin left France for the islands, he took with him an old photograph of an Egyptian tomb picture and he used to copy the faces and stylised postures. We also know that he took with him a photo of a Javanese temple frieze which Gauguin had bought at the Java pavilion during the great Paris exhibition. The photos still exist. They have appeared in several books. Gauguin didn't like painting faces so he copied the faces on the frieze. That is why they all look similar. So you see – '

I did see, unfortunately. I saw because, paradoxically, Vrinsky had blinded me with science. And I even remembered vaguely that Purvis *had* once told me why Gauguin painted faces from an old photo.

'But don't despair, Kit,' said Vrinsky gently. 'I know my way through the mazes of the art world – and I can tell you that the copies will excite great attention as curiosities. Dealers knew they existed but they've never been able to find them. Now they have. And what a furore they will create! I am myself a member of a New York syndicate which would be vastly interested in purchasing your collection – not, I fear for the price the originals would have fetched but for, say – ' He paused as if making some mental calculation. 'For, say, a thousand dollars each.' He let this sink into my mind. 'Indeed, I will offer you my personal cheque for that amount, knowing full well that my New York friends will agree.' He could see my bewilderment and he didn't press home the suggestion. Taking his jacket and slinging it casually round his shoulders he made for the door. Then, turning, he made his exit line.

'I realise, of course, that four thousand or so of your English pounds is scarcely enough to equip your hospital, but it will help. Do think it over, Kit. There is no hurry – not for a day or two. I will call on you early next week. But no longer, please!'

*

That same night I had invited Alec Reid for dinner and Jason and Miss Sowerby for coffee on the veranda after the meal. I had hoped for good news. Instead I poured out the whole sad story while Aleena spent the evening as though in a trance, almost in tears. The reactions of the other three were startling.

'I wish I could offer to help ye wi' a wee loan, Laddie,' said Alec. 'But as ye can see, I've nae got enough to buy meself a new belt. On the other hand, my guid lady is nae poor, nae mean. I'll write and ask if she'd like to offer us a loan for the hospital.'

'That's very generous, Alec.' I was touched. 'But the trouble is – she'd never get her money back.'

'I'm a Scot so I know that full well, Laddie, but she's a Sassenach, so she might be taken in,' he said sardonically, adding, 'and she's floating in money.'

Miss Sowerby coughed diplomatically as she fingered her port and lemon (which I noticed consisted these days of more port and less lemon) and started, 'I've got a small capital sum my father left me – '

'And I'm sure I could get *some* advance for my novel,' said Purvis.

I held out my hand. 'Thanks, thanks, thanks, one and all. But remember what Shakespeare said about good friends, "Neither a borrower nor a lender be". We are all friends here, don't ever let money come into that friendship. And don't worry. I've got some ideas.'

'Such as what?' asked Jason.

'We sometimes forget that we do already have the buildings for a hospital. We *have* got an offer of equipment at cut prices. I think we should consider taking Count Vrinsky's money if Aleena agrees – four thousand is a lot of pounds – and then I'll try to get Sam Truscott in California and maybe Mr Morris, the surgeon I met who lives in Boston, to organise some publicity and try to get some subscriptions. You know how good the Americans are at this sort of thing. I can see the headlines now.' I ran my hands in the air in front of me: 'BEAUTIFUL GIRL

GIVES PAINTINGS IN BID TO HELP HOSPITAL and then another headline underneath: BUT WILL IT BE ENOUGH? I'm sure that will bring in a few quid.'

I hesitated, and then added on a less cheerful note to Alec, 'I've got an unpleasant chore to undertake if you could let me have Nellie for a couple of days – and two days off.'

'She's yours if ye need her. For why, Laddie?'

'I've got to do the right thing and confess to Mr Petrie of Christie's. So I'd like to send a cable asking him to phone me at the Southern Cross on Friday if I can fly there. I'll have to spend the night in Sanderstown because they'll only accept London calls at six o'clock our time – too late for me to fly back.'

'Aye, that's all right, Laddie. Go ahead with the arrangements. And,' again with the sardonic voice, 'I'm glad ye're doing what you call the "right thing" and behaving like a gentleman, for there's one more thing ye'd best think about. Your precious Count Vrinsky. It'll nae be a bad idea to pour out all your troubles to yon Christie's man. He may offer you double the price for the copies.'

This had crossed my mind, for I was not that much of a fool. Vrinsky could easily play me for an art sucker, so I wasn't going to let him have the copies without checking first with Christie's.

The next day I got on the sked to Sanderstown, dictated a cable and finally arrangements were started for me to take a call from London at six o'clock on the Friday evening.

'Wish me luck.' I kissed Aleena as I prepared to leave.

'It's the first time we've been parted since we were married. Take care of yourself, my beloved.' She put her arms round me. 'You know, all this – paintings, forgeries, hospitals – *all* of it means nothing when I think of you. You're my heart and soul and I hope you love me as much as I love you. That's the only real thing that matters.' There were tears in the corners of her eyes and I said, 'Don't cry, my sweet. I'll be back soon.'

'I can't help it,' she smiled through her tears, 'my heart was never used for love until I met you.'

This time there was no delay in the call from Christie's. The phone bell in my room rang at exactly six o'clock.

'This is a very pleasant surprise,' began the agreeable if distant voice of Mr Petrie. 'I hope this means you have found a way to reach California.'

I hesitated before replying. 'I've solved the transport problem, yes. But I'm afraid I've got bad news for you and Christie's, Mr Petrie.'

'Sotheby's?' A whole wealth of meaning sounded in the one angry word.

'No, no, no.'

'Good!' There was, even over the telephone, an audible sigh of relief. 'What seems to be the trouble then, Doctor?'

'Worse than Sotheby's.' I had to use any words I could think of to cover up my sense of embarrassment, amounting almost to fear before finally I blurted out, 'I'm afraid they're forgeries. Copies.'

'Forgeries!' I almost felt that the shouting voice would jerk the phone off the bedroom wall.

'Well, Mr Petrie,' I started to explain. 'It seems that they're not originals, but copies by Vollard.'

There was a long pause. Petrie was obviously reflecting on the shattering news. Finally, almost carefully, he said, 'I know all about Vollard. There are many people who say he was an unscrupulous dealer. He certainly handled Gauguin and many of the Impressionists. And he *was* a talented copyist. But how do *you* know about Monsieur Vollard?'

'Well, Mr Petrie, a well-known art expert happened to visit Koraloona – '

'Doctor Masters, *please*! Famous art experts don't *happen* to visit desert islands.'

Koraloona was hardly a desert island, but I didn't have the heart to protest, for Petrie almost shouted, 'And this art expert – was he generous enough to offer to buy these fakes, notwithstanding?'

560

'Yes he was.' I hesitated. 'He made me an offer, but I put him off until I phoned you.'

'Thank God for that. Very intelligent of you, Doctor. You gave me quite a fright. Now, Doctor, remember that Christie's are paying for this radio telephone call. Not you or me. So let's forget that it costs money. Let's take our time shall we? Tell me what happened. Everything. Take as long as you like. I want to know every single thing that has happened – assuming that you can tell me you haven't entered into any obligations or promises to sell to anyone else.'

'I haven't.' I started to tell him the whole story. From time to time he interrupted me, and sometimes I asked him questions.

'Is it true that Gauguin visited Paris to raise money and met this Annah girl and went to see Mette, his wife in Denmark?' I asked. 'And that was *before* he met Aleena's grandmother, yet he painted Koraloona apparently on a previous visit.'

This was the key question that had puzzled me at first, until Vrinsky had told me how Gauguin had been to Koraloona on a previous occasion.

'I don't believe he made two visits to Koraloona,' said Petrie flatly. 'I just don't believe it. Almost everything that Gauguin did until the last year or so of his life has been documented by art historians. How is it that in many biographies I have studied, not one mentioned Koraloona until the brief details before his death in Tahiti?'

'That's what I said to the art expert, but he told me there were several gaps in Gauguin's life story.'

'Doctor Masters – ' even on the phone I could detect an edge of sarcasm as Petrie said, 'For someone who knew little about Gauguin less than a month ago, you seem to be remarkably well informed. May I ask how you came to learn so much so quickly?'

Rather crossly, I said, 'From the art expert who was staying with a rich friend of ours on her holiday estate.'

'I wasn't meaning to annoy you,' reassured Petrie, 'but

art experts are, in a sense, all members of a rather exclusive club. May I know the name of the gentleman in question?'

'Of course. His name is Count Vrinsky.'

Quite plainly I could hear a guffaw of laughter, hastily repressed, and less plainly an aside to someone who was obviously listening to our conversation on an extension, 'It's that old bugger Vrinsky up to his tricks again.'

'What did I hear?' I cried.

'Sorry, Doctor. It wasn't meant for your ears. It was my only way of expressing instant relief.' He laughed heartily. 'You see, we all know about your friend Vrinsky. And I won't go so far as to say he's a crook, because no one has ever proved that he is, but he's a rascal, and if anyone can pull a fast one in the art field, Vrinsky's the man. He's a genius at picking up bargains that, in some mysterious way, always turn out to be worth fortunes. Please, Doctor, *please* don't let him influence you.'

'You mean to say that he's a – a crook. Do you think that the Gauguins may be genuine after all?'

'I hope so. The very fact that Vrinsky has made a firm offer is an indication that they might be real. Copies by Vollard of any paintings aren't worth much.'

I had already told Petrie that Vrinsky had offered me a thousand dollars for each copy, and Petrie added with an almost urgent note, 'Whatever he offers, say no. If he doubles, trebles, quadruples the offer, say no, no, no. Every time he offers more money it's an indication that the paintings are genuine, not the forgeries he pretends they are. You do understand that? We are prepared to undertake the risk, to underwrite your expenses to New York so that we can have a chance to examine them, subject them to tests, then certify to all who attend auctions that they are genuine.'

'Don't worry, Mr Petrie. That's why I asked you to phone me. I first met Count Vrinsky before the war so, although I had my doubts, I felt that he *must* be trying to help as an old friend.'

The real crux of the problem, Petrie explained, was that

Gauguin's entire life had now been chronicled in dozens of art books. It *was* an established fact that he had been to Noumea – that was true – but he could not have broken his journey at Koraloona – because Gauguin's name was on the ship's manifest, and even the fact that on this particular voyage he wrote to a friend that he had changed from third to second class. That he had apparently not painted on Koraloona was put down by art historians to his being a sick man when he arrived there – again on a journey well documented. What made Vrinsky's story more credible was that, apart from mentioning the earlier visit to Koraloona, everything he had told me *was* true. There *had* been Annah the Javanese, there *had* been a failure to sell paintings in Paris, there *had* been a legacy which Annah had encouraged him to spend.

'The great skill of men like Vrinsky,' explained Petrie, 'is that they tell you so much truth that it makes one lie plausible. But, remember Vrinsky hasn't dwelt much on the texture of the canvases or on certain of the techniques that Gauguin employed. That's for us and our scientific advisers to study when we examine the paintings in New York.'

'I'm looking forward to seeing you,' I said.

'So am I. But remember, he's a very slippery customer, so I suggest that you play along with him. I'm sure that, as you told me it was a heritage, it might take time to make a deal – in other words you could invent excuses for delay. Why not suggest to him that you might contact the American Art Association in New York's Madison Square? If Vrinsky thinks they're genuine, you'll see how the prices he originally offered you will rocket up. Meanwhile, finalise your arrangements to fly to New York and when you're ready, let us know. The tickets for you and your wife will be ready for you in San Francisco, and we'll be waiting for you at Idlewild with a hired limousine and a reserved suite at the St Regis Hotel. We'll see you soon, Doctor. Good morning to you.'

*

Good morning! There he went again. The same mistake as last time. It was nearly seven o'clock at night, and all I wanted to do, but couldn't, was to fly Nellie and let Aleena know the good news at that very moment. As I couldn't, I did the next best thing, went down the stairs to the bar, humming, 'Oh! what a beautiful morning, Oh! what a beautiful day!'

It seemed the right tune for our changing time zones, this popular melody from *Oklahoma*, whose tunes had swept through every American camp in the Pacific (and thus Koraloona) since it was first produced in New York in 1943.

Yes, indeed, Oh! what a beautiful day!

40

When I returned to Koraloona and explained to Aleena what Petrie had said, Vrinsky's devastating assessment became replaced in a twinkling by a new-found feeling of confidence that all would now end well.

It wasn't that I had ever doubted that these were real Gauguins. But it was curious that, before Vrinsky appeared, I don't think I had ever worried whether they were genuine or not. When you suddenly see the contents of a treasure chest which can never be sold because it is a sacred trust, the question of their beauty is so breathtaking that – since they *are* unsaleable – the question of worth remains secondary to beauty.

And in a way, the same had applied when Tiare gave me the painting of 'Pink Street'. That magnificent picture might no longer be a part of the sacred trust, but I knew that nothing would ever induce me to sell it.

The curious thing is that if we had never decided to sell the paintings and build a hospital with the proceeds, and Vrinsky had come along with his shattering news, it wouldn't really have crushed any feeling. Wouldn't it? No,

I don't think so, because the paintings were just as exciting whoever had executed them. If, for instance, Vollard had been Tiare's father, would it have changed the beauty of the copies he might have made? Wouldn't they also have the same sentimental value? I may be wrong, but I don't think so.

Once the paintings, however, had become translated in our minds into items of merchandise, the situation changed entirely. Almost ashamed, I found myself regarding their beauty as second to their value. The canvases had become a substitute for money. If the paintings had never existed, yet had some rich benefactor offered to build the hospital and then, our expectations high, had withdrawn from the offer, would I have felt any worse than at Vrinsky's news?

But now it had all changed again, for it seemed as though they *were* genuine Gauguins. The fact that Christie's seemed convinced that they were genuine helped me to forget the blacker commercial thoughts.

Meanwhile, what to do about Vrinsky?

He wanted an urgent agreement; I wanted to delay any decision. I suppose I could just have told him to go to hell, but I was so angry at being treated as a sucker that I wanted to play along with him, not only as Petrie had suggested but also as a kind of revenge; it was only due to Christie's that my eyes had been opened, and they felt sure that, if Vrinsky increased his offer, it would be a further indication that the paintings were genuine.

I had only been away for the one night, and sure enough the next morning Vrinsky came round to see me after surgery, looking as immaculate and as spruce as ever, oozing confidence, the amber cigarette with its Balkan Sobranie cigarette held languidly in his left hand.

'Ah! You look well, Doctor. Did you have a pleasant evening in Sanderstown! A special patient you had to see?'

I hesitated – a simulated situation for I knew exactly what I was going to say, how I was going to give the impression of having played an underhand trick on such a 'trustworthy' man as Vrinsky.

'No, Count,' I muttered after I had offered him a drink which he waved aside. 'It wasn't a patient I went to see. I realise of course that these so-called Gauguins are only copies,' I lied. 'But my mother-in-law – the Princess Tiare – felt I should get what patients ask of a doctor when they are worried: a second opinion.'

'I don't quite understand.' His voice was guarded.

'Actually, I should have told you, but it was a spur of the moment decision, and I didn't have time – '

'I still don't quite understand – '

'I went to Sanders to telephone the American Art Association in New York. Madison Avenue. Just for advice, you understand.'

The only person I had phoned, of course, was Petrie and I was now doing only what he suggested. But at the words I saw Vrinsky stiffen, the languid air became replaced with a carefully controlled sense of watchfulness. He *looked* as casual and as languid as ever but, as a doctor, I could tell immediately that he was tense and worried beneath the calm exterior. I had seen too many patients trying to mask their fears when told they needed to have a dangerous operation.

'With what result?' he asked in a slightly sulky voice.

'They agreed that they were no doubt copies' – his face relaxed as I spoke 'because, as they pointed out, they would otherwise have been discovered and sold long ago. But they did say – '

'Yes?' asked Vrinsky eagerly.

'That though copies are not really valuable, they *might* have a certain value as they were done by Vollard, who is apparently more famous than I thought. They didn't make an offer of course, because they haven't seen them, but they asked a lot of questions and – ' I shrugged my shoulders. How fascinating to lie to order! To use lies to see the effect they have on another liar, each of us believing the other to be telling the truth.

I must say that at this moment Vrinsky displayed the quintessence of *sangfroid*. And I knew why. It was because

566

he thought I had told the American Art Association that they were *copies*. He assumed that I had believed his story that the paintings were only copies and (according to my lies) had never doubted this when talking to the AAA.

Without a trace of embarrassment, he looked at me with that frank open smile of his and said, 'What an extraordinary coincidence!'

'Coincidence?'

'Yes.' Suddenly, the tension gone, he lit another Balkan Sobranie. 'Extraordinary! While you were telephoning the Association in New York I was exchanging cables with *my* associates in America. You understand? I had to keep them in touch, of course, and that's the reason I really came to see you. When I first saw the copies I had to make what you call a snap judgment. So I said "A thousand dollars each".'

'And then?' For a moment I wondered whether he wanted to withdraw the offer.

'I received a cable back expressing the enthusiasm of the syndicate for the – ' he hesitated – 'for the Vollard copies, and telling me in no uncertain terms that I must be prepared to offer considerably more unless I wanted to let this unique – ' again that hesitation – 'Gauguin curiosity slip through our fingers.'

What a consummate actor he was! With hardly a moment's hesitation – he knew exactly when to hesitate and when not to! – he spread out his hands in a gesture of invitation and added, 'And you know, Kit, that I respect the worthy reason that prompted you and your wife to sell the paintings. And because it *is* such a worthy cause, I am prepared to double the original offer and pay you two thousand dollars for each copy.'

'But you mustn't let your heart rule your head,' I murmured.

'*Please*. My heart has always ruled my head. That is why I am not a millionaire. But we are in business, our consortium, and we won't make a loss, I promise you. But for a good cause, we are prepared to buy them at more than the

567

going price. And that will help you to build your hospital.'

What a smarmy, horrible creature he was! Half of me wanted to shout at him, 'You bloody liar!' But I couldn't do that. I had an oral assurance from Christie's that Petrie believed the paintings to be genuine, and especially if Vrinsky were to raise his offer. But Petrie hadn't even seen them. Who wasn't to say that Petrie wasn't another Vrinsky? In my heart I didn't believe that, but £8,000 or so payable now, on the dot! And the smooth way in which Vrinsky had doubled the figure! Mindful of Petrie's advice to play along with Vrinsky, I decided to do just that. And when I started wondering how to do this, fate gave me a helping hand.

I had agreed to think the matter over for twenty-four hours, using the pretext that I must consult both Aleena and her mother, and the next morning, driving her own car, who should be on the veranda of 'Harley Street' but Paula Reece.

Alec and I were both there, but Paula saw me first as Alec was inside, and she cried, 'So sorry to bother you, but poor Count Vrinsky is in agony. He's hurt his back – it seemed to go suddenly – and he can hardly walk. Could one of you come round to give him some painkiller or whatever you do for a bad back?'

'Of course. Hang on a minute,' I said, and inside I asked Alec, 'Would you like to go?' adding slyly, 'You'll get a free drink out of Paula.'

'He's yours, Laddie,' Alec replied, disappearing into the ward to do what we laughingly referred to as 'the rounds'. 'I canna stand the man.'

So I went, to find Vrinsky in bed and obviously in acute pain.

'My dear Doctor, this time you are coming to see me professionally.' Vrinsky's face showed his agony. Beads of sweat lined his face. 'I can't think how it happened. I was reaching to pick a branch of syringa for Paula's table decoration when – ' he snapped his fingers ' – pouf! It's agony.'

568

I examined him carefully, and found it was what I expected – a slipped disc which when it is out of place causes excruciating pain by bringing pressure on trapped nerves. But I wasn't going to let him get away with knowing it was anything so simple (though painful). I might not be able to match him in cunning where works of art were concerned, but I could easily blind him with medical science. I kept silent, tapped my teeth with a pencil as if mystified, wrapped the cuff of the sphygmomanometer above his elbow and noted his blood pressure (perfectly normal of course), prodded and tapped, listened through my stethoscope, looked grave, and told him he had a prolapsed intervertebral.

'And what? – ' he began.

'You will have to stay in bed for as long as it takes for the cartilage to ease itself back into place. It will be some days; and it will remain painful, I'm afraid.' From my medical bag, I shook some tablets into a small bottle, taking care to screen my action from him: I didn't want him to see that they were only aspirin. 'A couple of these will help ease the pain; but not more than three in any one period of five hours.' My tone implied that I was giving him some secret cure.

He was shaken; I could see that. But he couldn't forbear to hint at picture business. As I helped him on with his shirt he muttered through yelps of sharp pain, 'I had meant, my dear Kit, to bring to a close our – er – little business matter.' He sat down painfully. 'I have my cheque book with me – '

I dismissed the notion out of hand. 'You will leave matters of business entirely alone and concentrate on rest. Mental activity will only make things worse. No business,' I insisted firmly. 'When you're restored to a less painful condition, we'll talk. But now, rest.'

So, unfairly perhaps, I was able to delay matters. And then a further delay – this time a genuinely worrying one – came when Toma failed to appear with our early morning coffee and orange juice. I found him in bed, flushed and with an obviously high fever. His pallet bed was soaked with sweat and he complained that he felt 'stones all over, inside leg and arm, making alltime pain'. This was his way of saying he ached all over. I called Alec and we got Toma to the clinic in the ambulance, where Miss Sowerby bathed him with cool water and helped him into bed where he lay dry-mouthed and feverishly tossing.

Toma had barely been put to bed in Harley Street before five other men and women arrived, one being carried in a kind of fireman's lift by her father. All had similar symptoms – high fever, aches and pains, a dry mouth.

'My God,' I cried. 'I hope this isn't – '

'Aye,' Alec said, 'I ken what you're thinking.'

He was right. Was it the onset of a polio epidemic? We wouldn't be able to tell for several days since it began like any other virus infection. Was this the porodomal period before the stiffening of the limbs and the agonising pain set in? Or was it measles or hepatitis or just plain 'flu? There was no telling.

I watched constantly by their bedsides, especially Toma's, recalling with gratitude how he had so faithfully attended me when Mana had been trying to poison me. For three days the fever did not abate; then on the fourth morning when I took his temperature it was down to 100 degrees. 'This is where our real worries begin,' I said to Alec.

'Aye.' He shared my anxiety.

I kept making Toma and the other patients move legs and arms, fearful that, with the high threshold of pain tolerance common to Polynesians, they might not have reacted audibly. But as Toma's temperature slowly went down, he assured me, with the wan smile of a man exhausted by fever, that there was 'no alltime pain' and that his legs 'would walk about'. The others began to show improvement. But it was several days before Alec and I felt reasonably certain that the infection – all from the same village – had been no more than a savage attack of 'flu. By which time we were beginning to plan our departure for New York, still without anything being settled with Vrinsky.

But all thoughts of Vrinsky vanished when the last piece in the Gauguin jigsaw puzzle came to light in an extraordinary way.

Among the camp buildings which the Americans had left us – and which would form our new hospital – were some items of 'junk' (their description) which we would have to discard, and sometimes we would encourage a few cured patients to 'pay' our non-existent fees by taking away old chairs, broken tables, chipped enamel trays, items of no value, so that we could see better the lay-out of what we planned to do. Amongst the 'junk' about to be thrown away one day was an old filing cabinet which I remembered seeing in their admin quarters. It had four drawers and was painted dark green.

'We'll keep that,' cried Alec. 'It may be a bit large for our present hospital, but it'll serve us better than yon tin trunk of ours. And we'll expand, Laddie; we'll expand. Once the Gauguin Memorial Hospital gets going – '

We took the filing cabinet to Harley Street, then Alec volunteered to transfer all the folders to its roomy sliding drawers and index them.

The following day, Alec came puffing and sweating into my bungalow, waving a large slightly mildewed envelope.

'Relax on the sofa for a minute while I fetch some Old Rarity,' I suggested.

'I spent the afternoon,' he began between puffs and sips, 'at Harley Street. And I finished filing awa' our records in yon bonny filing cabinet. I was aboot tae tell someone to sling our empty tin trunk on the rubbish dump when – upending it, y'ken – I could hae swairn something slid aboot inside, though I could have swairn that I'd taken all the files oot.'

As always when Alec became excited, his Scottish accent took over completely.

'Now there's a wee mystery, I thought, and opened up,

571

thinking to find a file I'd overlooked. But nothing.' He held up his glass for emphasis. '*Nothing*, Laddie.' I poured a sizeable measure into the glass.

'So I set it down again, thinking that I was getting fey, hearing silence, y'ken. But no: each time I upended it, first one end then the other, there was this sliding sound; and each time I opened the lid there was nothing.' He paused and tapped his forehead with his knuckles. 'Then it struck me, Laddie – with the fer-r-r-ocity of a Shetland gale: there was a false bottom to the thing – nae doot for extra security against the ants and humidity, for private papers and the like.'

'Ah,' I said, still not understanding his playing the find up so dramatically. 'A trick box . . . a box of tricks.'

Alec winked. 'Now there ye have it. Tricks, the noo. A rare box of tricks.' He flourished the envelope. 'It took me but a couple of minutes to find the catch that released the spring holding the false bottom doon – '

'And you found that envelope. I take it there's something interesting in it?'

He leaned forward, put his legs to the ground. 'I tell you, Kit, *you're* the one that'll find it interesting.' He handed me the package and beamed at me with the beneficent smile of a cat that's enjoyed the cream. I took the package and shook from it a few letters, a miscellaneous selection of sheets of paper – some yellowed, some slightly foxed, some on which the ink had faded a little, as if they had been exposed to light before being hidden away beneath the false base of the trunk. I examined them, puzzled. They were all in French.

Alec saw my puzzled look. 'Aye, ma French is a bit rusty too. But it didna take me long to work out who they're from, and who to.'

I turned them over in my hands. In every case the signature was the same: Paul. I was thunderstruck. They were letters from Paul Gauguin to his lover Marama – Tiare's mother!

*

For a long, long moment I sat looking speechless – not with excitement so much as with memory and sadness – at the sight of the letters. At last! And yet I could picture in my mind's eye the penniless artist pouring out his heart to his lover; and the long road of destiny along which this love had led, first to Gauguin's beautiful daughter – the daughter he had never seen – and thence from Tiare to the beauty of Aleena, and now – to us, and soon to be lost. I knew the sale was for a good cause, yet, as I looked at the old documents, I felt a pang of – not exactly guilt – but a feeling that we were coming to the end of this long road. The letters made me realise how the pictures represented Gauguin's love for Marama, his Polynesian princess; the pictures had symbolised something that had been secret; and not tawdry, not some hole-in-the-corner affair, but a love on which Gauguin had lavished his last years, knowing (as he must have done) that he did not have long to live. And now the pictures would leave us for ever and we would probably never see them again; it was like grandchildren going through a box of old photographs, not knowing the people in the old-fashioned sepia reproductions, and in the end throwing them all away.

Finally I asked, 'This trunk – where did it come from?'

Alec knew the answer immediately. He must have been sorting out the past in his mind. 'It belonged to Tiare's mother, as ye know; and she gave it as a thanksgiving present when I brought Aleena into the world. Money didna matter, 'twas the thought that counted and I started using it to keep my records in.'

I will not dwell on the problems we faced in the translations. My French was poor, I only had old memories of lessons at school; Jason Purvis, however, was much better. And it was between us, with help from others who had a smattering of French, that we finally translated them into English. And it was purely for convenience that Aleena and I read them together only after the translation struggles had finally ended.

573

We pored over them, sitting at the table with the sheaf of papers between us, leaping on a phrase here and a phrase there, the yellow lamplight illuminating the sometimes painful words . . . *I ache with longing for you . . . even when I go away for a day to paint*. But they were by no means all letters of love and affection: some of them were extremely practical, concerned with trivia . . . *Please buy me some stamps, I feel too weak to leave the house today* . . . or with his theories of painting . . . *I wrote to Monfreid today, saying, 'All told, painting should seek suggestion more than description, as does music.'* There were perhaps twenty of them in all; and the interest and sadness of them apart, many contained references to the pictures – most delightfully to me personally to 'Pink Street'.

There is a saying among the English, something about viewing life through rose-tinted spectacles . . . I'm not sure; but I know you see the little main street as through a pink glow . . . so this is how I have done it for you – as I saw it in the first moment of my first sight of Koraloona.

It was evident that the gifts to Marama had been given on many different occasions, not in a collection as they had come to us. The letters were rarely dated beyond 'Tuesday' or 'my first day after my illness' or some indefinite time; and sometimes they hinted at Gauguin having come round to seeing himself in the wrong after some minor quarrel and making restitution in the form of a picture.

. . . this little thing of the boy with the load of bananas too big for his frail body will show you how I am burdened with guilt for my words, which I see now were cruel . . .

Sometimes, on the other hand, they were full of joy, as if in a burst of celebration he could not reward his mistress enough for her evident devotion to him:

. . . As I wrote to Mette [his Danish wife], *'There are two natures in me . . . – the humble and the arrogant [from my Peruvian ancestry]' . . . and today I am balanced as on a tightrope between the two, wanting at the same time to hurt you with lust (but you to love the hurt!) and to adore you with gifts . . . the Waterfall is yours because it is the biggest I*

could find and my heart says big, big, big for Marama and anyway it is you who stand there, even though it was done in the studio after a bout of love-making . . . The scrawny chickens are just a joke, they amuse me the way they scratch about for dear life, as if they have but an hour to live before departing from the idyllic joys of Koraloona . . . and the ship is yours too because it brought me to happiness here with you . . . ah, 'Oceanien', you can have had no idea of the task you were performing!

The most tragic letter of all was evidently one he had written when he was ill and perhaps (as Alec had once suggested) 'under the influence of a few sniffs of cocaine'. The handwriting was shakier than in the others; and although I had never much cared for the quartet of pictures that made up Gauguin's representation of 'The Four Horsemen of the Apocalypse', I at least now understood something of the anguish behind the painting of it:

. . . so in my mind the apocalyptic visions . . . the apprehensions of death that . . . [here his mind seemed to have slipped into another dimension altogether] *. . . YOU OUT OF MY CONSCIOUSNESS seem to come dreaming* [the mixed upper and lower case letters as mystifying as the jigsaw-jagged edges of the pictures were] *. . . the House of Pleasure is the lustre of the skull . . .* [then with a sudden return to normality] *. . . you will see what I mean, the pictures say everything . . .*

'And,' said Aleena, 'the letters say everything to us.'

It was true. And their discovery was entirely due to Alec. We owed him more gratitude than we could express. In the letters lay all the provenance anyone could demand.

Now we could go ahead, confident of success. I had already arranged with Alec to take two weeks' leave, deducting it from what was due to me. We had, anyway, never bothered much about leave. In theory the Mission in London allowed its doctors three months' paid leave every four years, but the war had prevented that. And we both loved

575

Koraloona so much that, during the war, we had got into the habit of not really wanting holidays.

But it was different now. Alec had explained to London in a long letter the peculiar circumstances – that I couldn't be sure when my presence would be required in New York or London in the event of an auction, but that I would first have to visit New York. The Mission was so excited at the prospect of a financial windfall that it gladly permitted Alec to make all the arrangements – and that included leave for me before Alec himself, although he was the senior.

'I dinna care when I take my holidays,' said Alec. 'Ye're the one who's going to raise the cash to build the finest hospital in Polynesia. Ye're not going on leave, ye're goin' working.'

I wasn't quite so sure of that – these comings and goings promised a pleasant diversion, and it looked as though they would allow me to take my bride to places as far apart as New York and London. But I knew what Alec meant. Someone had to handle the financial problem.

The next day I cabled Christie's again, saying DOCUMENTS LETTERS FOUND WILL CABLE ARRIVAL DATE SAN FRANCISCO. Then I got hold of Major Latimer, our cigar-chewing friend, and he quickly gave me a firm date on which to fly.

There was nothing left now but to prepare for departure. Aleena was so excited she could hardly even bother to help me wrap up the parcels of paintings into two packets protected by four layers of thick corrugated paper, most without their frames.

'We're ready,' I said to her finally. 'New York. We've never seen it – isn't it exciting?' And then I thought aloud. 'There's one unpleasant task I suppose I must undertake.'

'Who's sick now?' Aleena was tending to think more and more like a doctor's wife as each month passed.

'Count Vrinsky.' I had neglected him as a patient because I was more versed in detecting the possible symptoms of polio, my medical 'speciality'.

'But why should you go?' asked Aleena, almost angrily. 'He's a crook.'

'I think I ought to put him out of his misery. After all, I strung him along. It was a bit mean.'

I did go to see him, despite Aleena's protests. He was still in some pain, sitting down on an inflated rubber ring which had been made for him by Jim from some small inner tube.

'Sorry I haven't been able to come and see you,' I began. 'I've been occupied with a possible outbreak of polio.'

'Yes, Doctor Reid told me. But it's over, isn't it?' He squirmed and wriggled to try to ease the pain. 'Thank God it hasn't interfered with my smoking, but I don't know whether I'm more comfortable sitting up or lying down.' And then he really took the wind out of my sails.

'I do hope you are lucky at Christie's.'

My mouth fell open. Even when I was prepared to do the 'gentlemanly' thing and apologise for not being truthful, he had beaten me to it! 'Ah yes, I knew a couple of days ago. We get all advance information of major art sales the world over,' he explained. 'Everyone in the business does. No hard feelings, Doctor. I only hope you're right and they are genuine.' And then he added, smooth to the end, 'We all make mistakes, and I could have sworn they were copies.'

We shook hands on that and he never batted an eyelid.

Two days later we were sailing for Sanderstown on the first leg of our trip to New York.

41

'My goodness me!'

The first greeting from Christie's, after I had collected our baggage in New York, while Aleena stared disbelievingly at the carpet of snow, was of an astonished Mr Petrie saying, 'Somehow I thought of you as a middle-aged doctor, and instead I find this young man.'

As we shook hands in the hot – not warm, *hot* – central heating of the assembly hall at Idlewild, I asked laughingly, 'How did you know it was me then? You seemed to make a bee-line for me.'

'Not for you, Doctor,' Petrie gave an almost mischievous smile, 'I saw this beautiful black-haired vision, who obviously doesn't look American, and I made a bee-line for *her*.'

'You're very kind,' Aleena smiled, sharing his infectious attitude. 'Happy New Year, Mr Petrie. It *is* January.'

'And let's hope that 1946 is a very special year for you both,' he smiled back.

Petrie was in his late forties, I guessed, and he had such a charming smile that it made one feel 'at home' so to speak, belying the first impression of a rather stern face. Perhaps it was sterner when he was dealing with art crooks, for his brown eyes were restless, looking everywhere, missing nothing.

He had, as promised, provided a black rented car to meet us, and it was of the station wagon type which had become so popular in America. The porter called it 'a limo' as Mr Petrie placed the paintings – which I had personally nursed all the way from Koraloona – on the carpeted rear section of the car, and we squeezed comfortably in the large back seat. The driver closed the door and the car started to purr towards the skyline of Manhattan. On the floor of the rear seat were two packages, and with another laugh, Mr Petrie said, 'And here's something I thought each of you would need.'

Opening them, we discovered two pairs of galoshes. 'Thank you,' Aleena said and tried them on.

'Overshoes, they call them here,' he explained. 'The snow's not too thick and the weather's quite mild for the time of year, but when the snow turns to slush, you'll need them.'

'Where are we going now?' I was peering out at the streets and at the many (to me) quaintly shaped wooden houses, as we sped on our way towards the heart of New York.

'I know you are anxious to see New York, but we'll go first to the St Regis. It's on 56th Street,' Petrie suggested.

As we crossed the river the Manhattan skyline revealed a whole exciting new architectural wonder. Great concrete and glass towers pierced the sky.

'That's the Empire State building.' Petrie pointed to one skyscraper which boasted a spire. 'But the trouble is,' he confessed, 'that I'm as anxious to see *your* sights – in your packages – as you are to see New York.'

'Don't worry, Mr Petrie, we're just as anxious for you to see the Gauguins.'

Once over the bridge, the limo started to turn to the right towards the large straight lines of the main avenues and cross streets. The shops themselves were a bewildering sight. Huge signs promised everything from 'Charlie's donuts' to a running electric news bulletin where the words chased each other alongside a narrow band half way up a tall building. Because it was winter every corner semed to be filled with men selling hot chestnuts or crying 'Bagels', whatever they were.

It wasn't snowing, but very white on the pavements – and on the plots of open land, often made by demolished buildings. There was no sign of the dirty slush I remembered from London winters. We were crossing towards the centre of the city and finally turned left into an enormously wide road with room for four lanes of traffic in each direction, the two sides of the street down which traffic flowed in opposite directions, kept apart by the simple expedient of planting a wide garden fenced in with short iron railings.

Aleena goggled. The road itself seemed to stretch for miles, was slightly undulating, and ahead were scores of traffic lights, all turning from red to green at the same moment so that the traffic roared along past several streets before the green turned to red again.

'This is Park Avenue, and that's Grand Central station at the far end.'

Though the avenue had been cleared of snow, the

579

gardens in the centre were still white, and the grass central garden had been planted with large Christmas trees, dozens of them in a row ahead of us, decorated with hundreds of electric lamps – twinkling, dancing blobs of colour against the white. The buildings on either side were broken here and there by the staggering outline of a skyscraper, standing against the beautiful pure blue of the sky.

'It's it's breathtaking!' Aleena almost dropped her voice to a whisper and clutched my hand. 'I've never seen anything like it.'

'Almost there,' said Petrie more prosaically, 'but we have one final problem to discuss before anything else once we arrive at the St Regis.'

The car swung right into 56th Street.

'Only two or three blocks now,' and soon we saw that hotel sign.

'In front of you is the famous Fifth Avenue,' Petrie pointed ahead. 'The finest shops there are – Tiffany's, Cartier's and so on – and near it is Central Park – the Hyde Park of New York.'

A couple of bellhops – I had to master this foreign language quickly – carried in our bags. We stamped the snow from our shoes as we crossed the pavement and entered the hotel's small warm lobby, where we registered.

Our rooms were on the fourteenth floor, and we made for the lift.

'Sorry, no lifts,' said Petrie mockingly. 'In America they only have elevators.' We were whizzed up, expertly, taken to the suite which contained a basket of fruit, an iced bottle of champagne in a bucket and a discreet card, 'Welcome to the St Regis'.

'We can open the champagne as we talk business.' Petrie addressed both of us, as he untwisted the wire on the cork. 'Before we open the parcels of paintings, we have to make arrangements to be sure they are safe. You realise, Doctor, that if, as we believe, they are genuine Gauguins, they're worth a fortune. Nobody outside an art gallery has ever seen sixteen Gauguins at the same time. You can't leave them unprotected in your suite – even if you only pop out for a quick drink.'

'I was going to ask about that.'

'Here's what I suggest.' It was obvious that behind his cheerful demeanour, Petrie was a man who put first things first – and that meant business before pleasure. 'In America we work in conjunction with one of the world's foremost experts, Professor Norbet Huson, who specialises in the Impressionists and Post-Impressionists. He has a gallery on 53rd Street, and a kind of laboratory where he examines canvases to detect forgeries and – '

'And?'

'And a strongroom. He has to have a big one because he deals with a great many famous art works. I know that, at the moment, he's got a Van Gogh and a Monet. They were brought to him for authentication, but it might be a week before they are collected. So I suggest we don't open the parcels of pictures yet, but take them straight to the professor's. He's away for most of the day, but his assistant will be there and the professor will be back at six this evening, when we can meet in his studio. In the meantime I will contain my patience and take you out on a short tour of New York's main drag, as it's usually called.'

So we did just that. After we had washed in the marble bathroom, we took the paintings down, and deposited them, still wrapped, at the gallery, where Petrie insisted on watching the young assistant lock the strong door and made him give him a receipt for 'Parcels, the property of Christie's'.

After that we spent the first of several glorious days sightseeing in this most exciting of capitals. The first thing we did – it was so cold, we had to – was to buy cheap sheepskin coats, together with an item of clothing neither of us had seen before – Russian-style fur hats, mine with ear flaps that folded down.

It wasn't really *that* cold unless we stayed out a long time, because the moment we entered any shop it was like being hit in the face by the blast from a furnace. When we stayed in the open too long however, the cold started to seep into our bones. But the shops on Fifth Avenue were to us 'rubbernecks' exciting beyond anything we had ever seen.

'Right now,' Aleena pushed open the door to enter Saks, 'I feel as though we should sell all the Gauguins and spend the proceeds here.'

'You could – quite easily,' said Petrie.

We crossed Fifth Avenue almost opposite the slender beauty of the Rockefeller Center. In front of the main entrance a huge Christmas tree overlooked a skating rink on the Plaza on which were dozens of skaters – the girls in very short, flared, 'professional' skirts, almost like ballerina tutus, and twirling or dancing on the ice below a brilliant blue sky. Along one side of the rink was a café, warm and cosy, where people inside watched the skaters from behind huge plate-glass windows.

'Come this way.' Petrie led us from the Plaza through the revolving door where the sudden heat was welcome. Inside there was a long loop of shops where you could buy anything from shirts to shaving tackle, from sweets to suitcases.

'And now, let me invite you for a small ride.' We both looked mystified as we walked half way along the arcade to a bank of more than a dozen lifts, with twinkling changing lights showing where every lift was at that particular moment. Near them, large signs proclaimed 'Floors 1–10' or similar information, including express elevators to the top observation tower, seventy floors high. Petrie led the way to one lift which announced, 'Non-stop to 65th floor'.

'We're going in that!' For a moment Aleena looked positively frightened.

'I'm taking you to the Rainbow Room on the 65th floor, where we can sit down and have a drink and look at the view. It's only part of the way up, and the building isn't as tall as the Empire State anyway but it'll do for your first day.'

We shot up in the lift with such speed that when it

stopped at the 65th floor, and the attendant announced laconically, 'Rainbow Room folks!' I thought my stomach was going to hit the top of the lift. And the view *was* staggering.

'It's a mystery how it stays up.' I think Aleena was waiting a trifle nervously to be on solid ground again, and she wasn't reassured when Petrie explained, 'It's built on what I can only call an elastic principle. I'm told that the top of the Rockefeller Center sways up to twelve feet when there's a strong wind. If it was too rigid, it might snap.'

We did everything that afternoon, even – well-wrapped with fur rugs – a ride round Central Park in a horse-drawn carriage. When the drive ended, near the Pierre Hotel on Fifth Avenue, Petrie hailed a cab and said, 'Six o'clock! The professor will be there. Now it's your turn to give *me* a conducted tour.' Telling the cab driver the address, he said, 'I hope I looked patient this afternoon, but all the time I've been in an agony of impatience to see the real treasures when we unveil the Gauguins. Whatever they fetch, a collection of sixteen Gauguins is priceless.'

As the cab turned into 53rd Street, Petrie said, 'I think you'll like Professor Huson. For some time he was an associate of the art connoisseur Bernhard Berenson, so there's no doubt about his qualifications.'

The professor *had* arrived, and we all shook hands as we were introduced. He was a short man with very white hands and a contrastingly rubicund face. Round his neck was a black silk ribbon from which were suspended three gold-rimmed quizzing glasses – presumably of different powers of magnification. He sat toying delicately with these while I repeated to him as accurately as possible Vrinsky's assessment of the pictures. Every now and then a smile crossed his rosy cheeks and he nodded frequently as if in silent confirmation of his thoughts.

'That's about as accurate as I can recall, Professor,' I said when I had finished.

'And enough,' he raised a hand. 'Ah yes indeed, it all adds up. The count is not unknown to us.'

583

'So I gather,' I said.

'Very much so. A gentleman of considerable wealth, most of it amassed from – er – shall we say *inexperienced* owners of works of art, like yourself.'

'You mean he's a confidence trickster?'

'My dear Doctor! Perhaps that would be stretching it a bit. I think he's never done anything illegal; but some of his ventures, well,' he shrugged his shoulders. 'As soon as I heard that he asked you what you knew of Gauguin's life I suspected he was feeling his way, discovering how far he could go without arousing your suspicions.'

'But he offered me what seemed a reasonable price for the copies?'

'Ah! There we come to the heart of the matter. I am as familiar as anyone with the life and works of Gauguin.' He made gently deprecating movements with his hands.

'I appreciate that,' I said. 'Mr Petrie told me you're the number one expert.'

'Very kind. I dare say your count knows a good deal too – enough to sound convincing with a garbled story that has a basis of fact and which he touched up with technicalities.' He smiled broadly. 'French ultramarine not on the market indeed! Synthetic dyes not available! But don't bother your head with such things, Doctor. The fact is that there has never been in the art world any suggestion that Vollard ever made any copies of Gauguin's paintings. Vollard *was* Gauguin's agent and dealer, and actually supported him with money in advance of pictures in Gauguin's last years; Vollard was also a very good amateur artist. And Annah, it is true, *was* a Javanese girl he'd taken off the streets in Paris and she *did* ransack Gauguin's studio. But the rest is complete fabrication. Gauguin's life is heavily documented. Certainly Annah never made off with any of his pictures. Our friend has a fast-thinking mind and knew he had to get the paintings for a figure that would satisfy you and leave him and his syndicate with room for a handsome profit when the time came to re-sell. They realise that with the war over, there's going to be a big boom in art soon – and

584

the Impressionists and Post-Impressionists are going to be an important part of it.'

I suppose I must have looked relieved. 'What a good job I didn't sell them!'

'Certainly it is. Mind you, there's always the *possibility* that they may be forgeries. But before the war the appeal of "modern" artists was limited, so that with few exceptions their work wasn't worth forging. Collectors could buy originals for perfectly reasonable prices.'

I told him how I had read of Hugh Walpole buying a Gauguin for £145.

'Exactly.' He rose and his three quizzing glasses – like monocles – twinkled. 'Now let's undo the packages and have a look at them. By the way, Doctor, you've got the Gauguin documents?'

'They're in one of the packages,' I said. 'I thought it best to keep them all together.' I had sealed the large parcels with sticky hospital tape, and since I had known I would have to go through the customs at San Francisco I had brought a second roll of tape. Now I asked for a pair of scissors, cut the tape, tore off the four layers of thick brown corrugated paper, and slowly 'unveiled' the paintings.

'Be careful,' said Petrie with an anguished look. 'My God!' he breathed. 'What a find.'

'A splendid collection,' murmured the rosy-cheeked Huson. 'Really fascinating.' Between us we arranged the paintings standing against the walls of his 'laboratory'.

I thought with a touch of amusement of the way I had watched anxiously while Vrinsky had pored over the pictures and how I had been taken in with all his expertise. Now here was another 'expert' going to feed me with more jargon that no doubt would be just as incomprehensible – but, I hoped, more reliable. At least Professor Huson didn't take so long, no doubt because he didn't have to concoct a story that would convince me.

'Now here,' he said suddenly, 'is proof as good as you'll ever get that the pictures aren't copies.' He held the picture of the boy with the bananas and turned it over to show me the back. 'You see where the canvas is tacked to the stretcher and has received no paint?'

I nodded, and he handed me one of his quizzing glasses. 'See now the pattern of the warp and the woof. Peculiar, is it not?'

'Well,' I said doubtfully, 'I don't quite know what I'm supposed to be looking for. But it looks a bit different from the weave of my shirt.'

'Exactly. And that is because Gauguin used the local cloth for his easel pictures – the *tapa* that is made from the pounded bark of the mulberry, breadfruit, and other plants. As an artist who used anything to hand – wood, glass, paper, cardboard, fabric – Gauguin naturally used the local cloth, of which there was an endless supply, rather than order extremely expensive Roman linen, ticking, cambric, or other kinds of canvas from Paris. What would have been the point? *Tapa* is very strong, and being pounded with a grooved mallet gives it that unique weave. But suppose Vollard *had* wanted to make some copies. How could he have got hold of Polynesian cloth in Paris? But let us look further.'

He took the framed charcoal and wash sketch of the ship *Oceanien* and, after carefully removing the pins securing the thin wooden backing, revealed what he called the *verso* of the picture. I was surprised to see that the paper was printed with columns of figures like a balance sheet.

'There you are!' Huson cried. 'The date '99' that he's touched in under his signature is conclusive. That was soon after his legal daughter Aline died, and Gauguin attempted suicide – he overdosed himself with arsenic but his stomach rejected it. He worked for a time as a clerk in the Department of Public Works in Tahiti. He's ripped this heavy-quality paper from one of the department's ledgers. Probably the only thing he had handy. Vollard in Paris couldn't have got it any easier than Polynesian cloth. So you see, Doctor, you can forget any idea of copies.'

Again he made the little deprecating movements of his hands. 'As for forgeries, I would stake my professional career that they are genuine. True, any artist can in theory be imitated. But Gauguin's curious stylisation of eyes and mouths shown as almond shapes, divided by a horizontal line, and the feeling of *squareness* of the faces – because he copied so many photographs – these are characteristics difficult to imitate. The superficiality of such imitations would be instantly apparent – because style comes from *inside* the artist.'

He turned to the three self-portraits. 'You see the *vehemence* with which he's depicted himself, as if he's dissatisfied with what lies behind the features. In an imitation one would be immediately aware of the lack of that self-seeking vehemence. The tactile quality of the surface would reveal it, if nothing else did. A forger would be so intent on getting the lines, the proportions, and the colour-mixes right that the lack of inner feeling, of compulsion, would be evident in the lack of spontaneity of the brush strokes.'

'That seems to dispose of the matter of forgery, then,' I said.

'Certainly it does, Doctor. Especially as we have documents too. Mind you, artists with distinctive styles are easy to fake – El Greco, Van Gogh, Corot. It is a fact that there are more faked Corots in existence than real ones! And back in the early days of this century we had to rely on chemical analysis of the pigment to detect forgeries. But now – well, like you, we have X-rays to help us, and I will show you the final proof. We can see through a canvas – literally – to the foundations of the picture and see immediately whether it is a fake.'

'I wondered why you had a fluoroscope in an art dealer's.' I had noticed the fluoroscope machine immediately, standing on a table.

'Take a look, Doctor, and you'll see the non-medical value of X-rays and fluoroscopes.'

He switched the machine on, standing the painting of the boy with the red bananas against the machine, then beckoned me to look at the back of the canvas.

'Now you can see through the canvas. Notice how *clean* it looks. Untouched. It wouldn't look like that if it were a forgery. That's a genuine Gauguin all right. And I've no doubt that when I subject the others to the test they'll be genuine too.'

I began to realise what he was driving at.

'I can see that you understand, Doctor. As for Petrie here, he's probably seen more pictures with fluoroscopes than you've seen patients who need this magic machine.'

He explained the technical details in a fascinating manner. I had hardly realised that the most difficult problem a forger faces is to achieve the appearance of age, grime, patina, the cracking of the surface.

'The *craquelure* as we call it, needs great skill,' said Huson. 'Now let me give you another example.'

He went into the gallery next to his 'lab' and came back with an exquisite painting.

'I always say El Greco is the artist's artist. He painted superbly because he always felt he had to prove himself to his fellow artists. Now let's examine this through a microscope equipped with infra-red rays. Look at this.' I peered through the eyepiece. 'Notice anything odd?'

I had to confess that I didn't.

'Look more carefully. You're not looking at Greco at all. You're looking at a forgery. The infra-red shows that the forger has simulated *craquelure* by scratching lines on the surface, and then filling in the cracks with a hairline brushful of paint to tone down their freshness.'

'So that's a forgery.'

'I'm afraid so – though it was bought at auction. No, not Christie's,' he laughed.

'It looks so genuine.'

'I know. What this artist forger did was to treat the paint with a solvent that left it brittle when it dried, then wrapped the painting around a cylinder – wood or metal – so that the surface film was stretched and cracked. It's easily detected when put to the radiograph.'

'It's fascinating isn't it?' Aleena had been watching the

proceedings, and the cheerful professor at work, with astonishment. 'So you're satisfied?' she asked.

'Absolutely. I would like to study the documents,' said the professor, 'but I'm so sure of the authenticity of the paintings that any provenance is only really a formality, an added bonus. By the way, Mrs Masters, these letters and notes by Gauguin could be very, very valuable in themselves, but not to be sold yet. My guess is that in, say, ten or twenty years the prices of Impressionist pictures will soar to the skies. I know that you *want* to sell the paintings now for a good cause. But hang on to the letters and notes, because as the prices of paintings rise, so will the pieces of paper. I'll subject them to scientific tests, which will make me analyse the ink, paper and so on, and prove their provenance, but after that, keep them for ten years or more – a little nest-egg for the future, because selling autographs and letters is going to be big business one of these days.'

Petrie was of course delighted with the professor's seal of approval.

'Not that I ever doubted it,' he said, 'but in the art world Huson's word is law. And anyway, no forger could have imagined such a complicated plan. But it's always wise to have your instincts confirmed by experts.'

'Isn't it wonderful?' I hugged Aleena when we returned to the hotel. 'I still can hardly believe it.'

'I know.' She kissed me. 'And I'm so glad for you – and the hospital. And *everyone*! It's a kind of fear that's all past. The fact that we could never *really* be sure they were Gauguins. Now we know. It's like' – she searched for the right phrase – 'like a judge pronouncing the truth.'

'Now,' I said, 'we have a few hours to ourselves before we fly home. Tomorrow is our own sightseeing day!'

The trouble was, when we started seeing New York by ourselves we found the city exhausting. If we wanted to see a certain place we would be told 'It's only about five blocks'. But 'blocks' is an elastic term and though it didn't seem worth bothering to take a cab, we hadn't realised that in some mysterious way the 'sidewalks' were hard on the feet. Perhaps the snow made the sidewalks tougher to walk on. Perhaps it was the alternate switches from cold and blue sky to shops with neon lights and air so warm you could hardly breathe. Perhaps it was because we hardly knew *really* what time of day it was. The change in the hours between West to East – all the way from Koraloona – meant that we were ready to go anywhere or do anything in the afternoon and evening, but could hardly wake up in the morning.

'For me it's the other way round,' said Petrie when we met. 'Coming from London to New York, I gained five hours, so for the first couple of days I woke up at six in the morning famished because my stomach told me it was mid-morning. So what I've arranged for you both, in order to lessen the problem of time change, is to hold the conference in the late afternoon. That way you'll be at your best, and I won't be falling asleep.'

'Where are we holding it?' I was not looking forward to the ordeal.

'In the professor's gallery. The paintings currently on show are being taken down and the gallery will show only the Gauguins – just for the one afternoon and early evening.'

'And when?' asked Aleena.

'The day after tomorrow. Professor Huson is an old hand at arranging this sort of thing. The newspapers and photographers all turn up because they know from experience that he only handles important exhibitions. And because of the value of this particular exhibition, we've arranged for police protection.'

'Police!'

'You can't be too careful,' warned Petrie, while I thought of our single 'protection' back home in Koraloona – an old fish tank and some of Jim's putty! Suddenly, thinking of this, and the warm blinding beaches and the palms bending over and the surf breaking gently, I felt a touch of homesickness. New York, of course, was a wonderful adventure; so was the idea of the Gauguins being displayed properly for the first time in their existence. Yet Koraloona was *home*. Yes, home. Now and for ever. Nottingham and London – how far away, how long ago they seemed! It was seven years since I had first set foot on Koraloona, and even though I had suffered at the hands of Mana, I knew now that I would never leave the island. I was thinking, I'll be glad to get back home.

Our rubbernecking was interrupted by one chore which Petrie asked of Aleena before the press show.

'I want you to go to this address,' he gave Aleena a card. 'I've arranged for a limo to take you there and wait. It's one of the top dressmaking houses in New York. They will lend you an outfit for the show.'

'Lend?'

'Why not? It's a regular practice among the big fashion houses. And with famous clients. It's free publicity. And you will be famous. And this *is* midwinter. So we can't have you wasting money on a dress you'll never wear in Koraloona.'

'But will it fit? I mean, will it be clean and – ?'

'Don't worry your pretty head, my dear. They are all model dresses. The dressmaking house *begged* me to lend you clothes. Don't you realise that *their* dress will be in all the newspapers? What a free ad for them! So off you go when the limo arrives. Kit and I will make our own way to the show and you'll go there direct in the limo.'

That was how it worked out. By the time Petrie and I arrived at the gallery, the first of the press guests were drinking free highballs and munching sandwiches or canapés. Some were arranging their cameras so that they could get the best view. A newsreel camera was installed on a tripod in one corner.

Petrie and the professor had between them compiled what he called a 'press kit'. It had been copied by Roneo and contained not only details of the paintings, but potted histories of how they had been discovered; I squirmed a little when I read how I had saved a township from death during the cholera epidemic, but I forgot about that when I read of the beauty of Aleena and how she was happily going to part with the Gauguins to make sure that others didn't die from want of medical attention.

'It may sound corny to you,' Petrie apologised as he prepared to hand the leaflets to the reporters and photographers, 'but it stops reporters from asking too many questions, because most of the answers are already here.'

The gallery was soon crowded. The strip lighting cast an even glare on the four walls of the gallery, with a few cunningly placed spotlights to give special prominence to the larger paintings. Professor Huson darted round like a proud mother hen watching the people surveying the golden eggs on the walls.

Aleena, who had arrived by now, was waiting in the laboratory; Huson wanted her to wait until he gave her a sign so that she could make a dramatic entrance. 'Always good for a photo,' whispered Petrie. We remained two anonymous masks in a sea of faces and cameras until Professor Huson gave a nod to an assistant at the door, meaning that Aleena was ready.

Then Professor Huson, standing by a desk where normally assistants dealt with prices, catalogues and sales, banged with a gavel and the babble of voice abruptly ceased.

He made a brief speech to the expectant hush. 'Ladies and gentlemen,' he began. 'This is the greatest find of paintings by Paul Gauguin that the world has ever seen. It is of inestimable value and I hope you will read the fact sheet I have provided to show you how this hidden treasure came to light. Ladies and gentlement, may I present Aleena, Gauguin's granddaughter and the wife of Dr Kit Masters.'

At that moment Aleena walked in through the door from the lab and there was a gasp of astonishment. Even I caught my breath. I have never seen anyone more beautiful than Aleena was at that moment. And I doubt if any of the assembled reporters and photographers had either.

She stood there, slightly shy, wearing a white suit with a black blouse. The colour of the two-piece outfit not only framed her beauty perfectly, but the white suit enhanced the glossy polish of the blue-black hair hanging over her shoulders and half way down her back. She wore only a touch of lipstick round that beautiful mouth, and silk stockings on those long, slim legs and exquisite ankles.

As though someone had fired a starting pistol, the hush burst into a frenzy of applause, and then questions were shouted from every corner of the room, while flash bulbs popped from every angle.

'How old are you, Aleena?'

'How many people on the island?'

'Why did you marry Doc Masters?'

'Twenty,' she laughed, quite self-possessed. 'I'm not sure.' 'Because I love him.' Laughingly she answered all the questions she could. The queries were interspersed with cries from the photographers, all formalities forgotten.

'Can you stand next to the red banana painting, lady? A little to the left. Look straight at me and smile.'

Or: 'Can I have a photo of you and your husband, Aleena, in front of a picture? No, not *looking*, ma'am. How's about a nice kiss?'

They must have taken dozens of photographs but the one above all others that swept the country (as I was told later) and certainly made *The New York Times* the following morning was the one snapped just as we were about to kiss. I suppose that, analysing it, it combined all the virtues that were required for what read like a fairy story. It had an artistic background: newly discovered paintings, true love, and because Aleena was in profile, smiling as she was about to kiss me, it showed not only her face but her long black tresses, giving an added mysterious touch of the South Seas.

After that there was little left to keep us in New York, for not only had we done all we could, but we *were* the guests of

593

Christie's. We also had a daunting schedule of work ahead when we started to transform the camp into a hospital.

This, in turn, would be interrupted as we became more and more involved in the sale of the Gauguins, for it still took weeks to exchange letters, and the telephone service was difficult, yet we had to decide the date of the auction, and Christie's wanted us to be there when it was held – publicity again! Catalogues would have to be printed and approved; reserve prices would have to be agreed: Christie's would not take on the responsibility of arranging reserve prices without our approval.

Tentatively, with much hesitation, I had asked Mr Petrie whether Christie's might be willing to guarantee a bank loan in Sanderstown if we ran short during the hospital work. He had said that he must consult his head office on that. So altogether there was much to be done. He signed an itemised receipt for the paintings, together with a certificate of insurance, and I signed a contract giving Christie's all rights to conduct an auction of the Gauguins. And that was that.

Two days later we set off by air for the long return journey to Koraloona. We took with us a small suitcase of American gifts for friends, and we kept two souvenirs that we knew would make the islanders gape with astonishment – our galoshes.

42

Within a week of our return from the eventful trip to New York, I received a cable from Petrie announcing that arrangements had been made with the Chartered Bank in Sanderstown (where my modest salary was deposited monthly by the Mission) for Christie's to guarantee an overdraft of £10,000, providing they kept the paintings until after the auction as collateral. A letter followed from the bank confirming this.

Things were beginning to move quickly!

'We start buying and building straight away,' I said to Alec.

'We'll soon have nae time for doctoring,' he retorted.

'Come on, Alec! What's eating you?'

'I hope ye' nae goin' to spend all this new fortune tae quickly. Ye can be a bit impetuous, ye ken.'

'Don't worry.' I thought for a moment before suggesting, in a joking voice, but all the same a serious proposition, 'Tell you what, Alec. I'll be in charge of *selling* – pictures, of course. You'll be in charge of *buying* – building materials, of course.' He seemed pleased, and with a laugh I added, 'That way I'll get the last penny I can and you'll save the last penny you can. It's a deal?'

'Done!' he cried. 'I reckon I can save a copper or two here and there. But ye canna get away from one problem – and it's nae a wee one. We must have a generator powerful enough to guarantee that our hospital's electricity doesn't pack up in the middle of an op.'

'Of course,' I agreed. 'How will you go about getting one?'

'We've got help right here on our doorstep. A live, home-grown polymath. Know what a polymath is?' He screwed up his eyes.

'Sounds like a second cousin to a polypus to me. Doesn't it mean a great scholar? I seem to remember the Greek derivation from Oxford. But what do you mean?'

'It is that,' agreed Alec, 'but it's a man who can turn his hand to everything – and with skill, knowledge and attention to detail.'

'Sounds like a genius. Who is he?'

'Ye've nae met Walter Mitchell?'

I shook my head, but remembered of course that Mitchell had arrived on Koraloona just before we left for New York and so we hadn't met. Colonel Fawcett had appointed a second-in-command because at his age the burden was getting too heavy. Though younger than Fawcett, Mitchell had served with him in the Engineers, and I met him a few days later, a big man, with a powerful frame, a shock of red hair, size thirteen shoes, I would say – and a find in a million.

Mitchell could equally well make *papier mâché* ornaments or erect a Bailey bridge. He was an expert in joinery, bricklaying, and he displayed a remarkable knowledge of physics and understood everything from the internal combustion engine to drainage systems and electrical engineering. No mean hand as a quantity surveyor, he started to give us an accurate forecast of our needs in bricks and timber for the small ancillary buildings such as incinerators for hospital waste and the laundry that would have to cope with the linen; and was full of hints for cutting economic corners.

'But one thing you'll have to spend quite a bit of money on is additional generating power.' He emphasised again to me the point made by Alec. 'The island supply is pretty strained now, and I suspect that if every light and electrical gadget were switched on at any one time we'd have a power breakdown. To play safe, you need at least an additional two and a half thousand kilowatts, plus some sort of emergency supply for the hospital itself. Even in the tropics, storms can wreck overhead power lines; and of course it'd be impossibly expensive to lay underground supply cables.'

'And where,' I asked facetiously, 'does one pick up two and a half thousand kilowatts – whatever they may be – on Koraloona?'

He ignored my feeble attempt at humour. 'Units of electrical power. You don't find them: you make them – generate them.'

'Oh,' I said humbly. 'What with?'

He shrugged. 'Steam, oil, paraffin, petrol – whatever you have handy.' He made a dramatic gesture toward the cone of the volcano on High Island. 'It's absolutely infuriating that over there we've got an unending supply of terrestrial heat in the form of gas and vapour escaping from the fumaroles – '

'The *what*?'

'The safety valves – little holes in the ground from which wisps of steam escape. That's heat, Doctor – energy that we could use to drive the generators if we could get it here. Unfortunately we've got that little bit of the Pacific between it and us.'

'What about Pluto?' I asked brightly. Everybody knew about Pluto – Pipe Line Under The Ocean – which had supplied the invading forces in Normandy with a million gallons of petrol a day fed from storage tanks in England.

Mitchell shook his head sadly. 'Unfortunately the heat would simply warm the water en route; it'd be dissipated by the time it reached Koraloona. And pushing it through overhead pipes would mean a bridge you could never afford. No, I'm afraid we shall have to settle for an additional generator and a motor to drive it with.'

So in the end it meant the importing of an expensive Petter oil engine and a GEC generator from Auckland.

'Anyway, we couldn't have any fumaroles, or whatever they're called, because the volcano on High Island is extinct,' I said. 'Or, as Alec says, it farts once in ten years or so to relieve its feelings.'

Mitchell displayed yet another facet of his knowledge. 'No volcano is ever extinct, Doctor. The use of the word simply means it hasn't erupted in historical memory. "Inactive" would be a better description. When volcanoes are extinct the world will be too.'

'I only hope we have enough money in the kitty,' said Alec when I told him. It was Alec's recurring fear.

'Don't worry,' I promised him.

'And I'll start using my contacts to see if we can pick up a good second-hand one in Australia or New Zealand,' Mitchell promised.

We also had the help of Jim Wilson. As far as the buildings were concerned, very few alterations were needed. They could easily be adapted with few materials – beaverboard, corrugated iron, and timber – and we could get that in Sanders. And Jim Wilson could handle routine electrical wiring and elementary plumbing.

'But,' said Alec, 'we'll need a better system of drainage, with the effluent chemically treated before it's discharged into the sea. After all, it's a hospital we're building and we don't want any sources of infection. Elsan loos are out – we must have flush toilets and a water-purifying system. I know the polio outbreak and the cholera epidemic made a lot of islanders appreciate elementary hygiene; but a good many of the older people still defecate about the place if they know they're not being seen.'

Between Walter Mitchell and Jim Wilson, it wasn't too difficult. Mitchell had once been in charge of the flooding and draining of a dock. He could take the mere chlorination of piped water in his stride. He drew simple plans that could hardly go awry, checking with local labour periodically to make sure all was going well.

A week or so later I received a second cable from Christie's, announcing that they proposed to hold the auction on May 2. In my diary I saw that this was a Thursday, and I remembered a casual remark of Petrie's, 'Thursday is always a good selling day.'

So *that* was arranged. So was the little matter of getting time off to be present for this auspicious fund-raising project. Alec was very understanding – of course he was perfectly aware too that it was in his own interest for others to finance a magnificent hospital in which he was guaranteed the post of medical officer in charge. There had never been the remotest suggestion that I (or Aleena) would take advantage of the inheritance to further my own career, and he knew it.

So Alec fell in immediately with my proposal that I should take between four and six weeks of our allotted leave and spend it in England. Petrie suggested that I should arrive in London at least three weeks before the sale, and I agreed. If we spent three weeks before the actual

598

auction on May 2, we could go to see my parents, and the few old friends with whom I had kept vaguely in contact. I had promised to visit the publishers of Jason's novel; Mrs Reid in Wimbledon; and a number of other people. We also wanted *time* to enjoy one or two visits to the theatre, a concert perhaps, and short trips to almost forgotten sights like Covent Garden market or the river at Oxford. All this would be easier before the sale.

As it happened, Petrie had another reason for wanting us there early, but we didn't know about that then.

By now, with the world beginning to settle down to what we all hoped would be an era of peace, the *Sanders Sentinel* was reaching us regularly in Koraloona, usually in batches of two or three days at a time, and I read it avidly, not so much for local news, but for the agency reports of life in Britain, which seemed to be almost worse off than during the war, with rationing and shortages of every kind. They were even eating whalemeat! I reminded Aleena that as well as carrying the paintings to London, we must take stocks of food and other things, such as clothes.

'Well, we can't take local food – they'll hardly thank us for taking them some taro!' she said. 'Or Mother Hubbards if they're short of clothes! And there's not much tinned food here either.'

That was true; and that was the reason we decided to fly to London across the Pacific and America, rather than to Australia and back through the Far East. We would have a night stopover in either California or New York – and there was no shortage of anything there. We could take home – and leave – the sheepskin coats we had used in New York. We could buy food and clothes in abundance.

'Yes, we'll do that,' I said, absently skimming the inside pages of the *Sentinel*, when my eye lit on one fairly short item, merely because it was headed 'Bikini Atoll' – for Bikini lay to the north of our archipelago. President Truman, I read, was planning to explode two atom bombs, one on the atoll and a second underwater. Similar to the

Hiroshima bomb. I was thinking to myself why on earth should they mess around with such a dangerous substance as nuclear power, when I read the astonishing reason: apparently Truman wanted to give the world's press a demonstration of what it was like when an A-bomb exploded, and let them all see its extraordinary mushroom effect, from a safe distance, out to sea.

'They're crazy,' I said to Aleena, and threw the paper aside without really giving it a second thought.

'This is even crazier, and it's going to make you very cross,' Aleena said when she picked up the following day's paper, 'and the photo of me is horrible.'

'A photo of you? Why?'

Grabbing the paper I looked. It contained a half-page illustrated article headed: ISLAND PRINCESS' GAUGUIN FORTUNE.

'Oh no,' I groaned. It told the entire story – obviously based on clippings from the New York papers. I hadn't *really* enjoyed the publicity in New York but Petrie had assured me it would help, so I had put up with it. But New York was a long way off. Here, though! Among our friends! 'Fortune indeed,' I sniffed to Aleena. 'We'll be the laughing stock of the island.'

'I still think they should have used that lovely photo of the two of us just about to kiss.' She seemed unconcerned about the article, and I wasn't *that* annoyed as I grinned, 'All this publicity! That's what I get for marrying into royalty. And after all, we'll be in London before long.'

In fact with the good news from Christie's and the discovery of the documents, everything seemed to be going splendidly as we prepared for our trip to England – not because of the auction, but also because I was longing to see London again and also looking forward to introducing my beautiful bride to the family in Nottingham. But then, that newspaper article had embarrassing consequences.

Just as sharks seem to gather in shoals at the smell of blood, so sharks – no, that is unfair, they were friends and neighbours – seemed to gather around us at the sweet smell of success.

The news that we were about to dispose of the Gauguin heritage became common knowledge after the *Sentinel* appeared, telling the amazing story of the legacy, though the discovery of the documents supporting their authenticity was not yet known.

Almost immediately, we received pleas for help from several quarters. Two were not exactly pleas, more what was described as 'sound investments' for our sudden riches, even though the paintings were not yet sold, and when they were, the proceeds would, as part of the agreement, be going to financing a new hospital. All these facts seemed to be ignored. Or perhaps some of the locals were basing their 'knowledge' on rumour without any foundation; a feeling compounded no doubt by the fact that in Polynesia life was comparatively cheap and dying was a happy route to eternal bliss and ancestor worship. So what was all this fuss about needing a better hospital?

'What I says is that Harley Street's been good enough for all these years,' declared Johnson to Jim Wilson as he flicked a cigarette end off the porch. 'I don't hold with these new-fangled medical treatments. They only discover new illnesses, what we didn't 'ave before.'

Johnson was one of the first to approach me. To my surprise he stopped me one day when I was walking to the shipping agents just past his store and he said, still in his whining Cockney, 'Mornin' Doc. 'Ows about a beer? On the 'ouse. Nice and cold, been standing in a bucket of ice and water since before breakfast, it 'as. It's always the first thing I tell me better 'alf to do. Put the beer in the bucket!'

I was surprised. Johnson was hardly noted for his generosity, but I was thirsty, and I said yes, I wouldn't mind if I did. Johnson now had two old-fashioned wooden rocking chairs on his veranda overlooking Main Street, and as we sat there he opened two bottles with the crown cork opener which he kept on his key ring.

'Otherwise people pinch 'em all the time,' he grumbled,

'and that's the quickest way to chuck your profits out of the bleedin' window. 'Ere's to you, Doc!' I raised my none-too-clean glass to his toast.

'You must be doing well to give out free beer,' I teased, but the jibe was lost on him.

'Matter of fact' – he leaned forward confidentially – 'I'm thinking of expanding. Did you read in the *Sentinel* that some of them old Australian troop carriers is being converted into somefink new – cruise ships, they calls 'em. They plans to call in 'ere. If they do, we'll be quids in.'

I *had* read the report, which seemed to be a fairly accurate account of a new company being floated to run 'conducted tours' of the South Sea Islands, though my first thought was that they would call in at Sanders rather than Koraloona.

'Nah.' Johnson shook his head. 'It's the romantic stuff they'll want. Bare tits, excusing the language, and cheap trinkets.' Then he came to the point. 'There'll be a fortune to be made in the next few years, Doc, and I've got it all worked out. A big extension to the store. As a great favour I might cut you in on it. As a kind of partner, you might say.'

'I'm a doctor, and I'd be out of my depth in business.' I drained the last of my beer. 'Besides, plans like that need money.'

'That's what I mean, Doc,' Johnson said eagerly. 'A chance in a million on a fifty-fifty basis. We'd corner the market in grass skirts and set up dancing girls. Now that you're rich –'

'Me rich! On my Mission doctor's salary! You must be joking.'

'But what abaht them pictures by the froggie painter?' His voice took on an even more confidential air. 'They'll be worth a pretty penny – and you'd 'ardly miss what we need to finance a new wing to the store.'

'My dear Johnson,' I got up to leave, 'you must be crazy. All the money from the Gauguin paintings is being paid directly into a trust for the hospital. My wife and I don't get

602

a penny out of it. Why, we don't even get a bigger house to live in with all that money you've been going on about. Do you *really* believe we could touch that money?'

He looked genuinely astonished, and I found similar reactions wherever I went. Somehow the impression had gained ground that we would at least take *some* of the money for ourselves – I suppose because it was, after all, money that belonged to Tiare and Aleena, and also because they had seen how easily Aleena and I had gone off to New York and were now about to leave for distant London. You couldn't do that sort of thing if you weren't rich! That's how the story went, and nothing I could say would disabuse them. Most of the money might go to the hospital, but no one would miss a few thousands here and there!

I found the same thing when, having dined at Mollie Green's hotel for a change – lobsters again! – she made a similar suggestion. Not wheedling like Johnson, but sensibly because, after all, she ran the only hotel on the island, and she paid no rates, no rent or large upkeep. And she had a monopoly.

She wanted to enlarge her small veranda into a big open-air dining-room facing the sea, to cater for the new cruise ships, and said to Aleena, 'Wouldn't it be a wonderful way for passengers to see a small South Seas island on a beautiful moonlit evening? Only I don't have the capital. But you two – now that you're coming into a windfall. I read all about it.'

At least she had the grace to speak directly to Aleena as she heaved her vast bulk into her favourite tight-fitting wooden chair. She too seemed surprised when Aleena explained that we had no actual money.

Next on what I called 'the begging bowl list' came Father Pringle. And this was a more difficult problem, for after all, we had been married there, and he had agreed that Tiki should take some modest part in the service, and there was no doubt that his church – the cathedral as it was usually known – *was* poor. Father Pringle, though he did have a

603

free home, and free samples of whisky and gin, seemed to have no money other than the weekly collection and his commission on liquor for which he was an agent. Even so, sales were restricted to Johnson's, and Mollie Green's the only restaurant, and Mick's Bar.

We tried to explain the illusion that had grown up, but at least we were able to make one positive gesture. We might not have money, but we could give something in kind. The army camp which we had inherited had had an exercise field for baseball games behind the camp, and it included one hut of the standard size, large enough to sleep six. We agreed to give the land and the hut as a deed of gift to be used as a church hall and recreation ground for children who attended the village schools, and whose parents went to church regularly. The only thing Alec insisted on was that the gift be hedged in with safeguards against undue noise so near to the hospital buildings. At least this was a tangible way of helping, and would be a boon to youngsters who dreamed that one day they might play football for England – even in their bare feet.

Most irritating of all requests, though, came when Colonel Fawcett, blissfully ignorant too of the real facts, had the temerity to ask me privately whether Aleena and I would be prepared to make a gesture to celebrate our good fortune, as he put it.

'What gesture?' I asked, flabbergasted.

It turned out that the Union Jack Club badly needed £150 to redecorate and refurbish the club, which, I was the first to admit, was looking tatty after the war years.

'It's the annual general meeting the day after tomorrow, old boy,' he confided. 'And there's nothing like a spot of good news to brighten an AGM. It would be a damned nice gesture if we could announce it then, eh?'

'Out of the question,' I replied almost crossly. 'It's not our money to give away. It's part of a trust.' What I *didn't* say was that, in order to still this flood of ridiculous rumour, I proposed to raise the matter at the meeting. And I did.

When Colonel Fawcett, preparing to sit down as the

meeting drew to an end, asked his routine question, 'Any other business?' knowing that there rarely was any, I jumped up and said my piece. The meeting froze into rapt silence as I explained how I had unofficially been approached to finance the redecoration, and how sorry I was that it was impossible. I didn't mention the Johnson or Mollie Green approaches, but I wanted to make it clear that we could not give money to the church or the club.

At this, I sat down. Colonel Fawcett, obviously annoyed, again asked sharply, 'Does that conclude any more business?'

'No,' cried an obviously sceptical Paula Reece, as she jumped up. I could see she didn't believe me – and of course she didn't really like me or Aleena.

Now she said, in a very brisk tone, 'I do appreciate the problem that Doctor and Mrs Masters face, but sometimes there are ways round these difficult financial problems – ' she paused for effect – 'given good-will.'

I could see that she had decided to force me into a difficult corner, for she announced, 'Despite the difficulties, I will say this: if Kit and Aleena can find a way of helping our community's club and church, and I am sure they can, then I solemnly declare here and now that I will match any offer they can make.'

Almost with a smile of triumph she sat down, and there was a burst of clapping from the meeting as I whispered to Aleena, 'What a bitch!' and rose to explain our position again. As I stood there, a sea of faces turned to look at me, almost with hostility, though that is probably exaggerated. There was nothing for it, except to say how I wished I *could* take advantage of Paula's generous offer. Then a sudden thought struck me.

'Did you mean that, Paula?' I asked, trying to look pleasant. 'Anything I give to the club or church, you are prepared to match it?'

'I said so,' she agreed coldly, 'and I usually mean what I say.'

Nobody had discussed the church, though they knew the

605

club always raised any money for them, but I said, 'Thank you Paula,' and I felt Aleena tug at my trousers to sit down before I made a fool of myself, but she didn't know what I was going to say.

'I'm really sorry we can't help you with the redecorations of the club,' I began, 'but we *have* been able to help with the cathedral, and I'm very grateful to Paula for offering in front of us all, to give the same amount.'

Did she look a little pale and unsteady as she got up and asked, 'How much? What did *you* give the cathedral?'

As the members looked again at my face, their question a silent hush of expectancy, I explained, 'My wife agreed that we should make a legal document transferring to the cathedral in perpetuity an acre of ground and a large building to be used as a church hall and sports pavilion. And I need hardly say that Paula's generosity in doubling the size of our church sports ground will be very much appreciated.'

There was another outburst of clapping, and when I sat down it stopped, almost every clap ceasing at the same moment as Paula got to her feet and shouted almost angrily, 'You know I can't do that.'

'You made the suggestion, not me,' I said. 'If I were Doctor Shylock, looking for his pound of flesh – and no other kind of payment – I would argue that you *could*, Paula. All you need to do is lop off the end of your garden, which adjoins the land we've given to the cathedral, and we would have a magnificent sports ground.'

I paused, this time for effect. The stunned silence that had followed the clapping erupted now in a different noise – a titter. I saw that Paula was livid with fury. Embarrassed, Colonel Fawcett again tried to bring this eventful meeting to a close, but as he asked for the third time, 'Any more business?' I rose again to my feet.

'But ladies and gentlemen, I am *not* a Doctor Shylock.' There was laughter at that. 'And I don't for one moment suggest that Paula should ruin her beautiful garden – one in which we have all spent so many happy hours.'

I paused there, as the members waited expectantly. 'However,' I said slowly, 'when we decided to legalise the transfer of land and building to the cathedral, our chairman here, Colonel Fawcett himself, told me that some kind of evaluation had to be put on the deed. It seems that the sum of two hundred pounds was decided upon. Almost the same as the cost of renovations to the club. So why not,' I looked directly at Paula with what I hoped was a winning smile to match her controlled fury, 'why not let her match our gift of land worth two hundred pounds by paying for the one hundred and fifty pounds that we need for the club? That way she can keep her beautiful garden and we can call it quits.'

The clapping burst out again, and with as good a grace as she could muster, Paula – who would never miss the money – was forced to agree. For once I saw a smile of real pleasure on the taciturn face of Captain Baker!

We left in the first week of April on the first stage of our trip to London – which meant taking the overnight boat to Sanders, to catch the plane. As a gesture of thanks for our gift, Father Pringle gave the entire school population the day off and assembled those with the best choir voices to sing us a farewell serenade as the *Mantela II* edged away from the pier. All the local community seemed to have gathered to wish us Godspeed. The only missing face was Paula's.

43

It is almost impossible to describe our excitement as we finally prepared to land in London. Koraloona now would always be home to me, but still, parents, old familiar scenes, memories – they all crowded into my mind in a composite picture that made me tingle with anticipation.

New York had been exciting. But London – ah! – that was different; I would be able to show Aleena round myself; I would be the courier this time in a guided tour of a capital which I knew well, which had stood fast against the horrors of war, refusing to capitulate to the terrors of the blitz or the threat of invasion.

In a strange way, as far as memories were concerned, time had stood still for me during the eight years since I had departed for Koraloona. Though we had all read about the war and the way the people had endured heroic suffering, I had somehow not quite expected there to be any significant *physical* change; as though people had died, but the visible contours of the city had remained the same. We had time and again seen photographs of bomb damage in the *Sanders Sentinel*, but details had all been hazy and inconclusive, perhaps due in part to the censorship.

Even before we started the trip, I had been feeding Aleena with snippets like, 'You wait till you see St Paul's!' and 'There's no place quite like Bond Street or St James's!' or 'The real Piccadilly makes our Piccadilly in Sanders look like a poor man's imitation.'

False memories were overtaken by disillusion the moment we landed in the early morning at the grandiloquently named Great West Aerodrome near Hounslow Heath. We filed out to be met by a bus on the tarmac – just as we had been in New York. But what a difference! In America the bus had been brightly painted. Here it was drab, the wings dented, half the seats torn, almost as though someone had rescued it at the last moment from a scrap heap. Aleena had a seat, but many men had to stand, grabbing the few straps that weren't broken, or else clutching the stainless tubular rails overhead.

The bus lurched, and ahead of us I could see a long row of single-storey buildings where we finally alighted. They were obviously temporary buildings, but their flaky paint made them depressing, like the photographs I had seen of concentration camps.

We got through immigration quickly, for Aleena was

now a British subject by marriage. Nor did anyone worry us at the customs, or ask to open the suspicious-looking packages. But then we faced our first experience of life in the tough post-war world of London. There were virtually no porters. We had to carry our luggage to a taxi rank in two shifts. There I did see a man who seemed to be a porter, and asked, 'Where do I get a taxi, please?'

'Taxi! Blimey, you'll be lucky, mate!' he cried. 'We don't often get 'em all this way out 'ere. No petrol. But there's the bus,' he indicated where it was standing, waiting. 'It takes you to Victoria, and there'll be plenty of cabs there,' he said.

So we had to go through the drudgery of carrying bags and parcels again, and though the man in charge of the bus was helpful, Aleena, I could see, was exhausted. After all, we had come a long way, with only one good night's sleep.

At Victoria we didn't have to wait long for a cab, and ten minutes later we reached the Fitzgerald Hotel in Hanover Square, near both Bond Street and Oxford Street. Petrie had arranged the hotel for us because he said it was not only reasonably priced, but very comfortable and not far from his new office. (Although I knew that Christie's had been bombed, I did not realise that the building they had taken over was Derby House at the top of Stratford Place, off Oxford Street, where they used the ballroom as their main auction room.)

A note from Petrie was waiting for me, and it simply said, 'Sorry I couldn't meet the plane, please phone and we'll dine together if you wish.'

'Love to,' I replied on the phone. 'So long as it's not going to be a late night.'

'Don't worry. We've got a great deal of work to get through. I'll pick you up at 7.30 pm and take you to dinner at Claridge's. I've booked a table.'

'Claridge's!' I had never in my life been through its awe-inspiring portals – too impressive to use a mere word like door! – and asked, 'But isn't it terribly expensive?'

Petrie laughed, I could imagine his particular chuckle.

'Not too bad,' he said. 'Their set three-course dinner is five bob a head – plus wine of course.'

'Five shillings? You must be joking!'

'I'm not. It's all part of rationing – to make sure that rich and poor get equal shares.'

'Sorry. Must be the hangover of the long flight, but I don't understand.'

'Oh! You didn't know? Five shillings is the maximum charge any restaurant in Britain can make for lunch or dinner.'

I looked at Aleena, sitting on the comfortable armchair, puzzling about my repeated queries.

'It sounds wonderful – in principle,' I said. 'But what can you get for five bob in a place with overheads like Claridge's? Or the Savoy, or any expensive restaurant?'

'That's the rule, though you *can* pay supplementary prices for unrationed food like fish – if you can get them. But you probably don't realise, Kit, in many ways the shortages and rations are worse now than they were in the war.'

I didn't realise until we went out – to take our first look at London on foot. For sentimental reasons, I wanted to lunch at the old Lyons' Corner House where I had had my last steak and chips before leaving for the Pacific.

'There's no steak now,' I laughed as we studied the menu. The meal wasn't bad, but it brought home to both of us how desperately short of food Britain must have been during the war and the price she was now paying for having won it. All food prices were controlled, and I noticed the prices in the shops of basic food like bread, milk, meat and fish hadn't gone up. But as we soon discovered, food was very monotonous – dried egg, milk powder, snoek – a kind of compressed mixed fish – whalemeat, root vegetables. When I saw the cheese trolley it consisted only of inferior Cheddar.

'You've just arrived have you, sir?' the waitress asked almost sympathetically. 'This is the only cheese we have, sir. Mousetrap.'

The last thing I wanted to do was to paint a depressing picture for Aleena of the country where I had been born, but the more I saw in the first two days of 'sightseeing' the more dismayed I was at the greyness of the capital. It wasn't so much the bombed buildings, the ugly gaps in which you could visualise people who had been killed. It wasn't only unimportant items like the newspapers limited to four pages. It was more the general impression – which was certainly not the fault of the brave Londoners – that the whole city badly needed a lick of paint. Only poor old England didn't *have* any paint to spare, and no one was allowed to spend more than £10 on repairs to damaged property. You had to queue for everything – from permission to mend your bombed house to ration-free fish.

'Still, only "luxuries" have really increased in price,' I said to Aleena. 'But whisky and gin have gone up to fifteen shillings a bottle, and cigarettes, which used to be ninepence for ten in 1939, now cost a bob.'

Of course, there was another side to the coin, which both of us enjoyed to the full. The fun of a new world to Aleena, an old world to me.

People, cars, horses, trams, shops, pearly kings selling whelks – and a pride, not boastful but with head held high. Though everyone *did* complain about the post-war shortages, it didn't matter once we settled down. It was still a change, and whoever in the world had ever seen such a huge shop as Harrods? Saks had been big too, but we had been whisked round it in a few minutes. Here we could explore the mysteries and delights of Harrods (even though limited) all day – and return a week later if Aleena wanted to, because time was on our side.

Here, as befitted the more leisurely pace of England, of London, we had time to enjoy its elegance. Yes, London was an elegant city, with an astonishing number of parks and trees, the sweep of the Mall, Trafalgar Square, many beautiful buildings on Park Lane made more beautiful because it happened that we enjoyed such sunny spring and early summer weather most of the time.

After we had spent the first two days in London, struggling to overcome our time difference, and with nearly a month to go before the auction, we were summoned – asked in fact, but Petrie made it clear that it was a kind of summons – to a boardroom lunch at Stratford Place where several of the Christie directors would be present and who wished, as Petrie put it, 'to discuss a matter of grave importance before we start the publicity campaign and approve the catologues.'

Our arrival in London may have passed unnoticed, but the arrival at Stratford Place of a beautiful smiling raven-haired girl with a romantic background of the South Seas – *and* Gauguin's grand-daughter – delighted the directors and put them in an indulgent, happy, relaxed mood. As we ate our rationed but well-cooked meal, I thought we had just been invited out of politeness to meet several directors whose names, to be frank, I didn't catch. That was until they were passing the port, clockwise as is the custom, when Petrie got up, glass in hand, to make a speech. I had no warning, no premonition of the bombshell he was about to drop.

He led up to it gradually. Speaking to the dozen or so of us grouped round the table, but looking towards Aleena and myself regularly, he said, 'I'd like to have a round-table discussion. We have to admit that, although we are delighted to have the honour of preparing to offer the most unusual collection of Gauguin paintings known in England, the art market seems to be more interested in the old masters than the Impressionists, and Post-Impressionists. For instance, last year the Gainsborough "Harvest Wagon" was bought by an institute for over twenty thousand pounds – a great deal of money. And that, by the way, is the first time that a Gainsborough has made five figures since 1929.'

'Are you suggesting that the Gauguins are no good?' I interrupted. 'You told me that even before the war Hitler ordered the purchase for the German State Gallery of a Gauguin for eight thousand pounds. That too seems quite a lot of money.'

'Yes, it did fetch that price,' admitted Petrie. 'But in 1939, at the same sale, which was held in Lucerne, Hitler paid only two thousand four hundred pounds for a Tahitian picture similar to one we are hoping to sell.'

'But prices must have gone up since then?' I suggested. 'I know there has been war and death and misery, but there has been a lot of money made as well. New millionaires and so on, especially in America.'

'Doesn't that count for something?' asked Aleena.

'Don't worry, my dear. Of course we are going to do very well,' Petrie smiled to her with reassurance. 'But the real point I want to make to you two young people is based on one important factor: we are not here just to make a profit out of you and leave it at that. Christie's also wants to protect your interests.'

'But our interests and your profits – don't they go together?' I couldn't avoid sounding sarcastic.

'They certainly do,' replied Petrie equably. 'But that's only by chance. They *wouldn't* if you had left them in the hands of your friend Vrinsky. Do you know what he would have done?'

We both shook our heads.

'He would have paid you what he suggested, locked the entire lot of paintings in his storeroom for ten years, and then sold them at a huge profit. That's a danger we all face today – that the real owner of the paintings doesn't always get a fair return, because it's not only the genuine artistically minded people who will bid – it also includes rich entrepreneurs – tradesmen if you like – who are buying anything instead of holding on to their money, convinced that as the value of money goes down with inflation, the value of goods like art or furniture or porcelain is bound to go up. And what's more, it's true.'

'I wish I knew what you're driving at,' said Aleena quietly.

'Come to the point.' One of the directors whose name I hadn't caught, tapped the long end of cigar ash into a tray.

'I will.' Petrie drew a long breath. 'My colleagues and I

are firmly convinced that we are on the verge of an enormous increase in the value of Impressionist and Post-Impressionist paintings. On the *verge* – not yet, it hasn't arrived yet. It might take five years, ten, or at the very most fifteen. But one day it will burst. And we believe that in a few years a painting by Van Gogh or Gauguin will be worth ten times what people will have to pay for it today. Think of the Gauguin that Hugh Walpole bought for one hundred and forty five pounds in 1924. Now it's already worth, say, four or five thousand pounds. What will it be worth in ten years? Forty or fifty thousand pounds. Perhaps even more.'

'That's not possible!' Aleena looked almost unhappy.

'But it is, my dear; not just possible, nor even probable, but *certain*!'

'But there's one point you seem to have missed,' I said almost savagely, turning to all the directors, again with a touch of sarcasm. 'Everything goes up in price – but it just happens that we love the Gauguins and the only reason we are selling them is to build a hospital to save lives, and we want that hospital now. You don't realise, gentlemen, that the closing down of the British naval base hospital in Sanderstown is going to mean – and I *mean* – that people are going to die for want of medical help, for there won't be a modern hospital nearer than Auckland in New Zealand. That's why we are selling paintings that have been in the family' – I indicated Aleena – 'for decades, loved and cherished. What happens to them afterwards isn't our concern. We aren't really selling the paintings – we're exchanging them for human life.'

The man with the large cigar said, 'Hear, hear,' and actually clapped gently. 'A truly magnificent gesture,' he murmured.

'Forgive me, gentlemen,' I continued less passionately, 'but please understand that we must have this hospital. And please imagine the heart-searching this decision has caused to a family which, from the time of my wife's grandmother, swore a sacred vow never to sell them.'

'Of course I understand this,' said Petrie who refused to be ruffled. 'But let me ask you one thing, Doctor: how are you going to run your big modern hospital as costs mount in ten or fifteen years?'

'They won't rise on Koraloona.'

'They will, I'm afraid.' His voice was very firm. 'Inflation is infectious. It will rise all over the world.'

'Well,' I asked, 'do you have any solution to offer?'

'We – that is, Christie's – do,' said Petrie quietly.

'And you'll have your hospital, Doctor, never fear,' said the man with the cigar.

'Well, that's something,' I muttered, a little embarrassed by my outburst. 'For a moment I thought you were going to refuse to sell them for me.'

'We'll sell the lot for you if you tell us to,' said Petrie. 'But may I ask you another question, Doctor Masters?'

'Go ahead.' I could see Aleena look forward, concentrating as she waited for it.

'How much would you think – a calculated guess, I mean – it will cost to start your hospital?'

I reflected for a moment. 'Well, we've got the site free and the equipment cheaply. Our biggest expenses will be the generator and improved sanitation facilities, the salary of a couple of local nurses, and if we can afford it, another doctor. So you see – '

'Would you think that – say – forty thousand pounds would cover it?'

'Oh *yes*!' The enthusiasm must have sounded in my voice, for the rest of the table smiled. 'I'm sure that for a sum like that we could afford a third doctor – at least for a few years. By which time the Mission might be able to employ him.'

'Exactly!' cried Petrie, almost triumphantly. 'Now, here is what I suggest. Let us assume that we can get an average of five thousand pounds a picture. Let us put eight up for sale. That should give you forty thousand pounds,' adding with a discreet cough, 'less our commission. We might make even more if we publicise the romantic story of your wife's heirloom. Believe me, I only suggest this on one assumption: that you are not selling the paintings for money, but for the sole purpose of financing your hospital.'

'Absolutely!' cried Aleena.

I was so staggered that all I could blurt out was, 'And the other eight?'

Petrie didn't hesitate. 'Hold on to them! Instead of selling them, at the bottom of the market, to a dealer who would put them in store without looking at them for ten years, we'll store them for you,' Petrie explained. 'Without cost to you, in vaults with specially controlled air and so on. We will keep them for ten or fifteen years – the decision will be yours. You can sell when you wish. Though I must say that I hope you will let us advise you when we know that the art market is buoyant.'

'Ten or fifteen years?' I looked at Aleena questioningly.

'Really, Doctor Masters, they've been stuck in a fish tank for as long as that,' said Petrie. 'I don't see the difference, do you? And if your grandmother had sold them, she might have got five pounds each. Now, I'm confident that we will reach about five thousand pounds for each painting. And,' he paused before speaking very deliberately, 'I will stake my reputation that each one you don't sell now will be worth fifty thousand pounds in ten to fifteen years. Maybe much more.'

'It's not possible!'

'It isn't *possible*. It's probable. We *know* the market. You don't *need* the money. But later, as world inflation takes its grip, we'll sell again for you. You and your wife will make the decision as to when, of course. And the money that is invested will bring in as much income every year as the money you're going to get by selling only half of the heritage next month!'

He paused and I looked at Aleena.

'It sounds sensible,' Petrie smiled at both of us. 'By the way I checked and your Mission is registered with the Charity Commissioners.'

'I don't understand,' said Aleena.

'It's very important. All the income of a registered charity is paid free of tax. And you may smile, but with the mess that Britain is in today, we can see income tax going through the roof. Even up to fifty per cent.'

'Oh no!'

'Oh yes.' The man at the top of the table finally put out his cigar, and said, 'Even higher, I wouldn't be surprised, under a Labour government.'

A shocked silence greeted this heretical statement, broken only by Petrie who asked with a smile to both of us, 'Don't you think we've come up with a good idea?'

As we both looked at each other and then at him, we both knew that he was right, and we both nodded at the same time and everybody laughed when Aleena said in her soft, husky voice. 'You are always right, Mr Petrie.'

So it was arranged.

After lunch, and when the other directors had said their goodbyes and returned to their offices, Petrie asked Aleena and myself, 'What are your plans?'

'Go to see the Tower of London,' Aleena replied promptly.

'But seriously?' Petrie turned to me.

'Apart from the Bloody Tower,' I emphasised the word 'bloody' jokingly, 'I want to go to Nottingham on Wednesday – that's in three days – to see my family. I've phoned them already, of course. Aleena wants to meet them, but she feels I ought to go for one night alone first, then we'll make a second trip together. We've got plenty of time.'

'And Aleena? She'll stay at the hotel when you're in Nottingham?'

'Actually, no. Doctor Reid – he's my senior on Koraloona – he has a wife who prefers Wimbledon to the South Seas. I talked to her on the phone and she wants Aleena to spend the night with her. She'll pick her up at the hotel and drive her there.'

'Sounds fine,' said Petrie. 'What I really want is for you both to give me a couple of working days first.'

'If I can help,' I said doubtfully.

'Of course you can. First, I want you and Aleena to choose the eight pictures we've decided to sell. That's urgent because we have to prepare the catalogue and so on. It shouldn't take long.'

'And the next day?'

'The day after tomorrow we've got an auction. Not very important, but it occurred to me that if we popped in for a little while, to watch, it'd give you some idea of what to expect when the big day comes.'

'I'd love to. I've never been to an auction.'

'It's not *that* interesting – unless you're selling! But it's all over so quickly that sometimes it's hard for a layman to follow.'

'When do I report tomorrow? And where?' I asked.

'Here,' suggested Petrie. 'At the ballroom where we hold the actual auctions. We can decide on the pictures.' Then he added casually, 'If you don't mind, it might be a good idea if we asked Norbet for suggestions.'

'Norbet?'

'You remember him – Professor Huson.'

'He's in London?' I was astonished.

Petrie nodded. 'He comes here fairly often. He's flown over to examine some paintings for Sotheby's, and I know he'd be delighted to give you some guidance, if you think it's worth while.'

'Of course.'

And so Professor Huson was at Stratford Place the following morning when we arrived. It was like meeting an old and trusted friend one never expected to see again. 'I'm so glad you're here,' Aleena said impulsively.

'And me.' Huson was obviously delighted at the sincerity of Aleena's words. 'Especially as you are a prettier picture than all the rest put together.'

I, too, was glad of Huson's help, for I felt hopelessly out of my depth when choosing which eight to sell; Huson, however, was obviously pleased to advise us.

'We'll set up a little exhibition of our own,' he said,

entering into the spirit of the thing. Which is just what we did, Huson fulfilling the role of guide and entrepreneur.

'This one,' he began, tapping the picture of the skinny farmyard chickens with one of his quizzing glasses, 'I suggest we keep. It's insignificant in size – an important point unless you're dealing with a collector who lacks space – and it's not immediately appealing to the eye.' He took it from the hook and turned it over. 'On the other hand . . . an inscription in Gauguin's own hand, even if it's only about smoking cigars – "*je sais que je n'ai pas le droit de fumer, mais . . .*" It's likely to increase in value with time.' He moved on to the charcoal and wash sketch of the *Oceanien*. 'Much the same might be said of this little sketch. It's bigger of course, but very slight in inspiration.'

I remembered my own thought on seeing it for the first time. 'Like a writer making a note of something that might come in useful one day.'

'Exactly,' Huson agreed. 'And I think it might be more useful to your Trust, in a profitable sense, "one day" rather than now.'

There was no question about the painting of the secret pool. Huson stood back and nodded his head in appreciation. 'One of the stars of the sale – an immediate eye-catcher. Everything about it is right – size, subject, execution. I wouldn't be surprised to see it fetch the top bid. And that one too – ' he gestured at the picture of the boy with the bananas on his head – 'is going to make an immediate appeal to a connoisseur.'

Aleena looked at me, smiling but with a touch of sadness in her smile. 'I'll be rather sorry to lose that one. Don't you think – ?'

I looked at Huson, a question in my eyes. 'It's up to you of course, but – ' his leaving the sentence unfinished was as good as saying, 'There's little point in asking my advice if you don't take it.'

Of the four self-portraits, Huson suggested that we should not sell one of the pair that had background figures of native girls, but we should send for auction the other one of the pair, and the oddly erotic picture of the red wall against which the artist had painted himself full length with the tangle of vanilla sensually embracing him and the symbolic bird hovering in the green sky above the wall.

'To borrow an idiom of my American friends,' Huson said with a fluttering of his white hand, 'that'll knock 'em cold.'

The painting of the girls in their summer dresses with parasols shielding them from a paradoxically snow-filled sky was one that held a particular enchantment for Aleena and, after musing for some minutes, Huson agreed that at a time of post-war austerity it might strike too frivolous a note; while the portraits of Gauguin's wife and son were probably too conventional to attract the 'modernists' among potential buyers. They, on the other hand, would be immediately drawn to the four rather sinister 'apocalyptic' pictures which Alec Reid had felt had been painted under the effects of cocaine.

'Salvador Dali,' Huson explained, 'has influenced a lot of people's thinking on symbolic and surrealistic subjects; and I think these four are going to create something of a sensation. And sensation is something we want. Good-quality paper and high-standard colour printing are a bit hard to come by in England; but if I can get Christie's to have them on the catalogue cover, then these' – he waved at the quartet – 'these are going to arouse a great deal of controversy in the art world and a great deal of interest in the sale room.'

We agreed. The 'apocalyptics' had never been my favourites – perhaps because I found them too disturbing. The riotously happy picture of the Anani drinking festival, on the other hand, was a continual joy to Aleena and me, and I was delighted to agree when Huson suggested that, together with the girls with parasols, we should not sell – not yet. 'Pink Street' was of course my own; and with a benevolent hand on my elbow Huson smiled at both of us and said, 'An inheritance, eh? – for the next generation.'

*

The following day, Petrie had arranged to meet us an hour before the sale and, as we turned into Stratford Place, he was approaching too, a furled umbrella hooked over his arm, the catalogue held aloft like a flag. The courtesies completed, we made our way along Oxford Street to one of the government-subsidised British Restaurants that had been erected on the site of the bombed John Lewis store and was doing a roaring trade in self-service meals at tenpence a head. There, together with three cups of steaming urn-made tea at a penny a cup, we found a bench amid the weedstrewn rubble.

'I thought you ought to try it – for experience,' he explained.

The incongruity of the situation struck Aleena particularly. She had not yet fully adjusted to a war-torn land where incongruity was commonplace and the crowds took no more notice of us than they did of the bombed buildings.

'We must look very peculiar,' she said, laughing.

Petrie shrugged. 'The well-known English *sangfroid*, my dear,' he said. 'Now Aleena, what do you know about auctions?'

'Not a thing,' I replied for both of us, 'except that if you raise an eyebrow at the wrong moment you've bought a dining-room table you don't want at a price you can't afford.'

Petrie laughed. 'That seems to be the one thing that everybody's heard about auctions; and I can assure you it's absolutely untrue. The auctioneer is much too skilled to let himself be fooled by any but the most definite signs of bidding. Also, he's familiar with the faces of regular dealers and private buyers; and he knows too that a good many people attend auctions for the drama of the occasion.'

'We have settled down very well here,' he indicated Stratford Place, 'but we were lucky in King Street in St James's. There our main building was badly damaged, but the façade remained intact; so did the strongroom, where the most valuable stuff was stored. The premises'll be rebuilt in due course; but with building materials in short supply we don't know when. Meanwhile we've got the lease of Derby House.'

When we arrived in the ballroom, it was quite full of homburg-hatted men in groups chatting quietly and grasping catalogues which they used to emphasise remarks.

'I thought I'd bring you to this one,' Petrie said, nodding to one or two dealers, 'not only to give you some idea of what'll happen at the Gauguin sale, but because some of the main offers are of fetish idols and artefacts from the South Seas. Some dealers are trying to corner the market. But I doubt if we'll hear any startling bids: they're not keen on revealing their intentions by over-bidding.'

He flourished his own catalogue, pointing to the words 'At two o'clock precisely'.

'It means exactly what it says. That's why people get here in good time. It's frustrating to get here just as the hammer's falling on something you want.'

Petrie pointed to a row of chairs well forward. 'Representatives from *The Connoisseur, Apollo*, and junior reporters from the national press. They only send the juniors because nothing's likely to make the dailies in these days of paper shortage unless it's sensational – ' he nudged me – 'as I hope *our* sale will be.'

At 1.55 a clerk entered with a massive ledger under his arm and sat at his desk. It was the signal for everyone to sit down, as if the curtain were about to go up in a theatre. As I watched, the leading actor, the auctioneer, now entered from the wings, so to speak, stepped up on the rostrum and gave a little bow (friendly but also remote) and began at once:

'Good afternoon, gentlemen. Lot one. No doubt you've taken the opportunity during viewing days of handling this pleasant little figure from Easter Island. Nice patina, you'll have noticed. May I say thirty pounds?'

The porter held it aloft for all to see. Petrie scribbled on his catalogue, 'The first lots are a sort of apéritif,' and I gathered it was not etiquette to speak.

One by one the grotesque figures carved from native

woods – and the exaggerations of male and female genitals suggested they were mostly symbolic of fertility – were displayed and knocked down to different bidders.

I was astonished at the speed with which sales were completed – rarely more than a minute before the auctioneer was saying 'Are you all done, then?' and bringing his hammer down.

'An enlightening afternoon,' I said to Petrie, as we left an hour or so later. 'But I think I'm more at home in my surgery!'

44

Aleena had been quite adamant that I should go to meet my parents on my own for my first visit.

'Put yourself in their place,' she said. 'There'll be a thousand things they want to talk to you about, without the distraction of having to be polite to someone they've never seen. Give them a chance!' She added mischievously, 'And prepare the ground so they know more or less what to expect – a foreign girl who gets lost in five minutes in New York and this huge city of London.'

It was sensible, though I wouldn't have hesitated if Alec's wife Rhoda hadn't arranged for Aleena to stay the night while I was away. She would be well looked after in Wimbledon, and if I took a dislike to Mrs Reid when she came to collect Aleena, well, I could always invent some excuse on the spur of the moment to cancel the arrangement.

But I needn't have worried. One glance at Mrs Reid was enough to dispel any doubt. Rhoda Reid was not only attractive in middle age, rather tall with greying hair, but she arrived at the hotel exuding to the hall porter, who pointed me out to her, that special kind of presence which belongs only to women who, for want of a better word, have a kind of refinement. A woman used to the best of everything. She held out her hand and shook mine firmly, smiling, her eyes set well apart and frank.

Her height added to her air of distinction, and I could see that her greying hair had been arranged by an expert and not by herself. She had neat gloves, and slim ankles in the silk stockings which, during the forties, were supposed to be virtually unobtainable.

It was difficult to think that this elegant woman could ever have been attracted to the happy-go-lucky, sweating, fat little man she had married, and I couldn't help reflecting that Alec must have had many a secret chuckle as he wondered what I would think of his wife, for never once had he talked about her intimately.

She turned to Aleena and said, 'So you are Mrs Masters. Alec told me a little about you in one of his rare letters, but he didn't say how beautiful you were.' To me she added, 'My car is outside and as I gather that you're off this morning, Doctor, I'll drive your wife home and then we'll go for a walk on the Common to work up an appetite for lunch.'

With that she smiled warmly, took Aleena's arm almost protectively and, with a backward smile, promised, 'Don't worry, Doctor. I'll return her to you in good condition tomorrow evening.'

'Of course.' I returned the smile as the chauffeur helped the ladies into an old Rolls-Royce, and wondered in a casual way how she managed to get the petrol. Then I prepared to leave, packing up the presents I had brought for the family, but still thinking not so much of my trip to Nottingham as of Mrs Reid – and the extraordinary facts of marriage that could draw two such diverse characters together in holy matrimony who then, calmly and cheerfully, agree to spend their lives ten thousand miles apart, she with a Rolls-Royce and (I assumed) a large house, and he with a converted ambulance. How extraordinary, I was thinking as I packed, to imagine that these two people had ever been in love. Had they *really* been in love? What

624

on earth had attracted a sophisticated girl to a man like Alec?

For no reason, my mind went back to a moment when I was a young doctor in the East End. I had been called as a witness to give evidence in a wife-beating case, and the bedraggled wife seemed prepared to forgive her surly husband in the dock because he had beaten her only when drunk, and the magistrate had asked, 'Does he love another woman, do you think?' The wife had looked horrified, and the magistrate persisted, 'So the – well – er – intimate side of your marriage is all right?' and the woman had replied, 'Oh yes sir. He's very good and doesn't trouble me very often.' Perhaps Alec and his wife had remained married because he didn't 'trouble' her very often!

Ah well! As I settled down for the one-and-a-half-hour journey from King's Cross to Nottingham – which before the war had cost only 5s 6d, but now the return fare was over £2 – I started to think of my own family. I began trying to imagine what my parents would look like after eight years. We had spoken on the phone the day we arrived in London and Father's voice had sounded as strong as ever; so had Clare's, though Mother's had changed. But what would they *look* like?

The biggest change of all would surely be in Clare, for as people grow older the gaps of years don't matter so much provided they are in good health. There's not much difference between, say, healthy men of fifty-five and sixty-three, but it is different with the young. Clare had been a teenager the last time I saw her. Now she must be twenty-six.

Leaning out of the carriage window as the train puffed into the station, I recognised her immediately – bright, cheerful, pale auburn hair, waving as though she would never stop, then she half ran towards me as I climbed out. My heart gave a jump of joy – professional as well as emotional – for though she limped a little, I was thrilled to see that she could move faster than a normal walk. She had, I knew, long ago discarded the unsightly brace, and she

625

would always have a slight limp, but it wasn't as marked as I had feared.

'Clare! You look older!'

'Kit! You look older!'

We both laughed and hugged each other with the pure joy of meeting after all these years, five of them with hardly one intimate and personal letter because of the fussy, wartime censorship.

'Let me look at you!' I held her at arm's length. 'Quite a dizzy blonde!'

'Not in this old coat and skirt,' she sniffed. 'Dad doesn't need anything except shoes, so he lets me have some of his coupons, but I never have enough.'

'Wait till you see what I've bought you!'

She was as excited as a child and so was I, so I splurged on a taxi instead of taking the tram, and we set off for our home in Thorne Road. I was astonished when the taxi drew up. Age may not show in people you love, but buildings sometimes do. How insignificant our house looked! I had thought it such an important little house when I was young, but time plays strange tricks with memories, magnifying them in absence, and now it looked so small and faceless, no character that I remembered, just one in a row of terraced houses.

Mother must have been peeping through the net curtains of the front room, because the moment the cab stopped, the front door was pulled open, and out strode Father with Mother close behind.

'Welcome home, Doctor!' Father's handshake still had a strong grip.

'Glad to be back, Captain Masters,' I laughed, knowing that he didn't like to use the rank he had acquired in the first world war.

'By God, young man, you look damned well! Married life obviously suits you.'

Mother came fluttering behind, eyes moist with happiness as she put her arms round me – more frail now, her arms thinner after eight years, much of them spent with no help and indifferent food. 'It's so good to have you back home, son.'

'Must have a drink to celebrate.' Father ushered me into the sitting-room. 'The same as usual – a glass of beer?'

Without thinking, I said, 'I'd rather have a Scotch, Father.'

'Whisky!' He looked astonished. 'I've never seen you drink whisky before. You've always been a beer drinker. You remember the advice I gave to you as a young doctor – beware of a whisky breath.'

'That's nearly eight years ago, Father! I've changed.' His remarks were not in the least disapproving. He had simply forgotten the lapse of time, that I was now a grown man. 'I do enjoy a beer occasionally,' I explained, 'but I more or less gave it up because it makes you sweat so much in the tropics.'

'I see. Of course. Well, we haven't got any Scotch I'm afraid. It's very hard to find.'

'You don't drink a *lot* do you?' asked Mother anxiously.

'Very little – and very weak. But don't worry, Father, I brought a bottle for you. Bought it in New York.'

'New York! You are a globetrotter! I'd love to go to places like that.' Clare's voice was faintly envious. I noticed that she sat down almost immediately we entered the room, and understood why. The leg didn't actually hurt, but the standing on the platform, and then the unaccustomed run towards the train had tired the muscles.

'And how's your wife – Aleena?' asked Mother, hesitating before using her name. 'We're all so excited, waiting to meet her.'

'And she's dying to meet the family.' I explained where she was staying the night and why, but Mother said doubtfully, 'Do you think it's fair for a – ' for a moment I thought she was going to say 'a native girl' but she compromised, 'a stranger in a big city to be left alone?'

'Mother, dear, Aleena was put in a boarding school in a big city for years. And apart from the terrible ordeal when

627

she was taken hostage, she's a perfectly normal healthy girl; and believe me, she can handle herself. After all, she *is* the grand-daughter of a genius.'

Inevitably the talk veered from the lush fantasy world of the South Seas to my own particular ordeals – how I had nearly been murdered by 'witchcraft' and then taken prisoner, and the way in which I had been held hostage (though I spared them the details of the savage beatings) and how I had escaped death through the dummy land-mine.

'I was scared stiff,' I admitted. 'But at least after the first Japanese attack on Sanderstown, we were never bombed again until the land-mine floated down.'

Nottingham, it appeared, had not suffered as badly as many other cities; but even so, it had not escaped entirely because the flat Lincolnshire countryside to the north-east was dotted with military airfields like the one at Finningly where Father had for a time been posted as a Signals instructor. And sometimes the Germans hit the wrong targets.

'And what's going to happen to you now the war's over?' I asked, thinking of his age.

I had a feeling that in a way he had been waiting for the question, because as a man on the verge of sixty he exhibited none of the anxiety syndromes I so often came across in people whose jobs had finished.

But not with Father. Almost with a burst of pride, he announced, 'My boy, I'm going to earn more money than I've ever earned before. I've – '

'Really,' Mother murmured disapprovingly.

'I've landed a big job with a television company. I've been specialising on radar, sonar and advanced electronics for the last years and that, together with my previous expertise in radio, means that they leapt at the chance of getting me. Britain is going into major production in June when television restarts. You'll never recognise the roof-tops this time next year – a forest of metal masts strapped to chimney pots.'

628

'You do exaggerate,' Mother sighed, but I could see that she was proud that Father had landed such a big job.

That night we sat down to a real slap-up unrationed dinner – by far the best I had had in England: double helpings of roast pork with crackling, apple sauce, roast potatoes, and when I asked Mother how she had managed, she looked at Father who explained with a chuckle, 'It's perfectly legal – if you live near the country. Two of us bought a piglet from a farmer near Beeston. He looked after it, we paid for its food, and we had it slaughtered not so long ago – and our local butcher has done wonders with it – everything from roast pork to pure sausages and pork pies or bacon.'

After dinner I distributed the gifts, such as they were. But even though I was not very imaginative, everything was welcome in those spartan post-war days. I had brought half a dozen pairs of silk stockings for Clare, the two sheepskin coats, hardly used in New York, a dress for Mother, several pullovers of different sizes, pipe tobacco and the whisky for Father.

'That's great,' he said, 'and it's time to thank you for something else. The food parcels you sent us from Australia. They didn't all get through – neither did all your letters for that matter – but those parcels were a godsend.'

All in all, it was a very happy reunion and it was wonderful to think that I would be back in Nottingham in a few days, 'With your bride,' as Mother insisted on calling Aleena.

'I have the feeling,' said Clare as she took me back to the station the following day, 'that until you showed Mother your photos of Aleena, she wasn't really sure whether or not she was black!'

'I wouldn't have minded,' I teased her. Then I jumped into the train, and though I had bought the evening paper, promptly fell asleep. I wasn't used to talking half way through the night. I didn't wake up until the train jerked to a stop in Rugby, and then I did glance at the four pages of news, not that there was anything much of interest, for the front pages every day were filled with details of the Nuremberg trials; but in the way one's eye picks out a word in a small headline because you recognise it, mine alighted on 'Bikini'.

It was a story half way down page three and it read:

The world's press has been invited to witness the two explosions of the A-bomb at the Bikini atoll. The press will be taken in a warship to the observation point south of Wake Island. Sixty-seven expendable ships have been provided by the US navy and anchored at varying distances from Bikini, where they will be left and inspected after a long period, to see if they are contaminated.

A total of 42,000 soldiers, sailors, airmen, scientists, etc., will take part in the test. One of the expendable ships will carry a large collection of goats, pigs, and rats.

Two bombs will be used in the test, one of which will be dropped into the ocean to make an underwater explosion, the other on the atoll, from which the few inhabitants are being evacuated. President Truman, who created the Atomic Energy Commission, estimates that the explosion will be visible several hundred miles away.

How stupid men are, I was thinking as we drew into King's Cross. Messing about with dangerous stuff like nuclear power when they haven't the faintest idea how deadly it can be.

Aleena arrived back an hour after I reached the hotel. I didn't see Mrs Reid as she drove away immediately for another appointment.

'Have fun?' I asked.

'She was delightful,' Aleena kicked off her shoes with relief, 'but my feet! She never stops walking over the Common. Every day, she told me. But you, Kit – was it wonderful seeing the family again?'

'It *was*. And they're longing to see you.' I told her all about the trip to Nottingham, my father's new job and then, watching Aleena search for her slippers among her shoes in the wardrobe, I said, 'You look as though your feet hurt! I'd have thought our Mrs Reid, with her chauffeur, wouldn't bother to walk that much. She must like it.'

'I don't think she does particularly. But she told me she always walks five miles a day, rain or shine.'

'Seems crazy. What for?'

'To keep her weight down.'

'She seemed slim enough for me. Quite different from Alec. Don't you think that their marriage is incredible?'

'I did think so – until I found out the reason.'

'Ah! Tell me all.'

She smiled. 'It's nothing sinister. But I saw something you have probably never seen – a photo taken on their wedding day. It had been left – hidden and forgotten probably – in a drawer in my bedroom.'

'But why should it be hidden?'

'I think Rhoda was ashamed of it.'

'Ashamed?'

Aleena nodded. 'You should have seen it. There was Alec, slim, good-looking, a mop of hair, and he seemed tall as well.'

'Perhaps he was then. Some people seem to shrink in a funny way as they grow older,' I grinned, but was puzzled. 'But I still don't understand.'

'And there was Rhoda, the bride. Kit, she weighed a ton! Honestly, she was the original jam roll, fat, flabby, the only good feature was her face, and that was half hidden under a double chin and her cheeks. I was *horrified*! And I was just about to close the drawer and pretend I had never seen the photo when Rhoda walked in. Well, the door was half open, so she saw me.'

'My God!' I could visualise in my mind's eye that almost macabre moment. 'What did you do – say?'

'She blushed, and smiled slightly. Then she recovered her composure, as I said, "I just opened the drawer – "

' "I'd forgotten that photo." She smiled, adding sardonically, "I've changed a bit haven't I?" '

'I was lost for words. I didn't know what to say. It wasn't my fault, of course, I was just unpacking my few things, but afterwards she told me – and it was all very simple really, it explains perfectly why they married.'

Later that evening, over a quiet dinner, Rhoda had told Aleena that, when she was young, she was so much an overweight ugly duckling that her family were horrified with her, despite being educated at Roedean. She was the eternal wallflower, and when she became of marriageable age – in those days girls were desperately afraid of being left on the shelf, as they put it – no one would look at Rhoda, despite her rich parents.

Then Alec Reid, who worked in Wimbledon Hospital as a junior, came to treat Rhoda's mother, a widow, and according to Rhoda her mother was so impressed with the way Alec treated her that he became her regular doctor.

'And I'm sure Alec must have been impressed with her wealth and that huge house facing over the Common,' said Aleena. 'According to Rhoda, Alec played a large part in prolonging her mother's life, and the mother in turn encouraged Alec to be – well, kind to the overweight Rhoda. Rhoda's mother wanted to get her daughter off her hands, and of course I don't know the details,' Aleena added, 'but I suppose Alec was a bit overwhelmed by the whole rich background so finally agreed to marry Rhoda. And when the old lady died, Rhoda inherited the house and all her money.'

'Well, I'll be damned! But they went off to the South Seas,' I said. 'Why, I wonder?'

'It seems that this was part of an unwritten bargain. According to Rhoda, Alec had always wanted to travel, and now that they had enough money, she promised to go with him after her mother died. So they went there, but Rhoda hated it.'

'I see,' I said to Aleena. 'But why her handsome figure? Or rather, how?'

'The irony is,' Aleena finished her story, 'that when Rhoda returned to London, she felt so out of it that she decided to bant – that was the word she used – and she lost stone after stone. She still diets carefully, and she's never put the weight back.'

'And in the meantime,' I said, 'poor old Alec slipped into the happy-go-lucky ways of the islands, and started putting on weight! The supreme irony, I must say.'

Irony offered another twist a few days later, after I had made a 'duty' call at the Basildon Publishing Co., the firm which had bought Jason Purvis' novel. I had promised Jason that I would find out if the firm seemed sympathetic to new writers, or if they just regarded his first book as a casual business transaction.

Far from it! Alfred Beale, one of the directors, was a cheerful extrovert over six feet tall, broad-chested and sporting the largest pair of moustaches I had ever seen. Their offices were in Bedford Square and Mr Beale wanted to know everything about this strange unknown author. I tried to tell what little I knew, what he looked like, that we were friends and so on.

'But will his novel sell?' I asked.

'Sell? I'm sure it will. It's due out in July and we've already had an enthusiastic response in the trade – selling to the bookshops I mean.' He paused for dramatic effect, and I looked suitably impressed. 'I hope you'll tell Purvis when you see him to get busy and write another.'

I promised I would, and in fact, knowing how insecure Jason was where his book was concerned, I sent him a cable, telling him just that, and that I would take some early copies back to Koraloona with me.

A few days later, when we had returned to the hotel to wash and brush up before going to have what Petrie called 'a five-bob lunch', the telephone rang. I said, 'I'll get it, darling,' and picked up the receiver thinking it must be Christie's.

633

Slightly surprised, the operator asked, 'Are you Doctor Masters, sir?' And when I said that I was, she asked, 'Will you accept a long-distance reverse charge call, sir?'

In that split second which it takes to say yea or nay, or at least to enquire 'Who from?' the inevitable panic seized me that it could only herald bad news. And long distance! I suppose, analysing it, the reason was that we could not use the long-distance phone in Koraloona, so I had long since got out of the habit of answering anything other than local calls. All this rushed through my mind in that split second, and I realised that at least it couldn't be bad news from Aleena's family. They would never have bothered with the rigmarole of trying to reverse a charge.

'But where is the call from?' I asked, the split second over.

The reply really astonished me – and I started panicking again.

'It's from a town called Sanderstown in the South Pacific,' announced the voice in the casual voice of one saying, 'It's from Bournemouth.'

That started the adrenalin pumping! Nothing but bad news could warrant such a call. And the only news bad enough to cause this would be an urgent request for me to return to Koraloona because something must have happened to Alec Reid. But if he were ill, who would be making the phone call on his part?

'Will you accept the call?' asked the operator again. 'It's from a Mr Purvis.'

It *would* be Jason of course, though why he had travelled from Koraloona to Sanderstown to telephone me seemed crazy. He could have cabled.

'Yes, of course I'll accept the call,' I said, whispering to a mystified Aleena, 'It's Jason, in Sanderstown'. She turned round, hairbrush in hand, and *her* first reaction was, 'Oh God! I hope nothing's happened to Mummy!'

A minute or two later the voice of Purvis came through, loud and clear – and cheerful!

'Hello, Kit! Are you two lovebirds all right?'

'Are *you* all right?' I asked without preamble. 'What's the trouble? Carry on, I can hear you.'

'No trouble. I just wanted to thank you for the cable. Great news, isn't it, about the novel?'

'You mean to say – ' I began to feel an angry flush, but Aleena, with a smile, held out a restraining arm as I was about to explode. 'You're wasting my money – and –'

'Sorry old boy –' I could even hear the inflexion in his voice. 'It's *good* news. And I felt that you wouldn't mind paying for it.'

'What, for God's sake?'

It was almost uncanny, the way I could *feel* Purvis' hesitation and excitement across the thousands of miles, even before he spoke.

'You remember Lorna?'

'Of course I remember Miss Sowerby. What kind of joke is all this?'

'Well,' Purvis almost chortled, 'she's not Miss Sowerby any longer. She's Mrs Purvis!'

'What!'

'We were married at the cathedral in Tala-Tala a couple of days ago, and we're spending a three-day honeymoon at the Southern Cross Hotel.'

'Jason! Lorna! Wonderful news!' I beckoned Aleena, who, already sensing my excitement, was asking, 'What's happened?'

Holding my hand over the receiver I whispered, 'They're married. Here! You say hello.'

Grabbing the telephone, I heard her say, 'It's Aleena. Congratulations Mr and Mrs Purvis.' She laughed. 'Can I say a quick word to – your wife?' A pause, then, 'I'm so happy for you, Lorna. What does it feel like to be the wife of a famous novelist? Here's Kit.'

'Wonderful news, Lorna,' I echoed Aleena's words. 'I'm so pleased. But what about – '

'I'm staying on as matron,' she interrupted, the distance unable to disguise that rather prissy tone of hers. 'I could

635

never give up my work. Paula Reece is helping Doctor Reid out while we're here in Sanderstown.'

'Good. Tell Alec Reid that I've met his wife and she's in good health and sends her love. And now, can I have a last word with Jason? You're a rascal!' I cried when he was back on the phone. 'Doing this sort of thing behind my back. But when you return to Koraloona go round to Johnson's and get a bottle of champagne on my account to celebrate.'

Jason hesitated across the air waves before saying, 'Thanks for the thought, but I can't do that, I'm afraid.'

'Why not? I've told you, it's on my bill.'

'I appreciate that. But the fact is – well, I've stopped drinking. I've signed the pledge, as they say in the Sally Army. Half a sec. Lorna wants to talk to you.'

'I didn't want you to think that I forced Jason,' she said right away. 'You know, Doctor, he *is* a reformed character, and I'm so proud of him, and we both feel that, if he's going to write another book and be a good husband, we should put all temptation behind us.'

'Again congratulations,' and as an after-thought I took a leaf out of Mr Petrie's book and said 'Good morning!'

'Well I'm blessed,' I said to Aleena when I had hung up. 'Married. But, even so, poor old Jason. Teetotal! Who would ever have believed it?'

'Much better to be like us,' she gave me a hug, 'married and always ready for a glass of champagne.'

I was thinking as we walked towards Soho for lunch of how much Jason had changed over the years. In my mind's eye I could still see that emaciated figure in the garden of the cottage hospital looking as though he would drop dead from starvation and, as I pictured him later, seeming to enjoy music and alcohol in equal proportions, and whose only food was tinned stuff bought from Johnson's store on credit. In those days he had boasted that he would one day be a writer, but it seemed that he lacked the moral stamina to put his thoughts into words.

Perhaps I had helped him to a small extent, by offering

him a friendship (together with a square meal now and then) and not just leaving him as a beachcomber; but really it had been the missionary's daughter, lips pursed with disapproval if necessary, yet with a hidden heart of gold, who had slowly helped and encouraged Purvis to write until, finally, he had finished a book, was about to have it published, and they themselves had married – the ex-missionary and the ex-beachcomber.

'I do hope they'll be happy,' I said to Aleena.

We had hardly got used to the idea of 'Mr and Mrs Purvis' before it was time to return to Nottingham as Dr and Mrs Masters. Mother was a little nervous at first, perhaps because of the exotic nature of Aleena's beauty and her long black hair. But Aleena had such an uninhibited manner that the atmosphere quickly thawed, especially after Clare had taken Aleena's arm and hugged her, and Father had planted a firm kiss and said, 'Well, I must congratulate my son – he's picked a real corker.'

Father provided the whisky this time – my last bottle was almost empty, and I had no idea how to go about buying almost unobtainable goods – but we had roast pork again! I had forewarned Aleena, who ate it as though it was a great rarity, even though in Polynesia during the war pork and chicken had been almost our only staple meats after shipments of Australian beef or New Zealand lamb became infrequent.

We stayed two days in Nottingham this time. In a way it was a relief to get away from the business of the auction, and after our return to London, I had a few 'duty' calls to make: one to the only remaining nursing sister at St Andrew's where I had been an intern, and one to Dr Arnold Barton, who had been head of the governors when I was sacked – but who had softened the blow by getting me my job in Koraloona.

'And thank you not only for that,' I said when I met the elderly doctor, 'but you sent me to an island where I found a beautiful bride.'

'I've seen her picture in the papers.' Barton had lost none of his stern features, the years hadn't softened him much, and he still harked back indirectly to the unwelcome publicity I had received after the manslaughter case. 'I don't really hold with the newspaper reports of a doctor being involved in marrying an heiress – '

'I'm not advertising – '

'You weren't "advertising", as you call it, when you got into trouble with the press the last time. Still,' he had the grace to agree, 'I suppose if you look at it in the right way, misfortune can turn out to be a blessing in disguise.'

'I suppose so.'

'How furious you were when you were – er – relieved of your post at St Andrew's. Through no real fault of your own, you faced the end of a career you had already mapped out. But look what happened! If you hadn't gone to the aid of that old man being attacked in the street, you'd probably still be in a groove, doing the daily rounds, rain or shine. Instead – everything the heart could wish for.'

'And a fine new hospital, I hope,' I said.

'Of course. And anything to help the Mission is a wonderful thing. I hope the auction of these – er – unusual, modern paintings will fetch all the money the newspapers say.'

But would it fetch all that money? The days of pleasure, of anticipation, were rapidly slipping by. We had had our public relations sessions, based mainly on Aleena and, before I realised it, we had reached the eve of the much-heralded 'Auction of the Decade', as one newspaper named it. But would all this buzz of advance publicity make us realise our target of £40,000? I suddenly thought of Tiki's warning – would the gods on this occasion keep buyers away when the time came for the sale in a couple of days?

It was silly, I know, but two days before the auction I began to feel increasingly gloomy, sure in my own mind that the whole affair would be a dismal failure. I had awakened in the night with dreams centring round Tiki's warning about the revenge of Polynesian gods, and in the darkness I had found Aleena's arms round me as if I were a child with nightmares.

'You cried out – as though you were afraid. What's the trouble?' she asked.

I switched the light on. I could see myself in the mirror opposite the bed, looking bleary-eyed – which, as it was four in the morning, was understandable. But there was more to it than that.

'I suppose,' I said with a feeble attempt at humour, 'that I was dreaming that I was being marched off to Penal for debt if the sale's a flop.'

'Of *course* it won't be a flop,' she reassured me – but the mood persisted all the next day.

'I'm not by nature a prophet of doom,' I said; 'but it'll be a bitter disappointment to Alec and me if Tiki is right and we're wrong, and the hospital project fails.'

'Forget Tiki,' she urged me. 'After all, Mr Petrie and Professor Huson have never said a word that wasn't encouraging. And they're the experts.'

'Tiki is an expert at fate.' I tried to grin mockingly.

But the shadow of apprehension persisted. On the night before the sale, I dreamed that I was attending an empty auction room, or that people were offering ludicrous prices like five shillings because Gauguin wasn't a Royal Academician and his pictures were thought to be bad. And Mr Petrie was on the edge of it somehow, quite different from the Petrie I knew, saying very angrily that we must come to some arrangement about the repayment of the money Christie's had advanced.

45

On the morning of the auction I felt much better, less depressed. It was a crisp day with shafts of thin sun filtering through the bedroom windows. Perhaps my apprehensions had flown with the clouds that had made way for the sun.

After breakfast, Petrie arrived at the hotel about 9.30 and we had coffee in the downstairs lounge as he outlined the proceedings.

'And I want to tell you something about the cast of characters,' he said.

Aleena looked puzzled.

'By that,' Petrie smiled, 'I mean the characters who we hope will be bidding against each other. There are some intriguing names among them – rich names too, I'm delighted to say – but once we get inside I shall slip into the background. It would be most unethical for a director of the firm to be seen with the vendors.'

I nodded. I had been brought up on similar ethical considerations.

'I can tell you this. The two viewing days have been very well attended. Some interesting people – though that doesn't guarantee they'll attend the sale. Many were just scouting around, for themselves or someone else. Digby Cunningham, for example. He runs a smart gallery in Pont Street – a bit off the beaten track, but he has very good connections among collectors. Then I saw Claude Fournet, an exiled Frenchman who's known to have a great interest in Gauguin. And Leonard Brockbank of the Brockbank grocery chain – an American with flashy ideas!'

'But is he, for example, the sort of man who'll buy?' I asked.

'Well, he's just bought a vulgar palatial mansion in New York with enough wall space to take all the paintings we can offer. He's a millionaire ten times over.' Petrie paused. 'But there are others who are more interesting – including Mr John Smith – a rather obvious pseudonym. I'm told that he's representing no less a person – ' he lowered his voice dramatically, though it was hardly necessary – 'than Edward James.'

Aleena and I both looked blank. Petrie smiled again. 'Ah, you're mystified, not surprisingly. Mr James belongs to a social whirl you're not likely to have been in. Supposed to be an illegitimate grandson of King Edward the Seventh. Fabulously rich and very, very eccentric.' Petrie put a world of meaning into the word. 'He was married to the dancer Tilly Losch; but that marriage proved to be – er let's say *unworkable*. He collects modern paintings like schoolboys collect stamps; but lives in Mexico, so he has to have a representative wherever there's an auction he's interested in. I think Mr Smith is the man.'

'But is it possible for a man in England to buy a painting for a man in Mexico?' asked Aleena.

'Oh yes, it often works that way. The price ranges are agreed in advance by phone or cable. On the other hand, some representatives buy with a blank cheque, so to speak!'

'Anyone else of interest at the preview?' I asked.

'Yes. There was Pieter Stoephausen from The Hague, a wily old bird when it comes to scenting the unusual. And Monsieur Étienne Lamy who represents a syndicate making something of a corner in Post-Impressionists.' He waved an elegant hand. 'There were others of course, but – well, we shall see.'

He cleared his throat. 'Now: the auctioneer for the sale will be Mr Dickinson, a senior director. I've reserved a couple of chairs for you at the side with the press people – they always like to be near so they can write about eyes glinting with greed and so on – colourful, but not at all a true picture of the dignified proceedings.'

He turned to Aleena. 'Shall we proceed, my dear? I may say that, to my war-weary eye, your flowerlike grace brings a breath of spring and beauty to the occasion. And I wish you both, us both, good luck.'

It was a quarter to eleven when we took our seats and there was a much louder buzz of conversation and far more people than at the earlier sale I had attended. I nudged Aleena as we sat down on our gilt chairs. 'We're lucky. I can tell. It's more – dramatic, somehow. Quite a different feeling.'

People were taking their seats. The tang of drama in the air was exciting. We both looked down at our catalogues, Aleena with one hand lightly on the crook of my elbow.

'Lot one.' I read the entry for perhaps the twentieth time. 'A self-portrait in chalk and crayon, with marginal notes in the artist's hand, undated and unsigned but authenticated by the calligraphy. Probably a sketch for a later, more formal, self-portrait.'

As the porters brought in the easel, the conversation died. The porter gave the clerk's desk a swift once-over, and set the auctioneer's hammer slightly askew on the rostrum as if aiming it for action. The clerk at his desk peered down over half-glasses at his ledger then at the clock on the wall immediately opposite Aleena. There was complete silence when Mr Dickinson entered, without haste. With a springy step he mounted the rostrum. He was a very tall man with heavy eyebrows that gave him the look of a hooded eagle, but his dark eyes held a glint of humour. He nodded towards Aleena. 'Good morning, madam and gentlemen. I shall conduct the sale without preamble. Lot one. May I say a hundred?'

I gave a start. It was a long way below the reserve of £500 Petrie had suggested; then I remembered him saying, 'It's a sort of bait. An experienced auctioneer knows, having been told who the likely bidders are, that the little preliminary game simply means that he knows, and the interested parties know, and each knows the other knows,

642

that the opening bid will simply attract the small-time bidders who will quickly drop out of the race when the advances come in much bigger leaps.'

'– and twenty,' Mr Dickinson was saying in response to a raised catalogue; and a second or two later, '– and fifty.' He raised one of his impressive eyebrows. 'Two hundred from you, Mr Sorenson.' His glance seemed to dart everywhere. '– and fifty from the gentleman at the end of the row. Do I see three hundred from you, Mr Moresby? Thank you. Four? This is encouraging, gentlemen. I'm sure you haven't done.'

Petrie had told me that such semi-jocular remarks were often made to hint that the reserve hadn't yet been reached. Even before I had considered the thought, the bidding had progressed in leaps of a hundred to nine hundred, and there it seemed to slow down. But after an encouraging, 'Against you, Mr Sorenson. Another one? A thousand, I'm bid. And one. Eleven hundred, then.' He swept the room with his eagle gaze. 'Have you all done, then? Yours, Mr Moresby.'

As the picture was whisked away a porter replaced it with the companion self-portrait – for which, the catalogue said, the previous lot was believed to be a preliminary study. I looked at my watch in amazement: barely five minutes had passed and already we had – when the commission was deducted – £1,000. 'Let's hope it all goes like this!' I scribbled on Aleena's catalogue. She nodded delightedly. Would the next lot, on which Petrie had set a reserve of £1,500 'to show we mean business', go as quickly and with such proportionate leaps?

It didn't, quite. The bidding seemed to start sluggishly, with some hesitation before Mr Dickinson's opening suggestion of £800 was accepted – by M. Lamy as it turned out, who seemed disinclined to make any gesture when a man with a drooping moustache pushed it up to £1,000 – evidently it was understood that the higher the initial bid the greater the leap between subsequent bids. I was gradually beginning to grasp the procedures. A minute later someone said in a barely audible voice, 'And five in hundreds' – and our target was hit.

'Thank you, Mr Smith,' the auctioneer said with a quizzical smile. 'And may I expect something in the real bidding now?' – by which I assumed he meant advances of £500. They were a bit slow in coming, however. Still it had reached £6,000 when Mr Dickinson's hammer came down sharply in Mr Smith's favour. It was a quarter past eleven.

The 'apocalyptics', as I called them, had been catalogued as Lots 3 - 6. 'A quatrych of surrealist inspiration and powerful ambience' – and the green-overalled porters cleverly arranged four separate easels of differing heights to display the 'horsemen' more or less as they appeared in the printed catalogue. There was an edge of cunning to Petrie's insistence that the four should be offered as available separately or together, since none of them made much sense of the subject as individual pictures and the bidding would doubtless be held by the buyers with the greatest available funds. And so it proved.

Bearing in mind what Petrie had said about Edward James, I watched Mr John Smith very carefully. He was as unpretentious as his name, but, unlike most of the men who wore homburgs, he had a bowler hat, and the plain grey tie and suit of a City clerk.

Now he seemed uninterested, head bent as if contemplating his catalogue. The clerk entered the details of the previous purchase in his ledger. Mr Dickinson surveyed the room, his eyebrows raised in the manner of George Robey, the music-hall comedian whom I had been taken to see as a child.

'I shall test the temperature of the water,' he began. 'Perhaps I may have some indication of your wishes as to whether Lots three to six have your interest as single lots or as a parcel? The unique construction of this multiple work of art leaves it somewhat enigmatic in its separate components, but as a quatrych . . . I am at your service, gentlemen.'

There were murmurs, then a show of hands which seemed to settle the matter. 'As a parcel then, gentlemen. And may I say eight thousand?'

Mr Smith made no move. He seemed to have gone to sleep. A guttural voice answered from near the back.

So. Mr Stoephausen had opened the bidding. 'I'm sure some of you – ah! Monsieur Lamy raises me five. Any advance on eight thousand five hundred?'

Suddenly Smith was awake. He gestured with his catalogue. Immediately the man with the drooping moustache raised Smith's £8,750 to £9,000. I wondered if there was any significance in the fact that the advances had suddenly been reduced to £250; but apparently not, for a moment later Smith and Lamy were outbidding each other in leaps of £500 and with astonishing rapidity the figure rose to £13,000, with a new voice – that of the American, Leonard Brockbank, as it turned out – chiming in and the man with the drooping moustache being identified (rather surprisingly, I thought) as Mr Cunningham of the Pont Street gallery. I felt Aleena's fingers tighten on my elbow. She, like me, was beginning to be gripped by this curious kind of drama which depended on little but the basic ability to produce bigger and bigger sums of money from apparently bottomless pockets – money probably unearned, I thought, and as much as I was ever likely to receive in a lifetime of doctoring.

Suddenly I was jerked out of my thoughts as I heard Mr Dickinson say, 'Against you, M'sieur Lamy. Come now, I'm sure – Thank you, sir. And another one? The bidding is with M'sieur Lamy, gentlemen. And I'm sure – Ah! I suspected it. Thank you, Mr Brockbank. Fifteen thousand I'm bid.' Almost rashly, as though to close the bidding, Lamy cried, 'Eighteen thousand.'

Mr Smith raised his catalogue, and angrily cried, 'Twenty' – and even I could sense the note of finality in his voice – as, obviously, could Mr Dickinson, whose hammer was raised, like his eyebrows, in interrogation. 'And more? Have you all done, then?' The briefest pause and the hammer fell. 'To you, Mr Smith, for twenty thousand pounds, the quatrych.'

'Twenty thousand!' I gasped to Aleena.

There was a faint buzz of whispers as the porters removed the easels. Mr Smith seemed to sink into an attitude of indifference. I suspected that he'd either spent to his limit or that the mysterious Edward James had little interest in the remaining two lots.

I was evidently right. Despite Huson's prophecy, 'The Boy With Bananas' seemed generally to have considerably less appeal to certain types of bidders – as Mr Dickinson had obviously anticipated, for though he reached £1,000 fairly quickly, it crept up slowly to the final price of £3,000, and Dickinson had to use all his wiles to get it as high as that.

It seemed (as Petrie had suggested to me) that auctions mirrored prevailing tastes. Obviously the enclave represented by the Lamys and Smiths and Brockbanks were influenced by Surrealists and Dadaists. Others held more conventional notions. Connoisseurs of the 'primitives', as Huson had called them, seemed to be absent. At all events, enthusiasm had fallen at an alarming rate and I could see the press men wondering if this was the moment to escape to the nearest pub. They had been very busy with their pencils when the 'apocalyptics' had been on the easels and I suspected that, according to the different types of newspaper, some would praise the percipience of Gauguin, while others would write scornfully of men with money to waste on 'incomprehensible daubs'.

Aleena began to look worried. Like me, she had caught the excitement during the sale of the quatrych, and now we both wondered if we could reach our £40,000. It didn't look as though we would. A sense of failure was sneaking in, for we were £10,000 below our hopes.

'And now,' Mr Dickinson was saying, 'we come to the final lot in this most interesting sale. I'm sure the splendid support you have given it this far will be increased in your bids for what we may perhaps call the *pièce*

646

de résistance of the occasion. A masterpiece of immediate appeal.'

'Four thousand,' came Mr Cunningham's voice.

Mr Dickinson smiled warily. 'Four thousand I'm bid; but I know you can do better than that, gentlemen. Ah, I thought so. Thank you, sir: four five it is. And you, Mr Stoephausen? To six? Thank you.'

The tenseness in the atmosphere returned, increased.

'Against you, Mr Stoephausen. Will you advance? Thank you, sir. And Mr Brockbank? Seven thousand I am bid. And I feel you are far from done yet. Let me draw your attention to the picture again.'

As if by magnetism eyes were drawn to 'The Secret Pool'. I felt Aleena's hand grip mine as across the short distance to the easel she seemed to smile at our memories of the silvery waterfall.

'Ah, now we're approaching some worthy competition – as I knew we would. M'sieur Lamy, I hear you – and you, sir: ten, shall we say? Yes. And from Mr Brockbank again – twelve thousand five hundred. Can we raise it to the even sum again? Yes, against you, Mr Brockbank. Do you care to try again? No?'

The brisk look round seemed to confirm his sense that there was little more to be gained by forcing things. 'Are you all done, then? To M'sieur Lamy, then, Lot eight for thirteen thousand pounds.'

He set his hammer carefully down. 'And now if the purchasers will very kindly attend to the clerk's desk and settle your business I will bid you a very good morning.'

Amid the noise of chairs being scraped back Aleena and I made our exit.

She squeezed my hand. 'We did it!' she cried, exultantly.

I said, 'Let's go to the nearest pub. I'm dying for a drink!'

That night we held a quiet celebration dinner to honour our good friend Ian Petrie.

What a help Christie's had been! And what a wise

suggestion of the directors to persuade us to keep half of the Gauguins in store for a future sale.

We decided to dine at the Fitzgerald. We enjoyed the quiet little dining-room with its hunting prints and, always, a few non-rationed extras available. It had, for me particularly, a pre-war atmosphere. I liked the motherly waitresses in their starched white aprons, presided over by a correctly mannered grey-haired lady in bombazine whose dignity cried out that she had at some time been in service with 'the gentry'.

'It's rather sad to think that in a few days you'll be off and perhaps we won't meet until the next auction in ten years,' said Petrie. 'I've become very attached to you both.'

Aleena smiled dazzlingly at Petrie. 'We'll miss *you*. Thank you for everything.' She had her hand on mine on the table. 'Including the fact that at last you've helped to make Kit relaxed again. He was a bundle of nerves yesterday.'

Petrie shrugged. 'He had no need to be. But of course that's the sort of thing he tells his patients before whipping out their appendixes. They worry just the same – of course they do. But in the event, you have every reason to be extremely pleased, my dear Kit. And I'm sure you are.'

'With all that money in the Gauguin Memorial Hospital fund I could hardly be anything else,' I said. I might have looked smug, for I added, 'I see now that there's a great deal in the art of the auctioneer.'

'Mr Dickinson was marvellous,' Aleena said. 'He had me on tenterhooks several times, urging them to stretch just that little bit further to get over the reserve and then – well, sort of refereeing a tussle between the two finalists.'

Petrie nodded. 'Kit, you would call it the psychological approach: understanding what the patient is feeling inwardly. There's a famous auctioneer in France – Maître Rheims his name is – who watches like a hawk for people to betray themselves by looking apprehensive during the sale of the lot *previous* to the one they're after. Advance nerves, as you might call it. And he's usually right: sure enough,

they release the tension by being the first in the bidding –
and are prepared to fight to the end.'

'Did the sale bring any surprises so far as you're
concerned?' I asked.

Petrie paused a moment. 'I'd rather expected Claude
Fournet to make a showing. He's a great Gauguin man. But
when I chatted with him for a few minutes after the sale he
told me it was largely a matter of funds. An exile living in
England has great difficulty getting any money out of
France. Understandable. The economic situation in France
is pretty rocky. So regrettably he had to abstain when he
saw how the bidding was going. For the rest – no, I don't
think I had any surprises. "The Four Horsemen" went
exactly where I thought it would – to Edward James via
Smith. Smith's a very sensitive antenna for James' tastes
and earns his keep, whatever it is. As for Lamy – well, I
think his syndicate's likely to have more or less unlimited
funds, so they can afford to bide their time. And "The
Secret Pool" 's a picture I'm sure will double its value in,
say, ten years' time. By the way, talking of money, and to
be practical, Christie's will arrange for the money to be sent
to Sanders. Luckily there are no financial restrictions in the
sterling area. And now,' he paused, 'I think a toast is in
order.' He cupped his brandy glass in his hand. 'To the
Gauguin Memorial Hospital and the future health, wealth
and happiness of the islanders of Koraloona.'

As we all drank, Petrie added, 'Who would have thought
that the inspiration and work of a sick man would finally
lead to the treatment and cure of countless other sick
people? It is a paradox. But God works in mysterious
ways.'

They were words I was to recall with something
approaching bitter cynicism.

PART FOUR

46

We sailed on the *Mantela II* for the last stage of our journey to Koraloona. In Sanderstown we sent a message on the skęd to confirm that we were on our way, then sailed in the evening – the normal departure time – arriving, as always, the following morning.

How many times had one or another of us made that overnight sea trip across the bare hundred miles or so in the original *Mantela* with dear old Bill Robins ordering 'sticky green' nightcaps in the mahogany saloon? It was sometimes hard to realise that those days would never return. Yet now, time and people had passed but were not forgotten, and we were in the new *Mantela II*, with at least one experience we knew would never change: the beauty of awakening at sea and greeting the morning.

After quick showers, bacon and eggs and steaming hot coffee, we went on deck and leaned on the gunwale, gulping in the fresh air and drinking in the beauty of the scene: a pattern of tiny islets little more than treeless rocks that barely broke into white caps on the sea, as though spattered around by accident. In the distance, just as on that first day when Bill Robins had been my guide, I could see in one direction the flat smudge of Hodges Island, famous for its copra. To the right the white line of foaming, frothing water which marked the unseen barrier of coral that protected Koraloona; on the other side the water was as calm as a lake. At first I could barely make out the fringe of bending palms on the beach, but then, as the distance dwindled, the hills behind began to take on colour and shape – the greens of the trees smudged with red tin roofs or patches of blossom like an Impressionist painting and then, rearing even higher than the hills of Koraloona, was High Island, barely half a mile behind, standing straight up behind the foreground of 'our' island, steep straight hills, like a dunce's hat with a cone at the top where, when the earth was younger, fire had belched, and deep below which, according to Mitchell, lay the magma chamber where bubbled the hot molten rock material that would either be forced into the earth's core or extruded on to the surface.

Neither of us spoke for a while. Koraloona produced that magical desire for silence on many of those who loved the island. Words seemed almost an intrusion.

The *Mantela II* made her way slowly towards the reef, and soon the smudges of vivid colour became more defined, sometimes splashed with the white of a building edged with the faint red of trailing bougainvillaea. Once through the thrashing passage of the reef, and into the calm of the lagoon, we could make out a blur of faces, even waving arms.

'It looks as though there's a reception committee waiting for us,' Aleena broke the silence at last.

'Any excuse to give the schoolchildren a day off. I only hope to God there aren't any speeches,' I said as we approached the pier, where I could see a forest of waving hands and hear a faint chorus of cheers. We drew nearer, made out faces lining the wooden planks that were our link between sea and land, the pier supported by its heavy, slimy-green wooden supports.

'There's Mummy!' Aleena could see Tiare waving and, pointing her out to me, started waving back.

'And there's Alec!' I caught some of her enthusiasm as I saw the chubby figure in khaki shorts. Other faces joined in. One saturnine face waved almost as though operated by a mechanical device. It was Tiki.

Everyone in Anana and Tala-Tala seemed to be there, to say nothing of scores of locals from outlying villages or settlements, many of them, I knew, paying a kind of homage for the medical help they or their families had received over the years. Making the journey to greet us was their very genuine way of paying the fees for which they had no money.

Crewmen threw across the narrowing strip of water the thin lines attached to the heavy docking ropes. The *Mantela II* edged sideways, like a circus horse trained to prance that way. It was all very easy, really, in that warm, still lagoon, and almost before we realised it, we were back on dry land and Aleena was throwing her arms round her mother, and I was pumping the hand of Alec who said, 'Thank God ye're back, Laddie. I'm nae longer used to working seven days a week.'

'Sorry,' I laughed, 'but it was in a good cause.'

'Aye, I know that. But wait till ye go to Tala-Tala and see what we've done while ye've been gallivanting in the big city.'

'Where's Jason Purvis?' I felt I had to 'pay my respects' to the newly married couple before anything else, and I soon saw them, not really changed in such a short space of time – how could they be? And yet, had they changed in a subtle way?

As I shook hands and congratulated them, my diagnostic processes were thinking, almost instinctively, that they couldn't *really* be the same two persons they had been only a few weeks ago. They *looked* the same – though Lorna Purvis sported a much more summery dress – yet it passed through my mind that this prim and proper virgin now shared a bed – and I told myself, why not? It was all part of getting married. Yet if Miss Sowerby had allowed herself to go to the same bed just once with Jason Purvis *before* they were married, she would probably have committed suicide! Now, though, the same act in the same bed was sanctified and she had no qualms, and suddenly I realised that I *knew* what the difference was. She didn't have a smug look, far from it, but as she took my hand when I murmured a few words, she looked *satisfied*; and I flattered myself that I knew why: that she wanted something badly, and it wouldn't be long before she was coming to Alec or me to say that she was expecting a baby.

All this passed through my mind like a flash as I said to Jason, 'As soon as we unpack, I'll give you the best wedding present in the world. Three advance copies of your book.'

All the others were pressing around us, congratulating us, for news of the 'Sale of the Decade', sent out by Reuters, had been printed in detail in the *Sentinel*. The school choir, with Father Pringle struggling to keep time and tune, sang lustily, entangling themselves at times with melodies I could not always recognise. But it didn't matter of course. The effort, the occasion, was all that counted – to the schoolchildren as much as to the audience.

Colonel Fawcett had, as I feared, insisted on making a speech of welcome, but he was mercifully short. Finally, with the help of a couple of boys to load our bags we set off for our bungalow. Even the transport problem was made easy, for Jim Wilson, who had looked after my jeep, had brought it to the nearby pier to await my arrival.

'That's the kind of service you get on a small island.' He pumped my hand. 'Great news, Doc, and glad to have you back.'

'I just want to flop on my bed,' cried Aleena as we set off for the five-minute ride. 'I know it's only morning, but I feel as exhausted as though we've been dancing till five yesterday morning.'

'It's the change of hours,' I said. 'I'm as tired as you.'

I did, though, allow one visitor to follow us back to the bungalow – but then only for a moment. I didn't have the heart to keep Jason Purvis, author, waiting to see the advance copies of his first novel, to keep him in tortured suspense. He hadn't even seen the cover. I opened the suitcase, rummaged through my dirty linen.

'Here you are.' I handed the books to him and he accepted them almost with reverence, examining one to see whether he approved of the dust jacket, the type, and how many pages it made.

'It's taken a long, long time – and a few drinks – to get it off the ground to start with.' He looked at me, then added, 'I'd like you to have the first copy. Here it is. Hot off the press, as they say.' And he signed it.

Alec allowed us only one day of rest before I had to visit 'the sights'.

'What sights?'

'Not "sights", Laddie – S-I-T-E, site. The building site. Ye'll be amazed, the progress they've made.'

He wasn't wrong. Everyone was working, even at 8.30 am. Walter Mitchell was wearing a grubby naval duffle coat, presumably the acceptable wear for bosses 'on site', even if the temperature was in the seventies. Seeing my surprise, he winked and loosened the toggles. Beneath, he wore only a singlet and a pair of stained old slacks. 'Uniform of the job, Doc; but hardly suitable for the Union Jack Club, eh?'

On a conducted tour he showed us how the simple partitioning walls of asbestos hardboard had been erected and fixed with angle brackets, slotted and held in place with nuts and bolts so that they could be slid sideways to alter the area. The brick incinerator for the hospital waste and the tall chimney that lay alongside it were almost ready. I noticed the neatly stacked piles of brown earthenware drainpipes, all marked Doulton – shades of my early doctoring days in Lambeth. Many of the drainpipes were already laid in trenches which had been dug while we were in Europe.

Throughout the next two weeks or so, the hospital seemed to grow before our eyes. No one in Europe, with its workforce demarcation lines, could have ever erected a hospital so swiftly; for even though the buildings were, it is true, already on site, the size of rooms had to be changed, many had to be linked with corridors, and the ancillary services, like a laundry and the furnace, were almost ready. Mitchell had also found the answer to a generator for our electric supply. Instead of buying a new one, a large one to guarantee our power, he had bought from Australia a smaller one which could work in double harness with the existing one; this doubled our electric power and ensured a regular supply, even when used to capacity. Mitchell had also been concerned about fire precautions, but had overcome the problem by arranging in case of fire to use Paula Reece's diesel-driven electric pump by which she could bring water up from the sea into her pool. By buying 200 feet of fire hose, we would be able to uncouple the sea-water supply where it entered the pool – close to the hospital – switching it with a brass coupling to our fire hose, and pump all the water needed.

I had expected the generator to be enormous, but it turned out to be small enough to be transported in the back of my jeep. 'Not much for the money,' I remarked to Mitchell.

'But full of tricks,' he replied. 'The armature alone has several miles of wire wound round it. Don't be deceived: it's a remarkable technical feat and well worth the money. The engine to drive it is a different matter – you'll see.'

It certainly was. We needed a small crane to lift it from the vessel that brought it; and it took over an hour to lower it accurately on to the concrete base prepared for it in what Mitchell called 'the power house', which adjoined the newly built incinerator for hospital waste.

It also warmed my heart to see where all the equipment we had bought from Serpell was placed in different sections of the hospital – the Solus-Schall X-ray machine, the Drinker respirator, the oscillometer, and the anaesthetic apparatus.

By the last week in June, all was ready, and we prepared to move from the antiquated cottage hospital into the GMH.

We had decided to hold a dedication ceremony on July 1 – a Monday – when a plaque would be unveiled by Tiare – although no one had thought to consider that on this very day, hundreds of miles away, scores of ships were waiting to watch the explosion of two atom bombs in, on or near the Bikini atoll. Not that it would interfere with us.

And then, as we were almost ready to move in, we had an unexpected and welcome visitor.

Since the end of the war the *Mantela II* had called at Anani each Friday on its way round the archipelago, reaching Koraloona in the morning, as it had normally always done, and departing late that night. On the last Friday in June a passenger arrived on the island and checked straight into Mollie Green's hotel where, I was later told, he immediately downed the traditional courtesy shot of free Scotch that always greeted new guests, though I knew nothing of his arrival until I received a phone call in a voice I vaguely recognised, but had almost forgotten, a voice from the past: 'H'ya, you old son of a gun. What's cooking – and how's good-looking?'

'Sam! Sam Truscott!' I could hardly believe my ears. 'What the hell are you doing here? And where are you?'

'Got a chance of a free flip to Sanders. I'm in the American Reserve – so I thought I'd come over to Koraloona and see if married life agrees with you.'

'It does,' I laughed. 'And you? How's' – my voice stumbled on the name – 'Lucy?'

'Couldn't be better.' With a chuckle he added on the phone, 'Thanks to your magic, Sam, or Samantha, Truscott Junior is on the way.'

'Congratulations. That's marvellous. Now, I'll come and fetch you,' adding with a laugh, 'that's if you don't mind roughing it in one of those ex-army vehicles left over from the war. A jeep, I think it's called.'

'I use one all the time back home in Carmel.'

'I'll be straight round.'

After telling Aleena the news, and checking with Alec that it was his turn to take surgery and that he didn't need any extra help, I jumped into the jeep, waved to Jim Wilson as I turned right at the ship's chandler, and whizzed up Main Street, jerking to a stop with a squeal of brakes opposite the communal washing trough and Mollie Green's hotel.

Sam looked just the same. He was not in uniform of course but wore fawn slacks and a light brown leather jerkin that zipped up in front, giving the vague impression of off-duty flying dress.

On the way home he explained that, as part of serving with the Reserve Air Force, he had to do three weeks of duty a year, 'and the main reason I'm in the Reserve,' he admitted, 'is that I get one free trip a year on duty and there's a pretty wide choice of locations, and no real training, just a few flying hours to put in. Since Britain decided to close down its naval base, we maintain what's known as "a presence" on Sanders, so here I am.'

'I'd have thought you'd choose somewhere more dramatic for a free trip – Hong Kong or Singapore, at least a change of scene.'

'Nope,' he said, 'though I will admit that Sanders wasn't my first choice.'

'Which was?'

'I tried to get on one of the vessels that's watching the A-bomb tests at Bikini, but it was all booked up.'

'That's on Monday isn't it – first of July?'

Sam nodded. 'That's right. But not to worry. I'm just as happy looking up old buddies.'

When we reached the bungalow Sam looked admiringly at Aleena and said, 'The only pity is that since we're training for World War Three, with a capital 'W', officers' wives ain't among permitted cargo.'

Aleena was serving coffee on the veranda and Sam gave me a nudge and the nearest thing to a wolf whistle and grinned, 'We sure are good pickers, you and I.'

'We sure are,' I mimicked his American accent, slightly uncomfortable again as I had a mental picture of Lucy. I never felt any guilt about my earlier relationship with Lucy before Aleena grew up and before Truscott appeared on the scene, but I did have occasional twinges of guilt about not having told Sam when we all met in San Francisco that I had once been her lover, and even worse, I could never quite erase a pang of conscience at the memory of that one unforgivable lapse from grace, even though no one would ever know about it.

'Why not let's have lunch at the Union Jack Club,' I suggested. 'We'll reinstate your membership. Then on Monday, you can come to the dedication ceremony of the hospital – *your* buildings. It's really magnificent. Thanks to Tiare's generosity of spirit, and your help.'

'Let's ask Mummy for lunch, shall we?'

'Gee, she's a honey. I'd love to see her again.'

As we talked about the people he had known on the island, I said almost mischievously, 'I'm surprised that you're roughing it at Mollie Green's hotel when there are any number of beds at Paula Reece's place.'

'Shades of a murky past! Wouldn't dare! There could be lots of beds, but she's the one who decides which one you're going to use. I guess I'll have to go and see her, but oh boy! Remember that outsize bed of hers?'

'Not as well as you,' I laughed.

Tiare did come for lunch, but we arrived before she did, and even Truscott noticed the way the club had been smartened up since Paula Reece had paid for the repainting and the new basket chairs and other improvements. I had done my modest bit by bringing from London and New York a whole pile of the latest magazines for the lounge.

When Tiare arrived, and we all drank our gimlets, Sam said, almost with a sigh, 'I'd forgotten how beautiful you are, Princess. The girls in these parts sure know how to knock out a man!'

As Tiare thanked him, Sam added admiringly, 'I don't know why any man ever leaves Koraloona.'

'We don't,' I pointed out.

Sam greeted other members he had known, then who should arrive but Paula Reece, and Captain Baker. She rarely came to the club at lunchtime. 'Food isn't as good as at home,' she had once said.

'What a lucky break,' I said. 'Look who's here.'

'No luck,' she admitted frankly. 'I heard on the grape-vine that a handsome stranger was in town, so I guess I didn't want to waste time.'

Sam gave her a friendly peck on the cheek.

'I'd no idea it was you,' said Paula. 'Handsome, yes, though I'd hardly describe you as a stranger.' She managed to invest the words with a double meaning. And later, as we were about to start lunch, and she was leaving for her villa, she said with assumed nonchalance, 'But Sam – if you're going to stay a week, why put up with the hotel? You're welcome to a bed – '

Even Tiare couldn't resist a barb. 'Depends which one,' she said tartly.

'It's mighty kind, Paula, but now that I'm a married man and – well, maybe I'd better not.'

'I understand,' she said, 'so we'll make a party in your honour, Sam. Any excuse to welcome a new face – or an old one who's returned. How's about next Thursday? A buffet lunch. The day before you sail. Champagne all round?'

'Thursday suits me fine,' said Sam, as we nodded.

'Good. I'll start phoning around.'

The dedication ceremony was simple but impressive, and before Tiare unveiled the modest plaque, Father Pringle, sober for once, gave the hospital a blessing, followed by some arcane droning by Tiki. Tiare had asked for Tiki to be present, not insisting, but pointing out that it was in some measure due to his understanding and help that we had been able to sell the paintings.

'He did agree that we could dispose of them,' Tiare said. 'If he hadn't, it might have been much more difficult. So it'll please him – and the gods of the island.'

I didn't mind. It wasn't my affair anyway. Alec, resplen-dent for once in long trousers, but still with his MCC tie round his waist, was the doctor in charge.

'It's all the same to me,' he said. 'They can pray till

kingdom comes now we've got all we need for the hospital. And ye're the one to thank for that, Laddie.'

Tiare gave the only speech. She remembered her grandfather and the fame he had achieved too late to prevent his unnecessary death because he had not been able to call on the skills and facilities that the Gauguin Memorial Hospital would now be able to provide; then the 'unveiling' – little more than unpinning a coloured piece of the local cloth – revealed the neatly painted plaque Jim Wilson had done in blue lettering on a white ground:

GAUGUIN MEMORIAL HOSPITAL
Dedicated by Princess Tiare
of Koraloona to the health
and well-being of the islanders
July 1, 1946

Tiare added a few nicely chosen phrases about the care and devotion of Alec Reid, and of myself, which was slightly embarrassing because all the schoolchildren had been coached to cheer at that moment.

'Our dream's come true, Laddie,' Alec said as the crowd waved flags, and we started to make our way to the Union Jack Club where we were to have the celebration lunch.

'I'm hungry,' said Sam Truscott, 'but I'll admit there's something I want to do before I sit down for lunch.'

'What's that – drink?'

'Nope. The radio. We've all been so carried away we've forgotten what's been happening this morning on Bikini atoll. Geez, it's quite something. I'd like to hear the latest news.'

'We've got a radio in the bar, so we can sip alcohol and listen at the same time.'

'I'll drink to that,' he said.

Everyone else too was anxious to hear the latest news. We were rather cut off in Koraloona, and to many the atom test still seemed to smack of a cheap publicity stunt by President Truman.

'It's damned stupid, blowing up atom bombs just to get press coverage,' shouted Colonel Fawcett.

Once in the club, the drinks started to flow. George was aided by a second 'George' to dispense gimlets and whiskies while Sam twiddled the knobs to find the right station. Finally he found the BBC World Service, and there was dead silence as we all listened.

'This is the BBC,' began the calm voice of the announcer. 'I am sending this report from the United States sloop *Seattle* and we are anchored more than fifty miles west of the Bikini atoll in the Pacific. At precisely 8.30 am the B 29 Superfort *Gilda* unloaded the first of two atom bombs, in accordance with decisions made by President Truman.'

A note of excitement crept into the normal unemotional voice of the BBC: 'Even though we were some distance from the atoll, the vessel on which we watched the mushroom cloud effect almost took a nose dive. We had to hold fast to the gunwales or railings. Some people stumbled. And even though I am wearing inch-thick black goggles it was as though the sun had exploded.

'I am also wearing what is known as an anti-rad suit – rather like a diver's, but treated with some material that makes it proof against any radiation fall-out from the plume of black smoke that had a red lining at first and then spread out into a great brown and red flower – or more like a giant mushroom.'

The announcer hesitated and I could hear, over the airwaves, a kind of faint rustle; perhaps he was only collecting together his script. 'The second bomb,' he read 'being underwater made less noise but we were nearer and the sea for a moment spread red like blood all around us. In a way it was even more terrifying, because we know that, as it is underwater, it will probably end five miles down on the ocean floor and I have to say, it is going to make an enormous hole in the ocean bed if it reaches the bottom.'

When the announcement ended, and one of the 'Georges' switched off the radio, the silence gave way immediately to urgent cries for more drinks and both barmen were kept busy. It was only then that I noticed Walter Mitchell, Fawcett's assistant who had master-minded the building work, sitting alone in a basket chair, an unopened magazine on his knees, staring into space.

'You didn't like the opening ceremony?' I asked almost facetiously. 'And you haven't got a drink. What's it to be?'

'Gimlet, please. Thanks. No, the opening was fine,' he said in his slightly sing-song New Zealand twang. 'It's that bloody broadcast. Gives me the shivers to think of what's been happening this morning. Madness!'

'You're right,' I agreed. 'But thank God it's a long way off.'

'Sure.' He still seemed gloomy, even after a sip of iced gin and lime, served in the traditional champagne glass always used for gimlets. 'But distance is a darned funny thing. Specially under water.'

Sam had joined us, really to congratulate Mitchell on the fine job of work he'd done.

'Mitch' – his name had been shortened as we knew him better – 'is worried about the Bikini explosions,' I explained.

'Who isn't? But,' Sam echoed my words, 'it's one hell of a long way off, isn't it?'

'Even so – ' Mitchell began.

'But why the worry?' I interrupted. 'Bikini's not only hundreds of miles from here; but it's been evacuated anyway. Nobody's injured or killed. They've just blown the place up by dropping a bomb on top of it and another one in the ocean.'

'Exactly. That's what bothers me.'

'Making a big splash.' Aleena had joined us. 'Surely it can't do any harm?'

Mitchell gave a slightly lop-sided smile. ' "Making a big splash", as you call it, my dear, is somewhat understating the effect of the explosive power of what's the equivalent of several million tons of TNT.'

'But,' I said, 'there aren't any buildings like there were in

665

Hiroshima; except a few native huts maybe – with nobody in them or anywhere near.'

'No,' he replied drily. 'There is, however, the earth, what we used to call in geography-classes, the "oblate spheroid".'

'I never learned properly,' Aleena smiled. 'What's oblate?'

'It's the floor of the ocean – as far as we're concerned, the Pacific Ocean, where the bomb was dropped.'

'You're not going to tell me that *any* bomb, however big, is going to blow up the world – or even blow a hole in it!' I said.

'Perhaps not,' Mitchell shrugged. 'But there are plenty of damaging things it could do.'

'Such as?'

He paused again, and I could see he was trying to muster his arguments in a form that could be understood by a layman.

'I'm no geologist or a physicist or other "ists",' he said, 'but I've acquired a smattering of all those things due to working in different fields, and I hate like hell tampering with the structure of the earth.'

'But what the hell,' asked Sam, 'is tampering?'

'Well – putting it as simply as I can – and could someone get me another gimlet? – there's the solid core of the earth. That's believed to be iron – '

Sam drifted off to the bar. So did Aleena when someone called her name. I stayed for a few more moments as Mitchell tried to explain, in simple terms, how the iron as 'mantles' finally reached the *magma*, of heat-molten rock, just below the outer crust, the surface of the earth, and also explained how the layers – called 'plates' – are uneven and bumpy and tend to meld into one another, and how, if they move, you sometimes get earthquakes, volcanic eruptions, and disturbances of the ocean bed.

'But is this going on all the time?' I queried.

'More or less. But mostly without disturbing results. Though some places, like Japan and parts of the South

Seas, are affected more often. Which is what bothers me. That underwater explosion at Bikini probably won't set things off – but it's so bloody powerful that it *could* set off tremors that might shift the plates sideways.'

'A sort of delayed shock effect?' I said, thinking of a medical analogy.

'Exactly. And nobody really knows what explosions of the magnitude of today's bomb *might* do. That's what I mean by "tampering".'

A gong sounded.

'Lunch!' I got up, and so did Mitchell.

'I'm starved,' and with a grin I said, 'you may be a super builder, Mitch, but you're a bloody depressing geologist.'

47

On the Tuesday morning sked, Alec was called to the radio shack. Surgeon-Commander Ronnie Serpell (who, in my ignorance, I thought had long since departed) wanted to talk to him. It seemed that Serpell was on the *verge* of leaving. The base had been closed down. He was going on long leave before his next posting, and he wanted to see the hospital he had helped to equip. And though the newspapers were obviously filled with accounts of the Bikini A-bomb tests, he had read a short account of the opening of our new Gauguin Memorial Hospital.

Alec was delighted, especially as on Thursday Paula Reece was giving her champagne lunch for Sam Truscott, and wouldn't mind if Alec brought along an extra guest.

But how to get there? The boat only arrived at Koraloona each Friday morning, returning that evening, but, as Alec told me after he had spoken to Serpell, 'That's nae a problem. If ye'll be good enough to take the Wednesday surgery, I'll fly Nellie over early and be back with Ronnie before lunch. That'll give him a couple of nights on

Koraloona and he can catch the Friday evening boat back.'

The arrangements fitted in very well because we spent all Tuesday on the fairly painless change-over to the new hospital. Painless because, in fact, there was almost nothing to take from Harley Street apart from certain case records and the contents of the dispensary. Jason helped to pack and store things, Jim Wilson carried the few bits of furniture worth salvaging, though in truth we were now so well equipped that we left the old beds, sheets and blankets to anyone who wanted them.

Moving was exciting – leaving was a wrench. Silly really, I thought, but after all, Alec and I had spent eight years in the tiny shack with its makeshift operating theatre we called our 'hospital'. On my first visit I had been unable to hide my dismay, but we had beaten scourges like polio, with the help of a purse-lipped spinsterish missionary's daughter who was now a married woman. We had given vitamin pills to a half-starved beachcomber who had become a novelist; and all these years we had struggled, short of cash, short of equipment, fighting against all odds to conquer cholera, and I myself had twice nearly been murdered.

You couldn't just say 'So long!' and walk out of a place where every nook and cranny held a memory, many so tangible like the procedure I still recalled of the time I cured Jimbo. No one could ever erase pictures like that – or their background, to which we were now saying goodbye. It was sad to think we would never again see the queues of patient men, women and children standing in the garden waiting for their turn to be treated for a potentially dangerous illness – or to be dosed with the placebos that cured them simply because they had faith.

Now, in place of dear old Harley Street we were ready to start treating patients in a large, almost impersonal, hospital, helped by two local girls who were being trained as nurses by Mrs Purvis.

'Ye'll get used to it,' said Alec, 'and ye'll be glad of it.'

At least we had one thing which kept us busy: making

sure that everything would be in its proper place in view of Ronnie Serpell's sudden visit.

'After all,' I pointed out, 'he *is* a surgeon-commander. Even though it's a Mission hospital, he's so used to spit and polish, we'll have to play up to him.'

'Och, he'll just take it all in his stride,' said Alec.

When I met Serpell as Alec landed Nellie on our 'new' airstrip – left for us by Truscott – Serpell seemed to look exactly the same as the last time I had met him. I always find it difficult to realise that while we ourselves may have undergone traumatic changes of fate – after all, our auction had in a matter of weeks made us rich and in a way 'famous', and produced out of thin air a new hospital – all this had happened, yet to someone who was not involved, even a medical colleague, it meant little more than a couple of newspaper paragraphs.

Like Sam, Serpell was not wearing uniform and I found a certain (and unfair) gentle amusement in the difference that civilian clothes made. Divested of the gold braid and all the trappings that go with uniforms, he looked just a pleasant chap who, if you met him at a party, you would hardly remember if you met him a few months later. Yet as a surgeon-commander he had wielded the power of a local god, absolute master of a large hospital.

As we walked from Nellie to Alec's car, Alec suggested to both of us, 'We'll take a look at the hospital tomorrow if that suits everyone. In the meantime I'll take ye, Ronnie, to ma bungalow for a wee sip of liquid sustenance to get ye over the terror of flying with me. Here!' He turned to me, 'Surgery's done then? Good. Here's a wee batch of newspapers and magazines. Not a thing in them except stories about the bomb.'

'You're not joining us for lunch?' asked Serpell.

'Unfortunately I don't think I should,' I said a little awkwardly. 'Aleena seems a bit tired and she asked if I'd have a quiet meal with her in the bungalow. Perhaps tonight – ?'

669

Alec gave me what I realised later was a knowing look as he prepared to drive off. 'Take it easy, Laddie,' he said, 'and the wee wife too.' He handed me the newspapers and I made my own way back to the bungalow.

Once back there, in the basket chairs on the veranda facing the riot of blossom in the small garden, we shared the newspapers, devouring the printed pages as anyone always did in Koraloona. It wasn't so much that the atom bomb concerned us, more the fact that we had heard virtually no other news for day after day on the radio, constantly whetting our appetite. In fact the radio was rather like a meal which you are still enjoying when some unseen hand whisks your plate away and substitutes music as dessert for which you aren't ready. But with newspapers we could read items that fascinated us a dozen times if we wished.

I looked for the previous day's *Sentinel* – Tuesday's, the day after the test. For a newspaper which rather prided itself on being conservative and dignified, the *Sentinel* had gone to town. The entire front page consisted of one photograph, which had been radioed, of the bomb's mushroom cloud rising from the flat atoll, reaching to the heavens above it, writhing and curling and sinister. There were only five words on the page, in bold type: THE OTHER SIDE OF PARADISE

'What a picture!' I handed the newspaper to Aleena. 'You can understand why Walter Mitchell feels worried.'

'But it's such a long way off, darling. And it's only a couple of scientific tests. There's no *danger*.'

'Of course not.' I offered her a pre-lunch gimlet, but she shook her head. 'But what sometimes worries me is the future. It's one thing to drop a bomb on Hiroshima – '

'Poor people – ' she interrupted.

'Lucky for Britain and America,' I retorted. 'The A-bomb saved hundreds of thousands of Allied lives, and I'd rather a few thousand Japs died than countless numbers of our chaps who would have had to land on the Japanese mainland. They would have been slaughtered. But I *do* understand Mitchell's fears for the future. Who's going to

670

make the next A-bomb – and drop it? Listen to this.'

I quoted some of the newspaper reports verbatim, but for the most part showed her passages which I thought would interest her.

The *Sentinel*, quoting a news agency release, had built up a leading article around the possibility of Truman having sent the world hurtling to disaster by creating the Atomic Energy Commission. On the other hand, two New Zealand papers, quoted in the *Sentinel*, asked, in effect, 'Who will have to pay? The taxpayers of the world, though they were not responsible?'

The *Christian Science Monitor* had claimed that advances in technology could ultimately be for the good of mankind. The Archbishop of Canterbury retorted that this might be Christian Science but it wasn't Christianity. Nor was it Christian, said a letter quoted from the *San Francisco Examiner*, to sentence to death the collection of goats, pigs and rats that had been confined in one of the test ships; the San Fernando Goat Association had even organised a memorial service for the animals.

I almost gave a jerk of astonishment as I read one off-beat item linked with the tests.

'Trust the French!' I laughed to Aleena. 'You won't believe it, but they're actually naming a new bathing suit after the A-bomb test.'

'They can't. It's – it's blasphemous!'

'It's here in black and white, if you believe the newspapers. Listen.' I read out the paragraph:

'On July 5 Louis Reard, the French fashion designer with a *salon* in Paris, is to launch the tiniest, flimsiest two-piece bathing costume ever seen. Correspondents were given a sneak preview, in which a girl model showed an unprecedently abbreviated swimming pants and bra made of cotton, and imprinted with a newspaper design composed of a montage of cuttings about the test. Monsieur Reard announced, "I am going to call my new bathing outfit the Bikini because to me the A-bomb test on Bikini implies the ultimate."'

'How vulgar!' said Aleena.

'Maybe, but it would look rather good on you,' I grinned.

'Not for me – well, not for long,' she said as I went to pour out a second gimlet.

'Why not?' I asked. 'And what's all this business of not having a gimlet before lunch?'

'Well, you were talking about this horrible bomb and the danger in the future, so I waited a few moments and – well, Alec promised not to tell you – '

'Alec? Tell me what?'

She hesitated; it was the kind of hesitation that is born of pleasure, not guilt. Her smile was radiant as she leaned over and kissed me on the lips.

'You're the last person I need to tell that one can't be certain in the early days,' she whispered; 'but having missed the second month . . . well, I popped in to see Alec for a check, and he's just confirmed . . .'

'Darling! Why on earth didn't you tell me earlier?'

But I knew perfectly well. Mothers-doubtfully-to-be were the same the world over – they didn't want to raise false hopes. I'd seen them countless times, demurely blushing as they asked me if they could tell their husbands. And now Aleena wore that same demure look.

I was ecstatic. I embraced her, trying – unsuccessfully – to inflect my words with a hint of nonchalance.

'And if our baby's a girl she'll be as gentle as you are, darling. And as beautiful. At least' – I became mock serious – 'that's my prognostication as a medical practitioner.'

She took her tone from me. 'And if it's a boy he will as surely be like you. I speak with the authority of a medical practitioner's wife – and lover.'

Lover. Few words were needed. 'Shall we? Before lunch? To celebrate? Quickly?'

She nodded. 'Yes. Let's – because I'm so happy and there's no better way of showing it.'

I agreed; and we demonstrated our agreement.

Later, on a more practical level, and as we got our breath

back and started to put on our clothes, she said, 'And after lunch, I'll borrow the car and go to tell Mummy. It'll make her so happy too.'

For the first few hours I was so excited I could hardly think straight, and though we didn't drink much we might as well have opened a bottle of champagne for all the sense I made. I do remember thinking, Thank God I don't have to cope with a sudden operation! After coffee, Aleena gave me a 'motherly' kiss and drove off to see Tiare, waving and crying, 'Back soon, beloved.'

I lay on my long chair, the basketwork arms extended to give my legs a rest, happily humming a song until I sauntered down the hill. Near the pier Jim Wilson was tinkering with some machinery and gave me his usual greeting of 'Nice day, Doc!' and I walked closer and said, 'It certainly is. I'm going to be a father.'

He gave a look of astonished delight. 'Congratulations,' he said. 'I'd shake hands but I'm covered in grease so we'll celebrate when my hands are clean.'

And of course I had to go and tell Truscott. I walked along Main Street, but Truscott wasn't at Mollie Green's, so I told her instead – and was promptly rewarded with a double Scotch and, as she raised her glass, she toasted me: 'Let's hope it's the first of a dozen.'

Truscott, she told me, was having lunch at the club, and of course, I could tell *everybody* there! I walked back to our bungalow, left a note for Aleena, 'Gone to the club to celebrate!' then drove the five miles to Tala-Tala in my jeep.

At the club, I gave a large tip to the 'George' at the bar and ordered two bottles of champagne, because not only was Truscott there but so were Alec and Serpell who had just finished lunch. Near the veranda four ladies, including Mrs Fawcett, were about to start a rubber of bridge on the worn green baize table.

'So the wee wife's spilled the beans. It's plain in your face.' Alec gave a conspiratorial grin. 'Aye, congratulations, Laddie!' Then Alec announced the news to everyone who was there, and when the champagne was poured out and the froth allowed to settle into more polite bubbles, Alec said in a loud voice, giving a sideways look at Mrs Fawcett, 'And here's congratulations to ye, Doctor, to celebrate one of those rare occasions when ye can honestly combine duty with pleasure.'

'Three spades!' Mrs Fawcett cried ostentatiously to cover her embarrassment, and for a second I wondered, as I looked at her, whether she had suddenly had a mental and rather distasteful memory picture of the last time the Colonel and Mrs Fawcett had combined duty with pleasure. On Christmas and birthdays, I supposed.

Next I drove back to see Tiare, who was so overjoyed that her eyes were actually brimming with tears of happiness.

'I couldn't have asked for a better man to marry my daughter.' She kissed me on the cheek and spoke with the frankness of the island people who never get embarrassed at sentimentality. 'We often go on our knees to thank you, Kit, for the sacrifice you made when Aleena was held hostage.'

I tried to laugh it off. In England I suppose I would have shrugged an 'It was nothing, really', but I couldn't say that, so I just said gently, 'Thank God it worked out for the best in the end.'

It was like that all the rest of Wednesday, back-slapping from everyone. Jason came round; his wife – how odd that word sounded – was at the hospital doing her 'Sister Sowerby' chores.

'You've given me new heart, Kit.' Jason held his glass aloft in a rare and secret breaking of the 'Sally Army pledge'. 'I'm trying to follow your example.'

'It needs two,' I said slyly.

'Mrs Purvis is not averse to that kind of thing.' He put on a mock seriousness; but it was one which I could see was based on truth, and I was sure, not for the first time, that Lorna Purvis, rid of the shackles of virginity imposed by conscience, not only wanted a child, but now that she had been freed from restraint, was thoroughly enjoying the physical mixture of combining 'duty with pleasure'.

The following morning, before the party was due to start, Serpell made a long tour of the hospital and he was delighted with what he saw, especially the neat and workmanlike way in which we had arranged the apparatus he had so generously sold us. It tickled my imagination, though, to see the difference in his approach when he was out of uniform.

He watched every detail, made excellent suggestions now and then, but everything was in a much more relaxed way, with none of the austere discipline of a military hospital. I had once accompanied him on one such tour in Sanders, and I had had the feeling that everyone had been warned in advance that there was to be an inspection by the top brass – matrons and military patients smiled dutifully when they sensed that it was the right thing to do, then the matrons in particular would put smiles in their pockets and turn their faces into straight lines until it was time to smile again. Now Serpell was jolly and unrestrained and, as we returned to the reception area, looked at his watch and said to Alec and me, 'Thirsty work this. How long do we have before the party starts?'

'A half hour or so.' Alec also looked at his watch. 'So let's have a dram at the club while we wait.' And as we walked across – the hospital, the club and Paula's house were all so close to each other – he added, not exactly with a chuckle, but with the canny thriftiness so often associated with the Scots, 'Just a wee one, though. The drinks'll be copious at Paula's and there'll be nae question of payment.'

Alec was right. The drinks *were* copious, and everyone agreed, as the guests arrived, that this promised to be 'the party of the year'. Paula, it was obvious, had gone to enormous lengths to make sure of that. Her own servants were well trained, and she had also brought in the two

675

stewards from her yacht which lay in the tiny harbour of Tala-Tala. The fact that it was a buffet lunch didn't in her eyes mean that guests had precariously to balance a plate in one hand and a glass in the other. As she had once told me, 'I can't stand fork suppers. So vulgar.'

Tables and chairs were dotted round the pool area – but far enough away from the splashes of the few swimmers – or inside the long living-room where there were also two large makeshift tables, the trestles hidden under snowy tablecloths. One contained drinks and glasses, with a preponderance of champagne, the other was laden with food from which you could pick and choose – everything from stuffed breadfruit, curried bananas, prawns with ginger fried crisply, and other local delicacies, together with the inevitable pineapples, lobsters, and a sucking pig. But Paula had also introduced some American dishes – tinned pastrami and corned beef (prized because it was unknown on the islands); there was also turkey served with cranberry sauce as they eat it on Thanksgiving Day, with candied sweet potatoes.

By the time Aleena and I arrived the party was in full swing and there must have been twenty or thirty guests sitting at the various tables drinking or eating. Dick Holmes was having a quick dip in the pool and shouted to me, 'I'm allowing myself twenty minutes' eating time when I've finished my swim – then I've got to go back to the radio shack.'

'Mind if I join him?' I asked Aleena. 'I just want to feel cool water all over me to work up an appetite.' I kissed her as she smiled and nodded.

'You and Tiare carry on drinking for a few minutes. Champagne never hurt unborn babies.'

In the small bamboo changing hut, which almost backed on to the rear of the hospital, I stepped into my swimming trunks, then with a running dive, surfaced and joined Dick Holmes, who was a wonderful long-distance swimmer.

'What's the rush?' I asked as I did a slow crawl alongside him.

676

'Got a message on the sked an hour ago,' he gasped as we came up for air and both grabbed the tiled ridge at the edge of the pool. 'There's some minor flap on – been the tiniest earth tremor in the world thousands of miles away.'

'Small?'

'Insignificant, though oddly, I think I felt a kind of echo of it – if that's the right way to describe it – but I was sitting at my office desk before I came here when I saw – yes, I actually *saw* it, I swear to you – the framed picture calendar on the wall move at least an inch.'

As we jumped out of the pool and rubbed down before changing, I said, 'Sounds as though you had a thick night.' I reached for my trousers and started pulling them up.

'No,' he smiled, 'stone cold sober.'

'You might have imagined it. Better make sure the same thing doesn't happen to the champagne! Come on, Dick, let's join the ladies.'

'No question of panic,' said Holmes. 'It's a question of keeping in contact with any shipping in the area. Might be a hurricane far away or something like that. That wasn't a quake, of course, only a tremor. Still,' he almost whispered as we joined Tiare and Aleena, 'Colonel Fawcett is furious. He has to return with me. The New Zealand government authorities have told him to stand by.'

'Seems damned silly. If you're there, you could phone him if you need him and he'd be over in his car in ten minutes.'

'Sounds silly to me too,' he agreed. 'But that's governments for you. They never take a chance but always err, as they say, on the side of caution. I see their point of view, though.' The champagne was already on every table, so we were able to sit down and drink at leisure.

'I don't,' I said. 'It spoils a good party.'

'Well, it *is* a working day, and if any New Zealand ship sent out a mayday call and we didn't receive it because we were swilling champagne' – he grinned – 'I'd be looking for a new job damn quickly. Someone has to mind the shop.'

*

677

The lunch followed the pattern of all well-organised parties. Paula's resident pianist tinkled quietly in one corner behind the wooden square which she had installed years ago as a dance floor and was covered with an attap roof to shade it from the sun. Everyone mixed with everyone. Jason – neat in his white ducks – danced once with Aleena, and I took turns to foxtrot with Tiare and Lorna Purvis, though frankly I find after-lunch dancing hard work.

I do not recall the moment when I was first aware of warning signals of possible conflict between Sam Truscott and Paula Reece.

They came from Tiare. As guests mingled, Tiare came up to me and I could see her watching closely as Paula talked to Sam and appeared to indicate, with an inclination of her head, that she wanted to talk to him alone.

Aleena was dancing with one of the shipping-line men and, almost with a note of urgency, Tiare said to me, 'Kit, I'm going to ask you a very personal question. You don't have to answer it if you don't want to. But I think it's important. Paula looks furious – and my bet is that Sam's refusing her attentions.'

'And so – what's the question?' I had no idea of what to expect.

'You told me that Sam married Lucy. And how you helped her with medical advice. And how delighted Sam was because of what you did.'

'Well – ' I began to grow uneasy.

'Kit – does Sam know that you and Lucy were lovers? Did you tell him?'

I hesitated. 'No, I didn't,' I said slowly.

'But why not, Kit?'

'I was so staggered when I saw Lucy that first time in San Francisco – I couldn't believe my eyes. And there was Sam, anxious for help. And Lucy – it was such a long time ago – and she looked at me, begging me with her eyes to say nothing. And so,' somewhat lamely, 'I said nothing.'

'It's not for me to say whether you were right or wrong, medically or ethically or whatever. Fortunately – '

'Fortunately what – ?'

'Well, Paula has always hated Lucy – and the way Paula treated her was abominable. Luckily she doesn't have the faintest idea who Sam married. But what happens if she finds out that it was Lucy? After all, you said to me that Lucy had told Sam she met you when she was with Paula – '

'Tiare, I don't quite see what you're getting at.'

'Look at them. I'm afraid of one thing – that Sam, quite innocently, will tell Paula that he can't go to bed with her because his wife is an old friend of Paula's. That's what she said she was.'

'But then?'

'If Sam casually tells Paula that it was Lucy, you can imagine what Paula's reaction would be. Out of revenge for being "jilted", by both you and Sam, she'd drag Lucy's name in the mud; yours too, and indirectly, Aleena's. And your friendship with Sam would be ruined. I may be absolutely wrong, but I'm not going to take the chance. If any trouble does occur, I'm going to stop it.'

'I think you may be wrong, Tiare.'

'It's the most natural thing in the world for Sam to mention that Lucy was an old friend of Paula's. And look at them now.' Amidst all the crowded guests, Paula was obviously insisting on something.

'What can I do?' I asked helplessly.

'I'm going to stop her. I'm not going to allow Sam to be hurt, or Aleena made to feel embarrassed.' Then she added, almost with a smile, 'Aleena knows that you had an affair with Lucy years ago, of course. It was common knowledge. But the past is past, and every single man has a past if he's worth a present. But I don't want Aleena dragged in to a confrontation. Just when everyone knows she's going to have a baby.'

'Neither do I. But honestly, Tiare, I don't know what I can do.'

Then she outlined her suggestion. If – only if – Paula

insisted on talking alone with Sam – and after all, they had been to bed several times in the past – it would certainly be in what she called her master bedroom, the one with twin bathrooms. Each of those bathrooms had doors that led out to the first-floor landing.

'If I see her taking Sam upstairs,' whispered Tiare, 'you and I will make our way by the second stairs, and slip into one of those bathrooms. We'll be able to hear anything. If nothing happens, fine. But if there's any danger of a scandal, I'll burst in before either of them says anything stupid. Doesn't that sound sensible?'

'It sounds terrifying!' I forced a smile.

'Leave it to me. Act naturally, but watch them – and me – carefully. At the slightest sign they're going upstairs, you know where we'll make for – the bathroom.'

I nodded. I couldn't say another word. Hope said it was all nonsense, but common sense told me that, because of Lucy's association with Paula, it would be the most natural thing in the world for Sam to mention her name. And if he did! Well, it didn't need a medical diagnosis to know how that mixture of hate and revenge would boil up into the most unholy row.

I watched carefully, and then, suddenly, I knew that Tiare's warning was right. In fact I was dancing with Mrs Fawcett and managed to get close to Paula and Sam. They were almost arguing.

'Don't be so goddam straitlaced and stupid,' said Paula. 'At least come and talk to me. In my room – our room?'

'If you insist,' I thought I heard Sam say with a sigh.

'Excuse me – ' I stopped dancing with Mrs Fawcett. 'I'm not feeling too well –'

'Oh dear, Doctor,' she looked alarmed.

Before she could say anything more I nodded to Tiare and we actually rushed up the backstairs and reached the bathroom just as Sam and Paula reached the bedroom.

Then I heard the row start. It gave me an eerie feeling, Tiare and I hidden in the bathroom, deliberately eavesdropping on someone – and preparing to act if necessary.

Paula and Sam were obviously involved in a heated argument.

'Okay, so you got married,' I heard Paula say. 'But marriage has never stopped men from indulging in extra-curricular activities has it? Sure, you may love your wife, but marriage and fun – be your age, Sam!'

A little heavily, Sam muttered, 'Yeah, but my wife's pregnant – '

Almost sharply Paula retorted, 'Come on, Sam! You enjoyed it enough the last time. Remember? And it means nothing.'

'Well – ' I had the feeling that poor Sam, as sexy as ever, was hesitating.

'Come on. Don't be such a goddamn sissy.'

'I'm not a sissy,' he blurted out. 'But the girl I'm married to – she used to be a friend of yours, Paula, and – '

Here was the moment of danger. I felt Tiare grip my arm.

'A friend of mine? Who?'

'Lucy. Lucy Young.'

'*Lucy*. She wasn't a *friend* of mine.' Paula put a great deal of accent on the word 'friend'. 'Oh yes, we all knew Lucy. Pretty innocent freckled Lucy!'

'What do you mean?' Sam's voice was dangerously calm.

'My dear, uneducated idiot,' said Paula angrily, 'Lucy *worked* here. A holiday job. Temporary housekeeper if you like,' she sneered. 'So you fell in love with her! Well, you weren't the first. And I fired her, and do you really want to know why? You and your precious Lucy!'

I caught a glimpse of Tiare's face. It was contorted with fury. And then the next moment, her anger somehow disguised with a smile, she banged open the door leading from the bathroom to the bedroom, stalked up to Paula's face and without one word, without the flicker of an eyelash, slapped her hard on the face – and the Princess, for all her rank, was a Polynesian and she slapped hard – as both Sam and I watched goggle-eyed and (as far as I was concerned) terrified of what Paula would say next.

Paula screamed, four-letter words I hardly ever heard. She raised her hands and to me they looked, with their long nails, almost like claws.

'I'll kill you,' she screamed. 'How dare you – you a bloody princess. Balls!' She lunged towards Tiare still screaming, 'You bloody bastard daughter of a tart – get out of my house.'

'I know,' Tiare was breathing heavily, 'that you were going to tell Sam the truth about Lucy and – '

Now *my* heart was thumping with fear – no, not exactly fear, but apprehension.

'About Lucy and Count Vrinsky,' said Tiare remorselessly, as Paula looked baffled as well as angry. 'Well, just remember this, you oversexed whore – '

'*Get out!*' screamed Paula. 'Get out. You can't – '

'I can!' shouted Tiare. 'No, you're not a whore, you're a madame trying to force girls into prostitution. I wouldn't be surprised if you don't have a secret peephole so you can watch.'

Paula was alternately screaming and sobbing hysterically. 'Get out of my house, you illegitimate bitch.'

'I will – and never come back. But first tell Sam the truth – he's a decent man. Tell him why you kicked Lucy out.'

My heart almost stopped for a second as I waited.

'Get out!' screamed Paula as I felt the sudden heaving of a man about to vomit.

There was a moment's silence. I could see the cunning in Paula's eyes. She was as much in the dark as I was, she hadn't the faintest idea what Tiare was going to say. Neither had I – unless it was the truth . . .

Paula was gasping for breath. Her left cheek was a scarlet daub where Tiare had hit her.

'All right,' said Tiare, still seething with anger, but this time (I realised) more simulated. 'All right, I'll tell him. Look me in the face, damn you, or I'll slap you again.' Tiare looked at Paula with a glare of determination I had never seen in her beauty before, as though forcing her will on

Paula to agree, as she spoke with the slow, deliberate voice of a hypnotist who tries to force you to make you say what he suggests. It was beyond me!

'You kicked out Lucy who was a beautiful, sweet girl – because – '

I thought I would faint before Tiare added, again in that almost remorseless voice, 'because she refused to go to bed with the Count Vrinksy and other men who visited the villa as guests. That's true, isn't it?'

Before Paula had a chance to deny or admit to the lie, as she stood there glowering, almost as though she could no longer control her rage, Tiare added impassively, 'That's the truth, and it had better not come out. If I ever hear any rumours or distortion of facts outside this room – or lies from you – I warn you: I'll go straight to Colonel Fawcett and – illegitimate or not, I do have some say on this island – and when I tell Colonel Fawcett that you've been using this damned villa as nothing more than a whorehouse, he'll have you sent packing the same day on your precious yacht!'

All this time Sam and I had been stunned, silent onlookers at a slanging match, but I breathed a private sigh of relief as I realised the brilliant way Tiare had turned the tables – because Paula realised that this wasn't an empty threat. There was no law against enjoying sex with the girl of your choice, but Polynesian custom and local laws strictly forbade forcing girls to go to bed with men against their will. There was no such thing as a brothel in Koraloona (though morals were laxer, because of the soldiers and sailors, in Sanderstown). But Paula knew by now that if it came to a showdown, Tiare's word would be accepted against hers, and, even though Tiare's 'Princess' was an honorary title in some ways, she could easily, with the support of Tiki and men like him, force Paula to leave the island.

Finally Paula, still gasping, said, 'I wouldn't stay on this bloody island a moment longer than I have to, but I'm not going to be thrown off. I'll go when it suits me.'

683

'So you agree that this will never be mentioned outside this room?' Tiare's voice was quieter now.

'I agree – under duress from an illegitimate bitch.'

'Good. We'll leave the question of my father and mother out of this, and I won't ask any questions about yours. We have two witnesses here – shake hands on your promise.'

At first I thought Paula was going to refuse – in fact there was no reason why she should shake hands. But she did – grudgingly, panting, and with her face red and angry. And the matter might have ended there but for one deliberate – and to my mind stupidly unnecessary – final snub by Tiare. After they had shaken hands, Tiare turned towards the outsize double bed and with great deliberation wiped the hand which had shaken Paula's on the expensive bed-spread.

Never in my life – as a doctor or as an ordinary man – have I seen any woman's face turn really puce – not a blush, not a scarlet streak, but the entire face became a darker red, and then, after a kind of growl, and no other warning, Paula screamed and at the same time charged at Tiare crouching, head forward, almost like a bull who has been goaded by a matador. Before either Sam or I could do a thing, Paula butted Tiare in the stomach and *she* screamed, but with pain. As she started to lose her balance, Tiare grabbed at the expensive counterpane on which she had wiped her hand, but as she started to fall, the counterpane came off the bed and she landed on the floor. Unable to stop, Paula fell on top of her, and the next moment the two women were fighting, clawing at each other, kicking, with Tiare trying to get away, and with Paula doing everything she could to savage her.

'For Christ's sake!' I gasped to Sam, 'let's get them apart.'

We tried, both of us. But as I leant in towards them I got a sharp kick from a shoe on my shin. Sam received an elbow in his eye, and then all four of us were on the floor, trying to separate the two women.

'Stop it. *Stop it!* Please!' I could hardly get my breath as I

684

struggled to pull one woman from the clutches of the other. I wasn't even certain whom I was trying to tug away, because dresses were torn, shoes kicked off, I heard the ripping of silk, it must have been a blouse or something, then one screamed as the other grabbed her hair and pulled it. I slapped the hand that was pulling the hair. Paula loosed her grip, then the two women seemed to roll over, like wrestlers in a ring seeking a new position, and Sam pounced on one girl – it was Paula, I caught a glimpse of that angry face marked with a scratch across one cheek. Then somehow they got to grips with each other again. Each woman seemed oblivious to the damage she suffered, as though pain didn't count. With one last effort Sam and I separated them, and I was thinking that downstairs the noise must have been appalling, but why had nobody come up to see what was happening? I didn't realise that the house was empty but for us: except one man. I must have hurt my eyes, I thought, for I could hardly make out who it was in the suddenly dim light, but then the door of Paula's bedroom burst open and I recognised the Scottish burr of Alec's voice as he shouted one terrible word. It was 'Fire!'

As we all tumbled down the steps in near-panic, I glanced at the luminous dial of my wrist-watch. Half past three! Yet the bright sunlight had been replaced by a deep grey, as though a sea mist had clouded the entire house.

'What the hell's up?' I gasped to Alec as I scrambled to the door. It was almost dark outside.

'Look over there!' he shouted hoarsely.

'There' was the black conical shape of High Island, only half a mile away. From its sides I could make out sudden spurts of flame. They shot into the sky, disappeared – until one fell into the garden, narrowly missing us, and of such an intense heat that the few specks of black ash set fire almost immediately to a small patch of dry grass.

'Fumaroles,' cried Mitchell who was nearby. 'You remember them?' I did – the sinister word for the hot bubbles bursting on the side of a volcano which gave out hissing water or steam from time to time.

685

Then, without warning, the grey of the 'sea mist' turned into inky blackness. I couldn't believe it. Somewhere inside the house a light was turned on. Others followed, specks of light.

As though encapsulated in one moment of time, I caught sight of Father Pringle, staggering, obviously half drunk, holding his soutane knee-high; a terrified Mrs Fawcett clinging to the captain of Paula's yacht; Alec mopping his brow with a bandana; Mitchell standing startlingly erect as if listening to something nobody else could hear.

As day was turned into night, everyone was moving and screaming with the pressure of blind panic, the urge to escape. But escape from what? I felt myself forced through patches of murky light into beds of flowers – and as more lights came on in the garden something else startled me: the bright blossoms were coated with grey, as though turned to stone. I myself could feel the swirl of the 'sea mist' in the black sky. I heard Jason's voice from close by and turned to see him, his arms held out before him, his white ducks now as grey as the flowers. He cried incredulously, 'It's a cloudburst of dust!'

Then Mitchell loomed wraithlike through the murk. 'No! It's ash. Volcanic ash! Can't you feel the heat? Listen to the rumbling, roaring sound from High Island.'

It dawned on me at last: the volcano was in eruption!

Screams from the women mingled with the sound of panic-stricken feet as if everyone was instinctively fleeing from a scene of disaster. At the same time the heat suddenly became intense. Heat, yes, but deep within me I felt the icy core of horror.

For there was nowhere to flee to.

Then, almost as suddenly as it had vanished, daylight – of a sort – returned. Everyone turned faces skyward; but, blinded by the falling ash, they covered their eyes with their hands and stumbled about like puppets.

A great plume of black smoke hung over High Island, and it was this that had obscured the sun. It had moved now in an east wind and was passing overhead like a vast ship, its billowing sails ripped asunder by streaks of pink flame. The volcano itself seemed to have ceased its activity for the moment, as if taking breath.

The panicking footsteps halted. Everyone stood still again. No one seemed to be injured, though some spluttered and foamed at the mouth, trying to spit out the ash clogging lips, teeth, nostrils. Alec stumbled towards me, eyes heavy-lidded with dust. He looked up and yelled, 'Move, Kit, for God's sake! There could be fire!'

Just in time. A few hot coals rained down but they fell in the fields a hundred yards away. Most spluttered out with a hiss, but a few turned into a brief flame on dry grass.

'That's how we'll be needed, Laddie. Burns. And at any minute now if my prognosis is right.'

As it happened, he was wrong – for the moment anyway. No more coals fell, though I could hear what sounded like the dull thunder of stones or small rocks falling in the direction of Anani.

Mitchell materialised beside me, an ashen figure in every sense of the word. Figures moved in the half-light, faces begrimed with sweat mingled with the grey ash that coated everything.

As the realisation of what had happened came over them they registered shock in various ways – crying, mumbling, or standing rooted and dumbfounded.

'I think it's over,' I said as if I really believed it – perhaps more to quell alarm than for anything else.

Mitchell laughed harshly. 'Over! Not if I know anything about it. This is a mere sniffle compared to what that mountain's going to belch up. And all because of those sodding scientists and their bloody bomb! Didn't I tell you?' He reached out and grabbed my arm. He was almost hysterical. 'Didn't I tell you, now? Didn't I? *Didn't I?*'

Nearby Father Pringle took a deep swig from a bottle in the pocket of his soutane, then the next moment fell on his knees, oblivious to the heat of the ground, and clasping his hands and looking towards the heavens, began to pray.

'They'll be needing a shot of bromide,' Alec said matter-of-factly.

But Mitchell, regaining control of himself, apologised.

'Dinna fret, Laddie. We'll all be needing a shot the noo or sooner!'

I saw Alec walk up to Tiare, look at the scratch on her face and her hair all awry and tangled, and speak to her.

I suddenly stood away, my heart thumping. Aleena! Where was she?

48

As I looked around for Aleena, without success, Mitchell took one look at Tiare, hair tousled, face scratched, dress torn, and said, 'Are you all right? Can I help?' Sam Truscott stopped her too, and said, 'Gee – you're in need of running repairs. What the hell did that bitch think she was doing to you?'

'It's only a scratch.'

'Better let me take a wee look at it,' suggested Alec.

'There are others, much worse – ' Tiare waved her hand vaguely.

'Princess or nae, ye'll do as ye're told. If ye dinna cover that scratch, and ye get more ash dust in, it'll turn septic. And ye wouldna like to have yon pretty face spoiled, would ye now?'

'No Doctor,' she replied meekly, turning to me to say, 'Aleena's in the living-room in the house. Where's Paula?'

'Rotting in hell as far as I'm concerned,' said Truscott.

'Don't speak ill of people,' Father Pringle reproved him. 'You might be next on the list after this fellow here.'

He pointed to one of the few corpses lying around. There had so far been only a few deaths in or around Tala-Tala. This man had received a direct hit on his head from a large piece of stone, and according to those who saw it, it was so hot that it set fire to the man's thick hair so that it blazed; but he at least escaped the horror of fire, for the stone had killed him instantly.

'There'll be more,' warned Alec, while Serpell rushed around helping, filled with vigour. For the first time in years he was actually practising medicine instead of being a figurehead administering a large hospital.

'Thank God we've got plenty of acriflavine for bad burns,' he said. I was grateful, too. We had inherited from Sanders large stocks of tubes of the almost runny liquid ointment. 'I never thought we'd need it for a volcano!'

'But there'll be more.' Alec looked out over the flatlands where the taro crops grew, out towards the secret pool, pointing to the groups of foot-weary islanders trudging towards Tala-Tala from isolated settlements and villages like Tabanea, with its one main street.

In a sky darkened into a leaden chaos, they carried pitiful bundles of belongings – tin pans, a blanket, an ancient bicycle, porous earthenware jars to keep water cool – not that any of it would be of value now, but no one would believe that this was the end of a life; it was an interruption and soon they would start all over again, so they clung to everything they owned. They shuffled to their doctors, impelled by the conviction that men who had saved so many lives in the cholera outbreak would protect them again. In their bemused minds, we could work miracles, and so they made their way to the hospital, imploring, trusting, despair giving way to hope at the sight of us.

The worst cases of burns were mostly among young kids. Toddlers would see a stone fall, pick it up, burn their hands terribly. Other cases – people finding it difficult to see after looking upwards into ash clouds for too long – we put in Paula's house. She was nowhere to be seen, so we commandeered the house, to keep the hospital free for serious cases. But I could only treat the eye cases with Optrex.

Aleena was safe, but scared. She was not the sort to panic, and in order to help her I asked her to help me.

I knew how inactivity in moments of danger can breed fear.

'Will you look after these people with eye trouble?' I asked her. 'We need all the help we can. Lorna is busy with the burns, she and Serpell and Alec.'

'Of course,' she said almost gratefully. 'Tell me what to do.' I gave her some bottles of Optrex, each with its glass top in the shape of an eye bath, which they advertised in London with the slogan 'Eye bath every day, do you?'

'You can tell them in the local dialects better than I can,' I explained to her. 'They think that if you wash the outside of the eyes, they'll get better. It's inside the eye that has to be bathed – under the lids. So you can explain better than I can that you've got to make a patient tip his head back so that the solution in the eye bath really washes into the eyeball.'

'I understand. You go off and look after the more serious cases.'

'You're wonderful!' As I tried to wipe her lined, grey face, I said, 'But do be careful. Don't go outside. The corrugated-iron roofs of Paula's house and the hospital are slanting, so white-hot coals can roll off. In fact, that's our only hope of avoiding a large-scale fire, but if the tiniest stone touches your head, it'll burn that beautiful black hair of yours into a frazzle in a split second.'

She shuddered, holding me tight in her arms, oblivious to the men, women and children around us, crowded into the long living-room with its remnants of a party. One table was still littered with champagne bottles. I grabbed two or three unopened bottles which would be pollution free, for someone who might need liquid. On the other table the remains of the food still stood by the plates – lobsters, once pink, now covered with a coating of grey. I was looking at the tables thinking, as I held her hand, of the horrible speed with which life can change, when I saw the ancient telephone on the wall. I picked it up, cranked the handle, though I was convinced there would be no response.

For a moment there wasn't. The 'exchange' – such as it

was – was in a room near the radio shack and as I waited, listening to the bell stutter, I almost dropped the instrument when a croaking voice answered. 'Colonel Fawcett here.'

'Kit Masters. Are you all right?'

'Not bad myself. Losing my voice though. I sent most of the staff down to the beach. They can shelter in Jim Wilson's works, or in the shipping office, they're both fairly solid. I can't help, only tell people to skidaddle.'

'At least we've made contact. As soon as I can spare a moment I'll come to see you. Is the radio working? Does Sanderstown know?'

Fawcett had just started saying, 'I'm afraid –' when there was an almighty blast, and through the window of Paula's house I could see the sky turn blood red as flames burst up and out. The same bang – and its shower of molten rock – was the same one which had cut the phone link in Anani.

Aleena turned pale, ran into my arms, and cried, 'How can God be so wicked?'

'It may not be God.' The flame had died down. 'It may be man who has started all this. Mitchell's convinced it is.'

I swung round, leaving the earphone dangling on a twisted cord. 'It's bust,' I cried bitterly. 'The whole bloody world's going bust. How can you fight the elements?'

'You *can*, my beloved Kit. You *will*. I'm next to you. And remember. You've twice beaten a man who was just as merciless as this – as this devil from the underworld.'

As I ran back to the hospital, I saw a lone car approaching from the direction of Anani. Despite the greyness that made everything and everyone look the same colour, I recognised it as a jeep, and there was only one other jeep on the island. It belonged to the radio shack. It must be Dick Holmes.

It *was* Holmes. The engine was spluttering and coughing and, as he pulled up beside the hospital, it gave a final choke and died. We both knew then that we had an additional hazard to cope with: the fine dust was seeping into carburettors and under the seating of valves. It

691

wouldn't be long before it ruined all the mechanical apparatus on the island. *Nellie* would be grounded, Tiare's old Austin, my jeep and Ford, the hospital's generator, would all be penetrated by volcanic dust. Fresh foods would be contaminated and water was already muddy. Even the sea was rolling layers of cinders on to the shore. Coconut milk would have to replace water, and we would have to rely on whatever tinned food was stockpiled in Johnson's store and the Union Jack Club. But worse was to come.

As Dick stepped out of the jeep and wiped the crust of grey from his lips, he just blurted out, 'The radio's packed up. No contact.'

'But what – ?' I left the question suspended in mid air.

'It's that bloody volcano. The smoke and dust has been ejected upward by its own heat and has screened off the Heaviside Layer.'

'The *what*?' Alec had joined us. 'What the hell is that?'

Holmes jerked a thumb upwards. 'Up above, there's a layer of the ionosphere, atmosphere, whatever you like to call it, called the Heaviside Layer. Radio waves bounce off it; but if they can't get to it they don't bounce. And now it's screened off by thick layers of dust and we can't get a signal. Sorry, Doc, but that's the position.'

So we were cut off from the outside world. Neither help nor supplies could be summoned.

Holmes offered a mild ray of hope. 'There's a chance I'll be able to get it working again, but it'll take time. It's not only that I can't get a bounce, but the transmitter itself is clogged with dust. It's covering everything. I'll go back and see if I can clean out its guts.'

'How'll you get there?' I looked at his jeep, now nothing but a grey carcase.

'Walk I suppose,' Holmes said mirthlessly.

'Five miles! You'll never be able to make it. Every foot you take gets heavier with the ash. And probably burns the soles of your feet,' Alec said.

'I'll drive you back,' I suggested.

'If *your* jeep works?'

'I think it will.' My jeep and the old Ford 8 – as well as Alec's plane – were more protected than most vehicles because when the Americans built the camp and the strip for Sam Truscott's plane, they built a lean-to shed against a hillside, with a sloping corrugated-iron roof; it faced away from High Island and towards the sea, so there was a good chance that ash pouring down from High Island behind it would hit the roof and keep the vehicles clear. 'So it might just be in better shape,' I explained.

'Well, you both decide between yourselves what to do.' Alec sounded tetchy and I didn't wonder. His face was grey, not only with ash, but with fatigue. He looked done in. 'But dinna leave me alone for too long.' His voice had a sudden beseeching, begging sound. 'I couldna cope by mesel'!'

'Maybe I can be of help,' said a quiet American voice behind me. I turned to see Ron Baker, the skipper of Paula's yacht. Though we met occasionally, Baker was taciturn, no doubt because Paula tended to treat him as a highly paid servant and she expected to be obeyed at a moment's notice. Certainly she insisted that the *Nymph* always be kept ready for sailing.

'Doing what?' I asked, unable to keep the bitterness out of my voice.

Baker took no offence at my tone and managed a lop-sided smile when I mumbled, 'Sorry.' He turned to Holmes. 'We've got a shortwave transmitter and receiver on the *Nymph*.'

'My God!' Holmes croaked with sudden excitement, but his voice was drowned by a terrific roar, as sudden huge spurts of flame shot high into the sky.

'Take cover!' I yelled instinctively, but there was no cover in the world against this sort of onslaught. The huge roar stopped; it was followed by a hiss of steam like heavy, sinister breathing – or perhaps more like the sibilant hiss of a thousand snakes. Here and there rocks fell, but not near us, though I saw several small fires start in the distance.

'That's terrific.' Holmes gripped Baker's arm. 'If you've got short-wave and a good direction finder – '

'We've got the latest W-T,' said Baker. 'We've got a speech range of around two hundred miles, and morse keys for about twice that distance in case of emergencies.'

'My set's clogged up with shit – ash shit,' said Holmes. 'If you can help?'

Baker made an odd remark. 'It's the least I can do,' he grunted. Then he explained, 'It should be in working order because it's below decks. Almost like a sealed cupboard called a room. There'll be no ash in the radio cabin.'

Holmes turned to me.

'It's our only chance. I still don't know if we can get a signal through the Heaviside Layer, but it's worth a go. You agree? At least the *Nymph*'s got a radio. And if we sail eastwards – we'll be going in the opposite direction to the cloud.'

He looked up at the ugly spreading black drift of sulphurous smoke, then there was another sudden spurt of flame and this time we both actually saw objects fly into the air, thousands of feet, some flaming with intense heat, and then in a huge arc fall slowly, not on Koraloona itself, but over the island and past it, huge blocks of stone or coal or whatever they were, hurtling into the open sea. It seems incredible, and I would never have dared to say this had I not been with others who also saw it, but when the biggest rocks fell into the sea not far from Tala-Tala's tiny harbour, the water began to bubble and boil with the intensity of their heat.

'I'll have the goddamn engines ready in ten minutes,' Baker promised.

I could see the *Nymph* just below the incline leading down to the beach and the port, across the narrow coast road, with the nearby Union Jack Club apparently intact. A couple of figures were working feverishly.

'Brushing the coating of ash off the deck,' Baker explained as he started for the boat. 'It's a couple of inches thick in parts.'

'You've got enough – ?'

'Gas? Enough to get into the open sea and transmit.' Baker seemed to read my thoughts. 'Holmes can start trying to transmit a couple of miles outside the reef.'

I had a sudden thought. 'I know that making radio contact is a matter of life and death for all of us – but don't you think we should tell Mrs Reece of your plan?'

After a moment's hesitation, Baker said, 'That's okay. I've already spoken to Mrs Reece.'

'Good. I don't want you to lose your master's certificate' – I tried to smile – 'for taking a vessel away without the owner's permission.'

'All taken care of,' he said briefly.

'Where *is* Paula?' I asked.

'She's around,' said Baker.

'I knew she'd understand.' I had to force the words out because the disaster had struck us so swiftly after the fight when Paula attacked Tiare, that I would never forget the scene – so vivid, so recent that even now, with the threat of death hanging over us, I knew I would never be able to speak to her again – if, that is, we ever got another chance in life to exchange words. Because, now, with the ash falling like a grey pale drizzle, I could not but share the same thoughts I knew the others were thinking: would we all choke to death or die by burning?

This macabre line of thought was interrupted by a down-to-earth question from Dick Holmes. 'I'll be off then. But if it's possible, can someone let Colonel Fawcett know? I'm supposed to be in the radio shack and he'll be wondering.'

'I'll get a message to him.' It was a filthy-looking tousle-headed Jason who spoke. Looking at me, he asked, 'I could make it if I could borrow your Ford – or better, the jeep.'

I half nodded, doubtful. I didn't want to use the jeep except in dire emergency in case of breakdown: while she was in the 'garage' I felt that she was safer than on open ground. 'But hang on a minute, let's get Dick off first, then we'll see.'

As we walked down to the *Nymph* where the crew was ready to cast off, I suggested to Holmes, 'If you do get a radio contact with someone, ask Captain Baker to fire a Verey light so that we'll know.'

'Will do.' He climbed aboard. I heard the deep throb – the two 500-horsepower engines burst into life – welcome because the sound of the engines meant that, with luck, our own engines would work. The electricity was still functioning – and it was a sign that man's ingenuity might eventually triumph.

As the ropes were dragged on board, Baker was the last man to jump on to the vessel, but just before he took the wheel, there was a sudden almost unnatural silence, as though the volcano were sleeping, and the skipper shook hands and said, almost embarrassed, 'Never got to know you well, Doc. Sorry, but it's one helluva full-time job skippering a boat for a woman. And you know, orders is orders, but I've done what I could to help.'

I had never heard him make such a long speech – let alone at a moment of such stress. I looked at him, slightly baffled, as the elegant prow of the *Nymph* slid slowly through the ash-coloured water and towards the breakwater of the tiny harbour.

Walking back up the hill to the hospital, I saw an astonishing sight. The beach was littered with dead fish that had been thrown up as tortured waves receded. Not just dead. Boiled. A dozen lobsters lay there as though they had just come out of the pot, boiled by the water surrounding these heavy white-hot stones.

The *Nymph* was still visible, for the debris in the water made it imperative to keep the engine telegraph at 'Dead Slow'. But then I saw another sight that astonished me. A figure suddenly emerged from the saloon and stood on what Paula had once described to me as 'the drinking deck'. It was a woman. I could just see skirts flutter in the slight breeze. It was Paula Reece.

I knew now what Baker's last words had meant, 'Orders is orders, but I've done what I could.' For though Paula had decided that enough was enough and was bolting, Baker had at least smuggled Holmes aboard.

My first thoughts contained no anger, more relief that she had left. And after all, it *was* Paula's ship. She could sail when she liked.

'I can't say I blame her,' I sighed to Purvis. 'I've always disliked her, but if she makes it, at least it'll mean that Dick Holmes makes it too, and he's a good lad.'

I asked Purvis not to attempt the drive to Anani until we had seen a Verey light telling us that we had contacted the outside world. Much better to wait until we could give Fawcett good news. And, anyway, Jason could make himself useful helping out, trying to find room for islanders who were crowding in.

Though we didn't know how many had died – especially in isolated settlements – four people who had sought shelter in the Tala-Tala area had died so far – one from burns. But the living needed some sort of hope to cling on to. That and the eye suffering, where Aleena was doing a wonderful job helping to ease pain with Optrex. We attended to the burns.

Alec looked weary in spirit as well as physically exhausted – until children in need of help arrived. Then he mentally awakened, and his eyes brightened at the sight of the children he loved.

As bursts of noise and flames raged, the older men and women looked to us for medical help, but also to Tiki and a few fellow priests for spiritual guidance. Most priests were in the Anani area, and I have no idea why Tiki should, on this particular day, have been visiting Tala, but he was.

'It's a very grave matter, Doctor.' Tiki looked round me at people choking with dust; and I sensed that to him the gravity of the situation was due to a different reason. 'The gods cannot be fooled, Doctor. A vow taken in their sight – '

697

So that was it: Aleena and I had urged him against his deeper instincts to allow the paintings to be sold, and now the gods were having their revenge. As a rational human being I thought it ridiculous; but then Tiki was the leader of a world still affected by the traces of primeval instincts which missionaries had never really vanquished. I remembered Tiki and the ceremony of burying the dead during the cholera outbreak, when he and his fellow priest had led the islanders in their chanting supplication to their angry gods.

In the great pall of ash suspended over Koraloona, which gave an eerie light, Tiki, and his small gathering of priestly henchmen in their heavy ceremonial robes and masks, chanted as they prostrated themselves, facing what should have been the afternoon sun but which, through the thick smoke that shrouded us, was no more than a smudge like a yellow fingerprint on the sky.

Terrified villagers gathered around them, babbling pathetic pleas to their god. It would not have surprised me if Tiki had demanded the sacrifice of a human life on an altar of fire, or if he had ordered his flock to march like lemmings into the sea. But only the insistent beating of the ceremonial drums and the mingled rumblings from High Island marked the solemnity of the occasion.

My own thoughts, as I watched, were to let Tiki placate the gods if he would – or could. Unfortunately I knew better – that Mitchell's warning of trouble after the Bikini explosions was nearer the truth.

Time had no meaning now, but for the moment the mountain was quiet and most of the people were huddled in Paula's house or in the hospital wards. Some were so frightened that they refused to stay inside, but went out into the grounds, waiting, egged on by Tiki. More were coming in from the outlying settlements.

Knots of them gathered around, pitiful in their non-comprehension of the terror which had struck them. With their bodies coated with the grey ash – and on some, red weals where heat had touched them – they looked like statues to which some robot-like mechanism had been added. They looked imploringly at Alec and me as we shouted at them to follow us to the hospital.

'Burns'll be the main trouble,' Alec said breathlessly as he puffed along beside me. 'We'll need to radio for extra supplies of bandages and acriflavine, if young Holmes gets through.' He was sweating copiously and his face and arms were streaked with runnels of muddy grey. I gave a short, almost hysterical laugh, supposing I looked just as grotesque.

At the hospital Lorna Purvis' dedication to duty seemed to overcome any signs of physical exhaustion. She soothed and bathed the faces of bed patients, and I noticed that the quite pretty dress she had worn for the party was torn and stained with filth; and out of the corner of my eye I saw that one wall of the ward was blistered, its white paint bubbling.

Alec's glance met mine. We both felt the same pang of heartache. Was the Gauguin Memorial Hospital going to last for only a few days?

What we could see of the countryside was clouded with ash. Its weight bore palms towards the ground and their roots emerged from the sandy soil like fingers twisted with arthritis. The attap roofs of dozens of villagers' homes had collapsed, fatally burying or burning many of the inhabitants. Helpers were hard to find; their comprehension, slowed by shock, made them huddle together trying to comfort each other; but we managed to convey to them that they would be better at the villa, or the hospital, and Aleena or Lorna would deal with them as they arrived.

Even there – safe for the moment – they hardly spoke; their silence contrasted oddly with the efforts we were making to cope with the situation. The generators were still working, but only because they had been running non-stop instead of being allowed to idle and cool off, for continuous running prevented dust gritting up the works; but they would not run for ever unless cooled. And though we had plenty of fuel stored in drums and jerricans, the fuel tank had to be uncapped to fill the generator and the insistent dust and granules of ash would be bound to seep into the compressor sooner or later.

While we could, we dealt with burns and frequent outbreaks of coughing caused by infectious dust in the bronchial tubes.

'Everybody's so acclimatised to pure air here,' Serpell said hopelessly. 'Londoners with their fogs might be used to filthy air, but here it's a dangerous hazard.'

Aleena was badly affected by choking dust and I had to keep giving her expectorants to get some of it out of her system – for, as Alec had warned me, 'The bairn'll nae escape doon there in the security of the womb. It's his mither's breath he's breathing.'

As night fell, with the volcano still quiet, we tried to take stock of the position. The electricity was still working. We had a fair supply of uncontaminated distilled water in jars, to be used for serious cases; we had champagne to sip; and, praying that no burning rocks would set the jerricans alight, we had plenty of petrol and diesel in the 'garage'. We had stopped the taps of the fresh-water containers so that ash could not pollute the tanks which, as a hospital precaution, had been fitted with covers. They had come with some of the other material from Serpell, who, at action stations, was not wearing a jacket but one of the post-war 'Hawaiian' shirts made so popular by the Americans. He – a surgeon-commander – was doing anything that Lorna suggested, emptying bedpans one moment, the next trying to clean ash from the naked emaciated body of an old woman on the threshold of death. Had it not been so tragic, it would have been a wonderful sight – the art of the healer, the great equaliser.

At the same time we had to ration the water despite the insistent cries of those patients almost choking to death. Just about the only man who was able to roll a mouthful of liquid round his tongue was Father Pringle who was helping out magnificently, but also helping himself to his samples of whisky. He gargled in neat whisky to cleanse the dirt from his mouth, spitting it out, then swigging a mouthful, for at least it was ash-free.

I had asked 'Sister Sowerby' – the islanders could not understand why she should change her name – to depute one of the trainee nurses to keep an eye open for a possible 'signal in the sky' if Holmes did manage to make contact, for even if the *Nymph* were far out to sea a Verey light could be seen for miles, even in the ash-fog.

And then it came – but not from a faraway sea. Some of us were having a breather on what we called the 'convalescent veranda', overlooking the sea and backed by a rise of ground behind the hospital and airfield, so that the volcano was behind us. It also had a heavy sloping corrugated-iron roof, part of what had been a rest centre for the camp.

In the blackness of the night – with not a star visible, nor a wisp of moon – a Verey light shot up into the stars followed by three more, but this time they were star shells that linger, lighting up the skies in the way which, as I had seen in pictures, bombers lit up their targets over big cities. And in the sudden light I could see plainly the outline of the *Nymph* and – like a white ribbon because of the eerie light – the unmistakable sight of the reef. She had never left the lagoon.

It wasn't possible! It must have been hours since the *Nymph* had set off. Father Pringle, who was standing there, was just as astonished and without thinking, let alone asking, offered me a bottle and unhesitatingly I took a deep swig of Scotch.

'And what about a wee dram for me, ye auld heathen?' It was Alec's husky voice. 'What in heaven's name has happened?'

'I know, I'm sure I do,' said Mitchell in his usual gloomy voice. 'The motors must have packed up. Remember the *Nymph*'s been lying in the harbour, exposed to the full force of the ash cloud. She's clogged up. I'd stake my reputation on it. I hope she's got her sea anchor out or she'll be on the reef before long.'

'Well,' I said almost with satisfaction, 'it looks as though Paula's attempt to shanghai our radio operator has failed.'

At that moment, as the four of us and the girl trainee looked outwards, trying to pierce the greyness of the thin moonlit sky, a terrible roar broke out behind us.

'High Island again!' cried Mitchell. 'She's at it again, the sonofabitch.'

I had never heard a sound to equal it. A million lions roaring with rage at the same time, a dozen express trains colliding, would have been like the squeak of a mouse in comparison. The trainee nurse started screaming.

'Ye'd better brace yoursel', wee Lassie,' cried Alec as with a gesture of tenderness he gathered the cowering girl into his arms, so that she hid her face against him. It was as well that he did. Seconds later came a second roar, followed by a burst of flame so powerful and concentrated, and this time so prolonged, that even though our backs were to High Island and most of the hospital buildings shielded us, the heat was so intense I could feel my shirt about to catch fire; at the same time the flash was so blinding that I thought I would never see again.

It was, for those few moments, as though I had been forced to keep my eyes open and stare into the mouth of a furnace which was turning a river of red-hot, molten, liquid steel into strips. I closed my eyes. It made no difference. The power of the light made my lids ineffective. I could smell again the tang of burning flesh – it was the heat of my hair, not serious, but some of it on the crown felt frizzled when I ran a finger through it.

The flames searing miles into the sky lasted for – how long? – five seconds maybe, a lifetime, what difference was there in time? Out on the water, lit as though by arc lamps, I could plainly see the *Nymph* near the white froth of the reef. Then the glare faded.

Worse – far worse – was to follow. Without warning – and I was not looking back at the darkened mountain behind me – the volcano spewed out enormous blocks of white-hot stone and molten lava. The reason why I knew was because from the veranda I could see the debris passing overhead and away out to sea, hurtling shadows, vague outlines, some flaming like meteors, others stark black monstrous lumps of the earth's bowels, fearful against the sky.

They must have been heated to an intensity impossible to imagine because when some of the smaller fragments hit the ground not far away – but luckily not the hospital – many caught fire the second they touched a patch of dry grass or the roof of an islander's thatched hut. Those that hit the water made it bubble and froth, like water boiling in a kettle.

Then – and this we actually saw for a fleeting moment in a few seconds of flame – half a dozen enormous black boulders shot down from the sky on to or near the reef, smashing into it, then toppling into the hissing water on either side.

All but one. As far as we could see, it fell like a stone right on to the decks of the *Nymph*. The impact must have crushed the yacht into a thousand pieces, and we might never have realised what had happened in the thin moon, but almost at the same second a mighty explosion brought with it another bright, brief burst of fire. The *Nymph*'s fuel stocks must have exploded, and for a moment, but long enough – a second or two – I saw the remnants of the vessel hurled into the sky as she disintegrated.

'Holy Mother of God.' Father Pringle sank to his knees, and made the sign of the cross. 'May the mercy of God have saved them from suffering.'

They couldn't have suffered, I thought gratefully as pictures of Paula – poor, provocative Paula – and then of Dick Holmes flashed across my tired, encrusted eyes. No, as the phrase has it, they didn't know what hit them. Poor devils, yes – and yet, weren't they lucky? Perhaps their deaths were more merciful than the deaths that awaited many of the islanders doomed to an excruciating end.

In the middle of the night – I had no idea what time it was but it can't have been all that long since the *Nymph* exploded – I had just finished dressing some minor injuries when I returned to the 'convalescent veranda' for a breath of air. However sulphurous it smelled, it was better outside than in. Everything was so damned hot. I noticed more blisters on the paintwork in one of the wards. Even in Paula's house and in the hospital the heat of the air was so exaggerated that all of us – patients, doctors, nurses alike – were panting with the slightest exertion. When I flopped on to a rattan long-chair to try and decide what to do next, even the chair was hot to the touch. I could feel its heat through my thin slacks.

To make matters worse, I started being bitten by ants – or maybe fleas. I scratched and saw spots on my ankles. They weren't important, only itchy and annoying. But, as I sat there, unable even to enjoy a cigarette because everyone seemed to be coughing, I saw that they *were* ants. Two long columns marched across the veranda floor-boards, like two long rows of an invading army. I grabbed a broom – we always kept a broom in every room – and brushed them through the railings on to the ground below, wondering how they had surmounted the water traps that were attached to the piles supporting almost every building in Koraloona.

As I walked down to investigate, I saw a dreaded scorpion. The few that were supposed to be on Koraloona always stayed on the rocky outcrops of the hillsides. I kicked it before it tried to scuttle away, then went to see why the ant traps weren't working. It was revolting. The water of the traps was filled with thousands of dead ants, and live ones were relentlessly climbing over the drowned bodies and up the stilts. I had a photo-flash in my mind's eye of a picture which, painted soon after the first world war, had shown dead soldiers impaled on barbed wire, and their comrades, clutching rifles, climbing across the corpses to go into the attack.

It was while I was watching the ants that I heard a whimpered 'Help! Help!' from the beach on the other side of the narrow road. It came from the direction of the thin strip of sand between the club and the tiny port – the beach on which I had seen the dead lobsters boiled by the hot sea.

The stone-built house of Paula Reece was still the safest sanctuary, but some of the diehards were still sheltering in the club, though George the barman had long since fled. Yet there were plenty of drinks in the club – and quite a few drinkers, although I was sure nobody was signing chits any more. I hadn't seen Sam Truscott for some time – I had been too busy to look for anyone – and I felt that he might consider drinking himself to death a more pleasant alternative than being burned alive.

Again I heard the piteous cry in the dark – like the last gasp of a man in extreme pain, and I thought that perhaps someone had wandered out of the bar and had been injured or burned by a stray falling red-hot rock or burning ash. Nobody would have heard it in the club with all doors and windows closed against the ash. But someone might have left, for even though we had clean toilets, it was a time-honoured custom for the men late at night 'to water the garden' as they put it.

Once again I heard a faint cry and I was sure I was right. That was not the voice of a Polynesian. Brushing away the ants that were creeping up my trousers by the score, I ran across the road, flashing the small torch that I always carried on my evening rounds since the day, years ago, when the electricity had failed. I didn't really need the torch for the lights in the club were still blazing. But as I swivelled the inquisitive beam it picked out the point from where the cry had come – a body, still half in the lapping waves along the edge of the beach. A white body.

'Coming!' I cried. 'Hang on!'

Dashing across the strip of road, I reached the dripping, crawling form and, falling to my knees, carefully helped to lift the wet bundle of humanity, barely conscious.

It was Dick Holmes.

'Dick!' I cried, half weeping real tears on my ash-caked face at the sight. 'Thank God for you. How did you get here?' I knew he couldn't reply, for that final cry for help had exhausted his last ounce of strength.

'Don't worry, Dick.' I lifted him carefully, his weight increased by the water, though he wore only shorts and a shirt.

Somehow I carried him half way up to the hospital, and shouted, 'Alec!'

At first I didn't recognise the face of the man who rushed down the steps of the veranda to help me. He must have recognised mine, for a disembodied voice asked, 'Me help, Doctor. Me help.'

It was Lee Ho, the 'maid of all work' at Mollie Green's hotel, who had been borrowed as extra help by Paula to assist with cleaning up, washing up and any other chores needed.

'Get Doctor Reid,' I gasped as Lee Ho helped me to lay the body on the veranda steps, where, I noticed almost without realising it, the two columns of ants I had brushed away had now re-formed.

Alec appeared. 'It's Dick Holmes,' I cried.

'By God,' Alec breathed, his eyes streaming and smarting. 'How the devil did the laddie escape?'

'Don't ask me,' I said almost shortly. 'Look at him. He's been burned almost to death.'

'Can I help?' It was Ronnie Serpell.

Almost hysterically I laughed, 'Three doctors at once! First time we've ever had three doctors on duty at the same time.'

'Take it easy, Laddie.' Alec put a restraining hand on my shoulders.

'I'll take over.' Ronnie Serpell's voice had the authority I remembered of the man in uniform and I subsided on a chair for the moment as Serpell added, 'I've had more than my share of treating flash burns.'

Poor Dick Holmes – and I myself to a lesser degree – needed some mild sedative, and Alec managed to force a weak whisky and some precious distilled water through his lips, together with a pill. Then he gave me a drink too. 'Best medicine in the world, Laddie.' He held up the glass, and I sipped the golden liquid gratefully, though it made me cough.

'And Dick? He'll be all right?'

'I hope so,' said Serpell. 'I'm sure he will. He's got third-degree burns on his legs and arms, but he must have the constitution of an ox.'

I was all right after a few moments, the near-hysteria gone and, as I walked over to watch Serpell work skilfully, he said, 'He'll pull through. But we've got to use a basinful of your precious water, to cool off the burns and blisters. They've been caused by his suddenly swimming into patches of boiling water, that's why the burns are on the arms and legs. Swimming! Thank God he was wearing his shorts and underpants and a shirt, so most of his body escaped being badly burned when he swam into sudden patches of hot water. That's what saved him.'

'But he was thrown out by the explosion, do you think?'

'He couldna have been,' objected Alec. 'Not a soul this side of hell – and that's where we are – could'a escaped alive from yon boat.'

'Then what?'

'Give him a day to get over the shock and he'll tell us,' said Serpell practically. He was busy, even as he talked, making repeated applications of cold water on the burned skin – until the water was no longer cold. Then he covered the affected burns with a thick coating of cold cream, spreading it over wherever necessary, then lint and then thick pads of cotton wool, finally bandaging them, to try to keep any air from reaching the burns.

'That's the best we can do,' he said finally. 'I've given him some painkiller and a sleeping tablet and that'll stop him fidgeting for a few hours.' Then we put the four legs of the rattan chair in jars or mugs of water to stop the ants from climbing up and eating the half-dead man on the chair.

The rest of the night was – compared with the terror of the afternoon and evening – reasonably quiet. Sleep was virtually impossible, not only because of the innate fear that haunted every one of us, but because of the sporadic groans and grunts from High Island, but at least for several hours the volcano belched no flame.

With dawn, we could see the huge cloud, narrow at the top then swelling out, still being pushed away from us by an east wind. It looked like the gigantic smoke stack lingering behind a steam engine. Dick Holmes woke up, in some pain but much better though desperately thirsty. It was too early – and too difficult – to go searching for coconuts and we couldn't afford to dole out water, so I gave him the safest drink I could – a Coke, opened with a crown cork opener, pristine as far as contamination was concerned, and with such a narrow opening to the bottle that he was able to gulp it down from the bottle itself after I had washed away the ash-dust.

The burns which he had suffered when swimming through sudden patches of boiling water weren't as bad as they might have been and, after Alec had changed Dick's dressing and smeared on more cold cream, we were able to piece together the events that had led to his sudden appearance on the beach.

He had, as he explained, gone aboard the *Nymph* in the belief that she would sail through the reef into the open sea to try to transmit a short-wave signal, then return to the island to let us know that help would soon be on the way. Holmes then intended to try to repair the clogged set at Anani in the hope that, as the atmosphere cleared, he could get regular signals through.

Not until the *Nymph* had cast off and was half way to the reef did Baker tell him, in rather shame-faced tones: 'Mr Holmes, I felt I owed it to the people of Koraloona to give you a chance to save them, but,' he added heavily, 'I didn't tell Mrs Reece that you would be on board, and I didn't tell you that *she* would also be on board. So you can imagine –' the words tailed off – 'but I *did* feel that the most important thing, forgetting our ultimate destination, was for you to get a word to the outside world.' Baker had made it abundantly clear to Holmes that they were not returning to the island.

As we all knew, Holmes had a very strong sense of duty. It was duty that had persuaded him to board the *Nymph* – but only because he expected to return.

'And I promise you doctors,' he seemed to be apologising, 'even the prospect of freedom from this hell never entered my head. I was horrified.'

'Of course ye were,' Alec soothed his fears. 'Ye dinna need to tell us that.'

Confirmation came when, oblivious to the terror around her, Paula Reece stepped out of the saloon on to the covered deck on the stern of the vessel. That, I thought, must have been the moment when I saw the flutter of a woman's skirt. According to Holmes' recollection Paula turned to Holmes and said, 'Captain Baker has told me why he let you on board without my permission. I understand the reason, but you will have to remain with us until we reach the nearest safe island, perhaps Rarotonga.'

'But,' cried Holmes furiously, 'you're shanghai-ing me!' Sitting up in bed, he added, 'I was furious. I told her that I *had* to get back. She just looked at me, as cool as a cucumber, in spite of her torn dress and the hell all around us, and said, "Then you'd better swim back!" I didn't say one single word. I just went to the gunwale and climbed over it and I heard her shout, "Don't be stupid. I'm giving you a passport to life!" Then I dived straight into the lagoon. I'm a strong swimmer, as you know, and it was no distance, but by God, Doc, I never realised that in places the water was literally boiling.'

'You're lucky to be alive,' I said. 'That's what comes of doing your duty, Dick.'

'Aye, it is that,' Alec agreed. 'Had ye taken the easy way out, ye'd have been as dead as a doornail by noo.'

49

The following day Dick Holmes, at times almost in tears with a mixture of pain, fatigue and frustration, implored me to let Fawcett know that he had managed to get one weak signal through which had been acknowledged; and finally, with some misgivings, I agreed to let Jason go. He could drive my old Ford 8 – if it would start. I didn't want to risk using the jeep, which was sturdier, had a four-wheel drive, but which might be needed in an emergency more serious than just letting Fawcett know. But the old Ford started up with hardly more than its normal preliminary cough.

'More than can be said for us!' Nothing could dampen Purvis' spirit, though by now we were all coughing and spitting.

'But be careful, Jason,' I begged him, moving from foot to foot as I felt the soles of my sandals heat up. 'It's hell out there, and at least here most of our friends are with us.'

'Don't worry about me.' He climbed into the driving seat. 'I can still remember where the clutch is.'

'Honestly Jason, be *serious*. I'm giving you an *order*. If you smash my car up and I can't get the jeep to work, we'll be sunk. So go there – report – and I'll expect you back right away.'

Suddenly serious himself, Jason said, 'I'm not a complete fool, Kit. I'm also going in case anyone in Anani is ill, and I can bring them back for hospital treatment.'

As he was about to set off, Lorna, who must have seen us walking to the 'garage', rushed up, oblivious to the hot ash. It did my heart good to see how she kissed him on the lips with great love and said, deliberately loud enough for me to hear, yet not embarrassed, 'Remember, my husband, God will protect and bring you back to me.'

'I will,' he promised and then added, 'I love you, young lady, so God be with you too. And cross your fingers in case it's true.' He gave her a huge wink.

'Really, Jason!' If Lorna hadn't been covered in grey dust, she would have blushed. We both watched him drive slowly down the incline towards the main road, and then she said to me in her almost matter-of-fact, 'Sister Sowerby' voice, as though she was talking about a patient: 'It's possible that I am pregnant. It will make Jason very happy if it's true.'

I had hardly time to mumble 'Congratulations!' – this was no time for a jocular 'It seems to be catching!' – before she said, almost severely, 'I must get back to my rounds, Doctor.' The use of the word 'doctor' was her way of telling me 'I'm on duty now.'

The early morning passed in comparative calm. The mountain rumbled from time to time, and the black, sulphurous cloud, having drifted from the east, hung in a pall over the western tip of the island and for miles over the lagoon and beyond the reef.

There was nothing we could do but carry on, trying to help the injured, hoping that the early blast would not be repeated, knowing that we had to wait for our little corner of the earth to settle and cool down. Everywhere was desolation. Those trees still standing were dusted with a whitish grey, giving them an eerie resemblance to a Christmas tree covered with artificial snow to make it look more attractive. I could see that the road east to Tala-Tala, which led to Tabanea, was littered with either uprooted trees or large branches that had snapped off with the weight of ash.

Even our 'airfield' was cluttered with broken branches and something else – scores of dead birds everywhere and I couldn't tell how they had died. Some looked burned, others as though they had just dropped dead, perhaps too heavy to fly, or been tossed up in sudden bursts of steam, or struck by the jagged lightning which pierced the occasional eruptions of black smoke. It was some time before Mitchell, who came to join me and watch, realised that the slurries of ash and water, with occasional tiny rivulets of red-hot lava, followed pre-set paths.

Explaining the obvious – that 'what goes up must come down' – the sudden fires or surges of boiling water took the line of least resistance. 'It follows the undulations in the land, the small gorges on Koraloona.' He pointed out the sharp divisions between different hills around us. 'Those valleys get the left-overs of the eruption,' was his way of putting it. 'That's why Tala-Tala has mostly escaped any serious torrent of boiling water turning into mud. It goes somewhere else!'

It made sense. A few stragglers from the Tabanea area said that the settlement had been overwhelmed with a huge, swift tide of mud, molten ash, boiling water, which had hit the hills above Tabanea and swept down into the valley below. Those who escaped had been working in the fields, and some had been able to watch, powerless, for the few minutes during which the mud river rushed past them with a mighty roar and swept out to sea only a few yards from them. These lucky ones had escaped, though one worker in the fields nearest to the slurry died without being touched. His lava-lava and sandals unburned, he died instantly from the intense heat as the slurry swept past him. I could only wonder what other areas, on the opposite coast of Koraloona even nearer to High Island which it faced directly, had been overwhelmed. There must have been twenty or thirty settlements in that area which I had only visited occasionally, as during the cholera epidemic.

Soon we had to contend with a new and horrifying side-effect of the eruption, which had started with the death of the birds, and heralded the first panic in Koraloona's modest animal life.

We had never thought much about animal life on Koraloona. The villagers kept their scrawny farmyard fowls and goats, and there were a lot of semi-wild pigs; but though the pasture was lush there were no cattle or horses. Goats and coconuts replaced cows; and as for ploughing and sowing, teams of islanders took turns to pull primitive wooden ploughs.

Ants, though, had always been the most serious pest, together with a few small lizards and the occasional chameleon lurking invisibly among the leaves of taro.

Suddenly the larger animals were threatened by a new terror – not the volcano so much as the ants and scorpions. I could hardly believe it as I saw pigs, hens, goats in their scores stampede towards the water's edge, the pigs squealing with terror, and then, as I watched them, run straight into the sea.

It was only when a few half-crazed small piglets died before they reached the water that Mitchell pointed to them and explained: 'That's why they died – bitten to death by foot-long scorpions, or driven insane with ants and centipedes. Their only hope was to try and wash the insects off their bodies.'

Now I realised why the ants, as I had already noticed, were invading the buildings. The heat on the hillsides was driving ants, scorpions, centipedes, even a few snakes, away and down into the valleys. In their own fight for survival, the ants relentlessly attacked larger animals. They were trying to climb up anything that would free them from ground level – including animal legs and (as I saw later) children's legs.

Somehow we had to isolate the hospital and Paula's house – in effect, now the hospital annexe – from an invasion by insect life.

But how? My mind had been so bruised by events, and I was so used to scratching myself, that I hadn't realised, until I saw the pigs swimming to death, how the insect 'invasion' could overwelm us if we didn't take urgent action. Now, even as I looked around, the ants were swarming towards us in their millions and the scorpions in their thousands. I had only seen the vanguard.

The chance remark by Mitchell about the mud and lava rivers following the valley paths made me realise that animal instinct had made the insect world swarm towards Tala-Tala because it seemed to be safe. No valley led down to it, but there were dozens of valleys on either side, such as the ones down to Tabanea and the large one leading from the orange grove above Anani. We, on the other hand, were partly protected, and instinctively the ants knew this – and were about to overwhelm us.

It was Serpell who suggested the only possible course of action. We roped in everyone we could – including patients not too badly injured – to clean the hospital floors and all the ground around the buildings, by brushing them towards the sea. We had our own brooms, but we also made extra brooms from the few branches of coconut fronds, flailing the insects away. Those that refused, those that stuck to the brushes, were doused in the sea across the road.

This was only a temporary measure. New ants replaced the old ones in next to no time. We had to prevent any more getting in. Serpell said, 'We had an invasion of ants when we liberated a small island in the Pacific early in the war. Two men committed suicide because, during the night, after they'd taken sleeping pills, they were covered with ants the next day.'

'So what did you do?' I asked.

'How much lubricating oil and diesel oil have we got?' he asked.

'Plenty,' replied Alec. 'The last shipload brought us enough barrels to last six months.'

'Thank God for that,' said Serpell. 'If we can make a semi-circle around the back and sides of the hospital, with the sea completing the circle, we can use as many barrels as we can spare and douse the area around the buildings with a protective barrier, sticky and lethal, like a moat.'

I was wondering about our stocks.

'Don't be frightened to use almost all the stocks we've got.' Serpell read my thoughts. 'Even if the ants force their

714

way through the first layer of sticky oil, we'll pour on more and more.'

'And the generator?'

'Don't let it worry you. Help must be on the way, and anyway the generator won't last another week unless we cool it off.'

'Well, some ship or plane somewhere will have seen the activity and reported it,' said Mitchell. 'Sooner or later some plane or vessel will come and investigate. And of course the seismologists at their monitoring points will have detected the activity with their instruments and meters. So we're not isolated to all that extent. It's just a question of hanging on.'

I was too exhausted – and itchy – to agree or argue, but I did ask one last question: 'And the danger of fire?'

'Highly dangerous,' Walter Mitchell put an arm on my shoulder, 'but I agree with Commander Serpell. It's a risk we've got to take because, if this bugger erupts in our direction, we'd all be dead in seconds, anyway.'

'Aye,' Alec nodded when we all looked to him for approval because he was, after all, senior medical officer. 'Ye've got to take a chance if ye're nae going to lose out.'

So we did that. And though I knew that eventually the ants would willingly climb through the deadly oil and die on the sticky barrier, it would give us a respite, and then, if necessary, we would repeat the process; and, after all, Holmes had managed to get a weak signal through; and apart from that, the effects of the volcano must have been visible hundreds of miles away – and certainly in Sanders-town. Maybe planes would fly in and drop supplies, or at least signal us that they knew we were in trouble.

'Not yet,' said Truscott, who, after toiling at the hospital and snatching a few hours' rest, had rejoined us and was helping to pour out the barrels of oil. 'Too much turbulence to get near the island. One burst of flame or steam and that'd be the end of an aircraft. They'll have to wait a bit.'

In fact Truscott was wrong. Half way through the

morning when it was comparatively quiet, and I was trying
to force a slug of neat whisky down my burning throat – it
was the only breakfast I would get that day – I heard a cry
from outside the Union Jack Club and in dashed Aleena,
who normally never came to the club alone, and with dress
torn, face dirty and streaked with ash, shouted, 'We're
saved! A plane!'

Oblivious to the danger of unexpected fire-stones hitting
us, we all ran out to see what was happening. And on the
beach next to the club all eyes – shielded as best we could
from the dust – looked upwards.

Yes, there was a plane. It might not 'save' us as Aleena
had cried, for it could not land and there was no way we
could leave the roaring mountain that threatened us, but
still – people *knew* about us, were going to help us. It was a
sign. The plane circled out to sea, then dipped its wings in
turn.

'That sign's for us!' cried Truscott.

'What do you mean, sign?' asked Mrs Fawcett.

'The waggling of the wings. It's a sort of international
sign among pilots that they know about us.'

Suddenly, as we watched, the plane swooped low, almost
over the beach.

'The guy must be crazy,' cried Truscott. 'Hell! He must
have come down to two thousand feet. Look at him!'

The aircraft did seem to 'stagger' in the air, to halt, to slip
sideways, but it didn't dive into the ground as we feared.
Instead, nose up, it started to bank away from the island
towards the open sea, but just as it did so, just as the plane
turned away from us, something fell out.

Our eyes blurred, Father Pringle cried, 'The Lord
protect us. He's fallen out.'

'It canna be a man,' shouted Alex and as he spoke,
Aleena squeezed my arm, held my hand tightly with
excitement as Truscott shouted, 'Hell's bells – it's a
goddamn parachute!'

It was. The parachute floated down gently as the plane
flew away, and landed, a crumpled heap of silk holding

a large burlap sack within three feet of our protective anti-ant ring of oil.

In his excitement, Father Pringle led the way to retrieve the parachute, his soutane hitched up his bony legs. He wore his 'uniform' as he called it, because he had to be on hand all the time to bury people or console the dying. The men followed and between us we carried back a heavy bag into the clubhouse. It contained a message, 'Hang on. More to follow' and the most precious cargo of all – water, dozens of unbreakable bottles of pure water, together with antibiotic sulpha pastilles for sore throats and some new inhalers which the accompanying instructions advised us would help to disperse 'foreign bodies', which I took to mean ash-dust which all of us, despite trying to cover our mouths with handkerchiefs, still inhaled. There were some other items too, but it was the water we needed.

I noticed, back in the club, that Father Pringle was hobbling badly.

'What's the trouble?' I asked him.

'My feet,' he confessed. 'They're one mass of blisters.'

They were. He had walked without heeding the heat, which I tried to minimise by treading gently when I had to walk outside, so that it looked as though I was almost dancing. And of course I changed the position of my feet all the time. Father Pringle had not been so prudent, so I washed his feet in the coldest water I could find, applied cold cream and wrapped them up.

'We'll have to do something about all our feet,' I said to Alec. 'Or none of us will be able to walk.'

For it was only after the effort of carrying in the parachute bag that I realised how badly Father Pringle had been burned – and that if I didn't do something, my own feet would begin to burn badly enough to cause blisters – then I would be a patient, not a doctor.

Alec tried his best. 'I'll put a wee bit of cream on your feet, and ye can do the same for me.' He was gasping with the exertion of helping to carry the supplies. 'It's nae a solution but every little helps.'

717

'We need something different – stronger, to beat the ash.'

Alec looked at me, almost resigned. 'Tell me, Kit,' he wiped the cream on the soles of my feet, 'd'ye think we'll ever come out of this alive? Or is this the end of our world?' He was slurring his r's.

'Of course it'll be okay.' I tried to be cheerful. 'I don't know how, but we've *got* to, Alec. If only for Aleena.'

'Sometimes I wonder if it's worth it,' he sighed. 'Paula got out of it without knowing a thing about it. One moment alive, the next dead. That's the best way to gang.'

'Balls!' I said, knowing that in one way I did envy Paula's swift exit from life.

Yet it is astonishing, the ingenuity of man faced with impossible odds. It was – as might be expected – Walter Mitchell who devised a method of walking on hot ash.

'I've got the answer,' he croaked. 'Snow shoes!'

For a moment I thought he had gone out of his mind. More and more of the locals had become slightly deranged and soon it would be the turn of mature whites to lose their reason.

'Waiting for the weather to change?' Truscott asked facetiously.

'Stupid bugger!' croaked an angry Mitchell.

'Tell us more,' I asked him more gently.

'Enlarging the area of our feet – like snow shoes do, even if they're only made of strings like a racquet – enables you to walk *on* instead of *into* snow. And desert. And ash.'

'But even if we did have snow shoes, they'd burn,' I said.

'Not mine!' Though Mitchell was in agony because he had a burned throat, he was obviously so proud of his idea that he almost managed a leer of triumph.

What he said, even though it was interrupted by his protracted bouts of coughing, and by moments when he found it hard to breathe and had to spit blood, was, in plain language, as follows: 'We'll have to knock down the partition dividing the laundry from the dish-washing scullery.'

Again we all thought he was going crazy, and I saw an angry curl on the face of the impatient Truscott.

'Shut up,' I said to him, for all our nerves were jangled by now. 'Give him a chance.'

'Goddamn fool – and pessimist.'

'He *was* right,' I put in mildly.

The two rooms which he mentioned were adjacent because of the plumbing arrangements. They had been separated because obviously we didn't want soiled hospital linen mixed in with dirty dishes. Elementary hygiene. Though what a partition wall had to do with snow shoes was beyond me. Even Serpell asked, 'Why do you want to knock down a hardboard wall?'

Mitchell's explanation was brilliant. All hardboard walls – the sort we used for partition walls in the hospital – were in those days made of compressed asbestos – not only cheap, but useful against fire hazard. If we could cut a wall of hardboard up into rectangles, roughly two feet by eighteen inches, and find a way of using them as 'platform shoes', we would be able to move slowly but still less painfully across the hot ash, on it instead of sinking into it.

All of us must have contributed to the finished product. First we smashed down a wall by hammering out the angle brackets. No time for niceties like screwdrivers. Then we marked the wall into rectangles.

We had to cut or saw these into shape – and nobody seemed to know where the carpentry tools were – if there were any; usually we called on Jim Wilson for that sort of thing, but he was in Anani. Serpell obliged with the next best thing. He went into the surgery and returned with two bone saws – tougher than ordinary saws, for they had to be able to cut through anything when amputating major bones like the thigh. It was macabre, watching a surgeon at work, and I was glad that even 'Sister Sowerby' was not present. Soon we had a series of fireproof 'platforms'. Now we had to devise a way of fastening them to our shoes.

Alec thought that one out, by fetching two of the specially hardened surgical drills – rather like ordinary drills, but manually operated with a wheel and handle at the side. They have always been regularly used among other operations for drilling holes through shin bones in order to insert pins that stick out at each side of the leg in order to attach ropes and weights to put a leg into traction and slowly lengthen broken and shortened legs.

The drills were so tough that it was easy to penetrate half a dozen pieces of hardboard at the same time, on either side of where the ankle would be, then again in front of the toes. With a little stainless-steel wire, we could fasten the platform around a shoe.

It wasn't simple to walk, but nobody intended to walk far and as we shambled like creatures from another world, at least we prevented our feet from getting burned.

Everyone was exhausted, especially following the effort to surround the hospital grounds with oil, and most of the men made straight for the club – and a well-earned drink if they were still able to pass fiery alcohol through burned and clogged throats.

'You coming along?' asked Serpell.

I shook my head. 'Better do the rounds first with Alec,' I said, 'but I'll be in later.' All the same I did first help Father Pringle to walk across the street from the dispensary to the club.

It was strange, the feeling almost of unreality once you entered the club, as if the members were determined to carry on as though nothing – not even an earthquake – were allowed to interfere with their way of life. Lee Ho was helping at the bar, and all drinks were free while stocks lasted. Mrs Fawcett and three ladies were sitting in basketwork chairs. I seated Father Pringle down carefully – he found it difficult to walk because of the padding we had wrapped round his feet – and asked Serpell to give him a shot of Scotch.

'I'll be back in half an hour,' I promised. Not all one's promises can be kept, unfortunately.

Alec and I and Lorna were in the ward near the main road when suddenly the sky started to darken again.

'In the middle of the day!' I groaned. 'What will we ever do if the electricity packs up?'

'Dinna be despondent, Laddie. It could be worse.'

As I muttered 'I doubt it,' I was looking out to sea, when the darkness burst into the vivid scarlet of an eruption. The flames were blinding, the crash of thunder deafening. Almost at the same moment a white-hot boulder larger than usual hit the tin roof of the building opposite with a crash that shook our prefabricated wards.

'The club!' I cried and ran down the steps. The building was drenched with liquid flame. Though it did have stout stone walls, it had been filled with wood – basket chairs, tables, wooden veranda and so on, and in seconds it was a blazing inferno.

I saw a couple of figures stagger out, falling but apparently unharmed, followed by another, a man, then another, this time a woman, who was one sheet of flame from head to toe. The screams were terrible, mingling with the crackling of wood, the shattering of bottles of alcohol exploding, and I was so near the building that the heat singed me. Yet the speed of the catastrophe was such that, within a minute, it was virtually all over. I caught myself thinking, Thank God Aleena and her mother are in Paula's house, helping the coughing cases. But at the same time, all passing through my mind as I watched, almost spellbound, I was also thinking that, at any moment, this could happen to Paula's house too.

In the hospital, patients crowded to the doors and windows to watch.

'Get back to your beds!' I shouted, but they took no notice. They were afraid. I had seen the same fear on people's faces as they waited in hospital for the verdicts from surgeons who had been operating on mothers and fathers.

Only three people escaped, and they must have been the nearest to the door. The first, who fell out – or, it later transpired, was pushed out by Sam Truscott – was Mrs Fawcett. The second was Sam who had undoubtedly saved the woman's life. Mitchell staggered out, half in flames. All the others perished.

The remains of three other women were charred and unrecognisable. Father Pringle, Lee Ho, and Serpell had died too – poor Serpell, who had come to see the hospital which he had so generously helped to make possible.

I dashed in to get a blanket and somehow managed to stifle Mitchell's flaming body. As though it were a farce, I heard Mrs Fawcett, who wasn't hurt apart from her fall in the dirt, cry plaintively, 'My teeth. I can't find my teeth.' Sam was virtually uninjured, thank God. We needed him, and he helped me carry Mitchell into the hospital where Alec started to treat his burns.

Like all of us, Sam was filthy, his eyes scarcely visible beneath rinds of congealed dirt, his clothes smouldering where cinders had burnt them, his ankles swollen and probably infected with the mud that had entered through the weals left by burns.

Mrs Fawcett had lost not only her false teeth, but most of her hair, though she hardly noticed as she scrabbled around looking for her teeth. Once the undisputed female leader of the club, she had been transfigured into a toothless crone apparently resurrected from a tomb a thousand years old.

Lorna rushed in and fell into the sludge so that she too appeared to have been dragged from a dustbin; and her hair, moving like tentacles, had taken on a life of its own. But it was a bat. It had swooped in desperation and was trapped in her hair, squeaking furiously. I wrenched it from her and trod it on the floor with a shudder.

As for myself, God knows how ghastly I must have looked. There was congealed blood on my arms, face, and feet and an ooze of something was trickling down my forehead and lodging in my two-day growth of beard. It was that which reminded me of the time element; and as if in response Sam looked blearily towards a rift in the plume of smoke.

'Sun's kinda high. Must be noon-time.' Suddenly I thought: Jason's been gone two hours at least. I knew I

722

must go and look for him. Perhaps Sam would be able to help, but I could only make a quick dash, for the loss of Serpell had robbed us of a third doctor. I couldn't leave Alec alone for too long. If anything were to happen to him . . .

There was, however, one other thing to be done first. The fire at the club had frightened the wits out of me – the speed with which a solid building had burned down, until only one wall was left standing and on it, as I looked at the smoking remains, was the one notice: 'No singlets, no thongs'. The same thing *could* happen to Paula's house, or to the hospital. We must have some sanctuary against the wrath of the gods, some last place to hide until help came.

We knew now that help would be on the way once the volcano stopped erupting – and even Mitchell had at first said that this was only a minor eruption and wouldn't last long.

When I went into the 'annexe' to see how Tiare and Aleena were, I found them frightened but defiant. Does that sound ridiculous? They were no more frightened than I was – half of me was convinced we would die in the end – but they were not frightened enough to run away from their duty.

'How are the patients?' I asked.

'Much better,' Tiare replied. 'Me too. It's almost as though we've come to terms with the dust – acclimatised – or perhaps there's less dust.'

'There's more water. That helps. We've got plenty now, and we know that there'll soon be more on the way. But I'm frightened this building will blow up.'

'What can we do?' asked Tiare gently.

'How many coughing cases have we got?' I asked.

'Half a dozen coughing blood, but they're slowly getting better.'

'And you, Aleena. You're better too?' And when she nodded, I asked, 'The cough patients – can they walk?'

'They could,' said Tiare. 'But where to?'

I was not asking an idle question. I had had an idea.

'There's only one place in this part of the island – perhaps in the entire island – where you could be safe from fire – and probably breathe purer air.'

'Where?' asked Aleena.

I hesitated for a moment, then turned to Tiare. 'The secret pool that Gauguin and your mother discovered.'

'*The secret pool!*' Even amidst all the inferno, Aleena whispered as though it was sacred.

'Of course.' It was Aleena who spoke. 'Behind the waterfall, in the rock cave behind the waterfall. The water falls in an arc. It's dry in the cave behind the falling water.'

'And that water probably acts as a curtain against the worst of the ash,' I said. 'You see, it falls straight into the pool, and you and the women patients could shelter behind it. Will you lead the women there, Tiare?'

Looking almost bewildered Tiare whispered, 'I don't think I can.'

'Listen,' I urged her. 'I've got to go now and find out what's happened to Jason. He's gone to Anani to see Colonel Fawcett. But first, I'll drive you all in two loads along the road to the path leading to the pool. It's only half a mile. You can take all the asbestos shoes and fit them on when you start to climb the path. And each can carry a bottle of water and some tinned food. Could you do that?'

Tiare was almost beyond words. She just nodded, as though leaving fate in other hands. But Aleena knew that I was right. Apart from the foul air, the cave, with its narrow ledge leading to the cave under the waterfall, *was* the nearest thing we had to a fireproof dwelling.

I explained what I planned to do to Alec and Sam, then collected all the asbestos shoes I could find and set off with the first batch of six women crowded into the jeep. It started up straight away – as I had felt sure this sturdy workhorse would – and made light of the half-mile trip. The women managed to clamber out and as they marched off, almost like in a Biblical scene, up the narrow path, I turned the jeep round and set off again to collect the second load.

After they too had reached the path leading to the pool, I had to start thinking about finding Jason.

Once back at the hospital, and as I looked at the smoking ruins of our clubhouse – scene of so much happiness – I told Alec, 'I must go and see what's happened to Jason.'

Bewildered, the heart torn out of him, Alec just said, 'If that's what ye think best, Laddie.'

'You must give me permission.' I tried to jerk him back to reality. 'After all, you're the boss! I'm just afraid that Jason might not be able to get back.' Vaguely I added, 'The car – it's old. And there may be more patients.'

'Aye, best go and see. But take a bottle of water along. Ye might run into trouble with someone who needs a helping hand. And best have someone with ye.'

'I'll take Sam Truscott. He's still a bit groggy, but he's tough, and if the jeep does stall, at least pilots have to take a course in elementary engineering and he might be able to fix it.'

I explained the situation to Sam.

'Tiare's led the less injured to a safe place, and the jeep started almost at the first press of the button. What a machine! The greatest invention of the war.'

'Except the atom bomb.' Truscott tried to give me an ironic grin.

'Not funny,' I replied angrily. 'Don't joke about that bloody thing – with all these dead people around.'

'Jeez, I know. I'm sorry, pal.'

We set off slowly along the main road to Anani, and though the ash was thick, we could drive fairly easily, except that the road was littered with overblown, dead animals, even dead snakes, and every now and again we had to drive around corpses. I couldn't tell who they were. Many were burned beyond recognition. Others had their faces and bodies contorted with horror in the moment before death released them, so that their twisted features bore no resemblance even to patients I might have treated in the past. Anguish had stripped away their identities.

'Where the shit will it all end?' asked Sam helplessly.

'Maybe the worst is over,' I said hopefully.

'Maybe.' Then suddenly, 'Look – what's that?'

Even through the dust haze I could recognise it. It was my old Ford 8, half a mile or so ahead.

We had gone perhaps a very slow mile – even less – towards Anani, and I could clearly recognise the car, but I couldn't be sure if it was moving, though I prayed that it was.

'Can't be certain.' Sam shaded his eyes the better to peer ahead. 'But I guess it looks as though it's stalled.'

That was my worst fear. 'Come on!' I cried though I was doing the driving. I grabbed the green knob of the jeep's four-wheel drive lever. 'We've not a second to lose.'

As we bumped over the road, uneven because of rocks and torn branches, the distant image of the car came into sharper focus, as though I had adjusted my binoculars until they produced a bright, sharp, enlarged image. As I pressed the horn, I caught sight of a hand, held up for an instant in an attempt to wave. Then the arm fell down.

'It's Jason,' I cried. 'Thank God he's alive.'

Jamming the jeep to a stop with a mounting sense of urgency and foreboding, I lumbered across to the Ford. I knew one thing from that feeble wave: Jason was at his last gasp. Thank goodness the Ford was an open car with a hood which we usually kept up as a shield from the sun. I undid it in a moment and together we tried to lift Jason out of the front seat, into the back, where he wouldn't be trapped by the steering wheel. Without warning he opened his eyes, first with a blank look until I said, 'It's me, Jason. Here to take you back to Lorna.' I took out the bottle of water and held it to his lips. 'Take a sip of this,' I urged him.

He didn't have the power in his swollen, blistered lips to open them, and it was clear that his larynx was almost choked with ash. His breath came in great agonising gasps as he forced it out of his lungs through the blockage. I wiped his lips with a little water, tried to force some through. He didn't even notice, though he opened his eyes occasionally.

'Come and help me, Sam. I can't do this alone.' I, too, was gasping with the effort.

'He looks mighty bad,' said Sam.

I nodded my head. 'Our only hope is to try and force a passage through his throat with some water. Try and pull his mouth open.'

It needed rough treatment, but Sam did manage to wrench the lower jaw down and I poured in the equivalent of a glass of water. Most of it bubbled out of his mouth and down his shirt. The throat was partially blocked.

'He'll never make it,' I said to Truscott, holding up the bottle again and trying once more. At least the feel of water in his mouth must have soothed the agony. We stood there, helpless. My face felt as though it was drawn physically with the agony of watching the slow death of a man I had grown to love and admire, watching the lolling figure helplessly against a desolate backdrop of filthy water in the lagoon on one side, and stunted trees, burned undergrowth, dead animals all round us on the other. The agony of poor Jason, the effort each time to draw a miserable apology for a breath, made the salt tears come.

People talk about a doctor's impersonal tenderness, but seeing Jason now brought back the moment I had first seen him, a starving, bedraggled beachcomber in the garden of Harley Street. It was as though the wheel had turned full circle, for now he looked like that again, tall, emaciated through the effort of living. It was as though nothing had happened in between, as though all his achievements – as a reformed drunk, as a writer, as a happily married man – had never existed, as though it had all been a dream. But it wasn't. It *had* happened, it was true. It had been no dream. But now there was a nightmare. If I had carried my medical kit I would have given him an overdose of morphia immediately, to speed his death.

Jason opened his eyes and tried to croak out a few words.

I didn't have to tell him to prepare for death. He knew. But there was something he wanted to tell me. Sam Truscott stood holding one hand. I moistened his lips with water as he tried to speak.

I had to lean close to his mouth to listen to the few guttural, disjointed sounds. 'Forgot . . . publisher . . . dedicate book . . . Lorna.'

I understood.

'I will,' I promised him. 'I will write to tell them that you want the book dedicated "To Lorna with love."'

He was past words now, but he did manage to press a tired hand on to my arm to show his gratitude. Then I thought of the only words that might comfort his last moments of life.

'Will you let me be godfather to your baby?'

For a moment his eyes lit up with a sense of pleasure, happiness, gratitude, I'm not sure what. He stuttered, coughed, then he sighed and was dead.

I was in tears, I am not ashamed to admit it. No doubt the Dantesque eeriness of the scene, the helplessness, all contributed to my emotional instability and my lack of 'professional conduct' for I had seen so many people die but even now I knew that death had ended his agony, that I should be grateful he would no longer suffer, I couldn't stop the tears.

Truscott carried him into the back of the jeep as reverently as he could. I walked away from the Ford – and almost fell as I stumbled over something.

Half covered with a thin dusting of ash was a flat, thin rectangle. I brushed the ash away with my sleeve.

It was 'Pink Street', my picture, and incredibly it was undamaged. Poor Jason must have wasted precious minutes on his way back climbing to my bungalow to rescue my most prized possession.

We set off slowly, and then I suddenly realised that an extraordinary curtain of invisible heat in the atmosphere was stifling us. There was nothing to see – only a vague feeling of terrible anticipation, like an orchestra in the pit playing before the curtain goes up on a tragedy.

The windscreen was blackened with smoke and filth and I pushed it down with my fist. Along the bonnet paint bubbled in ominous liquid blisters. There was a smell of burning. I realised that the tyres had begun to melt in the heat and that I was driving on the rims of the wheels, though the engine kept going. Sweat poured from every pore in my body and I could feel my hair and eyebrows scorching. Yet there was nothing to see. I felt on the seat behind me for something to wrap round my head, hoping to prevent my hair from actually bursting into flames; but there was nothing there. I recall shouting to Sam, who was also panting, 'I'm an incandescent man and – '

I never finished the sentence because the most cataclysmic explosion of the eruption suddenly rocked the entire island. It was far, far worse than anything before. I felt the ground tremble, and the jeep's wheels leave the ground then settle back as a series of thunderous detonations nearly threw me out of the jeep, and the steam and smoke far above was seared by incessant jagged lightning. A fearful hot wind hurled itself across the island, tearing out trees by the roots, then tumbling in chaotic confusion on the ground between the jeep and Anani, gathering force and speed like a Cresta Run toboggan out of control. Then, further away – perhaps three miles or so ahead, I thought later – the searing fire spouting out of High Island seemed to be duplicated half way up the hillside above Anani. A roaring flame tore across the plateau and we both knew where it was – the large wild orange groves above the township.

The entire 'forest' of oranges was a wall of fire which engulfed the plateau. Gouts of molten lava fell, cooled by the air as they were flung free from the crater. Egg-shaped rocks, still white-hot, bombarded the town. And at the edge of the flaming grove, the earth – or what we could see of it on the hillside ahead – seemed to change into a red bubbling river as the molten lava flowed down the hillside on the surface of streams or beds of dried small rivers. From the distance I could see the menacing tides of fire approaching as gigantic bursts of flame curved across the water and on the land. Yet as I looked towards Tala-Tala, there was nothing but smoke.

Anani was different. I not only saw but heard the beginning of a scarlet avalanche as it poured a rain of fire, steam or boiling water down from the plateau, a red river, small at first, small as though poured out of the lip of a jug, but getting larger every second, down the valley along which, so long ago, Lucy and I had climbed up, and then down and into the warmth of our bed. How strange, sitting there in the jeep beside her husband, that, at this particular moment, I should have such a clear flashing picture of Lucy.

I could not see the actual downwards path of the hill, but I could remember it and realise what was happening. In my mind's eye I could see the slurry forming, the mud slide, the fire river.

'Let's get back.' I was trembling. 'I can't stand the sight of this.' But as we jumped into the jeep with our grisly cargo we saw what looked like the explosion of a gigantic fireball and then – though we could not see everything – I *could* see flames soaring from the wooden pier and hear the crackle of wooden houses in the heart of the town.

Both of us looked at the flames with horror. The whole of Anani seemed to be bursting with fire and explosions.

'Jesus wept!' Sam was almost in tears, the first to break the silence as though we had been too afraid to talk. 'That must have started in the goddamn orange grove and then – '

I knew what he was trying to say. It had started there, burning everything with fire, showering the town with white-hot stone and then it had started to cascade down, merciless fingers probing for an exit until in the end, rushing with increasing speed through the entire cleft in the hills above, ruthlessly hitting the town broadside on, it had

730

set fire to everything and suffocated or burned everyone to death in its path.

Unseen details – but sounds we could hear – filled in the gaps of the disaster from which there could have been no escape. Sudden explosions from ground level – they could have been oil drums or barrels of inflammable materials in Jim Wilson's shop, or tins of paraffin in Johnson's store. And from time to time there was a loud but distant sound of hissing.

'That's where the river of slurry has crossed Main Street,' I thought aloud, 'and hit the waves on the beach.'

'Any chance of helping?'

I shook my head. 'Not a hope. Apart from anything else everything would be too hot – even waves on the beach would be scalding. There'll be no way to get into the town for a few hours. It's the end of Anani. And everyone in it.'

Only a miracle had saved those still alive in Tala-Tala, for I realised that the filth and flames thrown up from High Island had to fall *somewhere* – and fate, in the shape of a deep ravine above Anani, had sent the wrath of the volcano in that direction, while we were protected because there was no easy way for any lava to settle above us and overwhelm us.

'There was a second miracle too,' I said to Sam as we drove off on the rims of our wheels. 'It's ironic but if Paula hadn't decided to hold her lunch party, most of her guests would have been in Anani – and dead by now. It was Paula who saved our lives.'

50

Four days had passed without as much as a grunt or grumble from High Island, and the smoke rising from its crater was whiter now, and slowly the air was becoming less sulphurous and the ash cooler except near the country trails where tiny rivers of molten lava had run.

Yet, though planes dropped supplies daily, we still couldn't believe that it was over. We had more supplies than we needed for the entire island – medical supplies, drugs, bandages, anti-burn ointment, plus gallons of pure water in sealed containers, together with powdered milk, tinned food for those who could eat it. Thoughtfully someone had sent in packet jellies and that old standby of invalids, the nutritious calf's foot jelly, which could easily slide down sore or burned throats.

Messages floated down too, though I felt an unfair irritation that parachutes couldn't send messages upwards! If only we could send word to worried relations! But the messages that reached us were reassuring, that ships were due to sail any day now, that scientists believed the worst was over, so that after the third day of inactivity, I drove my clanking jeep on the rims of its wheels to the secret pool, and in two trips brought out to Paula's house the women who had stayed there – all but one.

The cave of purer air had done wonders to improve the women's health but as I prepared to drive the second group back Aleena took my arm gently and asked, 'Could you manage a third trip in the jeep? So that we could drive back alone. I haven't seen you alone for so long.'

It was true. We had lived a lifetime of terror in a few hours, and I had hardly seen her except as one of a group, all of us wondering how much longer we had to live. I nodded, smiled, and stroked her cheek.

'Of course, wait here,' I whispered, and explained to a slightly mystified Tiare, 'You understand? This is the first time we feel *safe* – and we've never had a moment alone, but I'll be back in a few minutes.'

After I had taken Tiare and the others back to Tala-Tala, I returned to the pool, climbed up the now familiar path, and she was waiting – grubby perhaps, but still beautiful and, no words needed, I took her into my arms. We could not kiss, even clumsily, for my lips were badly blistered, but we held each other close and then I said, 'If only we could swim in Gauguin's secret pool – but I daren't. Even though it does run away from the waterfall into the sea, I'm afraid of contamination.'

Longingly I looked at the pool below. 'You see,' I pointed, 'there were always a few water lilies there, but now they're dead.'

As she nodded, I had a sudden moment of inspiration. 'But we *could* have a shower if you like.'

She looked at me, puzzled, and I pointed to a spot further along the ledge, beyond the dryness of the cave. There, the inside of the waterfall hit the rock while the outer edge of the waterfall cascaded straight into the pool.

'And if there's still any volcanic ash pouring down the falls from the hills above, it'll obviously be on the outer side of the waterfall.'

Hugging me, she said with mock seriousness, 'Doctor Masters, you are not only a wonderful husband but a genius. Come, let's.'

I had no thought but of the opportunity to try and cleanse my body, because the supplies we received by air had not so far included any clothing. And after all, we were an 'old married couple' now, my wife expecting a baby. Yet despite all that we had passed through, the agony of seeing people die, of losing one of my closest friends, I felt the impulse of physical love surging through me as, with the innocence of the Polynesian, she pulled the bedraggled dress over her head and then stepped out of her tiny American-style panties and stood there, arms raised and asked gently, 'Do you still love me – even like this?'

'More than ever,' I replied, but this time not croaking from dust and ash, but with the hoarseness of sudden passion. And because we were an 'old married couple' with no secrets I added, laughingly, 'You'll see for yourself in a second.'

With that as I prepared to walk along the ledge, I slid out of my tattered trousers and she whispered, 'Yes, you *do* love me. How beautiful.'

For a moment we stood, bodies touching from our faces to our feet, and as I stroked her thighs she let one of her hands drop to touch me and said, as she did so, 'It's so wonderful to be able to show your feelings like this. Do you remember that time in the Southern Cross Hotel before we were *really* lovers? Do you remember?'

'Of course.'

'It's like that now, isn't it?'

'Yes it is because, though it seems awful – terrible at a time like this – I *do* want to show my love for you. But we can't.'

'Because of the baby?'

'Yes. When this is all over. Alec will have to make absolutely certain that it is safe – for both of you.'

'I know, beloved. But,' shy, though the innuendo was, it was determined. 'Before we have your home-made shower, well – I did love what happened in the Southern Cross.'

Afterwards we stood close to each other, touching, while the inner curve of the waterfall poured all over us so that it not only cleansed our hair, eyes too, but sluiced its way between our bodies, running down them, both of us sharing the water so that we felt as though we were being stroked by each other's hands until, smiling with satisfied love, she touched my cheek with her lips and said, 'I suppose we'd better go.'

'In case people start talking!' At last I was able to make a joke and lovingly I slapped her firm little bottom as we dressed and prepared to return. The moment of bliss was already a memory of the past as we prepared to face the present, for I was still apprehensive that there would be more eruptions.

On the fifth day, however, I had a word with Mitchell. He, poor fellow, was a sad sight. Apart from other injuries, his forehead had been badly burned and Alec had treated him with a bandage, now stained, that drooped over one eye, making him look rather like a pirate. His pain was, of course, far worse than my minor injuries, for one of his shoulders had been badly burned too. He gave me a slightly sarcastic look as he said, 'So I was right in my prophecy, eh, Doc?'

'You were.' I thought it was best to say so, aware that it wasn't necessarily the whole truth. I *had* felt faintly derisive when he insisted that the Bikini test would bring disaster, just as I had felt that Tiki's plea to his gods to calm their anger would be useless. My cynicism was born of despair, for no one would ever *really* know whether Bikini had caused the holocaust, or whether it was a coincidence. And I wasn't going to probe further.

I didn't have to. Looking towards High Island, Mitchell said the most welcome words I could have heard: 'I think the old monster's exhausted itself.'

Through cracked and crusted lips I said, 'I hoped so when the planes started dropping supplies, but I couldn't be sure with that belching smoke still coming out.'

'Ah, but the fumaroles, the ordinary ventilation pipes – see how they've given up smoking altogether? To me, that's significant. And don't you see how the water's more tranquil than it was? As though the plates beneath the bed of the sea have settled themselves into a new arrangement.'

It was true. The water was still angry at times, and it was stained with debris and ash, but it was like a millpond compared to the torrent that had lashed the reef only three days ago.

'I only hope you're right,' I said. I tried to keep the touch of cynicism out of my voice, because I knew that he *was* right.

My mind went back to the moment of bliss above the pool, and I thought how it seemed like a small heavenly reward in our tortured lives. *We* were happy, but I experienced a feeling almost of guilt at being so happy, especially when I set off for Tabanea. I *had* to go there, but I felt like a soldier returning to the trenches from a wonderful spell of leave.

I took Alec Reid to Tabanea because we had worked so hard there during the cholera epidemic, and we both had a special affection for the village. In fact I wish now I had not

735

returned so quickly. The village was desolate beyond description. Not one figure was alive. Bodies lay rigid and coated with grey dust, like the distorted figures of crusaders lying on tombs in ancient cathedrals. The life had been choked out of them with burning ash and they lay twisted among the fantastically writhing crops of taro that seemed to embrace them with the ashen fingers of death.

Among these scorched and fallen crops, Jimbo had romped, and Toma's mother had gathered her small harvest. They were gone now, their frail huts torn apart by flame. The stench of sulphur filled the air. The village had been obliterated. It was no more now than a pile of cinders from which a few flames still hungrily licked the air.

There was no need to linger in Tabanea – no patients to treat, no dying to help in their last moments – and we returned with a sense of relief that we could get away quickly. Even so, I knew that another task, perhaps grimmer, faced me. Anani.

This time I went with Sam Truscott. Not only was Alec being kept busy, but I also felt more secure with Sam on the longer journey, for I was always scared that the jeep would suddenly stop. Even though it had no tyres, it clanked along marvellously, but for how long?

We set off with an uneasy feeling of despair, because Anani was not only bigger, almost a smallish town, but because it had been the centre of our lives and our work. I was stupefied at what we saw. It was so agonising that, at first, I could not take in the truth – there *was* no Anani. A few visible signs were all that remained to remind us that this had once been a happy, thriving, peaceful town where friends greeted each other casually in Main Street, where envy and bitterness were scarcely known.

Now, on the waterfront immortalised by Gauguin, a few charred stumps, sticking out of the slimy water like rotten teeth, were all that was left of the pier where – so long ago it seemed – I had first landed from the *Mantela*. And above the hill where once I had lived, a long solitary pole stood out like a mocking finger. It was the radio mast which Dick

Holmes had once proudly boasted was the tallest building in Anani. Now, everything around that area was buried.

A few half-demolished buildings still stood in and around Main Street, skeletons littering a landscape I could barely recognise – as though someone had erased all evidence of our world and redrawn the map as a desert, or rather a series of grey sand dunes.

'It gives me the creeps,' muttered Truscott.

'Me too.' I shivered. 'When I think of all the dead bodies no one will ever find.'

'Here died Anani,' said Truscott. 'It's the only goddamn memorial that suits the place.'

As we looked around in horror it was obvious that the red-hot lava had burst out in a torrent, engulfing the town, the hillsides, and pouring down until it reached the water's edge. Finally this corner of the island had cooled off, some of it to gritty dust, some of it set solid as pumice stone.

Opposite the remains of the pier, on the site of the ship's chandler, stood the grey silhouette of Jim Wilson's car, immovable, as though cast in stone for ever to commemorate some famous car race. A small opening of Jim's warehouse had been left uncovered, and as I peered into the blackness, it was like peeping into the corner of an Aladdin's cave, filled with treasure, but draughty in its desolation.

Somehow we managed to edge our way along the outline of Main Street, largely by following the wavelets fringing the beach. And then I saw that Mick's was still partly open, though the windows were smashed, the door off its hinges. Looking inside, I could see a wall along which rows of bottles stood in immaculate array. Hardly possible! But then I remembered that after the bombing of Sanderstown there had been equally ludicrous sights – an undamaged vase standing on a mantelpiece in a ruined house, a cat picking its way deliberately across rubble.

Further up the street a door banged – and the unexpected and eerie sound sent a shiver down my spine, even more when Truscott yelled, 'What the hell's that? I heard someone – yeah, over there, you bet I did.'

It was impossible of course, but Sam was right. A few steps further along Main Street, we ran into the half-demolished wreckage of Johnson's store. Its entrance and veranda had been partly saved because Johnson's main storehouse was behind the shop, and this had absorbed some of the damage. It wasn't the first time I had noticed how hot lava could curl round a building that was stronger than others around it. Molten lava seemed to take the line of least resistance.

But somebody was inside.

'Who's there?' I shouted, almost afraid as I started to creep through the wreckage into the shop. To my astonishment in this land of the dead a dozen or so men and women, all Polynesians, were hiding in the rear of the shop and as they saw me they gave a look of fear and started as though to run off – an impossibility for the only way in or out was through the small hole in the tangled wreckage.

'Goddamn looters!' cried Sam, seeing overturned bottles on the floor – and ignoring the fact that they might have fallen there during the eruption.

'What are you all doing here?' I cried. 'Where have you come from?' Though I was excited to see other human beings I wasn't really angry because I knew that most Polynesians had no mercenary instincts.

They weren't really looters, any more than were the members of the Union Jack Club, drinking the booze for which they should have signed chits. A few answers told me everything. They weren't even looking for goods, their desperate search was for liquid. They told me that several pockets of people in isolated settlements had missed the main onslaught of the volcano and this group had trekked along the coast road, paddling in water when it was cooler than the ash – all looking for something to drink. And they had found the only pollution-free liquid in unbroken, sealed bottles of Coke, squash, or even Johnson's favourite beer. These poor devils were just trying to keep alive,

738

huddling behind anything that would protect them, crouched against flimsy shelves or upturned tables.

Two of the women and one child were suffering from throats badly injured, and I promised to drive them over to Tala-Tala. I suggested to the others to walk there, if they could, for there they would find unlimited water and food.

The Polynesians were soon joined by others, and I noticed that, however much they suffered, their stoicism was enormous. I had seen this, of course, when we were treating youngsters for polio; they seemed to have a threshold of suffering or pain far greater than white people. As I examined the few new arrivals, I thought that many white men or women in that state would have died.

I told the three 'hospital cases' to lie down in Johnson's store while we took a quick look at the rest of the town. The others, who could walk, would try to make it to Tala-Tala. By chance I peeped behind a creaking door. And there were the bodies of Johnson and his jolly, overworked Polynesian wife. In the last desperate moments, when they must have heard the roar of the flames and ash that would end their lives, they had instinctively sought sanctuary in a sort of cupboard. Both had apparently been killed instantly as their roof caved in, but it was the way their bodies lay that made me think better of the mean and miserly Johnson, for he had placed his arms round her, as though to shield her in the moment of death. His last thought in life had been to protect his loyal wife.

Even more tragic was the scene at the radio shack and the Fawcett bungalow. In the graveyard that had once been Colonel Fawcett's dwelling, we looked for any traces of survival. It was in vain, and I had almost given up hope of even a sign of humanity when without warning, as we poked our way through loose ash, Truscott felt something solid.

'Jesus wept!' He recoiled physically as though in fear. He had stumbled against a man's hand, sticking out of the ash. It was clutching something, and we scrabbled away as much of the ash as we could from the hand and arm, though there was no point in trying to uncover the entire body. We didn't have the strength anyway. But again I saw that the fist was clenching something, and I recognised the wrist-watch on Fawcett's left arm. It was the colonel who was buried alive.

I managed to prise open the fingers, locked by rigor mortis. They contained a sheet of paper, crumpled into a ball. It was in fact the beginning of a letter. Aloud, but in hushed tones, as though the gallant colonel had risen from the dead, I tried to decipher for Sam the words on the crumpled paper.

It was in neat handwriting, obviously written as Fawcett prepared for death in the moments before the holocaust overwhelmed Anani. They were the final words of a brave man: 'We can all sense that we are on the edge of eternity, and we await our Maker with tranquillity, praying that it will be painless and swift and, as for myself, praying that my beloved wife will be spared and will understand that love lasts for ever. I hope that – '

And then it must have come, the catastrophe, for the last words tailed off, the last indecipherable letters the equivalent of a scream.

I do not know how long we took trying to find more traces of people buried in the town, but Alec's bungalow – and mine – had vanished, buried under countless tons of debris. Poor Bubble and Squeak must have perished instantly – at least I hoped and prayed that they had as I visualised one of them pouring out a Scotch. Alec would be lost without them.

The air was cleaner now and finally I suggested to Sam, 'Let's go back to the waterfront and have a free drink at Johnson's. I'm dying of thirst. Then I think we'd better pick up the three invalids and make tracks for Tala-Tala.'

'Okay by me.' We pushed our way into the store, then opened the bottles and wiped the necks on our shirts and forced our way back into the comparative freshness of the sea air.

Truscott went first, so I was still on all fours, crouching to

740

pass through the exit, when I heard Truscott cry, 'Ye gods! Ships!' As I reached the broken veranda, he was waving frantically like a shipwrecked mariner marooned on a desert island.

I stood stupefied, just looking. There, quite close in, were three small cargo ships – not just smudges of hope on the horizon, but already more than mere silhouettes, for I could make out figures, then action as boats were lowered over the side.

Of course we had known that rescue vessels would soon be on their way, yet the *sight* of them made my eyes smart – and it wasn't caused by volcanic ash. One forgets that, in moments of despair, we had so often been convinced that we would all share the fate of those friends we had already lost. And then suddenly – as I prayed silently – I saw the splashes as the tenders were lowered into the water, and heard the sound of their engines as they came puttering towards us. That really meant it was all over.

'I can't believe it.' I gripped Sam's arm with excitement. 'I just *can't* believe it.'

'They sure are real, though!' Truscott gave Churchill's 'V for Victory' sign, then waved – this time with reason, a different one from his first instinctive wave, for now the boat was approaching fast and someone waved back. The first tender was followed by boats from the other two vessels, and they were all making for the ugly stumps of what had once been the pier.

'Of course,' I cried to Sam. 'How could they know the pier's gone?'

'They must have seen it all through binoculars. That's probably why they anchored in the lagoon – to investigate.'

That must have been the moment, I thought, when they first saw what to them must have looked like two half-crazy men waving like mad.

The first boat veered away from the remains of the pier towards us, now half way along Main Street, still clutching our bottles of warm beer. It came in as close as possible, and someone shouted, 'You blokes all right?'

741

We shouted – but no shouts came, only the croak of voices that could not be heard against the background of the other boats' motors.

Suddenly the engine stopped and a man jumped overboard and splashed towards us. Excitedly I waded in, forgetting sandals, wet slacks (of which I only possessed the ones I stood in), and tried to run towards them, Truscott following.

I was so tense that all I wanted to do was throw my arms round the necks of my liberators. But the two men suddenly stopped their advance for a second or two and stood there, as though they had seen two ghosts.

'Poor bloody sods,' I heard one whisper. 'Poor buggers!'

It was the first time that I realised how awful we must have both looked. I had only half a torn shirt left, my trousers were ripped and torn, I was unshaven, filthy and above all *grey* – yes, still grey, even after my shower with Aleena. It was caked into the very pores of our skins. We had never realised it, when looking at each other, but we were all clothed by nature in exactly the same grey uniform.

The moment of horror I had seen etched in the men's faces passed in a flash, and a Cockney voice said, even though the cheeriness might have been assumed, 'You'll be all right now, mate! Come and have a cuppa tea – with summat in it.'

The other man, his face more puzzled than horrified, asked, 'Is this all that's left of Anani?'

I nodded dumbly, for the moment too emotional to speak, until finally I said, 'It's gone. Wiped out, but there's a lot of us in Tala-Tala.'

'We've just come over here to Anani for the first time, to see what happened,' explained Truscott.

I introduced him and then myself. 'I'm Doctor Kit Masters. Our chief medical officer is alive – he's in Tala-Tala where we have a hospital.'

'Glad you're okay,' said one of the men. 'We'll sail round

to Tala-Tala. Can you manage to get in? We'll give you a lift home.'

'No, no!' I cried in sudden – and quite unnecessary – panic. 'I've got to take the jeep back. It's the only car still working.'

'That old crock!' The man had stepped ashore now. 'It'll never make it. Can't you see it's got no tyres.'

'It's had no tyres since they melted, but that hasn't stopped us using it,' I said almost crossly. 'We can't abandon our only vehicle. Besides, we've got three invalids.'

The man must have thought I was going round the bend. He took my arm gently. 'We've got spare vehicles on the ship for you. Don't you worry. Just come on board – all of you.'

We did. We climbed up the gang-stair to the deck, and the equally horrified captain shook hands and, as the two men whispered, he said, 'We've not only got spare motor vehicles, but everything you need, including portable radio transmission equipment. Koraloona's been officially declared a disaster area. Once we get this mess cleared up, your people won't know what to do with all the materials we're getting for you.'

'Except – ' Suddenly I was thinking of poor Jason, and then of Fawcett's last message, as I gratefully sipped hot tea.

'I know, Doctor,' he read my thoughts and spoke quietly, 'but when you're dealing with war – and this has been worse than war for most of you – you gain a certain strength because it's not only one or two who suffer. It's everyone. It helps you to – but, as a doctor, I'm sure I don't have to explain . . .'

'To look forward,' I ended.

We up-anchored, and it took only a few minutes to reach Tala-Tala. We couldn't go in close, but lowered the boats again as soon as we approached, and we could see the entire able-bodied population of the village, and many Polynesians from villages which had escaped the

743

worst of the volcano, had gathered near the tiny harbour as they saw the ships approach. Even Walter Mitchell, head still bandaged, but hobbling around, was there. And in the forefront was Alec Reid, just as I remembered him on the day I landed at Anani, dirty old slacks kept up by his MCC tie, still taking off his battered topee, though his large bandana-type handkerchief had gone, and he had to wipe the sweat from his bald head with his sleeve.

As though rehearsed by a sudden signal, everyone who could waved and tried to give the rescuers three cheers of welcome as we all stepped ashore.

The first launches brought in hampers of clothes – in all sorts and sizes – and a team of experts. A scientist quickly tested the water and pronounced it safe for washing and rinsing teeth but not for drinking in large quantities. Other arrivals discovered areas virtually untouched by the volcano – areas where coconuts still flourished close to the coast of Koraloona nearest High Island, half a mile away. It seems that when the volcano spewed out its lethal cargo, the arc was so high before it fell that it often hit *our* coast, leaving the coasts nearest High Island cleaner.

Qualified engineers came to stop the generator and then, working twenty-four hours a day, stripped it down and thoroughly cleaned it so that, after two nights with paraffin lamps, our electricity was started again. Scientific agricultural experts armed with spray guns, rather like the ones strapped to the backs of vineyard workers, covered the semicircle 'ant barrier' with a powerful lethal liquid that would repel all the ants and insect life surrounding the hospital, the annexe and the cathedral which, though knocked around, still stood, alas without Father Pringle.

However, in addition to sending cables to loved ones all over the world, providing us with linen, better food, technical advice, an American chaplain arrived from an

American warship that had sailed to Sanderstown to offer help. After we had all been given time to wash and change and finally burn our old and stinking clothes, he conducted a service in the cathedral. I met the chaplain first on the boat, and led him to the small annexe of the church which Father Pringle had used as a 'changing room'.

The chaplain was a fine-looking man with an actor's presence and an actor's voice. He carried with him a large paper bag printed with the name Bloomingdale's, New York, as if he had just returned from some very worldly shopping spree. From it he took a black cassock, a white surplice, and a richy embroidered stole, which he deftly donned over his naval uniform, winking at me as he displayed the zip fastener that closed the cassock's full-length edges.

'A great benefit to the cleric, these zippers. Use'ta have to do up forty-eight buttons.'

With sudden tears behind my eyes I thought of Father Pringle, who had rarely bothered and whose soutane had billowed behind him like a voluminous cape.

But if the chaplain could be light-hearted about his vestments he could be equally serious about his immediate purpose, transforming himself with the actor's adaptability into the professional man of God.

Raising his arms in a gesture of supplication his voice rang out over the tranquil sea:

'Dear Lord, mankind in his concern for himself understandeth neither the will of God nor the forces of nature, which are God's to command, and seeth not the purpose behind the visitations of calamity. Give man the vision, O Lord, to see beyond his grief, and the spirit to fortify himself for the work of rebuilding, so that good may come out of seeming evil and that there may rise on this spot a new memorial dedicated in the name of Paul Gauguin to the comfort and care of the sick; and that elsewhere on this island, where fire hath wreaked havoc and destroyed and maimed and brought death to the people, there may be inspired in the survivors the will to be humble and contrite, and to build again to the glory of God, and to love their earthly paradise in preparation for the paradise promised in the life hereafter. For thy Name's sake, Amen.'

Epilogue

I have often thought about the disaster. It was almost as though Tiki had been right. Not that the gods had been angry with Koraloona because we had sold the pictures – in fact, sending them to Christie's had prevented them being destroyed for ever – but because most of us had avoided the dangers and deprivations of the war. As the US chaplain had said, 'mankind understandeth neither the will of God nor the forces of nature'; but the island is now so beautiful once again, and has become so prosperous, that one can but reflect, sadly, that it is only possible to build such happiness out of misfortune – or, you might say, on the other side of paradise.

Twenty years have now passed since the eruption all but destroyed Koraloona and yet, out of the tragedy, a new Koraloona was reborn and all of us who live here are so happy that I don't suppose I would have bothered to write this account of our lives had I not noticed a paragraph in the *Sentinel* saying that 'The Secret Pool' by Paul Gauguin had been sold by auction for an astonishing £170,000.

And how much had we sold it for, back in 1946? It was £13,000. How astute Ian Petrie of Christie's had been to advise us to sell only eight out of the sixteen canvases. We took that advice and now, with Aleena the mother of a boy and two girls (Kim, our son, is studying medicine at Oxford), I wrote to our old friend Petrie and asked him a few months ago, 'Is this the time to sell?'

In the new world, linked by international telephones and airplanes that fly anywhere, he replied immediately that he agreed. We did sell. In all, the eight remaining Gauguins realised nearly £800,000, more than enough to provide a new Trust to be used to increase the hospital facilities, rebuild old wings, employ extra doctors and nurses, since the GMH had become one of the most important medical centres in the South Pacific.

But how Koraloona has changed. Twenty years of peace and prosperity in the islands has brought in new residents, together with an ever-increasing number of people anxious to taste the magic of the South Seas in an island which, despite the structural changes, has retained its own special beauty.

Anani was never rebuilt. Engineers from Australia did, over the first few months, destroy the unsightly wrecked buildings, but nothing could remove the changed contours of volcanic hillsides – nor did anyone wish to desecrate the tombs of those who had died there.

Tala-Tala became the 'capital' and has vastly expanded so that, at the ripe old age of fifty-two, I can appreciate why the first missionaries who landed there so long ago, and named it by the Polynesian word for 'Preacher', chose wisely because of its sheltered position. Tala-Tala now has a large flourishing harbour whose vessels anchor in the lagoon. People arrive on the island by tender to see and sample the twin fascination of an 'unspoiled' island paradise, together with an excursion by road to the remnants of a volcanic eruption.

For Tala-Tala, despite its many innovations, even a daily air service to Sanderstown, *is* still very much a part of the past. True, there are a dozen bars and cafés on Koraloona where once there was only Mick's Bar, and there are three hotels, of which the most famous, 'Mollie Green's', is named after her ageless memory. It is a 'must' for visitors, mentioned in every Pacific travel brochure because Mollie's dream, of building a large dining-room jutting out on piles over the fringe of the sea, was realised when the new hotel was built. It now boasts the island's finest food – yes, there are still lobsters! – and one of the most romantic views in the South Seas.

There has been a fair amount of new building, for the

government grants given to Koraloona after the eruption enabled the island to build better roads, improve sanitation in the rural areas and generally improve the quality of life to such an extent that my medical skills have never been called on to fight another epidemic.

It has never entered *my* head to leave the island, especially as, with the passing years, it is possible to fly to England or any other place that is 'home', in a matter of hours; and with the hospital well endowed, 'foreign' doctors and their families (including us) get paid annual leave, with free air fares. Apart from the fact that I always knew Aleena would never really be able to settle down in England, any remote thoughts on those lines ceased when my father died a few years ago, followed a few months later by Mother. And any worry about Clare stopped when, to our delight, she suddenly got married to a respectable bachelor lawyer in Nottingham.

Quite apart from those considerations, I no longer liked England, except as a visitor. Whilst our life on Koraloona remained tranquil, I found the people of England had changed. Compared to the sun of the South Seas, England had given way to sullen clouds, and life there had become increasingly violent. It was different for Kim, our son, for he was cocooned in the world of Oxford, and he had a job to do if he wanted one day to succeed his father!

Many of the old faces have gone, of course. Dick Holmes left for another job, in England, I have no idea where Walter Mitchell is, and very soon after the first relief ships arrived twenty years ago, a sad and bereaved Mrs Fawcett left for New Zealand. I have never heard from her either.

Yet two stalwart comrades remain. Alec retired two years ago and I succeeded him as head of the hospital. But Alec did not, as we half expected, return to London. Rhoda, his wife in Wimbledon, had died some years previously, and that decided Alec. This was, and still always will be, 'home' to him, and he lives in a bungalow not far from us, so that we see him regularly.

The other one who will stay for life is Lorna Purvis, now

elevated to the status of Matron of the GMH. She bravely bore the loss of her husband, aided by a true Christian fortitude, and she named her son Jason after 'our' Jason; and the love she has for her son, combined, no doubt, with the zeal of a missionary's daughter, has given her a serenity many would envy. Jason Junior recently completed a special course in agriculture at Auckland, and is now superintendent – at the tender age of nineteen – of a newly developed kitchen garden designed to supply all the fruit and vegetables for the hospital, thus saving money to be used to buy imported drugs.

All these random thoughts and memories were passing through my mind the other night when we all met at our bungalow for a dinner to celebrate Doc Reid's birthday.

As Alec stood up, to say what he called 'a few wur-r-rds', I seemed to see him as he was all those many years ago when he welcomed me from the *Mantela* – his topee swept off with a flourish, his sweating forehead, his paunch still constrained by his MCC tie. Now he was, as he would say, 'a wee bit better dressed', the habits of retirement having invested him with a tidiness that came with leisure.

I looked round the table. At the far end, Aleena was looking beautiful – and as happy – as ever. She had all the grace and tenderness of happiness, so that, from time to time, tourists would turn to watch her in the street. Tiare, too, getting older now, along with the rest of us, had the same look of tranquillity. And on this evening Aleena signalled me surreptitiously to watch Lorna as she placed a reproving hand over her son's glass when he started to pour out more wine. The gesture reminded me so much of how she used to reprove Jason when he reached for a drink that I thought for the moment that the boy seemed to have become his father.

'Well, ye've all honoured me with your presence for ma birthday,' Alec started his speech, 'and I'll honour ye by being brief in turning the light away frae meself for a wee moment and shining it on Kit and Aleena. We all know what they've done to restore life to this island. Ye're a guid man, Kit, and a fine doctor, well trained by myself, if I do say so, but ye're also blessed with a wife and bairns who seem to grow more beautiful wi' every passing year.'

He paused and took a folded handkerchief from his shirt pocket and dabbed it to his forehead with the old familiar gesture, then he took up his glass of Old Rarity and embraced us all with his smile as he offered a toast:

'There's nae more to say, but tae gie ye a couple of lines from ma countryman, Robert Burns. "To see her was to love her, Love but her, and love for ever."'

I am still not quite sure whether he was talking about Aleena or Koraloona.

NOEL BARBER

A WOMAN OF CAIRO

A grand and passionate drama set in Egypt in the tumultuous decades culminating in World War II.

In the turbulent years when Egypt progresses from a corrupt monarchy to a fledgling democracy, Mark Holt and Serena Sirry grow up to discover a love for each other so strong that time, war, and even the wrath of kings cannot destroy it.

As the storms of war threaten this ancient and exotic land, the lovers – each trapped in loveless marriages – are forced to part. Even as fate seems intent upon separating them, an unbreakable bond carries them through to the powerful climax of this irresistible saga: Mark's defence of Serena in an Egyptian court – against a charge of murder.

'A story as majestic and fertile as its setting . . . always entertaining'

Publishers Weekly

A Royal Mail service in association with the Book Marketing Council & The Booksellers Association

Post A Book is a Post Office trademark

ALSO AVAILABLE FROM
HODDER AND STOUGHTON PAPERBACKS

NOEL BARBER

☐	37772 0	A Woman of Cairo	£3.95
☐	28262 2	Tanamera	£3.50
☐	34709 0	A Farewell to France	£3.50

CHRISTIE DICKASON

| ☐ | 41219 4 | The Dragon Riders | £3.95 |

MAEVE BINCHY

☐	38930 3	Echoes	£3.50
☐	33784 2	Light A Penny Candle	£3.50
☐	34002 9	Victoria Line, Central Line	£2.95

HILARY NORMAN

| ☐ | 41117 1 | In Love and Friendship | £3.50 |

All these books are available at your local bookshop or newsagent, or can be ordered direct from the publisher. Just tick the titles you want and fill in the form below.

Prices and availability subject to change without notice.

HODDER AND STOUGHTON PAPERBACKS,
P.O. Box 11, Falmouth, Cornwall.

Please send cheque or postal order, and allow the following for postage and packing:

U.K. – 55p for one book, plus 22p for the second book, and 14p for each additional book ordered up to a £1.75 maximum.

B.F.P.O. and Eire – 55p for the first book, plus 22p for the second book, and 14p per copy for the next 7 books, 8p per book thereafter.

OTHER OVERSEAS CUSTOMERS – £1.00 for the first book, plus 25p per copy for each additional book.

Name ....

Address ....

....